Writing Ireland's Working Class

Writing Ireland's Working Class

Dublin After O'Casey

Michael Pierse

First published 2011 by
PALGRAVE MACMILLAN

Palgrave Macmillan in the UK is an imprint of Macmillan Publishers Limited,
registered in England, company number 785998, of Houndmills, Basingstoke,
Hampshire RG21 6XS.

Palgrave Macmillan in the US is a division of St Martin's Press LLC,
175 Fifth Avenue, New York, NY 10010.

Palgrave Macmillan is the global academic imprint of the above companies
and has companies and representatives throughout the world.

Palgrave® and Macmillan® are registered trademarks in the United States,
the United Kingdom, Europe and other countries.

ISBN: 978–0–230–27227–9 hardback

This book is printed on paper suitable for recycling and made from fully
managed and sustained forest sources. Logging, pulping and manufacturing
processes are expected to conform to the environmental regulations of the
country of origin.

A catalogue record for this book is available from the British Library.

A catalog record for this book is available from the Library of Congress.

10 9 8 7 6 5 4 3 2 1
20 19 18 17 16 15 14 13 12 11

Printed and bound in Great Britain by
CPI Antony Rowe, Chippenham and Eastbourne

Contents

Acknowledgements

A book such as this is the product of many influences, encouragements and generosities that are impossible to condense into a single page. My journey to this point would have proved impossible without the assistance of many individuals and organisations, for whose time, advice and altruism I am forever grateful. I am indebted to my supervisor, Dr Paul Delaney, at the School of English, TCD, for his guidance, patience and indefatigable positivity during the course of writing the doctoral thesis on which this book is based. Equally, the encouragement and analysis of my viva examiners, Dr Aileen Douglas and Dr John Brannigan, allowed me to manage the thesis-to-book conversion. Dr Douglas's lively tutorials on working-class writing in my undergraduate years alerted me to the potential for a study such as this, and Dr Brannigan's advice and support over the past year can be traced throughout this work. Peter Sheridan, Paula Meehan, Lee Dunne, Heno Magee and Dermot Bolger, who gave generously of their time for interviews and provided otherwise elusive material, extended a helping hand that enriched the experience of writing the book greatly. Peter Sheridan, in particular, showed an enthusiasm for this project which helped confirm my own hopes for its possibilities. I am grateful also to Paul Mercier and Joe O'Byrne for access to unpublished plays, and many of these writers have provided critical insights that guided my writing and opened doors. I would also like to thank Mícheál Ó Heffearnáin, Seán Ó Haitheasa, Dr Eoghan Mac Cárthaigh and Máire Ní Bháin. I am grateful to Eoin Ó Broin for reading over part of this book prior to publication, but I must also stress that all of the mistakes, opinions and omissions in it are entirely my own, and that I look forward to seeing how others might correct and refute them into the future. Many thanks also to my friends, Mícheál, Damian, Aidan and Martin, for many interesting discussions and casual observations that guided me while writing. More than any others, I must thank my parents, Philomena and Mossie, for their faith and unconditional support, and my wife, Brenda, for her love and many incredible kindnesses. For the belief you had in me when I had none, and for the fun, laughter and unshakeable optimism, I am thankful and ever in wonderment.

Foreword

It is a critical time in the history of the disciplinary field known as Irish Studies. For two or perhaps three decades, Irish Studies has attracted a global range of scholarly interest, and several associations and societies draw hundreds of speakers and delegates together every year to discuss topics of Irish literary, cultural and historical interest. Many of the major academic publishers in the UK and the US have dedicated "Irish Studies" lists, and several major international journals are also devoted to the field. The nature of the relationship between this burgeoning academic subject and the rise (and fall) of the so-called "Celtic Tiger" economy deserves a materialist history of its own. Has "Irish Studies" been the vehicle of critical inquiry into Irish culture and history, or has it been too closely tied to the promotional energies of the supposedly "new" Ireland?

The social and cultural changes in Ireland in the first decade of the twenty-first century prompt important questions about the absence of class-based critique in Irish Studies. The Ryan and Murphy Reports of 2009 revealed the extent of child sexual abuse in institutions controlled by the Catholic Church, with particular implications for how class divisions manifested themselves in violent and abusive forms within Irish educational and religious organisations. The economic recession since 2008, which arguably marked the end of the "Celtic Tiger" economy, re-opened debates about whether or not the apparent prosperity which seemed to flow from Ireland's embrace of neo-liberal economics had, even temporarily, masked the fundamental, underlying structural inequalities and faultlines in Irish society. With unemployment, emigration and homelessness on the rise as I write this in 2010, questions about the pervasiveness of class divisions, and the significance of class as a material and cultural category, are neither merely academic nor merely political. They should be key questions within the field of Irish Studies, and within Irish society, and yet the critical record on class in Irish literature, culture and history is shockingly thin.

In the introduction to this book, Michael Pierse examines the reasons why Irish Studies has not adequately addressed issues of class, especially in relation to literature and culture. He rightly asks "why Ireland has yet to produce its own Richard Hoggart, Raymond Williams, or Terry Eagleton, and why, at third level, the working class remains underrepresented in terms of both participation and the curriculum". In providing some answers to these difficult questions, Pierse outlines the theoretical frameworks and critical tools which have been missing from Irish Studies on matters of working-class literature and culture. The book itself provides ample testimony to the existence of an important and continuous body of working-class literature in Dublin, from Sean O'Casey to Roddy Doyle. It includes rich, detailed analyses of some of the major writers in twentieth-century Ireland, including O'Casey, Brendan Behan, James Plunkett, Dermot Bolger and Doyle, but also celebrates writers whose work has been unjustly neglected. Pierse's chapter on Heno Magee, Lee Dunne and James McKenna, for example, revisits the forgotten mid-century tradition of working-class Dublin writing that forms a bridge between O'Casey and Doyle. The double oppression of working-class women is addressed in a chapter which attempts to account for the silence of working-class women in literature, at the same time as it explores how the representation of working-class women in the work of two male writers, Paul Smith and Peter Sheridan, embodies a disruptive potential. Chapter 4 examines the theme of industrialisation in novels by James Plunkett and Paul Smith, arguing that their work illustrates a subversion of the bourgeois form of the novel from within. In Chapter 5, the author examines how Brendan Behan, Peter Sheridan and Paula Meehan have used the setting of prison to examine themes of social inequality and injustice under capitalism. Sexual and cultural repression is the focus of Chapter 6, in which Christy Brown's *Down All the Days* (1970) and Dermot Bolger's *The Journey Home* (1990) enable the author to analyse the relationship between Catholic nationalist ideologies and social alienation. In the final chapter, the author focuses on Roddy Doyle's *A Star Called Henry* (2000), to interrogate the meanings of working-class political agency in the history of the Irish state.

The book consistently shows the inventiveness and subversiveness of working-class literary and cultural forms. Moreover, Pierse does not isolate this body of literature from its social and political contexts, but through a skilful and expansive consideration of a wide range of sources – labour history pamphlets, newspapers, interviews, unpublished plays, sociological studies and memoirs, to take a few instances – he demonstrates the social and public nature of working-class writing. For this reason alone, it is a valuable and timely intervention in Irish literary criticism in particular, and Irish cultural and intellectual discourse more broadly.

Yet, in true pioneering fashion, Pierse also goes further than this. He points out further avenues for research, sketches the possibilities for what questions might be asked, and what methodologies employed, to understand the history and currency of working-class literature and culture. Through astute readings of the Marxist critical tradition, and a wide-ranging critique of the theoretical paradigms dominant in Irish Studies, Pierse points the way towards an emergent field of cultural criticism fully attentive to class hierarchies and subaltern perspectives in modern Ireland. He also engages in sustained and detailed comparisons of the literature and criticism of working-class life in Ireland and England, comparisons which are made not for the purpose of establishing yardsticks of cross-cultural measurement, but instead to generate fruitful dialogues between texts which can sometimes seem to belong to different national traditions, at other times to echo common social and political experiences. His conclusion is nothing short of a rallying call to re-shape the values and methods of the discipline of Irish Studies.

JOHN BRANNIGAN

Introduction

"The 'working classes' have been the source of much disappointment and disgust for the middle-class observers who have studied them, and, in large part, this is marked out through the lack of legitimacy granted to working-class cultural capital," writes Steph Lawler. In orthodox academic and cultural terms, "they do not *know* the right things, they do not *value* the right things, they do not *want* the right things".[1] How, then, could the working classes *read*, let alone *write*, the right things? Since the development and codification of middle-class concepts of art and culture in Western Europe from the early eighteenth century, "taste" has been closely aligned with the attitudes and affectations of the middle and upper classes. In Terry Eagleton's enigmatic words, "only those with an interest [property] can be disinterested" – only those with a stake in capitalism can be truly capable of setting the standards for valid cultural appreciation. If the middle class governs the ruling ideas, it promotes and "discovers in discourse an idealised image of its own social relations".[2] Against this image, writing and culture generally of the working class is found wanting. This book aims to explore the development of a specific lineage of writing of the working class against the backdrop of such elitist practices. It seeks also to expose a particular legacy of neglect and snobbery in an Irish context, in the realm of literature and its appreciation, which resonates more broadly in the fabric of Irish cultural and social life to this day.

I. Class matters

The regressions of radicalism

Social class has, in recent decades, taken a back seat in the broad fields of cultural and literary studies, overlaid by a growing interest in the politics of identity, race, gender and sexuality. Sally R. Munt's recollection of a Queer Studies conference in Iowa – in which an unexpected "coming-out moment" occurred – powerfully illustrates the anxieties inherent in the contemporary relationship between the working class and academia, while also recalling an evocative personal epiphany:

> Someone had organized a workshop for working-class academics; a room full of us sat there, some cried. I hadn't really articulated until then the intensity of shame I had brought with me [from an English working-class background]. Silent, not speaking, I began to realize how my career as a lesbian academic had been prefaced by a professionalization which demanded that certain other identities had to be forsaken. Thus, I was caught between two forms of silence: that of the American identity politics context, in which having a "voice" seems so troublesome, and that of the British bourgeoisification of my perversity, which resulted in my feeling that in Huddersfield, where I grew up, I am ashamed of being gay, whereas in Brighton [as an academic], I am ashamed of coming from the northern working class.[3]

Despite the advances of progressive political opinions across university campuses, Munt's experience vividly conveys how class is a taboo subject in the contemporary academe. She had lived "through the years of lesbian feminism" in Brighton, but as the identitarian politics she espoused came to the fore of academic discussions, ironically "class became a wound" – "to articulate its concerns was to be labelled a spoiler, a guilt-tripper, a Manichean thinker, a fifth columnist".[4] As British society shifted cumbersomely towards the acceptance of sexual and racial diversity (and Irish society lagged ponderously behind), its new pluralism overshadowed the old class war, not least because class is not as blatant as skin colour or as clear-cut an issue as sexual equality. "As a butch lesbian, my sexual status was visible," Munt explains; "it was my (classed) history that feared exposure."[5]

In the same volume of essays, another Cultural Studies academic, Andy Medhurst, also extrapolates from personal experience to illustrate the evacuation of class from mainstream academic concerns. During tutorials on the study of soap operas, Medhurst confronted the hypocrisy of identity politics *sans* class consciousness. His students would "cluck like good white liberals about the paucity of black characters" in television drama, "but yet also make fun of the working-class accents, lifestyles and even names found in those serials":

> I even had otherwise impeccably progressive students distribute handouts to groups which give characters' names not as they are really spelled, but jokingly respelled in a mocking approximation of how these students hear the characters talk.

Thus, *EastEnders'* Bianca becomes "Beeang-urgh", and, while such juvenile antics may seem trivial or comic, Medhurst makes the point that "these students would be outraged if they saw an Asian or West Indian accent reproduced in such parodic terms by white people".[6] The use of working-class accents for humorous/deflationary effect in advertising, comedy, television and film has attracted some level of commentary in Britain, but in Ireland – while such uses are apparent, even widespread – they remain almost completely undocumented and untheorised.[7] The widespread capacity to unquestioningly accept this kind of snobbery illustrates the enduring prevalence of class prejudice and its counterpart, class shame. Even in the trendiest and most liberal of disciplines, "evidently class is fair game for the ideological exercise of linguistic condescension".[8]

In an article on the subject of the 2008 Beijing Olympic Games, a seasoned Irish commentator on class issues, Fintan O'Toole, also invoked comparisons from popular culture to illustrate how "social class" arouses "an underlying discomfort" in Irish society. After a number of boxers from working-class Dublin were fêted for their successes at the games, O'Toole rained on the proverbial parade:

> As so often in the past, national pride was salvaged by those of whom the nation generally feels least proud: young, working class men from marginalised communities. While the horsey set, with all their money and self-regard, were making a show of us yet again [amidst controversies over alleged doping in showjumping], the competitors who demonstrated honesty and discipline, pride and passion, were from the invisible Ireland that is represented only in court reports.[9]

Like Medhurst and Munt, O'Toole again draws attention to the role of popular culture in the marginalisation of the nation's proletarian *bêtes noires*. "Their accents are heard most often in caricatured advertisements, where they stand for criminality or stupidity," he observes: "Unless they become individuals by making waves in sport, they are skangers, chavs, hoodies, knackers." These social *Others* come from "non-place[s]", with galling levels of poverty and exceptionally low educational attainment. Stereotypes popular amongst Ireland's "well-to-do", of young men who "wear hoodies and white socks and throw shapes and sip cans of Dutch Gold lager on the back seat of the bus", allow for "a reassuring distance" from such places.[10] "Taste" again shakes its head contemptuously at the lower orders.

Candid discussions of class such as these chafe with postmodern sensibilities. The structural categorisations required for class analysis are the very anathema of the fixation on "slippage" and deconstruction that has emerged from the "linguistic turn". Class's invocation in contemporary academic discussions is thus hedged with apprehensions surrounding its rationality.[11] Gordon Marshall draws attention to the tendency towards opaque theorisation in postmodernism, noting that "the postmodernist critique of class analysis has largely detached itself from empirical reality".[12] That reality is essential in any understanding of the social aspects of literature, and class, as this book seeks to show, is still an indispensable tool in attempting to delineate the exploitative social relations and polarised cultural positions which characterise, spatially and socially, the contours of modern Irish society. My undertaking in this book is to explore how the working class is depicted in Dublin's literature and to argue that the body of literature examined represents a distinct, heretofore academically unrecognised lineage in Irish writing. In this introductory chapter, I will first examine the importance of class in general theoretical terms. I will then proceed to a discussion of Ireland's and Dublin's working class, its endurance throughout various economic changes and its relevance to Irish Studies. An outline of the principal theoretical approaches that guide the arguments of this book concludes the chapter.

Classifying class

Class exists objectively as "an empirical category, and its enduring subjective existence as lived experience". Relative deprivation "not only affect[s] life-chances (quantifiably), but also lifestyles, in the way that we measure and differentiate our social status (quantifiably). The gradations of such social status inform and prescribe our mobility through social space; they affect our bodily practices, circumscribe our ideational reality, our sense of self".[13] Why, then, has class become the elephant in the drawing room of so many disciplines, not least Irish Studies? Why, if class is inextricable from "aesthetic" matters, from our "way of life, appearance or language", has it become the unfashionable shibboleth of a hidden Ireland?[14]

In general terms, class encompasses not only the economic rubrics under which humanity is objectively categorised, but also a great deal of the quotidian social and cultural manifestations of subjective human experience. As E. P. Thompson put it, "class happens when some men, as a result of common experiences [...] feel and articulate the identity of their interests as between themselves", and class consciousness is "the way in which those experiences are handled in cultural terms: embodied in traditions, value systems, ideas and cultural forms".[15] But the theorisation of class often seems to refute such straightforward categorisations. Class analysis is notoriously prone to ambiguity, slippage and vigorous disagreement. As Joan Craig puts it in Ellen Wilkinson's English novel of the 1926 General Strike, *Clash* (1929), even amid the polarisation of industrial unrest, class is a "complicated business": "There must be a line between capitalist and worker somewhere, but whenever you think you've got it, it's always somewhere else. There's an obvious gulf between Harry Browne and the Duke of Northumberland, or Mr. Gordon Selfridge, or his own immediate boss, but where does the line shade off?"[16] Theory must strive to loosen the straitjacket of impossibly restrictive dogma, Wilkinson suggests, but it must also atomise the dynamics of exploitation in a way that can explain prevailing socio-economic relationships, on a basic, empirical level. In the gulf between the micro and macro, the typical and the particular, theories of class often come undone.

Thompson indeed warned against "a static view of class", postulating that it "is a relationship, not a thing".[17] Class is an organic, mutable concept, shifting according to the vicissitudes of historical change but nonetheless charting a solid continuity of human affairs under capitalism. "Class is never simply a category of the present tense. It is a matter of history, a relationship with tradition, a discourse of roots."[18] Whereas Thompson problematised theories of class structure – corresponding with more recent studies that re-evaluate class in light of the fragmentary and consensual nature of modern capitalist society – his essential achievement, nonetheless, was to delineate class's durability in British life.[19] This kind of task is of course fraught with various theoretical problems. As John R. Hall has put it:

> to come to terms with these challenges, it is necessary to avoid the twin modernisms – the Charybidis of historicism and the Scylla of reified formal theory. We need to acknowledge the role of theory in providing language that makes analytic discussion of classes possible, yet account for classes in their historicities.

The challenge, Hall contends, is to negotiate between the "structural holism" of certain Marxist approaches to class and the post-structuralist stress on "slippage between the empirical world and any 'structures' presumed to undergird or represent it".[20]

The roots of a discourse

Karl Marx's conception of class defined it in terms of evident economic disparities. In *The Eighteenth Brumaire of Louis Bonaparte* (1852), class is explained as a register of antagonisms, whereby, "insofar as millions of families live under economic conditions of existence that divide their mode of life, their interests and their culture from those of other classes, and put them in a hostile contrast to the latter, they form a class".[21] In *Capital* (1867), his three "great classes" are postulated as "the owners of mere labour-power, the owners of capital and the landowners, whose respective sources of income are wages, profit and ground rent – in other words, wage-labourers, capitalists and landowners".[22] Marx allowed for the existence of intermediate strata in *The Eighteenth Brumaire*, but these were mere anomalies in capitalism's irrevocable progress towards a "pure form".[23]

However, herein lies the rub: in those who fall between Marx's three stools, the question continually arises as to how occupational positions that have ostensibly contradictory or possibly conflated class interests are to be read from within structural paradigms. The exceptions threaten to destabilise the rule, and the endurance of this question – not least because of the failure of Marxism's predictions of capitalism's progress to a "pure form" – compounds the quandary for traditional Marxists. If capitalism allows for mobility, slippage, contradictory class locations, the modern consensual arrangements between unions and capitalists and the various other grey areas of the welfare state, how can stratification analysis stand? What happens when, in advanced capitalist societies, such as those of modern Europe, the development of service industries and white-collar jobs begins to fudge the barriers between the working and middle classes?

Reconceptualising class

According to Nicos Poulantzas, in *Classes in Contemporary Capitalism* (1975), two criteria can be employed to clarify the cleft between proletariat and bourgeoisie.[24] Returning to the determinist discourse, he defines the working class as those workers who produce surplus value and who are directly employed in material production; returning to tradition, he locates the division of proletarian and bourgeois between manual and mental labour. But Poulantzas's theoretical approach to stratification would seem to merely add to the confusion. Such a formula appears entirely outmoded in societies where the barrier between both definitions (profiteers/surplus value producers and mental/manual workers) is increasingly blurred.

Some neo-Marxist theorists, such as Serge Mallet in his *Essays on the New Working Class* (1975), readily acknowledge this blurring but proceed by contrast to a "proletarianisation" thesis.[25] They argue that traditional middle-class elements are in fact brought into a larger proletariat in modern Western economies.[26] Wage earners of all types are amalgamated into a "new working class" by the reduction of educational and technological hierarchies in workplaces and the clearer alignment of society into two conflicting class interests: the wage-earners and the profit-makers. But with highly paid professionals and trades workers earning far in excess of the cost of labour reproduction in advanced economies, can this alternative thesis really be sustained?

The proletarianisation analysis is refuted by some of the modern sociological approaches to class which stratify society into smaller groups, based not only on the division of wealth but also on educational attainment and social status. This analysis seeks to find the subtle lines of division "between capitalist and worker", which Wilkinson's trade unionist had found so exasperatingly elusive. From within this strain, Erik Olin Wright identifies twelve different class positions in the modern capitalist economy, which would seem at first glance to go beyond the old Marxist paradigm.[27] But Wright strives to resolve the debate over Marx's shortcomings by redefining the allegiances of seemingly anomalous positions in the modern class system *within* Marx's original mould. Managers in capitalist enterprise – who might well be wage labourers but who are also clearly allied with wage payers – are reassessed in terms of "organizational assets": their relative authority over workers and control of production. Professionals, who might equally confound the traditional classifications, are reconstituted in terms of "skill" and "credential" assets.[28] Wright posits "skill exploitation" and "organization exploitation" as new interventions in the Marxist tradition, new ways of conceptualising class divisions:

> In skill exploitation, owners of scarce skills are able to extract a rent component in their wages. This is basically a component of the wage above and beyond the costs of producing and reproducing the skills themselves [...] In organization exploitation, managers are able to appropriate part of the surplus through the power which they command inside the bureaucratic structures of capitalist production.

This understanding of exploitation explains

> those locations in the class structure which were exploited on one mechanism of exploitation but were exploiters on another. Professional and technical employees, for example, can be seen as capitalistically exploited but skills exploiters. They thus constitute "contradictory locations within exploitation relations".[29]

These workers very often receive stakes in businesses from employers keen to retain their indispensable assets; they are part of a "hierarchy of authority".[30]

But if Wright problematises old theories of class stratification, he also emphatically frames his innovations within the old tripartite model of owners, industrialists and workers. And while Hall argues that such analysis amounts to a shift towards the Weberian approach to class, "incorporating Weberian themes within a structuralist Marxist edifice", Wright rightly counters that the Weberian refusal to accept class warfare as a principle dynamic of social reproduction would not allow for his own adherence to a core Marxist precept – the centrality of the worker's exploitation to all economic understanding.[31] Wright thus conceptualises complex, modern social and economic relations, while "stubbornly working inside of Marxism".[32]

This accommodation of modern occupational and economic subtleties into a Marxist paradigm is attractive in theorising working-class consciousness and in attending to matters of culture. While it admits the deficiencies in outdated, Manichean concepts of class formation, it also allows for the enduring sense of class as a lived experience of wage labourers, with varying degrees of skills, education and earnings. For the most part, working-class people come from the same communities, are born into the same class as their parents (as studies show) and experience shared cultural, political and economic references (as studies also show). The challenge is to elaborate on Marx, as Wright puts it, "to explore a new way of adding complexity to the concept of class structure", which explains "empirical variations" and develops "within a broadly Marxist theoretical framework, a class structure capable of being used in analyses of micro-level processes at a relatively low level of abstraction".[33]

Within all this abstract sociological theory, Wright reminds us that it is imperative to remember that "class structures define a set of 'locations' filled by individuals subjected to a set of mechanisms that impinge directly on their lives as they make choices and act in the world", therefore "moving from the *abstract* to the *concrete*".[34] Taxonomies of class that draw on theories of historical development and structural antagonisms are only useful in so far as they represent lived experience. Classes "share common dilemmas with respect to collective action as well as individual pursuit of economic welfare and power".[35] The "experience of being forced to sell one's labour power in order to survive [...] does not simply define a set of material interests of actors, but a set of experiences as well".[36] Indeed, it is interesting in this context that when Irish people were recently asked what most defined class for them, "accent [was] regarded as the most significant indicator – more than house, job, clothes, car or schooling".[37] When class inflects things such as accent and idiom, when it affects a person's social status, cultural interests, gender relations and occupational prospects, it seems rather obvious that it is still a vital tool in exploring matters of culture.

In its focus on economic determinism, however, the debate between Wright and his detractors tends to obfuscate another important element in class formation: the extent to which the working class forms itself internally, *after the fact* of its exploitation. Etienne Balibar believed that "classes are *functions of the process of production as a whole*. They are not its subjects, on the contrary, they are determined by its form".[38] But this reduction of class to mere formula is something that a student of literature is likely to find unattractive, particularly in illuminating the study of working-class *cultural* and *social* life – and in attending to the organic formation of subjectivities from *within* that life. Thompson himself rebuffed Balibar's reductivism by stressing working-class *agency* in class formation. He lamented that, in Balibar's hypothesis, "the subject (or agent) of history [had] disappear[ed] once again" and "for the *n*th time, [was] re-ified". Since

> classes are "functions of the process of production" (a process into which, it seems, no human agency could possibly enter), the way is thrown open once again to all the rubbish of deducing classes [...] within a mode of production [...] conceived as *something other than* its eventuation in historical process.[39]

Crucially for Thompson, Balibar's view omits the consideration of class "self-activity" – his belief that "the working class made itself as much as it was made":

> We cannot put "class" here and "class consciousness" there, as two separate entities [...] since class formations and class consciousness (while

subject to determinate pressures) eventuate in an open-ended process of *relationship* – of struggle with other classes – over time.[40]

Being working class is not the same as being a passive victim of powerful social forces; it is part of a collective and active, organic and historical process of identity formation.

Thompson advocates the effective *humanisation* of the working class within the Marxist mould, which, he suggests, cannot be performed from within a narrow and "re-ified" framework of deterministic class analysis. The working class forms in *dynamic* struggle with other classes. It is the product of a dialectic of economic development and self-actuation; it has a culture, a history, a sense of its own existence, which renders theoretical debates about whether class exists or not irrelevant. Wright's and Thompson's respective conceptualisations of class – as both socio-economic empirical reality and intra-class cultural re-production – thus offer a fruitful and relevant continuation of the Marxist tradition in an advanced capitalist context. Wright overcomes the obsession with Marx as a reductive dogma by reformulating his theories to reflect the modern context, but the centrality of exploitation and antagonism remains. Thompson attends to the contingencies of history and economics while also highlighting the role of working-class *people* in creating class as a *social* and *cultural* phenomenon. My understanding of class in this book proceeds from these neo-Marxian concepts, and a contingent belief in the enduring relevance of the working class as a culturally, socially and empirically self-evident cohort. But following Thompson's stress on the importance of history, how has this cohort manifested and developed in Ireland's capital city?

Working-class Ireland

"Irish society is often thought of as a classless society", as Perry Share, Hilary Tovey and Mary P. Corcoran observe in *A Sociology of Ireland* (2007). Its people's legendary warmth and lack of reverence for status are sometimes proffered as evidence of a lack of obvious social stratification. Irish people prefer "to use first names even with relative strangers rather than titles and surnames", and the Republic, despite deep inequalities, is assumed by many to be a less hierarchical state than others. In the first decade of the twenty-first century, there has also been a general perception of increased opportunities for social mobility in the "Celtic Tiger" economy, which further problematises the clarity and application of class analysis here.[41] Drawing on Kieran Allen's examination of the lexicon of "social problems" – which frames debates on wealth distribution in public discussions about "poverty" and "disadvantage" – Share, Tovey and Corcoran convey how Irish views on class have shifted into a common perception of "gross differentiation between the majority – the 'more or less middle classes' – and an 'underclass' made up of the poor, the long-term unemployed, substance abusers and marginalised groups".[42] This, they argue, is a fanciful characterisation of class inequalities, but it is true that popular discourse and common perception often confute the Marxian dissection of Irish society along class lines. The two drug addicts in Leonard Abrahamson's film *Adam and Paul* (2004) are quintessentially "underclass" in this manner of thinking, as is the archetypal dodgy-dealer, Rats, in Ian FitzGibbon's film *Spin the Bottle* (2003), but where then, precisely, is the working class?

As Allen conveys in another publication (and as Share et al.'s analysis attests), the facts of Celtic Tiger Ireland themselves disprove familiar assumptions of classlessness and embourgeoisification. While the perception of generally increased wealth in Ireland has undoubtedly been embedded in a real, unprecedented increase in living standards across the board, it may be surprising for some to consider that, even in Ireland's boom years, "workers [were] receiving a lower share of the wealth they [were] producing than before".[43] Indeed, a widening chasm in earning levels accompanied the rising tide that lifted all boats, Allen notes, concluding, at the onset of the new millennium, that "class divisions and even class struggle have become more relevant than ever before".[44]

Perhaps this slippage between the rhetoric of public discourse and the glaring realities of Celtic Tiger Ireland betrays something more fundamental in the Irish psyche. As Share et al. attest, sociological research has shown that "despite common-sense assumptions to the contrary class inequality is and has been a highly significant feature of Irish social organisation".[45] Even at the height of Ireland's ballooning affluence in 2005, a survey conducted by Amárach consultants found that 30 per cent of the Republic's population still designated themselves working class.[46] Self-designation of this sort can be fanciful (although it generally tends to underestimate the size of the working class and to inflate that of the self-proclaimed well-off), but it conveys at least that a strong sense of class divisions still obtains in Irish society.

Questions of history

Peter Beresford Ellis's *A History of the Irish Working Class* (1972, revised 1985) provides a useful if at times theoretically flawed overview of working-class Ireland. It locates the development of the Irish working class within a broad field of historical evolution and pays particular attention to the conditions that led to the 1913 Dublin Lockout and the subsequent diminution of proletarian struggle in the Free State. It also accords due attention to the effects of Partition and the 1969–1998 North of Ireland conflict on working-class life. But Ellis's over-stressing of James Connolly's "Celtic communism", for instance, and his constant digressions from the matter of class itself overshadow his essential achievement.[47] Ellis often sacrifices a more detailed discussion of the social history of working-class Ireland for an inordinate focus on the macro-politics of decolonisation, relapsing into the standard discursive obsessions of Irish historiography – despite his stated intention of tracing a very specific history *of the working class*. This is not to eschew the key role of colonisation in the matter at hand; on the contrary, we shall see, later in this chapter, how David Lloyd (taking, after a fashion, Ellis's lead) engages post-colonial and proletarian histories jointly to fruitful ends. But Ellis fails somewhat in his stated objective; his focus becomes other than the nominal purpose of his study.

In terms of political developments, Brian Girvin provides an excellent analysis of the Irish working class from the 1920s to the 1980s in an essay published in *Saothar*, the journal of the Irish Labour History Society – a publication that has proved indispensable to my work.[48] But both Girvin's essay and the bulk of *Saothar*'s research concentrate mainly on the history of trade union and left *"political"* activity, as does Charles McCarthy's *Trade Unions in Ireland 1894–1960* (1977) and Emmet O'Connor's *A Labour History of Ireland, 1824–1960* (1992). Marilyn Silverman's *An Irish Working Class: Explorations in Political Economy and Hegemony, 1800–1950* (2001) is an exception to some extent, although its anthropological focus on the small population of Thomastown, County Kilkenny, is highly specialised, if admirably constructed. These works have contributed significantly to the growing body of scholarship on Irish Labour Studies, but, as Moira J. Maguire recently lamented, "overall, the field of Irish social history generally is significantly underdeveloped when compared with other European societies", and further, "issues of class are markedly absent from twentieth-century Irish historiography". Indeed, "much of twentieth-century Irish history seems to assume that social class distinctions did not exist".[49] Apart from the work of Kevin C. Kearns, discussed below, and a number of memoirs and local history books, social and cultural histories of working-class life are few and far between.

Dublin's working class

It should be prefaced here, as I have already suggested, that working-class politics and labour activity should not be taken as an encapsulation of the totality of working-class life. And even as regards the matter of class consciousness, it is important to attend to the nuances of how various historical configurations act to underplay – or indeed overemphasise – the actual lived experiences of class solidarity. Scholarship from historians such as Fintan Lane, Niamh Puirséil and Kieran Allen has shown how a very particular colonial and post-colonial history problematises any simplistic application of Marxist teleology to Irish working-class life.[50] Further, culture in particular must be grasped as a diverse and multi-layered area of activity that militates against simple political prescriptions. However, it is first essential to appreciate the complex political manifestations of Irish working-class life before we can proceed to a more nuanced understanding of how it manifested in broader experiential and cultural terms.

As Girvin notes, "the absence of industrial expansion prior to 1932 severely restricted the impact of the working class on politics and society" in twentieth-century Ireland, notwithstanding the 1913 Lockout and the execution of trade-union leader James Connolly three years later – occurrences that undoubtedly energised working-class activity and heightened class consciousness.[51] The relative paucity of a politically visible class struggle in Ireland undoubtedly has a great deal to do with the country's underdevelopment in capitalist terms. Although Dublin prior to the Act of Union was a thriving commercial centre with a growing population, half a century later it was outflanked by the new entrepreneurial and industrial heartlands of Britain and, in Ireland, Belfast. In a comparative analysis of Dublin, Belfast and Bristol, John Lynch shows how Dublin experienced a weak form of industrialisation from the 1820s onward, more a dipping of toes in the tumultuous waters of industry than a full-scale immersion.[52] The city suffered from severe and abiding poverty throughout the nineteenth century, lacking the stabilised working conditions that fomented class consciousness and political cohesion elsewhere, and Dublin's ill-fated economic plight persisted well into the following century. By 1913, the mortality rate in the city was the highest in Europe, and greater than that in Calcutta, and the city boasted little heavy industry and few factories. Apart from Guinness's brewery, Jacobs' biscuits and a number of distilleries, there was scant large-scale manufacturing – and it is notable that even these few exceptions were closely linked with agriculture.

Economy and consciousness

For our present purposes – the development of an understanding of Dublin's class character and consciousness – it is important to acknowledge that the city's tame industrialisation also presented difficult terrain for proselytisers of the labour movement. Lynch's analysis of the relative weakness of working-class social and economic movements – like the Workers' Educational Association and the co-operative movement – points to both the paucity of a well-paid body of tradesmen in Dublin and the consequent difficulty in building the necessary networks for proletarian social and cultural initiatives – organisations such as the Unity Theatre, Workers' Musical Association and Left Book Club, which made their mark on twentieth-century Britain.[53] This difficulty, in turn, facilitated little by way of thoroughgoing class consciousness – something that James Plunkett vividly depicted in his conjuring up of the early years of the twentieth century in Ireland's *Strumpet City* (1969). In this epic novel, most Dubliners exhibit an unthinking loyalty to their colonial masters during these years. But Plunkett also shows how that quiescence had dramatically reversed by 1913, when James Larkin, the "Prometheus Hibernica", galvanised a hitherto sleeping beast in a radical awakening to its own political power.[54]

The political eruption that characterised the Lockout had, however, more to do with the long gestation of appalling social conditions than any single, inspirational figure. By 1911, 118,000 working-class Dubliners were crammed into just over 5,000 tenement houses. And not only was official power seemingly oblivious to the plight of these festering ghettos – according to historian Diarmaid Ferriter, it had a vested interest in containing their conspicuous ills:

> Those intent on reform through slum clearance and new construction often found their plans were overshadowed by the desire to contain contagious disease within the slums and the continued ghettoisation of the poor, who were often depicted as being morally as well as materially in dire straits, by both state and charity organisations.[55]

But Plunkett's narrative indeed culminates in a metonymical collapse of colonial and capitalist hegemony: when a wealthy landlord's dilapidated tenements cave in on their inhabitants, there is a simultaneous sense that the authority of those in power is collapsing too. As Plunkett implies, the working class's subjection to material impoverishment and moral loathing undoubtedly served to fan the flames of radical thought.

In the preceding decade, Larkinism – the Irish variant of syndicalism – grew rapidly, culminating in the iconic dispute and exerting its hegemony over a large section of the Irish workforce. Allen enlists as evidence of this the fact that the *Irish Worker*, which Larkin edited at the time, "was easily able to outsell republican newspapers".[56] Such compelling evidence of the strength of the class, as opposed to the national, question in Irish life at the time is often glossed over in conventional histories – although Larkin's new Irish Transport and General Workers' Union (ITGWU), founded in 1909, also proposed the "Irishing of everything within the four seas of Ireland".[57] But the failure to accord adequate significance to the matter of class may have more to do with the diminution of labour issues in subsequent decades and the disappearance of such unbridled and unconcealed working-class solidarity after the foundation of the Free State.

In the revolutionary period from 1916 to 1923, workers played an important role in the decolonisation struggle, taking an active part in the Irish Republican Army (IRA) and using strike action to militate simultaneously against imperialism and capitalism. Union membership rose from 70,000 to 120,000 between 1916 and 1920, but, Labour leaders failed to consolidate the opportunities inherent in this period of grassroots political unrest, boding badly for their post-independence performance. As O'Connor remarks of the Free State dispensation, "while farmers, agricultural labourers and merchants all received something in return for their nationalism, urban workers got nothing".[58] In comparison with other Western European states, the urban working-class was admittedly small, with industrial workers accounting for a mere 13 per cent of those gainfully employed in 1926.[59] Furthermore, the establishment of the new 26-county state "coincided with a marked decline in union influence and activity".[60] A factor in the relative difficulty experienced by those organising this workforce was also, again, its largely deskilled nature, a consequence of a century's lack of economic planning, as one contemporary report implied: "The problem at present is really the outcrop of generations of vicissitude in the political, industrial, and social conditions of the people".[61]

While trade-union membership stood at 126,522 in 1924, it had declined to 70,573 by 1930, with marked losses in the transport sector, where Larkinism – the most radical strain in Irish labour – was strongest.[62] A number of trade-union defeats in the 1920s had also undermined confidence in the power of the organised workforce, and the consequent disaffection of radical elements allowed formerly quiescent, moderate union factions – which in the main represented smaller workplaces – to begin to take the movement's helm. A dramatic decline in the volume of industrial disputes ensued during the first decade of the Free State, with one-fifth of the annual number of workers engaged in strike activity at the start of the 1920s doing the same by the decade's end. Connolly was dead, and Larkin's career was now, and in the coming decades, bedevilled by imprisonment in America, chronic union infighting, a rift with the Soviet Union, a libel case and, at one stage, bankruptcy. He failed to revive the Dublin radicalism with which his name was once synonymous, despite some spells as a TD right into the 1940s. Anthony Cronin would later complain that "Big Jim" could not be counted among the "makers of modern Ireland": "And if his ghost stalks – as in one sense or another it will always continue to stalk – the streets of Dublin, it must be at least as much a disconsolate and forlorn as a triumphant or a happy spirit."[63] Whereas the increasingly sidelined Larkin had sought to preach the "gospel of discontent", the new union leaders, such as Tom Johnson, preferred "the gospel of faithful service – for the uplifting of the nation – materially and spiritually".[64]

Class cohesion became an expedient element in consolidating political stability at a time of national crisis, with the major political parties consequently eager to downplay social inequalities and to cement loyalty to the fledgling state. As Fearghal McGarry argues, "the legacy of the Irish Civil War, and the continued relevance of the national question in the interwar period, also militated against a political alignment based on social issues".[65] Labour was subordinated to nationalism, partly because it avoided taking a clear stance on the Civil War and largely because it agreed to toe the line in forming Free State hegemony. There was no place for revolutionism: as Johnson had also famously advised, "one revolution in a generation is enough".[66] That Labour continually spent its force after successful electoral campaigns – right up to its remarkable success in the "Spring tide" of the 1990s – by entering coalitions with centre/right-wing parties, seems almost now a truism of Irish politics. It also illustrates how class issues could be underplayed to form ostensibly irreconcilable right–left alliances.[67] Labour was condemned, it seemed, like Sisyphus, to forever roll its boulder up a hill, only to watch it trundle back down again, and, for the urban working class, which was anyhow largely behind Fianna Fáil, the politics of decolonisation led to a calcification of class conflict. Some dispirited leftists, from a traditionally stagist Marxist perspective, saw a postponement of that conflict as inevitable in a largely agricultural economy. Add to that the lack of leadership afforded by Labour and it is easy to see why the left underachieved. This complicated picture partly explains why the acute class consciousness of 1913 failed to find persistent mainstream political expression, regardless of trade-union strength. While the British working class flexed its muscles in both political and cultural terms, with a frenetic efflorescence of proletarian writing, for example, in the interwar years, the Republic's working class, by contrast, withered, in political, social and cultural terms.[68]

Sublimation and social expression

However, a temptation emerges at this point to overemphasise the impact and significance of political parties and other left-wing movements in the Free State, just as James Connolly's dramatic martyrdom often lends itself to an exaggeration of the influence of his Irish Socialist Republican Party (established 1896) and other socialist, Fabian or social-democratic predecessors prior to the state's foundation. While organisations such as Saor Éire (founded 1931) and the Republican Congress (1934) promised (the latter attracting in excess of 6,000 members) to channel left-wing republican and communist disaffection with the new state – particularly amongst disenchanted members of the IRA – their failure to achieve even a modicum of popular political success is emblematic, mostly, of the sway of insular Catholic values over the working class, of a culture that militated against recognition of obvious class divides.[69] Indeed, it can be argued that the power of Catholicism, aligned with capitalism, inveigling itself strategically into every institution and power block of the new state, was the principal reason why working-class consciousness was sublimated into more moderate forms.

This is perhaps also why a great deal of Dublin's writing of the working class aligns strongly anti-clerical opinions with a broader unease with the social and political trajectory of the state. An atmosphere of fear and zealotry effectively stymied the left. Church-inspired mobs and the St Patrick's Anti-Communist League went about intimidating and harassing socialists during the early 1930s, a precursor to the massive public shows of support for General Franco's fascist regime in Spain during the latter part of the decade, stewarded also by the far-right Irish Christian Front. As Niamh Puirséil remarks, at one point in the 1930s "the communist menace became practically the sole subject of [Catholic church] pastoral and sermon".[70] Again, predictably, the Labour Party and Irish Trade Union Congress remained aloof and largely neutral on the matter of the Spanish Civil War, facilitating by inaction the widespread propaganda of fascist apologists and enabling the establishment of Ireland's own fascist Blueshirt (Army Comrades' Association) movement. As McGarry observes, "the conservative social structure and political climate of interwar Ireland, characterised by militant Catholicism and nationalism, were not conducive to class politics".[71]

This suppression of working-class activism, at a crucial juncture in colonial and post-colonial history, emerges as an ongoing theme in the writing with which this book engages. The poet, playwright and sculptor James McKenna forges a link between poverty, politics and religion, in his sardonic 1970s poem, "Up Dev", castigating the Fianna Fáil leader (Éamon de Valera) for his theocratic leanings. So much literature of the working class harks back to the failures of the "revolution" of 1916–23 in this way. It is the nexus of religion and politics that McKenna implicitly holds responsible for the economic torpor:

> Tell me old dancer of Boland's Mill
> How did your army disperse
> And your car reverse on autonomy hill
> And a dream in religion immerse.

De Valera, McKenna charged, "lost [his] spade" – his commitment to industry, his closeness to the worker, to proletarian development – "in religion's chaff".[72] Policies popular with the Catholic Church – such as the banning of contraceptives in 1935 – increased Fianna Fáil's hegemonic sway (while creating insupportable burdens for many working-class families), and de Valera clearly believed that the function of the Catholic Church and that of the government were mutually reinforcing – "inculcating in the people that respect for lawful authority without which the continuance in their country of a Christian church and a Christian state would soon become impossible".[73] Implicit in this adjuration, of course, is a subtle threat: if you don't scratch our back, we can't scratch yours.

From the 1920s, "clergy now had the time, energy, and inclination to address, in a more formal and deliberate way, the morals, interests, and politics of working people", as Marilyn Silverman notes of this period of zealous religious activism.[74] The working class was suspended uneasily between the pressing reality of its material conditions and the demanding injunctions of its metaphysical beliefs:

> Indeed, the actions and views of the hierarchy, parish priests, and nuns divided families even as they proclaimed the sanctity of domesticity. They exacerbated class divisions even as they preached the unity of society. They divided individual psyches as labouring people had to reconcile their material experiences with their religious obligations. Finally, they divided workers as a class by fomenting and formalizing a contradiction between labour activism and godliness.[75]

Those who disagreed with the status quo were "essentialised", regardless of their political hue, under the habitual terms of Catholic contempt, as "auxiliaries of communism".[76] As Allen notes, the "culmination of this alliance" was the 1937 Constitution, in which divorce was banned, women were consigned to the home, private property was "deemed a 'natural right'", and "the most holy trinity" was invoked as the source of legal authority.[77]

The advent of the Second World War further bolstered this conservative state hegemony, with the frenzied clash of world powers – and the twin threats of Churchill and Hitler – inducing a fearful support for the nation-state amidst the horror beyond its borders. Furthermore, de Valera's economic policy of self-sufficiency had a logic to it in the changed circumstances, while international trade remained crippled. Tom Garvin also points to the cultural milieu: a "reinforced Victorian thinking" accompanied the "reversion to a Victorian horse-and-cart economy", which "entailed something of a cultural reversion as well".[78] Urban Ireland was again the poor relation, and Fianna Fáil again identified opportunities amidst the chaos, intensifying its attacks on communism as a means of stemming reinvigorated support for the Labour Party, following an upturn in trade-union activism during the early 1940s. At the start of this decade, all "foreign ideologies" – as evidenced by the contemporary butchery of millions – were to be feared, while the "neutral" Irish Catholic state, enjoying a measure of relative stability, could easily be portrayed as (and in the circumstances was) a benign alternative.

While after the war the rapid economic growth of formerly devastated European states provided a significant counterpoint to this logic – as Ireland suffered spiralling emigration and economic decline – the nominal left failed to recover or learn from the seminal failures of the 1920s and 1930s. This was despite the fact, for instance, that at the end of the war, as one Irish study showed, of the 10,500 Dublin families surveyed, 55 per cent were below the suggested minimum living wage; just two years earlier, another study had claimed that 71 per cent of children in working-class Dublin lived in homes which couldn't provide them with an adequate diet.[79] Conditions worsened in the 1950s, when Dublin's housing crisis meant that "accommodation was in short supply and families had to take whatever they could get, even if it meant living in rat-infested basements".[80] A 1949 newspaper reporter in the city's slums found "36 persons in a rat pit".[81] Hunger and squalor were at crisis proportions, with many children forced out of education, seeking to support their families from an early age. But while Britain was embracing the welfare state – its working class demanding a pay-off after years of war – Irish Labour's (and the unions' leaders') reticence about supporting Noel Browne during the Mother and Child Scheme controversy exemplifies just how much this movement was in thrall to, or in fear of, conservative Catholic values – and oblivious to, or afraid to broach, the desperate predicament of the working class. As Emmet O'Connor has put it, "the great puzzle of Irish history is the contrast between a relatively strong trade union movement and a weak political left".[82] But it might be argued that the great puzzle is how this left survived at all.

Justifiable frustration with the left in Ireland is indeed another facet of the writing I have explored. The irony of union politics cultivating division and disenchantment in working-class life is a theme for many writers, such as Robert Collis, in *Marrowbone Lane* (1943), with his criticism of the closed-shop mentality of sectional interest unions that "won't allow an apprentice unless his father's in the same trade".[83] Half a century later, Jimmy Murphy's *Brothers of the Brush* (1995) articulates a depressing commentary on phoney class solidarity, when one supposedly staunch trade unionist slyly manipulates a strike to get a workplace promotion over another. In Dermot Bolger's *Night Shift* (1985), labour activism again culminates in a depressing affirmation of internecine destructiveness, when a factory worker is almost killed in an "accident" contrived by disgruntled fellow workers targeting an alleged "scab" (strike-breaker); Donal, Bolger's protagonist, wonders at "the men who for all their comradeship had done this".[84] Such cynicism about political activity is also evident in Jim Sheridan's *Mobile Homes* (1976), when the decision of residents of a Dublin caravan site to band together for better services ironically also illuminates the cracks in working-class solidarity. Their attempt to gain control of the site fails because some residents refuse to support the campaign, one of them, Mrs Ogilby, betraying a marked disdain for anyone interested in fighting for workers' rights: "That's the trouble with you, you don't want to pay your way. Like the fellows with the beards refusing to pay the bus fare on their way to the labour exchange."[85] James Plunkett illustrates the dispiriting transformation of working-class political activism since 1913, in his 1977 short story "The Plain People". Tonman, a trade-union employee, "had known other days" in his union career, "when tough words and reckless courage were all that were required of a negotiator". By now he is reduced to "writing and telephoning, points of order and terms of reference".[86] Tumult has turned to torpor, and "trade unionism [...] is all a bureaucracy, nowadays", having adopted "the mode and outlook of the capitalist class".[87] His pessimism is a common expression of negative class consciousness in the work surveyed here – the consciousness that the class struggle has failed to manifest itself in the manner that the workers of 1913 might have envisaged.

An "urban subculture"

While it is often in terms of their devastation that Dublin's working-class communities are represented over the past century of writing, the city's class consciousness has in part intensified through isolation, punctuated by periods of frenetic activity like the 1913 Lockout, the Unemployed Protest Committee's campaign of the 1950s or the anti-drugs activism of the 1980s and 1990s. From the mid-century the visibility of this culture can in fact be seen to have grown. Abandonment of protectionism in the late 1960s breathed a new vitality into social and economic relationships across the country, and Charles McCarthy would characterise this period as a "decade of upheaval" in trade unionism.[88] While huge numbers of working days were lost to industrial disputes in 1961, 1964, 1965, 1966 and 1969, the more important underlying factor here was the changing *nature* of the economy, as it was transformed into an increasingly open, free-trading and industrialised financial system.[89] Seán O'Casey's urban proletariat was still there, with its distinctive "urban subculture":

> In particular, Dublin is its home; and to a lesser extent Cork. In Dublin it has inherited from its rich history a conviction of superiority, a conviction that one mile west of Inchicore, the bog begins. This is the subculture of the 1913 strike, of the O'Casey plays, and of the Irish trade union movement [...] is a tradition which has little place in our national histories, although there are few Irishmen who are not aware of it.[90]

Isolated from "the bog", this Ireland was "quite different from the Anglican – and the Gaelic" Irelands, and Alexander Humphries noted in 1966 that "the sense of class remain[ed] strong among Dubliners" who exhibited a "strong, continuing class consciousness".[91]

Joined by and incorporating displaced rural dwellers, Dublin's working class grew in voice and numerical strength.[92] Terence Brown comments that it was in the 1960s that the Republic became truly alive to the debates on class issues and social conditions that had long preoccupied the rest of modern Europe.[93] Following on recommendations made in the government's *Investment in Education* report of 1965, the 1967–8 free post-primary education scheme facilitated the attendance of poorer children at secondary schools. This was a key enabler for proletarians and is identified by poet Paula Meehan as responsible for bringing her (and her class) into contact with a formerly alien sphere of educational endeavour.[94] Supposed cultural certainties were also eroding, especially in urban Ireland. Garvin cites the late 1960s as a period from which there was "a steady increase in the post-Catholic and 'à la carte' Catholic segments of the population"; an increase, he adds, which followed a "class and urban-rural divide".[95] Indeed, in the 1970s, for the first time, more Irish people were living in cities and towns than in the countryside, and fewer people were working in rural occupations, such as farming and fisheries.[96] Many more were now engaged in electronics, engineering, the professions and office work, and the Irish population was increasingly concentrated in its capital.[97] Michel Peillon observed that the "rapid urbanisation which [had] engulfed" Dublin with a pace of "almost crisis proportions" made it less of a "Pale" on the periphery of the rustic and revered culture of the Gaelic peasantry, than a social, economic and cultural centre in which formerly dominant, conservative cultural norms were increasingly outmoded.[98]

Upwardly mobile?

While the 1960s engendered a renewed vitality in the city in demographic terms, the history of the working-class community it contains is best understood in terms of actual levels of class cohesion (or mobility) and the inequalities that have maintained (or mitigated) it. By the 1970s, 70 per cent of workers were wage-earners, compared with 48 per cent in 1926. Nonetheless, considerable poverty endured, with less than half of skilled manual and one-third of semi-skilled and unskilled households being owner-occupiers by 1973.[99] Moreover, while big business was beginning to thrive from the 1960s – and while this would suggest that conditions were emerging for increased social mobility – working-class people largely remained working class.

By the mid-1980s, nearly 75 per cent of working males were employed in businesses not owned by their respective families, and skilled manual occupations had increased along with the growth in managerial and white-collar jobs, but the Republic's proletariat still strangely suffered from chronically low levels of upward social mobility. Even in the late 1980s, 70 per cent of working-class men in the state were themselves the children of working-class men, and "in comparison with other Western European countries, the Irish figure for immobility [was] comparatively high".[100] Indeed, with 300,000 unemployed in the Republic by 1988, mobility was often downward in Dublin's most impoverished communities, where unemployment rates sometimes exceeded 80 per cent of the working-age population. Class inequality in Ireland since the middle of the twentieth century has remained gaping. Despite the considerable adjustment that "external dependent industrialisation" entailed, it seems that the prospects of mobility for (and the economic power of) working-class Dubliners actually *diminished* during this period.[101]

This paradox may be partially explained by the diverse quality of the industrialisation. While, again, in nearby Britain, the "enclave character" of major industry – mass local employment in coalmines or super-factories, for instance – led to an intensification of class solidarity and political activity, in Ireland a "very different structure" still prevailed.[102] Many branch plants in the Republic at this time employed small numbers of maintenance craftsmen and relatively large numbers of semi-skilled employees, but because of the specified nature of the work in such companies, "the experience of work [was] unlikely to militate in favour of a strong working-class identity – least of all the macho male type typified by the early 20th century Clydeside or South Wales".[103] This macho male type was perhaps akin to that associated with the brawny Dublin docker, but the port industries that employed Dublin's radicalised inner-city labourers were, by the 1960s, facing dramatic decline.

New industries were often, curiously, located away from the larger population centres that had an established trade-union tradition and that might have harnessed the new opportunities in different ways. Surprisingly, by 1974 "less than a quarter of new manufacturing employment was in the Eastern Region, although this contained nearly half of existing such employment".[104] In the period from 1973 to 1977, when manufacturing employment rose by 60 per cent in the western region, it actually *dropped* by 10 per cent in the east.[105] In 1980, James Wickham argued that, despite the increase in the relative size of the working class in previous decades, the growth of jobs dependent on large multinational organisations had actually further reduced the economic influence of that class.[106] The old industries, such as metal foundries, which had expanded to meet domestic needs during the state's protracted period of protectionism, were now also in decline. Plants producing items such as footwear or motor parts, with their "strong trade-union organisation [and] transferability of skills between plants" were "almost completely destroyed".[107] Dublin was experiencing a period of "deindustrialisation" – despite what is largely remembered as an era of *national* industrial (and local population) growth. Expansion in white-collar jobs and occupations traditionally held by women was availed of in the main by displaced rural dwellers, something that no doubt amplified the traditional rural–urban, as well as class, antipathies. Along with the construction of council housing estates and flats, which created ghettos of unemployment and disadvantage throughout the city – with little in terms of amenities and infrastructure – the decline in traditional working opportunities compounded the alienation of working-class Dublin in economic and social terms.

A further irony in all this is that despite widespread contemporary assumptions that the Republic has become a more meritocratic, classless society in recent decades, the rigidity of the class structure continues to confound overall economic indicators. The fallout from the Celtic Tiger's blistering demise remains to be comprehensively charted in terms of class mobility, though all indicators are that Ireland's current "social crisis" will result in a calcification of class boundaries.[108] As recently as 2007, Christopher T. Whelan and Richard Layte showed how misleading surface data can be. On the one hand, the number of Irish people in professional and managerial jobs "has grown substantially since the 1970s", "this trend has intensified over the past decade," and "the proportion of the population in low-skilled occupations has fallen steadily".[109] On the other, "those at the top of the class structure have enjoyed considerable success in maintaining an unfair advantage".[110] Where children from different social classes achieve what is ostensibly the same level of education, "working-class children are still less likely to attain the better occupational position than their middle-class peers".[111] Additionally, whereas in "absolute" terms social mobility has increased, "the offspring of working-class groups" are still "relatively disadvantaged in comparison to the offspring of middle-class groups"; the children of farmers and white-collar workers are on the move, but not so the children of the lower socio-economic strata.[112]

In 1982, Peillon noted how class lines were closely marshalled in Ireland by sclerotic social norms: few people from other classes married into the working class; office workers on low wages, despite their "transitional position", refused to recognise their shared interests within working-class people; social mobility for working-class children could be measured "over very short distances".[113] But despite the rapid economic changes of the past number of decades, aspects of this rigid inequality have endured. In the Celtic Tiger era, "even where working-class children [had] an identical IQ and educational qualifications to middle-class children, they [were] still less likely to make it into the most advantaged occupations and social classes" – in fact amounting to "a reduction in [...] equality over time".[114] Things were getting better, for some, but slowly, and the rhetoric of "modernisation", which assumes a corollary between overall economic growth and social mobility across classes, rings hollow in the light of empirical data. In 2002, Peadar Kirby observed that

> young people whose parents are unemployed or from unskilled manual groups tend to experience disproportionate levels of unemployment. The result can be clearly identified in the concentration of pockets of high unemployment and severe social problems in a number of urban centres, even at the height of Ireland's "Celtic Tiger" phase.[115]

Whether this social inequality that has persisted in the years of the boom will intensify in the years of the bust remains to be seen in the longer term, but all indicators, such as high, long-term unemployment, the return of emigration and reductions in wages across the board, suggest that class divides are widening, that the country's economic difficulties are "likely to lead to growing inequality".[116] Moreover, the endurance of stubbornly rigid social inequality and strikingly limited class mobility in Ireland, throughout the past century, suggest that class culture has a potent, if frequently underplayed, purchase on Irish life.

Education, the academe, culture and class

It is apparent nonetheless that working-class concerns have remained out of sight in terms of many areas of academic study in Ireland. Notwithstanding the work of sociologists cited above, class appears relatively infrequently as a topic of serious scholarship. As Wickham argued, and as I maintain here, "Labour history can no longer be equated solely with the history of the trade unions", and "traditions and subcultures must be studied seriously and not plucked out of thin air and used to explain everything else".[117] Kevin C. Kearns's 1990s social histories broke new ground in this regard.

His publication of *Dublin Street Life and Lore: An Oral History* (1991), *Dublin Tenement Life: An Oral History* (1994) and *Dublin Voices: An Oral Folk History* (1998) has provided an important resource. The richness and vitality of social and cultural life in working-class Dublin is deftly captured through oral testimonies that contribute significantly to the historical body of work on proletarian Ireland. But, as Lane and O'Connor remind us, in a 2001 appeal for research on "the 'everyday life' of workers", there was (and is) still a relative paucity of writing on "how and why were particular cultural practices constructed and deconstructed" in working life; "how did they spend their non-working hours"?[118]

A partial explanation for this absence is perhaps the classed nature of the Irish education system. Wickham argues generally that,

> if capitalism is a structure of economic domination, then it is also one of cultural domination. In any capitalist country, working class children "learn" in school that they are not suited to anything else but manual work – their values, their lifestyle, their very language, are not proper.

Furthermore, in such environments the lesson is "redefined by those on the receiving end": "manual labour for example becomes the only work that is really (men's) work".[119] But such cultural inequality runs far deeper than the inculcation of predilections around work. At the beginning of the 1960s, the children of the Irish working class were "less involved in post-primary education than children from any other social category".[120] And according to Patrick Clancy, in his analysis of school leavers in the early 1990s, parental backgrounds still had a pronounced impact on educational attainment over the last decade of the twentieth century. Of the 22 per cent of school leavers who left without a Leaving Certificate in the late 1990s, 47 per cent were from unskilled manual backgrounds, whereas only 3 per cent came from higher professional families. While over half of the children from this latter social stratum left school with more than five honours grades in the Leaving Certificate, only 4 per cent from the former did the same.[121]

Similar disparities were identified in terms of entrants to higher education, and despite significant advances since the early 1990s the gap is still particularly glaring in Ireland's most prestigious universities, fed by a massively disproportionate percentage of students from state-assisted, fee-paying schools.[122] While noteworthy advances in mainstream state education have occurred since the 1960s – when the *Investment in Education* (1966) report prompted a refocusing of educational provision on perceived economic and technological needs – as Denis O'Sullivan notes, "equality in the effects or outcomes of schooling was never a serious concern" for policy-makers. Economic expediencies often overshadowed "limitations and problems associated with the access dimension" of the system, leaving this concern "trivialised or obscured".[123] In Dublin, this inequality is intensified in ghettos of low educational attainment, such as Clondalkin, a working-class suburb in which only 4.5 per cent of children progress to third-level education – as compared to affluent Rathgar, where the respective figure is 54 per cent.[124] Joan Hanafin and Anne Lynch show that "social-class origins remain the greatest predictor of academic school success and failure" and of "future location in the labour market".[125]

Regarding curriculum issues, Honor Fagan additionally suggests that the failure of the Irish educational system to reflect the realities of students' lives is at the heart of broader class inequalities. Working-class experience is elided by schools' characteristic preoccupations, early school leavers feel. For example, "the curriculum and examinations are completely geared toward white-collar work. Thus the curriculum is divorced from the reality of working young people."[126] While research has not begun to scratch beneath the surface of how, for instance, the choice of literary works in school examination programmes is inflected with class and social biases, it is obvious at university level that Irish working-class culture has failed to be acknowledged in any significant, proportionate way.[127] Share et al. use Pierre Bourdieu's theory of cultural capital to hypothesise the effects of all this inequality on working-class children, on how they behave and on how they perceive the society in which they live, and education is continually linked with feelings of shame, inadequacy and alienation in the literature of working-class Dublin.[128] Persistent inequalities in educational attainment partially explain why Ireland has yet to produce its own Raymond Williams, Richard Hoggart or Terry Eagleton, and why, at third level, the working class remains underrepresented in terms of both participation and the curriculum.

In Britain, by contrast, working-class culture has received considerable (if not enough) attention in the academe, with many courses on proletarian literature and cultural studies, and the formal recognition of centres such as the Working Class Movement Library in Manchester, which holds thousands of books and pamphlets pertaining to working-class life (although Birmingham University's much respected Centre for Contemporary Cultural Studies was controversially closed in 2002). Munt notes that "Cultural Studies was a field formed by social class", being heavily influenced by Richard Hoggart, Raymond Williams and other leftist theorists such as Stuart Hall.[129] With the notable exceptions of the foundation of the Irish Labour History Society in 1973 and the Irish Labour History Museum in 1990, the Irish Republic has failed to value its working class in similar terms. As Lloyd writes, "we still have relatively few narrative accounts of Irish radicalism and even fewer that engage 'history from below'".[130] Campaigners such as Terry Fagan – who has worked for decades to establish a cultural centre for the study of inner-city history – have sadly made little material progress in their efforts to bring the celebration of that life onto an academic or state-funded footing.[131] Evidently, this lack of support for working-class culture has its consequences. As Ken Worpole put the case in Britain:

> The fragmentation of working class historical and cultural consciousness now fiercely debated [...] is not exactly surprising given the fragmentation and lack of concern for the material artefacts of that consciousness, that is to say the photographs, short stories, novels, autobiographies, histories produced by that historical class culture which were allowed to disappear through neglect [...] Such processes were not actively resisted, yet people are surprised that "consciousness" has become "discontinuous."[132]

How much more is this disregard the case in Ireland? Writers such as Brendan Behan, James McKenna, Paul Smith and Lee Dunne would all complain of the failure of governmental arts funding and institutional practices to support their work.[133] Indeed, the Irish government is often more likely to fund a sense of identity where there is no one to identify with it: the Burren gets a visitor centre, Ballybough gets short shrift.[134]

"A pole of differentiation"

But working-class cultural production, like its class consciousness, has endured in part as a response to outside influences. With the increasing and well-documented representation of working-class culture in British television, literature and media from the mid-century onwards, Dubliners took many of their cultural cues in music, sport and popular culture from across the water, as James McKenna was keen to emphasise in *The Scatterin'* (1959), or as Dermot Bolger stressed much later in *The Journey Home* (1990). In both works, young working-class Dubliners find themselves more at home in British than in Irish life. British television, for example, embraced working-class culture from early on, but as Helena Sheehan notes of the period from 1962 to 1987 in Ireland, the standard fare of Raidió Teilifís Éireann (RTÉ), which played a momentous part in shaping Irish identities from the 1960s onwards, was curiously oblivious to working-class, city life: "RTÉ had failed to come to terms with the real texture of contemporary urban life and particularly with its cutting edge [...] It had been most remiss with respect to its representation of working class life and strikingly negligent in relation to the most socially conscious and culturally advanced elements of urban life."[135]

As Peillon argued, the identification that Irish youths found in British culture was partly due to "a long tradition of emigration [that] created many close links", and a sense that the rural identity purveyed by domestic culture was out of sync with Ireland's "stark class contrasts, which reveal themselves not only in differences of status but also in differences of behaviour".[136] These differences of behaviour expressed themselves in "a specific lifestyle" that was radically averse to the norms of the Irish state: "the particularity of the working class appears from whatever aspect one studies it, and it asserts itself *as a pole of differentiation in Irish society*".[137] Terry Eagleton identifies such a phenomenon in British history, in the "counter-public sphere" character of working-class culture.[138] According to Peillon's research, by the 1980s working-class people were more open to contraception and less stifled by religious practices, and, while the size and economic character of poorer areas of working-class Dublin had changed significantly since O'Casey's 1920s writing, its social and cultural character had, again, endured:

> It would require few changes to bring O'Casey's portrait up to date: this social group still exists almost unchanged, and perhaps its persistence explains in part the fascination it continues to exert. But it exists very much on the periphery of Irish society and remains marginal in every sense of the word, situated on the edge of a stable society, and a constant source of embarrassment.[139]

Indeed, this "embarrassment" poured out onto the streets once again in the 1980s and 1990s, much to the chagrin of many media and establishment figures, when the Concerned Parents Against Drugs (CPAD) movement, "the largest working-class movement in Dublin since the 1913 Lockout", attempted to rid communities of the devastation of heroin dealing.[140] But, just as left-wing movements had been attacked as dangerous and destabilising in the 1910s and 1930s, the CPAD was treated by many in power as a threat to the very stability of the state. Those who dared, in modern times, to hurl the little streets upon the great, found about as much sympathy from the Irish middle class as they did seven decades earlier. This precisely illustrates Peillon's point about the "persistence" in Dublin's working class of a "marginal" "pole of differentiation", both as a recurrent, if often disorganised, source of radical activity in itself and as an object of continual disdain and embarrassment for the well-off.

Class, education and art

In the literature I explore in this book, classed behavioural and social differences are contextualised within this "embarrassed" ostracism of the working class. Official disdain for working-class people often manifests in encounters between their children and the state apparatus, particularly in terms of repressive educational machinery in which working-class concerns have been eschewed. As Catherine Dunne's carpenter, Farrell, recalls of his experience of education in inner-city Dublin in the 1960s and 1970s, "I hated school then. Brothers worrying about the margins in your copies when you hadn't even had a breakfast."[141] In *11 Emerald Street* (2005), Hugh O'Donnell's narrator recounts how his father had wanted to become a teacher in childhood until one violent encounter with a Christian Brother changed his mind. For his son also, his school days "certainly weren't the happiest days of my life."[142] In his similarly titled novel, *Emerald Square* (1987), Lar Redmond recalled the ritualised violence of school life: "One sum wrong – one stroke. Six sums wrong – six strokes. Not one exercise attempted – eight strokes. It was the same for algebra and geometry. I rarely escaped with less than six."[143] His educational experience vacillates between this early cruelty and the later lacklustre performance of vocational education: when Lar manages to secure his place on an architectural drawing course in Bolton Street Technical School (one of the vocational institutions in which many working-class men attained qualifications and trades) the quality of the education is poor. "No one cared whether you learned or not. One was [now] never corrected or caned."[144] The inequality of Ireland's two-tier education system was excoriated in Patrick Gilligan's controversial RTÉ drama series, *The Spike* (1978), which centred on the activities of staff and students in a Dublin vocational school of the same name. The Chairman of the Spike's Board of Management, Matt Magnier, is a wealthy businessman who envisions a very class-specific role for vocational schools:

> We don't like new ideas and we don't like problems [...] The function of the Spike is a containing one – you should know that. Its job is to contain the riff-raff of the town, while the other schools get on with educating the captains and the kings. Mix the two together and you get trouble.[145]

Thomas Kinsella expresses the feelings of such "riff-raff" confined by state education in his poem, "Model School, Inchicore", by narrowing the lines following a stanza that recalls the ritual of religious instruction. The child Kinsella feels that "the taste / of ink off / the nib shrank your / mouth".[146] His symbolism and form evoke the experience of being silenced by (the "ink" of) educational texts, and by extension, by the epistemic power of the system. Roddy Doyle's Paula Spencer also recalls being made feel "that I wasn't good at all" in secondary school, by teachers who "were all the same, cunts. Cunts. I hated them".[147] Paula's (mis-)education falls under a singular rubric of experience, "finding out that [she] was stupid", teaching her to be "rough" and "think dirty": "I had to fight. I had to be hard."[148] Her negative behaviour in class relates to her class of school, Doyle emphasises: "I wouldn't have done it if I'd gone to the Holy Rosary."[149] In his novel *A Walk in Alien Corn* (1990), Redmond again speaks of feeling "sunk" and "slotted for life" without a Leaving Certificate: "I was a blue collar worker, branded forever, as surely as an Indian Untouchable."[150] Unlike his younger brothers and sisters – who get the benefit of better schooling, after his father comes into wealth – Lar is restricted by his relative poverty in youth. The divide between siblings is emblematic of a wider class divide – a divide that is inextricable, for Redmond, from the general hypocrisy of the state. When he ponders on the blatant double standards of a publican who is a member of the temperance organisation "The Sacred Thirst", Lar considers how such glaring inconsistencies are integral to Irish life. The publican, "who hated drink" can yet "earn a comfortable living dishing it out" to labourers who can ill afford it, but his duplicity is "no worse than [that of] the clergy, Catholic and Protestant alike, who ran posh boarding schools for the sons and daughters of the rich, and belted the bejaysus out of the poor".[151] Working-class children, these works imply, have learned to recognise their inferiority in Irish society through the harshness and inferior quality of their education; this is precisely what the sociologists have found.

These inequalities can be made a virtue of by the subaltern class, and this tendency can act also to exclude that class from learning and art. If working-class experience is denigrated by formal education, then formal education, and its connotations, are often denigrated by the working class – part of the *othering* process by which classes distinguish themselves from other classes, "attributing negative properties", "in contrast to which their own identity is defined as normal and good", as Andrew Sayer puts it.[152] Redmond makes the point again. His largely autobiographical character loves literature and feels that in learning he is rebelling against all that the state has deprived him of: "I was a square peg in a round hole, born on the wrong side of the tracks [...] I was in the same league as Jack London and Charles Dickens, Emile Zola, and many other working class writers who had had to study, spare time, to appease the yearning inside them to express themselves." But although evidently inspired by this sense of following in hallowed proletarian tradition, Lar's yearning for knowledge is something he must hide from his peers. Education is the preserve of other classes, something his mates would frown upon: "I was trying to step outside my class, and so I belonged nowhere. I had two faces, one for the companions I found myself among, and then the secret one, the secret me, who would have loved to have been with the likes of Charles Lamb and his companions, and 'You, my darlings, my midnight Folios!' "[153]

Conflicted feelings such as these recall the depictions of indeterminate, educated working-class characters in British writing: in Kingsley Amis' *Lucky Jim* (1954), Raymond Williams' *Border Country* (1960) and *Second Generation* (1964), David Storey's *Pasmore* (1972), James Kelman's *A Disaffection* (1989), or as characterised by Richard Hoggart's "scholarship boy", cast adrift on the bourgeois terrain of academia.[154] However, in contrast with these narratives about the strains of British class mobility, Lar and other working-class Dubliners who harbour educational aspirations largely stay *within* their class, regardless of such yearnings.[155] The suffocating toughness of Lar's Liberties upbringing recurs in his thoughts throughout the novel – at times something to be proud of, at other times something to lament, but always he feels it has excluded him from the bourgeois world. Art is something effete and emasculating, something to conceal.

In Jim Sheridan's *Mobile Homes* (1976), Shea, a painter, experiences a similar sense of classed cultural anxiety. His profession makes him "another bleedin' headcase", a "waster" and a "bleedin' dosser", and an accidental attack he suffers at the hands of local vigilantes is symbolic of the internecine destructiveness of working-class life.[156] James McKenna was also deeply concerned with this classed aversion to art, which, he believed, was exacerbated by the location of cultural institutions and amenities outside of working-class areas – something that famously prompted him to stand for election in 1970s Ballyfermot with (hilariously) incongruous pictures of Grecian urns on his placards. "People feel the impulse not their own," one of his poems complained: "The Dance of Art – sounds like a dirty word."[157]

Such proletarian distaste for genres perceived as the preserve of an emasculated bourgeois domain might be enlisted to explain the relative lack of poetry in working-class life. To invoke Ellen Wilkinson's *Clash* again, there is a sense that such airy-fairy forms are taboo, for working-class *men* at least:

> Some of the miners were well read in economics and history, but poetry would have seemed too grim a mockery in the mining towns. The young souls who might be thrilled by it had to keep this a dark secret like some fearful vice, unless they could stand endless chaff.[158]

But in working-class Dublin, the long ballad tradition in particular is something to be proud of – or was at least before mass culture sent it to the margins. Articulating the discourse of prevailing political conditions in poetry and song, the ballad was part of a communal, folkloric culture. As James Stephens put it, "where but in Dublin will you meet the author of a ballad in a thousand limericks".[159] In his study of Irish street ballads and rebel songs, Georges Denis Zimmermann notes how the ballad was ideally suited to social and political commentary from people with limited educational attainment, acting as "a running commentary on Irish life seen 'from below'".[160] Ballads, a form of "subliterature", could transcend the pervasive problem of limited educational attainment, being "within reach of the virtually illiterate".[161] While it would be "ludicrous" to present "the bulk of these texts as poetry", he contends, some can be seen as such, and those that cannot – but which can still be heard in twenty-first century Dublin – surely form their own cultural repository of Dublin life and lore.

Other sources for further analysis in this regard can be found in Patrick Callan's study of O'Casey's political war ballads, John McDonnell's *Songs of Struggle and Protest* (1979), Mary Ashraf's *Political Verse and Song from Britain and Ireland*, Helena Sheehan's compact disk, *Songs of Labour* (1998), The Ballad Corner of the *Irish Socialist* in the 1960s and 1970s, and such individual pieces as Donagh Mac Donagh's "Dublin City, 1913", trade unionist Martin Whelan's "Talk to Me of Freedom" – a song regarding unemployment – and Ewan McColl's lyric on the Dunnes Stores strike of the 1980s, "Ten Young

Women and One Young Man".[162] The persistence of poet Michael J. Moran, popularly known as Zozimus in Dublin legend, suggests a further direction for future scholarly work. Paula Meehan's early poetry in particular explores the political and social alienation of her class, and the poetry of James Connolly, James Stephens, Seán O'Casey, James McKenna, Christy Brown, Dermot Bolger and Thomas Kinsella is inflected, however diversely, with class concerns.[163] I would like to suggest here that, while it is outside the scope of the present study, further scholarly research on working-class Ireland might benefit from assessing these poetry and ballad traditions.

II. Theory and writing the working class

Some explanation is also necessary at this point of theoretical terms and academic sources cited in the coming discussions. Even when critics herald the arrival of this or that working-class writer, they often implicitly fail to grasp exactly what their terminology might mean. There is a danger of speaking about working-class literature as a given, failing to specify exactly what it is. There is also a strange, related irony in becoming a "working-class writer". As Ken Worpole notes, "it is one of the paradoxes of writing – particularly for working-class people":

> The act of trying to represent the culture and geographical community in which the writer has grown up and lived is the first step by which the writer is separated from that life almost irrevocably. At the same time as many people acquire their first typewriter, they also acquire their first suitcase. The two are often connected.[164]

This irony of course questions the very sustainability of the term. If one starts out as a working-class author, when does one stop being one? Does promotion to a wealthier social class imperil the authenticity of one's work in one fell swoop? Additionally, can a writer not be middle class in origin but proletarian in his or her outlook, or *vice versa*? Can a writer from another class not write with authenticity, like the British author Nell Dunn did, of those whose experience is initially alien? Such questions have ever bedevilled those concerned with matters of literature and class.

This book is broadly concerned with writing *about* the working class, regardless of its provenance, rather than what is often a more narrowly defined and divisive concept of an organic "proletarian literature". But such a literature objectively exists, just as the proletariat does, and it is doubtless vital for our present purposes to define what it is and, more broadly, how writing of the working class is understood in this book. George Orwell argued (by no means clearly, as we shall see) that "proletarian writing" is literature that espouses left-wing politics, which seeks to further or to represent the struggle for the betterment of the working class.[165] However, in this study, and for reasons that will become apparent, the term is used to refer to literature that simply represents working-class life from within, regardless of its political standpoint. Writers such as Alan Sillitoe may have declared, from a self-professed "revolutionary" perspective, that "the Left and Right of literature [...] can never meet for compromise", but it would be just another form of glib exclusivism to suggest that only writers explicitly of the left in working-class life were worthy of study as authentically proletarian.[166] As we have already observed, some of Dublin's writing of the working class has indeed expressed grave disillusionment with the political left, and it is arguably just as valid and interesting for doing so. It will be argued over the coming pages that classifying working-class culture too narrowly is a disabling exercise for those who seek to promote it. Yet it will also be suggested that there are distinctive, common elements to working-class aesthetic tastes, which resonate throughout this broad body of writing, establishing common ground on which a thoroughgoing, but not exclusivist, theoretical analysis of literature in working-class life is made possible.

Form, formula and formation

The strictures of various dogmas can often prove incapacitating in discussions of class and cultural production. As Jeremy Hawthorn has argued, these dogmas often emerge from judgemental and condescending theoretical abstractions, whereby "middle-class critics have been rather too fond in recent years of explaining to working-class people how many of their values, aspirations and ideals are 'bourgeois'"; but the tendency goes much deeper than this superficial and irritating posturing, and it stretches back far beyond recent years.[167] Indeed, such attitudes are evident in and emerge from deeply ingrained notions of the relationship between "base" and "superstructure" in Marxist theory so that it is necessary, in dealing with the matter of cultural form and proletarian formation, to recover some of the ideological and political inflections underlying how culture is interpreted by left-minded thinkers. Filtering these concepts for what is truly useful, and what is evidently absurd, before we proceed to an understanding of the basic matter at hand, is a difficult but rewarding task.

Contentious classifications

A remarkable example of how utterly encysted in rickety ideological dogma these issues can become is a discussion, in 1940, between George Orwell and Desmond Hawkins, in which the former virtually declares the death-knell of working-class literature – along with the end of class itself. Hawkins voices concern over the term "proletarian literature", asking Orwell if there really is "such a thing [...] or ever could be". "You would expect it to mean literature written specifically for the proletariat, and read by them," he proffers.[168] Orwell, quite logically, dismisses such a narrow interpretation, arguing that to couch working-class literature thus would be to classify "some of our morning papers" as a form of proletarian writing.[169] He then elaborates his own view on the matter:

> What people mean by it, roughly speaking, is a literature in which the viewpoint of the working class, which is supposed to be completely different from that of the richer classes, gets a hearing. And that, of course, has got mixed up with socialist propaganda. I don't think the people who throw this expression about mean literature written *by* proletarians.[170]

So far, somewhat logical, but while Orwell rightly laments that the issue has "got mixed up with socialist propaganda", he ironically proceeds to ensconce his own argument in the most dogmatic of leftist terms. "The reason why I am doubtful of the whole conception", he opines, "is that I don't believe the proletariat can create an independent literature while they are not the dominant class".[171]

This assertion is a familiar, paternalistic refrain for those who study writing about working-class life, although Orwell's view here is perfectly reasoned in his own terms. It might even be called New Historicist, *avant la lettre*, for its insistence that nothing is free from the discursive reach of dominant social power and that all articulation therefore speaks, irrevocably, from within the ambit of that social power. Orwell at first refuses to see working-class writing as some sort of body of ideological dogma and refuses also to accept that it is "completely different" and "independent" from bourgeois values. However, when Hawkins protests that writers such as James Hanley and D. H. Lawrence represent something "new", "something at any rate that could not quite be said by anyone who had had the ordinary middle-class upbringing", he gets the issue half right; surely there are those who have added enormous value to literature by telling the stories of a class which is traditionally afforded little cultural capital? Surely such an authorial standpoint can be expressed as part of a literature *of* the working class?

While Orwell concedes that "there's no doubt that it was a big step forward when the *facts* of working-class life were first got on paper", his anxiety over what proletarian literature is – or *if* it is – vacillates revealingly throughout the remaining conversation.[172] At one point Orwell speaks timorously of "proletarian writers, or the people who are called proletarian writers". A few breaths later, he speaks with bold certainty about how *"proletarian literature is mainly a literature of revolt"*.[173] A few paragraphs on again, this ephemeral bubble of conviction is duly deflated. While optimistically predicting that working-class writing itself will soon disappear, because the age of revolt in nearly gone – because "capitalism is disappearing" and "we are passing into a classless period" – Orwell restates his rigid and bafflingly inconsistent contention that "so long as the bourgeoisie are the dominant class, literature must be bourgeois". Not content to be consistent for more than a few short breaths, however, he soon obfuscates yet again, conceding, confusingly, the "vitalising effect" of (yes) *"proletarian literature"*.[174] Apart from Orwell's spurious, teleological soothsaying, his befuddled denial, qualification, then reassertion of the central term under discussion is evidence of a lack of clarity in his own thoughts about the matter at hand – with which he yet speaks so authoritatively. Like a certain "ex-parrot" of the *Monty Python* variety, proletarian literature is dead, or is it just resting?

The conversation between Orwell and Hawkins is illustrative for a number of reasons: first because it shows to what degree questions of class in literature have given rise to deep-seated anxieties about class and literature themselves and the possibilities of classifying literature, or class, at all. Both men point forward to a crisis in Marxism, whereby the teleological certainty of socialists – that the path of capitalism leads *inexorably* to communism – has become, for many, an object of derision. The Orwell–Hawkins discussion is also salutary because it shows how indulging in the esoteric causality of political dogma can lead to a *cul de sac* of redundant conclusions.[175] But positively, and most importantly, from Orwell and Hawkins' wavering, meandering discussion, some ideas can be gleaned that might even now give a concrete expression to the genre of proletarian literature and its complex, disputed theorisation.

Orwell owes his confusingly difficult concepts of working-class literature to equally dogmatic and contradictory antecedents, the quintessence of which may be found in Leon Trotsky. In a study entitled *Literature and Revolution* (1923), Trotsky espouses a view of what proletarian literature is, should or could be, which sustains remarkable resemblances to Orwell's later hypotheses. Trotsky too canvasses a stagist notion of history in support of his formulations, and for him politics and culture are also separate, hierarchised realms, with the former taking natural precedence over the latter. Asking, rhetorically, "Can the proletariat in this time create a new culture?", Trotsky first prefaces his discussion with a typically Soviet caveat, that "the energy of the proletariat itself will be spent mainly in conquering power" – not, it should be inferred, through cultural (as he understands it) endeavours.[176] As the "non-possessing class", the proletariat subsists under a "bourgeois system", he elaborates, and, like Orwell, Trotsky seems to believe that this system is all-encompassing and ineluctable, refusing the proletariat "access to culture".[177] We are again plunged into depressingly fatalist territory as far as working-class counter-culture is concerned, for "all science, in greater or lesser degree, *unquestioningly* reflects the tendencies of the ruling class"; all science it may be noted, apart from that of blissfully transcendent adepts – "the upper stories" – such as himself.[178]

Thus, for Trotsky, culture is inevitably a secondary, supplementary area of activity, entirely removed from the political realm. For the worker, it is something to be put off for a future time:

> The proletariat, however, will reach its highest tension and the fullest manifestation of its class character during this revolutionary period and

it will be within such narrow limits that the possibility of planful, cultural reconstruction will be confined.[179]

Like Orwell, Trotsky believed that the working class would "free itself from its class characteristics" under revolutionary circumstances, thus enabling an entirely new dispensation in politics, culture and society; but Trotsky goes further than his later fellow-traveller.[180]

For Stalin's great nemesis, the (inevitable) victory of the proletariat will be a pyrrhic one of sorts, for once it has achieved a classless society, it will, by definition, "cease to be a proletariat".[181] In Trotsky's view, this necessarily leads to a syllogism of profound, futile finality for proletarian culture. As the objective of the politicised working class is an equal society, "in the degree to which it is successful it will weaken the class character of the proletariat and in this way it will wipe out the basis of a proletarian culture".[182] The proletariat writes its own epitaph in giving birth to its own emancipation, leaving very little time in the present or future for proletarian cultural endeavours. For working-class writers, the message is stark: take up your red flag and put down your pen. And for all classes the message is subtly menacing: in Trotsky's envisaged "completely harmonious system of knowledge and of art", where is the room for deviation, diversity or dissent?

Trotsky, it must be admitted, lends some recognition to the literature that had emerged from the Russian working class – with varying degrees of approval and disregard – but in doing so he mirrors Orwell's curious hypocrisy, assessing, albeit tenuously, the validity of something he does not nominally believe to exist. First, his confidence in the pervasive nature of bourgeois culture seems to slip. "Culture," he asserts, is "the organic sum of knowledge and capacity which characterises the entire society" – with a hasty qualification – *"or at least its ruling class"*.[183] Then, when he notes that "we have the literary works of talented and gifted proletarians", Trotsky is quick again to qualify that "that is not proletarian literature". But there is another awkward concession: "however, they may prove to be some of its springs".[184] À la Orwell's conceptual acrobatics, Trotsky then casually employs the term "proletarian poetry" when assessing the work of contemporaries some lines later.[185] It seems, despite the oppression of bourgeois dominance, and the befuddled conjecture of socialist dogma, working-class literature, in practice, concept and name, keeps winding its way past the censors and commissars.

There is a spurious division between politics and culture to be observed in Trotsky's terms: while the "proletariat has its political culture [...] it has no artistic culture"; thus, in a capitalist society, it is possible to be *politically* proletarian but not *culturally* so. This is the antithesis of a contemporary, Antonio Gramsci's advice, that "just as [the working class] has thought to organise itself politically and economically, it should also think about organising itself culturally"; indeed, "the mere fact that workers raise these questions and attempt to answer them means that the elements of an original proletarian civilisation already exist, that there are already proletarian forces of production of cultural values".[186] Trotsky allows (more confusingly again), in a mainly negative commentary on the literature of the proletarian Kuznitsa and Proletkult groups, that the work of Demyan Biedny is "proletarian and popular literature".[187] But this is while still maintaining that the "works of talented and gifted proletarians" is "not proletarian literature".[188] Like the parabolic doubting Thomas, he has seen working-class culture, has fingered its wounds and has spoken to its spectral presence, but Trotsky still refuses to believe it is actually there.

Misreading Marx

Beyond the comic value in all of this floundering dancing of angels on heads of pins, there is the more serious and lasting impact of negative theories of proletarian culture in socialist thinking. It would be easy to dismiss Trotsky's opinions on the matter if they were not so commonly held. Marx and Engels' more measured view in *The German Ideology* (1846), that the "ideas of the ruling class are in every epoch the *ruling ideas*", has been extended and distorted beyond recognition by what Raymond Williams characterised as a tendency to "overstatement" in the cut-and-thrust of Marxist polemics.[189] In particular, this overstatement has related to how the relationship between "base" and "superstructure" has been elaborated in Marxist cultural theory. Marx, in his preface to *A Contribution to the Critique of Political Economy* (1859), expounds that:

> In the social production of their existence, men enter into definite, necessary relations, which are independent of their will, namely, relations of production corresponding to a determinate stage of development of their material forces of production. The totality of these relations of production constitutes the economic structure of society, the real foundation on which there arises a legal and political superstructure and to which there correspond definite forms of social consciousness. [...] *It is not the consciousness of men that determines their being, but on the contrary it is their social being that determines their consciousness.*

If this is one of Marx's most oft-quoted passages, it is also the source of a wellspring of Marxist error. While it might be construed that base (the manner of economic production) and superstructure (the corresponding political and legal organisation that relates to forms of consciousness) are merely conjoined in a mechanical, causal manner for Marx – the base governing the superstructure, both determining consciousness – the father of modern socialism allows for a degree of human agency in this and other writings. While Marx rejects the idealist notion that people's inner worlds determine their outward beings, it is their *collective*, rather than individual consciousness – the consciousness of *"men"* – which is determined by their *collective* social being. This does not, emphatically, preclude individual will, or suggest that we are all automatons. He elaborates:

> It is always necessary to distinguish between the material transformation of the economic conditions of production, which can be determined with the precision of natural science, and the legal, political, religious, artistic or philosophic, in short, ideological forms in which men become conscious of this conflict and fight it out.

Base is an area of mechanical "precision", whereas the superstructure is a field of less knowable "ideological forms", where people "become conscious" of social conflict and take action on "such tasks as [they] are able to solve".[190]

As Williams points out, this relationship is further illuminated by a reading of Marx's earlier *The Eighteenth Brumaire of Louis Napoleon* (1851–2), in which he emphasises the difference between how base-superstructure manifests in "the whole class" and the "individual unit": "The individual unit to whom they flow through tradition and education *may* fancy that they constitute the true reasons for and premises of his conduct."[191] Williams interprets the conception of superstructure as meaning "the whole 'ideology' of the class: its 'form of consciousness'" – thus a collective rather than an individual form of seeing things; something to which individuals "may" in all likelihood subscribe.[192] As if thinking of Trotsky's monochromatic theorisations above, Williams also argues that, "in the transition from Marx to Marxism", the original understanding of base-superstructure became distorted, tending to indicate "relatively enclosed areas of activity". In turn, "these were then correlated either temporally (first material production, then consciousness, then politics and culture) or in effect, forcing the metaphor, spatially (visible and distinguishable 'levels' or 'layers' – politics and culture, then forms of consciousness, and so on down to 'the base')".[193]

Williams points to the irony in this revision of Marx, that "the force of Marx's original criticism had been mainly directed against the *separation* of 'areas' of thought and activity".[194] Marx, after all, had theorised an entire social and economic reality in which humanity and the epochal means of production create history through a *dynamic* and dialectical interplay. In the relationship of mutually constitutive – but by no means mechanically fabricated, entirely separate and causally transparent "areas" – one cannot discount or determine human agency as if it were a mere mathematical process. "Vulgar" or "determinist" Marxism therefore springs from a fundamental misunderstanding of Marx. In his or her effort to refute "reactionary" and "reformist" versions of socialism – and in a desperate dash to swerve past the unforeseen obstacles of real history – the vulgar Marxist doggedly pursues a blueprint which Marx himself never devised.

Williams returns us again to the evidence of Marx's texts. In Marx's original understanding, art in particular is clearly not reducible to the laws that govern economic activity:

> As regards art, it is well known that some of its peaks by no means correspond to the general development of society; nor do they therefore to the material substructure [base], the skeleton as it were of its organization.[195]

Here we find ample room for voluntaristic human agency: art and, by extrapolation, culture, cannot be entirely predicted and prescribed by nonetheless powerful economic influences, just as the individual human's disposition cannot be calculated exactly by recourse to a study of the "skeleton". "Social being", it can be said, "determines" consciousness, in so far as it foments or occludes a *general* consciousness of the *collective* plight of a class and its wider relations; it creates conditions for the dispersal and activation of ideologies, of certain ways of thinking. Humans enter into "definite relations which are indispensable and independent of their will", but implicitly they do have a *will*.[196] Engels was insistent when explaining how this materialist conception of history ought to be understood:

> The *ultimately* determining element in history is the production and reproduction of real life. Neither Marx nor I have ever asserted more than this. Therefore if somebody twists this into saying that the economic factor is the *only* determining one, he is transforming that proposition into a meaningless, abstract, absurd phrase.[197]

Engels would famously declare that "we make our history ourselves, but first of all, under very definite assumptions and conditions," and he added that "history is made in such a way that the final result always arises from conflicts *between individual wills*, of which each in turn has been made what it is by a variety of particular conditions of life [...] innumerable crisscrossing forces."[198] Social being – seamlessly and symbiotically linked with the base – inevitably interacts with and sculpts human ideas, but these ideas struggle wilfully from within. As Engels argued, "hence the interconnection between conceptions and their material conditions of existence becomes more and more complicated, more obscured by intermediate links. But the interconnection exists".[199] This is indeed a more nuanced paradigm of base-superstructure interconnections. Gramsci too said that the matter is "anything but simple and direct" and that "economic facts alone" cannot dictate history, for it "is not a mathematical calculation".[200] As Williams argues, the problem here is not that determinism's spurious divisions are too materialist, but that they are "never materialist enough"; as Gramsci put it, "'popular beliefs' and similar ideas are themselves material forces".[201]

In such an understanding of Marxist theory, it follows that not only can a genuinely proletarian literature exist but that it is itself part of the pervasive class struggle, never reducible to a singular dogma or illustrative merely of an economic paradigm but always imbricated with multifarious influences, in a complex engagement between social forces and individual volition.

Williams enlists various examples of how the narrow base-superstructure paradigm has been modified in cultural theory without losing its overweening determinist thrust. Ideas of the "typical", "correspondence" or "homology", as developed, diversely, by critics like Belinsky, Chernyshevsky, Dobrolyubov, Lukács, Goldmann and Adorno, can, on the one hand, be viewed as "crystallizations, in superficially unrelated fields, of a social process which is nowhere fully represented but which is specifically present, in determinate forms, in a range of different works and activities".[202] Culture, then, can be viewed as a primary activity rather than an afterthought or a consequence. However, as Williams argues, "on the other hand, 'correspondence' and 'homology' can be in effect restatements of the base – superstructure model and of the 'determinist' sense of determination [...] since in different ways they all depend on a known history, a known *structure*, known *products*".[203] This dualism is precisely the problem in Trotsky and Orwell. They can in fact be accused of reifying human consciousness itself, of presenting it as a "product" or a "thing". Williams refers to this problem elsewhere, deprecating that "fashionable form of Marxism which makes the whole people, including the whole working class, mere carriers of the structures of a corrupt ideology".[204] In making this criticism, he may leave himself vulnerable to the charge Terry Eagleton makes, of a "residual populism", which results in a "consistent over-subjectivising of the social formation".[205] Yet if we are to move beyond the reductive form of the base-superstructure concept, which views all culture in a capitalist economy as necessarily governed by bourgeois thinking, it is necessary too, with Williams, to move beyond the condescension and monism afflicting a certain strain of Marxist theory.

Returning to the kind of flexibility that Williams advocated, Eagleton indeed stresses that the idea of a dominant ideology should not be perverted into "an ontological carving of the world down the middle", but rather it should be viewed as "a question of different perspectives".[206] Undoubtedly the superstructure of various ideological institutions inculcates the dominant ideas, and, indisputably (for the socialist anyway), those ideas are most often those of the ruling class. Undeniably, the economic base has been the most singularly powerful instigator of social change. But within these structures, human beings, possessed of a limited but indisputable agency of their own, toil and struggle and create their own ideas. These ideas in turn change the course of history and reflect themselves in the operations of superstructure and base, returning to Thompson's point about how the working class forms itself internally. To the proletariat must be restored the agency of cognition, opening up the possibility of genuine counter- and alternative hegemonies, for which Williams scavenges hope in Antonio Gramsci's seminal writings.

Williams also finds affinity here in the work of Pierre Bourdieu, and I will also employ Bourdieu's concept of "habitus" – which refers to the acquired group mindset, behaviours and assumptions inculcated by social forces – to develop an understanding of how this key, complicated issue of social conditioning is depicted in the novels and plays explored in this book. In Bourdieu's use of the term, habitus refers to "durable, transposable dispositions" that are acquired by individuals in response to social forces in their environments, such as class, religion and education – which he collectively terms "field".[207] Habitus is "the system of dispositions (partially) common to all products of the same structures", and the parenthetical qualification is important here.[208] Bourdieu too refuses a rigid determinism, to see people as mere "products" of their environments. Indeed, like Gramsci and Williams, he side-steps the sociological conflict between determinism and individualism, subjectivity and objectivity, by postulating that what shapes the habitus is the interaction of individual will and social forces; that is, "the dialectic of the internalization of externality and the externalization of internality".[209] The habitus is not reducible to simple determinist rules; it is always subject to change and never complete. Like Gramsci's hegemony, it is "collectively orchestrated without being the product of the orchestrating action of a conductor", and it is *partially* available in all human products of the same structures.[210] Like Williams, it is crucial for Bourdieu to acknowledge, in theories of social conditioning, that "organic individuality [...] can never [be] entirely removed from the sociological discourse".[211] The "paradoxical product" of habitus is, he concedes, "difficult to conceive, even inconceivable", but "only so long as one remains locked in the dilemma of determinism and freedom, conditioning and creativity".[212]

Thus Trotsky's assertion, for example – that trying to create a proletarian literature is fruitless in bourgeois society – finds a stern riposte from within Marx *and* Marxism. Because the working class, as Williams puts it, "has, precisely, to become a class, and a potentially hegemonic class, against the pressures and limits of an existing and powerful hegemony", its cultural production is not only possible but *integral* to the struggle for a new society.[213] Cultural activity is "much more than superstructural expressions", is "never either total or exclusive", and this allows that the working class can develop its own alternative expressive forms, even if tunnelling, like an interloping worm, inside the golden apple of bourgeois art; new forms, which are "irreducible to the terms of the original or the adaptive hegemony, and are in that sense independent", always emerge.[214] As Gramsci argues, "the philistine sees no salvation outside the pre-established schemas [...] but history is not an oak tree, and men are not acorns".[215]

Modern modes: "the primacy of the social image"

John Fordham suggests exactly this in his analysis of a Liverpudlian-Irish writer, James Hanley, while elaborating how the habitus of working-class life might be seen to engender certain, common, distinctive features in the literature that emerges from it. Part of the problem in theorising working-class writing is that, as Fordham regrets, "no overall theory of working-class writing has been developed to cope with the multiplicity of forms which have evolved since the beginning of the twentieth century".[216] The result, he complains, is that "there has been a common tendency to suppress the inherent dialectic or ideological complexity in working-class texts in favour of their 'political accentuation' or their conformity to a prevailing political orthodoxy".[217] This is not to say that political analysis is somehow disabling: Fordham points to the work of various critics, such as Deirdre Burton, Tony Davies, Graham Holderness and Ken Worpole – who have introduced feminism and modernism to scholarship on working-class literature – to argue that at least this diversification moves beyond some Marxists' obsessions with *forms* of writing, forms that conform to tunnel-vision expectations of what proletarian literature *ought to* be (avowedly socialist/social-realist).

Fordham nonetheless suggests that "there is something qualitatively distinct about a working-class perspective which, because of its habituation to the extremes of social experience, finds adequate expression particularly in non-realist forms".[218] He proceeds to trace this tendency in Hanley's writing, arguing that "the working-class is not bound by the centrality of subjectivity, but rather has a life-experience which is determined by a perception of self as object and thus is uniquely able to comprehend the totality of capitalist society". As a by-product of their fundamentally alienated position in that society, working-class people are apt to "comprehend" how they have been objectified by capitalism. This seems nothing more than to state the obvious, after all – that working-class life brings with it material deprivation, and that this fosters a broadly counter-cultural perspective on capitalism. From Georg Lukács, Fordham takes the concept that in bourgeois thinking "all relations and values have been reduced to that of a commodity" because commodities are exactly what enable one to become bourgeois.[219] By contrast, the worker, in the act of selling labour power, is profoundly aware of the alienation inherent in this process, of his/her position *as* a supposed "commodity", and also of bourgeois realism's failure to represent the realities underlying this reification.

> Thus the writing itself, while it is often grounded in an ostensible realism, will nonetheless adopt descriptive or allegorical modes in which meaning does not so much depend on realist plausibility, but on a symbolic or metaphoric representation of a "re-ified" consciousness.[220]

Fordham associates this manner of writing in particular with expressionist forms. Eagleton, like Fordham, describes expressionism as a form that "feels the need to transcend the limits of a naturalistic" aesthetic that "assumes the ordinary bourgeois world to be solid". It endeavours "to rip open that deception and dissolve its social relations, penetrating by symbol and fantasy to the estranged, self-divided psyches which 'normality' conceals".[221]

Expressionism's refusal of "reality", its characteristic projection of a highly personalised vision of the world, contains within it the potential rejection of the doxa, of what society has taken for granted as the limits of the possible. In Strindberg's *The Dream Play* (1907), for example, with its action driven by dream association rather than a conventional, rationalised plot, or in O'Casey's depiction of war in stylised, expressive, dream-like form, during the experimental second act of *The Silver Tassie* (1928), there inheres a rejection of what is normatively constituted as "real". Expressionist forms emerged in part as a response to Europe's growing militarism, the attendant flourishing of totalising ideologies and, as O'Casey showed – for the many men who fought in its wars – the inherent irrationality and inhumanity that such ideologies masked. As "confident mid-Victorian notions of selfhood and relationship began to splinter and crumble in the face of growing world capitalist crises", such forms sprang organically from the inadequacies of realism's normative assumptions.[222]

Such writing thus works to "defy the conventional expectations of bourgeois plot or narrative development", Fordham comments.[223] In essence, while bourgeois sensibility tends towards the calculabilty and mechanisation of a *knowable* world – because it is by such knowing subjectivity that capitalism's *science* functions – the working-class subject comes into the world of work as the object of this alienating process and perceives, rather, the true relations belied by "functional" reality (which for O'Casey were vividly illustrated by war). Fordham suggests that an "episodic and metaphoric" form in writing of the working class can thus "suggest a less realist and more expressionistic level of reading consistent with the perception that human beings are determined by forces external to their individual will".[224] At first glance this might seem like yet another reductive account of how working-class life *ought* to look, but Fordham actually wishes to extend beyond overly prescriptive aesthetic taxonomies. He cautions that his view here is not to be taken as a rigid dogma – that there is a "dual relationship" between the working-class writer and the "priorities of the dominant class", in which can be discerned the marks of ongoing "struggle".[225] Shifting the characteristic terms of modernism in his analysis of Hanley's work, Fordham explores how Hanley conflates and confounds the opposition between social realism and individualist modernism, creating "an expressionist rather than an impressionist aesthetic, maintaining against the critical dominance of the feeling subject, of the unmediated impression, *the primacy of the social image through its subjective expression*".[226] In other words, and as will be argued in this book, writing of working-class life tends, as O'Casey's had, to exhibit a heightened awareness of the reification of capitalism, returning us relentlessly to "the primacy of the social image"; supposedly elitist modernist and realist forms are reconfigured from counter-hegemonic perspectives: "modernism, then, as transformed by the working-class writer, becomes a galvanic force, fuelled by the released energy of social oppression".[227] Interpreting writing "from a working-class perspective discloses the presence of a pervasive social conflict – a class struggle – which takes place both at the level of ordinary social reality (the 'life-world') and at the level of texts".[228] As my analysis, for example, of Christy Brown's modernist *Down All the Days* conveys in Chapter 6, class struggle is ever-present and ultimately predominant in Brown's proletarian aesthetic, even as his imagery becomes more esoteric and exoticised. As we shall see, it is there too, in various other forms, in all of the works surveyed.

While it has been argued that the engagement by working-class writers of "bourgeois" forms necessarily involves an acquiescence with or susceptibility to dominant discourse, Fordham argues that working-class writers "can significantly alter the generality of 'aesthetic experience' when, within that process of struggle, they 'illuminate the life-historical situation' and relate it to 'life-problems'".[229] Fordham is with Williams on the application of hegemonic thought to culture, asserting that those oppressed by dominant culture can nevertheless create subversive spaces within it, even through what are ostensibly conservative forms. Quoting Jürgen Habermas, he advocates "'the re-appropriation of the expert's culture from the standpoint of the life-world', an implicit refusal of modern culture's autonomy and a reforging of its links with 'everyday praxis'".[230] The "social function" of art, and the distinctive views of society and subjectivity that Fordham identifies as integral to working-class consciousness, will also recur in readings of the texts this book examines.[231]

Yet, as we have seen, there are some for whom the quiddity of working-class literature in "bourgeois" forms has always been a matter of hair-splitting and fractious debate. As Carole Snee advises, again in relation to realism, working-class writing "does not simply at best reveal and interrogate the dominant, unstated ideology, or exist uncritically within it, but can also incorporate a *conscious* ideological or class perspective, which in itself undercuts the ideological parameters of the genre, without necessarily transforming its structural boundaries".[232] Indeed, form, in all its various modes, is ever malleable and assailable, vulnerable to subversion from within. If a positive Marxist praxis is possible in other areas, it is possible too in literary pursuits, even when it comes cloaked in bourgeois apparel. As H. Gustav Klaus maintains, form is "not the only constituent of a text, and it is, above all, not some kind of cosmic, transhistorical category immune to change".[233]

The anti-Kantian aesthetic

Literature, like any area of cultural production, is riven with class struggle. In this regard, Bourdieu's theories of class, culture and capitalism again suggest how working-class culture exhibits particular, counter-hegemonic qualities, while conveying also how matters of "taste" are invariably loaded with inflections of class. Supported by extensive sociological research, Bourdieu maintains that class preferences suffuse dichotomies in cultural production, between the tautologous "good taste" of the elites and the easily dismissed popular culture of the working class. One might recall, for instance, the scene of disruption that occurs in the work of another Frenchman, Mathieu Kassovitz, to illustrate an extreme example of what happens when working-class culture meets with middle-class art. When three young men "from the estates" of Paris chance on some free refreshments at an art exhibition in the film *La Haine* (1995), their alienation from middle-class France is vividly illustrated by their utter incomprehension of the art on show – and the ensuing disintegration of their social graces, which results in them being ejected from the gallery.[234]

Abstract art of the kind exhibited makes little or no sense for these youths, and the "anti-Kantian aesthetic" of the working class – which prioritises the meaning and function of a work of art over its stylistic or formulaic abstractions – characterises the proletariat's preferred modes of representation, Bourdieu argues. Kant "strove to distinguish that which pleases from that which gratifies and, more generally, to distinguish disinterestedness, the sole guarantor of the specifically aesthetic quality of contemplation, from the interest of reason", whereas "working-class people expect every image to explicitly serve a function, if only that of a sign, and their judgements make reference, often explicitly, to the norms of morality or agreeableness. Whether rejecting or praising, their appreciation always has an ethical basis".[235] Moral purpose and utilitarian pleasure are to the fore in the preferred art of proletarians, Bourdieu contends; "judgement never gives the image of the object autonomy with respect to the object of the image".[236] This is precisely what Fordham argues of working-class writing – that however ostensibly abstract its aesthetic, it is always grounded in the social image, in moral concerns. It also approximates Hoggart's view of working-class art as "essentially a 'showing'" that "has to begin with the photographic" and be "underpinned by [...] moral rules"; however distorted that photographic element becomes, it is always there in projected form.[237]

Such a class predilection leads inexorably to typologies of aesthetic representation that tend to challenge social orthodoxies – art that is given, as Bourdieu put it, to "satisfy[ing] the taste for and sense of revelry, the plain speaking and hearty laughter which liberate by setting the social world head over heels, overturning conventions and proprieties".[238] In assessing the theoretical and stylistic innovations that undergird the writing in this book, this model of cultural production as something grounded in the distribution of "capital" in social and cultural life proves extremely useful.[239] And, as we shall see, Bourdieu's conception of a carnivalesque, comic "overturning" of convention in proletarian art also inheres throughout the literature, enriched by the particular counter-cultural tendencies of Dublin's working class.

Form and Irish society

But how can the specific history of the Irish working class be said to resonate with such concepts of aesthetics, culture and literature? David Lloyd's model of Irish working-class historiography fuses international post-colonial theory with the nuances of Irish historical specificities, in order to advance a broad theoretical framework, which illuminates how class and subalternity manifested generally in colonial and post-colonial Ireland. In doing so he also suggests how we might marry Bourdieuian theories of taste with the realities of Irish working-class experience. Lloyd maps the paradigms of Subaltern Studies – a movement of post-colonial theory and activism from South Asia – onto the topography of Irish social development. Borrowing also from Gramsci's writings, which heavily influenced the Subaltern Studies discipline, Lloyd provides a radically revised and highly influential paradigm for theorising both post-colonial and working-class Ireland.

For Gramsci, the term "subaltern" is a by-word for proletarian (partly because he was wary of prison authorities who monitored and censored his writing), yet it is also more than that. Subaltern is an enabling, emancipatory euphemism, which indicates those whom state hegemony does not incorporate – and for whom it holds limited attraction; it must liquidate or dominate these groups. The subaltern, consequently, is the field in which a counter-hegemony can be sown, a cohort, however internally diverse, which is ripe for iconoclastic and counter-normative ideas. After Gramsci, his subaltern is used to indicate, more generally, those who are subjugated by hegemony and who cannot express their common interests within it. For Lloyd, it is "that which the state does not interpellate, and therefore what lies outside it". [240] This extended use can "apply to groups that do not conform to a classical Marxist definition of the proletariat: as above, and potentially in Ireland, to a range of peasant groups [...] multiplying the significant domains of possible counter-hegemonic practice".[241] In the process of colonial extirpation, subaltern categorises those Wolfe Tone sought to engage, the "men of no property", who are dispossessed by the powerful and who are not subject to them as ancillaries, "uninterpellated as citizens and incomprehensible in mores and desires to the state's representatives".[242]

If it clarifies how hegemony works, however, this Gramscian term has also proven especially problematic. Gayatri Spivak has controversially argued that the subaltern cannot "speak"; that it cannot represent itself precisely because it is constitutively outside of hegemonic representation.[243] Discursively *othered*, the subaltern is other than discourse, and again we encounter a familiar, reductive determinism in another guise. As Lloyd puts it:

> The subaltern [in such terms] transforms the famous phrase "They cannot represent themselves; they must be represented" [which Marx used when

speaking of the peasantry in *The Eighteenth Brumaire of Louis Bonaparte*] from a determined declaration of the will into the expression of a certain despair. We might rather say, "They do not partake in representation; they cannot be represented."[244]

For Lloyd, subalternity should not "mean that a colonial underclass cannot be mobilised" in political action.[245]

Celticism, communism and counter-culture

As James Connolly had recognised, nationalism, far from being an ineluctable antagonist of the working class, could, especially in a colonial context, and not uniquely but favourably in an Irish context, accompany and enable agitation for social revolution. As his theory of Celtic communism suggested, it is partly because Irish nationalism had to conjure a primitivist sense of its own identity *vis à vis* that of the colonial centre and because Irish social organisation was so violently extirpated by colonialism that previous, anti-modern modes of thought also lingered in the collective memory, as stones to trouble the living stream. The memory of a Celtic communalism of the past proffered the possibility of a substantively different society in the future. "As Connolly seems to have grasped," Lloyd elaborates, "the coercive force" of capitalist colonialism's battle with Irish culture "produced as its differential counterpart a persistent if apparently discontinuous set of counter-modern discourses and practices".[246] The Irish subaltern hovered on the edge of "modes of living and apprehending the world that the state and colonial capitalism encounter as their constitutive limits".[247] Suspended, for much of their history, between poverty and emigration, the poor in Ireland were ripe for counter-hegemonic modes of thinking, and Connolly indeed suggested that some of these modes were, in what Williams might term "residual" form, latently present in the collective modern "memory" of Ireland's pre-colonial formations.[248]

In *Labour in Irish History* (1910), Connolly observed how "the coincidence of militant class feeling and revolutionary nationalism is deeply marked" in Irish history.[249] The Irish character, he argued, "has proven too difficult to press into respectable foreign moulds", the moulds of capitalist orthodoxy, because it sustained a memory of pre-colonial life, and thus he identified "the recoil of that character from the deadly embrace of capitalist English conventionalism".[250] The "Gaelic principle of common ownership", which in his analysis governed pre-colonial experience, made capitalism "the most foreign thing in Ireland". In the "Celtic revival", filtered through Connolly's terms, Ireland therefore steps outside the normative, Marxist, feudalism-to-capitalism paradigm of historical development, into new theoretical possibilities. For Connolly, hope for revolutionary change lay in the working class, which, because of its subaltern position – as "the most subject class in the nation" – was possessed of an intense "revolutionary vigour and power".[251]

As David Howell notes, such a romantic view of the past involved "a substantial accretion of myth", but is it not likely that Connolly was well aware of this?[252] Historical nostalgia was part of the cultural milieu, and such a twinning of romantic nationalism and scientific socialism "provided Connolly with a basis for deflating the pretensions of middle-class nationalist politicians", as within it "their support for the existing economic order" could be condemned, on their own terms, as "anti-national".[253] Considering how much communism has been denigrated in Ireland over the past century as a "foreign", un-Irish ideology, this historiographic revisionism was a deft sleight-of-hand. Celtic communism sustained a "tantalising claim": *Sure weren't we always communists?* Connolly seems to say.[254] Howell observes how the paradigm had its obvious flaws, like the fact that "'the democratic organisation' of the Irish clan did not include the slaves", but if the Irish subaltern memory of a prelapsarian society, in folklore, poetry, ballad and political discourse, was somewhat mythic and utopian, for an arch-propagandist it was a memory worth sustaining.[255] Seán O'Casey may have criticised Connolly for his combination of socialism and nationalism, but as Roger McHugh reminds, "Connolly's socialist ideas, operating within the changing circumstances of the Irish situation, had proved more practical and more flexible than O'Casey's."[256] The residual, combined with the emergent, in Irish nationalist and working-class consciousness, could prove a formidable force.

Lloyd makes this point in his defence of Connolly's seemingly counter-intuitive belief that the Irish proletariat was more fertile for socialist agitators than its English counterpart. In Celtic communism, "colonial damage and dispossession thus become the very basis both for resistance and for alternative notions of social transformation that do not demand that the Irish pass by way of full capitalist development in order to achieve a socialist society".[257] Connolly's theory, like Leninism, Maoism and Trotskyism, can be seen here also as an adaptation of Marxist theory to the actual, local conditions of socialist struggle – a departure from the teleology of Marx on the one hand, but a recommitment to the Marxist project on the other.

If it can be charged that Celtic communism contains elements of fancy and fabrication, it was also in fact rooted in real social and cultural conditions. Informing this theoretical departure, Lloyd notes, is Connolly's personal experience of how the vicissitudes of capitalism had shaped the collective consciousness of the Irish working class and its enormous diaspora. Due to the experience of emigration and displacement, which afflicted Irish workers in particular since the 1820s, and because Connolly had organised mainly "mobile and casual" workers of Irish birth or extraction in Ireland and the USA,

> his experience of Irish labour, then, signalled both the fact that it had, throughout its history and by virtue of its very mobility, been swept up

in capitalist modernity and that its very relation to that modernity, as a displaced and colonised population, could be productive of counter-capitalist formations that we might now call a "subaltern" kind.[258]

Indeed, the Irish working class had seen the worst of it for a century or more: it had manned imperialism's maritime ventures, had soldiered in its armies, had toiled at its most unsavoury and demeaning jobs, and had lived in filth and indigence in the most detestable of its slums. It was especially susceptible to counter-hegemonic thought, and if Celtic communism was somewhat mythic, it was also somewhat material. This point is implicit, for example, in Christy Brown's *Down All the Days* (1970), in which working-class characters sing maudlin ballads of "the ubiquitous underdog, the worm that turned, the berated beggarman roaming the streets with flapping uppers and bleeding feet"?[259] Celtic communism was rooted in empirical reality, in the fact that a "working class tradition of Irish nationalism has represented the obscured continuity of authentic anti-colonialism", the "'counter-culture' of the Irish working classes". It canvassed "the more substantial claim that a memory of an alternative system of property persist[ed] in the Irish consciousness".[260]

In a precarious world of emigration, exploitation and poverty, the Irish subaltern vacillates between extremes of despair and visionary zeal, Lloyd argues. Little wonder then, he opines, that while on one hand we observe countless reports of the masses of nineteenth-century Irish workers in England as a "dissolute and disease-ridden lumpenproletariat", on the other we find their presence "in the most 'advanced' social movements".[261] The emergence of Bronterre O'Brien, Feargus O'Connor and John Doheny amongst the vanguard of the Chartist movement; later, the international activities of the revolutionary Fenian movement; later still, Connolly himself and James Larkin; later again, the writing of Robert Noonan, James Hanley, Jim Phelan – are all evidence, for Lloyd, of the migrant Irish subaltern's radicalism. He notes also how Eric Hobsbawm marvels that the Irish "provided the British working class with a cutting edge of radicals and revolutionaries", and those who, in the cultural sphere, wrote the quintessential working-class anthem, "The Red Flag", and the classic British proletarian novel, *The Ragged Trousered Philanthropists* (1914).[262] As Alvin Jackson adds, "Irish people were simultaneously major participants in Empire, and a significant source of subversion."[263] It might be extrapolated that the fact that Ireland has never been fully decolonised has prolonged the cultural sensibility of residual anti-colonial lore as a bulwark of counter-hegemonic, anti-modern subversion.

Such a view of the Irish, locked between a backward, agricultural economy and the coalface of low-skilled capitalist production and acquisition, demands not only a rethink of how the Irish working class appears in history, but also a reconceptualisation of "the relation between political radicalism and social and economic development as it is generally posed".[264] As Eoin Flannery observes, Ireland "underwent intense and uneven experiences of modernisation via colonialism, rather than under the processes of a modulated history of industrialisation", leaving the country "culturally, confessionally and economically recalcitrant to the civilisational calculus of modernity".[265] The stagist approach that typically underlies a version of Marxist historiography "assumes, severally, that proletarianisation and politicisation correlate to the degree of industrial development". Thus, the political activities of the Irish subaltern are viewed as "merely reactive and spasmodic".[266] But the Irish case defies such logic, partly because "the Irish working class may be seen to have emerged as embedded at once in the long history of capitalism's becoming and in the no less drawn out process of resistance to that history".[267] Because the Irish dispossessed have been so integral to the development of Anglo-American capitalism, criss-crossing the globe as labourers, sailors and even slaves, or emigrating seasonally to Britain for short-term work, their experience of capitalism was highly developed, if not in the precise way of their British counterparts. As Lloyd concludes:

> In Ireland, perhaps more than anywhere, all that was solid melted into air. Only a historicism that discounts all that it has not already determined to be the most advanced historical experience could argue otherwise.[268]

In this formulation, it is questionable, for example, whether the ubiquitous Irish "peasant", "is in any way adequate to describe the historical experience of the rural, let alone urban, Irish poor".[269] Indeed, many of those labelled "peasants" in Ireland were amongst the most proletarian of proletarians once they ventured elsewhere. Equally, Lloyd's view of how the Irish working class developed radically counter-modern and counter-hegemonic characteristics – although it can by no means be argued that these were evenly felt or that they represented a comprehensive class view – presents some corollaries with Gramscian and sociological analysis of the working class generally, and specifically, with the "pole of differentiation" (Peillon) in Irish life with which this book is principally concerned. It may also explain why Ireland's relatively low level of industrialisation, and relatively weak left, are belied by an abiding pulse of working-class counter-culture.

Yet Lloyd's theorisation, like Connolly's, comes with some obvious caveats. Colin Graham allows that Lloyd, after Bhabha, produces a "re-avowal of intellectual agency".[270] But there is a danger inherent in his conjecture – in his Shavian tendency not to ask "why?", but "why not?" Graham notes the proclivity in Lloyd to scavenge "in the rubble of what preceded him in the (heroic) hope and expectation of discovery, until what is putative future becomes the end of criticism itself".[271] This rings true in particular when one considers how different Dublin's working class often *felt* itself to the rural "peasant", especially in terms of how both were accommodated differently to hegemonic national culture. Roddy Doyle deals with this vividly in his most recent novel, *The Dead Republic* (2010), in which Henry Smart's life story – that of a working-class Dublin rebel – gets diluted, distorted and sublimated into a saccharine film about rural life. Its director, John Ford, realises how little appetite there is for urban Ireland in Hollywood representations of the country:

> Dublin doesn't really count, [Ford] said. – Folks just didn't get *The Informer* back then. Because it was set in the city. It wasn't Irish. Dubliners aren't really Irish. They're scum.
> — And proud of it.[272]

As Flannery warns, "a taxonomy of postcolonial concepts has developed wherein the theoretical tropes have become signifiers for diverse sociopolitical groups" and thus "the facility to cast oneself as 'subaltern', 'hybrid' has become a *sine qua non* of post-colonial respectability".[273] Such romanticism can paper over considerable historical cracks. The subaltern can thus represent a purified, idealised cohort, apart from and counterpoised with the contamination of the state, "the site of cultural integrity and authenticity", and thus "pure because disempowered".[274] Like Yeats's idealised fisherman, a "wise and simple man" in "grey Connemara cloth" – "what I hoped 'twould be / To write for my own race" – the subaltern risks being "A man who does not exist, / A man who is but a dream".[275] Lloyd is, Graham rightly asserts, "perilously close" to a highly theorised form of nostalgia.[276]

Graham and Flannery question the possible overstatement of both the nation and the subaltern in Irish studies, and it is indeed important to distinguish between the enabling power of such an admittedly abstracted theory and its judicious application to particular historical conjunctures. However, it will become apparent throughout this book that a number of key aspects of working-class culture, as presented in its literature, suggest that Lloyd's subaltern is ultimately – accepting these judicious caveats – an enabling concept. His model of a form of nationalism that is opposed to the state may not be adequate to explain the counter-hegemonic tendencies of working-class Dublin – which often manifest as *anti*-nationalism – but it does go some way to theorising the embedded sense of counter-cultural recalcitrance that characterises much of working-class Dublin's attitude to the Irish Republic, as expressed through its literature, and how this recalcitrance relates to the past.

Lloyd enlists Connolly, just as Connolly had enlisted Celtic communism, more, perhaps, as an embodiment of a nebulous and disembodied idea, a point of reference for a residual counter-hegemonic impulse, than as a fully formed praxis in the great heterogeneity of working-class life. Terry

Eagleton interestingly does likewise in his novel *Saints and Scholars* (1987), where Connolly is revived and magically reconstituted as the agent of a history that might have been:

> Seven bullets flew towards Connolly's chest [in Kilmainham Jail, where he was executed], but they did not reach it, at least not here they didn't. Let us arrest those bullets in mid air, prise open a space in these close-packed events though which Jimmy may scamper, blast him out of the dreary continuum of history into a different place altogether.[277]

In Eagleton's mercurial work, Connolly evades death in Kilmainham, escaping from history's "dreary continuum" to fight another day. Eagleton suggests that such magical conjecture, such a sense of alternative possibilities, provides a space in which alternative concepts of the future and the past can emerge, and it is certainly true that orthodox histories often fail to account for the counter-cultural pulse in Irish life, of which Connolly was emblematic. While Spivak avers that "subalternity is a position without identity [...] where social lines of mobility, being elsewhere, do not permit the formation of a recognisable basis of action", Lloyd, like Williams and Gramsci, suggests that just because identity is outside hegemony, does not mean that it is silenced.[278] Indeed, in Lloyd this alienation might be seen as the very basis for counter-hegemonic culture, and in how Dublin's working-class is represented, and how it presents culturally in various forms, we hear the subaltern speak of an alternative conception of its own history and a radically alternative vision of Ireland from within. Just as Eagleton's Connolly may "prise open a space" through which to "scamper", the form of working-class culture in Ireland often punctures through the edifice of conventional wisdom, evading the clutches of epistemic orthodoxy. The proletarian appears in Dublin's writing as a conflicted figure, of commitment to community and dissent from orthodoxy, as a conduit for radical ideas and a disempowered, disenchanted pariah in its own state.

1

The Shadow of Seán: O'Casey, Commitment and the Literature of Dublin's Working Class

In a scene from *Inishfallen, Fare Thee Well* (1949), Seán O'Casey is reluctant to leave a pub with friends, to attend James Stephens' weekly soiree, because he is engrossed in the conversation between a man and a woman there. The woman, a street flower-seller, talks politics, criticising De Valera; the man talks about them both going back to his place, while slyly attempting to unbutton her blouse. "O Gawd," exclaims a disgusted member of the dramatist's companions, "let's go – it's too revolting". But O'Casey is enthralled:

> They led the way from the snug, Sean following slowly. He longed to stay where he was, watching common life unfolding on the bench opposite; smoky life, catching the breath with a cough at times, but lit with the red flare of reckless vigour [...] He liked James Stephens, loved him, really, and many fine people assembled there; but they were never themselves.[1]

O'Casey shuns Dublin's superficial "bohemianism", but the gritty, lively energy of working-class life – with its "smoky" authenticity and "reckless vigour" – absorbs him inexorably, like a moth to a flame. With lyrical nostalgia, the "slum dramatist" conjures here the impulse underlying his work, an impulse that this study also identifies amongst writers who emerge from his shadow. For O'Casey, his writing was inextricable from his affection for his own people – his commitment to the working class – and his unyielding advocacy of the cause of its emancipation. But, as Bernice Schrank has commented, "while there is growing acceptance of O'Casey's radical reinvention of the stage, there is less willingness to deal with O'Casey's ideological commitments"; those who do engage with the working-class politics that inform his writing are "lonely voices" indeed.[2] Few also attest to his relationship with later literature of Dublin's working class, and what follows is a brief analysis of O'Casey's importance for later writers of that class and the aesthetic discourse of communal engagement they share. As such, this chapter seeks to re-evaluate O'Casey's status in Irish literature – beyond his common acclamation as the great author of three iconic Dublin plays – and to argue for this dramatist's place as the towering figure in a distinct lineage of heretofore neglected writing.

The uses of literacy: the politics of O'Casey's aesthetic

For O'Casey, politics was inextricably linked with art. His tendency towards agitprop and consciousness-raising drama, and his success in having a political impact with his work, were examples that others sought to follow, and his significant contribution to Irish writing indeed began with political broadsides, letters to newspapers and propagandist pamphlets, such as *The Story of Thomas Ashe* (1917, the biography of a famous rebel friend, who died on hunger strike) and *The Story of the Irish Citizen Army* (1919), of which he was once a member. Early on, O'Casey developed a sceptical attitude towards the relationship between the political elite and the working class, his eyes opened to war's exploitation of the poor as he "thought bitterly" of Tom, his soldier brother, "risking all for England" and "for the gold and diamond mines of Johannesburg" (or so his later account would say).[3] And, while this revelation on the folly of blind loyalty did not stop the young Ó Cathasaigh (as he styled himself for a time) becoming a nationalist fanatic, later developments – such as Pádraig Pearse's defiant use of trams during the 1913 Lockout, and the Irish Republican Brotherhood's (IRB) failure to weigh in behind the Labour Movement after the event – sent the playwright on the path to disillusionment with nationalist politics and, eventually, outright hostility towards Sinn Féin.[4] His task ever after was mainly a narrow one: to defend the interests of the working class. But O'Casey nonetheless remained sympathetic towards republicanism and was an antagonist of Partition until his death, supporting IRA prisoners in England into the 1950s and 1960s, when such support would hardly have endeared him to his adopted home. (He had emigrated to England in the late 1920s and remained there till death.) He was also a lifelong communist, consistently refusing to acknowledge the failings and tyrannies of the Soviet Union, despite his declared humanitarian attitudes. Such complexity was the mark of the man.

O'Casey's life as an internal exile – a man forever on the outside of political structures staring in (nevertheless thoroughly absorbed by them) – mirrors the development of the working class itself in the Irish Free State. Both were central to Irish political life, but both were ironically ostracised by it. O'Casey, in Austin Clarke's opinion, became "in exile", "much more than Joyce [...] the 'conscience' of his country and the incessant critic of its indifference to social justice".[5] Working-class writers ever since have struggled to explain this curious sense of being simultaneously central to and peripheral within Irish culture. Following the Irish Revolution, "the class that thus came to power and influence was not a labouring class" but "a new middle class", O'Casey lamented.[6] The metaphor of the "flying wasp" – the sobriquet he used in a book of often caustic critical essays – is one that appositely encapsulates the consequent feeling, integral to Dublin's proletarian writing, of being one of a collective, yet also a breed of pariah, pestering the body politic, vigilant always lest a sudden sting can be administered.[7] This was a legacy O'Casey shared with later authors.

But unlike most of these other writers, O'Casey was also an ardent political activist. His membership in the Gaelic League, the IRB, the Gaelic Athletic Association (GAA), the St Laurence O'Toole (SLOT) Club and the Irish Citizen Army (ICA) was part of the kaleidoscopic political manifestation of his zealous support for various causes that would later, in his view, be subverted by some of the selfsame political activists who lent them their allegiance. After the emergence of the Free State, O'Casey was ever the waspish political outsider. He was a fierce critic of the colonial and capitalist establishment under British rule and perhaps an even fiercer critic of the Catholic and capitalist establishment obtaining thereafter. As a contemporary once recalled, this nettlesome man was "always complainin'. Always complainin'!", a penchant inseparable from his aesthetic.[8] Like Brecht, O'Casey married references to wider social upheaval in his work with subjective stories to create the sense of his class's real role in historical change. He often juxtaposed the reality of poverty in ordinary working-class homes with the hollowness of political rhetoric outside.

But this is not to suggest that, in his cynicism about Irish politics, O'Casey turned away from political life, nor did he seek to confine his concerns to a liberal humanist elevation of domestic life, as some have suggested. While a number of critics have focused on the gap between the domestic and political spheres in his work, Ronan McDonald has noted that the domestic realm in the early plays is by no means a settled concept and is rather subject to various forms of slippage.[9] From the very beginning, O'Casey's plays express the ironic sense of what I will call in this book an "alienation of the centre", by depicting the impoverished, anti-heroic Dublin poor at the epicentre of political tumult but simultaneously alienated by political power. This was a potent political intervention in itself. *The Shadow of a Gunman* (1923) evokes both the human frailty and the contrasting capacity for superhuman courage among slum dwellers, who are simultaneously bit-players in the anti-colonial revolution and disempowered observers of it. Donal Davoren, the poet who lodges with his friend Seamus Shields, is craven and opportunistic in exploiting the mistaken notion of his tenement neighbours that he is really a republican revolutionary in hiding, and there is comic bathos in his flirtations with Minnie Powell, who mistakenly idolises him as a rebel hero. There is, however, real tragedy, too, in her death at the hands of British soldiers. This ordinary heroism amidst the quotidian, with its realistic counterbalance of human folly, is a key dialectic of O'Casey's plays.

O'Casey's characters live on the margins of the main events of history, but their fates rotate inextricably around them. In *The Plough and the Stars* (1926), the eight tenement dwellers on whom the play's action centres are both central to and alienated from the locus of the Easter Rebellion, a message most graphically rendered in its public-house scene, where Pádraig Pearse's silhouette delivers a lofty message of ritualised martyrdom outside while some of those insulated from his public display in the bar will ironically bear witness to the worst effects of his rhetoric. Moreover, the rebels' decision to shoot at looters conveys their paradoxical contempt for the nation of real people they propose to liberate and foreshadows a sham revolution, after which Dublin's working class will still be treated as "slum lice".[10] O'Casey himself wrote of the courage of looters in their acquisitive zeal; that unethical and instinctual courage is conspicuous by comparison with the craven but politically reasoned logic of insurrectionaries.[11] The contrast is perhaps in part the reason why Fluther Goode, having imbibed his surfeit of looted alcohol, cares little for the nation or the city the rebels fight to liberate: "Th' whole city can topple home to hell, for Fluther!" he blasts.[12] But the message is socialist, not nihilist; the criticism of the Free State is always to the fore.

Such themes of working-class alienation, of subaltern counter-culture, recur throughout O'Casey's work. In *Red Roses for Me* (1942), Police Inspector Finglas's attitude to the "flotsam and jetsam" beggars (whom trade unionist Ayamonn manages to organise into political action) typifies what many later writers convey of the relationship between Dublin's underprivileged and its police who, according to writer and sculptor James McKenna, are "paid to walk in Dublin / and guard property like a dog".[13] But Finglas's abhorrence of the poor, his repugnance for their appearance and his violent vitriol when one of them accidentally spits on him, is also a metonym for the broader alienation of working-class Dubliners from official Ireland, from its state apparatus. It finds parallels also in writings by Paul Smith, Lee Dunne, Peter Sheridan, Mannix Flynn, Dermot Bolger and Mark O'Rowe, in which the forces of the state are often anathematised. McKenna's *The Scatterin'* (1959), Bolger's *The Journey Home* (1990) and O'Rowe's *Made in China* (2001) and *From Both Hips* (1997) all feature official abuses of power, by politicians, police and clergy. In O'Casey's *Juno and the Paycock* (1924), *Nannie's Night Out* (1924), *The Silver Tassie* (1928) and *The Star Turns Red* (1940), plots in which the political is intertwined with the personal, are constantly redeployed to show how working-class people make history but are denied its spoils, and, as such, these plays anticipate one of the major concerns of later Irish writing of the working class.

Theocracy

O'Casey is also a pioneer in his attacks on Irish theocracy from a class-conscious perspective and such attacks form another theme that suffuses this later literature. Although the young O'Casey embraced religion, the later playwright detested unquestioning religious fervour. Mrs Gogan's funereal fixation, her "thresspassin' joy to feel meself movin' along in a mourning coach" and her obsession with death and all its trappings in *The Plough*, is the peculiar expression of a morbid fixation with mortality that O'Casey exaggerated for comic effect. It is also, more seriously, the logical expression of her belief in the futility of human action. Gogan embodies teleology gone mad – a hyperbolic example of how faith in an omnipotent and all-controlling deity can make human agency seem pointless, with death the only desirable end.

A.P. Wilson had earlier castigated religion's role in the oppression of Dublin's working class, who "are told by priest and parson that there is a God of Love guarding the world's destiny" – a distortion of reality that protects the "cloud of commercialism" – and O'Casey followed this lead.[14] In *Red Roses*, he again ridicules religious folly, portraying Eeada, Dympna and Finoola childishly worshipping the idol of their patron saint and then unable to cope when the statue goes missing. To O'Casey, such unquestioning faith is an enemy of the proletariat, a contention supported by many later writers for whom organised religion's impact on the poor continues to cause concern. But O'Casey foresaw the descent of the Free State into fanatical religiosity long before others began to question religion's effects. With the increasing sway of the Catholic Church of the 1930s to the 1960s, and the state's consequent enforcement of stringent censorship laws, O'Casey's ire turned mainly on the theocratic nature of the state and its parallel recalcitrance towards modernity. For him, this too was a leftist mission, as the Church was now "the biggest and most unscrupulous enemy confronting communism".[15] Organised religion had eroded democracy in Ireland, and "an almost all-powerful clergy" was "*ipso facto* the Government of the country".[16] Ireland's was "the oldest civilisation in Europe, though she is still", socially and culturally, "in her teens", with a "people pathetically submissive to their clergy".[17]

Within the Gates (1933) was the first full-length play to feature religious hypocrisy as its central theme, but while it and a number of subsequent works on the subject of religion are set in areas outside of O'Casey's native Dublin, the essentially proletarian message remains. The play, which was highly praised by critics, derides the piety of an Anglican bishop who "never soiled a hand in Jesus' service", and whose "elegant and perfumed soul" studiously avoids "the stress, the stain, the horrid cries, the noisy laugh of life".[18] Modern organised religion is elitist and rarefied, the anathema of its Christian roots, O'Casey suggests. In *Purple Dust* (1940), this attack continues, with a celebration of sensual, pagan joy, what Canon Creehewel, a central character, dismisses as the "lower inclinations of the people". *Cock-a-Doodle Dandy* (1949) would articulate a similarly subversive commentary on religious hokum.[19] Father Domineer, the local priest of a rural town, attempts to retain control of his flock by exorcising the "Cock", a masque figure, who plays a symbolic, iconoclastic role in the play. Loraleen, a vivacious and sensuous young girl who arrives from London, seems to have precipitated a series of magical happenings – a commentary by O'Casey on the clash between modern England and regressive, superstitious Ireland. As the playwright was well aware, the emigrant working class of mid-century Ireland was adapting to modern modes of living elsewhere, which threatened the hegemony of the Irish church at home. In a comic scene emblematic of this social contrast, a statue of the amusingly titled "St Crankarius" is seen "standin' on his head to circumvent th' lurin' quality of [Loraleen's] presence", and an image of St Patrick makes "a skelp at her with his crozier".[20] The spectre of the Cock, personifying the pre-Christian worship of nature, is exorcised from the village, and with it go its youths (Lorna, Loraleen, Marion and Robin), who flee Ireland at the end of the last act. "Is it any wondher that th' girls are fleein' in their tens of thousands from this bewildhered land?" Loraleen asks, in an authorial comment on emigration trends.[21] The youths of *Cock-a-Doodle Dandy* emigrate from a barren society where "a whisper of love [...] bites away some of th' soul"; such a disenchanting vista would re-emerge with striking similarity just a decade later, in James McKenna's *The Scatterin'* (1959, see Chapter 2).[22] Both men excoriated the poverty and conservatism that forced their class abroad. Similar portrayals persist in writing of a more recent vintage, such as that of Dermot Bolger, with his vividly depressing meditation on the effects of mid-century theocracy in *The Holy Ground* (1990). *The Bishop's Bonfire* (1954), also set in a rural town, continued O'Casey's theme that, for Catholic Ireland, "joy, within the lights or under the darkness, is joy under the frock of death".[23]

In these plays and their echoes in later works by other writers, there is a dialogue between the working-class writer and Irish society, yet the rural setting O'Casey chose for his later writing indicates his increasing alienation from the urban Dublin of his youth – creating a gap which other authors, and not just Irish ones, would soon begin to fill. A year after *The Bonfire* appeared, Jimmy Porter, the brash, sex-charged, working-class antihero of John Osborne's *Look Back in Anger* (1956), caused controversy on the London stage, and it is interesting to note at this point (as I later explore in greater depth), the organic development of a proletarian literary rejoinder, British and Irish, to the increasingly staid and unrepresentative literature of the mid-century. The angry old man of Dublin and Torquay (where O'Casey now lived) was alive to the underlying currents of British and Irish life, and his legacy was that of an enabler who would create a space for equally angry, younger men (mainly) and women to vent their spleen. Indeed, as Christopher Murray notes, some young British writers of this time, such as John Arden and Edward Bond (though not, incidentally, Osborne), suggested O'Casey paved the way for their left-wing dramaturgy.[24] But O'Casey was, in his own words, looking "forward in anger".[25]

Ireland is greater than a mother: O'Casey and gender

O'Casey's stance on gender issues is another of the areas in which his influence on later writers of the working class can be traced. Women's plight in working-class life is a key, abiding theme of his *oeuvre*, as are the androcentric attitudes that he criticises unrelentingly. But what has been perceived as a gross caricaturing of gender roles along neatly dichotomous lines in O'Casey has courted the kind of criticism to which the polemicist playwright would have undoubtedly taken great umbrage. Seamus Deane argues that O'Casey's characteristic portrayal of gender roles results in a spurious and artificial division between personified ideas along male and female lines, men representing solipsism and vacuous ideology, women espousing a simpler, domesticated humanism.[26] Lionel Pilkington believes *The Plough* in particular "presents a sentimentalized version of patriarchal sexuality as the ethical norm against which all forms of political militancy are found wanting" and while he admits that the play celebrates sexuality, it is a "sexuality that is sexist to the point of misogyny".[27] Shakir Mustafa voices similar concerns.[28]

In contrast to these accusations of sexism, we find O'Casey described as a feminist by many other scholars.[29] But while this latter assessment may have achieved predominance in the general run of popular attitudes towards his writing, it might, as Nicholas Grene observes, be based on a selective reading of the plays. "O'Casey's cult of the woman went on to become a cliché in criticism of his work", but "it is noticeable that in this, as in many other respects, the three plays of the 'trilogy' are atypical of O'Casey's drama as a whole":

> Certainly nobody would think of O'Casey as a feminist on the basis of *The Harvest Festival* or *Red Roses for Me* with their positively Christ-like heroes, *The Silver Tassie* with its predatory wives and sex-object girlfriends, or the later plays in which male sexuality (*Cock-a-Doodle Dandy*) and male-led activism (*The Star Turns Red*) are so often associated with liberation.

Grene concludes that, even within the *Trilogy*, "the issue of gender is oversimplified in the traditional view of women as heroes, men anti-heroes".[30] O'Casey's own expressed view on the matter paints him as a *differencialiste* feminist. In an interview in 1958 with the *New York Herald Tribune*, he asserted his belief that women were more logical than men: "In life, yes. They're much more near to the earth than men are. Men are more idealistic, stupidly idealistic. They're not as realistic as the women."[31] This kind of dichotomy between idealism and humanism would echo again in Brendan Behan's astonished youthful ponderings on why his mother, an ardent republican, made sandwiches for British soldiers, whom she pitied: "And I lay on my bed that night and reflected and felt, in my opinion, that

that is what happens to make up a woman."[32] But O'Casey's own depiction of women is more complicated than his expressed opinion suggests, as any thorough analysis of creations such as Minnie Powell, Nora Clitheroe, Bessie Burgess and Juno will attest.

These women's heroism is repeatedly deflated by their self-interest and sentimental folly in the plays: Minnie Powell is brave in death but foolish in her awe-struck worship of Donal; Nora Clitheroe is brave in her bullet-dodging search for Jack, but her excessively self-interested, cocooned mind-set is shown to be dangerously oblivious to the reality around her when she finally goes mad; Bessie is heroic by misadventure, when she is shot while trying to save Nora, but the bullet that kills her comes from a British gun – inferentially, her jingoistic loyalism earlier in the play comes back to haunt her. Equally, Juno may in due course shirk the burden of her reckless husband, but her continual willingness to accede to his whims throughout the play – along with her excessive indulgence of the wily Bentham – leave her culpable in part for the general familial wreckage that ensues. As Herbert Goldstone writes, Juno is someone who "simply doesn't realise that she has let the very conditions of life which have victimized her become her ultimate standard of value".[33] And this is precisely O'Casey's point regarding all of these female characters: in their devotion to various illusory ideologies – whether it be the alternative utopia of domesticity, the nationalist fanaticism of British militarists or the patriarchal system itself – they have allowed themselves to become disempowered by capitalist hegemony.

But the characteristic and overriding mistake in O'Casey criticism in this regard is a tendency to always extrapolate the universal from the particular in any selection of his plays (normally *The Trilogy*); to suggest that a handful of female characters can stand in for the whole is misleading. The role of women in working-class life as a nurturing and heroic force is strong in O'Casey, to be sure. From the normally benevolent Mrs Henderson of *The Shadow*, with her righteous outburst against the British Army, to Minnie Powell, the martyr of that play, to later figures such as Ayamonn's nostalgically imagined mother in *Red Roses*, women often represent humanity at its best. And later writers follow O'Casey in showing how women's heroism in working-class life is often forgotten – a constant theme in this literature. Yet O'Casey, overall, depicts women in varied and often conflicting forms. Many are indeed portrayed as nurturers and subalterns to male protagonists – as when the writer acknowledges his own indebtedness to his mother in *Red Roses*: "you gave me life to play with as a richer child is given a coloured ball".[34] But this is only one type of O'Casey woman: Bessie's ultimate heroism stands in stark contrast to the avarice and callousness of the women of *The Tassie*, for instance, whose enjoyment of the advantages of freedom and finance that war brings is galling (and, as we shall see, is echoed later in Smith's *The Countrywoman* [1961]).

The breadth of O'Casey's life's work exhibits women in various states, ranging from the abject to the exalted, the heroic to the ignoble. Nannie, in his comic play *Nannie's Night Out* (1924), is the quintessence of this duality. A young "spunker", she is an alcoholic hooked on methylated spirit, who has just been released from Mountjoy Jail and who displays a hedonistic recklessness in her desire to pursue "a short life an' a merry wan". But there is also an underlying desperation in her suicidal threats to "make a hole in th' river".[35] Nannie would be at home in Paula Meehan's *Cell* (1999), as a Mountjoy inmate, or her *Mrs Sweeney* (1997), as a modern "junkie". She is the kind of contrast of outward gaiety and inner turmoil that Dunne sought to portray in *Does Your Mother?* (1970) and that Smith develops in *Summer Sang in Me* (1975), both novels in which degraded women, reduced to various forms of prostitution, upbraid the moral degradations of a sexist society. But if Nannie's social status is that of a pariah, she is also affirmed as a potential heroine. When she courageously helps the Widow Pender save her shop from burglary, three potential suitors of the widow's – heretofore occupied by boasting about their exploits – cravenly stand back in horror. Ironically, it is Nannie who is, in one version of the play, hauled off by the police after the robbery; again, the heroism of women is "arrested" by androcentric orthodoxy. But Nannie came to the stage at a time when "there was some public unease that O'Casey was dramatizing an unnecessarily sordid view of Irish life".[36] She embodies the ambiguity of O'Casey's women but again unambiguously asserts a proletarian message: if the working class of the new state has ostensibly become debauched through neglect, criminalisation and poverty, its great moral courage in defending that state (metaphorically, now a dowdy capitalist shop) is an indictment of Ireland's social failures.

Another "sordid" matter, the suppression of women's sexuality, is an acute concern in O'Casey's work that has also received scant attention. Again, this is a theme that echoes in Dublin's later writing of the working class and it too relates back to his essentially socialist message. In the daring *Within the Gates*, female protagonist Young Whore brazenly parades her sensuality before her bishop father. She confounds his hypocritical morality and upbraids English concerns (this play is based in Hyde Park, London) with outward shows of propriety. Two years later, a similar theme emerged in O'Casey's short story, "I Wanna Woman" (1933), illustrating once more his perception of women beyond a stereotypically maternal, nurturing role. In the story, a lively and uninhibited London prostitute teaches the sexually obsessed, misogynistic and immoral Jack Avreen a lesson when she charges him an extravagant fee for sex and takes for herself the expensive bracelet with which he had intended to seduce another woman; his moral self-deception, like that of the Covey in *The Plough*, is ironically exposed for the sham it is by society's quintessential personification of immorality, a "whore". *Bedtime Story* (1958), a play loosely based on the same theme, is set in a bachelor flat in Dublin. It depicts the haphazard efforts of a young lodger, John Jo Mulligan, to sneak a female friend from his room without being detected by his landlady, fellow lodger and parish priest, whose censure he desperately fears. The girl, who is again also uninhibited by her sexual antics or anyone's opinion of them, comes to despise her boyfriend's gutless shame. She deploys his "futile sense of sin" against him, threatening to expose his impropriety as she filches a number of his personal possessions.[37] It is notable in these works that propriety and property – the weapons that patriarchy uses to control women's lives – are symbolically expropriated by marginalised females. In taking what the men most treasure, these women highlight their own commodification and the reifying effects of capitalist relations. Refusing to be categorised by men as objects for exchange or objects of disgust, they turn the tables by revealing how hypocritical male characters themselves have become products of their own shallow value system.

The somewhat jaded tone of the morality play in these works is offset by their obviously risqué nature – particularly that of *Bedtime Story*, which ridicules Irish Catholic guilt. And again, the recurrence of such female characters offsets the common, stereotypical perception of women in O'Casey plays. These women are of a similar vogue to the liberated Julia Elizabeth O'Reilly of James Stephens' one-act tenement play (also a short story), *Three Lovers Who Lost* (circa 1913), who refuses her parents' control. The short play centres on a young man's attempt to secure Julia's hand in marriage by asking for her parents' consent to the union. Again, woman becomes symbolically and literally an object of exchange. However, this vignette ends with a perfunctory telegram from Julia – who never appears on stage – which curtly reveals that she has married another man without their consent. Julia is "a gad-about, a pavement-hopper, and when she has the tooth-ache she curses like a carman", according to her incensed father.[38] The "pavement-hopper" defies discursive orthodoxy by refusing to be dominated – by acting like a (car)man.

In regard to women's multiple forms in O'Casey's writing, it might also be salutary to consider the kind of contrast between Christy Brown's depictions of the dutiful mother/nurturer Mrs Brown, in *My Left Foot* (1954), and the bawdy and quick-witted prostitutes of Madame Lala's "house of pleasure", in *Wild Grow the Lillies* (1976). Such contrasts recur throughout this present study, as many writers of working-class life challenge normative Irish conceptions of gender roles. For every female character in this writing who conforms to society's (or men's) conventional expectations of how women should behave, there are other, ribald and uninhibited types who defy the sexist orthodoxy. Women who intentionally antagonise Catholic Ireland with hyperbolically outrageous antics pervade this literature, and other, later writers follow O'Casey's lead in this regard.[39] Moreover, the variety of O'Casey's female characters confounds simplistic attempts to totalise them as either representations of his putative "sexism" on the one hand or achromatic glorifications of womanhood on the other. O'Casey's women come in various, contrasting guises – from the deranged to the heroic, the deluded to the liberated – but always the essential message is the same. O'Casey stresses that capitalism and the theocracy and patriarchy with which it is aligned are ultimately responsible for the oppression of women and men. In succumbing to false ideologies, in allowing themselves to become interpellated by hegemonic mores, their human potential is curtailed, and it is often in those *most* subaltern types – those who live at the limits of social acceptability ("spunkers" and "whores") – that O'Casey finds his heroines. The "social image" of capitalist society is never far away.

"Is there anybody goin' with a tither o' sense?"

The other side of this gender coin is, of course, O'Casey's depiction of men, which has also come in for criticism as undeveloped, crude and stereotypical. This criticism has left its traces on subsequent generations of writers and the charge of anti-male reductivism bears greater scrutiny than those made against his depictions of women, for O'Casey often shows himself to be exasperated with men's inhumanity, narcissism and recklessness. Although there are levels of subtlety in his work that destabilise such claims, within them also is an irrefutable kernel of truth. O'Casey continually reduces men to caricature, obfuscating their political motivations and relegating them to convenient roles as mere egoists, with little self-awareness but a great deal to offer in terms of comic development. Another, later working-class Dubliner, James McKenna, even claimed that O'Casey had mounted "an assault on Irish manhood not seen since the Punch Magazine.[40] A reassessment of working-class manhood is integral to McKenna's play, *The Scatterin'* (1959), which is explored in Chapter 2.

Many of O'Casey's men indeed act as flawed foils for female courage. To look at the male *dramatis personae* of *The Shadow* is to anticipate the recurrence of similar caricatures in later plays. Adolphous Grigson, the corpulent, bourgeois, buffoon Orangeman of the play, shamelessly seeks to preserve his own safety during a Black and Tan raid. He functions as a contrast to his exhausted and emaciated wife, whose principal concern is her husband's care. Such odd couples recur in other works (Juno and Boyle, or Lizzie and Darry Berrill, for example), often illustrating male immorality through gendered contrasts – and through dramatic disparities between word and deed. Tommy Owens, for example, extols chauvinistic nationalism in principle but fails, unlike Minnie, to take a heroic role in the Tan War. Equally, many men are solipsistic in plays where selfless female heroism takes centre stage. Donal Davoren is peevish and whining, with Shelly's plaintive line – "ah me, alas! Pain, pain, pain ever, for ever" – his habitual refrain.[41] Bentham, in *Juno*, is treacherous and self-serving, while the dedicatedly unemployed Captain Boyle and his friend Joxer Daly are utterly absorbed in their own myopic egoism. Boyle's nickname, "Paycock", fits with his strutting rodomontade and unintentionally comic self-aggrandising. He is shown to be intellectually dishonest and hypocritical, at one time criticising the Catholic hierarchy for their treatment of Charles Stewart Parnell, then contradicting this view later on, when he acquires wealth and seeks to adopt the moral pose of the middle class. His comic *volte face*, contrived for audience mirth, is a classic device in O'Casey's mockery of shallow males. His weak moral calibre echoes in the young Labour leader Jerry's moralistic puritanism when he cannot come to terms with the prospect of Mary's pregnancy. Jerry's humanity "is just as narrow as the humanity of the others", Mary jibes, when his declarations of love quickly evaporate at the revelation that she may be having a baby for another man. Like the Paycock's, the rhetoric of Jerry's idealism echoes hollowly *vis-à-vis* the challenge of a real moral dilemma; he is The Covey, he is Jack Avreen, he is Harry Heegan.[42] He is perhaps who Robert Collis was thinking of when he created his trade unionist, Joe, "the great social reformer and all", who turns out to be a thief who cares little for his fellow proletarians.[43]

O'Casey's depiction of Pádraig Pearse in *The Plough and the Stars* crystallises the charge of male hypocrisy. The portrayal of the nationalist icon in silhouette is a parody of itself, a metaphor for O'Casey's ill-defined sketches of so many men. The contrast between Pearse's sanguinary exaltation of "terrible war" – the "homage of millions of lives" in "glorious sacrifice" and "shedding of blood" – and the awful reality of proletarian suffering is a biting condemnation of both warfare and its main instigators. In its ironic juxtaposition of rhetoric and reality, it filters O'Casey's composite judgement on the folly of man into one scene. The consumptive Mollser articulates the dramatist's own frustration with the futility of men's wars: "Is there anybody goin'", she famously asks, "with a titther o' sense?"[44] And such explaining away of political action is repeated at the end of the century in Roddy Doyle's revisionist *A Star Called Henry* (1999); it is why Seamus Deane asserts that the Dublin of *The Plough* "is not a city in which politics has any truly social or human basis. Instead, only in repudiation of politics can humanity express itself".[45]

There are also male characters in O'Casey who exhibit truly heroic traits, such as Fluther Goode, with his chivalry in defending Rosie and Nora. Indeed, the characters that are presented as obvious authorial stand-ins in the plays exemplify, in a crudely narcissistic way, how men can be selflessly heroic. Jack, in *The Star*, dies fighting fascists in the streets. In *Red Roses*, Ayamonn Breydon dies in an incident of brutal police violence. Ayamonn's relationship with the devout Catholic, Sheila Moorneen, his mother's similarity to the Mrs O'Casey that the playwright depicted in his autobiographies and other autobiographical events in the play (as well as the fact that in earlier versions Ayamonn's name is "Sean O'Casside") construct the young O'Casey as a stylised heroic icon: a painter, actor, intellectual and trade-union activist/martyr – a William Morris-esque ideal.

But men's self-delusion is a more potent and abiding theme in the plays, including short works such as *The End of the Beginning* (1934), a one-act farce, in which a domineering, pompous husband tries to humiliate his wife by betting that he can do her domestic work better than she can. Darry Berrill ends up enlisting his short-sighted friend, Barry Derrill, in this task, which results in a comic, Laurel-and-Hardy-esqe trail of carnage about the house. This slapstick vignette is, of course, a metaphor for what men do most in O'Casey plays: cause havoc in the domestic sphere because they can't see far enough beyond themselves. But this reductivism in the matter of male typologies in O'Casey's writing contrasts with more subtle and generous depictions of working-class manhood in later Dublin writing. Many of the male characters in this later literature are also egotistical and self-absorbed, but no subsequent writer conducts such a sustained attack on manhood. Yet it is true that there are (at times more disturbing) echoes of O'Casey's men in Smith's Pat Baines (*The Countrywoman* [1961]), Magee's Hatchet (*Hatchet* [1972]), Sebastian Barry's Joe (*The Pride of Parnell Street* [2007]), Doyle's Charlo (*The Woman Who Walked into Doors* [1996]) and a great many more depictions of deeply flawed and often violent working-class males. Doyle in particular exhibits a tendency towards the carica-ture of working-class manhood, as my final chapter shows. The relative complexity, however, of some of the male characters developed by later writers could be considered a reaction against O'Casey's stereotypes. The second chapter of this book illustrates how Magee, McKenna and Dunne – all of whom wrote for a new generation – develop male characters with far more subtlety and vision. This matter of conflicting male typologies, and the interplay of male subjectivity and working-class habitus, resonates throughout this study.

Commitment: the life we live

O'Casey's greatest influence on these later writers can be traced in terms of his style and aesthetic vision, and the most fundamental and abiding motivation behind these aspects of his work, as I have suggested, is a com-mitment to furthering working-class causes. Herbert Goldstone writes that the concept of artistic "commitment" is "closely related to, if not synony-mous with, community" in O'Casey's work, and "underlying this search is a deep conviction that the individual fulfils himself through involvement in some order larger than himself".[46] This returns us again to Fordham's point regarding the ubiquity of the "social image" in writing of working-class life. An early reviewer of *Juno* quantified the conceptual departure that the play signalled for the National Theatre in similar terms: "Democracy has at last become articulate on both sides of the curtain," he proclaimed, "with what the great public hungers after [...] the drama of palpitating city life."[47] Such enthusiasm captures the quintessence of what O'Casey was trying to achieve: the advancement of the proletarian struggle "through art and culture and the people of culture", as he was to tell Lady Gregory.[48] For him, this culture was not an assemblage of elite practices advocated by those with cultural capital; it was "the life we live", "far more than books on our shelves and pictures in our galleries" – something "that is within us".[49] Like Antonio Gramsci, O'Casey rejected the idea that a caste of cultural adepts, regurgitating established norms like "parrots" "possess the [hermeneutic] key to open all doors".[50] For Gramsci and O'Casey, "all men are intellectuals [...] but not all men have in society the function of intellectuals".[51]

O'Casey had many influences, and his milieu presented opportunities to emulate others who presented paradigms for writing of and for the working class. It is likely that Lady Gregory's *Workhouse Ward* (1908, produced in Liberty Hall in 1912), A.P. Wilson's *Victims* (1912) and *The Slough* (1914) and Oliver St John Gogarty's *Blight* (1917) – all plays about workers' suffering – would have affected O'Casey's evolving aesthetic; as perhaps would James Stephens' novel *The Charwoman's Daughter* (1912), his short story *Hunger* (1918), and St John Ervine's tragic play, *Mixed Marriage* (1911). Lady Gregory's and Wilson's plays were deployed as agitprop by the Irish Workers' Dramatic Company, under the direction of O'Casey's ally, and Jim Larkin's sister, Delia Larkin, and this manner of consciousness-raising through theatre was to influence O'Casey towards his ultimate vocation. In his comic-tragic, yet realistic portrayal of slum life, Gogarty too was anticipating O'Casey; *Blight* was one of a handful of Abbey plays that the "slum dramatist" saw before embarking on his literary career – and no doubt one that, with typical tenacity, the then obscure Dublin labourer had vowed to surpass.[52] Wilson's pre-Lockout play, *Victims,* had also vilified the "profit fiends" of Dublin, and his interplay of public and private lives amidst political tumult was a technique O'Casey may equally have observed and sought to emulate. But if he did "he kept quiet about it" – notwithstanding the comparisons Murray now draws with O'Casey's *The Harvest Festival* (1919), a play about a strike that also ends in violence.[53]

In the early plays that he did see, O'Casey had observed the possibility for localised dramatic propaganda. The theatre could present new opportunities for political agitation, and didacticism came naturally to the son of a proselytiser (his father worked for the Irish Church Missions). The Abbey theatre presented itself as a pulpit from which to pontificate, "the temple entered" for the "acolyte" in his "full canonical costume".[54] The Abbey's doors had been flung open to proletarian drama in the 1910s, having staged Wilson's *The Slough* in 1914.[55] But the theatre of the Gaelic Revival was still the domain of the middle classes that James Plunkett would mock in *Strumpet City's* (1969) riot scenes. In Plunkett's novel, a comic contrast is drawn between the polite theatre-going gaiety of Horse Show Week 1913 and the proletarian uproar on the streets outside the playhouse. After his sacking from the Great Northern Railway (GNR), O'Casey was very much one of these outsiders. He soon engaged in amateur dramatics with the SLOT club in Seville Place, which allowed him to hone his theatrical style but also brought to bear the sense of community and social interaction which pertains to amateur theatre, another key influence on his work. He indeed wrote a play for SLOT in 1918, *The Frost in the Flower*, which was lost, but had not visited the Abbey, he insisted, until 1917 – due partly to lack of funds and partly to social awkwardness. It is ironic to consider that less than a decade later O'Casey would make this theatre his own.

It is true also that the Abbey had a lesser influence on O'Casey than earlier, cheaper forms of entertainment, whose principles enabled him to develop an aesthetic suited to propagandist ends. Kiberd deciphers the trace in O'Casey's plays of conventional Victorian melodramas at the Queen's Theatre, which, at an admission fee of sixpence, the young John could afford.[56] There he learned the raucous power of stock situations and music-hall melodrama, the influence of which Beckett would laud in O'Casey's work as his "principle of knockabout", which "discerns the principle of disintegration in even the most complacent solidities".[57] This of course dovetails with the kind of proletarian artistic attitude that Pierre Bourdieu has identified, with its propensity for "setting the social world head over heels, overturning conventions and proprieties".[58] The young John had seen Boucicault's *The Shaughraun* (1874) in the Queen's Theatre in the 1890s, describing it as "a wonderful revelation" and he, like Boucicault, always wrote with an eye to entertainment, vaudeville and variety.[59] But the comedy, as Bourdieu suggests, could also turn propriety on its head. O'Casey's comic interludes and slapstick squabbles were undoubtedly also elements in the success of his earlier plays, and this lesson would again be passed on to popular working-class writers such as Lee Dunne, Christy Brown, Peter Sheridan and Roddy Doyle, for whom *divertissement* is indispensable. Comedy amidst tragedy may be a perilous path to tread, as Kiberd warns: "people, confronted with a sweetened propaganda pill, might learn how to suck off the sugar coating and leave the pill behind" (as critics who ignore O'Casey's socialism have done).[60] But comedy and its utility in his plays has left its traces on the writing of working-class Dublin, and it is often used likewise by later writers to voice social commentaries under a cacophony of laughter.

Irreverence of this kind, however, had other drawbacks; bawdy, comic treatments of contentious social issues often raised the hackles of conservative elements in twentieth-century Ireland, impeding the careers of many writers. O'Casey's and these other writers' attempts to reach out to their communities was stymied by state repression. Towards the end of his career, the "life we live" was increasingly elided from Irish literature by censorship, and what O'Casey saw as its evisceration of national culture. *The Bishop's Bonfire*, for instance, centres on the civic welcome for a bishop in which all heretical literature is to be burned, conjuring up associations with the recent past in Europe, and, by implication, levelling a serious accusation of literary fascism against the Irish government. This was prescient stuff indeed, for a great part of Dublin's working-class writing in the coming decades was to fall under the jackboot of Ireland's own cultural commissars. O'Casey stresses the class prejudice that underpinned censorship in an opinion voiced, in *The Bonfire*, by the Canon to Father Boheroe. The poor simply aren't capable of dealing with freedom of expression, he explains: "Can't you understand that their dim eyes are able only for a little light? Damn, it, man, can't you see Clooncoohy can never be other than he is?"[61] This concern with censorial snobbery was later voiced by Lee Dunne, who complained about the Irish government's banning of paperback editions of books (which the poor might afford), while letting the more expensive hardback editions through. "Economic morality" of this kind infuriated Dunne: "I mean, a book that's dirty at four shillings is clean at twenty five?" And such attitudes extended to other matters of form, Dunne notes: the indecency of Patrick Kavanagh's poem *The Great Hunger* slipped through the censor's net "because the working-class couldn't understand it", but his own moderately racy, but less difficult work, was banned because of the elitism inherent in state cultural practices: "*those* people, at that level – we can't unleash this upon *them*".[62] These issues of censorship, which O'Casey highlights in his broad concerns with the totalitarian bent of the state, recur frequently in later works. And within all of this – O'Casey's early "drama of palpitating city life" and later drama of palpitating pulpits – one observes the continual desire to combat aesthetic snobbery, and the promotion of an art form based on democratic principles, a literature *engagé*.

Appropriation

Nonetheless, as Schrank writes:

> A popular and pernicious perception of O'Casey's work is that the realistic "Dublin Trilogy" represents the high point of his achievement, and everything after *Plough* is one long, embarrassingly bloated falling away from his initial greatness. Despite its popularity, this view is gradually yielding to a more accurate assessment of O'Casey's achievement as a premature practitioner of the art of "total theatre".[63]

Some of O'Casey's most innovative dramaturgy emerged from the shadow of the Abbey controversy, yet much of it is barely known in Ireland today. In many ways, not only did O'Casey's career begin with the Abbey but so too did his cultural and political reappropriation. While the theatre refused *The Silver Tassie*, and largely neglected what came after it, the Abbey continued to reproduce his *Trilogy* works as a lucrative staple. O'Casey as "slum dramatist", who contrasted the diurnal poverty of the tenements with the otherworldly fantasies of nationalists, was welcome there. But the O'Casey who railed against the Catholic Church, the supposed heroism of the First World War and the intellectual and moral backwardness of the Irish Republic was less so.

This Irish cherry-picking of O'Casey's *oeuvre* is illustrated by the selective nature of his appearances in the Republic's post-primary educational system. While generations of Irish students became familiar with the canonical *Trilogy* plays, through the selection chosen for the Junior and Leaving Certificate curricula, most never learned anything of O'Casey beyond 1926, when his career had barely commenced. The trace of revisionist historical – and implicitly political – concerns (which I discuss in detail in Chapter 7) may be discerned also in this selectiveness. The avuncular voice of the poor, which perennially cautions against political fanaticism, is de rigeur, but the angry exile who heaps opprobrium on modern backwardness is derogated. In this regard, Herbert Goldstone made a number of telling suggestions for how O'Casey might be reinterpreted, in the historically significant year of 1972. Hazarding rather timidly that the "long-awaited (forty-four years)" contemporary Abbey production of *The Silver Tassie* might be a "promising sign" that O'Casey's "very substantial achievement" could now begin to become "more apparent" to his compatriots, Goldstone adds some contemporary reasons as to why the plays might prove their "timeliness":

> While as of this writing (summer 1972) the conflict in Northern Ireland hasn't reached the savage intensity of that of 1916–1922 in Southern Ireland, such an escalation remains possible. In that event the vision of the Dublin plays may take on a terrible, new urgency. At the same time in the south, the agitation for sexual and social reform (that the formation of a Women's Liberation Group reveals) may give the latest plays a comparable urgency.[64]

Here Goldstone is Janus-faced: looking back in fear, at the terror of insurgency and the intransigence of Irish society, while looking forward also, in trepidation, to what Ireland might become. And in his first suggestion, he may have been right: O'Casey's plays chosen for the national secondary-school curriculum served the inculcation of newly expedient ideas: the futility of war, the folly of nationalism, the inevitable suffering of innocent non-combatants; the supposed humanist universalities claimed by many to underpin this dogmatic Stalinist's work.[65] But in his second prediction Goldstone was lamentably wrong: what was especially socially progressive in O'Casey – his stance on Ireland's conservative mores – did not serve a state that was loath to embrace social reform, and thus what was of little political utility (and of great political embarrassment) was lost. *The Plough and the Stars* was dangerous in 1926 but useful in 1972, yet *The Drums of Father Ned* – dangerous and withdrawn from the Dublin International

Theatre Festival 14 years earlier, after criticism from the Archbishop of Dublin – was still a little too hot to handle, with its satire on civil-war politics and social puritanism. The old O'Casey was cosy in this view – his latter-day manifestation, cantankerous and disagreeable. As Schrank comments, "the narrative of O'Casey's neglect illustrates the degree to which socially created cultural artefacts create responses which are likewise socially created".[66] *The Drums of Father Ned*, "once placed in context, may be read metonymically as a more effective critique of the dominant culture than most of the Irish plays staged at the Abbey in the decades before its reopening in 1966", as Murray observes.[67] Yet how many Irish schoolchildren, or for that matter, English Literature graduates, have ever heard of it? Certainly, critics (especially Irish ones, and some Americans, many influenced by McCarthyism) could be caustic in their responses to some of these more overtly left-wing plays, but as Schrank argues, it seems that "the negativity of reviewers and critics alike is rooted in the plays' radical critique of the last days of Eamon de Valera, their attempts to subvert the status quo, and their efforts at political transformation and change through cultural intervention".[68] As Murray summarises of the National Theatre, the Abbey was a "sanitized clearinghouse of 'innocuous' ideas"; such was the emphasis generally in state-sponsored cultural fare.[69] By contrast, this was a time when British culture was opening up to radical writing about working-class life. Christopher Hilliard traces how a number of novels about that life in the 1950s and 1960s, such as Stan Barstow's *A Kind of Loving* (1960) and Barry Hines's *Kes* (1968), "had their readership buoyed for decades to come by the assignment of their books in school English courses".[70]

This history of O'Casey's reappropriation is not to suggest that the later writings were completely ignored. Indeed, the theatre practitioner and director Tomás Mac Anna led a crusading, solo campaign in favour of these works, affording many of them their first Irish productions.[71] But although Mac Anna worked as artistic director of the Abbey during the 1970s and 1980s, the theatre that O'Casey once hailed as his altar became a cold house for its one-time most lucrative asset. Despite its ongoing willingness to revive the *Trilogy*, in 1937 *The End of the Beginning* was the last of his plays to premier there. *Behind the Green Gates* (1962) did not appear in Ireland until 1975, directed at the Project Arts Centre by Frank Murphy. *The Drums of Father Ned: A Mickrocosm of Ireland*, rejected in 1957, did not appear in Ireland until 1966, and not at the Abbey itself until 1985. *The Star Turns Red* (1940) did not appear at the Abbey until 1978. Produced in New York in 1962, *Figuro in the Night* (written in 1959) did not see the light of day in Ireland until Mac Anna brought it to The Peacock in 1975. The exiled O'Casey had become, for Ireland, something of an unwanted pest, only to be smuggled in when least expected in the dark of night. Irish theatre was selective about what part of O'Casey it produced and when, in spite of the fact that he is, in the words of one critic, "not only a popular success; he has also achieved academic canonisation".[72] The plays from 1949 onwards, when *Cock-a-Doodle-Dandy* was first produced in Newcastle-upon-Tyne, are marked by a move towards increasing technical innovation; the juxta-position of vaudeville with lively polemics, dancing, costumes, the super-natural and the absurd. That these works have received scant attention in comparison with the earlier *Trilogy* is surely remiss.

Additionally, if there is a general shunning of the later plays, there is also "less willingness to deal with O'Casey's ideological commitments".[73] Critics such as David Krause have been eager to underplay the political element of O'Casey's writing.[74] Lowery and Mitchell, who take up this concern, are "lonely voices".[75] Critics in Ireland rubbished polemical plays such as *The Bishop's Bonfire* (1955), which attacked organised religion aligned with capitalism, despite generally positive reviews from English and American observers – and despite the crowds that thronged to see the play at Dublin's Gaiety Theatre.[76] In the Ireland that produced the fascist Blueshirt move-ment, the anti-communist Irish Christian Front and continual attacks on and denunciations of left-wing politics from church, state and even the trade union movement, it is unsurprising that a full appreciation of O'Casey's core aesthetic and political values failed to emerge in popular conscious-ness. It is surprising how the effects of this censorship endure. As Schrank laments, "this general reluctance to deal with O'Casey's socialism is unfor-tunate because it artificially isolates O'Casey's technical achievements from his political concerns".[77]

The slum dramatist

Another aspect of this distortion of O'Casey is that many of his biographers have misleadingly categorised the playwright's social standing. O'Casey played an important role in Dublin's working-class life. He posed questions of class's place in literature and literature's place in class, asking, for instance, "why should the docker reading Anatole France or the carter reading Yeats be a laughter-provoking conception?"[78] For this reason, and because his influence is so widespread, misleading assignations of the "slum dramatist" as an interloper on working-class culture must first be debunked if any case for the study of proletarian literature is to be fostered in Irish Studies. As Robert G. Lowery has observed, "most critics maintain that O'Casey was foremost a dramatist, before everything. Pushed into the background is the fact that he was first of all a human being, a product of an Irish working-class heritage."[79]

The O'Caseys' general economic status would seem to render suggestions that they were not working class mere mislead and pointless pedantry.[80] O'Casey was born into genteel poverty – if that is an appropriate description of what it is to be born to (self-) educated parents in the working-class Dublin of the 1860s. His father, Michael Casey, the son of a Limerick farmer, may have worked as a clerk for the proselytising Irish Church Missions (ICM) in Dublin, but he earned less than the average skilled tradesman at the time.[81] His mother, Susan (*née* Archer), was the daughter of Abraham Archer, an auctioneer, but her marriage to Michael ensured a life of bare subsistence. The young Seán worked as a despatch clerk in a wholesale chandler's office and also as a van boy at Eason & Son newsagents. Having no skilled trade, he later worked as a bricklayer's assistant on the GNR, from 1901 to 1911, was sacked for trade union activity and became unemployed and frequently malnourished, undergoing surgery for tubercular glands in 1915. His family always struggled to make ends meet and had lost at least three children in infancy. Life itself, as well as livelihood, was extremely precarious.

Seán's brothers worked at typical working-class jobs: Mick and Tom in the Post Office and later as soldiers, and Isaac toiling through 14-hour shifts as an office boy with the *Daily Express*. The dramatist's Gorkiesque descriptions of his mother scrubbing floors, "washing away the venom of poverty", have the ring of truth; his subjection to the tyranny of a hostile schoolmaster and his educational privations – having little money to see plays or buy books – all conjure up a bleak vista of working-class poverty in late nineteenth-century Dublin.[82] According to the first of his autobiographies, *I Knock at the Door* (1939), John (later Seán O') Casey was, like Roddy Doyle's Henry Smart in *A Star Called Henry*, the third child in succession to be given the same first name – the other two having died in infancy – and, as the first success after two false starts, he too was the embodiment of both his class's tenacity and its harrowing poverty. A family of eight children (or thirteen, according to O'Casey), living successively in cramped rented residences on Dorset Street, Inisfallen Parade and East Wall – on an income less than that of a carpenter, and then, after Michael's death in 1886, on whatever paltry earnings the children could muster for their mother – was not, by any economic index, "lower middle class".[83]

Restating this point seems superfluous, but it is necessary when so many critics insist on attaching this nebulous, "especially anxious" class assignation to O'Casey's family.[84] Furthermore, it is difficult to decipher from categorisations of his family as lower middle class precisely what the categorisers believe to be *working* class. This is not to discount the need to correct O'Casey's own misleading talk of being born in a "slum", or the need to point out that Susan Casey was from a bourgeois background, but it does indicate a level of unnecessary and unhelpful revisionism. Grene's assertion that O'Casey's parents were "lower middle class" because "Michael was a clerk" may accord with cultural inclinations of white-collar workers to *perceive* themselves as a cut above the industrial working class, but clerks on lesser wages than tradesmen, living in tenement areas at the turn of the century, were not necessarily much different from their more readily identifiable working-class neighbours.[85] Moreover, the education and occupations of his sons confirm that Michael's family largely affirmed rather than bucked the economic trends in working-class life. Grene stresses that Bella, O'Casey's sister, was "a trained National School teacher" – another "lower middle class" profession. But Bella only worked as a teacher for five years and was forced to leave her job because of the scandal of being eight months pregnant when taking her marriage vows; thereafter she was a charwoman, scrubbing floors for the better part of her working life. Bella indeed *personified* the sexist, economic disempowerment of working-class women at the time. Further, to argue that O'Casey's sister's work for a short period – while her family remained largely in poverty – partially renders the entire family lower middle class, is unconvincing indeed. It is even more so when one considers the actual conditions of female teachers at the time, who, according to John Lynch, were a "good example of the 'professional' working class". In real terms, having the status of a teacher was scant compensation for its lack of financial reward and the pervasive fear of "arbitrary dismissal".[86] Whatever way one looks at it, the O'Caseys were poor, but while Grene allows that Seán was "from a middle class family gone down in the world" (itself a questionable assertion), he does not allow that this descent made them proletarian.[87]

O'Casey's own opportunist, prolier-than-thou cultivation of the "slum playwright" tag inevitably plays its part in this distortion. An *Irish Times* reviewer maybe best synopsised O'Casey's six volumes of autobiography as "a strange rainbowed fantasia of fact, dream-fulfilment and paying off old scores".[88] In the *Autobiographies*, written between 1939 and 1954, O'Casey misrepresented his age, the chronological order of historic events, his outlook at different junctures, that of his family, his level of formal education, the street of his birth and the real facts of many different "rainbowed" events. His fabrications conform to the contours of a continuing effort on the author's part to reconcile the many antinomies of his life and to dramatise them in a flattering way. Perhaps also it is the general tendency to romanticise such writers of humble origins that arouses critical scepticism; O'Casey's frequent sobriquet of "slum dramatist" (one he was glad to accept as "suitable and accurate"), like that of Patrick McGill as the "Navvy Poet", or Francis Ledwidge as the "Scavenger Poet", is ripe for the kind of wry reception that inspired Flann O'Brien's parodic Jem Casey, the "Poet of the Pick" and "Bard of Booterstown", in *At Swim-Two-Birds* (1939).[89] In O'Brien's satiric commentary on the cult of the quotidian, the Bard's efforts to be close to his people are mocked in his own poetic travesty, "A Pint of Plain is Your Only Man".[90] One might also recall, in this regard, more recent controversies over the late Frank McCourt's gritty characterisation of childhood in working-class Limerick, *Angela's Ashes* (1996). The act of dramatising one's personal experience of hardship is sometimes met with incredulity, mockery or outright denial.

Concerns with hagiography and hackneyed, self-aggrandising autodidacts such as "Jem" might partially explain statements like that of biographer Garry O'Connor, that O'Casey's "assumption of poverty was, like a saint's, ultimately an act of will".[91] Christopher Murray also believes that the labouring class was "to be the class O'Casey *chose* to belong to".[92] But in all of this discussion of the playwright's intentions, it must be asked how much a poor, half-blind, trachoma-stricken, only slightly educated boy from East Wall at the time had any *choice* in the matter of his class.[93] Both economically and culturally, O'Casey was working class; why, then, the insistence that his fancies necessarily expose him as a Dickensian Bounderby?[94]

Kiberd's judgement of this "working-class realist" comes closest when he writes that "though O'Casey's family was nothing like the poorest of the poor, this was a life which he knew fairly well"; he was of the working class and close to its poorest members.[95] O'Casey's assignation as a (lower) middle-class interloper by critics is inaccurate and unhelpful and perhaps illustrates the pernicious and pervasive nature of the problem of the class concept in Irish studies with more clarity than anything else. As a trailblazing autodidact, O'Casey provided *the* towering example for other aspiring working-class Irish writers to emulate. He was an enabler of Dublin's proletarian culture, whose success would act as a beacon to later authors from impoverished backgrounds, such as Brendan Behan, Paul Smith, Christy Brown, Lee Dunne and Heno Magee. In interviews I have conducted for this book, with Magee, Dunne and Peter Sheridan, each cited this great Irish author as an outstanding influence. Unwittingly, the misleading critical reception of O'Casey is also an eloquent commentary on why these writers' commonalities of class (and so much else) have received so little critical attention, and perhaps also, on why the culture of Ireland's working class more generally has barely begun to attract scholarly inquiry.

2
Angry Young Men: Class Injuries and Masculinity

In "Rat Trap" (1978), the first Irish rock song ever to top the British music charts, working-class Dubliner Billy feels ensnared by his upbringing, and consequently needs to "find a way out" of poverty by "kick[ing] down that door" of social immobility.[1] His cry for a better life echoes the mood of the three plays that this chapter explores in a number of ways. Billy's vacillation between dreams of escape – from "traps [that] have been sprung long before he was born" – and the reality of poverty, in "high rise blocks", is a central dilemma for Dublin's own "Angry Young Man" generation of writers, who correspond with but differ in ways from the somewhat diverse "Angries" of mid-century Britain.[2] James McKenna, in *The Scatterin'* (1959), Lee Dunne, in *Goodbye to the Hill* (1976), and Heno Magee, in *Hatchet* (1972), are part of a movement in Dublin's writing which castigated the city of "closed doors" that The Boomtown Rats so pessimistically and poignantly portrayed.[3]

McKenna, Dunne and Magee articulate the emotional turmoil of detached young men who struggle to cope with the expectations and encumbrances that society foists upon them, and their plays share a parallel social function: to question Irish society's treatment of these working-class men and to unravel the complexities of their "habitus" – the acquired ideas, behavioural patterns and cultural tastes that characterise their environment.[4] All three writers present working-class Dublin men as a marginalised social cohort within the nation state, and each play presents emigration as their only prospect of escape from the "rat trap" of cyclical poverty. In this respect, they reiterate concerns voiced by the later O'Casey – particularly in plays such as *Cock-a-Doodle Dandy* (1949), where socially inhibited youths are forced to emigrate or to live at home in chronic boredom. However, whereas this later O'Casey, who was increasingly alienated from the Dublin of his youth, had largely focussed his plays of the 1940s and 1950s on rural conservatism, there is a sense in these later works of a new and unprecedented impetus in working-class, urban culture. Equally, while O'Casey had caricatured and lampooned men in a manner that McKenna, in particular, found offensive (see Chapter 1), these younger writers seek to explain, not *explain away*, the complex habitus of working-class masculinity.

As this chapter conveys, the plays' counter-cultural message – their criticism of state hegemony – is linked with the experience of emigration, influences from abroad and the contemporary proletarianisation of culture in Britain. Additionally, there is a key ideological change in how the working classes are represented. Departing from the focus of earlier writing, by O'Casey, A.P. Wilson, Denis Johnston, Oliver St John Gogarty, Joseph O'Connor and Robert Collis – which centred largely on the *material* privations of proletarian life – the post-1950s writers shifted the terms of class contention towards *cultural* and *social* deprivation, towards the "the hidden injuries of class".[5] In all three works, politics makes way for sociology and class angst is substituted for class warfare. Material realities of class inequality are indeed explored and deplored in the plays, but they act as secondary preoccupations to their authors' primary inquiries – into the cognitive and cultural inner worlds of working-class life. As such, these works venture into the realm of hegemony, into the subtleties of social power as it functions through multifarious discourses of repression, negotiation and consent. O'Casey's intensified concern with theocracy and social conservatism towards the end of his career also echoes in these writers' works.

Stylistically, the varied "realism" of this triumvirate is in itself both an aesthetic frame and a reaction against the unreal façade of social and literary discourse that, they suggest, has obfuscated the true nature of social conditioning. As we have already seen, it is often by subverting supposedly "bourgeois" forms that the most subversive counter-hegemonic messages are delivered, and this is often the case with these plays. We have also seen how, in Bourdieu's use, the term *habitus* refers to "durable, transposable dispositions" that are acquired and interiorised by individuals in response to social forces in their environments, such as class, religion and education.[6] Explaining the habitus of working-class life, the "system of dispositions (partially) common to all products of the same structures", is also key for Dunne, Magee and McKenna.[7] While it is often argued in cultural studies that such theories of social determinism can patronise the oppressed, assuming their (particular) inability (and presumably the theorist's/writer's ability) to see beyond the immediacy of their predicament, this tendency is also challenged by the countervailing aesthetic of Dublin's own collection of "angries".[8]

Richard Hoggart, in *The Uses of Literacy* (1957), criticised a cognate tendency in the middle-class Marxist's concept of working-class culture:

> He admires the remnants of the noble savage, and has a nostalgia for those "best of all" kinds of art, rural folk-art or genuinely popular urban art [...] He pities the Jude-the-Obscure aspect of working people. Usually

he succeeds in part-pitying and part-patronizing working people beyond any semblance of reality.[9]

Hoggart referred to Thomas Hardy's Jude Fawley, the hero of *Jude the Obscure* (1895), as the archetype of a working-class protagonist who functions as an "open book" for readers, a character who is determined sharply by his social conditioning and thus one who can be readily understood and explained in terms of his upbringing. The omniscient narrator's and implied reader's very act of "understanding" affirms their superior awareness and, by extension, their superior social standing. The working-class subject becomes a kind of puzzle, reified and readily understood by the astute bourgeois reader. As Andrew Sayer notes, "it is common for the behaviour of oppressed groups to be either pathologised or patronised", and Jude's function exemplifies perfectly this discursive condescension.[10]

According to Sayer, such an elitist view of socialisation proceeds from and supports a rigid sense of determinism that portrays individuals as mere products of their environments – devoid of what Bourdieu calls "organic individuality". As we have seen in the writings of Williams and Gramsci, which rebuff such simplification, reductivism of this kind is common to various theoretical strains of Marxism as well as to its bourgeois opponents. Illustrating this tendency in literature, there is, at times, a Manichean cleft between exceedingly good, "special cases" (the Jem Wilson of *Mary Barton* or the Frank Owen of *The Ragged Trousered Philanthropists*) and the unheroic, more plentiful and tragically corrupted denizens of their working-class world (exemplified in Gaskell's novel by Esther Barton, who becomes a prostitute through circumstance, and her brother John, who murders a tyrannous capitalist, and in Tressell's novel, by the class-unconscious plebeians Owen identifies as "despicable" and "dirt").[11] On the one hand, authors show how capitalism damages the poor; on the other, they choose to focus on protagonists who seem relatively – even implausibly – unscathed by those damages. Bourdieu's concept of social conditioning is useful in both contexts, in that, while it refutes the reductionism of the special case, it also refuses the temptation of determinism's extremities. Bourdieu stresses that "one cannot, in fact, without contradiction, describe (or denounce) the inhuman conditions of existence that are imposed on some, and at the same time credit those who suffer them with the real fulfilment of human potentialities".[12] His argument is neither "part-pitying" nor "part patronising"; it merely acknowledges the truism that poverty limits choice, but also, in stressing "organic individuality", refuses to represent those who suffer it as mere "products" of their environment. Bourdieu counsels that we "abandon all theories which implicitly treat practice [behaviour] as a mechanical reaction".[13]

The parallels between *The Scatterin', Hatchet, Goodbye to the Hill* and this analysis are salient, insofar as the plays wish to represent working-class characters as they are rather than in the manner a bourgeois writer might wish his/her representative "heroes" to be. This attitude is a marked departure from the discourse of pitying condescension that pervades writing on the working class. Like Bourdieu, these three writers seek to comprehend men's own imperfect construction of themselves *vis-à-vis* their environments, to depict what Walter Greenwood had termed "unpleasant people whose qualities, perhaps, are sad reflections of sadder environments".[14] But they seek also to show how their creations are neither completely determined nor "free", subject to a dialectic of self and society that remains a constant and inexorable negotiation.

Sculptor of words: James McKenna and his "book of liquid history"

James McKenna was an artist for whom the hidden injuries of class were an important theme, and perhaps also a deeply personal concern. Despite his acclaim as a sculptor, it was suggested that McKenna was deprived of Arts Council funding because "he [was] working class" and did "not fit in with the drawing-room atmosphere in which the Arts Council crew congregate".[15] McKenna worked in London for some years, partly with the London Underground, and would have undoubtedly witnessed the discontent from which some of Britain's Angries' writing arose. In 1959, at 26 years of age, he had written a play called *The Scatterin'*, and by that time he had emigrated to England four times – an experience that looms large in the play.[16]

The Scatterin' focuses on the bleak lives of four young Dubliners as they contemplate taking the mail boat for England. It explores their subjection to poverty, garda brutality and the consequences for one of them when he takes revenge for a brutal police attack. The play is set in June 1958, in the heart of working-class Dublin, "on the north side of the river Liffey", with players dressed in the contemporary "Teddy Boy" fashion that identifies them to the authorities as "dirty dressed-up gangsters".[17] Apparel of the Teddy Boy was indeed inherently subversive, mimicking the clothes of "the upper-class Edwardian dandy", but in an "imitation [that] was also an exaggeration, imprinting upon the styles of the upper-class original the signs of a different taste".[18] The Teddy Boys' youth, their modernity and their class alienates them from the backward, rural national culture of 1950s Ireland – a point the play repeatedly stresses.

McKenna wrote of Ireland in a poem of the same period as a place "forty years free; / Choked with ambiguity: / Surrounded by the sea", and the shabby surroundings of *The Scatterin'* emphasise the utter absence of the kind of affluence that was transforming working-class life in Britain: a house with a glassless fanlight, no door and "scooped out holes" for windows and a street described as "a narrow little canyon of dereliction" form the background to the opening act (*SC*, p. 7).[19] The dramaturgy, on one level, follows the familiar path of working-class social realism, portraying youth culture in an impoverished ghetto, but McKenna's stylised rock interludes and extraordinarily long monologues are defamiliarising features that hint at other theatrical styles. Moreover, the play works continually on the "metaphoric" level that John Fordham identifies with working-class literature. Fordham suggests that both realist and modernist forms operate, in working-class writing, with a constant allegorical edge. Metaphor and allegory are often used to subvert the fabricated "reality" of the work, showing how reality itself is reified, is alienated, by capitalism, and how the work's own surface reality must yield to the deeper veracity of common, barbarising capitalist relations. A critic in *The Spectator* lauded McKenna's play for its "many rare virtues", adding that his "lyrics have a bite and compassion which are the nearest things to Brecht I have seen written in English".[20] Indeed, the association with Brecht is apt, for McKenna constantly returns, as did Brecht, to an underlying political didacticism. The music emphasises *The Scatterin'*s modernity, and its experimental edge, but also harks back to (and modernises) the music-hall and variety tradition so favoured by Dublin's working-class theatregoers, in decline though it may have been by the early 1950s.[21] Ultimately, the play is a slice of contemporary working-class life – its final act set in the waiting room of a shipping company as its four central characters contemplate emigration, but there is always the deeper social message. The players are welcomed aboard their ship by a porter who represents the state – the prominent display of brass harp buttons on his coat invoking its official seal. His casual nonchalance about "the usual" (*SC*, p. 51) vista of a packed emigration ship invokes what McKenna later termed the "official cynicism" of a country abandoning its youth, or what Lar Redmond branded the "blood letting" of Ireland in *A Walk in Alien Corn* (1990).[22]

*The Scatterin'*s kitchen-sink quality was noted by reviewers, such as Gus Smith, for bringing "home the devastation of unemployment in the '50s" and being "relevant" socially, "particularly the brutality aspect".[23] McKenna himself said he had "drawn [his characters] as I see them" – "though", in keeping with Bourdieu's analysis, "not necessarily sympathetically"; "you probably won't like them", he cautioned.[24] The young sculptor was indeed explicitly associated with similar literary developments in Britain early in his career, when critic Denis Donoghue described him as "a young Irish 'angry'".[25] Although McKenna initially refused this appellation, it was one he would, on later reflection, accept.[26] Indeed, the play's anger speaks for itself, and McKenna's later description of its milieu of political indifference and social inequality exudes a still-palpable antagonism towards the state:

It is hard to convey the total official non-concern for the Irish people in the fifties. [...] We were a nation of demoralised men in gaberdines. Opposition, if only in dress, was offered by an increasing number of the young [...] who could find no other way of voicing their disgust at national official arrogance.[27]

Séamus O'Kelly, drama critic with the *Irish Times*, rhapsodically described *The Scatterin'* as "the most exciting Irish play since *The Plough and the Stars*", venturing that it was "above and beyond criticism".[28] Additionally, he again stressed its contemporary cultural significance, vouching that,

> If I were the Culture-Commisaar for Ireland (which heaven for-fend) I'd make Mr. Blythe [Ernest Blythe, former Government minister, then Abbey Managing Director] and his directorate attend "The Scatterin'" (in the Abbey Lecture Hall) every night, waited upon by all the politicians of all the parties in Ireland, with a repatriated (by force, if necessary) Sean O'Casey as train-bearer-in-ordinary. [...] It should show the Board of the National Theatre that young people *are* concerned with national problems and can write vividly about them [...] James McKenna's play could have been called "North-side Story".[29]

In his effusive praise, O'Kelly synopsises some of the main threads of the play – its counterblast to standard, Abbey-style plays, its affinity with O'Casey (despite McKenna's own reservations), its lessons for Irish politicians and its avowedly working-class, "North-side" flavour.

"Makin' little things seems so important": writing against the grain

Kelly's wish that *The Scatterin'* would become a Shavian lesson in youth sub-culture for the political classes suggests something that McKenna himself was keen to convey – the Irish state's elision of "North-side" (*read* working-class Dublin) narratives from literary and public discourse. This is a key point that links his play to the other works explored in this chapter and, indeed, this book as a whole. In *The Scatterin'*, references to the state's marginalisation of working-class people and their experiences abound. When the jocular Tony delivers his "monologue of self recrimination" – a story of his cheerless life of poverty and petty crime – McKenna juxtaposes suggestive, jarring references to Celtic Revivalism with the youth's own bleak memories. Tony announces himself sardonically, as

> Tony Riordan, the H.P. [hire purchase] Kid; ancient Druid in modern dress; livin' an' lovin' beyond his means. Been to all the high places in the city – Guinness's Brewery, Green Street Court House, and the Artane High School of Commerce. (I was in the Band, but they threw me out 'cause I hated the G.A.A.) Got me a flashy bike – me mother paid the deposit. And for a brief period of enchantment I took off like Oisin,

leavin' behind me the grim present an' went on a flight o' fancy – into the never never. (*SC*, p. 12)

Such "flight o' fancy" was the standard fare of Revival theatre, and the emergence of new theatres in 1950s Dublin (the Pike and the Damer) indicated a desire to move away from it. As Christopher Morash summarises, after the mid-century "constant comparisons with a sepia-tinged past generated a growing impatience with the theatrical heritage created in the early years of the Irish Literary Theatre"; the new Abbey unveiling of 1966 would itself provide "an opportunity of breaking with a certain tradition of writing", then director Tomás Mac Anna anticipated.[30] Fittingly, McKenna draws a vivid contrast between Tony's playful, self-aggrandising tone and his experiences of a "certain tradition" of Irishness to illustrate the inadequacy of that tradition.

The "never never" of "sepia-tinged" Ossianic legend is a far cry from the courthouse and the Artane School for Boys, and his "diabolically satirical" vision infers that Ireland's heroic narratives of primitivist fantasy are anathema to the stories of a generation of working-class men whose lives are so very unheroic. This was something McKenna expressed in a later poem that posited "the clash of past ideals and howling needs" in a country that had "paused too long before these graves".[31] The social image of reified social relations and a culture that alienates the working class breaks through in the symbolism of McKenna's jarring imagery. Irish lore fails to reconcile with the reality of "Dublin's frustrated teenagers, warped by an environment which can offer them only tenements, the street-corner, and the dole".[32] Tony's monologue continues less flamboyantly, but emphatically, in curt, brutal syntax, indicating how his life differs from that of the mythical Oisín:

Then one day the bogey man came knockin' at my door. He caught me with me trousers down. I was outa work an' hadn't a sou. None of us had. Jaze I'll never forget that day though. Me mother was cryin' her eyes out; me oul fella went for me with the razor. (I had forged his signature on the docket.) Anyways, the next thing I was in jail. (*SC*, p. 12)

Oisín goes to Tír na nÓg on his horse; Tony goes to jail for his "H.P." bike.[33]

Allusions to the young men as American Indians throughout the play are illustrative in this regard; talk of "General Custer" and "Sitting Bull", Jemmo's ominous stabbing and immolation of an effigy during the "portentous rhythm" of a mock tribal war dance in Act II (an illustration of which, painted by McKenna, adorns the frontispiece of the 1977 Goldsmith edition), and apocalyptic fears that "they'll stamp us out", as Tony's friend Jemmo predicts, that "one by one we'll disappear – like the Red Indians

from the Plains", all form part of a conceit that represents the forced emigration of poor men from their own country as a form of social cleansing (*SC*,
pp. 45, 32, 45, 23). By defamiliarising reality, these repeated spurts of experimentalism, in a mainly social-realist play, also serve to suggest how unreal
these young men's predicament should seem. The American Indian analogy
may seem exaggerated, but that is precisely what it is meant to be; after
talking about his problems in trying to court the interest of a girlfriend on
limited means, Jemmo dismisses his worries as "makin' little things seems
so important", but this is exactly what his creator wishes to do (*SC*, p. 54).[34]
McKenna's exaggeration seeks to develop a sense of how significant and
strange such commonplaces ought to be. Jemmo follows with an awkward
simile about King Cormac and an allusion to Brian Boru, which are not only
incongruous but superfluous; it is his own life of "little things", his hidden injuries, which take centre stage (*SC*, pp. 53–54). McKenna, like Patrick
Kavanagh in his 1951 poem "Epic", seeks to make his own importance.

   If the anti-hero of British Angry Young Man narratives challenged the
"conformity" of "affluent modern life", McKenna's men challenge cultural
conformity in a society that is failing to be either affluent or modern.[35]
Again, the unreality of reality is stressed. St Patrick's Day, the national feast
day, is "like a bleedin' funeral", with sepulchral floats like "dirty big industrial hearses streamin' along" (*SC*, p. 31). The youths mock Catholicism
and peasant rurality, inventing a parodic tribute to the national saint, "the
Wyatt Earp of ancient Ireland", and his "descendants, the farmers", who
bathetically "exterminated the rabbit for thirty pieces of silver" (*SC*, p. 31).
The tripartite analogy – to myxomatosis culling, St Patrick's banishment of
serpents and Judas's betrayal of Christ – is a blatant and sardonic pastiche on
the dominant cultural totems of rural, Catholic Ireland. Ireland embraced
a particularly austere brand of Catholicism in the twentieth century, as the
"blind man" character from James Plunkett's short story "A Walk Through
the Summer" (1955) implies, when he dismisses "foreign Catholics" as "notorious luke-warmers".[36] McKenna's young men lament the waning influence
of this Ireland with a satiric "Ochon is Ochon o!" (parodically invoking the
linguistic register of Gaelic Ireland typified by Peig Sayers), and while their
continual references to ancient figures, such as "King Cormac" and "Maeve
of Cooley", may seem surreal in a play about modern working-class life,
that is exactly their purpose (*SC*, pp. 31, 54, 55).[37] McKenna emphasises the
gap between different Irelands – mystical and quotidian, conceptual and
real – in order to question outmoded conceptions of national culture and to
foreground the internally alien counter-culture of working-class Dubliners.

"This is the story of nothing at all": Habitus and crime

McKenna also shows how the social inequality which has led to this alienation fosters dysfunctional behaviour in his protagonists. Whereas earlier

writers, such as O'Casey, Collis, Wilson, Stephens and Gogarty, had tended to avoid representations of crime in working-class life, McKenna follows Behan's lead in *The Quare Fellow* (1954) by charting its emergence as a serious urban problem. A criticism of such a limited focus might be that it overemphasises the untypical, lumpen elements of that community, but with the contemporary emergence of ghettoised working-class council estates and pockets of high unemployment – which led to the creation of crime black spots in Dublin – McKenna's theme was pertinent and prescient indeed.[38]

Characters in the play are trapped in a cycle of dole queues and monotony that engenders a disdain for life itself and leads to violent behaviour. The first words of the play, sung by Ould Rock – "this is the story of nothing at all" – infer both the boredom of the young men's lives and their social invisibility (*SC*, p. 7). The day is drawing to a close as the action begins – a temporal indication of its dispirited milieu – and Conn explains that he "never did a curse o' God thing [during it] but draw me money at the Labour". He and his young friends are already world-weary, "arseing about the length o' the day in idleness", with yet "another day gone to waste" (*SC*, pp. 8, 9). Conn (whose Gaelic name, recalling another Fianna warrior, forms part of McKenna's pastiche) sings about social alienation and crime – about being "clapped in a cell", haunted by the spectre of the "Big Black [police] Wagon", part of a life of "crawlin' about here in the sunlight like corpses on sick leave" (*SC*, pp. 8, 31). For Jemmo, his idleness is now preferable to work; social-welfare payments are "more than [he] used to get ridin' a carrier bike for them greasy ould bastards [one presumes he means businessmen] down town" (*SC*, p. 9).

Perhaps the one thing these young men share with the mythical Oisín of *Tír na nÓg* is that they too get trapped in a limbo of eternal youth, and again we find this allegorical rendering of Fordham's "social image". The youths shout "hurry, hurry" to John as he rushes to put another vinyl on his record player while the "sun is sinking", suggesting they live in fear of the future, of the ending of another day. Such a vista of disenchanted youth echoes decades later in Paul Mercier's Dublin play, *Wasters* (1985), in which a group of youths drink themselves to oblivion on waste ground near their council estate. Like McKenna's already world-weary Teddy Boys, Mercier's youths speak of not getting out of bed if the weather is bad, inflicting "tortures" on younger children for fun, robbing, gang membership, and living in a place where "nothing happens" and there is "fuck all to look forward to".[39] Evidently McKenna's point about the marginalisation of working-class youths was a far-sighted one. Roddy Doyle's Jimmy Rabbitte Sr encounters similarly alienated young men in *The Van* (1991), but these "Living Dead", as he terms them, only enter his world as "zombies", people to be avoided and pitied; "they'd be dead before they were twenty".[40] Mercier's play ends symbolically with a mock wedding, part of his youths' fantasy of growing up and an emblem of their tragic inability to do so; in the play's last lines, one character enquires "when does the sun come up?" and another responds, "does it matter?"[41] McKenna's use of the sun as an emblem of anxiety about the future echoes again in Joe'O'Byrne's play, *It Come Up Sun* (2000), based in a container yard in Dublin's docks.[42] Like Mercier's urban drama, O'Byrne's also (with curious similarity) ends in a mock wedding – yet another sardonic mockery of adult happiness. O'Byrne's Billy also fears the rising sun, symbolising the future, and the sound of the Docklands' crane that accompanies it, symbolising capitalist power. In *The Scatterin'*, a "children's chorus" intermittently sings in the background – its haunting and hopeful voices echoing dispiritingly in the failed adulthood that the play foregrounds (*SC*, p. 19). McKenna's dramatic emphasis, like Mercier's and O'Byrne's, is on the wistful feelings of lost youth and wasted life, the psychological indignities of poverty – its hidden injuries.

Additionally, McKenna refuses to gloss over the worst effects of poverty on his characters. In Act II they try to come up with stories to entertain each other as they drink in the rural surrounds of the Dublin Mountains, but despite this brief escape from urban decay, their depressing reminiscences show how trapped they are by the environment they have grown up in. Patzer castigates Irish moral conservatism, recalling the story of distraught, unloved, "poor ould Biddy the whore" (*SC*, p. 36), a local woman who had numerous children with different men and thus became a social pariah. One of her offspring dies in filth, sleeping with rats, another, thrown by the crazed Biddy herself from a moving train, is a product of what Nuala O'Faoláin termed "the whole dreadful, dreadful 50s thing that there was no sex and that nobody got pregnant before marriage [which] led to so many secret lives".[43] Biddy, like the characters in the play, is a complex, damaged personality, worthy of both pity and loathing.

In another long monologue, Jemmo excoriates the Republic for its scandalous abuse of children born to single mothers. His tirade anticipates Mannix Flynn's later novel *Nothing to Say* (1983) and play *James X* (2003), which fictionalised the author's sufferings in Irish "correctional" institutions. Jemmo recalls that, "after a short stay with the nuns, the kids were torn from their mothers an' sent in droves to the country" (*SC*, p. 38). These forgotten fosterlings were members of a forgotten slave class:

> The property of the State – the Free State [...] Kept starved; kept naked; kept terrified – an kept at home from school as soon as they could ride a carrier bike. They were also kept ignorant –'cause they teach nothin' in National Schools only Gaelic Games an' catechism [...] They were called nurse-childer, an' on farms especially they were tortured. (*SC*, p. 38)

Flynn would later castigate this abuse of mainly "working-class children" by "a Church that profited from the forced manual labour of 150,000 children, and a State that supplied them with these child workers".[44] McKenna also rebukes officialdom, business interests, the education system and the prevailing orthodoxies of Irish life, and his claims are perhaps one reason why John Ryan heralded this play as a "theatrical landmark in Dublin".[45]

But it is also telling that his stories of hidden terror are only utterable on the periphery of the city, in the isolation of the mountains. In a dramatic spatial metaphor, the city's limits speak to the city's cultural centre in parallel ways; the alienated and underprivileged criticise their country in the play-world, and they also confront the mainly bourgeois audience of the Abbey, the Pike and the Olympia in the world beyond the stage. Such dialogical, allegorical inter-class didacticism is a common tactic in writing on working-class Dublin, for example in Collis's *Marrowbone Lane* (1943), with its stated intent of "showing one section of society how the other lived".[46] The reflexive inter-class relationship continues to be deployed in later work, such as Val Mulkerns' *Very Like a Whale* (1986), with its focus on a middle-class character who comes face-to-face with working-class poverty – the "human scrap heap" of St Domenic's school, and the "living conditions that people this side of the river [the affluent south side] wouldn't believe".[47] Enda Walsh's *Sucking Dublin* (1997), which focuses on Dublin's heroin crisis, echoes these forthright addresses across class divides. Heroin addict Lep implicates his audience in his own degraded state: "What ya get is what ya deserve!! YOU DESERVE ME!! Forget me and I'll peep up and smash open your gaff [...] you left me with nothin cept this!!"[48] McKenna's Jemmo also excoriates Irish theatre's failure to address narratives of working-class life: "I've spoke enough about the jumped-up trollops o' Grafton Street [...] an' the Garrison in black over across the wall in Blackrock College hoistin' the keys o' the kingdom", he proclaims, before relating a "little story about little white youngsters durin' the war, an' the little concentration camps where many suffered for a time before enterin' into Artane" (*SC*, pp. 37–38). Anger is indeed a palpable element of the play.

These stories unearth a hidden Ireland unfamiliar in contemporary popular discourse and literature. Together with the brutal, unprovoked police attack on the youths, with which Act I culminates, the Teddy Boys' litany of complaint serves to explain their later exodus to England in Act III, and to frame our understanding of Jemmo's barbarous reprisal for police violence, in which he kills a policeman. As Jemmo attests himself, "we was on the wrong side o' the law from the start" (*SC*, p. 58). And when he tries to articulate his rationale for the brutal act, it is telling that he digresses into a monologue on his life thus far, and his subjection to capitalism's vicissitudes:

When I left school at fourteen I said I'd be a mechanic, like me brother [...] But the factory where me brother worked left off a hundred blokes, an' he was among them [...] not long after that the man I worked for got himself a new boy. I was gettin' too big for me bike – an' his wallet. Since then I've been scroungin' here an' there getting' bits o' jobs. I've been goin' around a year now without a bit o' work. (pause) I marched with the unemployed crowd onest...(*SC*, pp. 64–65)

Jemmo's meandering explanation here falteringly forages for meaning in an irrational act, attempting to reach beyond stereotypes of criminality and underclass thuggery, which pervade public discourse, by invoking economic and political realities, much as Hubert's intelligent reaction to the degradations of Parisian life in Matthieu Kassovitz's film *La Haine* (1995) offsets the awfulness of his murder of a policeman, also in reprisal for an unwarranted police attack on a friend. Jemmo might have perverted his anger at social conditions into a vicious and unjustifiable act of vengeance, but McKenna also suggests his previous potential for positive political activity with the "unemployed crowd" (which elected a Dáil member in 1957). Jemmo meanders on, explaining that his attack was "the only thing that I've ever done in my life" and that he is "not proud" but "not sorry", finishing abruptly, "that's it" (*SC*, p. 65). For him, this sad tale is the end of his life as he knows it, and it shows that the crime he has just committed emerges not only from his own twisted reasoning but also from the hopelessness of his habitus, the kind of bleak mid-century Dublin childhood that Pat Larkin more recently recalls in his collection of short stories, *The Coalboat Kids and Other Stories* (2007).[49] The murderous youth in McKenna's play is Bourdieu's "divided self" incarnate, a character whom audiences can both pity and anathematise, a young man trapped between his confused allegiance to his friends, for whom he kills, and his hoped-for escape through emigration, in which he fails.[50] McKenna imbues his actions with ambiguity, a sense of both their senselessness and their emergence from a distinct environment in which they begin to make sense.[51]

As such – and to return to Fordham's contentions on proletarian art – McKenna refuses the stereotypical bourgeois narrative of crime, whereby the criminal is exposed and simultaneously, perfunctorily anathematised and explained. In problematising Jemmo's act by reference to a multifaceted social milieu, and in rendering the complexity of the criminal's conception of his society with brutal honesty, McKenna chooses, as Fordham might put it, to "defy the conventional expectations of bourgeois plot or narrative development"; on the one hand, Jemmo refuses pity, for he is far from contrite or justified; on the other, he attempts to articulate some vague, ultimately confused rationale for his behaviour.[52] The impenetrability of his character refuses easy assimilation to the bourgeois presumption of a calculable world, but the difficult circumstances of his upbringing suggest that his is not the only crime in the play.

"Where they don't give a damn / Far, far away": going home

When the other young men of the play sail away, metaphorically they are sailing home. Irish culture is illiberal, doctrinaire, anti-urban and anti-working class. In Ireland, the youths can't even have sexual relationships, because Irish women are said to be "well trained in them women factories they call convents", where "the word MAN is handled with asbestos gloves an' holy water" (*SC*, p. 13).[53] By contrast, foreign cultures are vital and uninhibited. Jemmo says he wishes he "was in Mexico or somewhere now" as he partakes in a "mock-Spanish dance" (*SC*, p. 23). Music and dance were used similarly by Maura Laverty, in her 1950 play, *Tolka Row*, with its "awfully passionate" music of South American tangos and rhumbas emphasising the receptivity of working-class Dublin to outside influences.[54] (One must recall how radical such depictions were in the context of Irish culture: for instance, jazz music had been banned from radio stations by governmental decree in the early 1940s.) In *The Scatterin'*, Fats Domino himself seems to urge the youths to leave Ireland, singing "so long, I'm all tied up / An' know my way" (*SC*, p. 24). Suggestively, Tony would love to play his Anglo-American rock music "in every town in the country", which would make the "young fellas and youngwans" "dance till dawn" and cause the "ould fellas an' ouldwans" to "come out and shake the dust off themselves" (*SC*, p. 24). The dream of going to a liberal "Happy Land / Far, far away. / Where they don't give a damn / Far, far away" (*SC*, p. 51), is the youths' social salvation; it is also the antithesis of their surrounds, much as it is for Redmond in *A Walk in Alien Corn*, where Lar's excitement at the prospect of girls that "were a lot more givish" and a society that hasn't been "too well brainwashed by the Church" underpins his desire to leave home.[55] Lar's further exhilaration at "the distant roar of guns and explosions" shortly after arrival into wartime Britain is surely an ironic indictment of the boredom back in Ireland: even world war is better than Irish stasis.[56] A "curious thing about Ireland's manner of life," O'Casey noted in 1944, was that "while always standing haughtily apart from England, she has always been by her side".[57] British culture seems less foreign to these youths than that of their native country, and its world of sex, rock music and hedonism, to which the mail boat sails, is the modern world that Ireland eschews. England's cultural expansiveness finds expression in one of McKenna's poems about emigration to London, in which he repeats its title, "Oxford Street is Long", as a refrain that both illustrates the breadth of the new city and his own eager perambulation of its streets:

> But withal I have no nation
> And my only consolation is
> That
> Oxford Street is Long
> Oxford Street is Long
> Oxford Street is Long
> Oxford Street is Long.[58]

If Warley is a place "without memories" for John Braine's Joe Lampton in *Room at the Top* (1957), England is a place where McKenna can "have no nation".[59] For both angry young men, English and Irish, the possibilities of social mobility in post-war Britain present a revolutionary break with the past.

Hatchet: the monstrous mother

Like McKenna's Jemmo, Hatchet, Heno Magee's aptly nick-named angry young man, is also caught in a battle between social pressures and individual will. Like McKenna, Magee is deeply concerned with the process of socialisation. Hatchet is also forced to choose between the corrupting influences of his upbringing and the possibility of escape to a new life abroad – a choice that acts as the fulcrum for the tensions of the play. Burdened with the moniker he acquired for confronting the much-feared local "Animal Gang" (a real group that had attacked republicans and socialists in Dublin street battles) with a hatchet when he was 14 years old, Hatchet is a slave to his reputation for violence. In part, this reputation is also bequeathed by his notorious late father, the maniacal Digger (the root of his sobriquet, "dig", being local parlance for "punch"), and, with McKenna, Magee refuses to diminish the harsher aspects of working-class life by presenting likeable sorts or heroes who somehow surmount the privations of their difficult environment. But Magee's play has none of the light relief that musical interludes and dances yield in *The Scatterin'*. This is, in the words of one reviewer, "a play with a serious purpose".[60]

Magee develops an even grittier dramaturgy, in which the harshness of poverty and of those who live in it are presented with uncompromising veracity. His protagonist, Hatchet, is a liminal figure; ironically, however, he is also the quintessence of what his community expects a "man" to be. Torn between his reputation, his family and his own vacillating moral compass, he must struggle in vain to extricate himself from spiralling gang violence, and, like *The Scatterin'*, this play seeks a social and political understanding of the type of gang violence that is so often conceived of, in public discourse, as the inexplicable and irrational domain of "fiends with hair-trigger, violent impulses and reactions".[61] Magee's protagonist's actions are presented as those of a conflicted and complex young man, whose environment ultimately overmasters his basically benevolent impulses.

Heno Magee was born in 1939, six years after James McKenna and five years after Lee Dunne. He grew up in the tough working-class environs of inner-city Bridgefoot Street and left school at fourteen years of age to work as a messenger boy, later pursuing a career for five years in the British Royal Air Force. When Magee returned to Dublin, following various international tours of duty, he came back to a moribund economy and the enduring poverty of inner-city Dublin. Yet it was a place rich in dramatic potential, and the plaudits for Hatchet, his most successful work, question its exclusion from the canon of Irish studies. *Time Out* claimed that it had "kicked life and laughter" onto the London stage in its 1975 English production. The *New Statesman* found it "tersely written and brilliantly acted", and *The Financial Times* compared the work – in the mandatory parallel of those wishing to laud a working-class Dublin scribe – with that of Sean O'Casey.[62]

First produced in the Peacock Theatre, Dublin, on 27 July 1972, and a year later as a screenplay for RTÉ, Hatchet is set in 1970s "workingclass [sic] environs", in the Baileys' artisan home and also in their local public house.[63] Its later production in the Embankment, Tallaght, in 1981, matched the pub background on stage to the environment beyond it. Described in terms of proletarian authenticity, this production employed a stagecraft that tempered the austere tone of the theatre with more familiar working-class surroundings. "'Hatchet' was well attended," a reviewer recalled:

> [...in] the decidedly rough and ready facilities at the Embankment. The play is ideally suited to a pub venue such as this, with the raucous and energetic interplay of Magee's characters occurring quite naturally amid the clink of pint glasses and the plumes of cigarette smoke. "Hamlet" or "Death of a Salesman" just would not have gone down the same.[64]

In this respect and others, Magee's dramaturgy follows McKenna's, attempting to bring traditionally alien discourses into Irish theatre, but by 1981 Magee is more strident in his desire to bring alien audiences in as well. As the play opens, it is "late summertime" and – just as sunset imposes a gloomy sense of foreboding in *The Scatterin'* – Magee suggests that this is also ironically the late summertime for Hatchet and his new wife Bridie's fledgling marriage (*Hat*, p. 7). Magee's focus centres on the complex relationships that bind Hatchet, a docker in his mid-twenties, to his working-class surroundings: his almost Oedipal relationship with his termagant mother, Mrs Bailey, who moulds him into the role of protector and breadwinner, and his countervailing relationship with his exasperated wife, who wants him to leave home for a new life in England; he is bound by his friends, Hairoil and Freddie, who exhort him to engage in macho acts of violence, which, as in *The Scatterin'*, are partly a release from the monotony of vacant lives. Joey, a returned emigrant of about 60 years of age, and a factory chargehand in his adopted home of England, is Mrs Bailey's "fancy man", and he also unwittingly pressurises her son. His relative affluence and air of comfort, as well as his offer of a job in an English factory, suggest the benefits that might accrue for Hatchet from emigration.

With all of these pressures dragging at Hatchet's conflicted consciousness, the play is partly a psychological drama, with its main characters performing as personifications of his choices and the anxieties they arouse. Johnyboy Mulally, a hard man, has insulted Mrs Bailey in their local pub, before the action of the play commences, and the story starts *in media res*, moving through Mrs Bailey's galling attempts to pressure her son into attacking Mulally, Hatchet's helpless response and Mulally's reprisal, which closes the play. Dramatic tension centres on Hatchet's most fundamental dilemma: he must choose between the violent legacy of Digger, and the wealth, benevolence and comfort that Joey, an alternative father figure, represents.

"A man went out to find his enemies, and he found no friends": Machismo and class

Like McKenna, Magee attempts to rationalise his chief protagonist's destructiveness by constructing his entrapment in that classically working class, male "cross-fire" of "conflicting demands for fraternity and assertion of his own worth".[65] Even his suggestive nickname connotes Hatchet's severance from wider society, but, as already suggested, he also conforms with and excels at the expectations of male behaviour in working-class Dublin, engaging in ostentatious acts of bravado with his peers and taking a dominant role in the home. From his first appearance, Hatchet is an alpha male, "roughly" pushing the warring Angela and Mrs Bailey apart, asserting the primacy of his own needs: "Ah, shut up the lot of yis, I'm famished, where's me dinner, where's me dinner?" (*Hat*, p. 16). He spurns his wife's sister, ordering her to "sit down you, sit down", and asks his mother dismissively when she is "going to get sense" (*Hat*, p. 16). He flexes his power in the domestic and communal spheres, repeatedly associated with macho role-models, stretching out in his living room "like Tarzan", swaggering like "Clark Hudson, the way he swings them shoulders of his" (*Hat*, pp. 20, 12).

Beneath this posturing, however, we find a fundamentally weak and damaged individual, who struggles within the learned behavioural patterns of his habitus. As Andrew Sayer notes, "class lacks a moral justification" in itself, and therefore "people of different classes are likely to feel obliged to justify their differences".[66] This class affirmation results in what he terms "folk sociologies": internalised prejudgements, accepted norms and behaviours, which become normative, even prestige "folk" traits.[67] Working-class men oftentimes find "moral justification" in adopting a folk sociology of "laddish" masculinity; this, in turn, justifies their putative superiority to a supposedly effete middle-class male.[68] Economic distinctions become naturalised behavioural distinctions in class mythology; imagined distinctions of virility recoup prestige in male prowess for the working-class man – prestige which has been lost in comparisons of hard currency.

The internal battle with such powerful social and cultural forces is a recurrent theme in Dublin's writing of the working class. In *Night Shift* (1985), Dermot Bolger describes the habitual demeanour of poor young men who "strut about the place, each terrified of betraying signs of intelligence to the other [...] like CB headers, all tuning down to the one wavelength to conduct their conversations" – "boys who refused to admit feelings".[69] In Brendan Gleeson's *Breaking Up* (1988), this pretence of machismo is depicted as a social inhibitor. Frank takes pride in his image as a rough, tough labourer, a facile delight in being associated with manual work, as Deirdre, his girl-friend, scoffs: "you love that – wearing the working gear into the pub. Frank Bennett. The working man".[70] But the cultivation of this image demands that he eschew emasculating things such as education, which threaten to ruin Frank's contrived reputation. He is comically "affronted" when mis-taken for a student, and the play symbolically opens with one of his cohorts, Andy, kicking and upending books and study notes triumphantly as he cel-ebrates the end of school life: "Education, lads, edu-shaggin'-cation".[71] Such machismo is sometimes depicted as an attractive trait in working-class men, Roddy Doyle shows, a mixture of social clout and sexual prowess that Paula Spencer initially finds empowering in her abusive husband Charlo: "I was with Charlo now and that made me respectable. Men kept their mouths shut when I went by. They were all scared of Charlo and I loved that".[72] A thug in Conor McPherson's *The Good Thief* (1994) claims that such "power attracts women", and in Neville Thompson's novel, *Jackie Loves Johnser OK?* (1997), Jackie tellingly discovers her attraction to Johnser when she glimpses him triumphant in a fight, "standing over three bodies lying helpless on the ground".[73] Even in the softer working-class paterfamilias of Doyle's Barrytown Trilogy (*The Commitments* [1987], *The Snapper* [1990] and *The Van* [1991]), there is the ingrained fear of feminisation, of exposure amongst one's peers. In a moment of fondness, Jimmy Rabbitte Sr considers kissing his wife Veronica, "but no, he decided, not with the boys there. They'd slag him".[74] In all of these works, one observes this dialectic of pretence and insecurity; the act of masculine confidence is betrayed by a fear of expo-sure – the exposure of a softer side.

In *Hatchet*, Magee shows how this proletarian "folk sociology" of masculin-ity results in ruination for his central character, who finds himself unequal to its interpellating power. Hatchet is continually pressurised by his peers, to the detriment of his marriage. They cajole him into attending a boxing tournament, leaving Bridie trapped with Hatchet's cantankerous mother (*Hat*, p. 20). When Bridie chides, "tch, Hatchet, I thought ye were stronger, I really did, ye can't go running around with them all the time", he gruffly ignores her (*Hat*, p. 21). This is a culture in which women are degraded and despised, Magee emphasises. Freddie views his wife and children as a burden, always "moaning"; he brands his kids, in rhyming slang, his "god forbids" (*Hat*, p. 29). Hairoil later sings a tongue-in-cheek complaint against his wife, intoning "my wife's a cow, my wife's a cow, / my wife's a cow-keeper's daughter" (*Hat*, p. 48). His wife and family are the reason he spends little time at home, he says (*Hat*, p. 51). The relationship between Hatchet and Bridie underscores, in part, the reasons behind such negative attitudes; their lack of privacy and their failure to produce children are consequences of a lack of financial means. The sexual awkwardness caused by the lack of intimate space in Mrs Bailey's house makes Hatchet violent and resentful: "I'm mad to be putting up with ye, ye hardly let me near ye...I ought to give ye a bleedin' dig, that's what anyone else around here would do" (*H*, p. 22). Poverty denies them closeness, just as it does in Robert Collis's *Marrowbone Lane* (1943), where – in another domestic argument in a cramped inner-city dwelling – newlyweds Mary and Jim's relationship soon turns sour, she complaining about his devotion to the greyhound track and his friend Joe, while he complains about the lack of variety in his boring domestic life.[75] How many works of working-class life depict domestic discord as the microcosmic corollary of macrocosmic inequalities?[76]

But the ingrained culture of working-class manhood also plays its part. When Hatchet considers purchasing a present for Bridie's birthday, he reveals that he is beset by class and gender insecurities. He pathetically fears emasculation in the female domain of the clothes shop: "Ye didn't expect me to go into a woman's shop, did ye?" he protests; "I wouldn't mind but the way they stare at ye in those places, you'd think I was going to rob the bleeding shop" (*Hat*, p. 24). Such anxiety recurs in Jim Sheridan's *Mobile Homes*, when Larry refuses to seek contraceptives in a family planning clinic because, *pace* Behan's malapropism in *The Quare Fellow*, "they'll think I'm a sex mechanic". His wife Helen's riposte could equally refer to Hatchet: "It's the quare things you're embarrassed about".[77]

Like McKenna's youths, who are trapped in a juvenile social vacuum, *Hatchet*'s young men thrive on a childish culture of boyish adventurism. Hatchet and his friends' dialogue centres on such subjects as the "great goer" (fighter) at the boxing tournament, or whether actor James Cagney, "the head crook" in *The Roaring Twenties*, who "bleedin' milled everyone", would beat Humphrey Bogart in an imaginary fight (*Hat*, p. 36). This theme of impotent, infantile male fantasy is again recalled in other writing of the working class. In Doyle's 1992 play *Brownbread*, a group of adventurist young working-class men kidnap a bishop, seemingly because they've little else to do and, like Magee's hard-chaws, because they have been paying too much attention to the exploits of their silver screen heroes. "We're on the map now lads, wha' [...] this is the business, wha'", Donkey, one of the kidnappers delightedly enthuses. Another, John, *"puts his back very dramatically to the window wall; something he's seen done loads of times on 'Miami Vice'"*, later addressing gardaí in "a Harlem accent".[78] Beneath the comedy, Doyle suggests how violence is woven into the fabric of working-class male identity, accentuated by the influences of mass culture.[79] Beneath the farce in both of these works, there is a serious criticism of working-class masculinities. Working-class Dublin clearly reveres "hard-chaw" characteristics, and Magee posits their consequences.

Despite his firm rebuttal of his mother's repeated requests that he fight Mulally, Hatchet is ultimately unable to refuse the confrontation, a capitulation rendered all the more tragic by his late epiphany, in the final act, when he confides to the gentle Joey the wisdom of his former parole officer:

> A man went out to find his enemies,
> And he found no friends.
> Now,
> A man went out to find his friends,
> And he found no enemies. (*Hat*, p. 71)

The aphorism precedes Hatchet's rush into battle with Mulally, as his reputation and code of duty overmaster his common sense. As one reviewer wrote, "inheriting a code of blind, almost Sicilian honour, Hatchet himself is doomed as Anouilh, in his 'Antigione', predicted doom for so small a reason as waking up one morning wanting merely a little respect".[80]

Hatchet's mother knows, with cruel familiarity, the underlying codes of his habitus. It is implicit that Mrs Bailey is aware, when she takes a bottle in her hand after Ha Ha (Hatchet's brain-injured uncle) is attacked by Mulally, that Hatchet will act as expected, regardless of the consequences. Yelling "you can stay here if ye like" and "I'll do it for ye", she calculates that her son will soon revert to type. As he eventually emerges to face Johnnyboy, we observe the pitiable plight of a man torn between his friends, his mother, his wife and his own better instincts. His mother has "ruined everything", as Bridie yells, because Hatchet, like Digger, is incapable of being the man he aspires to be, the man "who found no enemies" (*Hat*, p. 75).

Like McKenna, Magee posits emigration from Dublin's working-class pressures as his angry young man's only hope of happiness, a message relayed most persuasively in the contrast drawn between Hatchet and Joey, the affluent visiting émigré. Mrs Bailey encourages her son's macho bravado, fearing that "everyone will walk over ye now", but by contrast she lauds her new "fancy man['s]" passivity. Joey is "real quiet, he wouldn't hurt a fly", she counters, when Hatchet questions what the older man did to defend her in a pub melee (*Hat*, pp. 73, 18). When Hatchet threatens Joey because he fears the older man is seducing his mother, the émigré neatly ducks out of Hatchet and his habitus's epistemic reach: "I don't know why you're picking on me, Hatchet, I'm not a hard man", he curtly retorts (*Hat*, p. 45).

Joey has escaped the normative masculinity of working-class Dublin, he implies. The code of the "hard man" is something he eschews now that he has come to wealth; indeed, since leaving home he feels a "stranger" with his "own" people (*Hat*, p. 58). "Civilised" by affluence, as Angela characterises it, Joey now acts as the voice of reason in explosive situations, warning Bridie to leave the house with her sister when Mulally threatens to attack it and urging Hatchet to "take it easy" when he becomes belligerent through drink (*Hat*, pp. 58, 65, 71). "I mind me own business, that's all I do", he professes.[81] Mrs Bailey's attraction to this wealthy, but gentle man – a contemporary of Digger but his symbolic antithesis – is evidence of her own ingrained hypocrisy and reverse class prejudice; she is charmed by his mellow ways but attempts to instil their opposite in her wayward son.

Hatchet complains, for instance, that his mother "keep[s] bringin' [...] up" the tale of his infamous attack on the "Animal Gang", lionising his exploits in having "cleared" the notorious roughians, leaving "a few skulls cracked" (*Hat*, 33). Yet, when Hatchet turns his ire on Joey, she protests that "Joe's A.1", admonishing her son's aggression, "a fine one you are, picking on me friends" (*Hat*, 46). The tragedy of the play, however, is that Hatchet remains ensnared in a pattern of learned behaviour that Joey transcends. He fails to emulate his would-be liberator and Joey leaves the stage almost unnoticed before Hatchet's final confrontation, ominously commenting "still the same" (*Hat*, 74). Walking away from his background and class, back into middle management in Middle England, he can leave without censure or shame, taking with him the prospect of a new life for his admirer's son. While even the innocuous Ha Ha is brutally beaten and "lacerated", Joey is an observer always, immune to the violence of the play (*Hat*, p. 74). In contrast, Hatchet is unable to take flight, as the symbolic sub-plot of his pigeon-fancying suggests.

While Hatchet is concerned "to get a racer out of" his pregnant pigeon Bella, his own prospects of fathering children are ironically waning. His uncharacteristic tenderness with the pigeons jars with his habitual persona, revealing a hidden sensitivity: "They need plenty of attention when they're like that, Bridie, ye have to be sort of tender, and treat them gentle" (*H*, p. 19). But if his pigeons always come home, Hatchet – in Magee's analogy – never leaves home. Rather in the manner that Sid Chaplin employs the metaphor of the sardine, in *The Day of the Sardine* (1965), the pigeon becomes the leitmotif of the play.[82] In Chaplin's novel of 1960s Newcastle, which also concerns gang warfare and a young working-class man's uneasy passage into adulthood, Arthur Haggerston is told how sardines in Norway "go bang into the nets like a hundred locomotives [...] all they know is the shoal"; like Hatchet's, Arthur's mother's lover (another alternative father) advises him, "don't be a sardine. Navigate yourself!"[83] But Hatchet, like his pigeons and Chaplin's sardines, is predisposed to follow the path set out for him, rather than "navigate" independently. As Mrs Bailey affirms, "Hatchet's like meself. Never leave the place we were reared in" (*Hat*, p. 28). The pigeon's death – which coincides with Hatchet's friends' fateful attack on Mulally – parallels the simultaneous demise of Hatchet's dreams of escape to a better life.

"They are *all* losers": nurture and nature

In this context, Magee's frustration with critics who characterised *Hatchet* as a play "about violence" is understandable. "What I'd like to point out is that it's about the *futility* of violence – there are no heroes in this play, no winners – they are *all* losers", he qualified.[84] Despite their various failings, Magee redeems his ensemble of proletarians with an underlying compassion, castigating their subjection to social and economic oppression even as they behave most horrendously. He attempts to reach beyond simplistic condemnations and vilifications, revealing the indelible marks of class injuries on human behaviour.

Despite Mrs Bailey's cynical manipulation of her son, even she is somewhat redeemed by a series of revelations. Ostensibly, Bailey is presented as a spendthrift, reckless and improvident debauchee – and narratives of the working class are littered with such Malthusian stereotypes of the improvident poor – but Magee only invokes the cliché in order to dispel it.[85] He suggests that Bailey could only subsist in the past by gambling effectively with the Digger's wages. Bailey complains that, "I couldn't have kept this place going only for it [...] your father was only casual on the docks for years now, don't forget that, and it was me kept this place going." (*Hat*, p. 32) Bailey also appears to correspond with another stereotype that pervades literature of the working class: that of the lubricious and sexually reckless slut.[86] In Britain, the topos is pervasive, instanced at the height of the Angry Young Man era by angry young woman Shelagh Delaney's slutty materfamilias, Helen, in her "kitchen-sink" play *A Taste of Honey* (1958). A decade later the type reappears, in Barry Hines' novel *A Kestrel for a Knave* (1968), in the figure of Billy Casper's feckless single mother.

But Magee presents Mrs Bailey in this cast, as a "brasser", a woman with a propensity, in her son's words, to "act the bleedin' whore", only to show how her lewd antics mask an inner pain (*Hat*, pp. 18, 47). Her suggestive songs in the play, "The Green, Green Grass", "Everyone is Beautiful" and "*Bouna Sera*", are chosen for their ironic metacommentary (*Hat*, 42). They speak, respectively, of the love of home, a naïve belief in the primacy of human goodness and the idyllic romance of young love. Such utopian subject matter could hardly be more discordant with the reality about her, and Hatchet's act of flinging his mother's wig on the floor, following her effusive kiss with Joey, is a symbolic confirmation of his own deep distrust of Mrs Bailey's artificial façade of happiness. She too admits that her antics are a mere papering over the proverbial cracks in an otherwise wearisome existence (*Hat*, p. 44):[87]

> I'm fed up in that room so I am, sitting and reading the wallpaper and counting me toe nails everyday. Browned off with it. [To Hatchet] I can't reach you anymore. And Bridie and her sister look down their nose at me so they do ... It's better than been stuck in like a statue anyhow. (*Hat*, p. 47)

Mrs Bailey's boredom, her increasing alienation from her son, her feelings of social inadequacy and her plight as a widow with little stimulation are the grim underside of her bawdy behaviour. As a working-class mother, she feels spent, unable to "reach" her grown-up son. She fantasises that she,

Hatchet and Bridie are "(*shouts*) one big happy family" (*Hat*, p. 43), but her motherly role – the essence of female orthodoxy in working-class life – is waning, and with it her sense of purpose. Mrs Bailey beseeches Hatchet to fight Mulally in a desperate, pathetic effort to keep him at home. "I don't care if he does ye", she callously tells him, "don't be afraid of him" (*Hat*, p. 74). As a woman, she is forced to rely on the men in her life for money and, lacking financial or social independence, she is also caught in an unnatural relationship with both her son and society. Mrs Bailey's charms result in Joey paying her overdue electricity bill, and Hatchet brands her a "brasser" because she elicits alcohol from local men by letting them "think they're on to a good thing" (*Hat*, p. 47). But it is her habitus that Magee condemns, for leaving women like Bridie and Mrs Bailey disempowered.

As with McKenna's play, this explanation of dysfunction is not in any way designed to evade the actual, ugly effects of capitalism on working-class life. As Lar Redmond says of the inner-city Dublin of his youth, "nobody ever spent a childhood here and escaped without being branded".[88] Magee wishes to faithfully convey the shocking "kitchen-sink" realities of Hatchet's environment and – to return to Bourdieu's point – the worst effects of capitalism on his characters. Such is this play's uncompromising bleakness that one reviewer of the 1972 production was even prompted (wrongly, in my view) to adduce that it "lacks the one redeeming merit of all such dark works – COMPASSION".[89] But the same reviewer added that "Magee writes with great honesty and, in the process, makes a desperate plea to release those trapped by their own violent environment".[90]

Hatchet's closest friends and his mother recklessly disregard his welfare. Freddie parrots whatever line of argument Hatchet voices when he thinks his "friend" is likely to explode into a violent rage, offering constant, calculated interjections of support: "absobleedinlutely", "the bleeder deserves a hiding" and "let's get him now" (*Hat*, pp. 45, 40, 39). Hairoil adds that, "if he slagged my oulwan, I'd dance on him" (*Hat*, p. 30). Yet when their nemesis, Mulally, arrives at the Bailey household, these erstwhile "friends" are reticent in Hatchet's defence. When Mulally asks if they are indeed Hatchet's friends, the pair only ambiguously respond, "ye could say that" and "we hang around together", before making a hasty retreat (*Hat*, p. 62). But their cowardice pales in comparison with Mrs Bailey's craven selfishness in the appalling crescendo of Act III. The monstrous matriarch's gently intoned encouragements to fight – "come on love", "I'm with ye" and "c'mon chicken love" – are the only such honeyed, motherly expressions she is afforded in the play, articulating, in this context, a perverse, ugly distortion of motherliness (*Hat*, p. 75). Hatchet suffers the burden of being an Oedipal replacement for his father in this bizarre relationship; he is ultimately trapped by his past, like the hero of Chaplin's novel, who objects to "being tied and knowing you were tied for life".[91]

In the context of Dublin's working-class writing, there is a new aesthetic confidence in this play – in its gritty naturalism and its faithful transcription of demotic – but there is insecurity too. Working-class life is depicted as something to be escaped from; Ireland itself is a monstrous mother. When Bridie plaintively asks her husband, "what's going to happen to us Hatchet ... All the plans we had?" his curt riposte encapsulates the desolation of the entire work: "We're here, aren't we, don't be dreaming." (*Hat*, p. 24) Emigration is their only, ultimately elusive, hope, while staying at home means not "dreaming". Living in working-class Dublin entails being brutalised by its poverty and cynicism. This, precisely, is the message of Lee Dunne's *Goodbye to the Hill*.

Goodbye to the Hill: "This country should be given back to the Leprechauns, with apologies!"

Dunne's most well-known play is an underappreciated Irish theatrical phenomenon, which illustrates, perhaps more so than any other work, how much censorship and exclusivist attitudes have prevailed upon the canon of Irish writing. Despite its great popularity – on the basis of attendance figures, this is probably the most popular play in Irish theatrical history – little scholarly criticism can be found regarding *Goodbye to the Hill* and its earlier manifestation as a popular novel in 1965. This neglect may have something to do with the tenor of early reviews of both, which were not always positive.[92] Yet, as Dunne himself notes, with no degree of overconfidence, "there is a growing opinion among those who decide these things that my novel is seminal to the 1950s" (the decade in which it is based).[93] Fintan O'Toole concurs: "With its colloquial tone, first-person narrative and bare-boned prose [the novel *Goodbye to the Hill*] is the first realisation that it might be possible to place Irish literature in the melting-pot of a transatlantic mass culture and still cook up something distinctively Irish."[94] But perhaps Mary Leland unintentionally captured something revealing in her assertion that "the Dublin of Lee Dunne is not the Ireland of anyone else", for the state continually banned Dunne's books as unfit for consumption in the Ireland of their time.[95] Evidently his Ireland was "not the Ireland" the state wanted to see.

Indeed, as Ireland's most banned author, Dunne should naturally stand out as an important focus for the scrutiny of scholars – and his enormous popularity should accentuate this importance. *Goodbye to the Hill*, as a novel, was a best-seller in Britain and the USA, selling over one million copies worldwide. It spawned a Hollywood movie, *Paddy* (1970), which was immediately banned by the Irish censors (only to be granted a 12A certification when passed by national censor John Kelleher in 2006), and in 1978 it ran for 26 weeks as a play at the Eblana Theatre, Dublin. In its most successful theatrical production, at the Regency Airport Hotel, from September 1989 until December 1992, *Goodbye* became Ireland's longest running play. This startling – because little acknowledged – accomplishment was achieved in

spite of the script being rejected by the Abbey Theatre and some other theatre companies who, improvidently it seems, "didn't think it stageable".[96]

Produced and directed by Dunne himself, the Regency sensation was
proof perhaps of John Fiske's assertion that bourgeois aesthetics are "naked
cultural hegemony", which "popular discrimination properly rejects".[97] At
the time, Dunne advertised his willingness to meet audience members per-
sonally at the theatre door after performances; he was keen to cultivate an
accessible, down-to-earth experience, free from any associations of preten-
tiousness. "That was part of my dream," Dunne recalls; "because I wanted
them to feel...there's too much putting the ordinary people down by people
in power – all my life I saw it. Looking down on them, and talking about
'those people, those people'. And I'd say, what do you mean *those* people?"[98]
This production would indeed attract people who did not normally frequent theatres, and the Regency, like Magee's Embankment, was conducive
to such egalitarianism. Its relaxed and breezy ambience created the kind of
conditions A.P. Wilson imagined when he hopefully penned the first known
play to depict working-class Dubliners, *Victims*, in 1912. Wilson envisaged
a "workers' theatre" that would draw "crowded audiences of workers" into
an atmosphere "free from the taint of class snobbishness".[99] Incidentally,
W.B. Yeats also flirted with a plan for just such a People's Theatre in 1903,
"along the lines of the working-class *Freie Volksbühne* in Berlin, but it came
to nothing".[100] Many decades later, and for a brief if spirited period, Dunne's
production of *Goodbye* echoed these ambitions. In a report indeed reminiscent of the description of Magee's play, one reviewer captured this aspect of
Dunne's setting colourfully:

> Many of the audience have never been to a play before or, if they have
> been, it was this one. During the interval, we all talk to each other. It's
> not like the Peacock or the Gate where people at the bar are comment-
> ing on the interpretation or the interaction. At the Regency, we're here
> to enjoy ourselves. Which is why you hear the occasional bottle being
> knocked over as someone makes his or her way out in the middle of the
> show for a natural break.[101]

Two hundred and eighty patrons a night, six nights per week, packed the
theatre. With an estimated total audience of circa a quarter of a million, the
play's success bewildered some, who found themselves aghast at the masses'
perceived lack of taste. One nonplussed critic, who prudishly objected to
Goodbye's "scatological pursuit of laughter", fumed comically that "certainly
it seemed at times that the only way to end its run might be to get a heavy
stick and beat it to death".[102]

Dismissive criticism of this kind typified the stance taken by a number of
contemporary theatre professionals, but for such unprecedented, irrefutable
success to be followed by such a parallel paucity of academic commentary

raises serious questions – not only regarding the play's reception – but also about prevalent predilections in Irish literary scholarship, and its relationship with popular culture. For his part, Dunne heaped invective on the cultural establishment for what he characterised as its unbridled elitism:

> Of course they didn't like me. I never joined the clubs; I never played the games. I never kissed ass [...] If you look at the artistic structure in this country, it is people who went to university together who are on the same boards, people that don't even rock the boat with a statement that's one degree starboard or port.[103]

But Dunne's enthusiasm for writing was far from stymied by this alleged partisanship. On the contrary, he remains one of the country's most prolific writers, having penned twenty novels, three feature films and countless plays – along with an astounding two thousand radio shows. He also shared writing credits in two major television soaps, *Tolka Row* (1964–68) and *Fair City* (1989–present), both of which played a significant role in bringing working-class Dublin into the nation's living rooms.

Reared in working-class, south-side Dublin, at the Mount Pleasant Buildings flat complex in Rathmines, Dunne left school at thirteen years of age and had been working on a milk round since the age of seven. Once described, during one of his many forays to the USA, as part of a *"Nouvelle Blague* first tidally waved by the bulk of Brendan Behan"*, Dunne, like his predecessor, was a conflicted figure; while not the conventional "scholarship boy", one of his short stories highlights his own dilemma with having ambitions beyond his means.[104] Leaving factory work in England, the narrator of "Is There Such a Thing As Serendipity?" describes being irked by feelings of class betrayal, recalling similar concerns in the "Angries" writing of 1950s Britain:

> There was just no way any amount of money could pay you for subjecting yourself to that kind of violence [of factory work] night after night. I'd sooner get thin, I decided and I quit, ignoring and trying to bury the judgemental quality in my attitude [...] Even then I knew I'd no right to look down on anybody. Thinking back on it though – my God – the noise and the stench of that rubber – and the slop served as food.[105]

The fifth child of warring parents in a "very unhappy home", Dunne suffered a difficult childhood and emigrated a number of times from his late teens to England and the Isle of Man.[106] As with McKenna, the experience left its mark on his work, and England, for Dunne, was also a revelation. Like Magee's Joey on his return to Ireland, Dunne also spoke of feeling alienated from his own people: "I took a look at the people, at the Irish, my fellow countrymen. Christ, I said to myself, we're all losers." The country he returned to was economically and culturally stagnant, and according to one journalist, Dunne was "struggling intellectually and physically to run from" his homeland.[107] This alienation was partly attributable to how he felt Ireland had treated its urban working class. In another of his novels, *Does Your Mother?* (1970), Dunne exposed the biting poverty of his youth, the squalor of tenements and its people's consequently deep, proletarian distrust of the state. He was particularly aggrieved by the TB epidemic in working-class Dublin, with Larry, the consumptive brother of the central character in *Goodbye*, representing "all the kids that died, who were eaten up by tuberculosis in those slums in the 50s. The kid would get diagnosed and be dead in 10 days, cough his lungs out of his own mouth, and I was so f****** angry".[108] Such frustration with tenement life is what drives Paddy Maguire away from his home.

"To make a sound, some kind of mark": social stagnation and working-class ambition

Dunne recalls how, "in 1964, I sat down one evening with the idea of writing a short story about a fourteen-year-old kid who rides his bicycle down this hill six days a week for three years, vowing in his own way: 'Someday real soon, I'm going to say goodbye to this place'."[109] Based in the early 1950s, in the flat complex where Dunne was reared, the play exudes class angst. Much more of that element of ribaldry – which characterises much of Dunne's work – is evident in the novel, but the play shifts its attention significantly more so towards issues of deprivation and class. Class, and its effects on a precocious boy's world, is indeed the leitmotif of *Goodbye*.

Paddy Maguire shares his name appropriately, but entirely coincidentally, with Patrick Kavanagh's rural youth of *The Great Hunger* (1942).[110] He too is a protagonist who struggles against Ireland's cultural, social and economic barriers. The son of a revolutionary, Mick Maguire, whose role in the Irish War of Independence renders his family's impoverished plight in the resultant political set-up all the more disenchanting, Paddy inherits a legacy of false hopes. Indeed, the stage absence of the *paterfamilias* is a metonym for the absence of working-class revolutionaries from transcribed Irish history, and their exclusion from the bounty of the state – an exclusion that echoes in Roddy Doyle's recent *The Last Roundup* collection of novels. Like Doyle's Henry Smart, who feels acutely alienated from the fanfare of the Republic's Easter Rising anniversary in 1966, Mick "was fierce. And a dreamer. Risked his neck for years", as Katy, his wife, recalls.[111] But, dispiritingly, "when the fighting was over it was love on the dole".[112] Like Smart, Mick Maguire is used and abused by "revolutionaries", then cast aside by the country he fought for. "Pride" once kept Mick "from going to England", when "he wouldn't work for the Brits", but now "he's in Manchester", serving his old enemy in exile (*GH*, 58). Mick's departure "like a lunatic", with he and his wife "screaming at each other like wild animals", is a far cry from the romantic dreams of his radical youth (*GH*, pp. 5, 6). The revelation that he has left "for Larry", his son, who is about to die of tuberculosis, compounds this contrast, and the memory of Larry "coughing his lungs up and [Mick] threatening to beat him" also accentuates the sense of the former rebel's – and metonymically working-class Dublin's – degradation (*GH*, p. 11).

Mick's family is threatened with eviction, they subsist on "buts of meat from the butcher" and 17-year-old Paddy is forced to "never stop working" at unrewarding odd jobs, because "Ma needs the dough" (*GH*, pp. 17, 28). Without an education, Dunne's alter-ego is "going nowhere fast", but despite this impediment he manages to become "the first white-collar worker [his] family's ever had" (*GH*, p. 58). His success in this regard is short-lived, however, as Paddy falls foul of an elitist boss and his own ingrained lack of self-esteem, but *Goodbye* charts his determination, despite these barriers, to defy the trammels of his habitus, "to make a sound, some kind of mark, something, anything, not just get sucked under without even trying to swim for it" (*GH*, p. 129).

"Between us and bullshit, we got you the job – evened things up just a little bit": Playing the class game

Dunne is at pains to stress the material privations of 1950s working-class Dublin, but like McKenna and Magee, he places greater stress still on its hidden "class injuries". Some of the play is indeed written in social-documentary style: when Dunne tells us in a stage direction that tuberculosis was "mostly fatal in Fifties Ireland", and Ma interjects that it "is killing children all over Dublin" (*GH*, p. 11), the author evidently wishes to highlight the real conditions of a world with which he was intimately familiar. Furthermore, he infers that Irish culture has failed to pay attention to this world, when, at the beginning of the play, Paddy's confidante, Harry Redmond, parodies the romance often attached to "dear, dirty Dublin" with his satirical rendition of "Molly Malone":

> In Dublin's fair city,
> Where the girls are so pretty
> And our architecture is Georgian and fine....
> The outlook is sunny for them that has money
> But what about us livin' on the bread line? (*GH*, p. 5)

But if Dunne stresses this background of socio-economic deprivation, he also foregrounds more so its cognitive effects. Throughout *Goodbye*, Paddy is demeaned by the circumstances of his upbringing. The "genuinely excited" relish with which the boy greets the present of new trousers from his middle-aged mistress – "Clare! Fantastic! Thanks a mill" – pathetically underscores the infantilising effects of poverty (*GH*, pp. 19, 18). And even as his father walks away from the Maguire household for good, Paddy cannot contain his gleeful anticipation of finally having a bed to himself: "Imagine! I'll have a bed all to myself at long last. What must it be like to have a whole room to yourself, with a bookshelf – a table to write on." (*GH*, p. 37) His limited means also affect Paddy's capacity to develop relationships. He admits that he has "never actually taken a girl out in [his] life" because he "never really had the money", and when his girlfriend, Maureen, asks "what kind of future have we got, anyway?" he can only reply, dejected, "I don't know"; Paddy later loses her and their unborn child to another, more wealthy suitor (*GH*, pp. 35, 89).

Dunne shows how hard it is for a young man to mature in circumstances that make the normal expectations of manhood financially unattainable. Paddy's job is demeaning and unskilled: "Twelve hours pushing meat deliveries around on a messenger bike" is "something I could live without", he complains (*GH*, p. 16). And while he longs to work at something more suited to his studious nature, he is inclined – through ingrained fear – to stick to low-skilled jobs:

PADDY   What's wrong with construction work? Good pay and I'm not equipped for much else.
HARRY   Ah the poor kid! He's underprivileged, no education.
PADDY   I'm educating myself with books and I'm smart. I can write too. But I've got no certificates, no formal stuff. (*GH*, p. 29)

Paddy's evident insecurity here is augmented by a sense that working-class people cannot comfortably enter the domain of white-collar jobs. His brother, Billy, dismisses his younger sibling's hopes that he is "going to set the world on fire cos you read books"; it is "about time you grew up", he admonishes (*GH*, p. 98). The Hill's stifling atmosphere retards their development, Paddy believes; a "fucking instant slum", it "should have been pulled down a fortnight before they built it [...] it's a kip to me. Gets in my way every day of the week" (*GH*, p. 93). Harry, his friend and confidante, tellingly upbraids Paddy's lack of enthusiasm when the latter acquires a post with an insurance company, advising that he "should be dancing after stroking a collar and tie job. Living on The Hill, that's a minor fucking miracle" (*GH*, p. 50). For Dunne it is not just economic inequality that curtails the ambitions of The Hill's residents – but also the associated social stigma, the injuries to human dignity and the lack of self-esteem that its habitus inculcates.

Like McKenna once more, Dunne emphasises, through a number of self-reflexive analogies, that writing about the people of The Hill entails writing against the grain of popular literary and cultural discourse. Paddy tries to draw a comparison between his parents' courtship and the romantic *affaires de coeur* he has seen in the cinema, for example, but the representational failure of Hollywood's standard fare emphasises the failure of popular culture generally to approximate their lives:

PADDY   Were you ever mad about him? Like they are in the pictures?
MA   Do you see a lot of pictures about the likes of me and your Da?
           (*GH*, p. 40)

Equally, when Paddy discovers that Maureen has been unfaithful with a more affluent "grocery guy from Rathgar", he tellingly "takes [his sister's] paperback from [the] table" and "then in fury throws it on the floor", intimating his frustrations at the gap between novelistic romance and social reality (*GH*, 100, 101). His brother Billy is also habitually engrossed in an escapist genre – *The Hotspur*'s comic-book world of boys' adventures – which he enjoys, symbolically, on the lavatory (*GH*, p. 14).

Dunne's implicit concern here, with the avoidance of reality that popular culture entails, echoes that of another Dubliner, Robert Tressell. In *The Ragged Trousered Philanthropists* (1914), socialist painter Frank Owen continually complains of his fellow Mugsborough workers' choice of reading material. For news they peruse self-explanatory titles like the *Daily Chloroform* and *The Daily Obscurer*, and Owen's attempts to educate these colleagues about politics correspondingly fall on deaf ears. Trivial diversions, like "a game of hooks and rings [...] football or cricket, horse racing or the doings of some royal personage", are always preferable to Owen's incessant Marxist didacticism, "a lot of rot about religion and politics".[113] Such scepticism towards mass culture re-emerges in Joe Comerford's 1977 short film, *Down the Corner*, when a boy and his friend sit rapt as their grandmother recalls her adventures during the Irish War of Independence. The old woman rubbishes some of the far-fetched fare that was served up on her television the previous night: "What was it that was on last night. Sure you can't even explain. Very stupid picture. Yer man was supposed to be dead, blown away." But a contrasting air of authenticity and redolent folk memory emerges as she recalls being "on the run" with an IRA man, while the camera flashes suggestively to a photo of James Connolly on her wall. For this former rebel, there is some room for popular culture – she concedes that she relishes cowboy films – but her own adventures in Irish history nonetheless take centre stage.[114]

Paddy's world is firmly set in modernity, a far cry from the independence struggle represented by his father and Comerford's elderly rebel. And in *Goodbye* Paddy's escapism is found in alcohol and casual sex, about which he continually lies, a mendacity forced upon him, he claims, because such things are part of the abounding silences in Irish life: "Lies, and more fucking lies, because nobody'll take the truth, not even you [his mother] could accept me as I am. I tried hiding in the bottle, women, but there's nowhere I can escape from me" (*GH*, p. 125). Walter Greenwood also lamented this habit of "inarticulate revolt in drunkenness" amongst his working-class men in *Love on the Dole* (1933)[115] and Paddy is forced to escape from "who he is" through drink because the stultifying climate of 1950s Dublin does not accommodate the "truth" of working-class life. Here Dunne echoes the recently deceased O'Casey's concerns with mid-century Ireland – and while Britain in the 1950s and 1960s saw "a golden age of working-class literature", Ireland, Dunne suggests, was still looking askance.[116]

At the heart of this concern with representation is an interrelated disquiet regarding masculinities. Paddy follows a typical Angry Young Man paradigm, that of the socially unmoored proletarian, like John Osborne's Jimmy Porter (*Look Back in Anger* [1956]) or John Braine's Joe Lampton (*Room at the Top* [1957]), whose aspirations and abilities set him apart from his peers, and part of Paddy's coming-of-age in the play is his realisation, *à la* O'Casey, that his conception of manhood is at odds with that common to his class – that any emulation of its expectations would result in the destruction of his true self, "as I am" (*GH*, p. 125). His relationship with the men about him is fractious: he "won't be shedding any more tears" for his father, "now [he's] over the shock" of his departure, because while he acknowledges that he "*is* [his] father", it is a "pity nobody told him that" (*GH*, p. 8).[117] Mick was unprepared for fatherhood and was "always [saying] the kids came between" him and his wife (*GH*, p. 8), and in Paddy's view, his own father – and it seems any father he knows locally – fails to accord with the expectations of popular (and we might read here, Anglo-American) culture: "I've read plenty of books where the father takes his kids to football, the seaside, the pictures. Are there really fathers like that?" (*GH*, p. 8) This forlorn questioning recalls the kind of paternal indifference Dominic Behan identified in his own father, who "hardly knew the difference between us and the other kids in the street"; comically, Christy Brown's paterfamilias also forgets the names of his tribe of children in *Down All the Days* (1970).[118] But as he speaks of this filial rift, Paddy is depicted in a suggestive movement that infers his own willingness to take on a traditionally feminine role: "Paddy brings cups to table. Paddy brings milk, spoons, etc. Goes back to the stove." By contrast, his brother Billy inherits their father's generally morose temperament; his selfishness regarding the tubercular Larry's suffering is galling when he asks, "is there anything you can do about his coughing [...] he kept me awake half the night"? (*GH*, p. 17). And he is equally unmoved by his other brother's impending emigration:

PADDY Someday, I'll send you a postcard from the other end of the world.

BILLY I'll put that in a frame. And throw sugar at it! [Pause] Anyway, good luck! (*GH*, p. 121)

His unemotional male pretence is again part of the cultural habitus of working-class life. It is the quotidian mien of a macho culture, which often overflows in the kind of violent brutality we see in *Hatchet*, as this folk song from *Goodbye* suggests:

> There's blood on the lino
> There's blood on the knife
> You bastard McBirney
> You killed your poor wife
> Rasher Ryan saw you
> You knew he would tell
> You bastard McBirney
> You killed him as well. (*GH*, p. 62)

The sanguinary ballad, lilted by a local prostitute, is harmonised with the melody of "Red Sails in the Sunset", a pastoral romantic lyric that depicts a young girl waiting for the sailor she is soon to marry. Like Magee, Dunne sounds a dissonant note in his choice of songs, highlighting again the contrast between Paddy's world of urban, domestic warfare and the popular narratives of romance with which his life cannot reconcile.

Dunne's contempt for phoney middle-class values – like that of Osborne in *Look Back in Anger* or Braine in *Room at the Top* – gives rise to some of the most comical and perceptive insights of the play. He also conveys how having to "play the game" of capitalism fundamentally undermines Paddy's integrity, fuelling his desire to emigrate (*GH*, p. 95). Forced to ingratiate himself with a middle-class woman in return for much-needed funds, Paddy, like Braine's Joe Lampton, finds that his acquisitive scheming ultimately corrodes his sense of self worth. Clare Kearney, a widow in her forties, with whom the teenager has a sexual relationship, pities him, and Paddy is initially only too keen to encourage her sympathies. She would "like to look after" him, to "make sure you had underwear, shirts, pants. You deserve more than you get" (*GH*, p. 19). Clare affords Paddy the first pair of trousers he has "ever had" and money that helps out at home, acting as a kind of surrogate mother, underscoring a certain perversity in their sexual relationship (*GH*, p. 18). Indeed, Clare's dual role as replacement mother and lover also hints at Paddy's corresponding feeling of being infantilised.

The theme of poverty and its infantilising effects on young men is another concern that recurs in writing of working-class life. In James Plunkett's short story "The Half Crown" (1955), recent school-leaver Michael is trapped in a similar developmental rut by unemployment, not having the money to go out with friends, to "stand a girl's fare and buy her ice cream". Like a child, he throws tantrums at his mother because of inadequate "pocket money".[119] When chided by his patronising father about not looking after a shaving blade properly, the symbolism of the borrowed razor – as an accoutrement of manhood – parallels Dunne's imagery of Paddy Maguire and his extended life in shorts. Michael's progress to manhood is retarded because of poverty;

he is referred to by his parents as "child" and "baby".[120] Standing "on the threshold of life", he cannot yet step over it, feeling "defeated and chaotic", left with "no words for anything except churlishness and anger".[121]

In Dunne's play, Paddy is stuck in a similar rut. He tells Clare, falsely, that there are "nine of us at home", which makes it "dead tough on Ma", in order to manipulate her sense of charity (*GH*, p. 21). But the exploitation works both ways: Clare's enjoyment of Paddy's sexual services is, she knows, dependent on their unequal economic status (*GH*, p. 19). When Paddy mentions that his mother is "in trouble with the back rent", and that he must leave Clare's bed to return to work, her offer to pay Mrs Maguire's arrears and suggestive prompt that he will "get plenty of chance to pay" her back equates their relationship with prostitution (*GH*, p. 20). When Paddy insists that he should leave, her subtle threat to revoke the offer – "so you don't want the fiver so?" – offsets the lewd comedy in his double entendre regarding his job "delivering meat" (*GH*, p. 22). Clare urges him to "help [his] mother out" by having sex – a transaction that gains more serious undertones in Dunne's autobiography, *No Time for Innocence*, in which Lee is somewhere between 14 and 16 years old when the real events on which this scene is based take place.[122] Dunne himself describes the relationship as a "metaphor" for exploitation and the taboo of child abuse.[123]

When Paddy connives with Harry's plans for the former's career advancement, he is again faced with the dilemma of whether he should debase himself for money. Hayes, a stuffy office manager in his fifties, is deceived by Paddy's adroitly delivered sob story during an interview – in a hilarious satire on sentimental bourgeois sympathy for the working-class "special case" of the "deserving poor".[124] Harry's interjected directions in the following dialogue are delivered as an aside, providing revealing commentary on Hayes's middle-class naivety:

HAYES   [Dons glasses, makes a note] Which Christian Brothers school did you attend, Mister Maguire?

PADDY   I won't lie, sir. I couldn't go to one, much to my regret.

HAYES   May I ask why, Mister Maguire?

PADDY   Things weren't too good at home sir.

HARRY   *My mother couldn't afford to send me.*

PADDY   My mother couldn't afford to send me, sir.
        It only cost a few shillings a week but she didn't...
        Paddy pauses

HAYES   Yes, I understand, Mister Maguire.

HARRY   *The invalid story.*

PADDY   You see sir, my father's been an invalid as long
        as I can remember.

HAYES   My goodness!

PADDY   And since we lost my brother Charlie, it's been more
        or less up to me to look after things.
HAYES   How did your brother die, Mister Maguire?
PADDY   He drowned sir. Over in Manchester. Twelve months ago.
HARRY   Remember Errol Flynn. Be brave.
PADDY   Things are beginning to bounce back, sir. At last. (*GH*, pp. 45–46)

The co-conspirators' interview masterstroke employs class prejudice
against itself; they know that Hayes will no doubt fall for the masquerade of
a part-pitied, part-patronised working-class hero who dreams of social betterment, despite various melodramatic impediments. He is the type of plucky
working-class youth that the middle-class man may recall from a Dickens
novel – the type of proletarian he wants. According to Thomas Halper's
study of prevalent bourgeois discourses of poverty, to become "deserving"
the poor must be "perceived as hard-working (and also as uncomplaining)"
(like Thomas Hardy's Jude Fawley), contract a "clearly incapacitating malady
or injury" (one recalls, perhaps, Dickens's Tiny Tim Cratchit) or just "cease
being – or appearing – poor" (like Daniel Defoe's Moll Flanders).[125] Paddy
aspires to the latter and overturns "the presumption of immorality [...]
sloth, intemperance or lack of ambition" that inheres in "deserving poor"
discourse by applying his mendacity in the other two areas – mentioning an
incapacitated father and being "brave" and uncomplaining.[126] But his con-
cocted story about the imagined drowning brother, if darkly comic, is also
undercut by the reality of his consumptive real brother, who lies dying of
tuberculosis at home.

   Such themes of pitying bourgeois hypocrisy are again common in writing of the working class – invoked, for instance, by a much earlier writer
of working-class Dublin life, Oliver St John Gogarty, in his depiction of
the interplay between tenement dwellers and a wealthy philanthropist. In
Gogarty's play, *Blight: The Tragedy of Dublin* (1917), Mrs Knox's talk about
poverty giving "occasion for fortitude", and her instructions to "practice
cleanliness", together with her frequent quotations from scripture, present
her as a quintessential condescending Christian charity advocate. She pat-
ronises the poor, pities them and luxuriates in her own perceived moral
superiority as a social crusader. But when Knox discovers that the object of
her charity, Mr Tully, has been drinking, she immediately begins to recon-
sider whether he is indeed deserving or not, branding him a "debauched,
deceitful wretch".[127] This middle-class hypocrisy was also ridiculed by
James Stephens in his short story "The Thieves" (1920), in which a wealthy
kleptomaniac sacks servants for stealing trivial items of clothing, because,
naturally, "laws are not framed against the wealthy but against the necessi-
tous class, and that which is acquisition in one becomes, by polarity, deprav-
ity in the other."[128] In Gogarty's play, Tully knows he must tug the forelock
if he is to secure a hospital bed for his nephew Jimmy, and so he resorts,

like Paddy Maguire, to sycophantic, if manipulative, pleading: "Surely ye wouldn't neglect your duty to extend a helping hand to the poor and weak and the weak-minded?"[129] Implicitly, both men know that they must make themselves "deserving" by being melodramatically pitiable.

In Dunne's play, when Hayes asks the underage boy (who claims to be 19) for his birth cert, Paddy unleashes "the big one", sobbing:

> I went to collect it on my way to meet you, sir. As a matter of fact, I nearly didn't come to the interview at all... It's not an easy thing to admit, sir. I just found out today, that when I was born, sir, my mother and father, they weren't married sir. (*GH*, p. 48)

As Harry advises, "they" – the middle class – "feel sorta guilty for being born in wedlock" (*GH*, p. 48), and so Paddy manipulates the "degrading Calvinistic assumption of immorality" in poverty – the sense the wealthy have "that the poor [are] repulsive: vulgar, crude".[130] In a recent study, Moira J. Maguire deciphers exactly this attitude in 1950s Ireland, where financial relief was only granted to working-class families "if the local authorities believed the family was 'worthy' [...] in ways that coincided with middle-class standards of respectability".[131] Paddy transcends this class condescension by using the "worthy poor" logic against itself, and Hayes duly identifies a "courageous young man" whose advancement will absolve his own middle-class guilt (*GH*, 48). While Paddy has little hard currency, he realises that he can manufacture plenty of the symbolic stuff. There is even a subtle egalitarian thrust to this skulduggery, as Harry infers: "Between us and bullshit, we got you the job – evened things up just a little bit" (*GH*, p. 49).

Harry's class-conscious mischief-making reveals a keen understanding of capitalism's underlying social and cultural dynamics. It also finds a salutary parallel in the ritual self-therapy that factory worker Jimmy indulges in "every six months or so when I'm a bit cheesed off" in Dermot Bolger's novel, *Night Shift* (1985):

> I take a day off and go for an interview for a really menial job that I know I'm going to get. And I sit and listen to all their shit and I answer all their questions, yes sir and no sir, and I wait until they have worked themselves up to doing me this great big favour with poxy conditions and lousy wages, and I suddenly stand up and say, "Excuse me, gentlemen, but would you mind taking your job and sticking it up your fucking arse."[132]

In Scottish writer Irvine Welsh's novel *Trainspotting* (1993), Renton achieves a similarly curious satisfaction by refusing the presumed cerebral superiority of his psychologist counsellor. Mischievously devising lies in order to "confuse" and "wind him up", Renton rebuffs society's efforts to pathologise his poverty – but this tomfoolery backfires on the Edinburgh heroin addict when it results in him being sent for more counselling.[133] Indeed, Dunne also stresses that Paddy's victory over middle-class conceitedness is a pyrrhic and tokenistic one. Hayes, Harry reminds his friend, is a capitalist and thus an exploiter – "Nice man me arse! He thinks he can use you or you wouldn't have got the job" (*GH*, p. 49).

In the final scene of the play, Paddy nonetheless rejects Harry's sagely advice, along with his cynical acts of self-effacement and debasement for money. When the arch-charlatan manages to manipulate a female American tourist's affection for the poetic Irish type – by writing poems for her and acting in a generally stereotyped, Behanesque manner – his antics make the younger man physically sick (*GH*, p. 128). Paddy recalls his mother's accusation that he himself is becoming a "phoney", but Harry attempts to comfort his friend by advising, "it's all a big bleedin game" (*GH*, p. 126). Harry's philosophy is simple: "Get what you want, especially sex and money. And don't ruin it by worrying about it afterwards" (*GH,* p. 51). To him, "this" – spending ill-gotten gains in a pub – "is the pinnacle, really living" (*GH*, p. 128). Paddy's subsequent dart to the toilet to vomit is, Dunne affirms, (in a somewhat superfluous stage direction,) "symbolic of his rejection, finally, of what Harry stands for" (*GH*, p. 129). The older man is a projection of Paddy himself, a man he might become if he does not realise, at this crucial juncture, that he has "got to make a sound, some kind of mark" (*GH*, p. 128).

In rejecting Harry, his own father and his environment on The Hill, Paddy echoes the agonised sense of conflicted allegiances that bedevils many such working-class males in literature, men who are impelled by ambition to reject their backgrounds. Joe Lampton does so in *Room at the Top,* but knows that he has lost himself in the process, observing his own dissolution, suggestively, in the third person: "I hated Joe Lampton, but he looked and sounded very sure of himself sitting at my desk in my skin."[134] This theme of class betrayal recurs in A.P. Wilson's *The Slough* (1914), when Jack Hanlon's social ambition severs him from the "baggage" of his family roots, and in Margot Heinemann's Welsh novel, *The Adventurers* (1960), when Danny Owen's intelligence leads to success as a journalist – success which allows him to escape the mines he once seemed destined for (or *doomed* to) but which also estranges him from his community and the politics it espouses.[135] Dunne lambastes the phoney sentimentality of middle-class ideology and the fawning, cynical abasement of working-class servility that characterises Paddy's best friend, suggesting that his protagonist, like Jemmo and Hatchet, must cut himself adrift from both if he is to forge a better future.

As with *The Scatterin'* and *Hatchet, Goodbye to the Hill* has only one alternative to Harry's demeaning subjugation: emigration. In Paddy's sexist vernacular, "drinking pints, telling old jokes, reciting poetry to pot wallopers and kitchen mechanics so you can screw them – there has to be more to life than that", and so he must "get away from The Hill" (*GH*, pp. 28, 94). His final decision to leave is forced somewhat by the fact that he has been sacked for drinking during office hours – something that foreshadows future problems if he stays in Harry's thrall.[136] But despite his promise early in the play to "never run out" on his mother, Paddy says, à la Joyce, that he will not serve and "settle for this" (*GH*, pp. 13, 43). Even his cunning in tricking his employers proves futile, because "Cahill [his immediate superior] hated me from the first day in that office. He was a snob, looked down his nose because he knew I came from The Hill" (*GH*, p. 123). The class snobbery that Wilson's Jack Hanlon had encountered in his office job in *The Slough* – where colleagues "taunt" him about being a "gutter snipe from the slums" – is evidently still in vogue in mid-century, class-conscious Dublin.[137] And while England has its rhetoric of affluence and post-war social mobility – something Paddy refers to obliquely in his ironic comment that an "extra shilling" on his paper round is indicative of the "Fabulous Fifties" – Dunne blasts his own country's contrasting economic and social gloominess, fuming that it "should be given back to the Leprechauns, with apologies!" (*GH*, pp. 9, 116) While angry young men like Sillitoe, Osborne, Braine and others criticise the social mobility of the British welfare state as a sham, for these Irish writers the escape to Britain offers a modicum of mobility that their protagonists could never realise at home.

Closer to Birmingham than Boston or Berlin

The achievement of these plays must be assessed in the context of theatrical as well as social and cultural history. Seán O'Faoláin wrote in 1962 – in a retrospective survey of the previous 50 years' writing – that there were a number of problems facing contemporary Irish theatre. On the one hand, he criticised "too much" of a "withdrawal-from-life" in the overshadowing sway of the Irish Literary Movement. Yeats, its central advocate, had "found inspiration in the ancient mind of his people, but not in a political mind, or a social mind, but a mystical memory."[138] On the other hand, O'Faoláin criticised those who superseded Yeats in the cultural ascendancy, the "new élite" of an "ambitious, hardfaced democracy" that "understood only 'realistic plays', political plays, representationalism, characterization, explanations, social comedies and tragedies", which were written in so "feeble" a manner "as to extinguish the value of the terms" he had just used ("'realistic', 'political', 'representational', 'social'").[139] "Because new audiences did not really want any of those things," O'Faoláin claimed: "they wanted those things in an *ersatz* form [...] They were not ready for plays that opposed what might be called, for short, the new synthetic orthodoxy." Concluding that "no social-realistic drama – whether comic or tragic – can thrive in this atmosphere", he cited as his main example the plight of Brendan Behan, who had been forced to seek his fortune in London and New York, because his modern perspective "could not have broken through" at home.[140]

Dunne, Magee and McKenna managed to make that breakthrough, with plays that avoided both Yeatsian "withdrawal" and Free State syntheticism, providing the kind of "socio-realistic drama" O'Faoláin had yearned for. In this, these three share a common bond as writers, but they also share far more. It is evident that this Dublin triumvirate of angry young men exhibit strikingly similar concerns. They articulate the emotional turmoil of a detached generation of men who struggle to cope with the expectations of masculinity and class that society foists upon them and to escape the legacy of poverty, violence and political failure bequeathed by their fathers' generation. Their plays share a similar social function also: to compel their audiences to question social conditioning and its limitations, to question how hospitable a place the Republic was for its urban working class and to what extent social exclusion contributed to delinquent and dysfunctional behaviour.

In this sense, these are political and proletarian plays; emerging from and expressing vehement social discontent, they conform to what Bourdieu terms the "anti-Kantian aesthetic" of working-class culture.[141] All three works were very much commented upon for their social utility, and when prisoners in Mountjoy Jail performed a production of *Hatchet*, directed by Frank Allen in 2001, their teacher spoke of the work as "addressing issues about offending behaviour", specifically "the issue of violence and the culture of the unemployed [...] about people trying to go against that trend".[142] The playwrights convey their central characters' subjection to subtle forms of oppression, through culturally inscribed domination and socially alienating elitism. They depict the complexity of class struggle, in a cerebral, emotional and deeply personal manner – presenting a masculine complexity that O'Casey often denied. Their young male protagonists also articulate an exasperated fatalism as regards the possibility of social advancement in Ireland, a sense that "there aren't any good, brave causes left," in Jimmy Porter's epochal words.[143] Caught in the "rat trap" of conformity, these youths suffer the kind of socio-economic disadvantage and internecine violence that recur in the stories of Barry Hines' Billy Casper, in *A Kestrel for a Knave* (1968), and Alan Sillitoe's Colin Smith, in *The Loneliness of the Long Distance Runner* (1959). Dunne, McKenna and Magee's writing thus insists on what Fordham terms "the primacy of the social image through its subjective expression"; while focussing on subjective lives, the social imprint of class struggle is always implicitly to the fore.[144] Along with Paul Smith and Brendan Behan, these writers represent a key period in Irish proletarian cultural development in a body of writing which, to borrow Sue's words in *The Scatterin'*, did not "fear to speak of '58, the new dead" (*SC*, p. 21).

3
From Rocking the Cradle to Rocking the System: Writing Working-Class Women

Fiction about working-class women is relatively plentiful, but fiction by them is not. With the notable exceptions of Maura Laverty and Paula Meehan, the vast bulk of writers within the scope of this book are male. Yet for most of these male writers, the predicament of working-class women is a significant, ongoing preoccupation. In writing from O'Casey to Doyle, working-class women's experience is a major concern. In regard to O'Casey it might even be argued that women more often than men convey the dramatist's own political views. Equally, in Plunkett's *Strumpet City* (1969), the neglected housekeeper, Miss Gilchrist, whose years of dedication to her wealthy employers are rewarded with a horrifying death in a workhouse, embodies a feminist castigation of the status quo. In Christy Brown's *Down All the Days* (1970), there is vehement contempt for a mother's subjection to her husband's bullying (see Chapter 6). And for Paul Smith, in *Summer Sang in Me* (1972, part of the focus of Chapter 4), *Esther's Altar* (1959, later republished as *Come Trailing Blood*, 1977) and one of the works I have chosen for analysis in this chapter, *The Countrywoman* (1961), there is an abiding current of complaint about women's suffering in working-class Dublin. Dermot Bolger, in *The Woman's Daughter* (1978), Peter Sheridan in *Big Fat Love* (2003, the other book I analyse in this chapter), and Roddy Doyle, most particularly in *The Snapper* (1990), *The Woman Who Walked into Doors* (1996), and *Paula Spencer* (2006), all focus on female subjection, in working-class life, to social conservatism and male aggression. These works are joined by some lesser-known writing – such as *The Pride of Parnell Street* (2007) by Sebastian Barry and *Sucking Dublin* (1997) by Enda Walsh – which also criticise androcentric norms in working-class settings. Indeed, a plethora of male-authored texts about working-class women's lives attest to a particularly striking preoccupation in Dublin's literature.

Carnivals and knockabout

This chapter discusses two novels that depict the harrowing experiences of abused women. Both works share a characteristic challenge to totemic social orthodoxies, and in terms of form, they enlist an attendant use of irreverent imagery and symbolism to make their point. In Bourdieuian fashion, they employ a typically "popular", proletarian aesthetic – what he terms "the plain speaking and hearty laughter which liberate by setting the social world head over heels, overturning conventions and proprieties".[1] O'Casey had employed vaudeville and music-hall devices to such ends; inflecting his own work with the preferred stagecraft of the working class (the only type it could often afford), he developed his "principle of knockabout", as Beckett put it.[2] O'Casey would puncture public pieties and oppressive ideologies with the power of deflationary laughter. Figures such as the Cock, Loraleen and Father Ned irrupt into O'Casey's plays as embodiments of joy and instigators of liberated thinking. They inspire and represent the free play of ideas; they harangue and harass religious virtue with Rabelaisian virtuosity. The primacy of the social image often emerges in working-class writing through such subversive interplay. Capitalist society's normalisation of reified relationships is challenged by comic iconoclasm and irreverent playfulness, which indeed sets "the social world head over heels".

A similar kind of polyphonic interchange was, for Russian structuralist critic Mikhail Bakhtin, the residual site of revolutionary potential in literature and culture. Bakhtin had traced how inherently subversive "relics" of popular festivities become "transposed into literature" that is "permeated with a carnival sense of the world".[3] Carnival's "free and familiar contact among people" from different social strata and their interplay in "half-real and half-play-acted" forms, produces an interanimation of supposedly "self-enclosed" ideas and ideologies in comic juxtapositions, in "carnivalistic mésalliances".[4] In Bakhtin's terms, the symbolic "crowning/de-crowning" of the "antipode of the real king" – the mock-elevation of the lowly that accompanied medieval festivals like "the saturnalia, the European carnival and festival of fools" – is carnivalism's mode *par excellence*; in Ireland this social subversion might be identified in the crowning of a goat as king during Killorglin's ancient (and still annual) Puck Fair.[5] But such ancient carnivalesque practices are also latent in organic popular culture and certain forms of literature, Bakhtin argued. In the "profanation" evoked by "carnivalistic debasings, and bringings down to earth, carnivalistic obscenities linked with the reproductive power of the earth and the body", and such forms of literary subversion as "parodies on sacred texts and sayings", social hierarchies and solemnities are sabotaged in intertextual forms of resistance.[6] Representations of this kind are simultaneously destructive and creative, deflationary and ennobling; but this subversion is no mere postmodern gaming, Julia Kristeva cautions, for Bakhtin's carnivalesque is always asserting "another law".[7] Indeed, to return to Lloyd's characterisation of the "popular" and "subaltern", and the space they create for counter-hegemonic rebellion, the dialogic levelling produced by the carnivalesque is precisely about foregrounding "that which the state does not interpellate".[8] Implicit within this concept of the carnival is a performative portrayal of counter-cultural revolt, in which the iconoclastic and taboo, the scatological and the bodily, come out to play. Characterising Bakhtin's carnivalesque, Nancy Glazener might well have been writing about Lloyd's subaltern discourse, in that both hark "back to a golden age in which 'the people' were clearly separate from official culture and therefore capable of making their critique from a conceptually pure 'outside'."[9]

Of course, such an untainted "outside" is problematic in the complex modern world, but it is interesting to note in this context that Jeremy Lane also deciphers an affinity between Bakhtin's carnivalesque and Bourdieu's modern sociological analysis of how "the dominant class's sense of social distinction" is used "to belittle and denigrate working-class tastes and life-styles": "Bourdieu employs both a heteroglot or polyphonic mix of con-flictual textual voices or genres and a peculiarly Rabelaisian image of the body which lends his work an unmistakably carnivalesque quality", Lane argues.[10]

> Having identified the series of oppositions structuring the canon of good taste – lower/distinguished; coarse/sublimated; vulgar/refined; venal/dis-interested; servile/gratuitous, Bourdieu's project throughout *Distinction* will be to highlight their essentially arbitrary nature, to locate their gen-esis in material class divisions.[11]

As such, Bourdieu's analysis "mirrors Bakhtin's description of the carnival as that which 'brings together, unifies, weds and combines the sacred with the profane, the lofty with the low, the great with the insignificant, the wise with the stupid'".[12] Such combinations are critical in interpreting the feminist, proletarian texts that this chapter explores.

Cognisant of feminism's abiding focus on the somatic aspect of women's experience, it is salutary also to consider how Glazener argues, albeit with some reservations, that Bakhtin's emphasis on the role of the body – in the "em-bawdying" character of carnival – is something that also "holds obvi-ous attractions for feminism".[13] Many "feminists have asserted the body's role in meaning" and "they have also called attention to the ways in which women play the part of the body for male subjectivity". Some feminists embrace this differentiated body after a fashion; others reject it altogether as something ineluctably inscribed with gender's politicised discourses. Moreover, a great many have "investigated the reduction of the body to part-objects: to the objectified female erogenous zones, and to the having and not-having of a penis [...] which becomes symbolically overwritten as gender identity". Another form of reification inheres in this discourse. In its obsession with the abstractedness of subjectivity, Western thought has "pro-jected many aspects of the body on to its margins: not only on to women, but also on to the lower classes (Bakhtin's popular culture of pre-capitalism, the proletariat of capitalism)". Women and working-class people thus have "an interest in integrating the body's semantic and organic aspects in order to free themselves from *embodying* the body, symbolically, for their cultures"; thus the carnivalesque, with its release of the corporeal and profane, provides a liberating, counter-hegemonic social space. Bakhtin shows how "profanation" of the body, often as an affront to the supposedly cerebral, is integral to carnivalesque form. As Glazener writes, it is thus claimed that the carnival event sutures the bodies of its individual participants into "a larger-than-life folk body, the emblem of material-based class consciousness for the people".[14] In this analysis, the taboo of the corporeal affronts the elevation of an abstracted subjectivity, which has subjugated both the feminine and the working class, as part of a broader consciousness of common subalternhood.

The carnivalesque, like the subaltern, is a realm in which the normative is sundered and reconstituted parodically, in which the interplay of radically subversive ideas reinscribes the body in discourse and challenges the discursive inequalities that characterise modern capitalist life. The novels explored below portray how, for working-class women, these inequalities are experienced in particularly acute terms. In Smith and Sheridan's accounts, women suffer from multiple social and economic impediments: as part of a disadvantaged economic class, as women in a male-dominated society, but also as women living in an especially androcentric working-class culture. In this context, carnivalesque forms of upending and interrogating normative behaviour furnish a powerful method of implicit social critique, and for both writers it is often through the Bourdieuian/Bakhtinian interplay of contrasting ideas and subversively comic juxtapositions that both capitalism and patriarchy are anathematised.

A century of change: gender and Irish society

Big Fat Love and *The Countrywoman* were published over four decades apart and are separated by over seven decades in terms of setting. They explore a broad and fertile field of historic transformation, and in approaching these books it is important to outline the changing social and historical contexts out of which they emerged. Both invoke major political and social upheavals in Dublin's inner-city life – the violent foundation of the Free State in one, and the demolition of Sheriff Street flats in the other – and in doing so they follow O'Casey's technique of interlacing historical and personal narratives to better illustrate both. There are also telling contrasts between these novels, which illustrate how life has changed for working-class women since the foundation of the state, but in some instances there are depressing continuities as well.

As the subtitle of a recently published study propounds, the twentieth century was generally "A Century of Change" for Irish women.[15] Since the foundation of the Free State, divorce has been banned and then reintroduced, and women's work outside the home has been curtailed by legislation, then later encouraged as a vital economic precept. A whole raft of official and unofficial impediments to gender equality have been created, then diminished or removed and Irish women have moved, in the words of a former Irish president, from "rocking the cradle" to "rocking the system"; they have emerged, from the domestic role assigned to them by the 1937 constitution, to play a vital role in challenging conservatism in Irish public life.[16]

Like all historic generalisations, however, such a broad analysis assumes a common experience that may not obtain in particular circumstances, as my earlier analysis of Ireland's post-1960s economic growth, for instance, had sought to show. In suturing the many socio-economic fissures in Irish society into the thread of homogeneous "national" experience, regardless of distinctions of class, location or demography, history can fail to acknowledge, in particular, the experience of proletarian life. In this regard, it may be true that Irish women have secured key advancements as an undifferentiated mass, but the extent and pace of change differs according to socio-economic context. Sadly, little has been written in terms of history about working-class Irish women.

While it is by now axiomatic to observe what Eavan Boland terms the "disproportionate silence of women" generally in Irish literature, the disproportionate silence surrounding working-class women is barely discussed in critical inquiry.[17] In recent decades, the issue of Irish women's history with literature has been the focus of vibrant academic and, indeed, public debate, with the publication of the three-volume *Field Day Anthology of Irish Writing* in 1991 being exemplary in this regard. Greeted with critical acclaim, but also assailed for its evident gender bias, the anthology was slighted by many critics for its inattention to women writers, and this criticism duly prompted the publication of two extra volumes 11 years later, which attempted to redress *Field Day*'s gender imbalance. But if *Field Day* generated much public and academic debate about the inattention to women in Irish Studies, it is noteworthy that there was scant attention paid to *working-class* women specifically and *their* history of silence.

An obvious explanation for this particular imbalance is the lack of writing from working-class women themselves, due, in no small part, to the general conditions that the class system imposes on their lives. Leisure time constraints and a lack of educational attainment have obviously curtailed working-class women's ability to express themselves in print, as Kevin C. Kearns has noted:

> Can one imagine any figure in Irish society with *less* time and opportunity to write letters and keep diaries than Ma's from the Liberties or northside – past or present – burdened with large families, financial problems, domestic chores, outside job duties and emotional strains?[18]

This observation does not entirely explain the fact that "Irish mothers have been woefully neglected by historians," Kearns cautions, "especially so the lower-income, working-class 'mammies' in Dublin's long-deprived, inner-city communities", but it does elucidate why little of their history has been recorded, or fictionalised, by the women themselves.[19] Additionally, neglect of this kind is by no means confined to academia or literature. It is telling that even the women's movement in Ireland has been criticised for its failure to explicitly include working-class women in feminist conferences and events.[20] In this sense, working-class women are doubly oppressed, by prevalent class *and* gender discriminations. The fact that most literary depictions of Dublin's working-class women have been penned by men parallels the utter lack of self-expression afforded to these women, more generally, in Irish public life, and it is fitting therefore that both Smith and Sheridan express a compelling sense in their novels of historic retrieval, of unearthing submerged female narratives. As in the writing surveyed so far, the individual stories narrated by these authors are allegorical reflections of a broader social experience, illustrations of a moral and social picture to which the subjective stories yield an immediate dimension.

Gender and poverty in Ireland

Maryann Valiulis identifies the oppression of women in the Irish Republic as the result of a typically post-colonial "gender ideology", and it is true that the post-independence era saw women's rights increasingly eroded.[21] Suffragette and republican Hanna Sheehy Skeffington criticised the gradual demise of gender equality issues in the Free State, observing that, "what was given at first with gladness has been gradually filched away". From her perspective, "equality [had] ceased to be accorded to us, save on paper".[22] Legislative change was key in this regard. A bill of 1927 proposed that women be exempted from jury service, undermining their sense of citizenship, and the "filching away" of equality that Skeffington lamented was particularly acute in the introduction of sexist labour laws. In 1935, the Conditions of Employment Act restricted the participation of women in paid employment, curtailing their access to factory work and also effectively excluding all married women from white-collar public-service work, including national-school teaching.[23] This exclusion had a "demoralising" effect, "sending out a clear message about the preferred role of women in Irish society".[24] In working-class life, where another adult wage might significantly increase living standards, these strictures were severely felt. Between the inception of the Free State and the 1960s, a falling number of women was consistently registered in censuses as "gainfully" employed (a fall of 16 per cent occurred between 1926 and 1961).[25]

Equally, women, particularly those on lower incomes, were badly disadvantaged by family law. For many, marriage became a trap, with divorce banned from 1937 right through to November 1995. Article 41.2 of the 1937 constitution also notoriously identified women's roles as confined to domesticity and motherhood, and it was not until 1956 that legislation gave married women equal legal status with their husbands. Women's disempowerment in the domestic sphere was further compounded by the state's tolerance for domestic violence, as evidenced by the fact that its victims had "relatively few rights until the mid 1970s".[26] The high number of female emigrants from the mid-1940s would suggest that women were increasingly, if quietly, uneasy about the direction of Irish society, and for Jenny Beale the half-century since independence amounted to "fifty years of inequality".[27]

To be sure, as the foregoing suggests, this inequality was compounded for less affluent women: the neglect of their health, grinding poverty and slum living continued and even intensified in the Free State. Because of the edicts of the Catholic Church, women were denied easy access to contraception, often giving birth to large families and consequently suffering sickness and premature deaths. Nevertheless, the state's advice was consistently in sync with that of the Church; in 1956 the Emigration Commission saw the downward trend in family size as "unwelcome", arguing, preposterously, regardless of the social consequences, that "every effort should be made to arrest it".[28] Bishop Cornelius Lucey even advised, in his submission to the commission, that Irish women's prodigious childbearing had a "salutary rather than deleterious" effect on their mental health.[29] It is a cruel irony that many of the middle-class officials who advocated Catholic policies on reproduction seemed curiously capable of evading their most obvious effects. As Tom Garvin wryly remarks: "Occasionally there were murmurings as to how it was that middle-class, relatively well-off people seemed to have relatively small families. They seemed to know something that the rest of us didn't." Stricter adherence to Catholic dogma by poorer families, or their inability to purchase contraceptives either way, are offered by Garvin as some "of the central reasons for Irish underdevelopment and poverty".[30]

Working-class women were also more likely to be entirely reliant on a husband's income, leaving them particularly vulnerable to manipulation and abuse. As oral testimony in Kearns's work confirms, these women had less control over economic issues in their homes than their wealthier counterparts and were more likely to suffer the scourge of alcoholic, macho, abusive husbands. They were equally more predisposed to clerical advice that they remain with such husbands and less likely to be equipped with the (financial and social) resources necessary to secure a marriage annulment. The twin despotisms of social and domestic abuse, as enabled by church doctrine and androcentric statutory control, made life a living hell for many working-class women. For Paul Smith, the story of this suffering was one of the hidden afflictions of working-class life.

Smith's realism in mid-century Dublin:
"this is not a nice book"

The *Spectator* thought Paul Smith "possibly the finest writer that Ireland has produced", and Anthony Burgess was "sorely tempted" to use the term "genius" to describe him, but refrained only because he claimed that such praise was too liberally ascribed to Irish authors.[31] Critics compared Smith to O'Casey, Joyce, Dickens and Dostoyevsky, and his novel *Annie* (1972) won the American Book of the Month Club Choice – lauded as a "masterpiece" by Kate O'Brien, a personal friend.[32] John Jordan compared *The Countrywoman* with the work of Emile Zola.[33] Its social realist style and political overtones even met with official Soviet approval, securing it a Russian translation and an inclusion in Volume III of the Soviet *Concise Literary Encyclopaedia* as a notable work of "social protest".[34] In 1978, Smith received the American-Irish Cultural Institute Literary Award, and he was also later conferred with membership of Aosdána. But, in a pattern that may by now be becoming familiar in this book, the reader is unlikely to have ever heard of Paul Smith. That little remains in either academic record or public memory of this enigmatic writer from the Dublin slums would seem to speak volumes of Irish society and his uncomfortable place within it.

Smith's own experiences of deprivation and marginalisation would prove inspirational for his work. Born in Dublin on 4 October 1920, he was the son of rural parents, on whom Pat and Molly Baines in *The Countrywoman* are believed to be based.[35] He grew up in two rooms off Charlemont Street in Dublin's south inner city, and although Smith could read at pre-school age, he generally suffered the educational deprivation common to slum children. In fact, Smith claimed not to have read any books in childhood because "there were no library books available to people like me. You had to be a householder, or know a householder, to get a ticket. And we didn't know any householders. Everybody like us lived in [rented tenement] rooms".[36] His mother's bad eye-sight had a silver lining for her precocious child; having no money for spectacles, she made him read newspapers out loud. This was Smith's closest brush with *belles-lettres* for some time, but it was also the making of yet another working-class autodidact.[37]

Such was the poverty of Smith's upbringing that he would later ask "what's working class?" because, "as far as I was concerned anybody who stayed at school till they were 14 was wealthy. I never knew anybody who did. I certainly didn't. At the age of eight I was driving a donkey cart for coal to Ringsend."[38] Just as O'Casey would hone his knowledge of working-class life while labouring on the railways, Smith's premature entry into the workforce, in a job in which "all life centre[d] round the roads", would furnish rich material for much of his later work.[39] The poverty he would encounter, and the righteous indignation it inspired, would stay with him too:

> "Why", [his boss] would ask, "did coal-dealers like us never have a summer lay-off?" "And why did the poor have to buy coal all the year round?" "And why in stones and halves?" "Because they can't afford hundred weights", [Smith would] tell him. I would then remind him how every kettle, every bit cooked in every room in Rock Street was done over an open fire.[40]

This precocious sense of materialism, of the subjection of the working class to basic but powerful economic forces, is integral to Smith's work. His first novel, *Esther's Altar*, is an epic study of the 1916 Easter Rising from the vantage point of tenement dwellers. Although the book was banned in Ireland, it secured his fame in the USA, and Smith was soon billed in England (in that by now hackneyed parallel) as yet another "new O'Casey".[41] But this and all of his subsequent endeavours – of which *The Countrywoman* was generally considered his finest – were banned in Ireland until 1975, despite translation into a number of languages and successful worldwide sales.[42]

His was a curious predicament, which illustrates the extent of Ireland's isolationism, and internal silencing, in literary matters: "Nobody knows me here", he complained that same year; "I'm like a dark stranger."[43] Such alienation was a tragic effect of censorship, which drove talent abroad – and, in particular, acted as a bulwark against the gritty kitchen-sink-style realism of writers such as Smith, which was sure to be proscribed. Irish isolationism could again be noted, for example, in RTÉ's decision to ban the Dubliners' rather trivial song, "Seven Drunken Nights", in 1967, despite its success in Europe and America and its achievement of a number five spot in the British singles' charts. While working-class Dubliners could achieve unprecedented success in Britain, the USA and even Russia, they could simultaneously be denied access to their community at home. But Smith, unlike the Dubliners, "was ever the outsider", and this isolation within his own country resonates in his depiction of a working-class woman's isolation in *The Countrywoman*.[44]

A "searing bitter picture"

A profoundly tragic novel about domestic violence, poverty, familial disintegration and the tenacity and courage with which one woman endures these ills, *The Countrywoman* is set in Dublin's tenements during and after the First World War, a period of growing social disenchantment and division. Robert Collis described this era in the preface to his 1943 slum play, *Marrowbone Lane*, in terms of vivid social inequalities:

> Here in Dublin lived two societies, one of which did not know how the other lived – did not know that 90,000 people lived in one-roomed

tenements and 10,000 in dwellings condemned as medically unfit for human habitation. Still less did they realise what this meant in pain, disease, cold and hunger.[45]

Sculpted in such a despondent social cast, Smith's book refused to efface its worst effects so that it might please the censor, and, as one reviewer assessed, "this is not a nice book"; that the novel was "as coarse and shocking as its background", however, was presented by this critic as a commendation. The naturalism of the work, its authenticity as a "searing, bitter picture of Dublin slums", was indeed its triumph.[46]

Set in Kelly's Lane, a tenement district in the south inner city, *The Countrywoman* charts the desperate travails of Molly Baines, a woman from rural County Wicklow, who comes to settle in the slums with her husband, Pat. Molly follows him around the country in his search for work, until they eventually settle in Dublin and start a family, but Pat becomes increasingly violent and abusive, and his enlistment as a British soldier in the First World War ironically comes as a respite for his wife and children. Their greatest fear thereafter is the "return of the brute" – to borrow from the title of Liam O'Flaherty's 1929 war novel. While Pat at first seems to have gone missing after the 1918 Armistice, his inevitable, dreaded homecoming ironically signals a renewed "war" on family life, but typical of her time and place, Molly is prevented from leaving this bullying husband by her adherence to the dictums of the Catholic Church, and her son Danny, who stands up to Pat and voices Smith's own radical views, is soon forced to flee to England. Danny's two older brothers have already emigrated to America, never to be seen again, and the novel centres on Molly's suffering, and that of her daughter Babby and sons Tucker Tommy and Neddo, as the family gradually disintegrates. War and national political upheaval provide a historical context to their private agonies, and, like O'Casey, Smith projects the social image through these subjective stories. His gritty realism was a direct attack on the failures of decolonised Ireland and is why the book was banned in June 1962 as "indecent or obscene", along with Tennessee Williams' *Cat on a Hot Tin Roof*, Edna O'Brien's *The Lonely Girl* and Aaron Bell's *The Abortionist*. Felicitously enough, the Censorship Board also banned a book innocuously titled *The Way to Happy Marriage* that same month.[47]

Rewriting women's history: "Voiceless because they would have been useless"

Molly Baines's unhappy marriage and her uneasy integration into the slums provides Smith with a number of useful contrasts. Her constant association with nature and traditional imagery of femininity clashes with the depiction of some of her more liberated, urban-born female neighbours – rather in the manner that rural ingénue Mary contrasts with her environment in

Collis's *Marrowbone Lane*, "like a caged bird in this [slum-ridden] place".[48] Molly comes to the slums of the 1910s with "great innocence", as a "breath of country air", and her naivety acts as a foil for the Gissingesque world of the tenements, which she fears might "all fall down on top of her" (*CW*, pp. 2, 1, 259). When Molly dies, it is noted that her window box is left "without the small splash of color for the first time for as long as [locals] could remember", the only splash of colour amidst the dreary "green darkness" of Kelly's Lane (*CW*, pp. 259, 272, 4). As such, she functions as an embodiment of the rustic purity that Irish culture had elevated to an obsession, but also its degradation in urban, working-class life. For most of the novel, Molly plays the archetypal, submissive Victorian housewife.

But for Smith this invocation of pastoral romance is a subversive ploy. Providing for a contrast between an idealised Irish womanhood and the dystopian dilapidation of tenement Dublin, it sustains a powerful social critique, implying a parallel contrast between the rhetoric of de Valerian Ireland and its reality as lived in the slums. Molly is indeed governed by such contrasts between public idealism and private realities. She rallies against her husband's brutality in her thoughts, but Catholic morality, aligned with "the fear in her mind reflected on [her children's] faces", prevents her from speaking out (*CW*, p. 101). Her protests anyhow are "voiceless because they would have been useless", in a society where women are disempowered (*CW*, p. 122). Molly observes subservience to supposedly divine rights; it isn't "her place to question the ways of God and His Church or His workings through a man like her husband" (*CW*, p. 34); the capitalised "His" might just as well refer to either male, but her embodiment of the "Angel in the House" ideal of female self-effacement is also a point of anxiety for Smith, as it is for her son Tucker Tommy – both a source of nostalgic affection and an exemplar of subservience he cannot abide.[49] Smith contrasts Molly's consent to male social power with her working-class neighbours' rebellious refusal of it, as a means of contrasting hegemonic Ireland with its *other*. In doing so, he accords with David Lloyd's suggestion that in subaltern Ireland – "that which the state does not interpellate, and therefore what lies outside it" – are the seeds of a radical cultural alternative.[50]

While Molly adheres with "patience and humility" to the tellingly nicknamed Father Rex Aurealis's advice that she should "stay with her husband", (the priest is otherwise known, equally suggestively, as Fr Tithe) there are those in "the Lane" and locally, in similar circumstances, openly "defying the teachings of the church" (*CW*, p. 2).[51] Molly's relationship with Pat is defined by male terror and control. When the swaggering, vainglorious soldier drunkenly returns after having "bollixed the whole Kaiser's army", he immediately strikes "fear" and "trembling" into even his grown-up children (*CW*, pp. 23, 27). He is, as Eileen Battersby describes him, "one of the most menacing figures in literature", exerting, like Frankenstein's monster, a kind of primal dread, even while he is away.[52] Pat assumes a graphically phallocentric dominance over the household on his return from war, ordering his wife to "wrap yourself around this" (his penis) (*CW*, p. 26), but Smith counterpoints this domestic male supremacy with the destabilisation of male power elsewhere.

In a juxtaposed scene at the beginning of Chapter 3, it is Mrs Slattery and Mrs Kinsella who assume dominance over a male aggressor, in an uproarious, comic female rebellion. Mr Bedell, a "relief man", whose job it is to decide who deserves special allowances for the poor, is driven from the tenements by the women's verbal assaults and threatened violence (*CW*, p. 28).[53] Cowed and emasculated, he shouts "feeble abuse" as a belligerent Kinsella advises him to "go an' stick your lousy seven-an'-six up your la-la!" (*CW*, p. 28). An implicit parallel between Pat's recent threat of female penetration and Kinsella's ribald counsel on where Bedell might deposit his money is suggestive; in a profanely carnivalesque contrast, the bodily violation is reversed. Bedell's miserly refusal to grant relief to Kinsella is based on his sighting of a baby's cot in her flat, an alleged sign of "full and plenty" and a symbol of female fecundity (*CW*, p. 29). His complaint is a metaphor for the barren, androcentric humanity he represents, the whingeing of a "dyin' lookin' puke" who has no "nature in him" (*CW*, p. 29). Kinsella and Slattery's vibrant, Rabelaisian "energy" thus contrasts with Bedell's calculating embodiment of capitalist power; the personification of a social disease, he is a "filthy Locke Hospital leavin's" (*CW*, pp. 28, 29). These women also contrast glaringly with Molly's submissiveness. Both take great pleasure at having made "short work of that pox bottle!" (*CW*, p. 28).

Just as O'Casey's feminist outlook is intertwined with his disdain for theocracy in plays such as *Cock-a-Doodle Dandy* (1949), Smith's feminism is inextricable from his views on religious power in Irish life. Molly's devotion to the Catholic Church suggestively mirrors her loyalty to Pat. In both relationships, she suffers the tragedy of being wedded to something that abuses her. While Molly builds a shrine in her tenement room to the Virgin Mary, it is constructed around a statue with a "lowered indifferent face hovering eternally in chalk-eyed blindness" (*CW*, p. 116). The icon becomes a symbol of religious remoteness, unsympathetic and unresponsive to her travails, even as it perpetually stares. It harks back to Eeada, Dympna and Finoola's idolatry in O'Casey's *Red Roses for Me* (1942), or, further still, to A.P. Wilson's *The Slough* (1914), in which Mrs Kelly opines that praying is "the only thing left for poor people like us to do".[54] Molly's object of prayer, Smith shows, is "impassive" and "pitiless to all appeals" (*CW*, p. 207).

Her tyrant husband, by contrast, identifies an image of his own interests in Christianity. After one particularly brutal scene, in which Pat's "drunken savaging flailed the room, crowding it with pain as he smashed his strength against his children and his wife", the family is left "like statues barely whispered into life in order that they might bleed" (*CW*, p. 136). Pat then nonchalantly reaches for his rosary beads and declares, without a trace of irony, and "in a deeply solemn voice", "The Joyful Mysteries" of the Rosary (*CW*, p. 137). Having left his wife with a "hacked body", his intoned reverence for maternal holiness is darkly ironic: "Holy Queen! Mother of Mercy, hail our life, our sweetness and our hope" (*CW*, pp. 139, 137). Molly pleads silently to the statue "in bewilderment", descending into "gradual disbelief" and "bitter resignation", as futile prayers issue through "a new gap where teeth had been" (*CW*, p. 137). But Pat's prayers and their responses are narcissistically self-affirming, punctuated by such megalomaniacal moments as "the Presentation of the Crucifixion, when" – outrageously, and in an irreverent attack of Christian patriarchy – "he might stop to liken his own travail to Christ's" (*CW*, p. 138). As Monica Mc Williams and Joan McKiernan write, "Christian women have been inundated with models which encourage submissiveness, modesty and suffering as Christian virtues", while organised Christianity has worked in "collusion with [their] abuse".[55] This religious hypocrisy is vividly realised in the contrast between the abused family Pat treats as "statues" and the statue of female benevolence which he treats as a deity. Inferentially, if Ireland, like Pat, honours a religiously inflected version of womanhood with solemn rhetoric and hollow ideals, in reality it desecrates its own vaunted morality by enabling men's tyrannical misogyny. Pat's battered son, Neddo, with his injured eye "closing like some exotic bud in the center of pear-shaped petals", symbolises beauty and innocence transgressed, but it is his transgressor, Pat, who draws greatest comfort from the Catholic Church (*CW*, p. 137).

The Church's abuse of women also obtains a more official and institutional level in the novel. Most perceived offences against religion in the Lane are blamed on women. Local woman Nancy O'Byrne becomes the victim of a veritable witch-hunt because of her sexual activities. Her father has died at war in France, leaving Nancy's mother madly distraught and depriving Nancy of parental care; she is already a victim of male violence, of the horror of war. But because Nancy has an abortion at 16, and a baby outside marriage at 18, she becomes, "in that district where neither incest nor rape caused any but a passing commotion [...] chased from hallway to hallway by endless relays of little men". These men are the enforcers of a frighteningly pervasive and Orwellian religious theocracy, and behind them, "at a discreet distance", is Fr Tithe (*CW*, p. 177). Nancy is "shadowed" by something akin to a Catholic police force, in a van "that resembled the Black Maria", and while such aggressive social monitoring may seem the product of a fictive hyperbole, Thomas J. O'Hanlon recalls how such a "block surveillance system" operated in Dublin under the auspices of an infamous archbishop, John Charles McQuaid (*CW*, p. 178).[56] As Tony Fahey notes, the Catholic hierarchy was "preoccupied with the sinfulness of sex [and] with its dangers outside marriage".[57]

Eventually Nancy is captured by Tithe's "hoor's ghosts" and taken surreptitiously to "Christ alone knows what sort of a place" (*CW*, pp. 181, 182).

And it is no coincidence that the priest suddenly appears just as Nancy is "kidnapped": "One minute that slieveen bastard wasn't there, an' the next he was" (*CW*, pp. 181–182). Mrs Baines is even "chastised" by a young nun, "a mere slip of a girl" for asking where her friend is being held (*CW*, p. 183). Working-class women's subjection to such religious tyranny was excoriated by James Stephens in his gripping short story "Sawdust" (1918), in which a Dublin woman, who has lost her husband and children to war and premature death, is denounced by a priest for drinking in a public house. She defies the clergyman, who predicts that she will "die roaring"; but his words are tragically prophetic, and Stephens' unnamed female subsequently dies at her own hand, another "Mrs So and So" who is "fished out of the canal".[58] Suggestively, she is deliberately never named. McQuaid operated as bishop from 1940 to 1972, and Smith's comments from the fictional vantage point of the 1920s bear testimony to the pervasive religiosity of the 1960s too – undoubtedly another reason his book was banned. Stressing this contemporary relevance, Mrs Kinsella even ominously predicts of the new Free State that "England's going to be in the halfpenny place compared to the way the priests an' the chapels are going to be running us before long"; without "Rome's and the sanction of the priests, ya won't be able to blow ya nose" (*CW*, p. 182).[59]

Nancy's shocking abduction may also partly explain why most young Irish women who had children outside marriage in the 1960s opted for adoption, and why so many of Smith's female characters are so belligerently opposed to Catholic values.[60] When Father Tithe denounces Nancy's supposed moral transgressions from the altar, liking her to the "Scarlet Hoor a Babylon", the response from Tessa Doyle is one of outrage, at "how he compares Nancy O'Byrne with that wan in Babylon [...] since she was an out-an'-outer"; the priest, Doyle vents, in a sacrilegious outburst, is a "dirty bad-minded oul' thing" for urging locals to "hunt out the fallen among us" (*CW*, p. 72). Her profanity is echoed in the heretical opinions of other women, such as Queenie, with her blasphemous thoughts regarding being "saddled with a baby", and the matter of getting the "five quid down and another five quid when it's over" for an abortion (*CW*, p. 167). Mrs Slattery's opinion on Molly's miscarriage being the "hand of God, and wasn't she saved the expense of going to Mrs Ennis to get rid of it" is a further provocative attack on Catholic dogma and state laws (*CW*, p. 31).[61] Even in (comparatively) liberal 1950s–1960s England, the treatment of similar issues in Nell Dunn's *Up the Junction* (1963) and Alan Sillitoe's *Saturday Night, Sunday Morning* (1958) provoked huge public controversy.[62] In Ireland, such concerns didn't even feature in (heavily censored) fiction, let alone in open public discourse.[63]

In a similar vein, the institution of marriage is assailed through disenchanting portrayals of married life. Again, as Kearns's study attests, "religious duties and a lack of life options" meant that many working-class women felt "trapped under the glass of [their] wedding photo frame[s]" – more so than their middle-class counterparts.[64] And notwithstanding the cruelty of domestic violence, "bad marriages" in the inner city "didn't justify 'broken homes'"; without "money, solicitors and contacts within the Church", annulments or separating in a "civil and socially acceptable manner" were unlikely options.[65] Molly's daughter, Babby, is thus naturally apprehensive about marriage to her lover Nick. Babby knows "there was no reason why they could not get married", but "even in her need for [Nick], she turned her mouth from his" (*CW*, p. 104). Feeling "released from her own body" in Nick's presence, she nonetheless tellingly fears being "imprisoned in his", with his "fire", his "dictatorial stream [...] like darkness pressing down" (*CW*, pp. 104, 105). Marriage, she infers, is about male control. Its oppressiveness diminishes a woman just as Vinny's battered mother, in Catherine Dunne's *A Name for Himself* (1999), figuratively seems to be "beginning to disappear" as her husband's violence intensifies.[66] When Queenie becomes pregnant, Molly urges her to marry Danny (the baby's father), explaining that "it's right the man that fathered your child should marry you", because "what other decent man is going to look you straight in the eye if he knows you've had a child by somebody else?" (*CW*, p. 168) Here, marriage is about sexual ownership and social shame, the fear of ending up "any man's fancy, an' the leavin's of all" (*CW*, p. 168).[67]

Even more subversively, for Mrs Kinsella marriage is about unadulterated sexual lust. "Sacrament, my arse", she blasts; "what's sacred about two people wantin' to go to bed with each other?" This supposedly sacred union is what happens when:

> we like the way the other fiddles, or when we see in them, or they in us, the shape of the thing we want [...] It's got hundreds of names [...] It's just not so good on a windy hill of a wet night [...] so they rush us to a priest or parson and have them say a few words over us, then head for bed. (*CW*, p. 35)

A license for sex, in these terms marriage is an agreement between two men (husband and priest), in which a woman is ceremonially disempowered.

This attack on religious oppression is crystallised in the words of Mrs Baines's eldest son, Danny, who, ruminating on how his anxiety about his imperilled mother keeps him in Ireland, protests that "*some*body ought to be able to abolish the power of the priests over the minds of the people" (*CW*, p. 112). They "teach people to accept" such things as "rule from England", "poverty as a way of life" and "the way things always have been instead of the way they might be [...] To accept and endure brutality in the name of God [...] submit like animals." (*CW*, pp. 112–113) The priests refuse "to face reality", he claims, "to deal with the reality of *our* lives", and it is ironic that while an oppressive male clergy enjoys a monopoly on moral virtue, women like Mrs Cogan, known locally as a "witch" – who is employed generally to meet "the [caring] demands of births and the laying out of bodies for wakes" – are the ones who are vilified (*CW*, pp. 113, 153). Conventional religious morality is skewed in favour of male domination and serves to demonise women such as Cogan or O'Byrne, but, perhaps more significantly, Smith shows that some working-class women have the temerity to question it.

Stigma and stigmata: Iconoclasm as social criticism

Smith's most subversive and obviously carnivalesque imagery of women accompanies depictions of female sexuality, which follow O'Casey's lead in plays such as *Within the Gates* (1931), *Cock-a-Doodle Dandy* (1949) and *Bedtime Story* (1958), by provocatively antagonising social conservatism. Moral backwardness is scandalised in stylised, semi-surreal comic interludes, and sexual desire is more often attributed to women than men in *The Countrywoman*, confuting prevailing gender constructions. Many of the women in the Lane openly parade their sensuality. Cocky O'Byrne, whose very name infers role reversal – and perhaps also hints at O'Casey's masque figure in *Cock-a-Doodle Dandy* – represents, to extend the metaphor, a new gynocentric dawn of sorts. In O'Casey's play, the Cock is exorcised by a priest in order to rid his village of sexual influences, and like O'Casey's symbolic interloper, Smith's Cocky also transgresses established moral boundaries.

When visited by the devoutly religious Mr Pughe, who attempts in vain to win her affections, Cocky rebuffs him by graphically illustrating a bizarre posthumous enjoyment of her dead husband's sexual prowess. The imagery here is astoundingly iconoclastic and instances Bakhtin's "carnivalistic obscenities linked with the *reproductive power of the earth and the body*", while also invoking carnival's *"parodies on sacred texts* and sayings". Spontaneously stripping off her clothes, Cocky tells Pughe that she wants him "to see the marks that came when she just *thought* of Peewee" – the marks, outrageously, of a sexualised "stigmata":

> When Cocky took off her blouse you could see on her arms and on her breasts the kind of new-dinge marks a man's fingers'd make...An' then she began to tell him how Peewee made love to her an' how he... well, you know, an' all. (*CW*, pp. 42–43)

This explicit association of Cocky's intensely felt sexual memory with a totemic, hallowed, Christian occult phenomenon is powerfully suggestive. "Peewee" may indeed even be a pun on Padre Pio, the famous stigmatic Italian priest who died in 1968, and had attained cult status by the time Smith wrote this novel.[68]

But if Cocky is an eccentric extreme, she is by no means an exception. Her carnivalesque theatrics typify a general "brazen vitality" amongst local women (*CW*, p. 74). As Smith observes, in a pointed authorial intervention:

> Apart from [the women's] enjoyment of sex, there was also pride in being able to brag about a husband's virility as well as one's own. And there was a continual race amongst themselves as to which of them could be pregnant in the shortest time and the most often. (*CW*, 73)

Florry Conors, for instance, explicitly contrasts her vital sensuality with religious morbidity. Having just visited a wake, she inauspiciously declares that, "when I grow up I'm going to commit every sin in the calendar", and then proceeds to steal the black bow adorning the mourning household's front door, transforming it into a sexualised accessory in a suggestive dance (*CW*, p. 128). "Under the skimpy dress, she contorted vigorously as she draped the black length of stuff around her head and across her shoulders. She laughed and began to strut, imitating the gyratings of grown women" (*CW*, p. 128). After previous scenes in which life is portrayed (*à la* O'Casey's Mrs Gogan) as a "trouble an' worry", and death as a "happy release" celebrated with lavishness that "was never given to the business of living", Florry's antics are a jarring, comic relief from Goganesque morbidity; emblematising the kind of contrasts that Bakhtin identified in carnival, she trails "the crumpled symbol of death like a pennant, triumphant after battle" (*CW*, pp. 16, 125, 124, 128).

Aggie Chance, who comically veers between extremes of puritanism and sexual voraciousness, is also illustrative in this regard. When she is "called again" (every "four or five weeks") to her intermittent "vocation" as a nun, the appearance of her navy-blue serge dress and coat on Mrs Chance's washing line comically signals peace of mind for the women of the area, as "for another while the girls' fellows were safe", while Aggie's allure is safely ensconced in the convent. But when Aggie returns again to the Lane, "what she's got she's offering with two hands" (*CW*, pp. 186, 41). Mrs Slattery and Mrs Kinsella also join in this general female irreverence, as they goad the religiosity of Aggie's mother, Mrs Chance, with iconoclastic remarks about the "ram" rebel hero Robert Emmet, who "ran that Sarah Curran bowlegged" (*CW*, p. 189). Even a local nun, Sister Eustace, is forced to "excessive self-imposed penances" by private thoughts of Pat Baines and Nurse Foley's "goings-on", and Pat's "hard dark voluptuousness which turned her mind from God and her hoped-for near promotion to the post of the Union's Reverend Mother" (*CW*, pp. 105, 94). As provocative affronts to orthodox morality, these images of female sexuality are powerfully subversive, and are made more so by Smith's narrative insistence that they indeed represent working-class *norms*. He would seem to corroborate Luke Gibbons's assertion that much of Irish culture's anti-urban inflections and attendant "idealizations of rural existence", which often sought to portray Ireland as a land of puritanical virtue, are "cultural fictions imposed on the lives of those they purport to represent".[69]

Indeed, such carnivalesque outrages are also the quintessence of what Bourdieu had identified in proletarian culture – in its penchant for "setting the social world head over heels". Cocky's untrammelled sensuality fails to make her a pariah and, indeed, parallels that of local women and the very architecture of the tenement world, which "held nothing back [...] exposing its great streel of a self" (*CW*, p. 74). When she again defies convention by exposing her nudity to the street, "big and buxom, doing a wild lament of a dance in the middle of the road", local women even applaud her, beginning "to clap their hands in unison and sing the song they always sang when they saw her coming". When the gyrating Cocky stops a tram, a symbol of the masculine, mechanised world, in its tracks, the "pale dirty remarks" of its "pale runt" driver elicit only laughter from the female observers. They celebrate her profanity, collude in her carnival crudity, and again there is an implicit overturning of orthodox virtue: when the tram driver attacks Cocky with a hail of tomatoes, Smith invites a jocose but again highly sacrilegious parallel with the stoning of an adulteress in the Bible's *Pericope Adulterae*.[70] Tellingly, the normally reserved Mrs Baines takes on Christ's parabolic role, venting her "fury" against this "mean cur" latterday Pharisee, which, "blinding her normal reticence", even prompts Smith's heroine to fling herself in the tram driver's direction. The scene depicts not only the conflict between real Christianity and false moral scruple, but also the clash between stagnant male authority and vital female sexuality. Cocky dances as if "by so doing she could still a hurt", the death of her husband at war; such untrammelled pleasure is her answer to war's man-made pain (*CW*, p. 75). She stands in marked contrast to the austere reserve of would-be suitor Mr Pughe, for whom (like the guilty nun) pain and repression are the inevitable responses to sex. Pughe "studiously" avoids the word love "as wicked and somehow lewd", and welcomes "the discomfort" of his tight shoes "as a private penance for doing something" – one presumes sexual – which "he secretly felt guilty about" (*CW*, p. 77). Cocky, by dramatic contrast, embodies the feminine *jouissance*.[71] Her orgasmic autoeroticism, without any need for corporeal male validation, is a challenge to prevailing orthodoxies of sexual behaviour. Smith's vignettes of subversive, sexually provocative female antics throughout the novel confirm Cocky's place in literature as an unlikely but significant agitator for women's social and sexual liberation.[72]

By contrast, Molly Baines' tragedy is that she never rebels, and that in meekly accepting the strictures of normative behaviour she is marginalised, but she too is a conduit for a feminist message. Molly suffers Pat's attacks to save her children, enduring "her own physical destruction in sanctified duress at the hands of a drunk" (*CW*, p. 271). Her life is sublimated in acts of giving, such as handing "over her own portion of food to the two boys", or working relentlessly to buy Babby a new shift, which she fetishises with "rose-ate thoughts", as if it were "a relic endowed with miraculous benefits" (*CW*, pp. 106–107, 98). Molly is "consumed with a desire to reach out protectively towards her child, to hold her forever in an impregnable armor against the butts and roughages of life" (*CW*, p. 97). But this self-effacement is tragically thankless. Like most of Molly's children, Babby is taken from her mother, this time by death. Her two eldest sons, then Teasey, Kitty and Danny, all emigrate, while Neddo is consigned to an orphanage. All Molly's letters to her children are "returned unclaimed and unopened" (*CW*, p. 176).

The ultimate irony of her "sanctified" martyrdom to family life is realised, again with the irruption of a wider social picture into the text, when the state accords Molly's neglectful and violent husband recognition as Neddo's authoritative guardian. When Neddo stops attending school and is threatened with institutionalisation, Smith shows how Pat has complete control over his young son's future. Neddo has "our hearts broke", Pat fallaciously whines to an official; "he's a liar and a cheat and a thief, an' not a day or night passes without him doing some harm" (*CW*, p. 222). While Molly gives an undertaking to ensure that her son will in future attend school, Pat's refusal to acquiesce leaves her powerless, because "if the child's father is alive, he is the person responsible" (*CW*, p. 224). Neddo's very reason for avoiding school is the shame caused by bruises that Pat habitually leaves on his face, yet Molly must witness "the passing of yet another of her children", as Pat "swear[s] his son's life away for six years [...] a son he had always, with no sense of it, hated" (*CW*, pp. 226, 229).

Molly's dedication and compassion in motherhood means little to the state, Smith conveys and, in a sardonic crescendo, she too is institutionalised, in a "madhouse", symbolically anathematised by society as insane (*CW*, p. 263). Tommy observes other dying women trapped in beds at the asylum, where they "moaned unheeded their mind's griefs" (*CW*, p. 264). Some are clearly mentally disturbed, some see "monkeys on the wall", but amongst them are "sometimes clearly audible sane voices craving attention" (*CW*, pp. 265, 267). Poignantly, Molly's position in her deathbed is reflective of the piteous self-abnegation that has become her lot in life. She makes "room for another",

> Tucker Tommy, perhaps, or one of the many children she had brought into the world, now scattered across a good part of it, leaving her to make her way from it alone, unhelped, unwatched. She lay slantwise across the bed as if to make a place in it beside her for one of them. Her arm crooked to hold a head. (*CW*, p. 270)

The pathos of Smith's imagery of the deserted and devalued mother, trapped in a mental institution to which a local alcoholic doctor has consigned her (despite her perfect sanity), is the apogee of Smith's tirade against sexist tyranny. Despite her "obedience, humility, [and] acceptance" (*CW*, p. 231), Molly is marginalised and rejected, an emblem of her society's hypocritical treatment of women. Not merely a foil for comparison with the more ostensibly subversive women of the Lane, she represents what Sandra Gilbert and Susan Gubar identify as the archetypal embodiment of the mad woman in literature, as the "author's double, an image of her [or his?] own anxiety and rage"; thus madness is employed as a metaphor for suppressed feminist revolt.[73] As "sanctified" martyr, his countrywoman personifies Smith's counterblast to male domination and his own abiding anger about how working-class women were treated by the Irish state.

Sheridan's Philo Darcy: the madwoman in the convent

Philo Darcy, the protagonist of Peter Sheridan's first novel, *Big Fat Love* (2003), is also a projection of authorial dissatisfaction with a patriarchal society, and Sheridan, like Smith, has exhibited an enduring desire to articulate the hidden narratives of working-class women. His play *Mother of All the Behans* (1987) is a dramatic adaptation from Brian Behan's (brother of Brendan's) biographical tribute to his mother. In *Women at Work* (1976, sub-titled "Same Sweat Different Pay"), Peter, along with his co-author and brother, Jim, produced an agitprop drama for post-primary students about the campaign for equal pay for women. *The Illusion* (1993) is a dramatic adaptation of seventeenth-century playwright Pierre Corneille's *L'Illusion Comique* (1636). It explores men's attempts to control women's sexual desires. *Big Fat Love,* as we shall see, develops a radical treatment of similar issues.

More broadly, a sense of social responsibility defines Sheridan's work. He identifies explicitly with Seán O'Casey's legacy, in fighting "a certain orthodoxy", and he believes "very definitely" in the power of the class system in Ireland, describing his background as "extremely working class".[74] Sheridan's aesthetic vision is informed by a conviction that his community's history and welfare has been denigrated in Irish cultural life. For him, "there isn't a great sense of the importance of preserving that kind of working-class culture that came out of the Docks", partly because there was a "form of apartheid that operated in this city", which imposed a cultural "stigma" on "lots of working class areas". But Sheridan also reserves some of his most damning criticism for sexism *within* these areas. Working-class Dublin was "bad for men", he argues, but "how much worse was it for women?" Physical force "somehow gave you stature" in working-class life, where "it was almost tolerated that a man could beat his wife". "I saw unbelievable violence against women in Sheriff Street growing up," he recalls.

This violence and its relationship with institutional discrimination is just one of the issues encountered by Sheridan's gregarious but deeply troubled Philo, who learns in the novel her own power and that of women generally in a male-dominated society. Like Smith's Aggie Chance, Philo finds sanctuary among nuns, after she escapes from her violent husband, but by contrast for her the local convent provides a new lease of life and an "escape" from domestic and social pressures, "in out of the world" (*BFL*, p. 3). It also, of course, provides Sheridan with a site in which to counterpoise aloof religion with social reality. Between the convent and Philo's home in the North Wall, "the contrast couldn't have been more profound", and this conflict between cloistered idealism and kitchen-sink realities again, like Smith's, resolves itself in a feminist message from below (*BFL*, p. 17). Philo emerges transformed by her experiences there, but Sheridan's tentative optimism is tempered by slippage and ambiguity about the position of working-class women in modern Dublin.

Philo's hatred of the "bucket of shit" society she has grown-up in is rooted in her experience as a disadvantaged woman, in a violent, male-dominated environment (*BFL*, p. 165). Feminism teaches us that patriarchal society "manages to convince itself that its cultural constructions are somehow 'natural'", and the world Sheridan depicts has a strong purchase on naturalised gender constructions.[75] Dublin's inner city has long been "famed for brawny dockers, hard-drinking pubmen, and rough and ready fellas of every ilk".[76] As Lar Redmond puts it, "the iron rule of this place had been forced on me: 'Never say your mother reared a gibber'".[77] Such stereotypes pertain to the hard men of Plunkett's *Strumpet City* (1969), or Magee's *Hatchet* (1978), just as they do to those who engage in a "riot of lootin' an' roguery" in O'Casey's *Plough* (1926).[78] The "hard chaw" echoes throughout Dublin's writing of the working class, instantly recognisable in Doyle's Charlo Spencer, of *The Woman Who Walked into Doors* (1996), or Paula Meehan's domestic despots, Franco and Benito, in *Mrs Sweeney* (1997). Such men are there too, more comically, in the form of Flann O'Brien's inner-city cowboys, in *At Swim-Two-Birds* (1939). A more brutal strain of this working-class male is typified by the father who is never seen "kissing" or "holding hands", but always engaged in "fights, shouts, police and partings", in Gerard Mannix Flynn's *James X*.[79]

In British working-class literature, there is a proliferation of similar rough-and-ready male types. Richard Hoggart described how the man in the working-class England of his youth was "the boss", who, "if something goes amiss [...] may 'bash' you, especially if he has had a couple of pints on the way home from work".[80] When Harry Hardcastle, of Walter Greenwood's *Love on the Dole* (1933), opts for a manual job at a local factory over his stable employment at Price and Jones's pawn shop, it is explicitly because he and his working-class peers view rough, physical work as more masculine than that of a "mere pusher of pens".[81] The writing of Nell Dunn, Pat Barker and Alan Sillitoe reiterates this distinctly physical and often violent aspect of working-class male identity.[82] As John Benyon notes, "for economically marginalized men or those in manual settings the threat of violence is the major vehicle for both [sic] establishing, retaining and asserting masculinity by placing other men on the defensive".[83] In *Mythologies* (1957), Roland Barthes argues that, since the working class has provided the physical manpower underpinning industrialisation from the nineteenth century, its identity has been subsequently associated with the physical realm.[84]

Sheridan conveys Philo's subjection to these class expectations of manhood through the dynamics of sexual attraction and the hailing power of habitus. Though she later suggests that she might have been better off marrying a woman (even, possibly, Sr Rosaleen, she jokes), Philo, like Roddy Doyle's Paula Spencer, is initially attracted to "rough men" (*BFL*, p. 167). Her husband, Tommo Nolan, is "good looking", but only "in the way boxers sometimes are", "well built, square as the lorry he drove" (*BFL*, p. 58). His job (like that of the tram driver in *The Countrywoman*) identifies him with industrial male power, and Tommo's proclivity for violence is also curiously alluring; his "flat nose" and "cauliflower ear that made him look like a man who'd been to war", are described as "manly" attributes, which Tommo uses "all his life to devastating effect" (*BFL*, p. 58). Philo is socialised to find such attributes attractive, Sheridan suggests, like Nell Dunn's Joy in *Poor Cow* (1967), who, after her violent husband has been sent to jail, finds love with Dave, another hard man, who soon also gets imprisoned for violent robbery. Sheridan infers in *Big Fat Love* that his protagonist has seen little else of men. When she enters the San Francisco Boys' Home after her son's move there, Philo is surprised to see a man in an apron for the first time. The benign Father Felix is a revelation – nick-named ET because he is so very alien in the north inner city.[85]

After Philo and Tommo marry, she takes her "dose of digs", implying a normative measure of domestic violence, a medicinal "dose"; and femininity itself is presented as a condition requiring male correction (*BFL*, p. 96). This mindset recalls Doyle's Angela, in his play *War* (1989), who ruminates that if her estranged boyfriend was to return, "I'd have let him hit me nearly". Philo inherits her submissive attitude from her mother, who also suffers her own husband's bullying, his constant propensity to "put [her] down".[86] She also inherits her acceptance of male violence from Sylvia, who suffers a lifetime of domestic abuse, and both Philo's husband and father are depicted as extreme misogynists. Tommo's terms for his wife and children are filled with venom – "fuckers, little fuckers, bastards, big bastards, pigs, dirty pigs, swine, elephants, big fat cows and fat cunts" (*BFL*, p. 109) – recalling also Pat Baines' similarly unpaternal vitriol, or the language with which Freddie and Hairoil dismissed their wives and "god forbids" in *Hatchet*.[87] Sheridan emphasises that Philo's predicament is no anomaly but part of a cyclical trend in working-class life. She has escaped from an abusive father only to meet "herself coming back wearing a different set of manacles" (*BFL*, pp. 115, 277). Philo has been conditioned to expect to be manacled by thuggish men.

Class, superstructure, sexism

Such explorations of a sexist habitus are integral to *Big Fat Love* – which repeatedly seeks to defamiliarise how male orthodoxy is maintained in working-class life. Philo's particular problem is paralleled with the wider social image, analogous, she infers, to the Catholic practice of the Eucharist, and again we observe a characteristic proletarian overturning of normative values. A priest, who Philo nicknames Buddy Holly, is depicted "stuff[ing] the host [of the transubstantiated Christ] into his mouth", then chewing on it "like he was eating a packet of crisps", which Philo characterises as a "vulgar and cannibalistic" act (*BFL*, p. 4). "She'd entered the convent to escape tribal warfare," the narrator explains, but is "surprised to be reminded of it, watching Buddy Holly munch his way through the Body of Christ" (*BFL*, p. 5). A metaphor for Darwinistic male thinking, the Catholic ritual reminds her how "life was a jungle and the Eucharist was part of it" (*BFL*, p. 4). Ann Wilson Schaef has written that in a "gynocentric", or female-centred society, relationships are prioritised over competition (which the Eucharist represents), but in Philo's world sexual relationships are characterised by adversarial behaviour.[88]

When she first attempts to escape from Tommo's violence, Philo surmises that her only power in the relationship lies in her ability to deprive him of her domestic services, that "he wouldn't be so quick to criticise and point the finger at dirty dishes and unwashed clothes" after she flees (*BFL*, p. 6). But Philo is soon apprised of her own social powerlessness when Tommo nonchalantly dumps their children in Goldenbridge Orphanage, getting "rid of them because he had to play a darts match" (*BFL*, p. 6). It is ironic that, when she attempts to secure their children's release, the Department of Social Welfare declares Philo "an unfit mother due to her abandonment of them", just as Molly Baines is declared mad after her husband sends his own son to an orphanage (*BFL*, p. 6). Not only is Philo "unfit", she too is "deranged", although "the only deranged thing was having to 're-establish the family unit'", as the state instructs her to do – returning her to Tommo's abuse. Like Molly, Philo is ostracised by society when she can no longer function in the maternal role that the state has prescribed for her.

Again, there is also a class element in this antagonism towards the state apparatus. Kearns speaks of the working-class woman's typical fear of institutions and forms, the "real feeling of interrogation" elicited by "degrading questions", asked by "men who surely never knew a day's deprivation in their lives".[89] In Brendan O'Carroll's *The Mammy* (1994), accessing benefit from the state is preceded by what amounts to another "interrogation" for Agnes Browne – "an exam of some kind".[90] Equally, in Neville Thompson's *Jackie Loves Johnser OK?* (1997), a newly separated wife finds accessing state accommodation a degrading experience: "some snotty fucking bitch sitting behind her desk asked all sorts of personal questions. Interrogated me like

I was a fucking criminal."[91] Confronted with a form from Sister Monica, Philo reveals that she too "hated providing information", and later we learn that it is "impossible" for her to "answer questions truthfully on a form" due to the "welfare system, where the simplest questions came fully loaded"; every answer is a "potential bomb" (*BFL*, pp. 8, 41). At Dublin Corporation offices, an official warns Philo "that false or misleading information would result in permanent exclusion from the housing list and/or a fine", leaving her wanting "to scream" (*BFL*, p. 123). For Sheridan's abused woman, every official document is another "black and white obstacle course". She senses that these forms have inscribed state domination onto her being – she has "filled in so many forms that they owned her, lock, stock and barrel. She was leasing her body from the State until she died" (*BFL*, p. 164). As Perry Share, Hilary Tovey and Mary P. Corcoran note, access to privacy is granted in Irish society in relation to personal wealth: "There is a sharp contrast between the lack of basic privacy accorded to recipients of state benefits (for example, queuing for the dole) and the privacy demanded by the wealthy and powerful when tribunals of inquiry of the Revenue Commissioners are attempting to investigate their financial affairs."[92] Sheridan's novel makes this point, with a feminine twist.

Reification and patriarchy

In very graphic and disturbing scenes, Sheridan also symbolises Philo's parallel appropriation by a male system of capitalist exchange. Her past is marred by the seminal actions of the man she calls "the devil", "Uncle Sam Harris", who sexually abused her as a child (*BFL*, p. 225). A local moneylender, Harris is not actually Philo's uncle, but the associations of his misnomer (Uncle Sam) with masculinity, violence and inequality hardly require elaboration. Sam embodies the worst abuses of a sexist and capitalist society. He causes Philo to make her memories "small" by piling on excessive weight. One of her father's "angels", she grows up in relative innocence until he falls into debt with Harris and begins to dispatch her with money owed to the loan shark every week (*BFL*, p. 225). Harris molests Philo during these visits, preying perversely on her childish innocence, using her love for "expensive lollipops" as an enticement, and intoning deformed children's rhymes as he abuses her:

> *Mary had a little lamb*
> *Its fleece was black as charcoal*
> *And every time that Mary stooped*
> *The lamb looked up her arsehole.* (*BFL*, pp. 225–226)

Such infantile resonances jar with grotesque imagery, a metaphor for innocence lost, and Philo's conception of sex is defiled by equally grotesque memories of how "he stretched it so that she would grow up to be a proper woman and when the time came she would deliver her babies without any pain" (*BFL*, p. 225).

But this abuse is also Philo's symbolic initiation into a society where women are traded as commodities, as metonyms for money and sex. When she refuses to visit Harris, we are told that her father, Jack, "clattered her", denouncing her as "a lazy pig, like her mother" (*BFL*, p. 226). Even though Philo eventually tells Jack that Harris taught her "to say bad words like arse-hole and cunt", her father is strangely oblivious, and does "not want to hear it" (*BFL*, p. 229). Philo surmises that "he must have suspected what was going on", but nevertheless "sent her there, week after week [...] just so that he could appease his blood-sucking moneylender" (*BFL*, p. 229). Economic and sexual exploitation are thus literally and symbolically inter-twined. Jack's paternal betrayal reduces his daughter, and sexuality itself, to a commodity between men, a means of mediation between classes; she repays "the loan with her flesh" (*BFL*, p. 229). Luce Irigaray has written of how phallocentrism constitutes a male economy of sexual desire in which women become reified objects of exchange, and Philo's narrative of abuse is a synecdoche for this objectifying system.[93]

Sheridan also correlates this female reification with Philo's obesity and self-abuse through gluttony and suggests a wider context for that abuse in linguistic and epistemic discourse. The "rocks" she covers with her "blub-ber" are memories of her past, which literally and metaphorically weigh her down (*BFL*, pp. 103, 196). "Her body had been perfect before Sam Harris put his finger in and started poking around," she recalls, but since then "she'd put on the fat to protect her secret", to "make herself an island" (*BFL*, pp. 230, 231, 260). This uglification-as-therapy recalls Kelly Brown's actions in Pat Barker's *Union Street* (1982), in which the sexually abused 11-year-old rejects the trappings of normative femininity, symbolically desecrating "a woman's room, a temple of femininity" in a house she breaks in to.[94] Kelly, like Philo, is taught through male violation to reject the female form, thinking the word "CUNT" is the "worst word she knew"; the rapist defines her – "she *was* what had just happened to her".[95] Equally, Dorothy Nelson illustrates this kind of disembodied self-loathing in her sexually abused teenager, Sara, when the girl begins to "hate being a woman [...] hate, hate, hate, myself". Sara imagines her "flesh peeled off in layers", floating about her, her "trapped rage scuttling along the ceiling and floor". She denies her subjectivity in order to cope with the trauma of sexual abuse committed by her father, and she thus becomes schizophrenically split between two per-sonalities, her own, and that of "Maggie", an imaginary alter ego, a "shiver-ing fleshless body" and ugly "mucus", onto whom she projects her pain.[96] For Philo, food becomes "her password to sleep" and the kitchen is "manna and heaven rolled into one". Uglification wards off her pain, because "the fat protect[s] her secret" (*BFL*, pp. 4, 10, 231).

"The divine mission of discontent"

But Philo eventually finds "redemption" – to use Sheridan's term – by forging a liberating and affirmative epistemology of self.[97] Ironically, her desire to step "in out of the world", "to make herself an island", is undermined by the convent's links with the community, and Philo's whirlwind immersion in community activities affords her a positive role in social action. A "banjaxed", "urban wasteland", the "dying world of the North Wall" has suffered the "devastation" of economic decline, and the convent's Day Care Centre is filled with "heads bowed, in silent reverie" (*BFL*, pp. 25, 17, 26). This inner-city world of economic stagnation and social despair is also captured in Val Mulkern's *Very Like a Whale* (1986), in which teacher Ben is posted in the Docklands, where "weeds [are] growing around and over the warehouses where the St Domenic's parents used to work". He is introduced to a school where "the futility of education" reigns – and local children are "doomed anyhow".[98] In such a dispirited milieu, Philo initially views the Sheriff Street area "old folks" as "worse than vampires [...] fucking monsters", but she soon finds herself reviving their spirits, leading the way in sing-songs, leaving even the nuns with "arms above their heads swaying disobediently to the insistent rhythm" (*BFL*, pp. 13, 29). Again there are traces here of a carnivalesque contrast. Philo engenders a "spirit reminiscent of the old days, when they'd had a village at their doorsteps, before progress had made rubble of their homes" (*BFL*, p. 47), and replaces the waning religious values of the past with a new ideology of collectivism, reminiscent of Jimmy Rabbitte and Joey the Lips' brother/sisterhood of soul in *The Commitments*: "We bring the music to the people," Joey says, when his band decides to stage their first gig locally: "We go to them. We go to their community centre. That's soul."[99] Such restoration of old working-class values in a contemporary, post-industrial setting was also the focus of British films of the 1990s, such as *Brassed Off* (1996) and *The Full Monty* (1997), in which hope and community triumph over social and economic crises. In an overtly religious lexicon, Philo nurses an ill, elderly friend, Dina, becoming her "saviour", and her welcome-home party for the ailing woman turns her home into a "grotto" (*BFL*, pp. 210, 203). Philo also obliquely revives Jim Larkin's hallowed memory, for she too has "come to preach the divine mission of discontent" (*BFL*, p. 203).

Sex and sensibility

If Larkin is remembered locally for his combative stance in the titanic Lockout battle, Philo too strikes out against social and economic norms, refusing passivity. In suggestive imagery that parallels feminist empowerment with sexual discovery, Philo's liberating social journey dovetails with the intimate sub-plot narrative of Cap and Dina's blossoming relationship. An elderly couple who initially refuse to communicate, the pair had become estranged following the fall-out from a mid-century industrial dispute, in which Cap and Dina's now long-gone husband took opposing sides, but now, in old age, they reconcile. Cap likens himself to "Ulysses on the stormy Mediterranean, chasing after Helen of Troy", and his ensuing exploration of Dina's and his own sexuality is indeed of epic proportions for the Irish male (*BFL*, p. 216).

Negative images and perceptions of sexuality have heretofore pervaded the novel. Philo must "endure Tommo, forever wanting to get up on her and put his thing inside her"; she hopes "her growing weight [will] put him off" (*BFL*, p. 41). Dina too has developed a distorted view of sex: "Despite three children, she'd never had an orgasm" and she "still carried huge guilt about taking pleasure from sex" (*BFL*, pp. 235, 251). This Catholic guilt is in turn associated with the kind of phallocentric sexual ideology Sister Monica naively repeats: "As a species, [men] had a stronger sexual drive than women – she'd been taught that as a novice. She had also learned that there were men who were roused by the thought that under every habit lurked a virgin waiting to be conquered." Her knowledge of sex, admittedly "in the abstract", illustrates how women in patriarchal societies are "taught to think as men, to identify with a male point of view" and thereby "legitimate a male system of values" (*BFL*, p. 79).[100] Catholic (and thus conventional) dogma constructs sex in terms of opposition and control, just as it had for Babby and Mrs Kinsella in *The Countrywoman*. Woman becomes "defined as lack, deficiency, or as imitation and negative image of the subject" as Irigaray sees it, capable of fulfilling sexual desires but deficient in terms of actually feeling them.[101] When Gerry speaks of Dina "like he'd won her in a raffle", he speaks for this phallocentric view of woman as a sexual commodity, as *Other* (*BFL*, p. 37).[102]

For Eve Ensler, author of the hugely successful and influential *The Vagina Monologues* (1998), such misogyny results in women "saying contemptuous things about [their] genitals" and this contempt, and its dissolution, is integral to the feminist message of *Big Fat Love*.[103] While bullying his wife, Tommo repeatedly uses pejorative slang terms for female genitalia: she is a "fat cunt" and a "stupid cunt" (*BFL*, pp. 6, 102). And Philo introjects this sense of shame, thinking, for example, that her abuser's (Sam's) "hairy hand had something to do with the blood" of menstruation (*BFL*, p. 226). In Nelson's *In Night's City* (1982), Sara also associates her first period with her own experience of sexual abuse: "If [her father, the abuser] had mutilated me [...] scarred me, it would have been far better than this red-rimmed cursed open sea of me."[104] Likewise, Sheridan's Dina has assimilated such misogynist perceptions, viewing "down below" as "something ugly, something that bled, something that should be hidden away" (*BFL*, p. 251).

The transformative epiphanies of both women nonetheless ultimately confute this self-misidentification.[105] For Philo, the word "gee" is significantly and curiously her "favourite word in the whole English language" (*BFL*, p.

18). It is a "slang term for vagina", she explains, and, rather like Eve Ensler's use of V-Day "outrageous events" to destigmatise terms like "vagina" and "cunt", Philo uses gee "mostly when she [wants] to shock people [...] especially hypocrites like her father, her husband and the clergy" (*BFL*, 18).[106] Her enlightenment in regard to what this linguistic rebellion might mean is, however, initially retarded by ambivalence. When Sister Rosaleen unthinkingly parrots Philo's idiom, thinking gee means "stomach" and agreeing that "I've a pain in my gee, too", it simply doesn't "sound right" to Philo, "like a corruption coming from her lips" (*BFL*, p. 18). Philo euphemistically explains the term to the erring nun, in revealing terminology: "it's your womanhood" (*BFL*, p. 18). However, when asked if she thinks gee is a "bad word", she doesn't quite know "what to think" (*BFL*, p. 19): are gee – and by metonymic extension, womanhood – "bad" words?

This tentative ambiguity, however, is gradually replaced as Philo's self-confidence develops. In order to get to sleep, she suggestively tries to "imagine all the wombs of all the different women she knew", putting "a fruit in each one", to pleasing, soporific effect:

> Josie Cullen was skinny so she got a banana. Dina was small so she got a grape. Red-faced women got peaches and fat-arsed ones got pears [...] The combinations went on and on and brought Philo to the deepest, fruitiest sleep she'd had in years. (*BFL*, p. 117)[107]

According to Ensler, misogyny destroys "the essential life energy on the planet" forcing "what is meant to be open, trusting, nurturing, creative, and alive to be bent, infertile, and broken".[108] Philo's dreamy gynocentrism correlates her emerging "open, trusting, nurturing, creative" life energy with positive imagery of female fecundity, or "fruitiness", as Philo might put it.

Her decision to rebel against her father by having the letters "M-A-M-M-Y" tattooed on her knuckles thus symbolises the beginnings of a feminist awareness, of a linguistic valorisation of maternity; "it should have been motherhood that was honoured" (*BFL*, pp. 82, 252). Women's "way of referring to experience", as Cora Kaplan writes, has been "suppressed in public discourse"; Philo's lived experience, her emotional openness, is neither reducible nor conducive to official forms but lies outside androcentric discourse.[109] Some feminists identify negative connotations in such essentialist imagery: Elisabeth Badinter regards the focus on biological difference amongst differentialist feminists as a dangerous reductivism, which "necessarily ends in separation and worse: oppression", and Bourdieu warns that "this feminism forgets that the 'difference' only appears when one adopts the point of view of the dominant on the dominated [...which] is the product of a historical relation of differentiation".[110] But Sheridan wishes to frame Philo's imagery of the female body in contrast to the misogyny of Tommo's hatred of "cunts" and society's vulgarisation of female physicality. He seeks what one feminist terms "a revolutionary linguism, an oral break from the dictatorship of patriarchal speech".[111]

Compounding this message, Philo's thoughts are again mirrored by Dina's, in the subplot of her discovery of clitoral pleasure. Heretofore, Cap (whose name, of course, itself infers repression) has "learned to live with his paralysis" in sexual matters, rising "to the occasional wank"; but now, in his 70s, he resolves to explore uncharted waters. Purchasing *"The Joy of Sex by Alex Comfort"* (*BFL*, pp. 213, 214), he proceeds to follow its instructions with Dina. Cap then "discover[s]" her clitoris, and she too "couldn't believe how beautiful it was to be looked at" (*BFL*, p. 251). There is an attendant sense of renewed spirituality for Dina, for "when he found it, she thought her soul was leaving her body and going home to heaven" and "when it came", she "felt like she'd been touched on the shoulder by God Himself" (*BFL*, p. 235). No longer is "down below" "something ugly"; Dina now feels that "her vagina *belonged* to her, that she *owned* it" (*BFL*, p. 251, emphasis in original). Her sexuality is repossessed from male vulgarisation; it becomes, suggestively, a new symbolic mouth: "She opened it out and displayed it. She even put a circle of lipstick around it as a surprise for Cap." (*BFL*, p. 251) Dina's lovemaking thus becomes a vagina monologue *par excellence*, a narrative of liberation that takes its place alongside Ensler's "outrageous voices", and the symbolism of epistemic reappropriation that Sheridan parallels in Dina's and Philo's dual explorations of self points to a new confidence in working-class womanhood.[112]

Emerging from silence

In a self-consciously farcical ending, Philo misappropriates the money collected by the recently deceased Tommo's friends – to pay homage to him by way of a phallic "tombstone" – diverting it instead into her own liposuction treatment (*BFL*, p. 281). The operation brings up "a lot of issues around her abuse at the hands of Sam Harris", but also affords her a symbolic retort to her former tormentor (*BFL*, p. 300). Armed with "two plastic containers of her fat", Philo resolves to "deal with her past" and, confronting Harris in his home, she accuses him of being the reason that she has carried the fat "around for twenty years" (*BFL*, pp. 301, 305, 306). When Philo proceeds to release the content of her "two bouncing babies" on Harris's lap, leaving him to scream "a desperate cry of pain, like someone drowning in a sea of his own vomit", there is a salutary parallel with how Hélène Cixous defines the truly "feminine" text, as "an outpouring [...] a fantasy of blood, vomiting, throwing up, 'disgorging'" (*BFL*, p. 301).[113] Philo literally disgorges her horrid secret of abuse in the manner of a cathartic fantasy.

Confronting this abuse is also an epochal departure from the enforced silence of abuse sufferers in Ireland, which Smith had referred to obliquely when Mrs Baines's daughter, Kitty, imagined a "little green boy disappear into the wall" of a tenement where "children had been raped" (*CW*, p. 118). In Roddy Doyle's *The Woman Who Walked into Doors* (1996), Paula Spencer also confronts the challenges of such silencing, when narrating her subjection to her husband's abuse: "I'm messing around here. Making things up; a story. I'm beginning to enjoy it. Hair *rips*. Why don't I just say He pulled my hair? *Someone is crying. Someone is vomiting.* I cried, *I* fuckin' well vomited."[114] Only in recovering her own story through the text can Paula move beyond being "the woman who wasn't there", and Philo too refuses to follow the spectre of abuse into oblivion.[115] Part of her achievement in this regard is also in regaining narrative control, in articulating the "unsayable" (*BFL*, p. 231).

Speaking with a woman's voice?

Both Smith and Sheridan tentatively suggest new possibilities for gender relations. Sylvia's death, along with Tommo's, marks the passing of an era in inner-city, working-class life and the emergence of new discursive possibilities. With this comes the kind of mix of inevitability and nostalgia that Pat Barker's octogenarian Liza Jarrett expresses, in *A Century's Daughter* (1986), for the wastelands of a once-thriving industrial Teeside: "In her mind's eye she saw this place as it had been [...] 'There's nothing left,' she said, and, although she'd known that it must be so, her voice was raw with loss."[116] In Sheridan's terminus novel, Sheriff Street's notoriously disadvantaged flat complex is pummelled with a "wrecking ball" as Sylvia, the matriarch, is simultaneously buried – their mutual demise symbolically paralleled (*BFL*, p. 261).

The bulldozer's *"danse macabre"* turns the locals' "past [...] to powder" as it overshadows Sylvia's funeral, "pounding" "the heart, liver and lights out of" the flats (*BFL*, pp. 262, 272). The smell of the conveyor belt moving under Sylvia as she is cremated is compared to that of Sheriff Street after a "bad Saturday night" of joyriding (*BFL*, p. 272). Her passing, in which the coffin that contains her corpse accidentally bursts open, is as ugly as the wrecking ball smashing through people's memories – yet it is somewhat liberating too. In her life, Sylvia has been a mere number, an unremarkable woman, whose ashes are tellingly marked "Sylvia Darcy, 102793", but as her remains are cast upon the wind, they now seem to take the "shape of a wing" (*BFL*, pp. 279, 282). Philo equally finds freedom in the death of her husband, darkly "delighted with her new status" as a widow – "the sight, sound and smell of it appealed to her" (*BFL*, p. 283). With the passing of one generation of women, new possibilities emerge for another, Sheridan implies, but his optimism is also fraught with uncertainty. It is, after all, only through death that Sylvia's mother can escape the cruelty of life, and through Tommo's demise and her improbable revenge that Philo can achieve her "new status".

In a similar vein, Paul Smith uses the war to suggest how women might live in a society less dominated by men – a temporarily gynocentric society – but he also suggests that it is only in men's absence that women can be happy. The ending of the First World War results in anarchy in the Lane, as men return brutalised by their experiences in Europe. Mrs Thraill's demobilised husband takes to "wearing a carnation in his buttonhole and, on Saturdays, setting fire to his wife". The wife of another returned soldier awakes one night to see him horrifically "devouring [their] baby" (*CW*, pp. 5, 69). Pubs ring "in a moithered orgy of fights and brawls and wild hooleys" and it is little wonder that Mrs Baines' children even sing songs in support of their father's enemies, advocating "Death to the Queen, an' her oul' tambourine," and a "hoorah for Billy Kruger!" (*CW*, pp. 5, 17). Women ironically enjoy their greatest period of peace during the war; as in O'Casey's *Silver Tassie*, it is a time of relative freedom.

Like *Big Fat Love*, however, this glimpse of women's liberation is tempered with uncertainty. The process of exhuming women from the historical graveyard is self-reflexively depicted by both writers as a struggle against the grain of powerful discursive forces, which, in the final analysis, they fail to surmount. Smith voices a metacommentary on the elision of female histories "from below" when Tucker Tommy frantically searches for Molly's grave, the location of which evades him. Analogously, Smith also grapples despairingly to recover the lost memory of his own mother and by extension the many women like her who are, as Sheila Rowbotham's famous study put it, "hidden from history".[117] There is "nothing to remember now", Smith narrates: Tommy "wouldn't be able to come and worry her, and neither would anyone else. She had gone. She had escaped" (*CW*, p. 281). When Tommy recalls that "she had given him the slip, given them all the slip", Smith speaks of poor, unremembered women in Irish history generally (*CW*, p. 280). Now an "empty city", a "vacancy" lies ahead of Tommy, a place whose forgotten women seem to cry out for recognition, one that is "ingrained with the sights and sounds of her destruction superimposing themselves over everything else by way of a sigh [...] echoing again her trials, tribulations and the emptiness of her going", like Philo's mother beneath Sheriff Street's wrecking ball (*CW*, p. 281). When Tommy touches his only remnant of Molly – the patch on his shirt "near the collar that she had put there", and "fingering the patch, he walk[s] into the coming night" – the garment represents a faded maternal trace, a creative fragment that, like the novel, only covers a gaping hole (*CW*, p. 282). The lost Mrs Baines is excluded from historical discourse forever: "And the earth was cold, all brown and empty," about her grave, Tommy recalls, "its face scarred with headstones stunted in dejection, and their weight held nothing beneath them, and so – they were meaningless" (*CW*, p. 281). Women's history is "meaningless" in the male world, because male textuality (the headstone) elides their existence – just as the male graveyard keeper's missing receipt, with "the number of the grave on it", leaves Molly's location "somewheres...could be anywheres" (*CW*, p. 280).

In both novels, then, there is a sense of over-reaching; their visions of women's freedom are enabled only by the artificial circumstances of war, or the unlikely *deus ex machina* of a contrived death, which Sheridan himself describes as a "fairytale ending" – "you kind of know 'this is not true'".[118] Sheridan also continually suggests that male control of the linguistic realm problematises his transcription of female history. Philo remarks that "it wasn't [Tommo's] fists she feared, it was his tongue" (*BFL*, p. 112). Tommo wields the phallogocentrism of language, for instance, to persuade the nuns that Philo is lying: "She abandoned them and she abandoned me," he tells them, in emotive terms, just as he later likens Philo to "animals who abandoned their young" (*BFL*, pp. 59, 95).[119] Philo, by contrast, continually struggles to articulate herself. Her frustration with language is repeatedly stressed, in her indecision about "a quiet noise – if there was such a thing", her inability to think of a word "offhand", or her failure to "remember the exact words" (*BFL*, pp. 4, 249, 152). She doesn't understand the term "circa", has "never written a letter in [her] life", and has never received a letter with the word "regards" before (*BFL*, pp. 297, 113, 168). Her longing for self-expression manifests itself symbolically and pathetically in the "bits of paper", containing secret messages, which she suggestively stuffs "inside the pillows and the eiderdowns" in Pownall's factory. These lost messages are a potent image of poor women's frustrated efforts to communicate, in a society that "sleeps" on their truths (*BFL*, p. 87). Philo's mother is also reduced to a number in the crematorium, a symbol of her absence from written history, her individuality elided from discourse, reflecting the kind of ontological anxieties Paula Meehan expresses in her poetic tribute to her own mother, "The Pattern", in which she wonders if, while waxing a floor, "did she catch her own face coming clear? / Did she net a glimmer of her true self? Did her mirror tell her what mine tells me?"[120] In Sheridan's novel, Sylvia's life of suffering is again also distorted by male linguistic appropriation on her headstone, which transcribes her husband's "hypocrisy". Its curt legend, "deeply regretted by her loving husband", would read "much better" as *"sadly forgotten by the one who never had a good word to say about you"*, Philo muses (*BFL*, p. 265). But her father assumes the power to write her mother's history.

Both Sheridan and Smith depict the end of women's stories in graveyards, where their voices have been lost (the lost grave) or warped (the misleading epigraph). Their attempts to ventriloquise the female voice are fraught with anxieties, they suggest. Xavière Gauthier writes that if women "begin to speak and write as men do, they will enter history subdued and alienated; it is a history that, logically speaking, their speech should disrupt".[121] Such disruption is what both writers perform – disruption of the bias of history – but they are conscious too that they do so inadequately as men. Smith's memory of his mother, like Tucker's plaintive search, is a longing for retrieval where there is only the memory of love, a longing for speech where there is only the trace of care. Sheridan's Philo is a woman who cannot write herself into history, whose speech is marked by evasion and struggle, whose own articulation is best in the symbolic mode, as a tattoo voicing maternal affection on a hand that struggles to write, as trauma projected into disgorged fat, or as messages stuffed in frustration into eiderdowns. Both authors are painfully aware of the lack in Irish working-class culture of an *écriture feminine* and that, if their words can "disrupt" history, they cannot change it.

4
Industry and the City: Workers in Struggle

In this chapter I will focus on two novels that depict the role of industry in working-class Dublin and on how they engage the overarching themes of alienation and counter-cultural radicalism, which this book holds to be integral to the city's proletarian writing. First, I will briefly consider their periods of historical reference. I will then examine James Plunkett's *Strumpet City* (1969) and Paul Smith's *Summer Sang in Me* (1972), as a means of exploring Dublin's proletarian consciousness. This examination will show how Plunkett and Smith manipulate a theoretically "national" and "bourgeois" form, the novel, in order to subvert its association with both the national and the bourgeois – in order, again, to intertwine a counter-cultural social image with the narratives of individual working-class lives.

As we have already seen, unlike Belfast, and the great cities of Britain, Dublin never experienced an industrial "revolution" of any comparative significance. In the early 1900s, it lagged behind many of its European counterparts, as "a commercial, distributive and shipping centre rather than an industrial city", and, as Desmond Harding notes, whereas the Europe of the nineteenth century "symbolised an age of capital and an age when imperial cities as metropoli underwent rapid urbanisation under the aegis of unprecedented industrial expansion", Dublin, "in contrast [...] progressively declined in the wake of its widely acknowledged and envied former Georgian splendour".[1] Perhaps the most tawdry of tributes to that diminished splendour was the city's populous Georgian tenement — its edifice harking back to a golden age of relative grandeur, its containment of the teeming human suffering of the slums a register of just how much Ireland's capital had deteriorated. Both of the novels examined in this chapter concern the inhabitants of these graphic symbols of Dublin's decline.

Few writers of Dublin's working class set their action in workplaces, or explore, specifically, issues that arise from the world of work, even after Dublin's later period of industrial development from the 1960s. Andrew P. Wilson's *Victims* (1912) and *The Slough* (1914), Oliver St John Gogarty's *Blight: The Tragedy of Dublin* (1917), and a number of O'Casey's plays, especially *Red*

Roses for Me (1942), depict the Lockout milieu. Dermot Bolger's *Night Shift* (1985) and *The Journey Home* (1989), Aidan Parkinson's *Going Places* (1987), Jimmy Murphy's *Brothers of the Brush* (1995) and Joe'O'Byrne's *It Come Up Sun* (2000) are amongst the very few works to represent issues of labour in working-class Dublin thereafter. Indeed, the *absence* of work has framed many depictions of Dublin's working class, although this experience is by no means in total contrast to that of British literature of working-class life. As Worpole attests – and contrary to the presumptions of those who wish to categorise proletarian literature in a particularly narrow fashion – the experience of heavy industrialisation was "by no means universal" to the British proletariat:

> For the many people brought up in single industry communities, with strong local traditions, there were as many for whom class was experienced as the dislocation of the generations, the rootlessness of city life, a succession of casual jobs and the constant search for employment [...] There was also often extreme psychological isolation.[2]

In Dublin, some writers engage this absence of work explicitly, like Roddy Doyle, with his comic-tragic portrayals of unemployment in *The Barrytown Trilogy*, or Philip Casey, with his fantasising lovers in *The Fabulists* (1994) – their tiresome lives on the dole inspiring them to create an alternative world in their imaginations. Many have indeed chosen to write about domestic and communal relations outside of the workplace, perhaps in part due to the inheritance of O'Casey's paradigmatic focus on domestic and community spaces. But conceivably it is simply because working-class people refuse to be defined by their work. It is fascinating, nonetheless, considering his decade of manual work on the railways and many years of frenetic agitation on labour issues, that O'Casey chose to situate most of his works *away* from work. More curiously still, it took a Dubliner, Robert Tressell, to write what many consider to be the classic British novel of proletarian labour, *The Ragged Trousered Philanthropists* (1914). What might Tressell have written had he stayed at home?

But Dublin's economic stasis before the 1960s bears its own peculiar fruit. Both Plunkett and Smith portray a city where capitalism is teetering on the brink of collapse and where those subject to its "deficient material progress" develop an acute sense of estrangement from its underlying ideology. For both writers, themselves children of the slums, this estrangement fosters a radical political consciousness. In this sense, the subaltern nature of the proletarian city they represent harnesses a basic conflict. Working-class Dublin is depicted not only at the forefront of modernisation and broad ideological change but also as a place in which modernity has produced multifarious failures. Since both novels were written during later decades of unprecedented industrialisation in Ireland, they can also be seen as timely political works that seek to illuminate the fundamental nature of capitalism, as the authors' city became increasingly proletarianised. In both Smith's and Plunkett's novels, the ghost of past neglect is resurrected in order to reassert the socialist vision that James Larkin personified and the working-class counter-hegemony that he played an enormous role in forming. This vision, again, would seem also to reaffirm David Lloyd's conception of a latent, post-colonial "memory" of a communal, pre-capitalist way of life, and its persistence in the counter-public sphere proclivities of Irish working-class people.

Strumpet City and the making of Dublin's working class: "The word of the modern, and the word *en masse*"

In marking the historic acme of class warfare in Ireland, the 1913 Lockout is an epochal event, which both captured the proletarian zeitgeist and resonated in working-class Ireland for generations to come. If E.P. Thompson situated the "making" of the English working class in the tumult of nineteenth-century Chartist emergence, the Lockout – as the culmination of a period of momentous political agitation – is surely the progenitor of Dublin's equivalent. This vexatious industrial dispute emerged from an acute sense of material and ideological alienation from both the colonial centre and the nation's home-grown captains of industry – something that can be adduced, for instance, from the title of Terry McCarthy's pamphlet on *Outcast Dublin, 1900–1914* (1980).[3] By 1913, average Irish incomes were only 60 per cent of those in Britain.[4] Dublin suffered far higher infant mortality rates and worse slum conditions in the first two decades of the twentieth century than those recorded in any British city.[5] That year, a decision by Dublin's biggest employers would plunge the city into industrial crisis for a period of over six months. Led by that most infamous plunderer of greasy tills, the business tycoon William Martin Murphy, the employers chose to "lock out" any employees who subscribed to James Larkin's Irish Transport and General Workers' Union (ITGWU). Twenty thousand trade unionists and their families were involved in the infamous dispute, in which 1.7 million working days were lost and severe hardship was endured.

Larkin, who is variously described as an inspirational and effective leader, an egomaniacal malcontent, or some combination of both, was vilified by the media, employers and the Church, leading to a pronounced polarisation of opinion in the city.[6] For the working class, he was something of a messiah figure; O'Casey portrayed him in biblical tones, as the herald of a new age, "the unfolding of the final word from the evolving words of the ages, the word of the modern, and the word *en masse* and a mighty cheer gave it welcome".[7] The playwright's depiction of his political hero as a champion of modernity and mass (read *working-class*) culture is apt, for in *Strumpet City*

Larkinism represents the *avant garde* of modernisation in Ireland. Larkin's brand of politics focussed on a belief in the power of workers, collectively, through sympathetic action, to take the economic and political life of the city into their own hands, and Ferriter indeed notes how important cultural leadership was to that project, for "trade union leaders [at this time] were keen to engender a sense of working-class hegemony".[8] Syndicalism and a cultural class consciousness were mutually reinforcing. As a political ideology, syndicalism relied on workers' willingness to partake in strikes that were not, strictly speaking, their immediate concern; its success therefore hinged on a heightened sense of solidarity, class consciousness and trust. This new ideology also transgressed national barriers, arriving like cargo onto the Dublin docks as part of an international solidarity of the working class.[9] At its heart, therefore, the syndicalist project was cultural as well as economic, corresponding with Antonio Gramsci's contention that "the concrete meaning of politics" is "its role in enlisting mass energies in the struggle for ideological hegemony", in establishing a new sense of "community".[10]

Emergence: "it's when all's quiet that the seed's a-growing"

In its panoptic fictionalisation of class warfare, *Strumpet City* is thus an originary tale of the emergence of a new community from capitalist subjection. This epic Lockout rebellion is all the more dramatic and surprising in the context of Plunkett's depiction of a placid Dublin in Book One of the novel, running from the period of 1907 to 1909, but its genesis is nonetheless implicit in his ominous hints of epochal change. Thompson cites the wizened phrase of a London costermonger, that "it's when all's quiet that the seed's a-growing", in describing how the ostensible political stagnation of 1820s England preceded momentous developments for its working class, and Plunkett likewise shows how the kernel of a working-class hegemony germinates even in times of outward political harmony.[11]

In colonialism and capitalism's complacent joint celebration of hegemonic power, Plunkett conveys how hegemony works through the kind of "relatively mixed, confused, incomplete, or inarticulate consciousness of actual men", which for Raymond Williams in part characterised Gramsci's fundamental conception.[12] The spectacular arrival of King Edward to a largely loyal and rapturous public reception (not unlike that fawning cacophony Henry Smart singularly attacks in *A Star Called Henry* [1999]) would seem, ostensibly, to affirm the city's unwavering subjection to the prevailing social order at the beginning of the twentieth century. And the monarch's confidence, in the steadfast power of Dublin's ruling classes and the subjugation of its working class, is registered fulsomely when he commends the "determination" of bourgeois Kingstown (now Dún Laoghaire) in providing small cottages "for the labouring classes"; such concessions to the poor are essential to capitalism's and colonialism's joint hegemonic preservation of consent, he implies: "the health and efficiency of the labourer depended to a great extent [...] on a happy home life".[13]

This implicit strain of Gramscian logic is again illuminated, more symbolically and revealingly, by the visit organisers' decision to dock a boardable prison ship, with "lifelike wax figures" of prisoners, close to Dublin's city centre (*SC*, p. 14). The floating museum crystallises the underlying dynamics of colonial and capitalist dominance, of a hegemonic order in which coercive violence must be celebrated, but need not always be enacted. Neither on land nor at sea, the vessel is also a portentous symbol of colonialism's coming demise; it is docking temporarily amidst Dublin's royalists, but, like the power it represents, it will soon be sailing away. The museum is also a spectral reminder of historic resonances. Its exhibition's representation of a brutal, museumised past, in which patriot rebels – and often people convicted of petty crimes – were shipped to the other end of the world, carries with it the implicit, anxious suggestion that this past is no longer relevant.

Mary – the domestic servant whose budding romance with dock worker Fitz consumes much of the beginning of the novel – seems to agree with this colonial revisionism. She is initially unperturbed by the museum; if she does "not care much" for its advertised attractions, she "might chance a visit" (*SC*, p. 14). The boat, like the king's sojourn, is "only a bit of excitement", and she finds it "hard" to fathom Miss Gilchrist's, an older servant's, "bitterness against the King" (*SC*, pp. 16, 28). Mary explicitly consents to colonialism's power, reasoning that the patriot heroes Gilchrist reveres, who were "put in gaol or banished to penal servitude", deserved what they got: one could "not expect a king or a queen to do nothing to people who openly threatened to take over a country themselves" (*SC*, p. 28). But her acceptance of this precept, Plunkett stresses, is intertwined with her lack of class consciousness. Just as Mary fails to question the quasi-feudal social stratification of "aristocrats and gentry and after them business people and then shopkeepers and then tradesmen and then poor people like Fitz and herself", she also accepts the imposition of social snobbery at a more basic, cultural level, patiently suffering Mrs Bradshaw's patronising and pedantic grammatical corrections (*SC*, pp. 28–29):

'I think it's me, ma'am.'
' "I", dear.'
'I, ma'am." (*SC*, p. 15)

For Plunkett's domestic servant, national, social, cultural and economic gradations of power have been completely naturalised.

But in Mary, as in the compliant city, there are also subtle signs of the potential for cultural and political change. When Plunkett's impoverished beggar Rashers Tierney falls victim to a pickpocket – and the ensuing ridicule of a city centre crowd celebrating the monarchy – he brands them "laughing loyalists" and is arrested for breach of the peace (*SC*, p. 29). However when a policeman subsequently assaults Rashers, Mary tellingly changes her mind about the prison-ship visit, because "the old man who sold me the ribbons was hit on the mouth by a policeman and his arm twisted until it was nearly broken. I don't want to see anything today that would remind me of that" (*SC*, p. 32). Plunkett suggests that while the abstract concept of colonial and capitalist power may seem completely rational to its oppressed subjects, its concrete reality in brutal repression leads even the most indoctrinated to question its ideology.

Equally, though Kingstown's wealthy may organise much fanfare for the coming of the King, when his arrival is announced with a "thundering salvo" from the royal party's ship, Mrs Bradshaw, the wife of an affluent landlord, suggestively spills tea over her tablecloth "for some seconds" in her "efforts to stifle a scream" (*SC*, p. 18). The violence that prompts Bradshaw's anxiety is an integral part of the symbolism that accompanies the King's visit, and it is violence, both epistemic (in the museum) and physical (the arrest and salvo), that implicitly facilitates his power. The King's government, in turn, facilitates capitalist power, allowing Mr Bradshaw to subject his slum tenants, over many years, to a tenement building that hovers on the verge of collapse. But the reality of this power, as it is palpably felt in these instances, ironically disrupts that relationship. With the sounding of the salvo, the link between reality and ideology is exposed; privately, Mr Bradshaw fears "what would happen to these five infirm shells of tottering brick and their swarms of poverty-stricken humanity when His Majesty's Navy blasted off a battery of heavy guns" (*SC*, p. 17). Metaphor, in this instance, becomes materiality. Plunkett's symbolic parallels suggest the vulnerability of hegemony to a battery of another kind – that in the need for capitalism and colonialism to assert themselves violently, as the policeman asserts himself against Rashers, its epistemic cracks will begin to emerge. In doing so, and despite his classically panoptic narrative perspective, Plunkett imbues subjective stories with a trace of the "life-historical situation" (Fordham), refusing the isolated individualism of bourgeois art.[14]

The alienation of the working class: *"We live and die like animals"*

These early, symbolic suggestions of the working class's alienation from both the Empire and its proponents in the bourgeois world of the Bradshaws are developed into a broader historical narrative of industrial failure and counter-cultural revolt. Yeats's characterisation of the malleable social milieu of late-colonial Ireland as "soft wax" resonates with Plunkett's depiction of a city ravaged by capitalism and primed for revolt.[15] The "world of industry", Plunkett asserts, "so long stable, so entrenched in its authority, was sliding on its foundations". The consequent "indiscipline of the working class" after "years of docility", which leaves Dublin's capitalists "frightened" and "confused", leads to the development of a radicalised sense of class solidarity (*SC*, p. 329).

In one particularly polemical paragraph, which stresses the extent of Dublin's industrial failures, capitalist colonialism is portrayed as a failed process of "cast offs". "Pinched and wiry" "ashbin children" (like Paul Smith's in *Summer Sang in Me*) live on "cast offs" (*SC*, p. 73). They come "each morning from the crowded rooms in the cast-off houses of the rich", "discarded" Georgian tenements, attired in clothes "cast-off by their parents, who had bought them as cast offs" (*SC*, p. 73). As Plunkett observes, in a direct authorial intervention, "if the well-to-do stopped casting off for even a little while the children would have gone homeless and fireless and naked. But nobody really thought about that. These things Were" (*SC*, p. 73). The author's capitalisation points again to the power of hegemony, its hailing and naturalised logic, but his depiction of the "cast off" system points to its vulnerability too.

Fitz's livelihood is susceptible to economic vicissitudes and individualistic caprices, rather like that of the inhabitants of George Gissing's bleak Clerkenwell, in *The Netherworld* (1889). He feels "people he did not know and would never meet decided its extent and continuance for reasons that suited only themselves", and this sense of precariousness is emphasised throughout the novel (*SC*, p. 171). When a number of pigeons break open a sack of grain, unwittingly causing an imbalance in a pyramid of sacks above them, they are left "crushed and dead", leaving Rashers in "shock", and "curs[ing] the pigeon, for its thievery, its unnecessary death" (*SC*, p. 317). The relatively trivial event emphasises the impersonal cruelty of "cold Sergeant Death", the "sad smiling tyrant" (*SC*, p. 318), but it also foreshadows the later climactic collapse of Bradshaw's tenement on its benighted inhabitants. This scene also occurs immediately prior to Yearling's encounter with a workman's "mangled and unrecognisable body" in his works yard (*SC*, p. 328). Capitalism's bestial debasing of human life is indeed one of the primary conceits of the book.

Imagery connoting slippage and transgression in the prevailing hegemony pervades the novel, also marking the re-emergence of a familiar form of stylistic subversion. Bakhtin's carnivalesque returns in axiomatic form. If it derives its life in literature from ancient public rituals, such rituals characteristically employ forms that blend "the lofty with the low". And in this comical act of levelling, the carnivalesque presents a potential for symbolic social subversion; again this method dovetails with Bourdieu's project of liquidating the arbitrary distinctions inherent in class-loaded conceptions of "taste". Plunkett exhibits a striking instance of carnivalesque's topos in his treatment of what is possibly his most famous character, the basement-dwelling, bin-raiding Rashers.

As Bakhtin had identified, "the primary carnival act is the mock crowning and decrowning of the carnival king", which is also the part of carnival "most often transposed into literature". He elaborates:

> Crowning/decrowning is a dualistic ambivalent ritual, expressing the inevitability and at the same time the creative power of the shift-and-renewal, the *joyful relativity* of all structure and order, of all authority and all (hierarchical) position [...] And he who is crowned is the antipode of a real king, a slave or a jester.[16]

Rashers, as such an antipode, is portrayed in richly suggestive imagery as the comic anti-king of *Strumpet City*, but for Bakhtin, as for Plunkett, this playfulness of *"joyful relativity"* has a serious purpose; in the act of "profanation", it is also "playing with the symbols of higher authority".[17]

Representing the lowest rung on *Strumpet City*'s socio-economic ladder, Rashers is continually and jarringly juxtaposed with his social superiors. Near the beginning of the book, we are told of an unlikely parallel with King Edward, who "rose that morning about the same time" as Rashers (*SC*, p. 20). Later, death is said to "do with us all [...] you and the sergeant before you, King Edward and Rashers Tierney" (*SC*, p. 34). Rashers reiterates the comparison during a bout of illness, ruminating that "if [he] was Edward VII he would be surrounded by doctors" (*SC*, p. 267). This humble rummager of bins is even imbued with an ethereal hint of holiness. While considering Rashers' affection for his dog, Fr Giffley opines that this benevolent animal lover and St Francis "would get on well together", and he proceeds to associate Rashers with a "religious picture which had hung somewhere, of a saint who wept for his ox" (*SC*, p. 217). Presently and tellingly, Giffley realises that he may be mistaken as to whether the man depicted in the painting was indeed a saint; its title might have been, "after all [...] 'The Peasant Weeps Over His Ox'" (*SC*, p. 217). In a similar manner, Rashers is even associated with Jesus Christ, while working as a walking advertising board for a shop. "Take up your cross right," he orders himself; "Here I come, Jesus, one front and back" (*SC*, p. 477).

Such hinted transgressions of totemic boundaries form part of a broader, carnivalesque motif for proletarian emergence from social and cultural domination in the novel – for working-class counter-hegemonic formation, in the "shift-and-renewal" of revolutionary fervour. Statutory and religious bodies in the book conspire to suppress the working class by social demarcation – the antithesis of carnival – but power continually fails to police the lines of class and social gradation. Fr O'Connor attempts to marshal the divide between his former parish, the affluent Kingstown, and his new parish and chosen focus of religious zealotry, in inner-city Dublin. He cannot countenance Mrs Bradshaw's trip to see her former servant, Mary, who lives in a tenement, arguing that these lowly dwellings may be "part of our city, but not necessarily fitting places to visit" (*SC*, p. 234). Equally, he is "irritated" when Rashers meets Mrs Bradshaw, and angered that this dishevelled boiler man should have been allowed to ring a church bell in public (*SC*, p. 240). Rashers must be kept in the boiler house *under* the church because he is "not very clean", a "bundle of galvanised rags", and it is not "seemly" to have such a man engaged in official church duties above ground (*SC*, pp. 246, 254, 246).

But the "small, smoothly enamelled world" that the Bradshaws inhabit, with perimeters policed so assiduously by their priest, is eventually shattered when the ramifications of Ralph Bradshaw's profiteering and corruption irrupt in the novel's dramatic crescendo (*SC*, p. 192). When the slum landlord's tenements (which were condemned but for Bradshaw's nefarious dealings with local councillors) collapse on their inhabitants, there is a shocking, parallel collapse of social boundaries.[18] While some of the tenement dwellers caught in the disaster fail to escape with their lives, the criminal Bradshaw escapes justice and guilt by travelling abroad with his wife. As Yearling tells an incredulous Fr O'Connor, the tenements "were condemned long ago – and then reprieved because Ralph knew the right people" (*SC*, p. 447). While O'Connor "refuse[s] to believe" this claim, trade union hero Mulhall's assertion shortly afterwards, that "there's a lot of ways of murdering people", is damning (*SC*, pp. 447, 460). Plunkett inserts a report absolving Bradshaw in the ironically named *Freeman's Journal*, which compounds the implicit accusation of ideology's role in supporting exploitation (*SC*, p. 448). Mr and Mrs Bradshaw go "abroad for an indefinite period", but while Plunkett invokes, in their escape, what Lukács identified as the novelistic convention of a restored social order, he undercuts it with a sardonic inflection (*SC*, p. 448).[19] Again, a supposedly "bourgeois" narrative trajectory is deftly undermined through allegorical and deeply political sabotage. Bourgeois order in the novel relies on human disorder, Plunkett suggests.

Ordinarily the "dialogic novel", as part of its concealed ideological unconscious, depicts a social order that is threatened but ultimately prevails. Part of a dialectical modulation between individual and society, this novelistic convention supports "the liberal goals of social reform": "the protagonist's character responds to the demands of their society while the society itself remains relatively unchanged, resulting in an uneven distribution of compromise".[20] Novels, in this mode, normally resolve social problems, reasserting the authority of a prevailing orthodoxy. But this narrative teleology is invoked only sardonically by Plunkett, in a self-conscious formulaic ironisation. Capitalism has been threatened by social slippage and transgression throughout the text, but the re-establishment of bourgeois power – the Bradshaws' public vindication, which parallels the failure of the strike – is all the more emphatically subverted in its own sordid undermining of moral authority.

This undercutting of novelistic convention is accentuated by the comic, carnivalesque resolution of another of the novel's subplots – the tempestuous story of love between union vigilante Pat and firebrand prostitute Lily, both social pariahs. An erstwhile radical socialist, Pat, in newly Fabian mode, following his union's defeat, believes that "expropriating the expropriators [is] a lifetime's work", or "the work, maybe, of many lifetimes", and he turns his interests, after years of class struggle, to the domestic sphere. In resolving his relationship problems with Lily, however, Pat ironically represents his class's epistemic break with conventional mores, even as he turns away from politics. Lily and Pat had encountered various difficulties on their way to domestic bliss, including his imprisonment and her contraction of venereal disease. They are a most unlikely pair for an orthodox novelistic love story, and in the scene that depicts them settling down, a portrait of Queen Victoria – representing Victorian convention and privilege – consequently stares "down at [them] with longstanding disapproval" (*SC*, p. 553). Yet again a subversive subtext emerges: Earlier in the novel, Pat had "dreamed fitfully" of "knocking on door after door in search of Lily", but had found that "each in turn was opened by Queen Victoria" (*SC*, p. 302). Symbolically and psychologically, the queen – and the conservative values associated with her – overshadowed their budding relationship. The success of Lily and Pat's courtship, under the Queen's disapproving gaze – and as an affront to conventional bourgeois narratives of "romance" – thus suggests the emergence of a new counter-hegemony, and does so in the manner of a typically carnivalesque upending.

Plunkett's narrative again subverts the novel's archetypal ending – its customary restoration of normality, quite often accompanied by a parallel, dénouement marriage, which naturalises that normality. Stressing this subversion, Pat takes another upending of social order as a positive portent. The success of his bet on a horse, "Revolution", which defeats, by a length, "Duke of Leinster" and "Prince Danzel", resonates with the Rashers-King metaphor; "the collapse of the aristocracy," Pat muses, "was a good omen" (*SC*, p. 556). Although the working class of 1913 fails in its short-term political battle against Dublin's capitalists, it succeeds in shedding the burden of conventional values, Plunkett hints. Larkin's achievement, in cultural terms, progresses towards what Jonathan Joseph terms the essential "task of revolutionary socialists": to "break the alliances with the bourgeoisie and the state [...] part of a general process in which the ruling class suffers a crisis of hegemony while the working class strengthens its counter-hegemony".[21] This "new partisanship" enables new social possibilities; if living is "sin" is "immoral" according to convention, for Pat, as for Paul Smith's tenement women, such dictums are the fabrications of "capitalists who invented marriage in order to protect the laws of inheritance" (*SC*, pp. 145, 102, 103).

"A visitation from the locusts"

Dublin's working class is therefore depicted in a cultural battle to replace the hegemony of the rich with a new hegemony of the proletariat, and a key element of this battle is its struggle to defy the alliance of religion with capitalist power. Religion's (like the bourgeois novel's) implicit assumption of an inherent, naturalised, universal order is indispensable to capitalism, just as it is to monarchy, Plunkett suggests. Fr O'Connor explicitly believes that socialism is "the worst enemy of the working man" because it "uproots his confidence in hierarchical order" and "it preaches discontent", making the worker *"covetous of the property* of his social superiors" (*SC*, p. 444, emphasis added). Throughout the novel, the young priest acts as an advocate for capitalist norms, just as the Priest Figure in *Talbot's Box* (1973) does when he prays for the beatification of Dublin worker-saint Matt Talbot because "in these troubled times the people might have a model of Christian loyalty and obedience, to fight off the false doctrines" of "subversive influences".[22]

In one passage from *Strumpet City*, which resonates with the famous, climactic scene of Elizabeth Gaskell's classic, *North and South* (1855), O'Connor again reveals how strongly allied his faith is to capitalist thought, but now his arrogance is affronted by a new proletarian counter-hegemony.[23] When the priest's tram is attacked during a strike, by rioters intent on discouraging "scab" employees from usurping their jobs, his exhortation to the crowd to "behave" emerges explicitly from his belief in the pseudo-religious rights of property over those of the workers: those in "rough clothes that smelled of dirt and poverty" about him "have been taught by scoundrels to *covet* what is not theirs", he admonishes, conflating scriptural archaism (God's command not to "covet") with the naturalised beliefs of the propertied class (*SC* pp. 390, 391, emphasis added).

In a moment of climactic rebellion, a brick grazes the pontificating O'Connor's head, leaving blood on the "stiff, white ring of his collar" – symbolically, the taint of red socialism on his rarefied, pure existence (*SC*, p. 390). A pebble thrown by rioters in *North and South* leaves them "ashamed" and "watching, open-eyed and open-mouthed," as "the thread of dark-red blood" has "wakened them up from their trance of passion", in one of the classic scenes of British fiction. The blood on Margaret's white skin symbolises the strikers' transgression of a social taboo through violence; the attack (albeit unwitting) by working-class men on a middle-class woman is enough to dissolve the "passion" of their entire protest.[24] The taint of blood on O'Connor's collar symbolises a parallel desecration of the priest's transcending role as spiritual advisor, another transgression of the social order, but by contrast O'Connor finds himself pilloried by the "hooligans" about him, who emit an "angry roar of agreement" with the offending stone-thrower (*SC*, p. 390). Plunkett infers that the taboos of Gaskell's world are no longer enough to mollify the rabble. Rashers, like a Shakespearean jester, is the voice of authorial wisdom, when he posits this diminished sway of social distinction in working-class Dublin rather crudely some time later, informing the "Reverend Gentleman", "God's holy anointed", that should he wish to find directions to the Fitzpatricks' abode he can "ask my proletarian arse" (*SC*, p. 488). His bawdy rebuttal conveys the extent to which the proletariat is beginning to reject the established social order of "the Clergy and the Castle" (*SC*, p. 512).

However, Rashers' blasphemy not only reflects the waning influence of religion, but also the growth of another, alternative "religion". Socialism becomes the new ideology of the awakened masses. Larkin's mobilisation brings with it a new belief system, a new brand of faith and a new messianism, which pointedly usurps Christianity's traditional role. Something akin to religious fervour possesses workers who march Dublin's streets, with "empty pockets", "bread and tea to kill hunger" and "no assurance of strike pay", when they cheer as their leader offers "nothing but hardship" (*SC*, p. 166). A sense of teleology, with religious undertones, engulfs them as they feel that "somewhere at the end of the road there was *a better world* waiting", "a feeling of movement that remained, a journey beginning, a vague but certain purpose" (*SC*, p. 166, emphasis added). Larkin inspires this "new, slightly incredulous hope" and, in a vividly suggestive episode, Rashers, again, with Hennessy, implies the clash of faiths that the Liverpudlian-Irishman personifies (*SC*, p. 97). With child-like wonder, Rashers asks his companion if he thinks "Jesus Christ is up there", comically surmising that it may be difficult for this god to see "through the rain" (*SC*, p. 100). But just as he doubts Christ's vision from afar, a new messiah approaches from nearby – a mystical "tall figure" (Larkin) who pauses to pet Rashers' dog (*SC*, p. 100). This as yet unknown earthly god is possessed of a Christ-like "magnetism" and resolve – becoming a "popular martyr" and "the most dangerous man of our time" (*SC*, pp. 165, 188). Fr Giffley even enjoins his new, socialist leader to "*lead Thou to God and His Presence – lead, through / Christ's Merit / Not to His Feet, but Their Print in the dews of His Meadow*" (*SC*, p. 226). Although he eviscerates Larkin's "evil doctrine", even Fr O'Connor realises that it is an "extraordinary thing" when he forgetfully imagines that he will see the union leader about Dublin, even though the man is jailed (*SC*, p. 208). Larkin, like a god, is omnipresent, and again hallowed social distinction is dramatically overturned.

Fitz feels "the inward drag of compassion and responsibility, linking him with the others below", when union activity begins to take hold on his imagination. "Some part of him had become theirs", Plunkett writes (*SC*, p. 122). This powerful, almost visceral sense of solidarity typifies the moral imperative created by trade-union activism. While pondering the nature of his attachment to the union, he ruminates on the links that Larkin's social upheaval has forged in his mind, and indeed contrasts them with religion:

> There were Farrell and the dockers and thousands of others throughout the city, some long resigned to perpetual squalor as the Will of God, others rebelling with recurring desperation whenever there was a leader to lead them. Never before had they stood so solidly together. (*SC*, pp. 415–416)

This emergence of the masses lends extraordinary power to the worker. When Mulhall returns from jail to his old employer, Doggett, the wealthy distributor is loath to refuse the militant his old job, because he fears he is "face to face with a movement", not just one man (*SC*, p. 286). Performatively embodying Plunkett's novelistic strategy, whereby collective, working-class experience is refracted through the prism of subjective narratives, Mulhall and his comrades are now never alone. Doggett's consequent fear of the "movement" resonates with bourgeois fears of working-class combination, which were themselves rooted in a sense that the "growth of the anarchic towns" had "shattered the controls on the working classes".[25] Such fears of an anarchic rabble are expressed more palpably in O'Connor's horror as he observes a trade-union march, "a tightly-packed array that had generated a soul and a mind of its own". For him the assembly is an animalistic, monolithic, menacing beast, "capable of response only to simple impulses, able to move itself, to emit a cry, to swing right or left, to stop altogether". It moves as one long, serpentine "unit driving the respectable off the sidewalks" (*SC*, p. 204). The priest senses the "near presence of evil" in these "agitators", a mere "mob" of "hooligans" (*SC*, p. 293). He is even "violently and repeatedly sick", because of an attendant sense "of infirmity, of uncleanliness, of corruption" (*SC*, pp. 212, 213). But there is an ironic, eschatological, biblical resonance to this empowerment of the working class in Yearling's foreboding that "they may yet come out of their hovels in search of a better living – all together, a visitation from the locusts" (*SC*, p. 202). In *Revelations*, apocalyptic locusts are instructed to punish "those of mankind who have not the seal of God".[26] Yearling recognises the capitalist order he has benefited from is being "bitterly assailed" by avengers who are in "search of a better living" (*SC*, p. 441). Cultural power –"the articulate city", the "respectable" – has condemned the mobilised working classes as an "evil" "mob", but the mob has begun to create a hegemony of its own (*SC*, p. 293). Although the strike is eventually defeated, Plunkett shows that this galvanised solidarity of workers, and, most importantly, the creation of an alternative, subaltern culture, is the Lockout's abiding achievement.

Child labour and the Bildungsroman:
"When have they had time to be childer?"

Tracing the development of a counter-hegemonic working-class culture is also a central preoccupation for Paul Smith. As with Plunkett's revolutionary slums of the 1910s, Smith portrays 1920s proletarian Dublin as a liminal and alienated social space, radically averse to the dominant orthodoxies of its time. In *Summer Sang in Me*, he also utilises formulaic subversion to make his point, deploying the classic form of the *Bildungsroman* – the coming-of-age novel – with ironic inflections.

Smith's tale is intimate and lyrical, centring on two children and their failed attempts to make sense of the adult world, making it an unusual and inherently subversive example of the *Bildungsroman* genre. Kari E. Lokke describes the traditional *Bildungsroman* as "a fundamentally conservative form, narrating, as it does, the growth of the middle-class young man from callow and idealistic youth to his integration into the societal *status quo* through bourgeois marriage and proper professional placement".[27] Ordinarily, then, this is an eminently normative genre of writing, but Smith parodies its classic narrative trajectory by portraying a *negative* emergence into the status quo. David Trotter notes how working-class writers, who "moved out of that class", have often "tended to write novels which justified their own displacement by devising voyages of self-discovery", utilising the *Bildungsroman* to depict a protagonist's identity developing "through [to] the rejection of allegiance" – through the rejection of their former (erring) working-class selves.[28] But the *rejection* of dreams of embourgeoisification by Smith's protagonist, Annie, results in her *acceptance* of the conventions imposed upon her by society and her working-class family, and in that acceptance Smith locates both tragedy and a *reversal* of "self discovery". In defying the coming-of-age novel's characteristic form, Smith conveys how capitalism suppresses the individuality of the working-class subject. With this allegorical, metaphorical reading, we are returned to that by-now-familiar preoccupation of proletarian literature, whereby the subjective story emblematises reification as opposed to normalisation. A social image of discord displaces bourgeois harmony.

Annie is a countervailing challenge to the *Bildungsroman's* archetypal humanist child, whose progression ordinarily dovetails with a positivist, linear narrative of capitalism and opportunity. Judith Plotz identifies just such a counterdiscourse in working-class writing generally, which eschews "*the* [archetypal literary] Child, who is unmarked by time, place, class, or gender but is represented as in all places and all times the same". In working-class writing, one more often finds the child that "declassifies and erases certain kinds of merely literal children by stripping them of that honorific label" (of the generic "Child"). Lives of "urban laboring children" are "clearly shaped and deformed by their environments", becoming "embedded in a thick social context from which they cannot be extricated".[29] Loss of child-hood innocence in lives "deformed" by a difficult upbringing is a theme employed continually by writers of Dublin's working class to represent more general social decay.[30] Dangers inhere in such narratives as, Carolyn Steedman notes: "The children of the poor are only a measure of what they lack as children: they are a falling short of a more complicated and richly endowed 'real' child".[31] Yet it is also true that what working-class children "lack" provides countless authors with a powerful metonym for the dispossession of their class.

Smith's Annie attempts to escape from the social context by which she is defined, to stay in the "summer" of youth, but ultimately capitalism steals this ambition away. Her fantasy of escape from factory work, by buying a street dealer's cart and becoming self-sufficient, provides the novel's chief complication: as her interview at the factory draws close, Annie must endeavour to make her dream a reality by earning enough money to start her own business, thus convincing her mother of the validity of refusing steady work. This device, of a proffered escape route, is again common in writing on working-class children, as Diane Reay observes, for "fantasies of escape are important tactics" in their "desperate efforts to separate out a worthwhile estimable self from a degraded, harshly judged context in which you are implicated as 'no better than where you come from'".[32] It is there in the recent Dublin-based film *Kisses* (2008), for instance, in which two working-class children from dysfunctional homes enjoy a fairy-tale escape from their dire lives into a world of ice rinks, canal-boat adventures and a chance meeting with Bob Dylan (or at least that is who they think it is), only to be eventually plunged back into the realities of child abuse and poverty that blight their lives. This refusal of a happy ending in Lance Daly's film echoes the essential message of Smith's novel. Annie is ultimately trapped by her environment, but it is in Smith's enthralling depiction of her *joie de vivre*, as she attempts to escape it – in her various escapades and schemes – that the tragedy of Annie's dashed potential is most powerfully conveyed.

"Her childish delusions of the solidity": the nightmare of working life

A historicised, demythologised child of the slums, Annie thus appears as the antithesis of the generic "Child" of the *Bildungsroman*.[33] She harbours no desire to seek external validation or achievement within orthodox parameters. On the contrary, she wishes to escape orthodoxy and doggedly refuses to conform to society's expectations. Annie resents the prefigured future of "a husband and the factory" that her mother envisages for her and ignores encouragements to act in a more conventionally womanly way – to "stop roughing about", to "quit whistling and sparring", and to "speak soft and sweet and give over running from here to the pump every morning bollicky naked" (*SSM*, pp. 12, 13).

Her rebelliousness is best articulated by her socially ostracised mentor, the sage street-trader Ellen Simms. Simms, who hopes to pass on her business to the sprightly youth, identifies the strength that has taken her protégée "this far without help or benefit from clergy or state" in the child's willingness to question authority:

> It's whatever it is made you face me when others your age were running the other way and crying "witch" [...] It's the thing that makes you brave the shopkeepers of Dublin day after day and risk five or six years in a reformatory [...] It's [...] what's making you stand up to your mother and her childish delusions of the solidity she thinks she can surround herself and them useless sisters of yours with, by condemning you to that hell-hole of a factory. It's whatever it is that makes you fight and go on fighting the way you do. (*SSM*, p. 115)

Simms anathematises the supposed "solidity" of mediocrity, the limitations of exploitative capitalism and the "clergy or state", and so too does her precocious charge, but it is in the ability of those limitations to curb "whatever it is" that comes to make Annie that the message of the novel is most forcefully rendered.

Throughout the text, Barker's factory looms over the child as a nightmarish vision of industrial imprisonment. Its workers are "skinny an bet an lonesome", so much so that Annie "could cry" (*SSM*, p. 15). With only a week to go before Barker's takes her on as an employee, she feels time is "shrinking at a nightmare rate" (*SSM*, p. 94). "Shadowing her like some creature of nightmares", Barker's is "black and terrifying and many-armed", she imagines (*SSM*, p. 120). The tone of finality and sense of imminent horror with which industrial labour is associated cultivate a sense of "feeling trapped and with no real prospect of getting the few pounds she would need" to escape. From the tales of her friends and acquaintances, it seems that Annie's fears are justified (*SSM*, p. 120).

Rose's story, of becoming a prostitute because she could not abide her work at a shoe factory, hints at the possible temptation of brothel-owner Miz Robey's invitations to Annie to join her "business". Another local girl, Florrie, escaped from slavish work earlier in the novel, when she "quit skivvying for the Jews on the South Circular, got a lend off wan a them and went to London an became a hoor", and this escape is explicitly given a "connection" to Annie's decision to give up her milk round and attempt to make money by cinder picking (foraging for and selling discarded cinders of coal, *SSM*, p. 16). Such tales of impoverished ingénues turning to prostitution through circumstance are common in depictions of working-class women, particularly in Dublin's literature. A.P. Wilson's consumptive Annie in *The Slough* complains of the "infernal factory" that is "killing" her, but her sister Peggy escapes from "slaving in a shop morning, noon and night for a pittance" by selling sex in Liverpool.[34] Oliver St John Gogarty's ironically named Lily, in *Blight* (1917) also escapes "*honest* work" in a laundry because of the lack of "*honest* wages", only to find work in a restaurant where, it is insinuated, she has a dubious relationship with affluent male customers, earning "seven and six a week [...] and free temptation".[35] Plunkett's prostitute in *Strumpet City* (1969), again (perhaps in tribute) named Lily, equally escaped from a factory by selling sex, and Rosie in Christy Brown's *Wild Grow the Lilies* (1976 – again alluding to metaphoric deflowerment), chose the same profession to escape "a tenement with two rooms and rats as big as kittens playing tick-tack all over the place".[36] Big Moll's tale of lost youth in *Summer Sang in Me*, from being "like a flower" in youth (to redeploy the now wilting cliché), to becoming a prostitute at "the end of her usefulness", highlights the narrowness of opportunity that working-class women were afforded in early twentieth-century Dublin. Patrick MacGill had also deployed this topos in *The Rat Pit* (1915), in which Norah Ryan progresses from the pastoral innocence of a Donegal childhood to her degraded death as an urban strumpet. Prostitution thus becomes a motif, an emblem of reification, of the barbarism of capitalism and its affront to human dignity. It is continually paralleled with the adult world of conventional industrial work and often depicted as a benign alternative to it. Coming of age thus becomes an object of anxiety for impoverished women, and Smith's city is full of such anti-coming-of-age narratives. The limited occupational choices available to working-class Dubliners are symbolically implied elsewhere in the novel, where jobless beggars and cinder pickers are ironically named "Brennan the Builder" and the "Plumber" (*SSM*, p. 124). Their misnomers derisively evince the city's lack of skilled work, and, from Annie's perspective, adult working life has nothing dignifying to offer.

Smith's precocious protagonist continually castigates capitalism's commonplaces of exploitation, profit and loss. She is perplexed by a moneylender's lack of conscience and wonders "how that woman can create the misery she does and still enjoy the comfort of her bed". Equally, Annie finds it "funny the way people who have money never believe others can be broke" (*SSM*, pp. 87, 84). She also feels "sickened and empty" when she listens to the "complaints or sagas of achievement" of local prostitutes, raging: "I just wish I could pull this whole, lousy street down" (*SSM*, p. 20). Her mother, Mrs Murphy, recollects how her daughter hilariously "banded together" a "mob of tramps", in order to "start a new revolution" (*SSM*, p. 9). Murphy is also dismayed at the trail of "foul-mouthed police" and children coming to her door, and "the shopkeepers whose tills [her daughter was] knocking off because you thought they were wallowing in profits they should never have made" (*SSM*, p. 9). Similarly, Annie's robbery of orchards – and risible attempt to "uproot the trees as well, then plant them along the banks of the canal" – reflects her redistributive, if risible, ideology (*SSM*, p. 9). Unable to fathom the logic of capitalist thinking, she links it, tellingly, with religion, arguing that the idea of a "living Christ" with "many houses" (as the Bible puts it) is "something I just don't believe [...] To begin with, why should one man have two houses" (*SSM*, p. 38).

But this "Annie who looked out for the maimed in mind and limb", who "gave to Jesus [a local beggar] and others like him, taking desperate chances to feck [thieve] the cigarettes they had to have", herself exemplifies a truly Christian kindness (*SSM*, p. 39). She sets aside "a stack of black cinders" for the beggar Scraps (*SSM*, p. 35). She loses the gains of her robberies by giving plundered goods away to the less fortunate (*SSM*, p. 82). It is through "her own weakness" – an impulsive generosity – that Annie affords Mary Doyle her robbed sugar, because she "will be needing it" (*SSM*, p. 83). Still a child, Annie nonetheless assumes the role of provider for the vulnerable in her community, the person "who put boots on their feet and kept the coats on their backs", "who scoured the streets in the depths of winter to get the eightpence that bought the beds in the night shelters" (*SSM*, p. 39). Annie is continually intolerant of injustice, voicing her "trumpet tongued resistance to wrong", excoriating the affluent dwellers of a "mean house" who pay a "mean, lousy half-dollar" for "a full day's scrubbing" (*SSM*, p. 26). The embodiment of a counter-hegemonic subaltern, as Tommy observes, she has "never shared in her life the general opinion on anything" (*SSM*, p. 78).

A young boy's death is a moment of epiphany in the novel that allegorises more generally the industrial crisis of Free State Dublin and the alienation of its working class which Annie personifies. Alfie, an unusually sensitive child of the slums, who secretly "likes dolls", is smothered by collapsed heap of "rock and stone and slidering slime" as the children desperately plunder coal from a store-yard – the kind of disaster that hovers in the background of Pat Larkin's *The Coalboat Kids and Other Stories* (2007), in which children of 1960s Docklands Dublin continually risk life and limb to steal coal, copper and other much-coveted scraps from the treacherous landscape of Dublin Port, in order to sell them to "the people in the posh houses" (*SSM*, p. 56).[37] But the tragedy of a child's death in Smith's novel is accentuated by what he hints is society's systematic elision of such stories. Here again we have an echo of O'Casey too, and a correspondence with the concerns regarding epistemic power that we have seen voiced so frequently by other writers. When Alfie suffocates under the slag, a policeman arrives and treats the children like criminals rather than witnesses. Subjected to "the questions, the chastisements" of his investigation, their playmate's death is rewritten by capitalist power, because of the "jobs that have to be made and kept":

> But first, the pad, the pen in white hands, and you look, from them up to the condemning stares, and from them to the pad again and the clever, sinuous movement of the finely fixed hand holding the pen, weaving lines over the lovely bare whiteness of the paper.
>
> (*SSM*, p. 57)

Smith's allusion to the textual power of state apparatuses, which collude in absolving the owners of the coal yard of blame, implies a corresponding elision of working-class history and hints perhaps also at the associated censorship that he had suffered as a writer.

For "trespassing on private property", the children, and not the system of private ownership that makes them risk life for coal, are deemed culpable for Alfie's death, and the link between capitalism and the accident is hinted at again in Tommy's simile for death itself, as "like the inside of coal" (*SSM*, pp. 57, 58). Tommy makes this comparison as a stacked turf boat passes him by, and it too is a reminder of the incessant demands of mere survival. Even as his friend lies dead, Tommy ponders, "if Annie and I hurried, we could get it at Leeson Street bridge, going through the locks. Lovely hard, red turf. I'd like to cry, but I don't. I'd like to move, but I don't move. Some things can't be lived with" (*SSM*, p. 58). As with Roddy Doyle's Henry Smart, in *A Star Called Henry* (1999), materialism is always to the fore in Tommy's thoughts. If Alfie is trapped under the coal, so too are the other children, whose lives depend on it, confirming Ellen Simms' assertion that "we are all of us trapped. We are born trapped and most of us stay trapped" (*SSM*, p. 117).

This Marxist, materialist theme also subverts yet again the discourse of the traditional coming-of-age narrative, which Paul Sheehan identifies as "the clearest link between the humanist tradition and the novel". Humanism's "central theme", he argues, "was human potentiality" – the idea that "man possessed latent powers of creativity, which could only be released through formal education".[38] The *Bildungsroman*, however, proposes that its protagonist must learn the universally obtaining humanist lessons of life "through self-forged learning on the streets, living by his wit".[39] In *Summer Sang in Me*, Annie learns her lessons in such a manner, on the hazardous streets of Dublin, but here "education" serves to undermine "human potentiality", to show how life under capitalism cannot be mapped onto the standard narrative arc of conventional bourgeois writing.

The triumph of failure

Annie fails to succeed as a *Bildungsroman* heroine conventionally ought to, despite how Smith courts our hopes that she might. Her mother sneeringly dismisses the girl's business "plans" as the "contrivances of a genius", but the mayhem they cause serves to underscore a valiant enthusiasm (*SSM*, p. 8). Murphy recalls her "plan to supply the shops of Dublin with fruit and flowers looted out of every garden you came across", which "brought [Annie's] poor father closer to the gates of Mountjoy [jail] than he had ever been", and left Tommy "with the spike of a railing up his guts" (*SSM*, p. 9). It is one of many failed, comic schemes to make quick money, such as her advertising venture for Miz Robey's brothel or her wholesale cinder-selling farce, which results in Annie being branded a "capitalist" and accused of

" 'arse nesting,' and 'ripe robbery' " (*SSM*, p. 124). But as each of these failures brings her closer to the dreaded factory, the novel depicts Annie's *unsuccessful* "entry into modern life". Like George Eliot's Maggie Tulliver (*The Mill on the Floss* [1860]), whose promise is continually frustrated by forces beyond her control, Smith's protagonist confounds the conventional, linear trajectory of the novel of formation.

In the classic *Bildungsroman*, the reconciliation of conflicts of ideology is often achieved by "the making of a gentleman and gentlewoman", but *Summer Sang in Me* ironises this characteristic, teleological pattern.[40] Rather like Behan's circular narrative in *Borstal Boy* (1958), in which the barely fictionalised author emerges unreconstructed from his experiences of "reformatory" life, Annie's story refuses to acquiesce in the affirmation of normative values. In the precarious world of the Dublin slums, she and her companion long for "the permanent in people and things and places", Smith conveys, but such permanence proves elusive (*SSM*, p. 17). Annie struggles with her inability to impose logic on a world in which "nothing is ever what you think it will be" (*SSM*, p. 104). Life's feeling of uncertainty defies language; she cannot "find the right word to tell of doubts in herself she had not felt before" and "I don't know rightly how to explain what I mean" (*SSM*, p. 104). Smith stresses her sense of awakening to a fragmentary modern world throughout the novel, analogously mirroring the working-class recalcitrance to modernity that Lloyd identifies with Irish subaltern consciousness. The novel's plot is predicated on a kind act by Ellen Simms – her generous promise, like a looming *deus ex machina*, to pass on her street-seller's cart – but the premature loss of Simms' life crystallises the sense of unreason from which Annie recoils.

Ellen has survived multiple ordeals. She has endured the death of her sweetheart, and her own ensuing insanity (*SSM*, p. 112). At one stage, she is unable to "check the drift" into madness, and becomes dislodged from any sense of purpose, walking ceaselessly and manically, without direction, finding solace amongst "Tinkers or Gipsies", whose nomadic lives are themselves symbols of her alienation, liminality and restlessness (*SSM*, p. 113).[41] But Ellen survives her institutionalisation and surmounts her psychological problems to become a woman of her own means. She achieves a kind of bourgeois coming-to-self. It is therefore all the more dramatically tragic, and thematically suggestive, when she is killed in a freak accident, run down by a horse and cart; Annie's hopes of salvation – along with her mentor – are ruined. Smith accentuates this tragedy when news of Simms' death reaches Annie and Tommy just as their most lucrative entrepreneurial venture has failed. The "lousy scurvy trick" of their fellow cinder pickers, in selling them bogus merchandise, thwarts the duo's budding business (*SSM*, p. 128). Annie's consequent epiphany, her realisation that life, in its manifold misfortunes, cannot be moulded to the contours of a teleological narrative, disputes middle-class logic, its promise of transcendence, which is integral to the archetypal discourse of "professional mobility" and "full social freedom", which "represent[s] capitalism" and its "new regime of accumulation".[42]

Franco Moretti characterises the English *Bildungsroman* "from Fielding to Dickens" as "one long fairy tale with a happy ending".[43] But after Ellen is "kicked to a pulp [...] be a horse and dray", Annie learns that "things happened [...] The world was big and mysterious"; "It can't be grasped at once [...] Everything can't be explained" (*SSM*, p. 129). Her positivist dream of an all-encompassing knowledge that would come with age is summarily invalidated:

> "I wish I was old," Annie often said. "I wish I was old because then I'd know things. When a person's old they know everything." But now, standing on the steps of the hospital, she said nothing, only looked until her eyes grew dim with looking. (*SSM*, p. 133)

In an elegiac ending, Tommy observes that "it was against humanity's and God's indifference that Annie cried" (*SSM*, p. 137). Again like Maggie Tulliver, Annie's obvious ebullience and talent are squandered. The concept that "things are [...] working themselves up into a state where they all come together like peas in a pod and finally show" is a sham (*SSM*, p. 107) and Smith correlates Simms' burial with this ideological defeat. Annie keens not just for the loss of her friend but also for the loss of her own naive faith, and the order of the funeral mass and the nuns who attend it contrasts vividly with the disorder of Annie's and Ellen's lives. Smith punctuates Tommy's recapitulation of their failed escapades, and Annie's "keen of grief", with the ritual Latin intonations of the mass, interweaving order with disarray, augmenting the children's sense of futility (*SSM*, pp. 135–136). Annie's cry is said to have "tore itself with the brutal authority of sorrow, right across the voices of the choir, who faltered indecisively, then ticked a minute like a clock, prim and slow, before they gave way altogether" (*SSM*, p. 136); the clock-like harmony of religion trundles to a halt under Annie's distraught screams, and "under the chapel's roof" – as if stabbing at the figurative structure of faith – "her crying fought and struggled with itself [...] and, scalpel sharp, found incisions where before none had existed" (*SSM*, p. 136).

Annie's lament echoes the sense of futility and orderlessness that Mary Makebelieve feels as her modest hopes of marrying above her class begin to fall apart in James Stephens' classic, *The Charwoman's Daughter* (1912). As hopes of matrimonial escape from poverty fade, Stephens depicts Mary walking away from a cleaning job: "She was very careful not to step on any of the lines on the pavement; she walked between these, and was distressed because these lines were not equally distant from each other."[44] Life's lack of geometric certainty projects itself into the uneven pavement, with its "unequal paces". Mary finds it difficult to negotiate life because, while "the physical and mental activities of the well-to-do person can reach out to a horizon", those "of very poor people are limited to their immediate, stagnant atmosphere, and so the lives of a vast portion of society are liable to a ceaseless change" with "no safeguards and not even any warning".[45] This, and not the farcical luck of her mother's inheritance of a fortune late in the novel, is Stephens' central message. One might recall here also James Hanley's persecuted child of the slums, Arthur Fearon, in *Boy* (1931), who is also forced into child labour by a bullying parent. When Fearon stows away on a ship to escape industry's hardship and his father's beatings, we might expect his courage and adventurism will, in classic coming-of-age fashion, lead to something better. But Fearon becomes a slave on the ship, beaten and sexually violated by older men. While Hanley's boy exhibits the same kind of mix of vitality and resilience that Annie embodies for Smith – eventually winning his place as an ordinary sailor on the ship through knuckling down and getting on with things – his contraction of syphilis and consequent agonised illness result in death, when the ship's captain kills him in an act of mercy. In such writing of working-class life, as in Smith's novel, youthful optimism turns sour with experience, and capitalist myths of meritocracy and opportunity are exploded by narratives of precariousness and poverty.

Annie's experience makes her suddenly aware of this "ceaseless change" that is the lot of the poor in capitalist society, particularly the unstable Irish kind, and with a volcanic outburst, "a crumbling, a scattering, as of ashes in an earthquake", her mouth is "filled with protest", echoing "the long barely subjugated cry of the lonely, the unwanted, the lovely who are not loved, whose expressions are of sleep, solitariness, savaged under the hobnailed boots of the selfish, the uncaring, the untouched" (*SSM*, pp. 136–137). Some time later, the now dejected girl is "beginning to accept the situation created for her by others" (*SSM*, p. 140). There is "a containment about her this morning that was not there before", Tommy worriedly observes (*SSM*, p. 142). His normally tomboyish playmate now asks him to kiss her, because "you're supposed to want to [...] All girls are supposed to" (*SSM*, p. 145). In a dramatic reversal, Annie indicates that she now wants to fit in; when Tommy counters that this kissing is something "only proper girls" do, she reminds him that she is "a proper girl", and now expects that "with lipstick on, a person should shiver like they have a fever" (*SSM*, pp. 145, 146).

In a classical allusion to the tale of Pyramus and Thisbe, whose forbidden, tragic love was inscribed by their blood on the mulberry tree, Tommy notices the "overripe mulberries" which "from a tree in the garden fell" and "stained black" the path before him.[46] Whereas the Thisbe of Roman legend had commanded that the mulberry tree would "ever bear fruit black and suited for mourning, as a memorial of the blood of us two" and, symbolically, their undaunted passions, Smith's trampled, mulberries, "walked [...] into the path", would seem to allude to the death of Annie and Tommy's passionate *joie de vivre* and with it the illusion of permanence that Thisbe longed for.[47] Presently, in an emblematic departure from childish pursuits, Annie disappears from a game of "Relievo", going home "without saying" (*SSM*, p. 147). Her mother now forces her into high heels and instructs her to eschew the "peculiarities" that might see her "ballsing up [her] chances below in Barker's" factory. Annie must now "try to behave like everybody else" (*SSM*, pp. 147, 148).

In an antithesis, also, of the classic "socialist *Bildungsroman*" identified by Lukács, whereby characters progress from false consciousness to class consciousness, through a series of epiphanies, Annie regresses from socially aware entrepreneur to socially constructed stereotype, through a series of social obstructions; but Smith's message is all the more subversive for it.[48] Annie's eventual accession to convention ranks with that of other female characters whose "progress" problematises the *Bildungsroman* form. Susan Fraiman identifies this phenomenon of formulaic subversion in the *Bildungsroman* "counternarratives" of Fanny Burney, Jane Austen, Charlotte Brontë and George Eliot.[49] Contradicting the linear progress of the traditional coming-of-age story, with plots that present "circularity" and "futility", these writers broach "dissonant ideas about just what formation is or should be".[50] Such a strategy is explicit, for example, in an authorial intervention in Patrick McGill's *Children of the Dead End* (1914), which reminds the reader that "in my story there is no train of events or sequence of incidents leading up to a desired end".[51] In *The Charwoman's Daughter*, Mrs Makebelieve's fear that her daughter Mary's life is being led "to a bleak and miserable horizon where the clouds were soapsuds and floor cloths, and the beyond a blank resignation only made energetic by hunger", represents the most likely prospect for working-class women in early twentieth-century Ireland.[52] In Smith's novel, conformity and acceptance – the normative features of a *Bildungsroman*'s resolution – are sardonically equated with Annie's sublimation as a character, her "blank resignation" to the horrors of child labour – a very significant issue for Dublin at this time.[53] In this way, society's injustices are indicted along with the ideological distortions of customary form.

Form and formation: subversion and the novel

For Benedict Anderson, the novel facilitates a union of the individual with the "imagined community" of the nation.[54] Historically, both concepts emerge about the same time in the eighteenth century, and both rely on the same idea of a coterminous, coextensive community, in which people living separate lives are tied together in space and time. Novelistic narrative links characters around a single plot, just as the nation links its "imagined community" about a single story of nationhood. As Anderson argues, the novel facilitates a sense of empathy in readers, which allows them "to visualise in a general way the existence of thousands and thousands like themselves".[55]

Both of the novels this chapter explores self-consciously promote such visualisations of commonality, but the visualisations of "thousands and thousands" that Plunkett and Smith focus on are firmly rooted in commonalities of class, not the horizontal comradeship of national identity. Both use a theoretically "national" form to challenge the association of novel and nation, a theoretically "bourgeois" form to subvert its association with the middle class. This formula is also remarkable in British working-class writing: David Trotter notes "the extent to which working-class fiction was able to represent working-class experience while still resembling bourgeois fiction", and that there were "advantages to be gained from adopting, without too much subversion, the literary form most likely to attract readers".[56] Both Plunkett and Smith engage the novel's capacity to reveal for readers the existence of many others like themselves and to portray the origins and persistence of a working-class counter-hegemony in private and public forms of rebellion. Both also subvert the novel's characteristic, ideologically inflected correspondence between form and content, narrative and social stability. Overturning the logic of normative practices, Smith and Plunkett forge a proletarian aesthetic that is all the more an affront to power for its adoption of traditionally "conservative" forms. As we shall see in the next chapter, such defamiliarisation of discursive orthodoxies recurs as a distinctive element in Dublin's lineage of working-class writing.

5
Prison Stories: Writing Dublin at its Limits

Declan Kiberd notes that, for the imprisoned Oscar Wilde "jail revealed to the writer the soul of man under capitalism, allowing him to 'see people and things as they really are'".[1] Exclusion from society paradoxically afforded Wilde a deeper awareness of its underlying realities, compelling the aestheticist *par excellence* to reach beyond "art for art's sake". Kiberd even terms Wilde's prison poem, "The Ballad of Reading Gaol" (1898), an "avowedly proletarian" work, because of its representation of prison suffering as a foil for the social decay of capitalist society and its existence of "living Death".[2] Prison, for Wilde, was a darkroom, a place in which society's negative could be developed into a crystallised depiction of its true social relations, and this use of what Wilde saw there as a mirror to life under capitalism resonates in the prison narratives this chapter examines. Brendan Behan, Peter Sheridan, Mannix Flynn and Paula Meehan's prison plays transfigure the carceral experience, developing it into a synecdoche for a failed society. Again we return to a mode of writing, which, "while it is often grounded in an ostensible realism, will nonetheless adopt descriptive or allegorical modes in which meaning does not so much depend on realist plausibility, but on a symbolic or metaphoric representation of a 'reified' consciousness."[3] In these plays, Behan, Sheridan, Flynn and Meehan follow Prisoner C33 (as the jailed Wilde was known), who smote the hand that "straws the wheat and saves the chaff / With a most evil fan".[4]

The Quare Fellow (1954), *The Liberty Suit* (1977) and *Cell* (1999) develop their commentary on life under capitalism by bringing those on its margins quite literally centre stage. In each, we are urged to envision, beyond the social and cultural boundaries of habitus, the commonality of mankind amongst those convicted of its greatest abominations. Viewers are asked to question the inequalities that lead to the sufferings of convicts and to witness their plight as a thematic defence of those who suffer the inequalities of society at large. Prison drama is exceptionally incisive in this regard, as it stretches the logic of the class system to its conceptual extremes. On one side of the theatrical divide are the (overwhelmingly) bourgeois theatregoers, with their privileged gaze; on the other are the (overwhelmingly) working-class prisoners, who endure the audience's surveillance.

One concern about this representation might, of course, be its focus on a small coterie of *lumpen* elements to illustrate the broader subjection of the working class. Marx's theory of the lumpenproletariat problematises the position of criminals from working-class backgrounds in that it suggests that those who commit crime are part of a distinct sub-strata of society, a generally unproductive class that is the surplus of all classes, or in Engels' opprobrium, "scum".[5] I will return to this argument later in this chapter, but it suffices to note at this stage that *The Quare Fellow, The Liberty Suit* and *Cell* develop a proletarian analysis of the inequalities of Irish life by representing jail as a mirror to society, a specular criticism of its socio-economic ills.

The prison as social laboratory

Inherent in the "realism" of these plays are the dramaturgical and ideological inflexions of a literature *engagé*. Their realism is only "real" in so far as it reflects the dynamics of socio-economic inequality. As Charles Baudelaire put it, realism is anyhow a "mot vague et élastique", but its elasticity is engaged in strikingly similar ways by all three writers.[6] Engels described a style of realism that elucidated both "truth of detail" and "truthful reproduction of typical characters under typical circumstances", later elaborated as "tipichnost" ("typicality") by Russian socialist realists; its aim, of capturing "typical circumstances", approximates the shared aesthetic vision of these plays.[7] The plays also employ, to varying degrees, some dramaturgical resemblances to the *Lehrstücke*, or "learning plays", of Bertolt Brecht, and his later development of the alienation theory known as the *Verfremdungseffekt*.[8] From the late 1920s, the German dramatist increasingly relayed overtly political messages by employing stagecraft that encouraged audiences to think outside of the immediate context of the action in front of them. Theatre, in Brecht's mould, resisted the traditional Aristotelian objective of engrossing theatregoers in narrative action, as if it were *really* transpiring before their eyes. Instead, Brecht sought to cause his audiences to reflect on political themes in a cerebrally removed manner. He encouraged players to act "in quotation marks" for instance – in a "gestural" style that called attention to the artificiality of what they were doing.[9] Drama, Brecht-style, doesn't so much "show" or "tell" as it "asks". As Terry Eagleton explains, it aims to "create contradictions within" audience members, "to unsettle their convictions, dismantle and refashion their received identities, and expose the unity of this selfhood as an ideological illusion".[10]

Othering the other fellow: Behan's anti-capitalism

Behan's political message in *The Quare Fellow* is developed through an elaborate pattern of such "unsettling", reflexive strategies and conceits. The play, which hinges on the plot of a murderer's execution and prisoners' reactions to it, depicts typical prisoners in typical prison activities. The foreboding caused by the looming execution, the prisoners' attempts to smuggle alcohol, their squabbles over food and bets and their mischief-making efforts to catch a glimpse of female prisoners all correlate broadly with the typicality of Behan's own prison experiences in *Borstal Boy* (1958). But, in Brechtian fashion, the play also refuses to allow its audience to be lulled into an unthinking immersion in the events on stage. Such experimentation is characteristic of Behan's dramaturgy, as exemplified more flamboyantly by Joan Littlewood's production of *The Hostage* (another Behan play, 1958), which diverged wildly from an earlier Irish language version, *An Giall* (1957), by including an array of defamiliarising devices. From song and dance to direct (and often drunken) impromptu comments from Behan himself on and off-stage, Littlewood's production engaged Brechtian theatrics with Behanesque flair.

But such strategies were not garnered from Littlewood (a follower of Brecht's drama) or indeed Brecht alone, as Robert Welch notes. Behan's uncle, P.J. Bourke, had written a number of patriotic melodramas for the Queen's Theatre, and the "songs, jokes, slapstick humour, and cross talk" of *The Quare Fellow* reflect Behan's "absorption of such techniques as he attended his uncle's shows". Again we see the trace also of the vaudeville aesthetic employed by O'Casey, who had greatly enjoyed these melodramas in his younger days and used their potential for upending and profaning orthodoxy to comical and political ends. Brecht is there as well in Behan, Welch argues, "but at a level much deeper than propaganda". To be sure, the experience of *The Quare Fellow* is about how it makes its audience feel; Behan "shows how the laws and ordinances of society condemn people to our rejection of them" and makes us consider our "collusion with these dictates".[11] Like Brecht, he seeks to throw the spotlight backwards, into the aisles, to criticise the structures of Irish society and those onlookers who support them. As John Brannigan observes,

> *The Quare Fellow* registered a growing sense of recalcitrance on the part of Irish intellectuals towards the dominant social, political and cultural trends sanctioned and policed in the Irish Republic, both as a powerful protest play against hanging, and as a satirical representation of the legacy of anti-colonial nationalism on the Dublin working class.[12]

As such, it is one of the first major pieces of writing in the post-war era to engage the central themes of this book and to carry O'Casey's legacy (still growing in 1954) to a new generation of Dubliners.

From the very beginning of its first act, *The Quare Fellow* endeavours to blur the conceptual boundaries between players and audience members, law-breakers and law-abiders, as a sign *"on the wall and facing the audience"*, in *"large block shaded Victorian lettering"*, imposes "SILENCE".[13] While fictionally the sign's intended readers are the *dramatis personae* of the prison, it is also reflexively read and enacted by the audience as it falls silent. Theatre etiquette and the imposing "Victorian" regime of the prison are thus performatively conjoined, as are the audience and the prisoners in their joint act of submission to institutional powers (theatre and prison). Only the singing prisoner in the solitary confinement cell disobeys the edict as the curtain rises and, when he sings that "the screw was peeping", and the warder retorts that "the screw is listening as well as peeping", the performativity of the play is emphasised again (*QF*, p. 40). The audience is reminded of its own parallel listening and peeping, its own collusion in the warder's act of surveillance.

In *Discipline and Punish* (1975), Michel Foucault explores the correspondence between surveillance in the "panopticon" prison and the control mechanisms of society at large, whereby the prison mimics the more general social surveillance of state apparatuses.[14] This "panopticism" is portrayed most vividly in another slice of working-class life, Pat Barker's *The Eye in the Door* (1993), when a British military intelligence officer, Billy Prior, spies on his own former comrades and neighbours, who are reviled as "conchies" – conscientious objectors to the First World War. Prior is consequently haunted by the spectre of the novel's titular "eye", which is painted on a prison door by his jailed neighbour and former guardian, Beattie Roper. For Roper, the eye is a reminder of the constant surveillance she endures, but for Billy it typifies his own conflicted duality, as a "watched" (by his own superiors) sympathiser with the radical conchies and "watcher" intelligence officer for those in power. Billy also feels conflicted as, on the one hand, a functionary for the capitalist state and, on the other, the son of a socialist who wanted to "raise the status of the working class as a whole".[15]

This feeling of duality is similar to what Behan harnesses in unsettling his audience, in dramatising Foucault's assertion that "we are neither in the amphitheatre, nor on the stage, but in the panoptic machine, invested by its effects of power, which we bring to ourselves since we are part of its mechanism".[16] The prison play implicitly enacts such a feeling of doubleness – giving audience members a glimpse of the conditions they themselves enforce – and Behan specifically distances the normativity of bourgeois society through a number of reflexive, comic scenes. When Prisoner A suggests that it is a "nice day for the races", Prisoner B responds that he has "too much to do in the office", juxtaposing his comic estrangement from "office" society with the idiomatic small talk by which it is ironically invoked (*QF*, p. 40). Dunlavin's assiduous shining of his "little bit of china" – a prison chamber pot – also contrasts the proprietorial pride of homely, bourgeois curatorship with the ignominies of prison life (*QF*, p. 42).

More pointedly, Behan also reasons that prisoners like Dunlavin have been drawn further into crime and degeneracy by the "corrective" institutions of justice themselves and, by extension by the society that runs them. When two young prisoners come "singing softly" to see a different kind of hanging – the "mots [in an adjoining women's prison] hanging out the laundry" – their vulnerability and energy provide a vivid contrast to the morbid meditations of the older, hardened prisoners (*QF*, pp. 47, 48). The youngsters flee their own wing, where death, in the form of a carpenter bringing up a coffin for the Quare Fellow, is the antithesis of their youthful concerns. "I'd sooner a pike at a good looking mot than the best looking coffin in Ireland", Young Prisoner 1 declares (*QF*, p. 48). He is nicknamed "scholara", the Irish term for scholar (properly *scoláire*), inferring a reputation for erudition, but Behan posits the kind of "education about screwing jobs, and suchlike, from experienced men" which he may well end up getting in jail (*QF*, pp. 58, 48). Two such "experienced men", Dunlavin and Neighbour, portend the boys' probable future as lumpenproletarian outcasts, "too old and bet for lobbywatching and shaking down anywhere, so that you'd fall asleep on the pavement of a winter's night", waiting for the "market pubs to open", on "hard floorboards", with "a lump of hard filth for your pillow" and a "wish that God would call you" (*QF*, pp. 60, 61). Implicit in this depressing vista is the question of how society has let its prisoners down, as opposed to the more familiar concern of how they have let down their society.

Prisoners "A", "B", "C", "D" and "E" may appear alphabetically and pointedly as anonymised members of a degenerate social cohort, but they question the social inequalities that have depersonalised them in public discourse and do so emphatically on a class basis. In an interchange between Dunlavin and Prisoner A, they infer the absurdity of social distinctions. Dunlavin speaks with veneration of "the fellow [who] beat his wife to death with the silver-topped cane, that was a presentation to him from the Combined Staffs, Excess and Refunds branch of the late Great Southern Railways", his verbosity approximating a comical reverence for petty social status (*QF*, p. 42). Equally, Prisoner A reserves a certain regard for the upper-crust murderer, who deserved his death-sentence reprieve because,

> well, I suppose they looked at it, he only killed her and left it at that. He didn't cut the corpse up afterwards with a butcher's knife [...] a man with a silver-topped cane, that's a man that's a cut above meat choppers whichever way you look at it. (*QF*, p. 42)

This risible (if gruesome) hauteur is just an exaggerated echo of the snobbery that pertains outside the prison, a point conveyed by Behan's linguistic connotations of conventional elitism: the symbolic associations of a "silver-topped cane" and the presentation of it by a quasi-distinguished institution, to a man who is, in comical wordplay, a "cut above" his peers. It correlates with Ciaran McCullagh's analysis of crime and class in Ireland, which suggests how society skews justice according to ingrained, snobbish predilections.[17] In his scrutiny of "getting the criminals we want", which McCullagh supports with some considerable research, prison itself reflects class bias, and criminality is associated with the working class in general public perceptions. As Leslie J. Moran notes, "middle-class men are not culturally associated with violence as there is an assumption that violence (as pathology) is a characteristic of the criminal 'Other', the working and underclass".[18] One character suggests how this system operates in Mannix Flynn and Joe Dunlop's RTÉ prison drama, *Inside* (1985): "Money talks. If you have the bread you can build your own courts. Buy the judges. The lot."[19]

Dunlavin and Prisoner A's parroting of class snobbery is extended into an absurdist conceit in the interplay between the comic pair and two new prisoners, the middle-class Other Fellow and Lifer, the "silver-top" killer. While Dunlavin has excused Lifer's crime as a "natural class of a thing could happen to the best of us", he is deeply perturbed by the "offence" for which the Other Fellow has been jailed. The unmentionable abomination of this "dirty beast [...] dirty man-beast" is of such an odious nature that even Dunlavin (who has just recently outlined, with little delicacy, various methods of assassination, from poisoning to mutilation) fastidiously refrains from naming it (*QF*, pp. 43, 42). Invoking the sacrilegious irony of J.M. Synge's Christy Mahon, Lifer is "only" in for "murder, thanks be to God", but this loathsome Other Fellow is of "that persuasion" (*QF*, p. 42), which suggests he is imprisoned, like Wilde was, on charges of homosexual acts. What Dunlavin disparagingly terms the "dirty animal on me left" is so far beyond human decency that he even advises Lifer, the "decent murderer", to get away from the Other Fellow's cell, lest he be "getting [himself] a bad name" (*QF*, pp. 43, 51). But the "sex mechanic", as it happens, has a "good accent", has never been in prison before, is in early middle-age and wears a suit – probably looking and sounding much like the patrons of an average theatre (*QF*, pp. 64, 49). This *othered* fellow even fears that he will have to endure the company of "murderers and thieves and God knows what": "you haven't killed anyone, have you?" he asks in hysterical tones (*QF*, p. 52). Again, the bourgeois theatregoer is forced to question class loyalties, and here society's ostracism of gay men is also probed. When Dunlavin finally relents in his persecution of the new arrival, reasoning that the Other Fellow is "someone's rearing after all", he hints again at the theme of class antagonism, surmising that the "sex mechanic" "could be worse"; "he could be a screw or an official from the Department" (*QF*, p. 64).

Kiberd argues that Behan's plays "owe more to the absurdist theatre of Ionesco, Genet and Beckett than their forerunners in the Irish dramatic movement", but like Ionesco's utterly absurd *Rhinoceros* (1959), which carries a subtextual critique of conformism, or more appropriately, Genet's *Deathwatch* (1949), set in a prison cell, and depicting three men trying to "kill each other off", Behan's absurdity comes loaded with serious undercurrents.[20] He questions the nature of class and moral prejudice in particular, and their role in the classification of crime.

Capitalism as crime: "What's a crook, only a businessman without a shop"

Behan's use of metaphors for cannibalism and spectatorship compounds this theme, lambasting capitalist society's moral compass. Developing into an elaborate conceit in the play, this imagery symbolises and excoriates society's parasitic, voyeuristic and inhuman treatment of its most alienated citizens. Talk of food and animal imagery evokes humanity's blood lust; men are depicted bestially feeding off each other, just like Lefranc is accused of "feed[ing] on others" in Genet's prison play.[21] In explaining the ministerial decision to spare one death-sentence recipient, Dunlavin says "enough is as good as a feast" (*QF*, p. 43). When Young Prisoner 1 objects to Neighbour ogling his girlfriend, Prisoner B jokes that "he's not going to eat her" (*QF*, p. 57). Neighbour terms the prison doctor a "vet", and he and Prisoner E (the jail bookie) bet their Sunday bacon on whether or not "the quare fellow will be topped", equating the devoured spectacle of hanging with the devoured Sunday meal (*QF*, pp. 61, 77). Indeed, the prisoners obsess about the Quare Fellow's final dinner, "two eggs, the yolk in the middle like [...] a bride's eye under a pink veil, and the grease of the rashers [...] pale and pure like melted gold", but they will pass on the "rope stew to follow, and lever pudding and trap door doddle for desert" (*QF*, p. 85).

In Prisoner B's story of a hanging, warders "have their breakfasts and don't come back for an hour. Then they cut your man down and the doctor slits the back of his neck to see if the bones are broken" (*QF*, p. 45). As he arrives to oversee preparations for the execution, the prison governor tellingly appears in "evening dress" – dressed for the spectacle and dressed to consume (*QF*, p. 110). During his execution, the Quare Fellow is even said to have a "white pudding bag" over his head, and the play abounds with many more instances of such imagery, which Behan adroitly employs to impose a general sense of moral nausea (*QF*, p. 120). We are made to "taste" the noxious reality of hanging as something that society has cannibalistically gormandised, to see, as prisoner James X does, in Gerard Mannix Flynn's play, that prisoners are viewed as "only animals savaging each other".[22] Akin to Peter Sheridan's use of the Eucharist – the symbolic eating of the body of Christ – to symbolise capitalist competition in *Big Fat Love* (2003), Behan defamiliarises society's dog-eat-dog ethic by estranging everyday practices and by showing how they make humans no better than cannibals.

Behan is not merely critiquing capital punishment here but, emphatically, the ideology of capitalism – of fractured, competing and unequal human relations. Imagery of gaming and entertainment is used to associate the execution explicitly with economic exploitation. Aleksandr Pushkin reminds us that "drama was born in a public square, it formed a popular entertainment [...] The people require strong sensations – *even an execution is a spectacle for them*", and the audience is here reminded of its own participation in such "entertainment", and the capitalist ideology Behan associates with it.[23] Indeed, Warder Regan sardonically argues that the hanging's "show" quality merits its staging in the form of a public sport, "put on in Croke Park; after all, it's at the public expense and they let it go on. They should have something more for their money" (*QF*, p. 114). The words of the Home Office memorandum on hanging etiquette accentuate this gaming motif at the end of Act II. While providing company for the condemned prisoner in his final hours, the warders are instructed to deport themselves with "an air of cheerful decorum [...] and a readiness to play such games as draughts, ludo, or snakes and ladders [...] A readiness to enter into conversations on sporting topics will also be appreciated" (*QF*, p. 104). This association of sporting pleasure with death is paralleled with the worst *Schadenfreude* of the prisoners themselves. Prisoner A recounts a spell in Strangeways jail, Manchester, where, "during the war, we used to wish for an air raid"; when "a bomb landed on the Assize Court next door, and the blast killed twenty of the lags", he recalls, "we all agreed it broke the monotony" (*QF*, p. 85–86). Neighbour's bet of his Sunday bacon may sound like something uttered by someone "in a week-end pass out of Hell", but his casual callousness merely reflects the cruelty of society at large (*QF*, p. 104).

Felicitously, Behan's hangman is also a publican, who serves both entertainment and intoxication to his customers – and who profits from each as he does from his public executions (*QF*, p. 111). The prisoners may seem crass and opportunistic when they squabble over profits from the stolen Quare Fellow's letters – which they hope to sell to Sunday papers – but they remind us that such self-interest is the business of commerce on the outside. "There's no need to have a battle over them," Prisoner B interjects, during their argument over the spoils, and Prisoner D concurs: "Yes, we can act like businessmen. There are three. One each and toss for the third. I'm a businessman" (*QF*, p. 124). Prisoner A acquiesces too, articulating again the play's subtext: "Fair enough. Amn't I a businessman myself? For what's a crook, only a businessman without a shop" (*QF*, p. 124). As they toss for the final letter, using its envelope rather than a coin, D's casual enquiry of A, as to "what side" he is on, "the blank side or the side with the address", is the last comment before the curtain falls, and a profound piece of wordplay. The tossed envelope, with its "blank side" and "side with the address", is an emblem of the false division between the prison and the society that surrounds it. Official society, "the side with the address" (i.e. with property), is a reflection of its flip side, the elided and propertyless "blank side". Despite their division, both are made from the same substance. The criminal avarice of these prisoners is merely a reflection of the appetite for sensationalism that the newspapers feed. If the prisoners view the hanging as a game, then society does too; if they profit from the "business" of reified humanity, they only replicate the processes of capitalism elsewhere. It is notable too that the year of this play's production was also that of Ireland's last hanging.

Marx's theory of reification, *"Verdinglichung"* – which literally means "thing-ification" – is, as I have already argued, apposite here, for the reduction of man to an object of consumption implies a wider social process of reified human relations. The Quare Fellow who "bled his brother into a crock, didn't he, that had been set aside for pig-slaughtering", who used his "experience as a pork butcher" to commit fratricide, is hypocritically murdered like a pig by the society that condemns his brutality (*QF*, pp. 76, 97). He, like it, and the man he killed, is "thing-ified".

Prisoner D, a white-collar criminal, who embodies the interests of the political and business classes, stresses that class solidarity is a threat to this corrupt system, which he supports. He is embroiled in the murky world of electoral politics – jailed "for embezzlement", "there were two suicides and a bye-election over him" (*QF*, p. 94). But whereas Prisoner C and Crimmin (whose name is, of course, suggestive) come "from the same place" and show a parochial and, inferentially, a class solidarity by being "for hours talking through the spy hole, all in Irish", Prisoner D sees this fraternising as "most irregular" – a threat to the stability of social gradation: "How can there be proper discipline between warder and prisoner with that kind of familiarity?" (*QF*, p. 95) Equally, when Warder Regan broaches a left-wing perspective on the class makeup of prisons, it is Prisoner D who strongly objects. The prisoners are "good boys only a bit wild", according to the warder: "[they are] doing penance here for the men who took us up, especially the judges, they being mostly rich old men with great opportunity for vice" (*QF*, p. 93). Emerging symbolically from a freshly dug grave, Prisoner D counters with what is inferentially a moribund way of thinking. Risibly professing his middle-class credentials "as a ratepayer", the affluent criminal can't stand these "libellous remarks about the judiciary"; "property must have security", he retorts (*QF*, p. 94). If implemented, the benevolent warder's disdain for punitive justice would result in middle-class people being "innocent prey of every ruffian that took it into his head to appropriate our goods [...] Hanging's too good for 'em" (*QF*, p. 94). D's defence of punitive justice is therefore allied to the logic of capitalism, while Regan's class consciousness points the way forward in threatening the limitations of both the jail and the society around it.

"Scrub some of the Dublin scum off yourselves": *The Liberty Suit* and social defecation

Peter Sheridan makes the importance of this kind of social image – of his aesthetic "tipichnost" – explicit in his author's note to *The Liberty Suit*: "In short, the aim [of the production] has always been to move from the typical individual to the social environment [...] beyond the experiences of one individual former inmate".[24] The individual former inmate referred to is co-author Gerard Mannix Flynn, whose own experiences of confinement informed the writing of the play, but, as in Behan, theatre's task here is not merely strict mimesis. *The Liberty Suit* is designed to encapsulate the macrocosm of a "social environment", to go beyond the particular of its immediate action, and again, a socialist analysis of class strife is also apparent throughout this play.

As with *The Quare Fellow*, social control and surveillance are emphasised from the start of Sheridan and Flynn's drama, but in *Liberty Suit* this control is framed explicitly in terms of a conflict between rural and urban Ireland. Warder Martin, otherwise known as "Diarrhoea Powder", echoes Behan's imposing "screw" in the opening act of *The Quare Fellow*, but this time the tone is specifically anti-urban (*LS*, p. 8). Prisoners are ordered to "get into them showers and scrub some of the Dublin scum off [them]selves", to which Curley – Sheridan and Flynn's central protagonist – retorts by calling the warder a "culchie bastard" (*LS*, p. 8). But the playwrights are not merely criticising the ascendancy of the rural over the urban in Irish culture here. Joe Furey, the "silent itinerant", is also mocked and jeered as an outsider by the Dublin prisoners, a counterpoint to their own marginalisation that suggests deeper concerns (*LS*, p. 10).

The Liberty Suit is essentially about class consciousness, and the failure of class solidarity within the prison manifests itself in Furey's persecution. As a Traveller, he is continuously bullied as an *Other*, branded "Joe Shite" by Curley due to his willingness to participate in the most odious of prison jobs – collecting and disposing of the faeces that other prisoners have ejected from their windows (*LS*, p. 60). Here Sheridan and Flynn convey the senselessness of intra-class strife. Metaphorically and socially, Furey is at the bottom of the pecking order, suffering the "excrement" of others who needlessly make life difficult for an "othered" member of their own class. Behind the scatological crudity is hidden suffering, and following an uproarious strip-show, and the ensuing farce of a prison riot, there is an "extremely slow fade-up" that jars dramatically with the levity of the previous scene: "As the light grows the figure of BILLYBOW is seen facing GER's cell. In the cell FUREY is hanging from a rope. Dead" (*LS*, p. 59). O'Flaherty, another Traveller and Furey's friend, emphasises that intra-class strife is to blame for the suicide. He points to his and Joe's social exclusion as Travellers, shouting that "youse don't understand him [...] he's only a travelling man", but turning on Curley – the man he now perceives as a murderer – O'Flaherty ironically parrots the kind of pointless othering that has killed his friend: "He was only a travelling man ... Ye dirty Dublin ..." (*LS*, pp. 59, 60).

Despite the other prisoners' culpability in this tragedy, however, Sheridan and Flynn refuse any easy vilification; as with the plays of Heno Magee, Lee Dunne and James McKenna explored in Chapter 2, *The Liberty Suit* endeavours to explain the complex habitus from which its characters' dysfunction has emerged. Sheridan and Flynn emphasise that their working-class Dubliners have a great deal in common with the persecuted Traveller.

Even though Curley had bullied "Joe Shite", he too suffers hidden despair. When he asks Ger, "did you ever try [suicide]?" both show their scarred wrists, admitting to "depression" and "loneliness" (*LS*, p. 60). Echoing the symbolism of Behan's prisoners' betting on death, the playwrights' imagery suggests that life is cheapened by a form of currency exchange. Ger had taken the rope subsequently used for Furey's suicide from the work yard, because he "thought [he] might be able to swop it for some tobacco" (*LS*, p. 61). Curley too had smuggled medicinal anti-depressants for Furey and had a rope smuggled for himself. Those with shared class interests, and who have suffered similar social exclusion, nevertheless choose to trade in misery – something Joe's demeaning job had also implied. As with Behan's play, *The Liberty Suit*'s prison mirrors fragmented social relations on the outside.

Class consciousness and political action

This focus on the failures of working-class people to fully comprehend their own common plight is essentially also a critique of how both institutional and social influences have moulded the prisoners' false consciousness. Beginning the play as a "fire bomber" – in terms of both his crime of arson and his generally volcanic disposition – Curley risibly claims to be the "innocent victim of Irish law" (*LS*, p. 5). He has heard and adopted the rhetoric of the ongoing North of Ireland conflict but shows no real understanding of it. Because he has also seen and envied the benefits accorded to IRA prisoner Lane, he is "claiming political status" for what seems to be an act of unadulterated vandalism – the burning down of a factory – and melodramatically threatens "hunger strike" to attain it (*LS*, pp. 21, 27). Opportunistic charade and farce as this may be, there is nonetheless a tentative political consciousness in Curley's posturing, though we are never privy to his reasons for setting fire to this symbol of capitalism.

Curley's progress towards obtaining his "liberty suit" is depicted as a process of advancement towards class consciousness. Like Behan's chokey singer, he often uses songs to express his experiences, and his lyrics gain an increasingly polemical tone as the play progresses. They form part of a distinctly Brechtian technique, in which music voices authorial metacommentaries on the action of the play itself. Curley "started to rob" because he "could not read nor write" one song claims (*LS*, p. 34). When he is isolated in the "chokey", and degenerates into a subhuman state, the "come day go day" world of solitary confinement induces introversion and near-madness, which is articulated in metaphoric ramblings that emphasise his reification (*LS*, p. 53):

> Small, hard, rounded, lumps of black brittle shite...on the mattress, the blankets, the floor, the window, the walls, the plastic cutlery, my

body...My body, mi-wadi. Body, biddy, billy, baddy, bandy, randy...on me biddy, billy, bandy, randy body. (*LS*, p. 49)

His breakdown here manifests itself in a desperate grasping for language and meaning, in what seems mere bland alliteration and assonance. But in suggesting how Curley's world is reduced to the scatological – his "black brittle shite" – and the libidinal – his "biddy, billy, bandy, randy body", Sheridan and Flynn emphasise his depersonalisation, which was also hinted at when Warder Martin numbered him "8072" (*LS*, pp. 49, 6). Indeed, it is notable that the authors randomly and frequently switch their protagonist's name from "Jonnie" to "Curley" in the script, eroding and destabilising even this paratextual nominative certainty.

But if Curley is dehumanised by the prison, it also gradually affords him a new political awareness. Speaking of the scars he bears from beatings at Daingean Reformatory School, a children's correctional institution, he attempts to find some pathological rationale for why he has been incarcerated in institutions all his life. Although the prison describes him as having "no distinguishable features" on an official report, it belies the inner injuries of the state's "reform", due to which he is physically and mentally "L-A-C-E-R-A-T-E-D" (*LS*, p. 49). During his time in these institutions, Curley was forced to deny his very identity, again in the language of rural dominance: "I'm sorry for being smart, Sir. I hate Dubliners" (*LS*, p. 49). He also shows that he has introjected the social stereotyping of the "'dangerous' classes" (Marx) by praying insanely to a dead rat:[25] "Oh Satan...say it. Oh Satan...good. For all the sins...of my past...and present life...I am truly glad." (*LS*, p. 49) This self-vilification is repeated by Flynn's protagonist in *James X* when, skirting near madness, he thinks of Satan and becomes "alive with power, the power of destruction, destroy, smash, rip apart".[26]

But in beginning the process of rationalising how he has descended into crime, Curley also begins to understand the set of social, cultural and economic factors that have blighted his youth. He is aware from the start of the play that he has been "las.er.ate.did", though his poor spelling is a metaphor for his limited self-awareness (*LS*, p. 8). Having had "enough of schools in Daingean", he is ill-disposed to educational instruction, and we see from the actions of Warder Martin, who ironically "punches [Curley] across the room" when he misspells the word "reformatory", that institutional instruction is equally ill-disposed to learning (*LS*, pp. 17, 8). When Curley expresses his budding artistic talent by penning amorous poems for his teacher, his creativity is again repressed by the prison regime. Martin confiscates the rhymes because "anything to do with prison life is prison property" (*LS*, p. 54). As Curley's lyric expresses, the prison is a stifling place:

> Now your nerves will go when you hear the blows,
> And the scream from the prisoners down below,

> And you beg the Lord to let you go.
> Oh no … oh no. (*LS*, p. 32)

However, in a dramatic epiphany at the end of the play, Curley exposes the programme of vocational and rehabilitative learning in the prison as a charade. He realises he has been "sawing the same log since [he] came here. The same fucking log, Ger". "Nothing changes" in prison, and even though he has "only three days to go", Curley sardonically questions "what [he is] suitable for […] sawing logs on the outside?" (*LS*, p. 67). Gesturing to his fellow inmates, as if performing a surreal benediction, he then points his axe at each of the other prisoners in turn, punctuated by the now correctly spelled letters of his angry refrain, "l … a … c … e … r … a … t … e … d. *On the final letter he smashes the axe into one of the logs*" (*LS*, pp. 67–68). This "laceration" is what Foucault terms "the branded existence of delinquency".[27] In Foucault's view, "the prison cannot fail to produce delinquents. It does so by the very type of existence that it imposes on its inmates: whether they are isolated in cells or given useless work [… it is] an unnatural, useless and dangerous existence".[28]

But in such an existence Flynn (now a Dublin City councillor) had honed his political consciousness, and Curley's progress to socialism elaborates the central message of the play. Early on, Lane speaks of Warder Carson as a fellow proletarian and another "oppressed victim of the system", just as Behan's Martin and Crimmin indicate their common class position with prisoners (*LS*, p. 22). But Curley incredulously dismisses this class analysis, scoffing, "so we're all victims then" (*LS*, p. 22). For much of the play, Lane's politicised logic (inflected here with Behanesque bestial imagery) indeed falls on deaf ears:

GER: Some of the screws treat us like animals.
KAVA: All of them. That's why they're called pigs.
LANE: But if it's yous that are being treated like animals then you're the pigs, not them.
KAVA: Who are you calling a pig?
LANE: Forget it, Kava. You wouldn't understand.
KAVA: Who wouldn't understand? I forgot we were all stupid except for Che Guevara here. (*LS*, pp. 42–43)

As the action unfolds, however, Curley arrives at a qualified understanding of Lane's ideology, soon advising Kava that, "all screws are not bastards … That's shite talk" (*LS*, p. 36) and he even adopts Lane's systematic view of prison violence, continuing: "I don't blame the screws for being the way they are […] The violence breeds itself." This progress to an understanding of hegemonic processes lends some credibility to Lane's assertion of the potential for political radicalism amongst his fellow inmates. "People like them have the right to rob, steal, march, organise," Lane argues, " 'cos they've nothing. And they've nothing "cos the comprador classes left them with nothing. And they left them with nothing" cos they sold out to monopoly capital" (*LS*, p. 42).

But Curley also transcends the somewhat flawed analysis of his political mentor and, in doing so, articulates a more authentic understanding of socialism. Although Lane may profess to be "in here because [he] tried to better the lot of people like Kava", his patronising, pontificating deportment reveals a Coveyesque unease with the people he seeks to radicalise (*LS*, p. 11). This scoffed-at "Che Guevara['s]" imperious attitude of "you wouldn't understand" is remarked upon by Ger when he asks "how come, Lane, when you talk about screws and prisoners it's always them and you. You never include yourself" (*LS*, p. 43). Similarly, Lane's class solidarity with the warders is betrayed as hollow rhetoric when he misinterprets Carson's offer of a cigarette as a "bourgeois trick" (*LS*, p. 36). As his name suggests, Lane may offer a route into political awareness, but it is a narrow one indeed. Reminiscent of Harold Heslop's Welsh trade unionist Joe Tarrant, in *The Gate of a Strange Field* (1929) – whose education only sullies the initial purity of his political convictions, allowing him to "lord it over the rest of his workmates" – Lane's polished erudition actually becomes an impediment to class solidarity in the prison.[29]

Curley, who initially prefers "wanking and football" to politics, at first comically suggests how his immersion in popular culture jars with Lane's socialist rhetoric:

JONNIE: And what's the badge, George Best?
LANE: No. That's Lenin.
JONNIE.   Where's Yoko Ono? (*LS*, p. 15, 14)

However, this preference for pop culture begins to develop into a politicised exploration of his own misfortune later on. As Curley sings the words of Queen's "Bohemian Rhapsody" – "Mama, uh, uh, uh, uh, I didn't mean to make you cry" – pop-singing suddenly turns to personal revelation: "Why did you send me away, Ma? I was only eight years old. I wasn't a criminal" (*LS*, p. 50). Another song again indicts the prison, along with an "old" society:

> Hey warder, I was down on my knees
> I was begging you to stop your blows and to let me go
> But now I know what freedom means,
> It's not a dream, it's not obscene,

> It's in my heart and my soul
> You'll never find it
> Cos you are blinded
> And growing old. (*LS*, p. 57)

Lane, unlike Curley, is aloof from and dismissive towards popular culture. Ger and Flaherty enjoy Victor magazine, but Lane accuses Warder Michael, who kindly provides them with an edition, of using pop culture as a pacifier, a "solution to prison problems" that aims to produce Orwellian proles: to "get the prisoner stupid enough to read the Victor and the Hotspur? You won't find them handing out copies of James Connolly's 'Socialist Ireland', 'cos then the prisoners might really ask questions" (*LS*, p. 42). But whereas Lane trivialises his fellow inmates' "stupid" cultural tastes, Curley, in his song-writing, fuses "high" and "low" culture in a manner that mirrors his creators' own aesthetic practice.[30] Near the end of the play, he may have packed a "dirty book" for his departure, but tellingly he packs a "Connolly poster" as well (*LS*, p. 68).

The man who dubiously posed as an "innocent victim of Irish law" arrived in prison as a parody of heroic political posturing, but his new-found political praxis suggests the possibility of real social engagement (*LS*, p. 5):

LANE: [...] *Taking him aside.* Are you going to join the Movement when you get out?

JONNIE: *After some thought.* I'll tell you what, Laner, I'll think about it. (*LS*, pp. 68–69)

If Lane preaches class solidarity, he excoriates a prison informer as a "rat face" (*LS*, p. 43). When he seemingly advocates a fight between Curley and Kava, Curley retorts that, "if Kava smashed my face in and I kick him in the bollox, what good is that for your struggle?" (*LS*, p. 37). Curley is proselytised by Lane to a new faith that urges him to "rob, steal, march, organise", but he also transcends Lane's elitism. Sheridan and Flynn thus suggest that leftist politics is vacant if aloof from working-class culture, and when Curley, with his common touch, wins the prison's "Entertainer of the Year" competition by writing a political ballad, he exemplifies how art can forge a link between the lived experience of the disadvantaged and the complexity of socialist politics. His song exemplifies the *narodnost* ("ready accessibility to the people" in socialist realism) aesthetic of his creators' play and its words are the kernel of the play's political message – that capitalist society has fostered criminal activity through inequality and that it is only through political consciousness, through knowing "what freedom means", that Curley can wear his "liberty suit".[31]

Cell: "An intensified microcosm"

It is apt, then, that Paula Meehan immortalises her days of theatrical collaboration with Peter Sheridan with an image of him preparing a theatre set while also implicitly preparing for revolution:

> I saw
> A man once hammer Connolly
> Into a picture of our history.
> His anvil rang sparks into the dark.
> Some must catch, take fire.[32]

The young poet's symbolism of hammer and anvil, her invocation of James Connolly and her portentous "sparks" of revolutionary fervour reflect the enthusiasm for social change that underpins both writers' work. But Meehan's hope that art can feed the "fire" of socialism is undercut by her acknowledgement of the cultural exclusion of the working class in Irish life. In the same poem she criticises a perceived elitist emphasis in Irish literature by mocking a man who stands at its core. W.B. Yeats's own self-deprecations, in his epic encomium to the Easter Rising rebels, "Easter, 1916", echo sardonically in Meehan's assessment of cultural class biases. Yeats had himself admitted to having lived outside the main concerns of Irish society, "where motley is worn"; the austerity of his rebel acquaintances was but fodder for a "mocking tale or a gibe" at his "club", something he later regretted.[33] But for Meehan this admission is, moreover, symptomatic of a cultural malaise; the poet who "spied motley / From high Georgian windows" with his "literary crew" is the representative of a legacy of cultural inequality, whereby "the poor become clowns / In your private review".[34] Meehan might dismiss too easily the man who famously and fancifully sought to ally the peasant and aristocrat against the acquisitive mediocrity of bourgeois values (or so he characterised it), but the sentiment stands. Yeats and the literature he represents have conceded little to the subjectivity of the poor, she argues, in a pointed reference to another of his poems, "Among School Children":[35]

> But when all is done and said
> Your swanlike women are dead
> Stone dead. My women must be
> Hollow of cheek with poverty
> And the whippings of history.

Like Sheridan and Flynn's men, Meehan's women are "lacerated" by their circumstances, moulded by material reality, and if Yeats's "Quattrocento" portrait of a Ledaean beauty "bent / Above a sinking fire" is of a universal, ahistorical and idealised transcendence of the political (it is posited as a reverie that diverts him from his senatorial duties), Meehan's women are, by contrast, particularised, historicised "sparks" to light a *rising fire* of discontent.[36]

First performed in the City Arts Centre in 1999, *Cell* is the most recent prison play of the three explored here and the only one to focus on female prisoners. Like the other two, it is a politically charged, social-realist work, and it also employs techniques of audience estrangement to unsettle discursive orthodoxies on class and crime. Furthermore, *Cell* is both temporally and thematically about breaking new ground. The play's first production came a timely 22 days prior to the opening of the new women's prison at Mountjoy Jail, which was named the Dóchas (Hope) Centre and billed to herald considerable changes in the prison regime. Meehan's cellmates continuously refer to the much-anticipated new prison, and her original audience was alive to the political resonances of the action on stage, its propitious link with reality. As a former tutor to both male and female inmates, Meehan had taught impoverished inner-city women, who were mostly jailed for drug-related crimes, since early 1980s. She had also encountered the questionable effects of prison "reform": in her first educational workshop in Mountjoy, Meehan had tutored 12 female prisoners, but when she attempted to track them down over a decade later, only one was still alive.[37] Prison had clearly failed to correct their downward spiral; in all likelihood, it had hastened it.

To be sure, *Cell* indicts society at large for such failures, from the first moments of the first act, when, as in *The Quare Fellow*, the action on stage reminds its audience of their own intrusive presence, and their empowerment vis-à-vis the players. Echoing also the scatological shock value of the Sheridan and Flynn's "shite party" – and Wilde's description of prison as a "latrine" – the first "articulation" of the play is a prisoner's "strong stream of piss into a galvanised bucket", engendering a palpable, physical awkwardness between audience and stage.[38] As obtrusive voyeurs, theatregoers are again part of the prison surveillance system, of its graphic infringement on the prisoner's privacy.

Delo, the woman whose urinating we hear, plays a key role in revealing the perverse results of the justice system which contains her. Due to the communal fear of spreading AIDS, it is vital that the women in her cell synchronise their menstrual cycles.[39] As the cell matriarch, she monitors this synchronisation and is apoplectic when someone has upset it by falling "out of sync with the heavenly cycle", breaking their "pact", their "solemn promise" of "no blood" and "no faecal matter". Menstruation – a metonym for the natural cycle of reproduction, and femininity itself – should be curbed and controlled due to the expediencies of containing "the big V", but this bodily containment is not just about avoiding contamination (*Cell*, p. 9). Delo speaks of nature itself having "failed to get the message" of the daily morning call in the prison. "The sun still sleeps", she says, as if natural time is somehow subservient to the jail's regime (*Cell*, p. 10). Lila, her cellmate, later echoes this sentiment when she disjointedly articulates her estrangement from the real, natural world outside her window. Her automated, stylised delivery echoes Curley's staccato monologue in *The Liberty Suit*: "Lovely roundy moon, check. Weeping willow, check. Leaves falling, check. Yellow, check [...] Black clouds away over the canal, check. Dark blue clouds too, check. Rain, check" (*Cell*, p. 47). In a rigidly inhuman jail, there is little room for natural feeling, Meehan infers. As with Behan's imagery of metaphoric cannibalism, her symbolism illustrates prison's and society's dehumanisation of human affairs.

Delo curbs her own maternal talk of her children's funny lingo lest she might arouse any unwanted emotions: "He-highls. That's what my girls used to call [high heels]. When they were only little. They'd dress up in my old stuff and...Ah fuck it" (*Cell*, p. 14). Echoing Curley's delusional conversation with a Satanic rat, she too indicates that she has succumbed completely to the psychological branding of state correction, intoning a similarly malevolent and parodic creed of the *bête noire*: "For I believe in the one true apostolic church of God Almighty. Who has four hooves and a flying mane. Or a scaly body and he breathes fire" (*Cell*, p. 11). Satanic undertones recur when Delo manipulates Lila's drug addiction, forcing the younger, more vulnerable woman to pay for heroin with sex. As Lila fondles Delo, the drug dealer speaks in a grotesquely distorted, incestuous maternal lexicon, urging her cellmate to "snuggle in there. Oh yes. That's the spot. X marks the spot. Sex marks the spot. O I like that"; "who's my girl...won't I mind you...who's your best pal?" Delo refers to the tattooed, satanic snake on her arm, again in a perversely parental, infantilised tone – "and Snakey likes it too! [...] Snakey loves it" – and later, in a more overtly incestuous register, she intimates that "mammy loves Lila", that "mammy loves her little titties", while molesting the helpless drug addict and making her "want to throw up" (*Cell*, pp. 15, 19). Lila has "no choice in the matter" of her subjection to this horrific abuse and, as Martha (another cell mate) warns, if she does not obey Delo she will "end up with Tracey fucken Dunne farting in your face while you suck her off" (*Cell*, pp. 20, 22).

This grotesque imagery is part of an extended metaphor in the play, indicting the prison's pretensions to maternal care – a theme which emerges in the subtext of Martha's bizarre cannibalistic nightmare, again echoing Behan. In it, she searches madly for her daughter Jasmine:

Only I couldn't find her anywhere and there was this strange smell coming from the kitchen. I went in and there was a pot on the gas boiling away like mad. I lifted the lid and there was Jasmine all chopped up. Like a lump of meat she was. There was a bit of her face and the eye; and then another chunk with her mouth; all rolling around in the boiling water.

And do you know what I did? I turned the gas down to simmer and put the lid back on. (*Cell*, p. 10)

These bizarre scenes again invoke the theme of perverse motherhood to illustrate the real role of punitive justice. Jasmine, the flower, is the Hindu symbol of love (Meehan uses other Hindu symbols in the play, as discussed below). The "chopping up" of Martha's daughter is the perversion of that love. The conflict between the ostensibly benign, motherly tone of Delo's "baby-talk" and the transgressive, rapacious aggression of her sexually predatory actions not only foregrounds Delo's malevolence but also, like Martha's fantasy, refers to something vile in the prison and society outside. In calling Martha and Lila her "little piggies", with her their "mama sow", Delo invokes Joyce's axiomatic analogy of warped nationhood, the "old sow that eats her farrow" (*Cell*, p. 7).[40] Delo may contend that she is "like a mother", with her "family" in her "nest", but the cell matriarch, as Mother Ireland, continually abuses her disobedient charges, torturing them, making them stand in their bare feet "for thirty bleedin hours" (*Cell*, pp. 10, 13, 23). An analogy is drawn between this "monster" mother and the monstrous society that facilitates such horrific abuses (*Cell*, p. 43).

Meehan stresses this thematic synergy between cell and society by continually invoking the lexicons of political and religious discourse. As the general election from which the prisoners are "disenfranchised" takes place outside, Delo poses as an election candidate, assuring her cellmates of "my un- un- wavering, yes, that's the word, unwavering support": "In any way, on any day, say but the word, and Delo will do her utmost [...] We should tackle this together as a community. Community action against drugs" (*Cell*, pp. 37, 60). Mark O'Rowe invokes a similar parallel in his play *The Aspidistra Code* (1999), in which ruthless criminal loan shark Drongo parrots the language of conservative politics, in order to justify his amoral attitude towards customers who fail to make repayments: "Rules are what keep society in shape, keep it from getting flabby. Rules are what prevent anarchy [...] What are we worth *if* we break them? Nothing. We are people without laws and without a code. We're animals."[41] Ironically, this criminal would-be conservative parrots the lexicon of "zero tolerance" on crime; ironically also, it is the would-be politician who does the drug-dealing in Meehan's prison, and it is a typical pillar of "society", her solicitor, who supplies the drugs.

Meehan echoes here her allegory of an earlier poem, "She-Who-Walks-Among-The-People" (1994), which further elucidates the theme of the play. In fairy-tale language, the poem describes two unequal sets of "tribes": firstly, "the tribes who had nothing were broken in spirit. Nobody cared about them, and nobody listened to them." Their children were "charmed by strange potions, bad visions, grew thin [...] were locked away in dungeons."[42] This tribe, of course, is the urban working class, in which heroin addiction had reached epidemic proportions. The other tribe, by contrast, "had many, many tokens", but "few [amongst it] were the lawgivers / who cared about justice, few were the doctors / who cared about healing, few were the teachers / who cared about truth".[43]

This allegory of class warfare has echoes in *Cell's* structure of prison exploitation. Delo's political parody is accompanied by bourgeois talk of being a "humble trader", her "motto" being "fair trade", and like Behan's "businessmen" gamblers, she imbues the language of commerce with a criminal inflexion, suggesting that her parasitic preying on other cellmates is an organic part of the system outside (*Cell*, pp. 30, 10). Audience culpability in this system is again hinted at in another cryptic invocation of Hindu symbolism. When Alice asks Lila if her name is an abbreviation for Delilah, Lila pointedly informs her that it is actually an Indian name: "My Ma was into a lot of Indian stuff when she had me [...] meditation, the Guru" (*Cell*, p. 25). Sometimes spelt "leela", this Sanskrit term relates to a Hindu concept that sees the universe as a cosmic puppet theatre and plaything for the gods.[44] Literally meaning "play", and referring in religious texts to "divine play", the idea is employed as an oblique analogy for Meehan's own dramatic strategy. In Indian drama, the term refers to a dramaturgical act of transcendence in the "play of God":

> According to Hindu thought, Man and the World are but images in God's dream; consequently, Man's sense of reality is nothing but an illusion (maya). Only when Man transcends the physical and material bounds of existence does he encounter God. *Lila*, then [...] is a limited revelation of the mystery of God's eternal dream.[45]

Meehan's version of "divine play" is one that puts the theatregoers in the seat of the divinities, affording a godlike insight into their "puppets" in a place that is often far removed from public consciousness and concern. Utilising the same dramatic principles as *The Quare Fellow* and *The Liberty Suit*, *Cell* thus allegorically questions its audience members, probing the extent of their own participation in the real conditions to which events on stage refer. They, like the *lila's* "gods", play a vital part in the creation of prison norms, in creating the "puppets" on stage, and for Meehan, society and its prisons are illuminating reflections of one another:

> You can learn an awful lot about your culture by looking at how prisoners are treated. It is a good barometer of what's happening in the culture outside. And it's a microcosm – an intensified microcosm – of the forces that are at play in the greater culture.[46]

Again a proletarian aesthetic projects the social image through the subjective tale, subverting "given" reality with metaphoric invocations of capitalism's (puppeteering) reification.

Meehan's analogy achieved further resonance in an Austrian staging of the play in 2004, which harnessed the defamiliarising potential of the *lila* by staging it in a more familiar Brechtian format.[47]

> Characters wore tee shirts that labelled them: thief, dealer, murderer, junkie [...] The effect was to make people ask about their own/society's labelling of people they wish to imprison. [...] The Austrian production had a subtext which was developed in the director's staging – that the real prisons are in the mind. It was a very free, body-oriented production. Even with my minimal German I got it because it was almost danced rather than performed.

This production was more "philosophical" and sought to "imply that we are our own warders".[48] In *Cell*, as in Foucault's panopticon, the act of "surveillance" is thus imbued with a broader social meaning.

The burden of responsibility: "My city's million voices chiding me"

Meehan's poetry abounds with references to the political valence of literature, which parallel the preoccupations of this play. The poet and playwright reveals an almost tribal sense of kinship with, and responsibility to her class, a burden of accountability that infuses the very essence of her work, propelling her relentlessly towards social engagement. In "Intruders" (1984), Meehan graphically portrays how the "voices" of her community petition her, when she envisions them as pleading and unrelenting phantoms of a ghostly past.[49] During a holiday to the Shetland Islands, impoverished Dublin appears as a reproving interloper on her serene isolation, and although Meehan tries not to "hear / My city's million voices chiding me", she cannot extinguish the spectral images of inner-city life:[50]

> Then the boys appear by the dyke lobbing
> Stones at passing cars and plundering
> The small grimy shops of country merchants
> That hold their ma's to ransom.[51]

Not only does this imagery attest to an abiding sense of social responsibility, it also again invites comparisons with Sheridan and Behan. As with *The Quare Fellow*'s equation between business and crime, and *The Liberty Suit*'s exhortation to "rob, steal, march, organise", the notion of criminality is problematised by Meehan's vandalising class warriors. Bourgeois "country merchants" hold the boys' "ma's to ransom", not as a literal, physical act, but as part of a general class analysis. The boys avenge themselves on the bourgeoisie through "plundering" shops and stoning cars.

Like the ransom-taking country merchants of "Intruders", drug dealer Delo personifies the corollary between capitalism and crime in *Cell*. She also adopts the language of a busy entrepreneur in battling rebellious proletarians, outlining her "work to be done. Deals to be struck. Profits to be made. And the drones mutinous" (*Cell*, p. 10). Self-styled as a "humble trader", her drug dealing is part of the system of "fair trade", she argues, which is "the principle" of her business (*Cell*, pp. 30, 10). Like a publican, her "company motto" is "do not ask for credit as a refusal often offends", and Delo also promotes social snobbery and class division in the prison (*Cell*, p. 13). Annie, a deceased Traveller who had previously shared her cell, was bullied by Delo as a "knacker" and an "awful eejit" (*Cell*, p. 21). Just as "Joe Shite" is rejected as a social contaminant in *The Liberty Suit*, Annie is said to have had a "smell", and is even, in similarly scatological tones, blamed for Delo's constipation (*Cell*, p. 22). Delo sat with a clothes peg on her nose as a way of tormenting Annie; like Joe, Annie ends her suffering by killing herself.

Delo also explicitly associates her bullying with politics: the Traveller's suicide reflected "a woman's right to choose" (*Cell*, p. 34). Equally, she is "proud" that crime is the election's "big issue"; parroting the lexicon of the Peace Process, she opines that "they want us kept off the streets", to "make them safe for peace and reconciliation" (*Cell*, pp. 37, 18).[52] But whereas Delo would vote for a "general amnesty ticket", Alice, another prisoner, is given the voice of authorial intervention, opining that she would not close prisons but "open a sight more of them" and "put the real crooks in", starting "with the politicians themselves" (*Cell*, p. 37). As in *The Quare Fellow* and *The Liberty Suit*, pillars of society are here indicted as part of a criminal and corrupt system. Delo's exploitation of her "family's" drug addictions is framed in the same linguistic terms as conventional commerce, suggesting an association between orthodox capitalist activity and the unorthodox, illicit "business" of crime.

Radicalising and reclaiming Marx's "refuse"

"This scum of the depraved elements of all classes, with headquarters in all the big cities, is the worst of all the possible allies. This rabble is absolutely venal and absolutely brazen."[53] This was Engels' advice to anyone who thought that the lumpenproletariat could serve in socialism's march to victory. In it, and in Marx's often caustic descriptions of the "dangerous classes", one can locate a broad social cohort to which the prisoners depicted in these plays could be said to belong, but in it too we find a problem at the heart of socialism and Marx.[54]

Meehan, Sheridan/Flynn and Behan's depictions of society's pariahs convey that it is difficult, if not impossible, to attach any consistent, singular paradigm of class to their fictional prisoners; Behan and Meehan are particularly eager to show the class divisions the prison's hierarchised relationships highlight. Marx viewed lumpens as categorically undifferentiated and benighted parasites on bourgeois society, and therefore he aligned them to middle-class (not working-class) interests. But that did not make them fully middle class either; rather, they were "the refuse of all classes", he argued, "swindlers, confidence tricksters, brothel-keepers, rag-and-bone merchants, beggars, and other flotsam of society".[55] This heterogeneous fusion would equate James Plunkett's indigent Rashers Tierney (with his chimpanzee and organ-grinder) with Roddy Doyle's Dolly Oblong (as affluent brothel-keeper): an odd class alignment indeed. And many modern Marxists would no doubt recoil in horror from easy equations between the "underclass" and the criminal underworld. Moreover, in this crudity, Marx's writing "reflects the morality of his times", Lydia Morris argues: "Here in the lumpenproletariat we are presented with an entirely blameworthy, immoral and degenerate mass, a category which differs from the surplus cast off by the industrial machinery of capitalism, standing apart from the 'real workers' of the proletariat."[56]

But it was Marx and Engels, after all, who retrieved the term "proletarian" from ignominy. Dr Johnson had defined this word, in his *Dictionary* of 1755, as meaning "mean; wretched; vile; vulgar", and, as Peter Stallybrass notes, "the word seems to have had a similar meaning in France in the early nineteenth century, where it was used virtually interchangeably with *nomade*".[57] Marx and Engels thus transvalued a negative term, and the retrieval of "proletariat" was thus revolutionary in the true sense of the word: "They inverted the meaning of the term, so that it meant not a parasite upon the social body, but the body upon which the rest of society was a parasite."[58] For this reason, the *lumpen* and the proletarian perhaps have something in common.

The prison plays examined here strive to explain the debasement of a pariah social cohort in terms of broader social culpability. They suggest an alternative way of understanding criminals, not as a distinct mass – or a heterogeneous class – but as a reflection of the basic binary of working class and middle class, another part of capitalism's inescapable dynamic of class warfare. Behan's betting prisoners, Sheridan and Flynn's traders in mutual misery and Meehan's dealer in death all represent the worst individualistic tendencies of capitalism, but they do so, suggestively, in the ubiquitous symbolism of "business" and "trade" that the plays draw on – as fully fledged capitalists themselves. On the other side of the social divide are those prisoners like Dunlavin, Neighbour, Curley, Kava, Martha, Alice and Lila, whose capacity to engage in society has been diminished by the privations of capitalism, by the *crime* of economic inequalities. These suffering prisoners are represented as part of the general working class that society has failed, and just as Marx had redefined the proletariat as preyed upon rather than preying, these playwrights redefine their prisoners, more as *victims* of society's superstructure than offenders against it.[59] Changing, indeed "inverting", perspectives in this way is precisely what these plays are about. Estranging the mundane and everyday world, they correct what Marx himself termed the "camera obscura" of ideology, its capacity to misshape and distort the real powers at play in capitalist society.[60] The Quare Fellow may be a murderer, but, as Behan puts it, on the scaffold he will be "surrounded by a crowd of bigger bloody ruffians than himself" (*QF*, p. 101).

6
Return of the Oppressed: Sexual Repression, Culture and Class

In this chapter I will discuss issues of sexuality, culture and class with reference to two texts, Christy Brown's *Down All the Days* (1970) and Dermot Bolger's *The Journey Home* (1990).[1] I will show how these novels employ sexual repression as a metonym for cultural repression and advance this theme as a criticism of hegemonic norms. I will also outline the historical and cultural context out of which both works emerged and the relevance in particular of Ferdia Mac Anna's apposite and influential essay identifying a "Dublin Renaissance" in Irish literature.[2] My thesis here, as elsewhere, is that literature of working-class Dublin places that community in conflict with dominant cultural norms, expressing its alienation within the capitalist state through symbolism, form and the unearthing of submerged narratives from Irish history.

Sex and the "Dublin Renaissance": "Individual rather than state freedom"

In a seminal essay, Mac Anna identified an avant-garde of writers as the harbingers of a new Irish revival – and a new canonical genre – conceiving the term "The Dublin Renaissance" to describe their collective emergence. This revival was firmly grounded in experiential reality, he contended, and many of its rising stars would write slice-of-life depictions of working-class people and their communities. Starting with the "less-than-steamy sex" and "punchy hard-nosed" realism of Lee Dunne's *Goodbye to the Hill* (1965), a renewed "freshness and vitality" infused the city's literary scene. Its emphasis was on the hyper-local, individuated and anomalous narratives of those who confounded the expectations of a stultifying national culture. In their work, the "Renaissance" writers conveyed that liberation could be "redefined in terms of individual rather than state freedom".[3]

Identifying Dunne as progenitor, Mac Anna proceeds to delineate a chain of writers who wrote against the grain of rural dominance in Irish culture. He charts the emergence of a popular aesthetic. Dunne's liberal dose of ribaldry and down-to-earth reality suggests the kind of "anti-Kantian aesthetic" that Pierre Bourdieu propounds as quintessentially working-class, and this kind of writing reverberates throughout the "Renaissance" literature.[4] The importance of Dunne's work was both cultural and stylistic; Mac Anna relates, "that it was the first book we had read that dealt in a realistic and believable way with the realities of modern Dublin life".[5] His invocation of Dunne, James Plunkett, Heno Magee, Peter and Jim Sheridan, Mannix Flynn, Roddy Doyle, Paul Mercier, Dermot Bolger and Paula Meehan also suggests, although not explicitly, that there was a strong class bias to the "Renaissance". Rock band Thin Lizzy, Heno Magee's *Hatchet* and the work of the Sheridan brothers in theatre, fiction and film all contributed to a new aesthetic of "social consciousness", authentically relating the gritty realities of urban life.[6]

To this extent these writers paralleled developments in British working-class writing, particularly the disenchanted post-war work of "kitchen-sink" social realists such as John Osborne, whose *Look Back in Anger* (1956) seemed to answer the exasperated complaint of Arthur Miller that year, in *Encore*, that "British Theatre is hermetically sealed against the way society moves."[7] John Braine's *Room at the Top* (1957) depicted a sexually promiscuous young man of working-class origins inveigling his way into bourgeois England by seducing the daughter of a rich businessman. Alan Sillitoe's *Saturday Night, Sunday Morning* (1958) delved into the thoughts of another promiscuous and angry young man, Arthur Seaton, and issues such as abortion and marital infidelity. Nell Dunn's episodic *Up the Junction* (1963), with its casual sex and graphic depiction of abortion, caused a furore when it was screened as a television drama by Ken Loach.[8]

Notably, sex was to the fore on both islands in representing the fissures between orthodox, calcified, bourgeois cultural production and the characteristically more abrasive and experiential variety favoured by the working classes. But British society in the mid-century was progressing at a far greater pace than that of its near neighbour, not least as regards matters of sexual openness. John Messenger's 1960s study of the remote Inis Beag, in which he concluded that "probably the most prominent trait" of the island, and of the Irish personality generally, was "sexual Puritanism", found that this outward aversion to all matters sexual engendered a characteristic, inward psychological cycle of sexual fantasy and repression, and indeed this cycle features strongly in both of the novels with which this chapter is concerned.[9] In his 1966 study, *New Dubliners*, Alexander Humphries specifically identified such containment in city men, finding that, "though more open than the countryman on the subject of sex, [the city men] too feel that sex is somehow evil and suspect".[10] This puritanical frame of mind led to particular social evils, Tom Inglis argues, including violence, alcoholism and fanaticism.[11] Much of this experience found perhaps its most concrete expression in Ireland's infamous network of industrial schools, which virtually imprisoned thousands of working-class children.

As Diarmaid Ferriter illustrates in a recent study, institutional abuse was also heavily implicated in Ireland's pervasive "class discrimination", and when complaints were made about the treatment of children in state care, "the class background of inmates clearly affected the seriousness with which their complaints were taken", with those from "socially disadvantaged communities" suffering most.[12] But the industrial school was not just a place in which to contain social ills such as juvenile crime; it was, moreover, the most brutal expression of a class-inflected cultural apparatus of domination. It was not just another inevitable consequence of post-colonial poverty, but, as Ferriter argues, the work of "more calculated and sinister forces [...] who were obsessed with the visibility of those whose behaviour or existence challenged the notion of the Irish as more chaste, pious and respectable than people elsewhere".[13] As Paul Smith's depictions of slum Dublin in *The Countrywoman* (1961) and *Summer Sang in Me* (1975) or, for instance, as James Plunkett's romance between prostitute and vigilante in *Strumpet City* (1969) show, the place where this "visibility" of the unchaste was most likely to find expression was amongst Dublin's working class.

Ferriter indeed enlists Lee Dunne's often coarsely sexual novel version of *Goodbye to the Hill* (1965) in his analysis of how Catholic mores were on the wane in the 1960s, at least in the back seats of cinemas, and how this adulteration of Irish sexual purity had a curiously classed edge. Working-class boys, such as Dunne's roguish protagonist Paddy Maguire, would seek out "the load[s] of mots that were on the look-out for a good neck and a grope", although "to look at [these young women] in the queue you wouldn't think butter would melt in their mouths". For Dunne, the irony was not just the contrast between public propriety and lust let loose in the dark, but also that many of these girls would shun working-class boys like himself in the outside world. In the "three rows from the back" of the Stella cinema such class divisions disappeared:

> Publicans' daughters, policemen's daughters, girls from all over Rathmines and Rathgar and Terenure, girls who wouldn't talk to you if they knew you came from a place like The Hill. But they didn't know, they didn't even know your name, and they forgot their class consciousness, anyway, and opened their brassières for you in the darkness.[14]

Inferentially, these girls associated a more *risqué* Ireland with working-class life, in a furtive world where class differences melted away. The people Michel Peillon fashioned as a social and cultural "pole of differentiation in Irish society" were those most likely to embrace "foreign" ideas and eschew native insularity, as many of the works explored thus far have shown.[15]

It is unsurprising, then, that writers of working-class Dublin were developing a broader critique of conservatism in Irish society by returning its repressed sexual monsters to the forefront of literature. From Paul Smith's gritty portrayals of sex in *Esther's Altar* (1959), *The Countrywoman* (1961) and *Summer Sang in Me* (1975), through James Plunkett's questioning of church teachings on birth control in *The Circus Animals* (1990), to Peter Sheridan's challenge to social taboos in *Big Fat Love* (2003), sex and its suppression are employed to criticise a sclerotic culture more generally. Roddy Doyle also confronts the issue of pre-marital sex in *The Snapper* (1990) and uses sex to poke fun at nationalism in *A Star Called Henry* (1999), by having his protagonist, Henry Smart, make love amidst the making of war in the hallowed birthplace of the Republic, Dublin's GPO. The link between violence, psychological angst, social disease and repressed sexuality is a major conceit in both of the novels I assess in this chapter, and this link is shown to resonate within a larger body of writing of the working class. Brown and Bolger use it to develop a proletarian counterblast to state norms, to what Liam O'Flaherty had termed "the dour Puritanism of the young generation, arisen since the revolution".[16]

Cultural anxieties and reproduction in *Down All the Days*

Christy Brown delivers this counterblast in the form of an Oedipal rebellion against the old, sexually repressed world of his father, Patrick, whom he "never loved and often hated".[17] Brown's attitude to the paterfamilias, and the cultural zeitgeist he represents, evokes a strange and symbolic mixture of love and loathing in *Down All the Days*. He even figuratively *fathers* himself in the novel, depicting his coming-of-age as artist, as we shall see, in a self-induced "birth". The curious manner in which Brown fictionalises his own childhood in novel form (just as Dunne does in *Goodbye*) is indeed an expression itself of a rejection of reality and, implicitly, of the legacy of his father's generation.

A major conceit of the novel is its use of sex and reproduction as metaphors for artistic fecundity, while sexual repression is correspondingly associated with perversion, mental angst and violence. Brown charts the beginnings of his aesthetic consciousness – in a world with which, as a severe cerebral palsy sufferer, he cannot communicate – to his emergence as artist from a long, painful, but ultimately enabling gestation.[18] Throughout his story, which depicts childhood in a bustling working-class family, the Kimmage writer also links the rise of his own aesthetic, symbiotically, with his father's decline into death. While his art seeks to represent what is depicted as an authentic, historically grounded proletarian culture, he shows how, in order to render that culture veraciously, this artist as a young man must first flee the nets that have been imposed on working-class life.

Class consciousness and culture: "He sat entranced by it all"

Down All the Days, then, reflects both continuity and change in working-class Dublin, and despite his reservations about its ingrained conservatism, Brown also wishes to portray the cultural richness of the Dublin of his youth. His ambiguity echoes the preoccupations of writer and academic, Richard Hoggart, who critiqued mid-century changes in English working-class life in *The Uses of Literacy* (1957). Hoggart eulogised the cultural influences of his own upbringing, the "full rich life" – as he termed it – of working-class Leeds: the social networks of workplace and neighbourhood, the closely knit, familial feel of working-class areas and their pubs, working-men's clubs, typical sports, publications, interactions and vernacular.[19] His vision of an organically authentic proletarian culture undoubtedly resonates in Brown's reminiscences regarding the local fair, cinema, bookies, pubs, childhood adventures, sports, wakes, ballads and local history. And in this the Dubliner also illustrates his community's sense of an enduring tradition of proletarian counter-culture.[20]

The young protagonist of the novel, an autobiographical figure, is engrossed by his mother's sense of connection with the past, as she recalls the lore of the tenements, where, in a previous existence as eighteenth-century Georgian houses, "men had died violent deaths at the hands of patriotic assassins in the great upsurge of national identity and pride" (*DAD*, p. 53). Class consciousness, twinned with nationalist sentiment, is to the fore in these tales of an age "so genteel and exquisite for some, so brutally impoverished and unbearable for the vast majority of others" (*DAD*, p. 53–54). This sense of class is strong elsewhere in Brown, as when, in *Wild Grow the Lilies* (1976), Luke Sheridan – a working-class boy who becomes a journalist – is accused of becoming a "classless parasite", no longer "fitting in anywhere because you turned your back on your own people – !"[21] Such "fitting in" is integral to the communal life of *Down All the Days*. A shared sense of disadvantage inheres in verse and song, such as in this excerpt from a ballad regarding love thwarted by social inequality:

> For he was from the Rathmines district
> And I from James's Street
> And like the west and the far, far east
> Never the twain could meet. (*DAD*, p. 139)

Men link arms and sing "We'll Keep the Red Flag Flying High", and Father reminisces nostalgically about his trade-union hero, Jim Larkin. A communal kinship is stressed in the novel, with many scenes – like those of Maura Laverty's *Liffey Lane* (1947), or Pat Larkin's collection of 1960s short stories *The Coalboat Kids and Other Stories* (2007) – depicting the ready, genial social interaction of a working-class community (*DAD*, pp. 48, 142).

On the Kimmage bus, passengers intermingle and banter in the kind of "dramatically intimate" and "almost unavoidably congested and familiar" mode that Brendan Kennelly identified when he termed Dublin "more a stage than a city".[22] A mouth organist on the bus entertains with "Mexicali Rose", while a "bearded youth" starts to tearfully recite "My Dark Rosaleen" (*DAD*, p. 227). Amongst other spontaneous entertainments are two elderly men discussing poet James Clarence Mangan as a "turkey-faced woman" who shares her whiskey with other commuters (*DAD*, pp. 227, 228). They carry to the suburb the community culture of the tenements, where, as Laverty described it, "all the families made one family".[23]

Participatory street culture appears also in the antics of working-class boys in the carnival and cinema, just as it does in Dominic Behan's memoir *Teems of Times and Happy Returns* (1961), Lar Redmond's *Show Us the Moon* (1988), and Billy French's *The Journeyman: A Builder's Life* (2002). The uproarious, bustling exuberance of the movies is captured in one long passage of poetic enjambment, describing a "long beehive, serpentine rows of lumber-suited, short-trousered, butt-smoking boys [that] wound sinuously up the narrow sideyard of the picture house [...] a surging, elbow-digging throng of barracking boys whistling, cat-calling, jostling, sly-pinching" (*DAD*, p. 42). But even as they are immersed in the "vicarious" entertainment of the silver screen, the activities of "slapping, clapping, whistling and applauding", with "fierce yells of encouragement and glee when there was shooting" and "loud boos and catcalls when there was kissing", all form a greater part of the communal diversion (*DAD*, pp. 43, 44). The spillage of cinematic violence into real life vividly culminates in fisticuffs when Mr Brown assaults a notoriously vicious usher, in the manner of boxer "John L. Sullivan" (*DAD*, pp. 45–46). Although the spectacle of mass culture captivates, it is their ability to make a participatory, social occasion of it that characterises its sense of fun for these boys, questioning the left-Leavisite concerns of Marxian scholars, typified by Hoggart or the Frankfurt School (Theodor Adorno and Max Horkheimer), about the supposedly corrosive influences of mass culture on working-class cohesion. Brown presents a local culture that is enriched by mass culture and it is difficult, in this context, to sustain R. Brandon Kershner's contention that "the vitality of Dublin's workers is drained in drink and brawling" in the novel.[24]

Lively parties, such as that after the protagonist's sister Lil gives birth, punctuate the social scene of Kimmage life with nights of song and communal engagement. The hordes of alliteratively "gobbling, guzzling, swearing, singing, shouting, bawling, calling" locals entertain with spoon playing, bawdy horseplay, recitations, song and gossip – hardly a loss of "vitality" (*DAD*, pp. 89, 89–99). Class consciousness is again stressed, in decidedly Lloydian, subaltern ways: in verse and song they identify with "the ubiquitous underdog, the worm that turned, the berated beggarman roaming the streets with flapping uppers and bleeding feet" (*DAD*, p. 98). Moreover, the emphasis on experience and usefulness, whether in extolling political values or in creating communal fun, correlates with Bourdieu's identification of working-class culture with aesthetics that "perform a function" or have "an ethical basis".[25] This experientially linked realm of cultural exuberance thrives alongside modernisation, informing some of the most poetic passages of the novel.

However, there is an ambiguity also in Brown's inheritance of working-class traditions, hinted at in the symbolic link between his own work, as artist, and that of his father, as builder. Brown portrays the labour of the skilled tradesman dubiously, with a conflicted sense of both affection and fear. He regards his father's "large, loose, knuckle-jointed, work-roughened hands", tellingly, with "terror and yet a strange burning unnameable longing". Like Seamus Heaney, who draws an evocative parallel between his father's digging for potatoes and his own symbolic "digging" for knowledge in the eponymous poem ("Digging" [1966]) – or Thomas Kinsella, who draws inspiration from the discovery of his father's tools with their almost alive "soft flesh", which endures after the elder man's death in "His Father's Hands" (1979) – Christy parallels his writing with the physical labour of Patrick Brown, imagining:[26]

> those hands alert and agile with the bricklayer's trowel and chisel [...] magically moulding a patchwork pyramid of cemented rectangles to enclose the lives, loves, labours, passions, despairs of innumerable strangers; those master craftsman's hands turning deserts of empty spaces into jungles of human dwellings. (*DAD*, p. 130)

Awe of the "master craftsman", with his "patchwork pyramid", is powerfully redolent; it lauds his diurnal achievements, links them with hallowed ancient art, and also hints at the ambitions of Christy's own aesthetic – his parallel "moulding" of material to "enclose the lives, loves, labours" of "innumerable strangers". Like Heaney, with his metaphor of the "digging" pen, Brown intimates a sense of continuity with his own family tradition of labour, invoking also potent signifiers of class in trowel and chisel. However, that this analogy incites "terror" in the young Brown is also revealing. If his father represents something he seeks to emulate, he also symbolises something Christy deeply fears.

Catholic guilt: "Blissful burning melting of will"

Where both Patrick Brown and Irish society meet on the figurative plane of the boy's emotions is in their dual role in repressing the young Christy's sexual feelings, inducing expressionist, Freudian, dreamlike bouts of neurosis throughout the book. Brown posits this repression as the locus of more generally regressive, conservative tendencies and thus shows how the habitus of working-class Dublin impacts on his own agonised development. For Patrick's generation, sexuality is something of a curse, "so bloody unfair" (*DAD*, p. 185). Its result, the scatter of children about him, is more to be endured than enjoyed, evidence of "God taking it out on him just because what he had down there between his legs was warm and real and alive and not entirely useless" (*DAD*, p. 185). This libidinally induced misery, he knows, is also partly the result of his own class position; the unmanageably large family is inextricable from "the way the poor people live and they say the grace of God shines on us each time we make a child" (*DAD*, p. 185). Sex and poverty, along with religion, have conspired to destroy his and his wife's lives, he ruminates: "Poor bloody him. Poor bloody her [...] There was this wildness in him that got in the way of everything [...] crucifying him with a blood-red, beer-black, sperm-thick uproar" (*DAD*, p. 185).

In Lar Redmond's *Emerald Square* (1987), he describes this era of Catholic containment and its effect on working-class women who are told, despite dire poverty, to "obey your husband and multiply in the sight and love of our dear creator".[27] Maura Laverty also ironised Irish society's attempts to deny sexuality by depicting how tenement children were forced to pretend that they didn't know anything about sex, or reproduction, even as their mothers approached labour. "This hush-hush policy in defence of innocence was always put into fullest operation when a mother's time became due [...] it was an unwritten rule that all these signs and portents" – including the mother's bump – "should be ignored". Such feigned innocence was ironic, "living as they did", in claustrophobic, overpopulated poverty, where children knew all about sex from an early age.[28] As Neville Thompson's Jackie fumes, in *Jackie Loves Johnser OK?* (1997), "God's wish" was the dictum that impelled women of a previous generation to have larger families, but it was also "God's wish that none of us ever had a pair of trousers with an arse in them. God's wish that Santy always brought us broken toys. Some wish."[29] Georgina Hambleton has observed how Christy Brown saw this "poverty lock his family and himself, especially his father, in a social jail cell".[30]

In embracing his sexuality and the experiential world it is part of, Brown thus also rebels against the underlying religious and cultural influences that confined his family to a life of struggle. His imagery continually illustrates an almost instinctual refusal to internalise "the appalling messages of society or the Church", as Nancy J. Lane terms it.[31] One early passage, at the local fair, where his brothers and friends find adolescent pleasure in the pornographic images of a "picture box", suggests the crucial role sexuality will have in the author's aesthetic development. He is "utterly absorbed in watching" a woman undressing rhythmically, which is initially depicted as a pure, even *high*, artistic experience – "melodic, like a ballerina", a "Picasso-like distortion of reality" – but repression, fear and shame are never far away (*DAD*, pp. 8, 9). The woman's gyrations arouse the protagonist, triggering an illicit memory, which, "before he could grasp it, identify it, it darted away, back into the subterranean cave where such things remain hidden most of the time" (*DAD*, p. 9). Despite the flamboyant sexual horseplay of the boys, "winking and making obscene signs with their fingers", the imperative of keeping "such things" "hidden" is omnipresent (*DAD*, p. 7). Christy's tormented recollections of glimpses of his teenage sister in their cramped bedroom resurface with "painful, ecstatic, guilty feelings" and, in a "haze of anguish and pleasure", the boy's inevitable arousal is unspeakable, unprintable, and only intimated in the reactions of the others about him, accentuating his acute "shame and guilt" (*DAD*, p. 15). His juxtaposition of the *higher* inclinations, invoked by Picasso and the ballet, and the *lower* inclinations, of sex and voyeurism, is of course subversively carnivalesque in itself, for "the denial of the lower, coarse, vulgar, venal, servile – in a word, natural – enjoyment [...] implies an affirmation of the superiority of those who can be satisfied with the sublimated, refined [...] pleasures forever closed to the profane". Such a separation of *high* and *low* culture fulfils "a social function of legitimating social differences".[32] But Brown's consequent feelings of "rage" and "betrayal" are tellingly the "only clear articulate thing left in him" (*DAD*, p. 15). His art and his "articulation" emerge from his struggle with these "lower emotions".

Just after Brown has depicted his protagonist's terrible ignominy at the fair, he ironises the shameful spectacle by mischievously intimating Freudian sexual connotations in the religious symbolism all about him. Again we discern the carnivalesque interplay of the saintly and salacious. There is a conspicuously phallic obviousness in the local church's architecture, in which the "blue veined pillars of marble", which "rose steeply to the huge dome", infer subconscious sexuality's irruption through moral piety. Outside, the boy observes "moist fingers and fronds of moss twined around the gnarled barks of ancient trees" and "against the linen-white clouds of autumn the church spire glinted reddish in the sunset, sharp and slender as a pared pencil" (*DAD*, pp. 16, 17). Sexual repression only makes sexuality more pervasively, if subliminally, present in his thoughts, and it is notable that his unconscious projections take the form of a phallic creativity: in the architecture of the church, an "arrowhead" of life-sustaining sunlight, the fertile body of a tree, and the writer's tool, a "pared pencil" (*DAD*, p. 15).

When Brown relates his sins of "solitary dark communion with himself" through a series of contrite grunts in confession, a young priest advises the boy "to think of the Holy Virgin" whenever "bad thoughts" enter his head, but this injunction only serves to underscore the futility of sexual repression (*DAD*, p. 27). Inglis notes such "inculcation" of the "teachings of the Church" in twentieth-century Ireland, "through a series of strategies based on creating shame, embarrassment, guilt and awkwardness about sex".[33] Lar Redmond also explains how "a perfectly normal young man" growing up in the mid-century is made to feel like "some kind of sex maniac" because of "information via the Church".[34] But, in a redolent sexual dream, Christy's inherent sexual subversiveness conjures a seductive "Virgin Mary [who] kept coming and going all in her gown of Reckitt's blue" (*DAD*, p. 19). The association of Reckitt's, a brand of sky-blue-coloured washing soap for whitening clothes, accentuates the contrast between religious sanitation and its unintentional effects.[35] Such iconoclastic sacrilege is repeated, for example, in Gerard Mannix Flynn's James X's recollection of his first sexual arousal in a Christian Brothers' institution, when he "fought hard to get the image of Holy God and Mary and Joseph out of [his] head" as he "began to stroke [him]self", or more grotesquely, in Dorothy Nelson's *In Night's City* (1982), when Sara's abusive father places a picture of the Sacred Heart over the bed in which he molests her.[36]

Brown's iconoclasm achieves a similarly sacrilegious register when one of his dreams transfigures a "fat, simpering" breastfeeding neighbour into a symbolic vision of religious iconography, "with a knitting needle stuck through her huge bare breast and drops of blood oozing out of it instead of milk" (*DAD*, p. 37). This warped deformation of the Virgin of the Seven Sorrows – with her heart depicted as a symbol of persecution, pierced by swords – encodes another subversive message.[37] The "knitting needle", symbolising creativity, is turned perversely on the woman herself. It sears through her breast, a source of sexual attraction and reproductive sustenance, producing blood instead of milk. The tortured Virgin is transformed into an image of warped sexuality and perverted creativity, and Catholicism's most vaunted icon of female chastity becomes a motif for sexual angst. *À la* John Messenger's 1960s study, the more Christy attempts to deny his sexuality, the more of an obsession it becomes; his thoughts are consequently suffused with guilty and violent horrors.

Exorcising Old Ireland: "Cry and be cleansed"

Christy is continually tempted and tormented by satanic forces, devils "dancing around him, their bodies writhing grotesquely, their private parts hanging and swaying lasciviously and hideously" (*DAD*, p. 63), yet these images also chart a cultural and aesthetic pilgrimage. When a she-devil displays her pubic hair, her groin area also appears as a "flaming arrow [...] like a little goat's beard", the recurrent "arrow" symbolism (of needles, spears, obelisk, church spire and pencil) suggesting a journey, pointing somewhere (*DAD*, p. 61). As Kershner notes, the invocation of the goat can also be taken as one of many allusions to Joyce and the terrifying "lecherous goatish fiends" haunting Stephen's dreams in *A Portrait of the Artist as a Young Man* (1916); it hints also at the kind of artistic emergence that Joyce's *künstlerroman* conveyed.[38] Explicitly, Brown shows that these dreams emerge from his Freudian unconscious, as the return of his repressed desires, for "a dream is just as real as the five fat fingers on my hand or the hair growing out of my nose holes [...] merely the irrational and totally unbound side of reality. It is, if you like, the absolute reversal of the external experience" (*DAD*, p. 195). This authorial intervention finds a corollary in his poem "Multum in Parvo" (1971), in which a sexually liberated woman is associated with mental health: "She has enough to carry her [...] no neurosis complex / believing religiously in sex."[39] Here, sexual liberation is linked with mental well-being; in the novel, the protagonist's contrasting sexual repression is linked with deranged dreams. But this repression is also tellingly associated with the social ill-health of his father's generation.

In the same dream, the spectre of Christy's "father's face", a "large thorny murdered head", invoking the crown of thorns on the crucified Christ, enacts the climax of a rape fear, as a "muscular forearm" appears, "gripping a white-hot poker with pulsating circles of heat extending halfway up its length" (*DAD*, p. 195). In its ghostliness, it also brings to mind Joyce's theme of the false father in *Ulysses* (1922), particularly in the novel's many references to Shakespeare's *Hamlet*. As he feels the phallic poker "embedded in his flesh", Christy hears his father's words hailing him: "My son breathes in me as I in him. Brave, oh brave. He never uttered a whimper" (*DAD*, pp. 195, 196). Symbolically, the author's dread of what amounts to a symbolic rape in this interlude is also a perceived violation of personal integrity to be committed by his Christ-like father and, by extension, a tyrant Christianity. The boy fears that he will become as one with his father, and by extension the Catholic orthodoxy he obeys, breathing "in me as I in him". Linking sexuality, sin and silencing – "not uttering" – it is in the oblique symbolism of horrific dreams that Brown's anxieties about Irish life find their most graphic expression.[40]

Patrick is associated with sexual and emotional repression, inverted moral prurience and misogyny throughout the book. His hatred of women, in its utter barrenness, is portrayed as the antithesis of his son's creativity. Lil's shame at her pregnancy, feeling "awkward" around her brothers, conveys how reproduction is taboo in the household (*DAD*, p. 176). Patrick blasts that his daughter "couldn't keep her legs shut", despite her apparent chastity (*DAD*, p. 71). Further imagery suggests that Lil's sensuality is "cropped" by Patrick's oppressiveness.[41] Lil's "fine dark under-hair" gives the protagonist "a peculiar throb of pleasure", and symbolically it seems "cruel and barbaric when later she shaved her armpits with Father's safety blade" (*DAD*, p. 101). Violence against women is also a recurrent feature of domestic life in his household – a fact entirely omitted from *My Left Foot* – and, as such, a fact that Brown had surely found difficult to represent in the memoir's sanitised form.

However, when Christy ventures to glimpse inside his father's mind, he discovers an essentially pathetic vulnerability behind the oppressive, macho façade of a man who was, despite his son's loathing, "a very real person indeed".[42] The elder Brown beseeches himself to cry, but fails to, lacking "the gift of tears": "Oh cry, damn you. Cry and empty yourself of the hard dried-up concealed grief lying in your heart like dead blood. Cry and be cleansed, be purged [...] for some unnameable thing unnameably lost down all the speechless years" (*DAD*, pp. 189–190). It is no coincidence that this excerpt contains the first coded reference in the text to the novel's title. Father's internal monologue is in fact an imagined dialogue from son to father, a painful wishing away of his father's emotional and expressive shortcomings, his "unnameable" loss of communication, "down all the speechless years". As his virility ebbs, Father considers bitterly his pathetic envy of the female body: "A wide lonely landscape pitted with hidden ravines [...] A woman's body the endless plain over which a man strayed all his life and sometimes lost himself. Theirs the power and the glory, the triumphant pain" (*DAD*, p. 191). This longing is expressed in terms not only of his loss of sexual potency, and his loss of words, but also as an absence of femininity. The elder Brown's rage towards his wife is fuelled by jealousy and fear; he has wasted years "raging against her tenderness, her knowledge of him, the terrible innocence and clarity of her through which he saw finally his own utter weakness" (*DAD*, p. 191). The "cascade of senseless violence" against women in the novel is something of a "God-given duty" for men of his background, but repressing women is also about repressing a hidden aspect of his own identity (*DAD*, pp. 68, 69, 191). The real problem with his wife is that she exposes a lack, "probing to the final level below which lay nothing but the dense dark and desolateness of self" (*DAD*, p. 192).[43]

In this regard, Patrick articulates a barren conception of reproduction, thinking that "a deeper part of" a man's vitality is lost with each new child, that "each kid that came kicking and bawling into the world took a part of you with it, made you less and less, weaker and weaker as a man" (*DAD*, p. 181). Seeing a "nest of baby mice" that makes him "bloody sick", he reflects nauseously on his children, "nothing but glistening lumps of boneless raw flesh. Rabbits. Mice. Rats. Kids." In horribly pouring "the scalding contents of his billycan over [the mice], almost hearing them bleat", he repeats his visceral fear of creation and new life – linking it again with his fear of women: "take away the womb and you're okey-dokey" (*DAD*, pp. 181, 182). This rejection of the corporeal and the sexual is reiterated by the Matt Talbot character in Thomas Kilroy's *Talbot's Box* (1973), in which the Dublin "workers' saint" adheres to the biblical concept that the body is a "garment of shame", which "shall be cast off'n there will be no more male'n female".[44] One of Dorothy Nelson's characters, the physically abused Esther, suggests a similarly besmirched conception of sexuality in her constant characterisations of sex and reproduction as degraded and filthy; her child's "first stirring" in the womb representing "filth and dirt inside".[45] Patrick Brown's repression of sexual feeling, his author-son shows, is also a stifling of fecundity and, metaphorically, creativity. In this, Christy echoes the concerns of the later O'Casey with a barren and joyless Ireland.

Sex and aesthetic emergence: "Show us the way to go home"

It is therefore fitting that Brown's literary coming-of-age is represented from within the same lexicon of sexual reproduction, as a "birth". He dreams of a giant pregnant woman, whose stomach is "transparent, like a sheet of plateglass", and inside he sees "the unborn infant curled up within her" (*DAD*, p. 199). The child is "shaped like a question mark" – a metaphor for his own questioning (which he uses several times) – the impetus behind his art.[46] The face staring out at him, "to his unique surprise", is his own, and this metaphor of vaginal emergence is employed also in another dream, during a real-life surgical operation, in which the boy is "crawling down a long, dark tunnel of pain" where "the walls seemed about to collapse, to fold in upon him; everything seemed to be breaking up, dissolving, disintegrating; he seemed to be stuck, submerged in a sort of gum mucilage" (*DAD*, pp. 199, 37). Both images correspond with his infantilised state as a cerebral-palsy sufferer, unable to talk, emitting only "mumbled grunts and semi-said words", expressing himself – in his own disdainful words – with "twisted ugly faces [...] like a pig" (*DAD*, pp. 27, 60). His envisaged rebirth, he suggests, is also about articulation.

As Christy descends into the flames of hell in another dream, he can only make "grunting noises", prompting laughter from ubiquitous devils, who mockingly request that he make "more funny noises" (*DAD*, pp. 62, 63). Disability becomes a symbol of personal and cultural struggle. As Kershner attests, "the protagonist's immobility becomes the perfect metonym for the paralysis of everyone surrounding him. If he is reduced to primal grunts and uncontrollable bodily reactions, so to a degree is everyone else in his world".[47] The symbolism of the sin book in Chapter 10, when "red Indians" and "glowing little devil-figures" dance around as his sins are disclosed from a text, conveys Christy's fear of being textualised by others – by priests, doctors, nurses, neighbours and his father, who impose their views upon him throughout the novel (*DAD*, p. 62). Against this fear, Christy discovers his literary voice, his vocation to speak, not just for himself, but for others, for those he "fishes" for in a dream, caught in "huge barbed-wire-strung nets in which [...] human infants wriggled and squirmed in lieu of fishes, their soft pink limbs plucked asunder and harpooned by the dagger ends of wire" (*DAD*, p. 210). The author himself is a Christ-like proselytiser, a fisher of men.[48] In the dream, trapped babies implore someone to lead them, to "show us the way to go home" (*DAD*, p. 210). They beseech their saviour to write the stories of those who lie under the "black engraved lettering" of tombstones, the victims of textual tyranny: the boy is asked to tell "the dull short histories of those who lay recumbent beneath them [...] revealing the closed little volumes of their lives" (*DAD*, p. 212).

Brown suggests his role in unearthing the submerged narratives of those precluded by history, just as he yearns to reach out artistically, to "share a single intense moment of his existence with" his family: "as long as he had known the moment, stepped over the threshold, savoured the warmth, touched their uniqueness with his own, free of the muteness that chained him" (*DAD*, p. 118). He senses his community, his family, calling for representation in literature; that which was "tiresomely real" can be "made dream-like", he envisages, "the dream descending and putting on ordinary garments, an ordinary face, dancing on ordinary feet, beckoning him, saying there was no longer need to hold back from the loud laugh and lusty stamp of careless life loving". The social image and modernist aesthetic pilgrimage are part of the same artistic journey, he implies.

Brown's repetition of "ordinary" here infers the predisposition of his art, his desire to share in the experientially linked world about him, "that he might enter their dusty bellowing arena, partake of their bread, share their rough warrior kit, their brawling, bruising, belligerent world" (*DAD*, p. 123).[49] In another late reverie, a climactic epiphany, he conceives this fusion in an image of classical art. Set in a Grecian courtyard, an enlivened marble statue of a woman, a "naked female figure, resting on elbow", with "a laurel crown girding the smooth forehead", is the quintessence of his woman-as-creativity conceit. She also invokes the sites of origin for Eurocentric high art (in ancient Roman and Greek cultures), and its connotations of permanence, which modernist art often celebrated (*DAD*, p. 207).[50] But Brown's vision of the sublime, like that of the earlier "pyramids", is suggestively set in his native city – what seems to be the Docklands and quays area of the inner city where his family originated – near a "compact toy-like train", "tall blackened roofs of factories, warehouses, churches, the squat flattened domes of gasometers, the phallic spires of electric pylons" (*DAD*, p. 207). Juxtaposed with a panoptic vision of the urban, industrial modernity of working-class Dublin, the statue surveys "the grit and grime and gangrene of living". The antithesis between the two is emblematic of a dialectical conflict between the urge for individuality and transcendence in modernism and the mechanised, urban experience of modernity. Christy associates his aesthetic vision with revered cultural antiquity, but inflects it with his desire to represent ignored urban reality, suspending his focus between the sublime and the social. Before the "unseeing, all-seeing, the unparalleled eyes" of the statue, which "gazed far out beyond his own fitful little life crackling dully inside him like a damp fuse", he begins the process of self-articulation (*DAD*, p. 208): "And he heard his voice, his words, moving like deep waves within him. 'Who are you? Where am I?'" (*DAD*, p. 208). In her "all-alive and lifeless perfection", the statue represents a paradox of aesthetic practice; she symbolises not only the "lifeless" eternal verities of high modernism but also an "all-alive" art of the masses, "facing towards chaos" and the city "of industry" (*DAD*, p. 208). As John Fordham notes, "while there is a tendency [...] in modernist writing to privilege the individual will to isolation, to represent the self as socially transcendent, there is also a consciousness of regret, of nostalgia for what [...] has been painfully suppressed, not entirely forsaken and denied".[51] For Christy this dialectic leads not to the transcendence of sublime isolation, but to the raw reality of his community's urban environment.

Like the black hawks that clamour all about him, Christy enjoys a piercing, panoptic spectacle of Dublin, while suffering also the brutal restrictions of cerebral palsy, his and "their wings strapped cruelly to their bodies" (*DAD*, p. 209).[52] Film director Jim Sheridan's observation that talking to Brown was "like watching a 747 prepare for liftoff" is apt here; he was "a massive energy and presence at once grounded and struggling for flight".[53] Brown's dialogue with the statue, its representation of sexuality and its transcendent values of artistic excellence, represents this struggle for "flight", and his artistic emergence, in speech, is also emblematic of a broader cultural break with Irish mores. He hears his father's voice "rolling over the lost sandcastle years of his childhood like a giant breaker flinging aside the delicate debris of his dreams", but staring at his now-dead father before his funeral, the rebel son narrates that "nothing stirred inside him now save the need to be done" (*DAD*, p. 237).

Christy still fears the stifling sway of cultural restraint; the black tie that "lay coiled about his neck like a soft silk noose or a snake curling tighter", is "a burning scapula round his throat [...] lighting in his heart a tiny voiceless dread": the Catholic scapula is, paradoxically, associated with the satanic biblical snake (*DAD*, p. 238). But now, as the elder Brown begins his final journey, his son reveals also his final epiphany; a "light [is] snapped on inside his head" as "the negative side of reality flared suddenly into relentless black-and-white planes blazing into his mind" (*DAD*, p. 239). An earlier motif is resurrected in Glasnevin Cemetery – the ambiguous symbolism of phallic power in the "gracious stone obelisk pointing like a giant finger skyward under which reposed the broken bones of the man who had set this land of green fields and squalid cities breakneck to bitter freedom under the lash of his silver tongue" (*DAD*, p. 245). Dedicated to Catholic emancipator and patriot, Daniel O'Connell, this obelisk invokes again the symbolism of androcentric, Catholic cultural hegemony and its repressed sensuality that irrupts conspicuously in artistic form.

But this time the symbolism precedes scenes of pilgrimage and rebirth. It is Easter, Brown reminds us, and the plangent bells of the risen Christ toll "out over the risen city" (*DAD*, p. 248). Passing the "cold shadow of the obelisk", there is a sense that his life can only begin, can only "resurrect", by leaving behind his father and the past; the phallic building is also a "pointing" "finger". Brown obliquely recalls Zozimus, the famous, blind, Dublin street-poet Michael J. Moran (circa 1794–1846), in his reference to a "blind juggler of words and images" and the "gold plaque inscribed to the memory of a blind Irish poet" in a local pub, hinting at his own emulation of another disabled artist (*DAD*, pp. 250, 241). Joyce writes, in *Ulysses*, on the return journey from Dignam's Glasnevin funeral, that "it's the blood sinking in the earth gives new life", and after his visit to the same cemetery Brown feels, at the "long narrow last-supper table" in Brendan's Bar, that his own new life is emerging, Christ-like, from death (*DAD*, p. 251). The cognac he drinks is "anointing" his flesh, "with a fiery touch" (*DAD*, p. 243).[54] Despite the "titanic tyrannic tormented shape" of the elder Brown "throwing its ubiquitous shadow over his life", he looks at himself, ominously, through a "tankard by his side" and sees, in the last words of the novel, "his own face, thin as a hawk's and his eyes already voyaging, rising to meet the world" (*DAD*, pp. 254, 255).[55] Christy's "rising to meet the world" invokes Dedalus's declarative "welcome" to "life" and "the reality of experience".[56] The shadow of Brown's father's "tyrannic" shape is resonant also of Dedalus's "fear" of the Gaeilgeoir Mulrennan, "just returned from the west of Ireland", and the metaphoric resolution to a "struggle" with him "all through the night till day come, till he or I lie dead".[57] Brown, like his father, will encapsulate the lives of his fellow city-dwellers with his art, but, unlike his father, he will "build" on his own terms. In this "burial", the artist is "born", no longer "so much a cripple endeavouring to overcome his handicaps, but rather an adult faced with the far more intimidating problem of overcoming himself after his handicap".[58]

"To make people look up": Bolger's bleak suburbs

Dermot Bolger expresses similarly conflicted views of his native city, albeit with a more mordant inflection, in *The Journey Home* (1990). Bolger's vision of Irish life is riven with conflicting allegiances, polyglottal voices and an unremitting sense of the nation as a deeply divided society. As Ray Ryan writes, his "work is the most sustained attempt to thematise the divisions of country and city in the Republic", and these divisions are heavily inflected with issues of class.[59] Like Brown's novel, *The Journey Home* shows how sexual repression projects itself into disturbing psychological anxieties, and it also uses this theme to illustrate a broader social malaise: the subjection of Finglas's working class to a rural-centric, nationalist and corrupt bourgeois elite, whose sexual perversity is the symbolic outworking of their repressed humanity.

But Bolger's Dublin is less knowable than Brown's, less a community than a site of cultural and generational conflict. The difference between their cities marks a Hegelian break in the history of working-class Dublin. Lynn Connolly recalls the latter period in the life of a working-class suburb as one in which the notion of community began to break down. In her memoir, *The Mun, Growing Up in Ballymun* (2006), "apathy" "took over" the area's high-rise flats; "within ten years Ballymun had gone from being a model estate, filled with respectable families, to becoming a place where only the desperate wanted to live [...] somewhere that nobody seemed to care about any more".[60] As the narrator puts it in Bolger's 1999 novella, *In High*

Germany – ironically set amid the patriotic fever of the Euro 1988 soccer tournament – "Home? Where the hell was home for us any more?"[61] Whereas Brown had evidently enjoyed the authentic, organic working-class traditions he so enthusiastically documented, Bolger's characters come to loathe their cultural heritage. They live in an alienated, individualistic Ireland, one Bolger had documented in the dystopian *Night Shift* (1985), when, in a bus scene that seems almost a direct counterblast to Brown's depiction of the Kimmage bus camaraderie, Donal recalls how "two schoolboys had hurled a seat down the stairs, laughing at the top of their voices", but now "nobody looked up from their newspapers" and "nobody cared".[62]

Declan Kiberd identifies such a characteristic "bleakness of tone" in plays and novels of this period, and Bolger's *The Journey Home* compares strongly with Paul Mercier's play *Wasters* (1985), for instance, which articulates its desolate tale of petty crime, poverty and emigration in the dialogue of teenagers who socialise on waste ground at the edge of a council housing estate, where there is "fuck all to look forward to". [63] In Jim Sheridan's play of the mid-1970s, *Mobile Homes* (1976), Shea, his principal character, watches aghast as his father shatters a mirror to pieces, invoking again the ubiquitous trope of mirror to nation in Irish literature, this time to represent a young generation that is "shattered into a thousand fucking pieces all over the kip".[64] In James McKenna's mid-1970s poem "Crisis", he too asked "what has gone out of men?"[65] These decades are typified in writing of Dublin's working-class as a time of worsening social, economic and cultural malaise, and in this regard, *The Journey Home* is typical of its milieu. The novel captures the general mood of a country "mired in an economic depression from which there appeared no possibility of escape".[66] It harnesses and exaggerates social ills, representing working-class Dublin as a profoundly alienated social space, and it precipitates also the emergence of revelations about institutional abuses and political malpractice whose shock waves are still reverberating throughout Irish society.

Church-state abuse and social class

When the report of the Irish Republic's Commission to Inquire into Child Abuse (CICA) was published on 20 May 2009, its writers' mammoth achievement was commended by the seismic effect it had on public consciousness. Six months later, the furore caused by the CICA (or "Ryan") Report was compounded by the release of the Murphy Report into child sexual abuse in Dublin. Both investigations, and the many years of research of which they were the culmination, were of course preceded by many other works, of fiction, drama, historical research, poetry, television production and biography, which incrementally took the lid off Ireland's most pernicious can of worms.[67] Taken as a historical epoch, this process of disclosure and excavation became an integral part of the Irish *Zeitgeist* from the 1990s, and has left the country irrevocably changed. As we have already seen, part of that change has been the realisation of how class and institutional abuse were intertwined. *The Journey Home* interweaves the question of class antagonism in Ireland with the country's inveterate tolerance of institutional sexual abuse. In doing so the novel presages the discoveries of recent years.

While it may seem peculiar to associate such recent events with a novel that has been, for many years, firmly embedded in the canon of Irish writing, these revelations of the past revise the history of the times Bolger was writing about in such a radical way that they recommend the reappraisal of not only this and many other literary works but also of many aspects of Irish historiography since the foundation of the state. In what is often regarded as Bolger's most daring work, he had sought, in *The Journey Home*, to jolt the public into a new awareness of hidden abuses. For this reason, and because the novel has been so heavily criticised for its monstrously surreal and exaggerative depictions of official misconduct, a new reading now seems a salutary exercise.

It was not that the Murphy and Ryan reports' revelations of widespread institutional and clerical abuse were entirely new, but that their collation in such a comprehensive form, supported by such rigorous and patient research, crystallised myriad tales of individual torment into a damning indictment of how those in power in Irish society had dealt with a problem they knew to exist but chose to ignore. The experience of survivors, their complex personal tales, was sutured into a single narrative, a forceful condemnation, by the revelation of many parallel sufferings, many similar stories of horror. But despite the ensuing feeling of collective expurgation, of a cathartic coming together of survivors in a fellowship of victimhood and defiance (as evidenced by the dramatic march of 10 June 2009, in which children's shoes were symbolically tied to the railings of Parliament Buildings), perhaps the most obvious commonality shared by these sufferers has received less attention than it deserves. Bolger had emphasised this key aspect of Ireland's hidden institutional abuses, as I shall show: the question of the victims' social class and its role in their collective torment.

A more personal and concrete example of the nature of the relationship between Mother Church and the children it mistreated most is captured in the vivid individual recollections of Christine Buckley, a well-known campaigner for abuse victims and herself a survivor of the St Vincent's institution at Goldenbridge, Dublin. In the wake of the Ryan Report, Buckley remembered how she and her fellow incarcerees suffered a surreal daily ordeal of ritualised cruelty:

> There was babies in Goldenbridge; there was babies turned upside-down, beaten to a pulp because they cried. There was babies strapped to potties and we, as children, were forced to push their rectums up [...] While we starved and ate rabbits' faeces, we now find today the surplus that these

abusers were making [...] There was a monkey in Goldenbridge – Jenny. That monkey lived in a palace as far as we were concerned: the nuts, the bananas, the whole lot. And that monkey was taken on that one's [a nun's] shoulder and brought into the dining room each day, masturbating and jumping on top of all of us, and if we budged we were beaten stupid. They had a dog, Tusa, who took lumps out of children's legs; it was ... words will never, ever express what they did for us.[68]

Such hideous imagery might seem so outlandish as to meet with immediate incredulity, if it was not borne out by so many other testimonies – and this phantasmagoric, almost surreal aspect of Ireland's stories of institutional suffering also plays an important role in the coming discussion of Bolger's novel. Buckley's experiences seem less unreal when paralleled with those of many of the 170,000 other former residents of such institutions, some of which the *Irish Examiner* presented in a dramatic front-page display. One survivor's account reads: "I overheard somebody say that my mother had died the night before. When I asked about it, I was ignored and dismissed." Another recalls: "We were all lined up naked and slapped in the face a lot. We had to drink water from toilets and were all washed in the same bath water." Yet another remembers, most shockingly: "I was tied to a cross and raped whilst others masturbated at the side".[69] Such appalling memories paint a picture of nightmarish maltreatment across the institutions involved.

But Buckley and others also stress that there was a broader, systematic, socio-economic aspect to the abuse, which reflected general power relations and class interstices across the society that tolerated it. Buckley conveys how the religious orders themselves were acutely aware of this power imbalance and relied upon it as a justification for their behaviour. A "very deep personal letter" she sent to her former abuser in 1984, seeking an apology or an explanation for the years of mistreatment she suffered, elicited a very revealing response from an unrepentant nun:

What she said to me on the phone floored me to bits [...] She told me that I was going to end up like my mother, who was "in a room with a red lamp", and she was very surprised that hadn't happened to me. In other words, that's what they said to us in these hell holes – that our mothers were prostitutes. She told me my father didn't work *on* the buses in CIE, he worked *under* the buses [...] "You remember, you're third-class citizens".[70]

Framed in such explicitly classed terms, the nun's feeling of empowerment vis-à-vis her accuser again correlates broadly with the central findings of the 2009 reports, and Fintan O'Toole is one of the few commentators in recent times to highlight this aspect of the abuse – the matter of social power, how it was distributed in Irish society and how it affected and explains the experience of survivors. With the degree of outside knowledge regarding what was going on in the institutions for decades, O'Toole reasons that "the internal culture of brutality should not have survived". It did so, he suggests, for three basic reasons, "power, sex and class":

> The perpetrators abused children because they could. They drew that power from the immense stature of the church, its ability to command deference and to intimidate dissenters. The majesty of the church became, in the hands of the abusers, a cloak of impunity.[71]

Attesting to Ferriter's analysis above, however, this mystifying social power was derived from something more fundamental than subservience inspired by religious devotion:

> This was a society in which the middle classes expressed their insecurity about their own status in a hysterical contempt for the poor. The function of the industrial schools was to punish poverty. The great majority of the 170,000 children were incarcerated, not because they had committed any crime, but because they were categorised as "needy". The needy were dangerous. In society as a whole, the violent reputation of the institutions served as a general warning to the poor. Within the institutions, violence was justified on the basis that, in the words of one Brother in Letterfrack, without it "there would be chaos".[72]

Barbarity of this sort was thus excused by a draconian and perverse philosophy of social harmony; the anarchy of mindless violence was explained away by the perceived need for social control, rooted in the kind of hysterical "respectable fears" that Geoffrey Pearson identifies in British bourgeois discourse: ingrained fears "of imminent ruin, reprocessed and embroidered for generations", fears which rely upon "a cluster of themes bearing upon the production and reproduction of consent and social discipline among the working class".[73] The dehumanisation of working-class children was rationalised in Ireland within a more widely prevalent distaste for the "lower orders". "Children from working-class backgrounds were told their families were 'scum', 'tramps' and 'from the gutter'," O'Toole observes.[74] After all, girls like Christine Buckley would probably end up on street corners anyway, her abuser surmised.

Mary Raftery and Eoin O'Sullivan made this compelling point in their comprehensive 1999 study, *Suffer the Little Children*, in a chapter titled "The Myths". While many of the industrial schools have – at first glance innocuously – been categorised as "orphanages", they note that this misnomer harboured sinister, strategic intent. "The description of the children as 'orphans' was far more likely to elicit sympathy for both [the children] and their religious carers"; but very few of these children were actually orphans. Like O'Toole, they stress the other, more pervasive and sociologically manifest reason for which the children were incarcerated:

> The reality – namely that thousands of children were detained in a State-funded system essentially because their parents were poor – would not have produced the same levels of either sympathy or charity from the wider community. Had there been a proper understanding of the true nature of the system, [its basis in class,] it is likely that it would not have survived for so long [...] The orphan myth essentially meant that the obviously preferable option of giving that same funding to families to allow them to keep their children was never publicly debated.[75]

Raftery and O'Sullivan proceed to point out how the *real* orphanages run by religious orders mostly charged fees and catered for "the children of the middle-classes who had fallen on hard times". Furthermore, these institutions – which were sharply distinguished from the industrial schools sector in practice, if not in the popular imaginary – "served a very specific purpose in *maintaining a rigid class divide* between children from different backgrounds".[76] The industrial schools were "designed for the children of the poor, who were perceived as a threat to the social order"; they were never merely intended to contain the chimera of social disease, but rather to cloak the reality of a diseased social order.[77]

Bernard MacLaverty's *Lamb* (1980) is one of the most prominent examples of this broader consciousness in fiction, stressing repeatedly that "the whole system was totally unjust" and furthermore, that it had the "backing" of the "state".[78] As Michael R. Molino puts it, all of the evidence points to "a concerted effort of both Church and State to criminalise poverty, hide and punish the children of the poor, and exploit the young for commercial gain".[79] Thus class was not incidental but integral to the functioning of this system and, moreover, to the maintenance of the state in which it prospered. This capitalist interrelation between the vilified working class and the dominant bourgeoisie in Ireland, as well as the horrific sexual and social abuses it contained, is something Dermot Bolger was keen to elucidate at the onset of the "Robinsonian" era in Ireland, before it was popular or profitable to do so.[80]

Remembering to forget

Christine Buckley and her fellow survivors recall being told by professionals employed by the Church that they were suffering from "false memory", and it is this kind of pathological shovelling of uncomfortable truths under the sacristy carpet, on a wider, societal level, which prompted Bolger to write his most iconoclastic work. One of its characters, Katie, indeed repeatedly invokes the idea that "you do not allow yourself to remember" (*JH*, p. 19).[81]

The Journey Home hovers on the precipice between memory and fantasy, exaggeration and truth, but does so performatively, as a reflexive illustration of a surreal social context. Correlating with the monstrous display of church snobbery that Buckley recalls, the novel shows how the trinity of "power, sex and class" manifests itself in working-class Dublin.

Like Brown, Bolger illustrates how sexual repression projects itself into disturbing psychological anxieties, and he too uses this theme to illustrate a broader social malaise. Based in Bolger's home suburb of Finglas, "a country village populated by an influx of families from both the old city and the country, all in search of *Lebensraum*", *The Journey Home* portrays a divided and uncertain Ireland.[82] It tells the story of Hano, a young man from the area, his relationship with Katie, a young heroin addict, and his friendship with the charismatic Shay, another local youth, whom Hano comes to idolise. Charting the events leading up to and immediately following Shay's death at the hands of a local parliamentarian's son, the novel culminates in Hano's vengeful murder of the prominent politician's brother, the local corrupt businessman, Pascal Plunkett. The rest of the narrative charts Hano's flight from the authorities with Katie, illustrating their sense of homelessness – of being socially and culturally unmoored in an alien Ireland. Most of all, *The Journey Home* represents the political rot that was beginning to emerge in media revelations of the time, when "the sense that politics was a corrupt affair, peopled by self-serving members of the bourgeoisie" had "accumulated to public life".[83] Ferriter observes that the following decade saw the frequency of general public scandals escalate, heralding a "growing awareness of many of the failures in independent Ireland", and Bolger foreshadows this period of disclosure by illustrating the sense that Ireland's dam of secrets was about to burst.[84] In his novel *The Woman's Daughter* (1987), which concerns a Finglas girl born of an incestuous relationship and hidden by her mother from the world outside their home, Bolger ventured beyond the closed door of sexual taboos. In *The Journey Home*, his graphic images of sexual perversity are even more arresting, coagulating both major strands of media revelations – the sexual and the political – into a caustic indictment of the failures of Irish society.

Representing the repressed: "Both menacing and menaced"

An anecdote of the Plunketts' Machiavellian bid for political power in the 1960s is emblematic of middle-class Ireland's reconstitution of history to suppress the working class, a revisionism that Bolger later links with sexual containment. The fiftieth anniversary of the Easter Rising in 1966 – a landmark event in the history of the Irish Republic – is recalibrated as a landmark in the consolidation of corrupt business interests, "the making of" the Plunkett brothers, who comic-tragically take advantage of its outpouring of nationalist sentiment by having their ailing grandfather "dragged up" as an election gimmick (*JH*, p. 214). In *The Dead Republic* (2010), Roddy Doyle's republican hero sneers at the jubilee marches, in which men who failed to partake in the 1916 fighting nonetheless make use of the occasion to pretend they were there.[85] In *The Journey Home*, Eoin Plunkett, one of Henry Smart's contemporaries and an elderly war hero from Mayo, is deployed by his grandsons as evidence of their own supposed republican credentials. Although, as a "confirmed socialist", Eoin had "joined with Connolly's men" in the workers' Irish Citizens' Army – and later fought on the socialist side in the Spanish Civil War – the proletarian rebel is ironically enlisted as a form of cultural currency for his capitalist grandsons. Eoin's working-class politics are silenced by the opportunistic pair who, "each evening before they took him on their rounds of the estates" of Finglas, "would remove his false teeth so that the people mistook his tirades against the smugness of the new state for the standard pieties they expected" (*JH*, p. 214). Such cynical distortion of the past to suit the present is echoed again in Doyle's novel, where Smart is "show[n] off" as one of "the ancient activists, the man from song", a "living saint".[86] In Bolger's hands, the muzzled rebel grandfather is an equally cartoonish device, but he too is an emblem of the disaffection of the Republic's dispossessed, and of the alienation of rebels, like Lar Redmond's father in *Show Us the Moon* (1988), who had played their part in winning "freedom [...] all the freedom in the world to starve".

Redmond uses the analogy of Dáil deputies raising "a laugh by laying bunches of rhubarb, carrots and cauliflowers at Queen Victoria's statue on Leinster Lawn" to illustrate the growing gap between their tokenistic anti-Britishness and the material realities of Irish working-class life: these "jolly little offerings" would "have been swiped in two seconds had her statue been in the Liberties", he surmises.[87] O'Casey's disenchantment with the Free State echoes here again, his contempt for the supposed liberators in *The Plough and the Stars* (1926) who dismiss tenement dwellers as "slum lice".[88] Such ironic contrasts are central also to *The Journey Home*. Eoin Plunkett's legacy is repressed and revised to bolster his acquisitive, bourgeois grandsons' efforts to take power – in an analogy for the convenient historical revisionism conducted by the *nouveau* elites of Irish politics. But, poignantly, Eoin also dies "as the first bombs exploded on Derry's streets", underscoring both Ireland's failure to resolve colonial and class conflicts, and the ultimate folly of trying to repress the truth of the past (*JH*, p. 214). The episode evinces the central theme of the novel: that repression makes more monstrous that which it seeks to repress.

The Plunkett brothers – Pascal the politician and Patrick the businessman – who represent the alliance of both spheres in a mutually beneficial social pact, are utilised to link the social and political degeneracy of Irish life with its endemic culture of sexual repression. This repression is projected into all areas of society in the novel, which, like *Down All the Days*, plays out social problems on the psychological plain. Bolger associates "rural traditionalism" – which, as Conor McCarthy observes, is culturally "upstairs and implicitly dominant" in *The Journey Home* – with hidden sexual perversity.[89] And the brothers personify a monstrously Freudian "return of the repressed" in the twisted, violent and bizarre details of their sexual lives.

A rapacious gay sexuality is repeatedly associated with fear, danger and corruption. The Phoenix Park, a notorious meeting point for male prostitutes, is "dangerous at that hour when furtive men sought each other" and Hano recounts how, "often their footsteps would follow yours, you'd glance over your shoulder to see their eyes, both menacing and menaced" (*JH*, p. 149). This homosexual threat achieves its full realisation in Pascal's lust for Hano. Moving from the "veiled but unmistakable dropping of innuendoes", the older man's suggestive overtures culminate in a graphic and violent rape (*JH*, pp. 224–5). Having pinned Hano to the floor, Pascal then molests him, his "insistent, animal-like" voice repeating the lustful mantra: "I want! I want! I want!" (*JH*, pp. 225, 226). An extremely troubling scene follows, in which Pascal forces Hano to perform oral sex, while the latter feels "vomit about to rise" (*JH*, p. 226). And while this incident might seem an isolated horror, society's role in cultivating Pascal's perversity is emphasised some pages later. "Nobody ever let me be who I am. How could I …" he trails off (*JH*, p. 229).

Pascal proceeds to recall a homophobic attack he suffered on a building site, after a youthful gay liaison with another worker. He explains how the attack affected his mindset from then on: "That taught me Francis, taught me gentleness was a luxury for the likes of me." Accentuating the associations of capitalism and repression in the election episode, Pascal then links his own sexual repression with his success as a businessman: "I switched cities [after the attack], another site, worked my back off, rose to foreman, never let anyone see me weak again. Then I undercut, got contracts myself." (*JH*, 227) The sublimation of secret sexual feelings fuels a ruthless capitalist greed, Bolger suggests, and the mantra "I want! I want! I want!" encapsulates both. As Linden Peach notes, "menace, theft and violence are not simply signs of the underbelly of Dublin" in *The Journey Home*, "but interleaved with negative aspects of capitalism: greed, exploitation and selfishness".[90] By sacrificing his identity, Pascal takes what he "couldn't have by force", but spends the rest of his life trying to "to bury the poverty of his youth" (*JH*, pp. 230, 264).

This "burial" of powerful traumas – sexual and social – and its consequences, are paralleled with Pascal's brother Patrick's encounter in Amsterdam with Shay. There the politician feeds the youth to the point of gluttony in a restaurant and then pleads with his surfeited guest to "do it on me … [defecate] on my face, on my chest, please" (*JH*, p. 337). Graphically, Shay listens to Plunkett "squirm to get his face directly below" him in a bath (*JH*, p. 338). He has "sold" himself by engaging in the act (for which he was paid), he later tells Hano, and has "never felt clean again"; they both "carry the sins of the Plunketts" (*JH*, pp. 338, 339, 254). But this sub-plot scene also again works on a deeper level. The scatological act represents the politician's association of sex with humiliation – his need to confront repressed feelings of filth, weakness and abjection in order to become aroused. The Plunketts repress who they really are (grandsons of a working-class socialist, and gay), in order to achieve success in bourgeois society (as capitalist and politician). Repression of this kind, Bolger's symbolism infers, results in and emerges from a perverse society.

Hano's murder of his rapist is thus a cathartic act in the novel, which represents a release from the clutches of this sexual *and* social oppression. "Everything in his house made me feel unclean except the blood that was caking my flesh," Hano says, depicting the brutal slaying as a purgative liberation (*JH*, p. 384). The murder is also a figurative attack on the accumulations of affluence: "I started pulling out the suits and the neatly folded shirts and jumpers. I was filled with fury as I ripped them, as though his possessions were mocking me" (*JH*, p. 384). Hano also sets fire to the house, and, just as the earlier burning of his father's garden overgrowth reflected a rejection of the rural ideal, this later fire represents the young man's release from social trammels, hinted at by the "bondage magazines" that fall from Plunkett's bed, and remembered perhaps also in Pascal Plunkett's stare, "which seemed to say: *Soon I will own you too*" (*JH*, pp. 385, 163). Hano ultimately refuses to be owned, to be prostituted like Shay, and in doing so refuses subjection to the orthodoxies that the Plunketts embody. Juxtaposed with the subplot of Mooney, an office manager's sexual harassment of a young trainee, the story of Shay and Hano's abuse at the hands of the Plunketts is part of a caustic attack on the sham morality of bourgeois Ireland (see *JH*, pp. 301–311). As Shay comments, "when something is dying it rots all over" (*JH*, p. 366).

Shock tactics

For Bolger, this narrative technique – of correlating bizarre tales of sexual abuse with capitalist exploitation – is more about consciousness-raising than strict verisimilitude. Disdainful of Irish people's tolerance for political corruption, he recalls feeling compelled, on writing *The Journey Home*, to shock his readers into recognising a malaise that had been normalised – that they had come to accept: "As a writer I had to find a way to suggest [political corruption], to make people look up."[91] However, whatever sympathy one might have with this exasperation, it is notable that sexual perversion is, in the main, homosexual in the novel, and that homosexuality is repeatedly associated with political corruption and capitalist exploitation. True, at a more subtle level, there is a suggestion that Shay and Hano's "intimacy" is something more than friendship on a number of occasions – that Hano, in particular, is repressing unwanted feelings (*JH*, p. 5). A work colleague

questions, "are the pair of them bent or what?" and Hano's romantic characterisation of his relationship with Shay, which is "as close to love as I had
ever known", hints at something more than platonic friendship (*JH*, p. 95).
Shay is Hano's "hero", his "other half", but there is never an outright expression of romantic love, the suggestion being enough to rouse curiosity, the
omission enough to underscore the code of silence surrounding gay Ireland
(*JH*, p. 303). But at a time when "homosexual acts" were unlawful in the
Republic – and when many were actively campaigning for their decriminali-
sation – it is questionable if Bolger's consciousness-raising efforts were progressive in this regard.[92] Such reservations are compounded by the fact that
homosexuality is "a very rare theme in working-class writing", and Bolger
misses a rare opportunity indeed to treat it with the complexity and respect
it deserves.[93]

In representing Ireland's development from *"Gemeinschaft"* to
"Gesellshaft" – from organic to corporate community – Bolger's general failures of subtlety and coherence have indeed been criticised, by many commentators, as stylistic slips that diminish the strength of his tirade.[94] Declan
Kiberd sees "something overdetermined" in the novelist's attack, making it
"considerably less subversve than it sometimes took itself to be":

> In its underlying sentimentality about its youthful subjects as victims
> of social tyranny, it grossly exaggerated the malevolence and the impor-
> tance of priests, teachers, politicians. [95]

Despite Hano's advice that "it's a mistake to ever get sentimental", the
sheer emotionalism of Bolger's attacks on society's superstructure, throughout the novel, leaves his message seeming somewhat overcooked (*JH*, p. 329).
Patricia Craig summates that "at his best, Bolger is a forceful social critic, but
his portrayal [of Dublin in *The Journey Home*] might have been fashioned
with greater sharpness, less bludgeoning."[96]

Undoubtedly this text is surfeited with melodramatic sequences and over-
wrought symbolism. Bolger's didacticism is ever-present and often obtuse.
The control the Plunkett family exercise on business and politics in Finglas,
for example, reads like a bad conspiracy theory. Plunkett Auctioneers,
Plunkett Stores, Plunkett Motors, Plunkett Undertakers – "the crucifixion"
of Plunkett enterprise – plus, for good measure, their "name on every second
shop front", is a grossly exaggerated departure from any monopoly on commercial affairs in any Dublin suburb (*JH*, pp. 100, 313). Justin's (Patrick's
son's) depiction as "the angel of death" is clichéd; the "Nazi salutes" that
mock him behind his back are part of an inflated pattern of caricature (*JH*,
pp. 107, 108, 116). A comparison Bolger draws between young Dubliners
and victims of Nazism and fascism on a number of occasions in the novel
is equally belaboured – a "tasteless absurdity" (*JH*, pp. 15, 327).[97] McCarthy
argues that this "overblown polemical linkage of Irish state-nationalism and

totalitarianism" does the novel a disservice.[98] Pascal Plunkett is, indirectly at least, responsible for Hano's father's untimely death, as he is "afraid to go near a doctor [...] You know how Pascal Plunkett is about sick days" (*JH*, p. 150). The attack by gardaí on Shay is, inevitably and surreptitiously, orchestrated by the politician – and his death is Justin, Pascal's nephew's, handiwork. The Plunkett trio are the Prosperos of Finglas, a suburb refashioned as an autocracy; Hano's claim that "to hundreds like my mother, [Pascal] was a deity who controlled their lives" is patently outlandish (*JH*, pp. 263–264). Like a caricatured villain of the Boucicault variety, Pascal is even heartened to know that people with degrees are sweeping floors, leaving power to "just me and my kind now" (cue the villainous guffaw, *JH*, p. 192).

The outlook Bolger presents us with seems to lose "some of its impact because it is simply too exaggerated [...] it is too outrageous to be taken seriously."[99] His late and rather clumsy attempt to rescue the novel from accusations of homophobia, contrasting the good gays, as it were, with the bad gays (i.e. the Plunketts), is so cumbersome that it even exaggerates his own inflated insensitivity. Smuggling a "gay couple", who befriend Shay, into the text in a later chapter, Bolger relates, with contrived back-pedalling, that "watching the lads, relaxed and open as they leaned against each other on the sofa and laughed with Shay, it seemed impossible that men such as the Plunkett brothers had ever existed" (*JH*, p. 348).

All of these concerns, however, about the strident hyperbole of Bolger's narrative, must be tempered by our cognisance of the outlandish reality that the work sought to engage. There is a sense that form and theme combine in the discourse of repression that frames the novel. In his expressive sketch of the Plunketts, of sexual containment and capitalism's sublimation of character, Bolger emphasises that repression only intensifies that which it represses. As with the dysfunctional young men who kidnap a bishop in Roddy Doyle's *Brownbread* (1992), or, as with Christy's maddening dreams in *Down All the Days*, the repressed in Bolger's novel turn on the orthodoxy that represses with a horrific fantasy of vengeance. An argument that therefore retrieves Bolger's credibility, in the face of his constant overstatement, is that his amplification is effective hyperbole, his embellishment is exaggeration for effect – reflexively enacting the kind of excessive outpouring of repressed feelings that the novel so often depicts. This is something John Ardagh suggests when he describes *The Journey Home* as "a kind of fable, a psychic history of Dublin in the 1980s".[100] The sheer, exaggerated aura of disenchantment is so provocative that it seems to directly address the community the novel represents. Indeed, when Justin's father, Patrick, delivers a speech, it goes so over the top that Hano actually admits, "okay, okay, maybe I've embellished it slightly. I'm exaggerating, but it was some such shite" (*JH*, p. 109).

Bolger implies that Hano's retelling takes poetic licence, according with Jim O'Hanlon's contention that "one of the central tensions" in Bolger's work is "that tension between poetry and realism".[101] Bolger indeed admits that the novel's assembly of caricatures "are not particularly realistic", but cautions that "the Plunketts were never meant to be real people"; in this regard, he points to the influence of Italian communist writer and film director Pier Paolo Pasolini's controversial film *Salò, or the 120 Days of Sodom* (1975).[102] The Italian's film depicted fierce, outlandish scenes of mutilation and sexual abuse that are symbolically linked with the last days of Mussolini's fascist regime. Deranged sex was presented in a deliberately removed and unerotic manner in the film, and *The Journey Home* owes some debt to this symbolic grotesquery. Bolger's most gruesome scene, in which representative bourgeois figures – a doctor, a chemist, a draper, "a few big farmers with sons at college" and "the local councillor with his fainne" – rape "retarded girls" in an asylum, is clearly based on Pasolini's representation of a duke, bishop, magistrate and politician kidnapping and raping young men and women at a palace (*JH*, pp. 69–70). It is also redolent of the combination of "power, sex and class" that enabled the systematic abuse of disadvantaged children in Ireland for the best part of a century.

When passing Portrane asylum, Katie is reminded of her own local, rural, asylum, which, as "a former workhouse", is symbolically linked with the historical marginalisation of the poor (*JH*, p. 67). In modern times, the asylum was not "just for the sick", but "a dumping ground for anyone they didn't want" (*JH*, p. 68). This symbolism of the mental asylum is also used in other writing of the working class, such as Paul Smith's *The Countrywoman* (1961) and Paul Mercier's *Drowning* (1984), to reflect a sick society. Both works portray working-class women whose deteriorating mental health results from domestic and social persecution; society abuses them in the outside world, then it abuses them inside institutions – ironically under the cloak of compassion.[103] Bolger's Katie recalls a rural neighbour, Mary Roche, who spent 25 years in the asylum. At 20 years of age, Roche had become pregnant to a Dublin carpenter. Again, class inequality is to the fore in Bolger's concerns: "It wasn't just what she was doing but who she was with," Katie explains: "If it had been the doctor's son they would have all been indignant and yet delighted" (*JH*, p. 69). Because of the young woman's love for a working-class Dubliner – and her frantic attempt to find him again in the city – she is wrongly committed, with the acquiescence of a corrupt local doctor who would "have signed over his granny's corpse for a brandy" (*JH*, p. 69). (We may recall here Paul Smith's similar depiction of an inebriated committal in *The Countrywoman*.) This repeated emphasis on bourgeois corruption is, again, a common theme in writing of the working class, from Oliver St John Gogarty's *Blight* (1917), with its condemnation of local authority land rezoning in Dublin, Robert Collis's *Marrowbone Lane* (1943), with its attack on the system of "special introductions" and "special lists" for those who wish to secure council housing, to *Strumpet City's* (1969) piercing condemnation of the profiteering Bradshaw and his bribery of council officials.[104]

The theme is extended, rather hyperbolically by Bolger, when Katie recalls the Pasoliniesque paedophile ring:

> They [local dignitaries] unveiled a statue to some poor wanker who'd been shot at eighteen by the Black-and-Tans. They'd a pipe band, a priest and altar boys, the usual old shite [...] The organizing committee had a row of seats on a raised platform. As each of their names were called out I could hear my mother trying to hush Mary Roche as she intoned like the response to a psalm, *He had me! He had me! (JH,* p. 70)

Repressed sexual trauma, which Bolger links to class repression, inevitably reveals itself, even in the sanitised lexicon of the religious psalm.

For Pasolini, sexual abuse was a metaphor for a degraded society, for the broader dehumanisation that accompanied fascist rule, and Bolger employs *The Journey Home's* sexual debasement to parallel ends: "I used that sort of *deviant* sexuality, it's not *gay* sexuality. I don't think the couples are gay," he argues. The Plunketts "were vampires, they were like the undead [...] They were metaphors," he adds, linking his dark surrealism with the Dublin gothic tradition, and, in particular, Sheridan Le Fanu.[105] "I wanted to suggest a culture of political corruption that was prevalent at the time. I mean, everybody knew that Charles Haughey was corrupt at the time, and *people didn't mind* [...] It was trying to shock people." Indeed, as Molino has quipped regarding the ambiguous recognition of what was happening in industrial schools, "abuse suffered by children [...] has been for years a problem hidden in plain sight".[106] Frustrated by this bewildering societal relationship between truth and recognition, Bolger "deliberately made [the novel] slightly cartoonish".[107] Sexual abuse, corruption, exploitation and cultural revisionism are contorted, dismembered, disfigured and reconstituted with a kind of magic realist horror that speaks poetically of Ireland's degraded moral state. Moreover, in light of recent revelations, it must be asked if Bolger's imagery of representative pillars of Irish society raping and exploiting its most vulnerable citizens is not a little closer to the truth than some might like to admit.

If this shock-poetic technique can be argued for, it is of course somewhat botched by overuse. Bolger is adamant that his depiction is veracious in a selective sense, stressing that "the interesting thing about *The Journey Home* is the fact that there is nothing in it that didn't happen to somebody I knew at the time of writing".[108] Yet, while "every part of the book happened", he concedes that "this does not make it realistic".[109] Indeed, when I met Bolger for an interview, he had recently reread the novel for the first time since 1990, due to its impending publication in a new American edition. On this reading he found the work "quite scattergun". In particular, the scenes surrounding the asylum were "very caricaturing" – "even though it was based on something somebody told me". "There are bits in there I would like to take out," he admitted, but editorial temptation yielded to judicious historical concerns – the sense that the novel was, of its time and place, an authentic, if somewhat indiscriminate expression of a legitimate youthful exasperation. "It's an angry book and it's a young person's book and therefore parts of it are going to be a load of bollocks", he bluntly concedes.[110]

In the final analysis, Bolger's assertion of the novel's historical value may (along with its popularity) be the most convincing argument for its enduring relevance. And as I have already suggested, it seems – in light of tales such as Christine Buckley's of abused children eating rabbits' excrement while being physically assaulted by nuns and their pets – that such bizarreness is no mere fabrication. This sense of a surreal reality resonates with the title of Colm O'Gorman's influential account of institutional abuse, *Beyond Belief* (2009). The intentional nature of Bolger's consciously unrealistic "style as cynicism" does not make *The Journey Home*, at times, any less tedious for the reader, but there are flashes of literary brilliance that presage his startling success as a writer.[111] As Neil Corcoran argues, the novel "has its melodramatic elements; but these pale in comparison with what it manages in the way of analysis and suggestiveness."[112] If the author shouts sometimes, it is because of the quiescence about him. His anti-representational exaggeration demands a reaction and poses a provocation, urging his community beyond apathy, to realise its own potential and to reassess the corruption of Irish society, to understand its subjection to political malpractice and social marginalisation. In not fitting in to Irish society, Hano and his peers represent its repressed side, the working class. Their "exile", as Hano puts it, is that of a cohort whose welfare has been neglected yet whose marginalisation all the more forcefully recommends its place at the forefront of Ireland's narrative of modernisation (*JH*, p. 387). This narrative, as the recent reports show, is still being radically rewritten and revised.

Dublin "with the lace curtains off"

Like Brown, Bolger stresses working-class Dublin's accommodation of mass cultural influences, but the later writer's protagonists are trapped between two cultures, one old and rural, the other new, urban and increasingly cosmopolitan. Nonetheless *The Journey Home* and *Down All the Days* share striking thematic correspondences. As Terry Eagleton writes, "the consensual or hegemonic in political life lies very close to the aesthetic", and for both authors forms of aesthetic subversion are employed to challenge the hegemonic and consensual.[113] Both write provocatively in an attempt to stir their readers from an ideological slumber. Brown also courted criticism for his effusive anger, "often interpreted by others as a deadly power, unleashed unfairly and certainly in ways that made others very uncomfortable."[114] The discomfort with sexuality in Irish society indeed becomes the novelists' "deadly power", a motif for that society's fundamental discomfort with modernity. Brown's novel had "pointed out the hypocrisies of the Irish culture in its attitude towards religion, sex and tradition."[115] In his own assessment, he had wished to write "about Dublin working-class life as I know it, with no great plot or even melodramatic situations". His novel would depend "ultimately upon its relation to life and its concern with the truth of that life".[116] This was a Dublin "with the lace curtains off", as William Trevor put it, "a snarling, yelling world in which the language may be good to listen to but yet is the language of sadness".[117]

Bolger also employs his exaggerated attacks on orthodoxy to forcefully render the social and cultural deterioration of Dublin life, creating an eerie sense of imminent social liquidation. But whereas Brown envisages rebirth, Bolger foresees social cataclysm. The authors correspond in how they portray Ireland's social and cultural degeneracy metaphorically through sexual motifs, and in this they parallel other authors in this book who use their work to represent what Brown terms "the unbound side of reality" – that which has been repressed by the social milieu. In both works, the realities of working-class life find expression in powerfully subversive and profane conceits. When Hano thrashes violently at the overgrowth in his father's back garden, with "every blow" becoming "like an act of finality, a foretaste of separations to come", he aggressively asserts his refusal to submit to the old Ireland that his father represents, repeating Christy Brown's Oedipal metaphor (*JH*, pp. 170, 17). Both men reject the orthodoxies of the past, and in their writing we again find the emphatic insistence on the social image, the irruption of hidden narratives and unseen class relations through iconoclastic imagery and subversive textual tropes.

7
Revising the Revolution: Roddy Doyle's *A Star Called Henry*, Historiography, Politics and Proletarian Consciousness

LORD MAYOR:	Yeth, yeth, boyth; but remember what the Purple Priest said: an honest day's work for an honest day's pay.
1ST WORKMAN:	To hell with the Purple Priest.
LORD MAYOR:	Remember the example of our ancient warrior forefathers: strength in their arms, truth on their lips, and purity in their hearts.
1ST WORKMAN:	Well, we're the young warriors, and we're different.
2ND WORKMAN:	A helluva lot different.[1]

Like Seán O'Casey's socialist workmen in *The Star Turns Red* (1940), Roddy Doyle's republican rebel, Henry Smart, is "a helluva lot different" from the "ancient warrior forefathers" of Irish nationalism. An unconventional, irreverent working-class hero, the protagonist of *A Star Called Henry* (1999) is, like O'Casey's radicals, pitted against the status quo of Irish cultural mores. He also challenges deeply ingrained notions of Irishness and the nobility or wisdom of political martyrdom. In this chapter, however, I will argue that if Doyle's *fin de siècle* work challenges these and other nationalist discourses with a radically unconventional, proletarian history "from below", it also glibly reasserts many debilitating, hackneyed historical discourses "from above". This hugely successful novel continues to assert the politically charged themes of marginalisation that have characterised depictions of Dublin's working class in the other works explored in this study, and Henry Smart's tall tale continues to elaborate the exclusion of that class from the national narrative in his most recent instalment, *The Dead Republic* (2010). Doyle rearticulates the paradox of an urban community simultaneously eschewed by and central to the development of the Irish Republic, but he also questions the relevance of political action generally to working-class life. As such, at the end of the twentieth century, and as the most compelling elaboration of Doyle's literary aesthetic and political ideology, *A Star* provides for a useful survey of the themes that characterise the most prominent modern author to engage with Irish working-class life.

"Revisionists and 'revisionists'": the troubles with historiography and class

Doyle's questioning of the dominant ideologies in Irish culture dovetails continually with the vexatious debate over historiographic "revisionism" – a debate which continues to provoke crucial interchanges in the development of Irish Studies. Cognisant that the necessarily terse reflection that follows cannot possibly do full justice to the nuances of this gargantuan issue, I nonetheless wish to elaborate a number of key concerns with revisionism that are vital in assessing the historical resonances of this novel. My principal concern here is to show that contemporary revisionism has become more of a political intervention than a historiographical precept, and that this political intervention buttresses anti-nationalist concepts of history. In *A Star*, Doyle's own revisionist stance problematises his outwardly socialist pose, because the heavily politicised, anti-nationalist ideology he adopts carries with it also a dismissal of the socialist, proletarian thrust of the revolutionary period from 1916 to 1923. In proffering the ultimately misled involvement of Henry Smart in the national liberation struggle – which he refashions as a capitalist coup – Doyle's remaking of the uprising also undermines the possibility of working-class political activism more generally as a vehicle for social change.

While the term "revisionism" is often employed with great conviction and certainty in contemporary debates about politics and history, it is by no means a unitary or settled concept, and in the enigmatic words of one eminent Irish historian, "clearly, there are revisionists and 'revisionists'".[2] It is widely recognised that Irish historical revisionism has evolved considerably since its inception, and for many the new "revisionism" has been far more politically motivated than its 1930s progenitor.[3] While early revisionism sought to professionalise Irish historical analysis by grounding it in academic principles of sound research and objective scrutiny, later "revisionism" has in part subverted this methodology through tendentious, overtly anti-nationalist interventions – many of which are inspired by the lived experience of contemporary political developments.

When Theodore William Moody and Robert Dudley Edwards included a special category entitled "Historical Revisions" in their seminal journal, *Irish Historical Studies*, in 1938, it was certainly a courageous decision in academic and historical terms. The periodical would refute received wisdom and widely held assumptions regarding well-known figures, periods and events, not by resorting to other, equally unfounded assumptions but by analysing the raw data of new historical and archival research. In the interests of probity, Moody, Edwards and their contributors would sear through mythic and misleading versions of Irish history with the dispassionate lance of rigorous and principled academic research. Historians such as F.S.L. Lyons, Conor Cruise O'Brien and D.A. Thornley would show how the predominance of constitutional movements in Irish nationalist history refuted what John Hutchinson terms "the republican conception of an apostolic succession of revolutionary leaders from Tone to Pearse".[4] Their work showed how common perceptions of Irish history were being distorted by the process of state hegemonic formation in decolonised Ireland.

Considering this originary ethos – revisionism's fundamental determination to treat of history with an even hand – it is all the more disappointingly ironic that modern-day, second-wave revisionism has adopted a stridently political, biased tone. If early revisionism embarked upon an "innocent" journey of charting historical topography – correcting, revising and reinterpreting its contours according to objective data – later revisionism seeks to change the political landscape itself. Early revisionism endeavoured to distinguish between good history, "which is a matter of facing the facts of the Irish past, however painful some of them may be" and "mythology", which is "a way of refusing to face" these facts.[5] But after the resumption of the British-Irish conflict in the North of Ireland post-1968, revisionists became more concerned with "the dire past still overhanging the dire present" and the expedient "need to go back to fundamentals and consider once more the meaning of independence [...] revolution [...] nationality [...] history".[6] Renewed conflict renewed political expediencies, or as Henry Smart puts it pithily in *The Dead Republic* – as he surveys the damage of the Dublin-Monaghan bombings – "the new damage had brought new life to the old damage".[7] While both revisionisms sought to question established metanarratives, the latter's "present-mindedness" – its engagement with contemporary political concerns – was an explicit reaction to disquieting modern events, signalling its shift into a new, more overtly politicised role.[8] This engagement would become a constant in new revisionism's moral and political compass, its dial thereafter pointing north – to the carnage that once again made historiography and ideology matters of life and death.

Moody set the pace with his multivolume *New History of Ireland*, which, although first mooted in 1962, did not begin to come to fruition until the end of the 1970s.[9] But other second-wave works that sought to rationalise (or irrationalise) the contemporary political crisis would begin to emerge in the meantime, such as Owen Dudley Edwards' tellingly titled *The Sins of Our Fathers: The Roots of Conflict in Northern Ireland* (1970), followed two years later by major monographs that would establish the politicised trend: future Taoiseach Garret FitzGerald's *Towards a New Ireland* (1972) and future unionist Conor Cruise O'Brien's *States of Ireland* (1972). Both works argued that the true tradition of Irish nationalist politics lay in finding an accommodation

with Britain through constitutional reform – not in fighting with it for independence, as the Provisional Irish Republican Army (PIRA) was then doing.
These new revisionists articulated a new academic reaction against the re-
emergence of a tradition of armed republicanism. T.W. Moody's compact *The
Ulster Question, 1603–1973* (1974) illustrated this tendency glaringly, with its
division of the history of the province into two separate eras. In his segmen-
tation of the book into pre- and post-Civil Rights histories, Moody weighed
the previous six years (1968–1974) heavily, both in volume of pages and
import, against the previous 365. Distinctly present-minded in outlook, the
book even offered a formula for resolution of the ongoing Northern conflict
(a formula which, with visionary prescience, forecast much of the content
of the Belfast Agreement), but in so doing Moody's metacommentary was
surely going beyond any objective notion of history as it is commonly understood.[10] Despite its broad titular scope, *The Ulster Question* was an overt challenge to modern politicians, an explicitly politicised, present-minded work.

Further revisions in the epistemology of Irish nationalist history emerged
with extraordinary efflorescence in the decade to come, with studies such as
Ian Adamson's *The Cruithin* (1974) and F.S.L. Lyons's (very different) *Culture
and Anarchy in Ireland* (1978) adding to the body of academic knowledge in
politically powerful ways. Later works, such as R.F. Foster's towering *Modern
Ireland, 1660–1972* (1988), would establish revisionism as *the* historiographical orthodoxy in Irish studies, supplanting the predominance of the "traditional" nationalist view, which had previously held sway. Some of the
second wave's analysis emerged from a left-wing rejection of the sectarian
aspect of the northern conflict, but, as Kevin Whelan has noted, "many of
those active earlier in espousing these allegedly left-wing views – Paul Bew,
Conor Cruise O'Brien, Eoghan Harris – have followed the logical evolution
of their arguments by ending up as unionist advisors in the 1990s."[11] In
second-wave, or what might be more fittingly termed "post-revisionist", discourse, the lines between politics and scholarship are repeatedly blurred.

But to criticise revisionism for simply being "political" is not my purpose here. Indeed, it would be misleading to suggest that any version of
history, or the theories that underpin it, are entirely apolitical. In this
regard, Brendan Bradshaw's essay, "Nationalism and Historical Scholarship
in Modern Ireland" (1989), adroitly encapsulates the anti-revisionist case
while refusing to deny his own tendentiousness. Bradshaw's linkage of his
own stance with an admiration for the republican tradition again muddies
the waters between history and politics, as Paul Bew has noted. But such
a criticism misses Bradshaw's essential point, that "espousal of the value-
free principle may simply result in practice in value-based interpretation
in another guise."[12] Bradshaw does not eschew partisanship per se, just
partisanship *masquerading* as even-handedness. Edward Said had famously
made this point in *Orientalism* (1978), when he challenged "the general
liberal consensus that 'true' knowledge is fundamentally non-political

(and conversely, that overtly political knowledge is not 'true knowledge')". This common pretence of dispassionate commentary, in theory, literature and historic narrative, is a fallacy, Said contended – an intellectual deceit used "to discredit any work for daring to violate the protocol of pretended suprapolitical objectivity".[13] While both Bradshaw and Said nonetheless fail to specify any universal approach that could supplant this "protocol" of supposed objectivity, Bradshaw's view that later revisionism has failed to live up to its originary aims – as a pretended suprapolitical practice – is easily substantiated.

The temporal analysis by Bradshaw and others of political shifts in revisionist thinking is perhaps the most convincing criticism of this discourse. Scholars critical of revisionism show how its leading luminaries, such as Cruise O'Brien and Lyons, shifted their analysis of key periods of Irish history towards a less nationalist and more pro-unionist stance post-1968, suggesting the significant impact of contemporary events on their views of the past.[14] D.G. Boyce instances a typical example of the revisionist hypersensitivity to political ideology: T.W. Moody's "embarrassed" attempt to attribute militaristic sentiments in a letter written by Michael Davitt (whom he admired) to "the state of excessive mental stimulation and physical exertion in which [Davitt] was living" is a curious feat of interpretive contortionism.[15] Terry Eagleton cites another similar example from L.M. Cullen's *The Emergence of Modern Ireland 1600–1900* (1981), whereby Cullen, "anxious to assure us that middlemen, if not grandee landowners, enjoyed close bonds with their tenants, offers in evidence the fact that they occasionally abducted their daughters".[16] Clearly such strained psychological and social judgements across centuries are reasoned with an eye to the ubiquitous contemporary dilemmas of political violence, part of what Whelan terms "a specific ideological response to the needs of the southern state in coming to terms with a major political crisis".[17] Like Freud's *Nachträglichkeit*, "the process by which past experiences may be revised to align them with one's current psychic state", second-wave revisionism is very much about the now.[18]

Later revisionism, then, is acutely aware of recent violence, and its interpretation of earlier conflict nods continually towards the political present. Such a politically loaded awareness of contemporary conditions is abundantly evident in *A Star Called Henry*, and it is for this reason that I have also chosen to analyse the novel in the context of more recent cultural and political influences. In this regard, it is apposite to note that while much of what might be termed historicist criticism of this novel has appraised it in terms of the revolutionary period it depicts, the notoriously conservative period of Irish history it presages or the (post-)modern Republic that its author actually inhabits, none has attended to another salient context – that of "Troubles" literature and film. John Hill, Martin McLoone, Patrick Magee and others have documented the impact of the recent Northern conflict on modern perceptions of political violence in writing and film; such a pertinent context – one that "devastated a whole society, scarring two generations of Irish people" – is indispensable to any evaluation of modern retrospectives on earlier Irish "troubles".[19] *A Star Called Henry* reflects the long shadow this modern-day conflict has cast in its adoption of some of the most notable tropes and themes of its milieu, as the coming analysis will show, and these influences heavily inflect how Doyle portrays proletarian political consciousness.

Poking fun: A "shocking substitute" for history

But if such historical significance is at play in *A Star*, it is important to note that to simply contrast its meandering, playful narrative with "objective" historical record and to lambaste it for contradicting some irrefutable "reality" would be grossly unfair. Doyle's aim was, after all, to "take liberties and mess around and poke fun" with this blatantly satiric work, to usurp reality with a "shocking substitute" – Henry's own revealing description of himself.[20] In his use of a magic-realist technique, Doyle treats history with a flippant, irreverent nod towards comedy, and his lively, unconventional narrative should certainly not be viewed as an attempt to achieve *conventional* verisimilitude. Critics such as Rüdiger Imhof and Brian Donnelly have all too readily dismissed the novel on the assumption that such realism was Doyle's intention and that in this context the narrative is simply "too good to be true".[21] Donnelly finds Doyle's magic realism trying, observing that he employs the technique selectively and that it "jars against the pervading naturalism" of the book.[22] An "execrably bad novel", Imhof admonishes, *A Star* evinces "too much Doyle codology [...] to be convincing".[23] Producing some examples of how Henry Smart is, unrealistically, "physically almost perfect", he concludes that our narrator "beggars credulity". Why, he wonders, has the novelist "seen fit to people his novel with so many grotesques"?[24]

Such an unfair critique arises, not from any failure on Doyle's part to "be convincing", but from Imhof's own refusal of the logic (or anti-logic) of the novel's experimental style (this, despite his own pioneering work on John Banville's experimentalism).[25] "Grotesques" are of course integral to a genre typified by a mingling or juxtaposition of the realistic and the fantastic or bizarre, skilful time shifts, labyrinthine narratives and plots and instances of the horrific or inexplicable. Improbable occurrences are treated as rationally as more ordinary events, just as they might be in a conventional fairytale, and while it is difficult to fully define magic realism as a genre, its potential for "poking fun", for inspiring iconoclasm and parody, is obvious. Not only does it distort legitimised reality, magic realism unashamedly juxtaposes improbable narratives with probable or widely accepted ones – something that Imhof and Donnelly fail to acknowledge. Salman Rushdie employed this ambiguity in *Midnight's Children* (1981) – on which some of the episodes in Doyle's novel are clearly based. Gabriel García Márquez had also utilised the technique in his imaginative take on Latin American history, *One Hundred Years of Solitude* (1967). Through the interpolation of real events into both novels' explorations of tyranny, the historic fantasy achieves a curiously profound "realism". Like the television mockumentary, magic realism thrives on creative ambiguity. Allowing the novelist to rebuff the criticism that he or she is distorting "reality" (because he or she does not pretend to accurately represent it), it thus irks those who might expect a more conventionally realist approach. *A Star* is highly self-reflexive and engages the postmodern confrontation between assumptions of representational transparency and an acute, denaturalising awareness of the processes of narrative creation. The "codology" of history – and its related histrionics – is what magic realism finds "grotesque". *A Star* "slips and slides all over the page [...] neither completely believable nor completely unbelievable", as Jennifer M. Jeffers observes, and this might explain why it is "doubly upsetting" for some.[26]

The slippery, counter-intuitive form of the novel precisely endeavours to "blur and skew our sense-making capabilities".[27] As Doyle himself puts it, "magic things happen in *A Star Called Henry*".[28] Consequently, Dermot McCarthy may justifiably caution that "veridical concerns" are "inappropriate" here.[29] The reader's task must lie with extrapolating the subtext of the novel, with looking beyond while presumably enjoying the outrageous literary fabulation it presents, with divining instinctively to the underground streams of theme that flow beneath the slippery surface of the text – as Henry's symbolic forays beneath the city's surface, into the sewers of Dublin, suggest. Self-conscious reader participation is invited, and Doyle is, as he has himself advised, taking "liberties with reality".[30] The reader is thus made aware of his or her own hermeneutic agency in the process of *creating* historical meaning. Could Éamon de Valera have "smelt of shite" and have worn red socks at the moment of his dramatic arrest by British soldiers, the novel asks (*SCH*, p. 139)? Why would one consider such a prospect unlikely?

Thomas Kilroy makes a similar point in his play, *Talbot's Box* (1973), in which the memory of Matt Talbot is contested by contradictory accounts of his life, from the Church, capitalists, socialists and Talbot himself. Talbot, for his own part, professes to be a far simpler man than posthumous controversies would allow: "To tell yus the truth, I never wanted anything but to work wid timber," he admits.[31] The point is reiterated when Countess Markievicz appears in the play, complaining that the Church "manipulated the home, manipulated the family to oppress" women, and one character protests that she "never said that!"[32] History, Kilroy suggests, is whatever we want it to be. This, too, is why the working-class Henry, who "wasn't important" – for whom history has "no room" – is airbrushed from a photograph of de Valera's surrender (*SCH*, pp. 138, 139).

Doyle indeed flaunts his disregard for historical linearity with the inscription of part of an Irving Berlin lyric (*Cheek to Cheek,* 1935) as the epigraph to his novel and tantalises those expecting historical veracity with a bibliography (a most untypical feature in a novel) citing many straightforwardly historical texts. Such "deliberately awkward" paratextual conventions are, as Linda Hutcheon notes, common in postmodernist writing, and it is as if, to mischievously rile irate historians, Doyle is claiming to have produced a historically accurate work.[33] *A Star* thus parodies the "fetishising of the archive" of history, destabilising the supposed dichotomy between the fictive and the real, unpacking and "denaturalising" the authority of history – including its potential to elide the history of the working class. George Moore, in *Hail and Farewell* (1914), asked if "reality can destroy the dream, why shouldn't the dream be able to destroy reality".[34] Doyle too treats reality in terms of possibilities, not certainties, but crucially this is not to suggest that the novel eschews political concerns.

Anomalous violence

"With the possible exception of greenness," writes David Lloyd, "no quality has more frequently and repetitiously been attributed to Ireland than violence".[35] Depicting the country's most explosive era of anti-colonial struggle, *A Star* is replete with political violence, but it is in what is shown to motivate this violence that we are most aware of the compellingly political thrust of the novel. The author proffers many motivations for the Irish insurgency: poverty, gangsterism, egomania, conservatism, xenophobia, greed and abstract idealism are just some of them. And Henry Smart, though well meaning, becomes an unwitting conduit for all of these native ills – as a dupe, a child of the slums, made violent by circumstance and led astray by the sinister machinations of others. A foil for the politically inspired revolutionaries of the history books, he unthinkingly succumbs to the romance of being a nationalist icon (or being told he is by the propagandist Jack Dalton). He unquestioningly also follows orders that are secretly issued by his lifelong nemesis, the gangster TD Alfie Gandon. In seeking to extirpate injustice in the old regime, Henry tragically and ironically buttresses it in the new one.

The novel's form indeed reflects and compounds this dramatic conclusion, with what Doyle himself has termed its "circular quality".[36] In a subversive deployment of that grand novelistic tradition Georg Lukács termed the "glorious 'middle way' " – whereby the bourgeois hero typically restores order from chaos – the status quo is imperilled, in this case by the novel's protagonist and his comrades, only to be reconfirmed by the plot's ultimately cynical conclusion.[37] Again the novel of working-class life confounds its own historically ideological form. Henry brands his father a "slave" and a "gobshite", a "puppet [...] Pinocchio Smart" with a "stupid, saturated heart", for slavishly serving Gandon, his villainous capitalist master, but the younger Smart unwittingly follows in his father's footsteps, becoming another naïve "puppet" for the very same man (*SCH*, pp. 43, 61, 43, 49). Symbolically, both Henrys wield the same weapon and phallic emblem of disability, their trusted wooden leg; for them violence is both a weapon and a metaphoric crutch – a means of defence and a symbol of their underlying weakness. Correlating Henry's nationalist violence with the gangsterism of his father, Doyle also underscores an ironic parity between the IRA's new regime and the old one it has ostensibly sought to overthrow, by portraying Gandon – the quintessence of capitalist cruelty – as the nexus that links them both. Both Henry Sr's servility and his son's rebellion ironically enable Gandon's corrupt authority, as a criminal in the old regime and a TD in the new one. In this context, the abstract ideology and political vision Henry has served seem irrelevant to the needs of the poor.

Conditioning and ideology: "Ireland was something in songs"

At the outset, however, Henry's rebellion against the capitalist system is not based on any ideological perspective but on his experiences as a youth growing up in grinding poverty. A neglected "Street Arab", he "fell in with the crowd", and was made "at home in the rags and scarcity, dirt and weakness". "We looked and learned", Henry relates, he and his brother Victor becoming "little packs of enterprise and cunning", habituating themselves to an arduous life of petty crime (*SCH*, pp. 45, 63). Foreshadowing his future as a violent insurrectionist, Henry steadily becomes inured to various barbarisms, killing rats and cows, reduced, like his father, to violence, by the vicissitudes of economic necessity:

> I felt [a cow's] scorching blood on my head before I got away and I heard the life charge out of it and felt the weight of death as it fell. I made lines of the blood down my cheeks with my fingers and Victor copied me. (*SCH*, p. 68)

Like the savage children of William Golding's *The Lord of the Flies* (1954), the Smarts are socially conditioned in a way that makes them prone to barbarous behaviour.

As an untainted "glowing baby", Henry exuded a sense of optimism that drew lines of local mothers to marvel at his beauty – rather like Rushdie's Saleem. But later, after exposure to Dublin's rough streets, Henry becomes corrupted and barbarised through experience, developing also a curious, exaggerated aversion towards anything outside of his immediate struggle for survival. While awe-struck Dubliners observe Halley's Comet's apparition in 1910, for Henry it is "just a big star" (*SCH*, p. 67). He ignores the celestial spectacle but is alert to its potential rewards and instead conducts the more terrestrial business of picking star-gazers' pockets. While he and his fellow Street Arabs contract their expertise in animal cruelty to nationalists who commission them to maim the cattle of "absentee bastards who were pushing the small men off the land", they are nevertheless uncomprehending of the politics for which their cruelty is contracted (*SCH*, p. 70):

> – Do you love Ireland, lads? Said one of them.
>
> They got no answer.
>
> We didn't understand the question. Ireland was something in songs that drunken old men wept about [...] I loved Victor and my memories of some other people. That was all I understood about love. (*SCH*, p. 69)

Henry equally rails against his mother's abstract and excessive sentimentality – her devotion to another star "called Henry", a real star that she delusionally believes to be a heavenly embodiment of one of her dead sons. This earlier Henry had died in childhood, driving Melody to madness, and her obsession with this ethereal child is pointedly indulged at the expense of the tangible one by her side. While Melody fixates on her imagined, celestial son, blood flows from the nose of the living infant, "in a rush that failed to shock her" (*SCH*, p. 34). Oblivious to the sufferings of the "pale and red-eyed" real Henry, "held together by rashes and sores", with "a stomach crying to be filled, bare feet aching like an old man's", she indulges a delusory obsession that eventually drives the family apart (*SCH*, p. 1). Henry Sr becomes embittered towards the newly born Henry, for reminding his wife of her dead child, and the new Henry increasingly resents his dead brother, for whom he becomes a "shocking substitute". By metonymic extension, the real Ireland is also a shocking substitute, an ersatz replacement for the imagined utopia of nationalist fantasists. Henry tries desperately and in vain to divert his mother's attention from the "twinkling bollox": "I beat her. I climbed onto her hair. I pressed into the breasts that were no longer mine," he declares; "I scratched my sores and bled for her" (*SCH*, pp. 35, 34). But he eventually becomes completely estranged from Melody, rejecting the otherworldly fiction into which she pours her tears.

As in other magic-realist works, this implicit parallel between family and nation in *A Star* is a conceit that dominates the novel. Melody, as Mother Ireland, is obsessed with the dead past, oblivious to that which is still alive, the neglected, attention-seeking baby that "puffed and shook and spat" (*SCH*, p. 34). Abstraction is implicitly at odds with the interests of the working class – whether it be that of the nationalist agrarian activists who "love Ireland", of the men who gaze gob-smacked at Halley's Comet, or indeed of a neurotic mother driven insane by her traumatic loss. Doyle is also taking a side-swipe at religion here, in a climate in which "most Irish people lived, until quite recently, in a world where the hereafter was very close and as real as the landscape around them".[38] Henry does not love "Ireland", but he does love Victor; his mother fails to love him, but obsesses about an image of her past. Doyle correlates the devotional, sentimental nonsense of nationalism, as he views it, with Melody's excessive grief. Both deflect attention from the difficult "here-and-now" of working-class life.

Henry, by contrast, is acutely conscious of these conditions, of the strictly material world in which he struggles for survival. In his early interchanges with his schoolteacher, Miss O'Shea (who will later, preposterously and comically, become his wife), Henry's inability to conceive of the abstract except in terms of the material is vividly emphasised when she broaches some basic arithmetic:

> – Twenty-seven and twenty-seven.
> – What?
> – Bottles.
> – What's in them?
> – Porter.
> – Fifty-four.

He cannot add *abstract* numbers, the episode conveys, but is a "genius" when calculating *tangible*, useful things, such as bottles of porter (*SCH*, p. 73). Likewise, Henry explains that an immaterial concept such as Home Rule means "nothing to us who had no homes" (*SCH*, p. 70). "Imagined communities," as Benedict Anderson has argued, are the preserve of those *with* property, *with* a stake in society; nationality means nothing to those without it – like Henry and Victor, who sleep beneath a sheet of tarpaulin by a canal.[39]

This dramatic conflict between abstract ideology and concrete poverty is typified in the allegory Doyle constructs around the visit of the English monarch, King Edward VII, to the second city of his empire. When the king jaunts past Dublin's obsequious tenement dwellers, the uproarious sequence of events that unfolds recalls another literary attack on abstraction – that of Hans Christian Andersen's classic fairytale, *The Emperor's New Clothes* (1837). Henry is intuitively averse to the king, the "fat man", the "eejit" who "didn't belong", and he ejaculates a "treacherous roar" that sets the adoring crowd against him. "Fuck off!" he tells the monarch, "fuck off with your hat", prompting "the king's loyal subjects" to scramble to "box the ears" of this treasonous "angry little man" and his brother. Like the sagacious fairytale boy, however, Henry's objection reminds his pursuers of what they secretly know, and consequently he surmises that they "admired our guts" (*SCH*, p. 51). But if Doyle tantalises with the suggestion that this plucky rebellion foreshadows Henry's future republicanism, he is quick to dismiss such a conclusion. "Was I a tiny Fenian? A Sinn Feiner?" Henry rhetorically asks: "Not at all. I didn't even know I was Irish" (*SCH*, p. 52).

Henry may not know that he is part of an "imagined community", but he is acutely aware of the reality of his social and economic exclusion. He simply looks and instinctively scorns "the fat man at the centre of it". He reviles "the wealth and colour, the shining red face, the moustache and beard that were better groomed than the horses" (*SCH*, p. 52). He may be unaware that this magnate, who anyhow "didn't come from Dublin", is the "king, or that the floozy beside him was the queen", but he intuitively brands him an "eejit", because the monarch "didn't belong". This is not, again, because of any abstract, republican notion of sovereignty but because the vista of obscene opulence inside the king's carriage galls the child in its stark contrast with "the cart that had carried us from house to house to basement" (*SCH*, p. 53). Abstract ideals are, like the proverbial "emperor's new clothes", mere imaginary adornments that attempt to cloak reality in a fantasy – to obscure socio-economic disparity with an elegant lie.

But if this allegorical lesson seeks to prioritise the true conditions of the working class, Doyle's didactic portrayal of Henry's social conditioning undermines the possibility of a truly conscious reaction to those conditions from within that class. Henry is portrayed as a reactionary, not a revolutionary, a boy capable of understanding and reacting *only* to those issues directly pertaining to his individuated, material world. He cannot understand complex political ideas that pertain to the macro-economic, to the national or even to his own class consciousness. "Not capable of discerning situations", for him "there is no possibility of measuring the distance to normal, rational meaning", as Jeffers argues.[40] Veena Das, of the Subaltern Studies movement, has proposed that such distancing of the subaltern from "normal rational meaning" should be rejected as a regressive representation of the colonised. In any focus on "the historical moment of rebellion", she avers, it is imperative that "the subjects of [colonial] power are not treated as passive beings, but are shown at the moments in which they try to defy this alienating power".[41] Henry is repeatedly portrayed as just such a passive being, incapable of "discerning", reacting to and pre-programmed by highly personal grievances and traumas.

The 1916 Rising, to which Doyle flashes forward *in media res* following Victor's death, must thus be conveyed as a function of the narrator's personal experience. It is indeed telling that Doyle elides the seven-year period leading up to the Rising, emphasising the link, for Henry, between Victor's premature demise from neglect (only a few pages earlier) and his own later role in the insurgency, as well as creating a sense of the spontaneity of the Rising itself. Ranajit Guha notes that many historical narratives of colonial insurrections evince such a sense of their spontaneity, giving "the lie to the myth, retailed so often by careless and impressionistic writing on the subject", of colonial rebellions "being purely spontaneous and unpremeditated affairs".[42] In a certain view of Irish history, Lloyd argues similarly, "resistance to capitalism and colonialism tends to be seen as merely reactive and spasmodic, an inarticulate and usually violent upsurge".[43] Doyle elides the reality of decades of working-class agitation – collective urban strikes, protests, agrarian campaigns and social upheavals – instead proffering multifarious localisable roots of the Rising in individual grudges and complaints.

Henry's desperately impoverished state is stressed in the first part of the novel, and likewise the Rising is refracted through the individuated prism of his childhood privations. The once barefoot boy symbolically reserves his first bullet of the insurrection for Tyler's shoe shop, more specifically "its special corner for children's boots", and continues with a barrage on a cakeshop, tobacconist, clothes shop, servant's registry office and the Pillar Café (*SCH*, p. 99). All of these outlets become metaphors for his marginalisation. Of the latter he remarks, "I'd been thrown out of there before I was properly in the door, me and Victor". The memory is, amidst the chaos of insurrection, nonetheless powerfully redolent – he can "still smell the manageress's breath" (*SCH*, p. 105). Past degradations are the primary, if not the only, motivation for Henry's particular armed struggle, Doyle suggests, and he "shoots" and "kills" "all that I had been denied, all the commerce and snobbery that had been mocking me and other hundreds of thousands behind glass and locks" (*SCH*, p. 119).

This analysis finds affinity with Denis Johnston's in *The Scythe and the Sunset* (1958), a play which is, propitiously, set in the Pillar Café that Henry shoots at during the same events. When a Cumann na mBan rebel expresses exasperation at the failure of an assembled crowd to cheer the reading of the IRA's Proclamation – "Don't they know they're free," she blasts – a bemused character, Dr McCarthy, infers the real concerns of the working class. Just as those in the café hear a crack of glass and "scattered cheering" at a nearby sweet shop, a waitress excitedly asks what has happened, to which McCarthy wittily quips, "the Birth of a Nation".[44]

As for Johnston's looters, shops and what they symbolise are Henry Smart's enemies, but in truth the proletariat is not his cause. Henry's crusade is, emphatically, a personal one, and "while the lads [take] chunks out of the military", he occupies himself with more avaricious concerns. "The Empire was collapsing in front of us," he relates, but it is still alive in his pockets: with "the last of the [stolen] money" from the post office secretly deposited in his trousers, Henry hilariously declines to "join in the victory dance; I didn't want it to jangle" (*SCH*, p. 106). Ostensibly serving the "august destiny" (as the 1916 Proclamation has it) of the Republic, the working-class rebel is quite literally weighed down by his less-than-august concerns. He is portrayed, not as an active vehicle for historical change, but as a highly determined and self-absorbed product of environmental factors. An unthinking malcontent who wants "to shoot and wreck and kill and ruin" (*SCH*, p. 109), he is summarily depoliticised. The non-explanation of personal grudges and a bad childhood replaces the intricacies of history and the complexities of hegemony.

A materialist view: "The greatest fuckin' eejit ever born"

Henry Smart's simplicity here may indeed proceed from a "materialist view of history", but Doyle's is a sharply reductive, determinist type of materialism.[45] This is the "vulgar" travesty of Marx that we have already encountered, in which the reification of capitalism becomes a kind of ultimate value. Doyle certainly stresses the impact of material conditions on political events but does so from within a rigid conception of the relationship between the two. It is as if Henry has no mind of his own – a depiction that is certainly at odds with the dialectical materialism propounded by Marx. As Cliff Slaughter puts it, Marx "could not proceed from a theory which simply saw men as the product of something called 'the environment'"; indeed, his "scientific socialism meant a break from mechanical materialism".[46] This issue of the "role of ideas" in working-class consciousness and in relation to Marxist materialism has indeed constituted one of Marxism's greatest debates since the nineteenth century. However, as Anthony Giddens has noted, a position which "apparently removes man from his own history [...]" leads to the endemic difficulties faced by orthodox dialectical materialism in recognising the active and voluntaristic character of human conduct".[47] Human consciousness, and particularly that of working-class people – who often appear in discourse as the section of society most determined by their social conditions – is undermined by a strict, mechanical base-structure paradigm. This fails to recognise that, in Erik Olin Wright's contention, while "the limits of social structures are real [...] they are transformable by the conscious actions of human agents".[48] Giddens in part popularised the idea in sociology that structure should not be conceived of as having complete control over agency. Both must be understood as interlinked, dialectical phenomena, whose relations are complex, and only partially symbiotic, he argued. As we have observed early on in this present study, this is an argument expanded upon considerably by Antonio Gramsci, E.P. Thompson, Raymond Williams, and Pierre Bourdieu.[49]

In Liam O'Flaherty's evocative 1925 novel, *The Informer* (later a film, 1935), Gypo Nolan, the eponymous IRA informer, lives in an impoverished Dublin, where there is little social mobility or choice for those on the bottom rung of the socio-economic ladder, but there is still "resplendent idealism in damp cellars, saints starving in garrets", "thigh to thigh, breast to breast" with "the most lurid examples of debauchery and vice".[50] Slum idealism is something O'Flaherty, as a founding member of the Irish Communist Party, was acutely aware of; he portrays it cheek-by-jowl with the desperation of those more familiar in Doyle's novel, with "the most degraded types of those who dwell in the crowded warrens on either bank of the Liffey". In *The Informer*, women fall into prostitution, men into debauchery, Gypo into treachery, but there is still the articulate and visionary idealism of the working class – the disdain for the "publicans and bishops that were always

top dog in this country", the self-sacrifice for, and intellectual commitment to, the "Irish Worker's Republic" of "sincere revolutionist" and socialist worker Bartly Mulholland. He dreams of an Ireland of "no slums, no
hunger, no sick wives, no children that got the mumps and the rickets and
the whooping-cough with devilish regularity". In fact, Mulholland's lofty
idealism is the antithesis of Henry's simplistic materialism (or the simian
Gypo's brute selfishness, for that matter); it "never worried him" to think
of his impoverished family's material want, because "the 'cause' was above
everything" and "it was his wife who often urged him on to give all his time
to the 'cause' whenever he became slightly despondent".[51]

Doyle's lack of analysis also stands in stark contrast to the idealism of
Dublin train driver Dan in Ken Loach and Paul Laverty's recent film, *The
Wind that Shakes the Barley* (2006). As the IRA begins to embrace middle-
class supporters, Dan reminds fellow volunteers that they are "paupers just
like" him; "the IRA are backing the landlords and crushing people like you
and me".[52] This set-piece scene is the culmination of Dan's role as trade
unionist turned revolutionary, and, though it portends of capitalism's sway
over the emerging state, it also reveals the sway of reasoned ideology over
Dublin's radicalised working class. Bartly and Dan are thinkers, *in spite of*
the material privations that their ideology brings them. Henry is a revolutionary in spite of himself.

The "endemic difficulties" Giddens identifies in orthodox materialism
are evident in Henry's socially conditioned behaviour and compounded
by Doyle's portrayal of Gandon, Dalton and the other representatives of
bourgeois Ireland as sinister but quick-witted, active and controlling agents
in Irish society. In contrast with their proletarian foot soldiers, Doyle's
bourgeois nationalists are never deprived of an "active and voluntaristic"
consciousness. Dalton, the nationalist propagandist, befriends Henry and
converts him from the socialist Irish Citizens' Army to the more narrowly
republican cause of the IRA. As a proponent of "green" nationalism, his
calculating cynicism correlates unmistakably with the reductive gangster
typecasting of "Troubles" discourse, which film critic John Hill identifies
as part of a general "bias against understanding" – or what we might term a
discourse of depoliticisation – in depictions of conflict in Ireland.[53] Martin
McLoone sees this discourse as a means of accusing the Irish of an innate
tendency towards violence, which evades political explication – using "dominant negative stereotypes to deny the politics of the situation and to blame
the Irish themselves for their own proclivity to violence".[54] It is their "pathological fault" that they fight, not the consequence of imperial intervention
or ideological belief.[55] Such logic is inherent in many "Troubles" films, such
as the revealingly titled *Nothing Personal* (1995) and *The Devil's Own* (1997),
both of which portray combatants as cynical and psychopathic killers.

Dalton's own psychopathic disposition is of a type that is prepared to
kill Royal Irish Constabulary (RIC) members while admitting that they are

"all decent men" (*SCH*, p. 254). He also has the cynical audacity to write a Machiavellian article in Gandon's name, outrageously claiming that the late convert to republicanism – and erstwhile criminal – fought in the General Post Office (GPO). He treats foreign journalists to staged tours of the city that demonise the British forces, and his deeply sinister aptitude for "spin" ensures that the grisly, wanton murder of an innocent man with seven children will be "made heroic by night-time" (*SCH*, p. 247). The Neil Jordan film *The Crying Game* (1993) exemplified this paradigmatic Troubles reductivism by using the classic fable of "The Scorpion and the Frog" to illustrate how evil is "in [the scorpion's] nature" and terrorism, analogously, is in the terrorist's.[56] In Troubles parlance, Dalton is a "scorpion" *par excellence*, and Henry becomes his frog, an unsuspecting dupe who assists a creature of greater sagacity and malevolence through the hazards of war, later confessing himself to have been a "slave, the greatest fuckin' eejit ever born" (*SCH*, p. 318).[57]

Dalton, for all his villainy, is acutely aware of what is going on, of how to manipulate the press and the working class, suggesting that his social cohort has a purchase on politics that evades poor, Orwellian proles like Henry. Dalton's world of "wheels within wheels" eludes the witless Henry for most of the novel. He is always the intangible, shady villain, and such themes of "vulnerable individuals" falling foul of "an amorphous and superficially drawn terrorist presence" are, again, as Eve Patten notes, paradigmatic in Troubles writing. This narrative paradigm, which "has supplanted the novel's function of critique with a kind of literary compensation", has also "obliterated the need to examine the complexity and ambiguity of social conflict, while an elevation of the individual sufferings has largely obscured the exploration of community, identity and motivation".[58] Brian Moore's *Lies of Silence* (1990) and Benedict Kiely's *Proxopera* (1977), thrillers that focus on hostage situations, are illustrative in this regard, with their action-based narratives of individual sufferings perpetrated by malevolent and amorphous terrorist forces.

As Richard Hoggart noted, "the corollary of successful 'personalisation' is constant and considerable simplification", and Henry, as we have seen, is constantly simplified.[59] Later in the novel, he succumbs to egomania, Dalton's lyrical flattery – "*the pride of all Gaels was young Henry Smart*" – luring him into fighting for the cause of separatism, for "a version of Ireland that had little or nothing to do with the [socialist] Ireland I'd gone out to die for the last time" (*SCH*, pp. 170, 171). These irrational impulses are again implicitly comparable to those of his father. Asserting his fervour for killing policemen, Henry reminds us that this proclivity is (as the title of the "Troubles" film goes) "nothing personal"; "I came from a long line of cop killers [...] They were never people, the rozzers" (*SCH*, p. 193).[60] One of Doyle's rebels, Ivan Reynolds, becomes, and is actively fostered by his superiors as, the quintessence of psychopathic native brutality. He is yet another cliché of the "Troubles" canon, what Martin McLoone terms the "Paddy", "the simian primitive – a violent and irrational character who came to represent the Irish as a whole".[61] Owing to a dearth of enthusiasm for the IRA's campaign, Doyle's guerrilla army is forced to adopt a conscious strategy of promoting and intensifying terrorist savagery: "Collins himself said that there were never more than three thousand fighting. So, savages like Ivan did the work of hundreds" (*SCH*, p. 235). Evening-up the odds with his titanic malevolence, "Ivan the Terrible", "later to become Ivan Reynolds T.D.", is thus a typical simian rebel – one of "our own Mad Mullahs" – committing and commissioning countless acts of horrific political degeneracy (*SCH*, pp. 236, 253). As a "local warlord" he breaks the knees of a 12-year-old spy – an overt reference to more recent acts of IRA vigilantism (*SCH*, p. 311). Indeed, Doyle takes a light-hearted side-swipe at the revisionism of "Old IRA" sentimentalists here and in his latest book, in which an aged Henry and his Cumann na mBan wife discuss PIRA punishment beatings. "They didn't have that in our day," Henry unthinkingly remarks:

> – What? she said.
> I pointed at the telly.
> – That, I said.
> It was 1980. We were watching the news.
> – Kneecapping, I said.
> – No, she agreed. – We didn't have that.[62]

Doyle's point here is not merely that the old and new IRAs are the same political animal but, moreover, that they are the same deranged, depoliticised beast. Ivan, Doyle's old-new IRA man, is not alone in his seemingly instinctive proclivity for violent acts. Dan Breen – author of the book *My Fight for Irish Freedom* (1924) – is said by Jack to have "half the population terrified" (*SCH*, p. 252). Similarly, Doyle's hatchet-carrying dockers, "who came into work armed with blades, iron bars, bale-hooks, their own knuck-ledusters" (*SCH*, p. 159), are of a far more brutal breed than the politically conscious 1913 Lockout activists in James Plunkett's *Strumpet City* (1969). In yet another evocation of undifferentiated thuggery, even the police are the same as the pimps: "Costello cracked Dublin heads for a living. So did my father" (*SCH*, p. 14). Violent acts in the novel are denied any depth of meaning, their perpetrators any political intelligence. It is salutary to note that the only political ideology of any kind associated with Doyle's most monstrous and psychopathic creation, the criminal wife-beater Charlo Spencer, is militant republicanism: "Charlo was big into the H Blocks. He knew all the names [...] He'd have loved to have been in there with them."[63] This, in some ways, typifies the logic of Doyle's representation of political violence. What we are left with in *A Star* is yet another glib resistance to the historically particular and a typically universalising liberal-humanist denunciation of "the men of violence".

But Doyle's denunciation of political violence is a political intervention in itself, one that buttresses the imperial view of anti-colonial resistance as something beyond logic and beneath integrity, as perpetrated by "creatures" let "loose on the country" (*SCH*, p. 252). As the term "terrorism" suggests, the violence would seem to thrive on its own merits, as an over-arching ideology in itself – a doctrine of terror – rather than the result of any historically situated, ideological and material conflict. In the "freezing, dripping darkness" of a sewer, the child Henry seeks comfort in his father's blood-soaked coat, even though it stinks of death. He smelt and "liked the smell of animals and blood", we are told; "I didn't know that I was inhaling years of violence and murder" (*SCH*, p. 56). Later, with the "worst scum of the slums", he would kill cows and smear blood on his face, boil baby rats and smear the "soup" (*SCH*, p. 66) of their decaying bodies on his hands to madden their trapped parents. Having paid for that "blooding" – that initiation into savagery – he is loath to pass it on. Rejecting his father's legacy, Henry later denies his newborn daughter a taste of *his* coat, the blood-drenched war vestment within which the child is symbolically "looking for a nipple" (*SCH*, p. 330): "I held her out before she could suck at its history [...] I stood up and took off the old coat. I took it to the door and threw it in the yard" (*SCH*, p. 330). One is reminded here of Yeats's description of his own political zealotry as the creation of a "fanatic heart", which he took from his "mother's womb".[64] Ireland's legacy of violence, Doyle's reductive symbolism suggests, might be explained away by a "taste for blood" – an animalistic, visceral barbarism induced by the most specious of circumstances, the most individuated of conditions.

As Seamus Deane has noted of revisionist historiography, "theory always seems to be apart from, not of the Rising. The other stock opposite to theory – instinct – is also invoked".[65] More universally, the omission of a thinking insurrectionary is, Guha discerns, "dyed into most narratives by metaphors assimilating peasant revolts to natural phenomena: they break out like thunderstorms, heave like earthquakes, spread like wildfires, infect like epidemics".[66] While Henry's revolt is not a peasant uprising but a proletarian one, it too seems to infect like a disease. Unlike him, Saoirse, his daughter, will be truly "free" from this malaise. Only in the rejection of an old, barbarised Ireland, it is implied, may a new narrative of peace begin, but the reality of colonialism is conspicuously absent. As Deane also acerbically deduces, "sometimes Henry Smart seems like one of those stalwart heroes from a Dick Francis thriller; sometimes he's just another blarney-blathering id that believes it's an ego".[67] As his crutch again suggests, he is crippled by some fundamental absence, and it is with a similar logic that Joey "The Lips" of *The Commitments* (1988) could opine that "the feuding Brothers in Northern Ireland [...] wouldn't be shooting the asses off each other if they had soul."[68] Like the crassest caricatures of "Troubles" writing, Doyle's proletarian revolutionaries are emotionally and intellectually deficient clichés – bereft of "soul". His stereotypes confirm widely propagated non-explanations of "senseless violence", reducing the labyrinthine complexity of history to the facile commonplaces of counter-insurgency propaganda.

Kleptocracy, Catholicism, nationalism: *"un marché de dupes"*

In another sense, there is a nonetheless profoundly proletarian thrust to this novel, as with much of Doyle's work, and there can be little doubt that his repudiation of Irish nationalism, and its all-too-comfortable relationship with capitalism and Catholicism, conveys more of his ire for the claustrophobic political milieu he has lived in than for the formative period that the novel depicts. Doyle has made no secret of his distaste for the conservatism of the state in which he lives – if the second divorce referendum of the 1990s was not passed, he threatened to leave it, and his harrowing television series, *Family* (1994), played a significant role in public debate on the issue at the time.[69] Doyle has also been a regular contributor to the immigrant newspaper *Metro Éireann*, with a book of short stories he wrote for it published as *The Deportees* (2007). A collaborative centenary retelling, with Bisi Adigun, of J.M. Synge's *The Playboy of the Western World* (1907), in which Christy Mahon becomes Christopher Malomo, a Nigerian, was staged in the same year – and both works were obvious efforts to begin the integration of immigrants' stories into the fabric of Irish literature. Doyle has indeed consistently championed the causes of Dublin's most disadvantaged and marginalised communities, having worked as a teacher in one of them for many years. He joined the Socialist Labour Party at one point, "read a lot of Trotsky" and currently identifies himself as a socialist.[70] Indeed, for him, Dublin's working-class culture is something implicitly at odds with the establishment norms of Irish life; he tries to "capture and celebrate crudity, loudness, linguistic flair and slang, which is the property of working class people."[71]

In *The Snapper* (1990), Doyle explores the shame and social embarrassment suffered by working-class teenager Sharon Rabbitte and her father, Jimmy, when she becomes pregnant to a local married man whose identity she refuses to reveal. Jimmy battles with his own shame, but eventually surmounts it, rejecting the religious and cultural conventions that leave him anxious and embarrassed. In *The Woman Who Walked into Doors* (1996) Doyle deals with domestic violence and a society in which women are disempowered. In *The Commitments* (1988), working-class Northsiders embrace soul music, discovering – as the "niggers o' Dublin" – an affinity with the USA's alienated black community: "Say it loud, I'm black an' I'm proud," Jimmy Rabbitte, the novel's chief protagonist, exclaims.[72] Indeed, the film version (1991), directed by Alan Parker, which had a huge impact in popularising working-class culture in Ireland, stressed the importance of ideology to the fabric of working-class life. When the soul band falls apart, Joey the Lips reminds his dejected "soul" brothers and sisters that:

> the success of the band was irrelevant! You raised [local people's] expectations of life, you lifted their horizons. Sure, we could have been famous and made albums and stuff, but that would've been predictable. This way it's poetry.[73]

In all of Doyle's work, there is a sense of irreverence towards and radical alienation from hegemonic values that chimes with other writing assessed in this book.

In a similar vein, *A Star* evinces the sense of betrayal that exasperated many erstwhile working-class revolutionaries in the bourgeois Republic. Doyle's narrative underscores the process by which their stories have been historically elided. Consequently, his history, the one in which Henry plays "The Last Post" at O'Donovan Rossa's grave, in which de Valera "smelt of shite", is one that is intentionally at variance with official record (*SCH*, p. 139). In the real world, Henry, and others like him, are written out of history, whereas the "gurrier" Dan Breen, "who lived long enough to write the book and so became the man who fired the first shot for Irish freedom", is written in (*SCH*, p. 128). As an uneducated proletarian and "one of Collins' anointed", Henry may be useful fodder, but he is "actually [...] excluded from everything" (*SCH*, p. 208). A new political dispensation finds little use for the working-class activists who risked life and limb in the military engagement that brought it about. Unlike the bourgeois Gandon and rural Ivan, they have "no stake in the country [...] never had, never will" (*SCH*, p. 327). The regime once "needed trouble makers", Dalton explains, but "very soon we'll have to be rid of them", a purge presaged by the strictly hierarchical system of Sinn Féin electioneering, whereby Henry and "none of the other men of the slums and hovels ever made it on to the [candidacy] list" (*SCH*, pp. 327, 208). Subjected to some of the more unpalatable expediencies of revolutionary warfare, they "carry their cross for Ireland" (to paraphrase a frequent mantra from Doyle's sequel *Oh! Play That Thing* [2004]), while bourgeois opportunists cynically capitalise on their gains. "Gandon got Commercial Affairs and the Sea," Henry wryly remarks, while "Henry Smart got wet" (*SCH*, p. 209). O'Flaherty's McDara also evokes such anger on behalf of the soldiers "of the common people [...] the nameless ones", who are eschewed as "the backwash of revolution".[74] Equally "nameless and expendable", Henry and his fellow "decoys and patsies" are unceremoniously extirpated from the Irish body politic, and the omission of their histories poses one of the central questions of the novel (*SCH*, p. 208): if conventional history has elided the working class, why then should this unconventional novel of the working class pay tribute to conventional history?

In this invocation of the theme of history "from below", Doyle attempts to cleave a neat division between socialism and nationalism, between the altruists "from below" he wishes to lionise and the bourgeois radicals "from above" he wishes to vilify and debase. James Connolly's socialist politics – which were renowned and often criticised for their affinity with nationalism – must thus be revised in light of the novel's particular ideological standpoint. In personal terms, Connolly is portrayed as an antitype of Pearse, nationalism's most revered icon. While Pearse parallels the stargazing Melody, pontificating absently from a podium or mumbling aloofly from a high chair in the midst of carnage, his abstract disposition is a foil for Connolly's unpretentious, practical humanity. Connolly "wasn't just a man," Henry explains, "he was all of us" (*SCH*, p. 127). A tangible, humane figure, he profoundly impacts upon Henry's youthful development, teaching him to read and write and, most importantly, explaining the relevance of social revolution – "why we were poor and why we didn't have to be" (*SCH*, p. 127). He and Larkin are portrayed in an almost Messianic light: Henry, "Paddy and Felix were the same, and the rest of the Citizen Army men. They'd all been *made* by Connolly and Larkin" (*SCH*, p. 127; emphasis added). Reclaiming Connolly as a socialist, not a nationalist, is perhaps understandable in light of how he "lives on in official memory as a Fenian martyr rather than as a Marxist revolutionary", but Doyle's depiction is ultimately light on politics, and rather more given to accentuating Connolly's "human condition".[75]

He therefore eschews the actual politics that Connolly espoused, in which nationalism and socialism, "the two currents of revolutionary thought in Ireland [...] were not antagonistic but complementary".[76] The revolutionary who would declare "to all the world, that the working class of Dublin stands for the cause of Ireland, and the cause of Ireland is the cause of a separate and distinct nationality", is conveniently remoulded, like so many other aspects of the Rising, to accord with Doyle's revisionist views.[77] In doing so, the author is ironically open to the very charge he makes against the emergent nationalist hegemony, that of rendering Connolly, who was "dangerous alive", "more useful washed and dead" (*SCH*, p. 318). The novel traduces Connolly's political vision, supplanting it with a liberal-humanist ethic of eternal verities – of a benevolent essence, which he comes to characterise. Here we have an instance of what Slaughter identifies as an "increasing influence on world literature", the "philosophical resignation to what is taken to be 'the human condition' ".[78] Connolly's "humanity" conveniently transcends politics, becoming an innate "condition", rather than the product of a complicated ideological vision.

A Star suggests that such political complexity is somewhat irrelevant to Henry, who is ultimately a mere cog in the overarching and imperturbable capitalist system. Capitalism in the novel can manipulate political unrest,

killing Climanis or torturing Miss O'Shea, ostensibly for political expedi-
ency, but really because their behaviour is "interfering with free trade",
and, one by one, the capitalist criminals of Doyle's pre-revolutionary
Dublin opportunistically embrace the incoming regime (*SCH*, p. 316).
Once a clandestine gangster, Alfie Gandon becomes a noted political
activist, then a TD, retrospectively and falsely placed among the rebels at
the GPO. Like the stevedore who demands sexual favours from employees, or Henry's newly converted republican landlord, he now becomes
assimilated as "one of us" (*SCH*, p. 169). A "Home Ruler and a Catholic",
he is purportedly "not like one of the tail-coated fuckers who robbed the
people blind and called it business" (*SCH*, p. 165). The revolution has
changed Gandon's style, not his substance, has changed Ireland's flag,
but not its financiers. "Sinn Féin had very quickly become respectable,"
our narrator recalls, "the party of the parish priests and those middle-
class men [like Gandon] cute enough to know when the wind was changing". They are curiously "outlawed by the British, but cosy", representing
the kind of schizoid quality that Gandon, as both gangster and politician,
so chillingly personifies (*SCH*, p. 207). Ivan too represents this triumph
of human avarice over idealism. He articulates the calculating cynicism
that Henry has unwittingly assisted all along, advising that "all the best
soldiers are businessmen", that "there had to be a reason for the killing
and the late nights, and it wasn't Ireland". "Control of the island" has
surely been the point of all this mayhem, he reasons, "not the harps and
martyrs and the freedom to swing a hurley" (*SCH*, p. 314). His acquisitive
vision echoes that of the Volunteers in the GPO, who are concerned at
the fate of money left unattended by fleeing staff. The Volunteers and
ICA men alternately dreamed of stamping money with harps or starry
ploughs, but while they haggled over symbolism, the capitalist system of
monetary exchange remained unquestioned. Rejecting that "old Jewish
shite" called socialism, the new state rushes to affirm that capitalism's
practices "will go on without the English. And that they'll go on even
better without them" (*SCH*, pp. 172, 178).

All of this disappointment leaves Henry feeling a "complete and utter
fool" and emphatically revises the "revolution" as a capitalist coup in which
stupid proletarians, led by Machiavellian middle-class forces, caused a lot
of trouble for no good reason (*SCH*, p. 317). Our protagonist has murdered
many supposed enemies, yet now he wonders if any of his victims "really
[were] spies" (*SCH*, p. 327). In a moment of depressing clarity, the zealot
who would have even killed Connolly, had he been given his "name on a
piece of paper", now begins to question his years of "revolutionary" warfare (*SCH*, p. 318). But Doyle's conclusion is not quite as much a critique of
conservative politics as a capitulation to them. For him, it is Henry's idealism that was unwise, not the logic of the conservatives and capitalists.

Reviewing his years of warfare, Henry articulates a rather bleak evaluation of the results of his toil that summarily depoliticises a period of profound political importance:

> Everything I'd done, every bullet and assassination, all the blood and brains, prison, the torture, the last four years and everything in them, everything had been done for Ivan and the other Ivans, the boys whose time had come. (*SCH*, p. 318)

Invoking the sloganeering of more recent Troubles – in a parodied invocation of the IRA maxim "tiocfaidh ár lá" (our day will come) – Doyle suggests the continuing futility of political violence, and we return to the present-centredness of revisionist historiography.

In Doyle's latest novel, the last in *The Last Roundup* trilogy, this present-centredness is reconfirmed. History and filmography are again magically revised as Henry teams up with another host of unlikely narrative conduits, including film director John Ford and the PIRA army council. Henry becomes a consultant on Ford's 1952 film, *The Quiet Man*, which, it transpires, was originally intended as a warts-and-all biopic on the working-class revolutionary's fight for Irish freedom. The film, however, becomes nothing of the sort, as Henry's story – and, by extension, the history of proletarian Dublin – is dropped in favour of a less controversial romance between John Wayne and Maureen O'Hara, in which Ireland itself is romanticised. While Henry is accorded a greater degree of agency in this later book, the novel nonetheless concludes with his realisation, yet again, that he has been "such a fuckin' eejit".[79] The IRA, he discovers, had seen his gritty script and has baulked at its realism. It needed a fantasy of "a place worth fighting for" in order to keep the conflict with Britain going, and though Henry's tale was "exactly as it had happened", its narrative of the Free State's foundation, depicting "the fight and the ultimate betrayal", "the failure of the revolution", was inconvenient if compellingly real.[80] Doyle undoubtedly chimes here again with one of the major themes of Dublin's writing of working-class life, once more representing the elision of working-class history from nationalist narratives. A cynical IRA volunteer tells Henry that such counter-proletarian propaganda and mendacity are what nationalism is made of: "Ireland was *The Quiet Man*. Not Dublin or Belfast, or the slums or the queues for the boat out. Or the true story of Henry Smart. That'll be a different day's work. A different film altogether."[81] Henry had earlier inferred the nationalists' modern logic was inherently bourgeois. Observing the 1981 IRA hunger strike, he and a confidant discuss its historical resonances:

> –A bad business, he said.
> –Yeah.

–Like in your day, Henry, eh?
–I never went without food, I said. –If I could help it.
I'd go for his head and knock out any doubts he had about me.
–I knew hunger all my life, I said.–And it was never a fuckin' strike.
Only the middle class could come up with starvation as a form of
protest.[82]

But while nationalism may be dismissed by some socialists in this manner as "a bourgeois abstraction", as Eagleton writes, "it is equally a matter
of passionate popular sentiment [...] Like gender and ethnicity, nationalism
has no obvious class bearing, but is itself, as Connolly recognized, the site
of a class struggle".[83] Moreover, if late-twentieth-century Dublin is worse
than ever, "killing everything young", its poverty "just atrocious", Henry
fails to envisage any hope of political betterment for his class.[84] Derek Hand
came to a similar conclusion in his review of *A Star*, arguing that Doyle's
analysis finds "that all ideology – be it nationalist or socialist – is in the end
quite useless in altering the facts of working people's lives". The novel "is
more concerned about reading the Irish past from a very present-centred
perspective".[85]

Doyle's proletarian rebel is not just inherently stupid, but wilfully so.
His people are not just caught up in a violent conflict but, in *The Dead
Republic*, "prone to violence" itself. "It was an old story," as Doyle himself
puts it.[86] Alternatively a comic farce or a deeply sinister capitalist *coup d'état*,
A Star's "revolution" also resists any sense of the little man, Henry Smart,
having had any significant or substantive political impact. Foreign tyranny
is replaced by native tyranny, the possibility of proletarian political resistance – "from below" – is undercut by the reality of irrevocable dominance
"from above". In Dermot Bolger's *Night Shift* (1985), Donal ponders on how
"there were no statues of how those who didn't make it into the corridors of
power looked twenty years after the truce", and how pathetic such statues
might have looked, of men "squabbling over the details of inflated attacks
in pubs". Henry is perhaps the unmoulded statue of one of these unheeded
proletarians, "staring out from dead-end jobs over a stagnant Free State".[87]
But in a typically postmodern fashion, the "facts" of his history become provisional and slippery, comparable, as E.H. Carr has put it, to "fish swimming
about in a vast and sometimes inaccessible ocean; and what the historian
catches will depend, partly on chance, but mainly on what part of the ocean
he chooses to fish in and what tackle he chooses to use."[88] *A Star* is not
merely a novel about the revolutionary period, it is also about the present,
in which the authority of history and the history of authority has become
increasingly destabilised. It is a novel that yearns for a future in which
Ireland's "obstinacy", as Michael Hartnett termed it, "its constant connection with the past", may be broken, or at least reconfigured with a sense of
ironic detachment.[89] But ironically too, *A Star* would seem to affirm that

the possibility of such detachment has not yet arrived, for, in its invocation of some of the most depoliticising thematics of "Troubles" writing, Doyle's novel admits a pressing connection with the past and its own choice, in Carr's metaphor, of a particular part of the ideological "ocean" in which to "fish". Political violence becomes the dehistoricised by-product of personal suffering, avarice, egotism and instinct and, moreover, it is the proletarian protagonist and his working-class comrades who are denied the cerebral capacities of their bourgeois betters. This suggests a rather depressing belief in a very rigid materialist determinism, which curiously only applies to the working class. Correlating the mistakes of criminal father and rebel son, Doyle parrots a depoliticised discourse of undifferentiated barbarity and infers the pointlessness of proletarian political agency. To Yeats's spectral question, "Was it needless death after all?" he rejoins with a resounding "yes".[90]

Conclusion

Doyle has remarked that being invited to see Paul Mercier's play *Wasters* (1985) was a decisive moment in his own artistic development. The production was "fast and funny and wonderful but that wasn't it: for the first time in my life I saw characters I recognized, people I met every day, the language I heard every day [...] I'll never forget it."[1] His sense of excitement at seeing contemporary working-class Dublin depicted on stage was a measure of how little that community was served by literature and popular culture. It echoes the frustration of another, earlier writer, Brendan Behan, who quipped in 1951 that "cultural activity in present-day Dublin is largely agricultural". Behan complained of the "feeling of isolation one suffers writing in a Corporation housing scheme", while relating that contemporary Irish authors wrote "mostly about their hungry bogs and the great scarcity of crumpet". "I am a city rat," he continued. "Joyce is dead and O'Casey is in Devon. The people writing here now have as much interest for me as an epic poet in Finnish or a Lapland novelist."[2] Both he and Doyle started out as writers in environments that afforded them little encouragement for their own brand of art, and yet they would achieve a great deal in representing the Dublin they knew but rarely found in contemporary texts. Both writers expressed the sense of a lacuna in Irish culture, and it is out of a similar concern that this book has emerged.

The reading of 13 individual texts in this study has explored issues of gender, nationalism, class "injuries", culture, industry, work, imprisonment, sexual repression, historiography and political agency. It has revealed a continuing tendency towards subversive literary forms, which often invoke bourgeois logic in order to confute it. It has engaged these issues in order to explore how the fiction and plays of working-class Dublin sustain common themes, and found that a number of central ideas emerge. It has also discovered many echoes of O'Casey's central concerns and parallels in the fiction and plays of writers such as A.P. Wilson, Oliver St John Gogarty, Robert Collis, Joe O'Byrne, Paul Mercier, Sebastian Barry, Thomas Kilroy, Ken Harmon and Enda Walsh, whose writing on working-class Dublin

suggests great scope for further scholarly work. Most of the works examined here have received little or no academic attention to date. Despite their
striking resemblances, they have heretofore failed to secure the status that
they clearly deserve as part of a distinct literary heritage, which represents
the "people [that Doyle and others] met every day".

Further, the central concern here, of charting a continuity of writing
that is embedded in the lived experience of working-class people, is mirrored in the preoccupations of the writing itself. The failure of predominant
aesthetic practices to reflect the lives of the poor remains a central theme
since the earliest writing. In Act III of Oliver St John Gogarty's *Blight* (1917),
a meeting of Dublin Corporation's Hospital Board is used to contrast the
aesthetic aloofness of the middle class with the material realities of proletarian life. City councillors opt to avoid reading a letter from the Local
Government Board, "calling attention to the urgent necessity of adopting
some scheme for preventing the spread of the hidden plague" in the tenements, because of "considerations of good taste".[3] Instead, they pointedly
turn their attention to lofty musings about Dublin's architecture and the
building of an ornate mortuary chapel.[4] Gogarty's message could hardly
be clearer: in Dublin's corridors of power, the aesthetics of death are more
important than the proletariat's misery in life. The dichotomy he draws
between the reality of working-class experience and the aloofness of bourgeois aesthetics is not just a figurative comment on social divisions but also
a challenge to the world of culture. The term aesthetic itself is "shorthand
for a whole project of hegemony, the massive introjections of abstract reason
by the life of the senses", as Terry Eagleton writes.[5] Predominant aesthetic
practices affect how we express ourselves through art and how hegemony
expresses itself in everyday "abstract reason".

Consider, for instance, James Wickham's contention that working-class
Dubliners have been on the receiving end of forms of "cultural discrimination", which pervade basic assumptions about behaviour and status and result
in their social invisibility. Wickham observed 30 years ago "the paradox that
while it is often claimed that there are no class accents in Ireland, nobody
expects someone with a 'Dublin accent' to come from Foxrock: working class
language apparently does not exist."[6] His contention is still valid today. Yes,
there has been immense progress in this regard since Donagh MacDonagh
thought it necessary to include a glossary containing 69 words of working-
class Dublinese at the end of his farce play *Happy as Larry* (1946).[7] MacDonagh
explained vernacular words such as "bowsey", "gas" and "hoosh", and other
idiomatic expressions such as "fair enough", "ball of malt" and "ould ones".[8]
Evidently, he felt hearing and seeing these terms would be a new experience
for much of his largely middle-class audience and, as such, his translation
suggested gaping class divisions. In Heno Magee's play, *Hatchet* (1972), a glossary at the start of the published text explains the meaning of colloquial-
isms such as "oulwan", "oufella", "youngwan", "brasser", "slag", "slagging"

and "burst".[9] Magee admits such translation was necessary, given the likely middle-class makeup of his audience.[10] Later writers, particularly Doyle, have shown far greater confidence that their demotic will be comprehensible to readers. Doyle's novels are replete with working-class language, not to the extent of an Irvine Welsh work perhaps, but certainly more so than most Irish fiction. But in the 1990s Doyle related that this idiom still occupied an uncomfortable space in Irish culture. In *The Snapper* (1993), Jimmy Rabbitte's working-class accent impedes his chances of becoming a radio presenter. His attempts to develop a (bourgeois, Southside) radio voice – "Hoy there [...] This is Jommy Robbitte, Thot's Rockin' Robbitte" – may make him "sound like a dope", but his attendance at elocution lessons in order to develop this ridiculous middle-class twang is indispensable in his view:

> – I've a gig in a few weeks; Soturday, he told Sharon.
> – Stop talkin' like tha', will yeh.
> – I'm tryin' to get used to it.
> – It makes yeh sound like a fuckin' eejit.
> – Here maybe, but not on the radio, said Jimmy.[11]

Becoming acceptable in society is partly about losing the markers of a working-class upbringing, Doyle suggests. In *The Van* (1991), Jimmy's father observes the "confident" voices of those, on Dublin's affluent Grafton Street, who are "used to money": "they shouted and didn't mind being heard – they wanted to be heard. They had accents like newsreaders".[12] His son's sense of class shame echoes in Catherine Dunne's *A Name for Himself* (1999), when Farrell checks his accent in front of a middle-class friend:

> Christ. He was making himself sound like a common labourer [...] suddenly, painfully conscious of his dark blue overalls and his Dublin accent. No matter how careful he tried to be, broad, unguarded vowels still slipped to the surface of his speech in moments of stress.[13]

Anxieties of this kind are a curious part of the suppression of proletarian culture through elitist practices and predispositions. Joe Duffy, the well-known Irish radio presenter from Ballyfermot, might be furnished as a near anomalous example of a successful Irish media broadcaster with an identifiably working-class accent, but the much-laurelled *Liveline* presenter reveals, in a recent newspaper interview, how he struggled against class snobbery both within RTÉ and previously as leader of the Trinity College Students' Union. Duffy's election to the Trinity position was heralded by an *Irish Times* headline that noted the unlikelihood of his provenance – "Ballyfermot man gets Trinity post" – making him feel like "I'd come from outer space". He later feared rejection as an RTÉ applicant, because his voice wasn't "trained"; as interviewer Patrick Freyne comments, "the elephant in the room, of course, was class. Working-class accents were then (as now) not the norm on national radio broadcasts".[14] Duffy agrees, recalling:

> Thinking when I was growing up in Ballyfermot that all the ads on radio and television were middle-class ads [...] It was all "take the car to..." and we never had a car, or "ring this number ..." and we never had a phone. We had a rented television with a two-bob slot in the back [...] It was a completely working-class world.[15]

Such lazy replication of social snobbery as televisual reality has been a chronic failure of the "national" broadcaster. Helena Sheehan probes the almost surreal elision of working-class people from RTÉ's flagship soap opera, *Glenroe* (1987–2002), in which "nobody even worked for a wage" – incredibly – for the first five years of its production history.[16] While the Dublin-based soap opera *Fair City* (1989–present) did much to redress this concern, Sheehan considered the paradox that "although most characters were supposed to be of working class origins [in this later soap], hardly any of them have been wage labourers"; indeed, "an extraordinary number of characters have owned their own local businesses".[17] In this phantasmal "Fair City", people with Finglas accents still had Foxrock bank accounts, all classes intermingled cosily in the local pub, and the everyday issues of class stratification, or of living on working-class wages, received scant attention.

This baffling aversion to the working class, in everything from accent to television drama, is a curious comment on Irish culture. It is part of what Peter Sheridan identifies as a "certain orthodoxy":

> Particularly if you look at the whole legacy of de Valera and this rural idyllic notion he had of Ireland being a place of "comely maidens dancing at the crossroads", a kind of rural utopia. For those of us who were coming from a working-class background this was so far out from where we were coming from, where, obviously [...] whole communities were abandoned [...] What a thing for a country to do to people – to take away who they are![18]

Sheridan's writing, and his work in theatre, is partly about a historic and cultural retrieval of "who they are", about giving "Irish society [...] a good kick up the backside", as he puts it, and the writers this book has examined all try to unearth the submerged narratives of a Dublin that became a non-place in national culture. They equally endeavour to challenge that culture *from below*.[19]

Retrieval, revision and renaissance

To be sure, retrospection and disclosure go hand-in-hand in the fiction and plays of working-class Dublin. Works such as Christy Brown's *Down All the Days* (1970), Dermot Bolger's *The Woman's Daughter* (1987), *April Bright* (1995) and *The Passion of Jerome* (1999); Mannix Flynn's *James X* (2003), Peter Sheridan's *Big Fat Love* (2003) and Sebastian Barry's *The Pride of Parnell Street* (2007) all retrieve meaning from past events, which they perceive as historically distorted or unaccounted for. This was central to O'Casey's aesthetic in the plays for which he is most famous, the *Trilogy* and *The Silver Tassie*, in their return to the site of unfinished historical business to dig up the unrecognised histories of working-class life. Historiography and its misrepresentation are abiding themes from O'Casey onward, as my readings of Roddy Doyle's *A Star Called Henry* (1999), James Plunkett's *Strumpet City* (1969) and Paul Smith's *Summer Sang in Me* (1972), in particular, seek to show. In his surrealist play on the "worker saint" Matt Talbot, *Talbot's Box* (1979), Thomas Kilroy intimates the role of texts in the diminution of working-class history. He parallels the historical revisionism attendant on Matt Talbot's memory – which either diminishes his reputation locally as a "scab" and "strike breaker", or lauds him among businessmen as a "model" to "all Christian workers", who "never complained" – with the historical revisionism of capitalist state hegemony.[20] The "Priest Figure" of the play brings forward Talbot's book collection, which Kilroy uses to emphasise the shared interests of capitalism and the Catholic Church:

> Priest Figure: The remarkable library of a simple saint, found after his death. *(Title.) Socialism* by Rev. Robert O'Kane, S.J. Several books by Mr. Belloc on the Church and Socialism. Studies of the illustrious Father McKenna, S.J. on the workers' problems...
>
> First Man [businessman Mr D.]:   That will be all, father. Thank you, the point is made. (Priest Figure *retreats*.) Meanwhile, the Servant of God digested these works of Christian direction and advised his fellow workers on their rightful place in society.
>
> Second Man [worker]:   Ay. Down on their uppers!
>
> First Man: Well, now. That's it. Law and order restored. It didn't work. Consult your history books.   Police exonerated. Disturbances exaggerated. The usual protesters. They're all down in me little book. Enemies of Church and State.[21]

History books exonerate the powerful of wrongdoing, Kilroy suggests, while fostering meekness, acceptance and social stagnation in the working class.

Kilroy criticises this process of silencing through discourse, which was highlighted too in the women's stories explored in Chapter 3. Sheridan's Philo and Smith's Molly speak, albeit problematically, for all those working-class women whose histories have been forgotten, and both writers show how the institutions of the state are particularly dismissive towards working-class women, who have little social power. Hiding of the truth of institutional abuse was also a key concern for writers such as Sheridan, James McKenna, James Plunkett, and Dermot Bolger, as we have seen. Working-class people were particularly prone to ending up in state institutions because of their lack of access to legal and social power, and for some, such as Mannix Flynn's James X, the truth of this is simply too painful, a site of anxiety and ambiguity.[22] "Somebody tell someone. They make us squeal and dance like little pigs," James writes of his sufferings at the hands of the Christian Brothers. But his underlying uncertainty about his own history mirrors his society's refusal to recognise it: "Let me hide away from my memory, remember? It happened! It happened! It happened! It happened! Didn't, did, didn't. Did so! No! No! Yes OK".[23] A similar articulation of psychological embattlement and ambiguity over past sexual trauma (and, by extension, society's own inadequate response to sexual abuse) arises in Dorothy Nelson's depiction of a harrowing memory in the opening of her novel *In Night's City* (1982). When Sara recalls her father molesting her at four years of age, she first obliquely describes the act, then displaces it onto a phantom alter ego, Maggie: "I felt the Dark touchin' me funny an' I was cryin' so Maggie came an' he touched Maggie funny not me. Not me. Not me."[24] Sara's coping mechanism in recalling such events is to pretend they are happening to someone else, that she "wasn't there"; her mother's method is to pretend it is all a "dream".[25] A similar attitude allows Sara to deny her poverty: when out in town she pretends not to know her brothers, "scruffs" whose general appearance betrays the family's penury; "you'd be able to tell right off I was a nothin' when you'd see them".[26] Mannix Flynn's protagonist also proclaims his sense of classed cultural exclusion while part of a punk band. At a gig, he evidently feels utterly alienated from the crowd "and their fucking student cards", and from the Arts Centre itself, "this poncy middle of the middle of the road, middle class's centre".[27] His surname, "X", is indeed a register of his enduring anonymity, his disfigured, branded subjectivity. The scars that society inflicts on its most vulnerable, and the role of class inequality in dehumanising working-class people, was again a potent theme in the prison dramas of Chapter 5, in which the prison is a microcosm that reflects macrocosmic human relations under capitalism and brings those from the margins of society centre stage.

In my introduction I drew attention to a comment by Michel Peillon, in which he characterised Dublin's working class as a community opposed to hegemonic norms – "a pole of differentiation in Irish society".[28] The sense of this social stratum as an alienated cohort throughout this study, in both cultural and socio-economic terms, dovetails with the radical outlook that Peillon identified, and with Terry Eagleton's "counter-public sphere" of working-class radicalism.[29] In the literature this book has examined, Dublin's working class is simultaneously at the forefront of national social change and excluded from the epicentres of superstructural power: Henry Smart is perhaps its crystallisation (if problematically so, as I have argued) with his central role in Irish history systematically airbrushed and distorted to suit hegemonic power. This alienation is identified in more general terms by Ferdia Mac Anna, who grounds his "Dublin Renaissance" in a counter-hegemonic reaction from the city. Like Sheridan, he argues that the emphasis on rural life in Irish culture caused an "exile" of the capital city, and young Dubliners have felt culturally displaced within it; it "was like living inside a fossil".[30] Mac Anna pays particular attention to the obsession of "Renaissance" writers with the "ignored or officially invisible suburbs", the "gurrier chic" which provoked much public criticism and debate.[31] Writers were "now indicting the society that spawned them, a society rooted in corruption, laziness and indifference to the problems of contemporary Ireland".[32] Their "Dirty Dublin Poetic Realism", in which the "myth of a single Ireland is no longer true", marked the emergence of a literary challenge to hegemonic modes of thought.[33] What is most important about Mac Anna's appraisal, for the purposes of this present study, is his identification of a number of common ideas and themes in "Renaissance" writing: pointed social disenchantment, the desire to unearth hidden narratives of impoverished Dublin life and an almost obligatory attack on the orthodoxies and norms of bourgeois Ireland.[34] However, his failure to specify *class* as a key factor in this paradigm is remiss, even if it is strongly inferred.

In Doyle's *Brownbread* (1992), a typical "Renaissance" work, young working-class Dubliners are depicted in a surreal confrontation with rural Ireland and the religious and cultural ideals it espouses, when they kidnap a bishop and goad rural gardaí with cries of "go home, you, and milk your cows!"[35] One of the kidnappers, Donkey, has a "tattoo he did on himself at the back of the class" which proclaims an "Eire nua. Eire bleedin' nua".[36] But Donkey tellingly eschews patriotism:

JOHN: You'd die for Ireland, wouldn't yeh?
DONKEY: I would in me brown.[37]

Donkey yearns for a new Ireland, but he is not a conventional nationalist. His envisaged Ireland, the plot suggests, is one in which rural superiority and Catholic teachings no longer subordinate the urban poor. Marshall W. Fishwick writes, in his study of popular culture, that the proletarian is "chiefly marked by being cut out from the vital functions of his own society. He is the aggregate of outsiders, the fringe-dwellers."[38] The ironic sense of being a "fringe dweller" in one's capital city is a major theme of this writing – in Bolger's *The Journey Home* (1990), McKenna's *The Scatterin'* (1959), Dunne's *Goodbye to the Hill* (novel, 1965; play, 1976) and Heno Magee's *Hatchet* (1978), to name but a few examples. Working-class Dubliners occupy an estranged space in the nation-state, but act as a vanguard of modernisation. They are alienated from national culture, "this glorious shagging kingdom you were excluded from", in Bolger's words, despite their enormous role within it.[39] Paula Meehan, in her poem "A Child's Map of Dublin", captures this exasperated feeling of exclusion in symbolic terms: "I wanted to find you Connolly's Starry Plough, / the flag I have lived under since birth or since / I first scanned the nightskies and learned the nature of work", she tells the porter at a museum. "That hasn't been on show in years" the porter replies; "They're revising at the National Museum". In the "revised" history of Ireland, Connolly, his Plough, his progressive politics and the people he represented, are displaced.[40]

It is unsurprising, therefore, that the forms employed by writers of working-class life are often as subversive as their themes. Realism is always inflected with expressive tropes and content that challenge the reality of the status quo. Sheridan again highlights the dichotomy between the De Valerian fantasy of hegemonic Ireland and the disenchanting reality of its inner-city dwellers' lives in *Finders Keepers* (2004). The play commences as a conventionally realist work, and its central complication is the realistic dilemma of young would-be dock worker, Pancho, regarding his father's drunken sale of a "button" – a work permit passed on by dockers to their sons, which secured their "inheritance" of a job. If Pancho has no button, he may need to emigrate, but the play ends with Pancho and his friend saving the button and thus avoiding the mail boat to England. However, the late transformation of Pancho's headmaster into the form of a frog emphasises the ironic improbability of Sheridan's happy ending. Moreover, it suggests the farcical inappropriateness of the conventional, fairytale, coming-of-age narrative to the precarious poverty of working-class life.

This juxtaposition of utopian fantasy and dystopian reality recalls many other works: it is apparent in writing of the working class since James Stephens' *The Charwoman's Daughter* (1917), with its unlikely *deus-ex-machina* ending for the implausibly lucky "Makebelieves". In Plunkett's *Strumpet City*, Father Giffley's bibulous buffoonery in attempting to revive a parishioner, Lazarus-style, from his coffin, is a satiric comment on the irrelevance of religion, and its fantastic claims, to the tragedies of working-class life; Plunkett's love story between prostitute and vigilante, as Chapter 4 shows, is his way of ironising such a conventional, bourgeois realist, all's-well-that-ends-well discourse. The contrast is again apparent in Sheridan's fairy-tale ending for *Big Fat Love* (2003, as discussed in Chapter 3), and it is there in Paula Meehan's *Mrs Sweeney* (1997), where Mr Sweeney recoils from the horror of his daughter's death through heroin abuse by transforming himself into a mock-legendary bird-king. In Paul Mercier's play *Drowning* (1984), working-class fantasist Luke imagines himself as "Ozzy Stench", the lead singer in a rock band, but his recurrent dreams of fame are comic-tragically interrupted by the realities of his family's horrible dysfunction.[41] In Philip Casey's novel *The Fabulists* (1994), unemployed lovers Tess and Mungo regale each other with fabricated stories of foreign travel that mask the boredom of living on the dole; their unromantic lives themselves are not "interesting" enough for a novel, Casey suggests. Throughout the writing, subversive literary forms and reflexive metacommentaries are deployed with striking frequency to show how culture and literature share a difficult relationship with working-class reality. Lee Dunne's *Goodbye to the Hill* had inferred this with its contrast between the glossy images of cultural production (films, books and magazines) and the Maguires' dystopian existence. Smith's *Summer Sang in Me*, Bolger's *The Journey Home*, Behan's *The Quare Fellow*, Sheridan and Flynn's *The Liberty Suit* and Meehan's *Cell* also estrange the familiar in order to show how cultural representation has failed to reflect proletarian life. Often it is by overturning reality that we paradoxically come to see society as it is.

New writing

While recent writing of Dublin's working class shows that the fabric of communal life has been damaged by social and economic change, the persistence of old themes and ideas is evidence of the continuing relevance of class analysis to the study of Irish literature. Alienation has grown as a theme: Sheridan's happy ending in *Big Fat Love* is undercut with worries about how redevelopment in Sheriff Street will affect the community that its demolished flats contained. This concern with redevelopment returns in Bolger's *From These Green Heights* (2005), which concerns the proposed "rejuvenation" of Ballymun. Uncertainty about what the future holds for another deprived community is the central theme, and his more recent play, *The Consequences of Lightning* (2008), also based in Ballymun, shows how poverty and social deprivation continue to have consequences for its characters. The play conveys how an old, established community is being destroyed by "redevelopment", and, like *Big Fat Love*, it also ends with the death of a central character who personifies his community. Such concerns about the breakdown of social ties are evident again in Conor McPherson's *Dublin Carol* (2000), where Mark and John, who work in an undertakers' office during the Christmas period, exemplify how human relations are increasingly problematic in the city at the beginning of the new millennium:

> JOHN: You know if you're listening to the radio and there's all static and you put your hand on it.
> MARK: Yeah, you earth it.
> JOHN: Yeah and there's a clear signal. It'd be great to be able to do that, wouldn't it? To people, I mean. To people.[42]

Yet it is also important to acknowledge the desire to counter popular discourses of social breakdown and alienation in working-class life. bell hooks identifies a problem of representation in *Outlaw Culture* (1994), whereby when "intellectuals, journalists or politicians speak about nihilism and the despair of the underclass they do not link those states to representations of poverty in the mass media". In order to "change the face of poverty so that it becomes once again, a site for the formation of values, of dignity and integrity, as any other class positionality in this society, we would need to intervene in existing systems of representation".[43] In Joe O'Byrne's *It Come Up Sun* (2000), in which an Eastern European woman emerges from a container in the Docklands, Joe, a security guard, is faced with the dilemma of whether he should report this illegal immigrant to the authorities or help her in her effort to gain entry to the country.[44] In this way, he must also decide whether to align himself with his employers and the state or with the dispossessed and the foreign. His common class interest with the woman is inferred a number of times:

> ANA: Like country, no want to leave.
> JOE: No want to leave. Your brother, he left.
> ANA: Life hard. He leave, yes, brother, he leave.
> JOE: Life hard. Who're ye tellin'! You think I want to be doing this job? You can have it! If it wasn't for my three kids ...[45]

Joe's feeling of worthlessness in the play is derived partly from the tedium of his job and partly also from the dissolution of his sense of family. His children "make fun of" him, and his wife is "disappointed" in his achievements.[46] But his decision to help this refugee is depicted as part of a cultural shift, the genesis of a new Ireland, which Billy, Joe's friend, hints at when he meets Ana: "it's like you just, you know took one of your ribs and made her".[47] Joe finds validation in asserting his common class interests and in taking the woman's side, refusing to report her even though the "security" of capitalist property is essentially his job.

In Ken Harmon's *Done Up Like a Kipper* (2002), the Tallaght working-class family of a taxi driver, Gino, enjoys the affluence of the economic boom. There is much talk of sun tans and holidays, Dyson washing machines and recreational drug use, but the local community is also ravaged by drug abuse and anti-social behaviour from "good for nothing cunts. Have the place gone mad. With scumbags. Overrunning the kip".[48] Despite newfound wealth, old class injuries remain; Gino's son, Eugene, a student of psychology, assesses his father: "You know what your underlying fear is, under all your working-class bullshit – you're terrified that people don't take you seriously as a person. And the truth is that people don't".[49] Gino's family is also falling apart, and he fears his daughter's alliance with a black man, Nathan. However, with the revelation of Gino's horrific stabbing with a syringe, the family rallies round, and the play ends with Nathan singing "Dublin in the Rare Oul Times", symbolising again the integration of a new working-class into the "rare old" one.[50] The family finds affirmation in "stick[ing] together", and Gino pointedly renounces his own newfound consumerism when his Mercedes Benz is burnt out: "It's only a fuckin car anyway".[51] Both O'Byrne and Harmon use the arrival of immigrants to stress enduring commonalities of class, and a pointed disdain for bourgeois values.[52]

In Bolger's 1999 play, *The Passion of Jerome*, there is barely veiled anger at the middle-class Clara's contempt for the people of Ballymun as "only consumers at the lowest end of the market", not a genuine community, part of a real social class.[53] Her businessman lover Jerome's stigmata, caused by a ghostly boy who committed suicide in the flats, symbolises the return of that community's suffering as a spectral indictment of middle-class Ireland, and it also suggests how that community, and its hidden narratives, refuse to go away. The writers I have explored in this book carry O'Casey's legacy: his insistence on the essential, if spectral, place of the working class in history and literature. To return to Herbert Goldstone's point, they continue to assert his sense of "commitment" to a neglected community.[54] Peter Hitchcock identifies a similar impetus in working-class writing generally, which he extrapolates from Mikhail Bakhtin's early essays that use "answerability or responsibility to describe the relation between art and life: they should be answerable to each other or else both run the risk of being ineffectual". This concept, like those cognate concepts of Hoggart, Williams, Fordham, or Bourdieu, adds "an ethical dimension to aesthetics [...] a form of social responsibility that allows workers to 'speak' to one another across a range of discourses, discourses of memory, of experience, of alienation, of solidarity". Answerability, as an aesthetic precept, "underlines that working-class Being is more than the content of such lives or the aura of dispossession that this content implies."[55]

O'Casey's use of agitprop, his valorisation of a counter-culture, his defamiliarising, experimental and irreverent literary craft, his desire to reveal the hidden relations of society and to counter the elision of working-class history, endure as central elements in the writing that I have analysed, affirming a sustained sense of class and community. His desire to reveal the shared interests of working-class people and to forge with them a hegemony of their own – a "working-class Being" – is a project that continues. So too is the urgent project of revising the historical and cultural formations of the Irish working class, of recognising, as David Lloyd has insisted, that "the Irish, and in particular the Irish working classes, were always in relation to the most profoundly transformative effects of capitalist development".[56] The fiction and plays of working-class Dublin after O'Casey represent an enduring lineage of class struggle through art, a literary disruption, contestation and subversion of the established order. While this is not an exhaustive study of the literature of working-class life in Ireland's capital city – and my research conveys the possibilities for a great deal more scholarly work in this area – it has identified a continuity of writing that demands further academic attention. Asserting that working-class history has been "conspicuous by its absence from undergraduate courses within Irish academia" and noting the "complete absence of a rigorous Marxist historiographical tradition in this country", Fintan Lane urges historians "to finish building the skeleton on which we can construct a generalized socio-political history of the Irish working class".[57] Irish working-class culture has equally barely begun to get the recognition that its energy and complexity clearly demand.

Notes

Introduction

1. Steph Lawler, "Escape and Escapism: Representing Working-Class Women", in *Cultural Studies and the Working Class, Subject to Change*, ed. Sally R. Munt (London: Cassell, 2000), p. 116. [Emphasis in original.]
2. Terry Eagleton, *The Function of Criticism, from "The Spectator" to Post-Structuralism* (London: Verso, 1984), p. 16.
3. Sally R. Munt, "Introduction", in *Cultural Studies and the Working Class, Subject to Change*, ed. Sally R. Munt (London: Cassell, 2000), p. 9.
4. Ibid.
5. Ibid.
6. Andy Medhurst, "If Anywhere: Class Identifications and Cultural Studies Academics", in *Cultural Studies and the Working Class, Subject to Change*, ed. Sally R. Munt (London: Cassell, 2000), p. 29.
7. See Guy Cook, *The Discourse of Advertising* (London: Routledge, 2001), p. 95; See also Beverly Skeggs' essay, "Classifying Practices: Representations, Capitals and Recognitions", in *Class Matters: "Working-class" Women's Perspectives on Social Class*, ed. Pat Mahony and Christine Zmroczek (London: Taylor & Francis, 1997), p. 125.
8. Medhurst, "If Anywhere: Class Identifications and Cultural Studies Academics", p. 29.
9. Fintan O'Toole, "Boxers offer a window into our marginalised society", *The Irish Times*, 26 August 2008, p. 13.
10. Ibid.
11. For a detailed discussion of the relationship between postmodernism and class, see Scott Lash, *Sociology of Postmodernism* (London: Routledge, 1990), pp. 25–30.
12. Gordon Marshall, *Repositioning Class: Social Inequality in Industrial Societies* (London: Sage, 1997), p. 17.
13. Munt, "Introduction", p. 3.
14. Ibid.
15. E. P. Thompson, *The Making of the English Working Class* (London: Penguin, 1980), p. 8, 9.
16. Ellen Wilkinson, *Clash* (London: Virago, 1989), p. 297.
17. Thompson, *The Making of the English Working Class*, p. 9, 10.
18. Medhurst, "If Anywhere: Class Identifications and Cultural Studies Academics", p. 20.
19. See, for example, Jan Pakulski and Malcolm Waters, *The Death of Class* (London: Sage, 1996); Marshall, *Repositioning Class: Social Inequality in Industrial Societies*; or more recently Nick Cohen, *What's Left? How Liberals Lost their Way* (London: Fourth Estate, 2007).
20. John R. Hall, "The Reworking of Class Analysis", in *Reworking Class*, ed. John R. Hall (London: Cornell University Press, 1997), p. 9.
21. Karl Marx, *The Eighteenth Brumaire of Louis Bonaparte* (New York: International Publishers, 1963; orig. 1852), p. 124.

22. Karl Marx, *Capital: A Critique of Political Economy*, trans. David Fernbach, 3 vols. (London: Penguin, 1993) III, p. 1025.
23. Ibid.
24. Nicos Poulantzas, *Classes in Contemporary Capitalism*, trans. D. Fernbach (London: New Left Books, 1975).
25. Serge Mallet, *Essays on the New Working Class*, ed. Dick Howard (St. Louis: Telos Press, 1975).
26. See for example Rosemary Crompton and Gareth Jones, *White-Collar Proletariat: Deskilling and Gender in Clerical Work* (London: Macmillan, 1984).
27. Erik Olin Wright, *Classes* (London: Verso, 1985) and *Interrogating Inequality: Essays on Class Analysis, Socialism and Marxism* (London: Verso, 1994).
28. Erik Olin Wright, "Rethinking, Once Again, the Concept of Class Structure", abridged by Maureen Sullivan, in *Reworking Class*, ed. John R. Hall (London: Cornell University Press, 1997), p. 55.
29. Wright, *Interrogating Inequality*, p. 251.
30. Wright, *Classes*, p. 80.
31. Hall, "The Reworking of Class Analysis", p. 13.
32. Wright, *Interrogating Inequality*, p. 13.
33. Wright, "Rethinking, Once Again, the Concept of Class Structure", pp. 42–43. While Wright himself conceptualised the theory of "contradictory [class] locations" in the late 1970s, which allowed for the anomalies that gradations of management and self-employment, for instance, highlight within Marx, such contradictory locations only show that "people in certain locations within the class structure are simultaneously exploited through one mechanism of exploitation but exploiters through another mechanism". Ibid. pp. 53–55. Notwithstanding this complexity, "classes are fundamentally polarized around processes of exploitation". Ibid. 60.
34. Ibid. 44. [Emphasis in original.]
35. Ibid. 48.
36. Ibid. 49.
37. David McWilliams, *The Pope's Children: The Irish Economic Triumph and the Rise of Ireland's New Elite* (Hoboken, NJ: Wiley, 2008), p. 27.
38. Etienne Balibar, "The Basic Concepts of Historical Materialism", in *Reading Capital*, ed. Louis Althusser and Etienne Balibar (London: New Left, 1972), p. 267. [Emphasis in original.]
39. E. P. Thompson, *The Poverty of Theory and Other Essays* (London: Merlin, 1978), p. 298–299; for further discussion of the contrast in approaches see Ira Katznelson and Aristide R. Zolberg, *Working-Class Formation: Nineteenth Century Patterns in Western Europe and the United States* (Princeton, NJ: Princeton University Press, 1986), pp. 9–11.
40. Thompson, *The Poverty of Theory and Other Essays*, pp. 298–299.
41. Perry Share, Hilary Tovey and Mary P. Corcoran, *A Sociology of Ireland* (Dublin: Gill & Macmillan, 2007), p. 170.
42. Kieran Allen, "The Celtic Tiger, Inequality and Social Partnership", *Administration* 47:2 (summer 1999), 39; Share, Tovey and Corcoran, *A Sociology of Ireland*, p. 170.
43. Kieran Allen, *The Celtic Tiger: The Myth of Social Partnership in Ireland* (Manchester: Manchester University Press, 2000), p. 71.
44. Ibid. 2.
45. Share, Tovey and Corcoran, *A Sociology of Ireland*, p. 171.

46. 50 per cent saw themselves as middle class; cited in McWilliams, *The Pope's Children*, p. 26.
47. Peter Beresford Ellis, *A History of the Irish Working Class* (Dublin: Pluto, 1989), pp. 11–26.
48. Brian Girvin, "Industrialisation and the Irish Working Class Since 1922", *Saothar* 10 (1986), 31–42.
49. Moira J. Maguire, *Precarious Childhood in Post-Independence Ireland* (Manchester: Manchester University Press, 2009), p. 12, 13.
50. Fintan Lane, *The Origins of Modern Irish Socialism 1881–1896* (Cork: Cork University Press, 1997); Niamh Puirséil, *The Irish Labour Party 1922–1973* (Dublin: UCD, 2007); Kieran Allen, *Fianna Fáil and Irish Labour: 1926 to the Present* (London: Pluto, 1997).
51. Girvin, "Industrialisation and the Irish Working Class", p. 31.
52. John Lynch, *A Tale of Three Cities: Comparative Studies in Working-Class Life* (Basingstoke: Macmillan, 1998).
53. See Lynch, *A Tale of Three Cities*, esp. pp. 40–57.
54. John Newsinger, "'In the Hunger-Cry of the Nation's Poor is Heard the Voice of Ireland': Sean O'Casey and Politics 1908–1916", *Journal of Contemporary History*, 20:2 (April 1985), 223.
55. Diarmaid Ferriter, *The Transformation of Ireland: 1900–2000* (London: Profile, 2004), pp. 52–53.
56. Allen, *Fianna Fáil and Irish Labour*, p. 27.
57. Quote from the *Irish Worker* cited in O'Connor, "Labour and Politics, 1830–1945", p. 33.
58. O'Connor, "Labour and Politics, 1830–1945", p. 33.
59. Richard Dunphy, *The Making of Fianna Fáil Power in Ireland, 1923–1948* (Oxford: Clarendon, 2005), p. 40.
60. Allen, *Fianna Fáil and Irish Labour*, p. 27.
61. *Dublin Civic Survey*, 1925, qtd. in Cathal O'Connell, *The State and Housing in Ireland: Ideology, Policy, Practice* (New York: Nova Science, 2007), p. 21.
62. Allen, *Fianna Fáil and Irish Labour*, p. 27.
63. Anthony Cronin, *An Irish Eye* (Dingle: Brandon, 1985), p. 27.
64. Qtd. in Allen, *Fianna Fáil and Irish Labour*, p. 30.
65. Fearghal McGarry, "Radical Politics in Interwar Ireland", in *Politics and the Irish Working Class, 1830–1945*, ed. Fintan Lane and Donal Ó Drisceoil (London: Palgrave, 2005), p. 209.
66. Qtd. in Emmet O'Connor, *A Labour History of Ireland, 1824–1960* (Dublin: Gill & Macmillan, 1992), p. 121.
67. See Ferriter, *The Transformation of Ireland*, p. 710.
68. For an outline of the growth in British proletarian literature in this period – and the surprising willingness of publishers to actively seek out and encourage working-class talent – see Christopher Hilliard, *To Exercise Our Talents: The Democratization of Writing in Britain* (Cambridge: Harvard University Press, 2006), esp. Chapters 4 and 5.
69. For an assessment of the Republican Congress, see Eoin O'Broin, *Sinn Féin and the Politics of Left Republicanism* (London: Pluto, 2009), pp. 135–140.
70. Puirséil, *The Irish Labour Party 1922–1973*, p. 48.
71. McGarry, "Radical Politics in Interwar Ireland", p. 224.
72. James McKenna, "Up Dev", in *Poems* (Dublin: Goldsmith, 1973), pp. 22–23.
73. Allen, *Fianna Fáil and Irish Labour*, p. 46.

74. Marilyn Silverman, *An Irish Working Class: Explorations in Political Economy and Hegemony, 1800–1950* (Toronto: Toronto UP, 2001), p. 278.
75. Ibid. 378.
76. Ibid. 379.
77. Allen, *Fianna Fáil and Irish labour*, p. 46.
78. Tom Garvin, *Preventing the Future: Why was Ireland So Poor for So Long?* (Dublin: Gill & Macmillan, 2004), p. 81.
79. Moira J. Maguire, *Precarious Childhood in Post-independence Ireland* (Manchester: Manchester University Press, 2009), p. 21.
80. Ibid. 23.
81. Qtd. in Ibid. 24.
82. Emmet O'Connor, "Labour and Politics, 1830–1945: Colonisation and Mental Colonisation", in *Politics and the Irish Working Class, 1830–1945*, ed. Fintan Lane and Donal Ó Drisceoil (London: Palgrave, 2005), p. 27.
83. Robert Collis, *Marrowbone Lane: A Play in Three Acts* (Dublin: Runa Press, 1943), p. 33.
84. Dermot Bolger, *Night Shift* (London: Penguin, 1993), p. 116, 118.
85. Jim Sheridan, *Mobile Homes* (Dublin: Irish Writers' Co-operative, 1978), pp. 44–45. Some unemployed Dubliners at this time had taken to refusing to pay their bus fares to labour exchanges.
86. James Plunkett, "The Plain People", in *James Plunkett, Collected Short Stories* (Dublin: Poolbeg, 2000), p. 264.
87. Ibid. 270.
88. Charles McCarthy, *The Decade of Upheaval: Irish Trade Unions in the Nineteen Sixties* (Dublin: Institute of Public Administration, 1973).
89. Working days lost due to strikes were at 377,264 in 1961, 545,384 in 1964, 552,351 in 1965, 783,635 in 1966, and 935,900 in 1969; See Teresa Brannick, Francis Devine and Aidan Kelly, "Social Statistics for Labour Historians: Strike Statistics, 1922-99", *Saothar* 25 (2000), 114–120.
90. McCarthy, *The Decade of Upheaval*, p. 7.
91. Ibid.; Alexander Humphries, *New Dubliners* (London: Routledge, 1998; orig. 1966), p. 196.
92. Despite the growing profile of the urban working class, with its "subculture of the 1913 strike", and despite the growth in industrial unrest during the decade, the assertion of working-class issues in the political sphere was hampered again by a divided left. Political splits, characterised in the 1960s and 1970s by a proliferation of socialist organisations – such as the Workers' Party, Sinn Féin, the Socialist Labour Alliance, the Socialist Party of Ireland, People's Democracy, the League for a Workers' Republic, the Limerick Socialist Organisation, Young Socialists, the Communist Party of Ireland and Saor Éire – created confusion rather than cohesion.
93. Terence Brown, *Ireland: A Social and Cultural History* (London: Harper, 2004), p. 94.
94. Interview by present author with Paula Meehan, 11 May 2005.
95. Tom Garvin, "A Quiet Revolution: The Remaking of Irish Political Culture" in *Writing in the Irish Republic*, ed. Ray Ryan (London: Macmillan, 2000), pp. 187–203.
96. In 1961, half of Ireland's employed men worked in farming; by 1981, the figure decreased to one fifth. I use figures for men here and below, as figures for women's work tell us less about their social position than that of their male partners

does. From the 1930s to 1961, the number of Irish women in the paid workforce actually decreased; See Share et al., *A Sociology of Ireland*, p. 262. Even as late as 1971, only 8 per cent of married women in the Republic were involved in the paid labour force, with the figure rising to (only) 17 per cent in 1981. However, the period 1951 to 1991 overall saw a seven-fold increase in the number of married women in the paid workforce; Ibid.; Kieran A. Kennedy, Thomas Giblin, and Deirdre McHugh, *The Economic Development of Ireland in the Twentieth Century* (London: Routledge, 1988), p. 71, 148.

97. See Brown, *Ireland: A Social and Cultural History*, p. 246. In 1966, the population of the Greater Dublin area was 840,900 according to the national census; from 1971, for the first time, more than half of the population of the Republic was living in urban areas. By 1981 the population of Greater Dublin was 1,091,900 and ten years later it was 1,139,700. Growth declined in the county during the following fifteen years, stabilising at 1.2 million in 2006, but this masks the rapid growth of the "soft" commuter belt in Meath, Wicklow and Kildare.

98. Michel Peillon, *Contemporary Irish Society: An Introduction* (Dublin: Gill and Macmillan, 1982), p. 1.

99. Ibid. 117.

100. Ibid. 175. Richard Breen and Christopher T. Whelan also observed an "extremely low level of upward mobility" from the working-class into middle-class jobs at this time; Richard Breen and Christopher T. Whelan, *Social Mobility and Social Class in Ireland* (Dublin: Gill & Macmillan, 1996), p. 169.

101. James Wickham, "The New Irish Working Class?" in *Saothar* 6 (1980), p. 84.

102. Ibid.

103. Ibid.

104. Ibid. 85.

105. Ibid.

106. James Wickham, "The Politics of Dependent Capitalism: International Capital and the Nation State", in *Ireland: Divided Nation, Divided Class*, ed. Austen Morgan and Bob Purdie (London: Ink Links, 1980), pp. 53–73.

107. James Wickham, "The New Irish Working Class?", p. 85.

108. See Micheál Collins, Seán Healy and Brigid Reynolds (eds), *An Agenda for a New Ireland: Policies to Ensure Economic Development, Social Equity and Sustainability, Socio-Economic Review 2010* (Dublin: Social Justice Ireland, 2010).

109. Christopher T. Whelan, and Richard Layte, "Opportunities for All in the New Ireland?", in *Best of Times? The Social Impact of the Celtic Tiger*, ed. Tony Fahey, Helen Russell and Christopher T. Whelan (Dublin: Institute of Public Administration, 2007), p. 67.

110. Ibid. 68.

111. Ibid. 72.

112. Ibid. 77.

113. Michel Peillon, *Contemporary Irish Society*, p. 29, 32, 31.

114. Whelan and Layte, "Opportunities for All in the New Ireland", p. 81, 85.

115. Peadar Kirby, *The Celtic Tiger in Distress: Growth with Inequality in Ireland* (New York: Palgrave, 2002), p. 172.

116. Collins et al. (eds), *An Agenda for a New Ireland*, p. 2, 9.

117. James Wickham, "The New Irish Working Class?", p. 82.

118. Fintan Lane and Emmet O'Connor, "Speed the Plough", *Saothar* 26 (2001), p. 4.

119. James Wickham, "The New Irish Working Class?", p. 85.

120. Michel Peillon, *Contemporary Irish Society: An Introduction*, p. 36.
121. See Patrick Clancy, "Education Policy", in *Contemporary Irish Social Policy*, ed. Suzanne Quinn, Patricia Kennedy, Gabriel Kiely and Anne O'Donnell (Dublin: UCD, 1999), pp. 72–107.
122. See recent front page reports in Ireland's two main daily broadsheets for example: John Walshe, "Fee schools stretch lead in race for top courses", *Irish Independent*, 4 December 2008, p. 1; Seán Flynn and Gráinne Faller, "Over 60% of top schools limit admission to certain groups", 4 December 2008, p. 1.
123. Denis O'Sullivan, "The Ideational Base of Irish Educational Policy", in *Irish Educational Policy: Process and Substance*, ed. D. G. Mulcahy and Denis O'Sullivan (Dublin: Institute of Public Administration, 1989), p. 262. As Kirby notes, "educational policy has given priority to the needs of the economy rather than seeing education as a means to generate greater social equality and mobility"; Kirby, *The Celtic Tiger in Distress*, p. 152. See Terence Brown, *Ireland: A Social and Cultural History*, pp. 237–242, for some discussion on the effects of fee abolitions following the *Investment in Education* initiative. Emer Smith and Damian Hannan find that despite continuous increases in formal educational participation in recent decades, "educational inequalities by social background" persist. Emer Smyth and Damian F. Hannan, "Education and Inequality", in *Bust to Boom? The Irish Experience of Growth and Inequality*, ed. Brian Nolan, Philip J. O'Connell and Christopher T. Whelan (Dublin: IPA, 2000), p. 117. At third level, the comparative gap between entry levels of children from professional and unskilled manual backgrounds has grown over recent decades. Clancy's study of third-level access across class divides in 1998 found that 58 per cent of higher education entrants were from middle-class groups – the higher and lower professional, farming, business and managerial backgrounds – despite these groups constituting only thirty-seven per cent of the relevant population. Clancy, Patrick, "College Entry in Focus: A Fourth National Survey of Access to Higher Education" (Dublin: HEA, 2001) <http://extranet.hea.ie/uploads/pdf/Clancymaster%20.pdf> [accessed 2 December 2008], p. 82.
124. Share, Tovey and Corcoran, *A Sociology of Ireland*, p. 233. In contemporary Ireland, a rural bias also persists: "The Dublin region, with its high concentration of working-class people, has the lowest participation rate in tertiary education, while the western counties, such as Galway, Sligo and Leitrim, have the highest"; Ibid. 233.
125. Joan Hanafin and Anne Lynch, "Peripheral Voices: Parental Involvement, Social Class, and Educational Disadvantage", *British Journal of Sociology of Education*, 23:1 (March 2002), p. 36. As Tovey, Share and Corcoran put it, "three decades of educational reform [...] have left patterns of class inequality in education largely unchanged"; Share, Tovey and Corcoran, *A Sociology of Ireland*, p. 219.
126. Honor Fagan, *Culture, Politics and Irish School Dropouts* (London: Bergin and Garvey, 1995), p.100.
127. Apart from a module entitled "Working-class communities in Dublin," under Dr Laurence Cox at the Department of Sociology, NUI Maynooth, there is little evidence of formal academic interventions specifically tailored to the culture of one of Ireland's largest social cohorts. Professor Helena Sheehan's Dublin City University course on Social History and TV Drama put a strong emphasis on class in the history of Irish television (she has recently retired). Dr Aileen Douglas's module on British working-class fiction at Trinity College Dublin – which played a significant part in inspiring my own interest in and awareness

of the possibilities for analysing literature in class terms – is the only module of this kind I am aware of across English departments in Irish universities.

128. Ibid. p. 235.
129. Munt, "Introduction" in *Cultural Studies and the Working Class*, p. 1.
130. David Lloyd, *Irish Times: Temporalities of Modernity*, ed. Seamus Deane and Breandán Mac Suibhne (Dublin: Field Day, 2008), p. 111.
131. Fagan has been attempting to secure a local history centre in the North Inner City since the 1970s; a survey of his work can be viewed on <http://www.dublinfolklore.ie> [accessed 8 December 2008].
132. Ken Worpole, *Dockers and Detectives: Popular Reading: Popular Writing* (London: Verso, 1983), p. 10.
133. The latter pair's careers have been marred by state censorship, which of course affected writers of all classes. Dunne is the most banned author in Ireland and Smith's domestic market was almost completely wiped out because his major works had to be published abroad during the censorship era.
134. The prospect of class-based cultural initiatives is no mere fancy, Worpole argues, citing for example a 1970s initiative by the Swedish government which saw the publication of working-class writers in a series of cheap books available on news-stands – and saw these writers become a new part of popular national literature in a matter of months; Worpole, *Dockers and Detectives*, p. 26.
135. Helena Sheehan, *Irish Television Drama: A Society and its Stories* (Dublin: RTÉ, 1987; re-published in a revised edition on CD-ROM, 2004), p. 131. This is not to underestimate the influence of domestic television about working-class life, such as *Tolka Row* (1964-68, which Maura Laverty had first written as a play in 1950), *Babby Joe* (1966), *Shadows in the Sun* (1967), *The Testimony of James Connolly* (1968), *I'm Getting Out of this Kip* (1973), *Hatchet* (1973), and *The Spike* (1978). *Tolka Row* was a particularly important intervention in working-class consciousness, as Sheehan observed: "For the first time, with Tolka Row, it was people like themselves on the screen whose lives were seen as having dramatic significance. It made them feel differently about themselves and their own lives and they warmed to it greatly. When it was gone, they missed it, not perhaps because it was irreplaceable, but because nothing comparable did replace it for many years"; Ibid. 34.
136. Peillon, *Contemporary Irish Society*, p. 2. Michael P. Hornsby-Smith and Angela Dale noted, in their study of the assimilation of Irish immigrants in Britain, that by the 1960s survey evidence suggested an increasing affinity with British cultural mores – something that would inevitably impact on the Irish back home. They found that Irish emigration to Britain resulted in cultural and social changes for those who chose to leave the Republic. Research from 1967–1976 showed that "Irish-born women adopted 'reliable' methods of contraception during the decade" and "by the mid-1970s their contraceptive practices were approaching those of the population generally". Endogamous birth rates decreased since at least 1970, indicating the increase in marriages between Irish and non-Irish and assimilation generally, as did the convergence of religious opinion between Irish and non-Irish. While it was apparent that the Irish in England enjoyed far less social mobility than the indigenous English, "time-space analyses have suggested [...] a process of economic embourgeoisement and geographical mobility outward from the inner-cities into the new suburban estates" for Britain's largest immigrant group. Michael P. Hornsby-Smith and Angela Dale, "The Assimilation of Irish Immigrants in England", *The British Journal of Sociology*, 39:4 (December, 1988), pp. 524–525, p. 526.

137. Ibid., p. 35. [Emphasis added.]
138. Terry Eagleton, *The Function of Criticism* (London: Verso, 1990), p. 36.
139. Ibid. 39.
140. Brian Gray speaking on the *Today with Pat Kenny* radio show, RTÉ Radio One. Gray, with Jim Davis, is co-director of a recent documentary, *Meeting Room*, on the subject of Dublin's working-class anti-drugs movement in the 1980s; "Meeting Room". *Today with Pat Kenny*. RTÉ. Dublin. Thursday 18 February 2010.
141. Catherine Dunne, *A Name for Himself* (London: Vintage, 1999), p. 41.
142. Hugh O'Donnell, *11 Emerald Street* (London: Vintage, 2005), p. 37.
143. Lar Redmond, *Emerald Square* (Dublin: Glendale, 1990), p. 259.
144. Ibid. 286.
145. *The Spike*. Dir. Noel Ó Briain. RTÉ. January 1978.
146. Thomas Kinsella, *A Dublin Documentary* (Dublin: O'Brien, 2006), p. 62.
147. Roddy Doyle, *The Woman Who Walked into Doors* (London: Penguin, 1997), pp. 25–26.
148. Ibid. 28, 35.
149. Ibid. 41.
150. Lar Redmond, *A Walk in Alien Corn* (Dublin: Glendale, 1990), p. 7.
151. Ibid. 9–10.
152. Andrew Sayer, *The Moral Significance of Class* (Cambridge: Cambridge University Press), p. 58. Sayer elaborates, "the excluded may feel torn between envying the better off and associating with others with whom they have more in common to avoid feeling a sense of lack [...] it is common for those who are refused certain goods to refuse what they are refused"; Ibid. p. 121.
153. Redmond, *A Walk in Alien Corn*, p. 61.
154. Richard Hoggart, *The Uses of Literacy: Changing Patterns in English Mass Culture* (Boston: Beacon Press, 1961), pp. 238–249.
155. I am thinking here of Lee Dunne's Paddy Maguire, Peter Sheridan and Gerard Mannix Flynn's Curley, in *The Liberty Suit* (1977), Brendan Gleeson's Frank, in *Breaking Up* (1988), and the doomed inner-city students of Val Mulkerns' *Very Like a Whale* (1986).
156. Sheridan, *Mobile Homes*, pp. 16, 26.
157. Illustration for month of January on *The Goldsmith Press Calendar*, 1975.
158. Wilkinson, *Clash*, p. 249.
159. James Stephens, "Dublin, A City of Wonderful Dreams, Silent and Voluble Folk", in *The Uncollected Prose of James Stephens: Volume 2*, ed. Patrick McFate (London: Gill and Macmillan, 1983), p. 159.
160. Georges Denis Zimmermann, *Songs of Irish Rebellion: Irish Political Street Ballads and Rebel Songs* (Dublin: Four Courts Press, 2002), p. 2.
161. Ibid. 9.
162. Patrick Callan, "The Political War Ballads of Sean O'Casey, 1916-18", *Irish University Review*, 13:2 (Autumn, 1983), 168–179. See Helena Sheehan's website for further information on Irish labour songs: <http://webpages.dcu.ie/~sheehanh/hsheehan/lsongs.htm> [accessed 8 December 2008].
163. Less known writers like Rose O'Driscoll, (*Rose of Cabra* (1990)) and Sheila O'Hagan (*The Peacock's Eye* (1992); *The Troubled House* (1995)) might also provide scope for scholarly research.
164. Ken Worpole, *Dockers and Detectives*, p. 94.
165. George Orwell, "The Proletarian Writer", discussion between George Orwell and Desmond Hawkins, broadcast 6 December 1940; published in *The Listener*, 19

December 1940, re-published in *Orwell and the Dispossessed*, ed. Peter Davison (London: Penguin, 2001), p. 288.
166. Alan Sillitoe, *The Writer's Dilemma* (London, 1961), pp. 70–71.
167. Qtd. in Eddie Wilson, *A Different Story: The British Working Class Novel between 1914 and 1939* (San Francisco: Free Press, 2004), p. 39.
168. Orwell, "The Proletarian Writer", p. 283
169. Ibid. 284
170. Ibid.
171. Ibid. 284.
172. Ibid. 285.
173. Ibid. 286. [Emphasis added.]
174. Ibid. 288. [Emphasis added.]
175. Perhaps it was because Orwell hardly believed what he was saying at all that he flip-flopped so readily. More recent revelations of his covert work for British Intelligence, spying on "crypto-communist" writers and "fellow travellers" who were "not to be trusted" by the British government (such as George Bernard Shaw, the "stupid" Seán O'Casey, and C. Day Lewis), suggests a more complex picture of the man, and his ideology, than that enshrined in socialist lore. In July 1996, public records released by the British government revealed that Orwell had "supplied a secret propaganda unit in the Foreign Office" with intelligence on writers, artists and intellectuals, many of a left-wing hue; See Arthur Mitchell, "George Orwell & Sean O'Casey: Two Prickly Characters Intersect", *History Ireland*, 6:3 (Autumn, 1998), pp. 44–46 (p. 44).
176. Leon Trotsky, *Literature and Revolution*, trans. Rose Strunsky (Michigan: Ann Arbor, 1971), p. 185.
177. Ibid. 191.
178. Ibid. 197, 198. [Emphasis added.]
179. Ibid. 185.
180. Ibid.
181. Ibid.
182. Ibid. 193.
183. Ibid. 200.
184. Ibid.
185. Ibid. 201.
186. Antonio Gramsci, *A Gramsci Reader*, ed. David Forgacs (London: Lawrence and Wishart, 1988), pp. 70–71.
187. Trotsky, *Literature and Revolution*, p. 214.
188. Ibid. 200.
189. Karl Marx and Friedrich Engels, *The German Ideology*, ed. C. J. Arthur (London: Lawrence and Wishart, 2004), p. 64. [Emphasis added.]
190. Karl Marx, "Preface to *A Contribution to the Critique of Political Economy*", in *Karl Marx: Selected Writings* (Indianapolis: Hackett, 1994), p. 211. [Emphasis added.]
191. Karl Marx, *The Eighteenth Brumaire of Louis Bonaparte*, p. 26. [Emphasis added.]
192. Raymond Williams, *Marxism and Literature* (Oxford: Oxford University Press, 1992), p. 76.
193. Ibid. 78.
194. Ibid.
195. Karl Marx and Frederick Engels, *The German Ideology*, p. 149
196. Karl Marx, "Preface to *A Contribution to the Critique of Political Economy*", p. 211.

197. Frederick Engels, "Letter to Joseph Bloch", in *Cultural Theory and Popular Culture: A Reader*, ed. John Storey (London: Harvester Wheatsheaf, 1994), p. 71. [Emphasis in original.]

198. Ibid. 71, 72. [Emphasis added.]

199. Frederick Engels, "Dialectical Materialism", in *Ludwig Feuerbach and the Outcome of Classical German Philosophy*, ed. C. P. Dutt (New York: International Publishers, 1996), p. 55.

200. Antonio Gramsci, *A Gramsci Reader*, p. 45.

201. Williams, *Marxism and Literature*, p. 92; Gramsci, *A Gramsci Reader*, p. 215.

202. Williams, *Marxism and Literature*, p. 106.

203. Ibid. 106–107; Adorno, for example, rejects vulgar Marxism for its totalising, teleological concept of history as a pre-determined material process. On the other, he speaks of "our totally organized bourgeois society, which has forcibly been made over into a totality"; Theodor W. Adorno, *Philosophy of Modern Music* (London: Continuum, 2002), p. 25.

204. Raymond Williams, "Notes on Marxism in Britain since 1945", in *Problems in Materialism and Culture: Selected Essays* (London: Verso, 1980) p. 241.

205. Terry Eagleton, *Criticism and Ideology: A Study in Marxist Literary Theory* (London: Verso, 2006), p. 32.

206. Terry Eagleton, *Ideology: An Introduction* (London: Verso, 1991), p. 83.

207. Pierre, Bourdieu, *Outline of Theory of Practice*, trans. Richard Nice (London: Cambridge University Press, 1977), p. 72.

208. Ibid. 85.

209. Ibid. 72.

210. Ibid.

211. Ibid. 86.

212. Ibid. 95.

213. Williams, *Marxism and Literature*, p. 111.

214. Ibid. 111, 113, 114.

215. Gramsci, *A Gramsci Reader*, p. 49.

216. John Fordham, *James Hanley: Modernism and the Working Class* (Cardiff: Cardiff University Press, 2002), p. 2.

217. Ibid.

218. Ibid. 3.

219. Ibid. 4.

220. Ibid.

221. Terry Eagleton, *Marxism and Literary Criticism* (Los Angeles: University of California Press, 1976), p. 24.

222. Ibid. 26.

223. Fordham, *James Hanley: Modernism and the Working Class*, p. 4.

224. Ibid. 4–5.

225. Ibid. 5.

226. Ibid. 89–90. [Emphasis added.]

227. Ibid. 100.

228. Ibid. 235.

229. Ibid.

230. Ibid. 235.

231. Ibid. 6.

232. Carole Snee, "Working-Class Literature or Proletarian Writing?", in *Culture and Crisis in Britain in the Thirties*, ed. Jon Clark, et al. (London: Lawrence and Wishart, 1979), pp. 168–169.

233. H. Gustav Klaus, "Introduction", *The Socialist Novel in Britain: Towards the Recovery of a Tradition* (Brighton: Harvester, 1982), p. 2.
234. *La Haine.* Dir. Mathieu Kassovitz. Canal. 1995.
235. Pierre Bourdieu, *Distinction: A Social Critique of the Judgement of Taste*, trans. Richard Nice (London: Routledge, 1998), p. 5.
236. Ibid. 42.
237. Hoggart, *The Uses of Literacy*, p. 100.
238. Bourdieu, *Distinction*, p. 34.
239. Alain de Botton's popular analysis of status as the social reproduction of economic distinction and control, in *Status Anxiety* (2004), and Michael Marmot's similar analysis, in *Status Syndrome* (also 2004), have renewed interest in this interrelation of class, status and power. Alain de Botton, *Status Anxiety* (New York: Pantheon, 2004); Michael Marmot, *Status Syndrome* (London: Bloomsbury, 2004).
240. David Lloyd, "The Subaltern in Motion: Subalternity, the Popular and Irish Working-class History", *Postcolonial Studies* 8:4 (2005), 422.
241. David Lloyd, *Anomalous States: Irish Writing and the Post-colonial Moment* (Dublin: Lilliput, 1993), p. 126.
242. Lloyd, "The Subaltern in Motion", p. 424.
243. Gayatri Chakravorty Spivak, "Can the Subaltern Speak?", abridged in Patrick Williams and Laura Chrisman (eds), *Colonial Discourse and Post-Colonial Theory: A Reader* (Hemel Hempstead: Harvester Wheatsheaf, 1993), pp. 66–111.
244. Lloyd, "The Subaltern in Motion", 422.
245. Ibid. 426.
246. Ibid.
247. Ibid.
248. See Raymond Williams, *Culture and Materialism* (London: Verso, 2005), pp. 40–50.
249. James Connolly, *Collected Works*, vol. I (Dublin: New Books, 1987), p. 174.
250. Ibid. 21, 21–22.
251. Ibid. 22, 23, 24.
252. David Howell, *A Lost Left: Three Studies in Socialism and Nationalism* (Manchester: Manchester University Press, 1986), p. 32.
253. Ibid. 33.
254. Ibid. 32.
255. Ibid.
256. Roger McHugh, " 'Always Complainin': The Politics of Young Sean", *Irish University Review*, 10:1 (Spring, 1980), p. 96.
257. Lloyd, "The Subaltern in Motion", p. 429.
258. Ibid. 429.
259. Christy Brown, *Down All the Days* (London: Pan Books, 1972), p. 98.
260. Ibid. 109.
261. Lloyd, "The Subaltern in Motion", p. 431.
262. Ibid.
263. Alvin Jackson, "Ireland, the Union, and the Empire, 1800–1960", in *Ireland and the British Empire*, ed. Kevin Kenny (Oxford: Oxford University Press, 2004), pp. 123–153.
264. Lloyd, "The Subaltern in Motion", p. 432.
265. Eoin Flannery, "External Association", *Third Text,* 19:5, p. 450.
266. Lloyd, "The Subaltern in Motion", p. 432.
267. Ibid.

268. Ibid. 433.
269. Ibid.
270. Graham, *Deconstructing Ireland: Identity, Theory, Culture* (Edinburgh: Edinburgh University Press, 2001), p. 29.
271. Ibid. 53.
272. Roddy Doyle, *The Dead Republic* (London: Jonathan Cape, 2010), p. 89.
273. Eoin Flannery, "Outside in the Theory Machine: Ireland in the World of Post-Colonial Studies", *Studies: An Irish Quarterly Review*, 92:368 (winter 2003), p. 366.
274. Ibid. 110.
275. W. B. Yeats, "The Fisherman", in *W.B. Yeats, A Critical Edition of the Major Works*, ed. Edward Larrissy (Oxford: Oxford University Press, 1997), pp. 68–69.
276. Graham, *Deconstructing Ireland*, p. 110.
277. Terry Eagleton, *Saints and Scholars* (London: Futura, 1990), p. 10.
278. Gayatri Chakravorty Spivak, "Scattered Speculations on the Subaltern and the Popular", *Postcolonial Studies* 8:4 (2005), p. 476.

1   The Shadow of Seán: O'Casey, Commitment and the Literature of Dublin's Working Class

1. Seán O'Casey, *Autobiography Volume 4: Inishfallen Fare Thee Well* (London: Pan, 1972), p. 204.
2. Bernice Schrank, *Sean O'Casey: A Research and Production Sourcebook* (London: Greenwood, 1996), p. 11.
3. Seán O'Casey, *Mirror in My House: Autobiographies of Sean O'Casey*, 2 vols (New York: Macmillan, 1956), I, p. 361.
4. This disillusion with constitutional nationalism was illustrated by the message of an early play, since lost, *The Crimson in The Tricolour*, which Lady Gregory feared would "hasten the attack on Sinn Fein"; Garry O'Connor, *Seán O'Casey: A Life*, p. 131. O'Casey later launched a blistering attack on Pearse's political credentials, pointing out that: "This leader of democratic opinion consistently used the trams on every possible occasion, though the controller of the Dublin tramway system was the man who declared the workers could submit or starve" – qtd. in John Newsinger, " 'In the Hunger-Cry of the Nation's Poor is Heard the Voice of Ireland': Sean O'Casey and Politics 1908–1916", *Journal of Contemporary History*, 20:2 (April 1985), p. 231. Newsinger relates that the Lockout was a watershed in terms of O'Casey's relationship with socialism and republicanism, between which he had always tried to find a synergy of political ideology, but "Larkin's fiery oratory, together with Shaw's *John Bull's Other Island* won him over to the left [...] experience showed him republicanism's feet of clay"; Ibid., p. 228. Newsinger also shows, however, that although O'Casey withdrew from the IRB – which feared upsetting its more affluent elements by any outright alignment with socialism – he was afterwards to show great admiration for Pearse.
5. Austin Clarke, "Tales from Dublin", *The Times Literary Supplement*, 6 September 1963, p. 674.
6. Herbert Goldstone, *In Search of Community: The Achievement of Seán O'Casey* (Dublin: Mercier, 1972), p. 16.
7. Seán O'Casey, *The Flying Wasp* (London: Macmillan, 1937).

8. Roger McHugh, " 'Always Complainin': The Politics of Young Sean", *Irish University Review*, 10:1 (Spring, 1980), p. 91.

9. Ronan McDonald, "Seán O'Casey's Dublin Trilogy: disillusionment to delusion", in *The Cambridge Companion to Twentieth-Century Irish Drama*, ed. Shaun Richards (Cambridge: Cambridge University Press, 2004), p. 148.

10. Seán O'Casey, *Collected Plays: Volume One*, p. 232.

11. Seán O'Casey, *Mirror in My House: Autobiographies of Sean O'Casey*, 2 vols (New York: Macmillan, 1956), I, p. 684.

12. O'Casey, *Collected Plays: Volume One*, p. 237.

13. Seán O'Casey, *Red Roses for Me: A Play in Four Acts* (New York: Macmillan, 1943), p. 95.

14. A.P. Wilson, "Tom Robinson's Part Acts II and III", *The Slough* (Dublin: Abbey Theatre Papers, 1914; National Library of Ireland Mss. Dept.), p. 14.

15. Christopher Murray, *Sean O'Casey: Writer at Work, A Biography* (Dublin: Gill and Macmillan, 2004), p. 284.

16. Goldstone, *In Search of Community*, p. 157. The original comment was made in O'Casey's own notes for the Mermaid production of *The Bishop's Bonfire*.

17. Seán O'Casey, "They Go the Irish", in *They Go, The Irish*, compiled by Leslie Daiken (London: Nicholson & Watson, 1944), p. 7.

18. Regarding the play's critical reception, see Schrank, *Sean O'Casey: A Research and Production Sourcebook*, p. 9, 79; Seán O'Casey, *Within the Gates: A Play of Four Scenes in a London Park* (London: Macmillan, 1934), pp. 69–70.

19. Seán O'Casey, *Selected Plays of Seán O'Casey* (New York: G. Braziller, 1954), p. 582.

20. Seán O'Casey, *Collected Plays: Volume Four* (London: Macmillan, 1951), p. 124.

21. Ibid., p. 194.

22. Ibid., p. 219.

23. Sean O'Casey, *The Bishop's Bonfire: A Sad Play Within the Tune of a Polka* (London: Macmillan, 1955), p. 35.

24. Murray, *Sean O'Casey: Writer at Work*, p. 374.

25. Ibid., p. 375.

26. Seamus Deane, "O'Casey and Yeats: Exemplary Dramatists", in *Celtic Revivals: Essays in Modern Irish Literature 1880–1980* (London: Faber 1985), pp. 108–122.

27. Lionel Pilkington, *Theatre and State in Twentieth-Century Ireland: Cultivating the People* (London: Routledge, 2001), pp. 99, 102.

28. Shakir Mustafa, "Saying 'No' to Politics: Seán O'Casey's Dublin Trilogy", in *A Century of Irish Drama: Widening the Stage*, ed. Stephen Watt *et al.* (Bloomington: Indiana UP, 2000), p. 110.

29. See Garry O'Connor, *Seán O'Casey: A Life*, pp. 153–155. Marianne Peyronnet makes a forceful argument for O'Casey's categorisation as a feminist writer; "Was O'Casey a feminist playwright?" in *Times Change: Quarterly Political and Cultural Review*, 12 (Winter 1997/8), pp. 23–26. Paul Kerryson, who directed O'Casey's *Trilogy*, takes a similar view of O'Casey: See interview with Kerryson in Victoria Stewart, *About O'Casey: The Playwright and the Work* (London: Faber & Faber, 2006), pp. 94–95. Jules Koslow equally describes O'Casey's portrayal of women as "ennobling"; Jules Koslow, *The Green and the Red: Seán O'Casey... the Man and His Plays* (New York: Arts Inc., 1950), p. 43. Neil Blackadder argues of *The Plough* – which received a hostile response from suffragettes – that "ironically, [O'Casey's] play can more justifiably be considered feminist than the protests [by suffragettes] against it"; Neil Blackadder, *Performing Opposition: Modern Theatre and the*

Scandalized Audience (Westport: Praeger, 2003), p. 128. One production of *The Plough* that might put this controversy in a new context is the 1991 Abbey revival by Garry Hines. In this modernised version, the stage was stripped bare and the actors were depicted in punk style, with female players' heads shaved bare. This had the effect of refocusing the action away from its emotive historical resonances and towards its more fundamentally liberated, humanist portrayal of its women.

30. Nicholas Grene, *The Politics of Irish Drama: Plays in Context from Boucicault to Friel* (Cambridge: Cambridge University Press, 1999), p. 125.
31. Reprinted in Stewart, *About O'Casey*, p. 64.
32. Brendan Behan, *Confessions of an Irish Rebel* (London: Arrow, 1990), p. 98.
33. Goldstone, *In Search of Community*, pp. 39–40.
34. O'Casey, *Red Roses for Me*, p. 13.
35. O'Casey, *The Complete Plays of Sean O'Casey*, 5 vols (London: Macmillan, 1984), V, pp. 508–509.
36. Schrank, *Sean O'Casey: A Research and Production Sourcebook* (London: Greenwood, 1996), p. 10.
37. O'Casey, *Collected Plays: Volume Four*, p. 228.
38. James Stephens, *The Lover Who Lost* (National Library of Ireland: Abbey Theatre Mss., microfiche, n.d.), p. 9.
39. Less exuberant but equally engaging depictions of female suffering with brutal men are there in O'Casey, too. "The Star Jazzer", a short tenement story about rape within marriage, and "The Job", another, which depicts a woman being sexually harassed, were both published in the collection *Windfalls* (1934), and they illustrate a darker aspect of female experience that becomes a major preoccupation for writers like Paul Smith, in *Esther's Altar* (1959) and Roddy Doyle, with *The Woman Who Walked into Doors* (1996).
40. James McKenna, *Abbey Ambiguities* (n. p: n. pub., May 1980, pamphlet), p. 2.
41. O'Casey, *Collected Plays, Volume One*, p. 156.
42. Ibid., p. 81.
43. Robert Collis, *Marrowbone Lane: A Play in Three Acts* (Dublin: Runa Press, 1943), p. 75.
44. O'Casey, *Collected Plays, Volume One*, p. 191.
45. Seamus Deane, "O'Casey and Yeats: Exemplary Dramatists", in *Celtic Revivals: Essays in Modern Irish Literature 1880–1980* (London: Faber, 1985), p. 111.
46. Goldstone, *In Search of Community*, pp. 5–6.
47. William J. Lawrence, in the *Irish Statesman*, 15 May 1954; cited in Hogan, Robert and Richard Burnham, *The Modern Irish Drama: A Documentary History VI: The Years of O'Casey, 1921–1926* (Gerrard's Cross: Smythe, 1992), p. 193.
48. Murray, *Seán O'Casey: Writer at Work*, p.165.
49. Seán O'Casey, *Blasts and Benedictions: Articles and Stories* (London: Macmillan, 1967), p. 77.
50. Antonio Gramsci, *A Gramsci Reader*, ed. David Forgacs (London: Lawrence and Wishart, 1988), p. 393.
51. Ibid., p. 304.
52. Yet there was obvious emulation too, as James F. Carens notes. The "general resemblances" between Gogarty's Tullys and O'Casey's Boyles include crippled males (Jimmy Foley and Johnny Boyle), peevish whiners (Tully with his backaches and the Paycock with his notorious "pains"), boasting male leads, and while "Mary Foley's roots in reality go not so deep as Juno's", nonetheless "they

go deep". James F. Carens, "Introduction" to Oliver St. John Gogarty, *The Plays of Oliver St. John Gogarty* (Delaware: Proscenium, 1973), p. 11. Add to this the *deus ex machina* of compensation from a construction site accident – which catapults Tully into unexpected wealth – and also Tully's Paycockian bravado as paterfamilias, and one can delineate the extent of O'Casey's borrowing for *Juno*.

53. Wilson, *Liberty Hall Plays No. 1*, p. 15; Murray, *Seán O'Casey: Writer at Work*, pp. 95–96.
54. O'Casey, *Mirror in My House*, p. 139.
55. Robert Hogan describes it as "the first notable play about the Dublin working man" in *The Modern Irish Drama: A Documentary History IV: The Rise of the Realists 1910–1915* (Dublin: Dolmen, 1979), p. 342.
56. Declan Kiberd, *Inventing Ireland* (London: Vintage, 1996), p. 220.
57. Qtd. in Kiberd; Ibid.
58. Bourdieu, *Distinction*, p. 34.
59. Murray, *Seán O'Casey: Writer at Work*, p. 44.
60. Declan Kiberd, *Inventing Ireland*, p. 221.
61. O'Casey, *The Bishop's Bonfire*, p. 79.
62. Interview conducted with the present author, 27 November 2007.
63. Bernice Schrank, "Sean O'Casey (1880–1964)", in *Irish Playwrights, 1880–1995: A Research and Production Sourcebook*, ed. Bernice Schrank and William W. Demastes (Westport, CT: Greenwood Press, 1997), p. 262.
64. Goldstone, *In Search of Community*, p. 195.
65. See Bernice Schrank, "Performing Political Opposition: Sean O'Casey's Late Plays and the Demise of Eamon de Valera", in *BELLS: Barcelona English Language and Literature Studies*, 11 (2000), pp. 201–202.
66. Schrank, "Performing Political Opposition", p. 202.
67. Christopher Murray, "*O'Casey's 'The Drums of Father Ned' in Context*", in *A Century of Irish Drama: Widening the stage*, p. 118.
68. Schrank, "Performing Political Opposition," p. 200.
69. Murray, "*O'Casey's 'The Drums of Father Ned' in Context*", p. 118.
70. Christopher Hilliard, *To Exercise Our Talents: The Democratization of Writing in Britain* (Cambridge: Harvard University Press, 2006), p. 286.
71. Mac Anna revived *Purple Dust* in 1973, at the Lyric theatre Belfast, *Roses for Me* in 1967, at the Abbey, *The Star Turns Red* in 1978, also at Abbey, and *The Drums of Father Ned* was produced for the first time in Ireland by Mac Anna, at the Olympia Theatre, but did not reach his Abbey until 1985.
72. Colbert Kearney, *The Glamour of Grammar: Orality and Politics and the Emergence of Sean O'Casey* (London: Greenwood, 2000), p. x.
73. Schrank, *Sean O'Casey: A Research and Production Sourcebook*, p. 11.
74. See his criticism of C. Desmond Greaves and Jack Mitchell, for example, in David Krause, "The Risen O'Casey: Some Marxist and Irish Ironies", *The O'Casey Annual*, 3 (1984), pp. 134–168.
75. Schrank, "Sean O'Casey (1880–1964)", p. 262. See Robert Lowery, "The Socialist Legacy of Seán O'Casey", The Crane Bag, 7:1 (1983), pp. 128–134, and Jack Mitchell, *The Essential O'Casey: A Study of the Twelve Major Plays of Seán O'Casey* (New York: International Publishers, 1980).
76. Schrank, *Sean O'Casey: A Research and Production Sourcebook*, pp. 19–21.
77. Ibid., p. 11.
78. Terence Brown, *Ireland: A Social and Cultural History*, p. 32.
79. Lowery, "The Socialist Legacy of Seán O'Casey", p. 128.

80. Some years after O'Casey's death, Seán McCann's *The World of Seán O'Casey* (1966), and later, Martin Marguiles' *The Early Life of Seán O'Casey* (1970), questioned the writer's working-class credentials.
81. Murray, *Seán O'Casey: Writer at Work*, p. 15.
82. O'Casey, *Mirror in My House*, I, p. 216.
83. Only eight children were recorded or spoken about, leading O'Connor to doubt the truth of O'Casey's recollection; Garry O'Connor, *Seán O'Casey: A Life* (London: Paladin, 1989), p. 4.
84. Andy Medhurst, "If Anywhere: Class Identifications and Cultural Studies Academics", in *Cultural Studies and the Working Class, Subject to Change*, ed. Sally R. Munt (London: Cassell, 2000), p. 19.
85. Grene, *The Politics of Irish Drama*, p. 111. See John Lynch, *A Tale of Three Cities: Comparative Studies in Working-Class Life* (London: Macmillan, 1998) for some discussion of petty snobberies in Irish working-class culture at this time, esp. pp. 93–109.
86. John Lynch, *A Tale of Three Cities: Comparative Studies in Working-Class Life* (London: Macmillan, 1998), pp. 107–108. Lynch writes: "Although female wages in the profession were good compared to other areas of employment they were still lower than men's [...] The female teacher was expected to dress to a 'ladylike' standard and the daughter of a prosperous Birmingham tool maker had to spend £10 a year on clothes to maintain appearances. As some contemporary commentators pointed out it was difficult for a female teacher to live even on comparatively high salaries."
87. Ibid., p. 112.
88. Anon., "Recent Paperbacks", *The Irish Times*, 26 March 1971, p. 10.
89. O'Connor, *Seán O'Casey: A Life*, p. 4; Flann O'Brien, *At Swim-Two Birds* (Dublin: Penguin Books, 1992), p. 76.
90. Ibid., p. 77.
91. O'Connor, *Seán O'Casey: A Life*, p. 5.
92. Murray, *Seán O'Casey: Writer at Work*, p. 18. [Emphasis added]
93. As Murray has noted, the class ambiguities of the 1901 census form filled in at their Abercorn Road home are instructive in this regard, with Susan making a "very political statement" by denominating her family "Church of *England*" (aligning them with the imperial centre), but their occupations are unequivocally working class, with Mick a "telegraph labourer", Tom a "postman" and John a "Junior Delivery Clerk"; Murray, *Seán O'Casey: Writer at Work*, pp. 54–55. O'Casey would later subvert his mother's social snobbery in the 1911 census, mischievously describing himself in Gaelic as "sclábhaidhe do lucht an bhóthair iaranais", or "slave for the railway crowd"; Ibid., p. 79.
94. Ibid., p. 20. True, in 1881 and 1882, Michael Casey was listed in *Thom's Directory* under "Nobility, Gentry, Merchants, and Traders" as the lessee of a tenement building, but whatever the circumstances of his short and failed spell in property management, Michael's membership of such an esteemed group was doubtful, and in any case short-lived.
95. Kiberd, *Inventing Ireland*, pp. 218, 220.

2   Angry Young Men: Class Injuries and Masculinity

1. Boomtown Rats. Rat Trap. A Tonic for the Troops. Ensign. 1978. Geldof was inspired to write the song from his experiences working in the bleak environs of

an abattoir in Dublin where, "there was this guy called Paul who used to measure the value of his weekends against how many fights he'd been in. It was pretty much what I thought of Dublin at the time". Tony O'Brien, "What about Bob...?", *Irish Independent*, 17 August 1994, p. 26.

2. Harry Ritchie argues convincingly that the Angry Young Man "movement" was a rubric that contained many, underestimated contrasts and was largely "invented by the media"; Harry Ritchie, *Success Stories: Literature and the Media in England, 1950–1959* (London: Faber and Faber, 1988), p. 207. See esp. pp. 184–219.

3. In reference to *Goodbye to the Hill*, I refer to the theatre version. Dunne's earlier novel of the same name appeared in 1965.

4. Pierre Bourdieu, *Outline of Theory of Practice*, trans. Richard Nice (London: Cambridge University Press, 1977), p. 72. See also Pierre Bourdieu, *Distinction* (London: Routledge, 1998), esp. pp. 101–103.

5. Richard Sennett and Jonathan Cobb, *The Hidden Injuries of Class* (Cambridge: Cambridge University Press, 1977); Sennett and Cobb wrote, like Bourdieu, of feelings of duality in working-class men, whereby, due to their subordinate position in class relations, they feel divided within themselves as to their identity in the class system and their feelings of dispossession. This was an existential problem, they concluded, that "subjects a man internally to a cross-fire of conflicting demands for fraternity and assertion of his own worth"; Ibid. 118. Bourdieu's landmark study, *The Weight of the World* (1999), has equally emphasised not only the material injuries accruing from capitalism, but also the related lack of self-esteem and respect suffered by those from working-class backgrounds.

6. Bourdieu, *Outline of Theory of Practice*, p. 72.

7. Ibid. 85.

8. Harold Perkin wrote, in a somewhat acerbic but salient essay, that "the sociology of the well-heeled Marxist intellectuals of the old and new 'new left' would make a fascinating study, if they would allow someone to pursue it – they believe in studying the social conditioning of everyone but themselves [...] the trademark of the middle-class intellectual 'labour historian' is his condescension toward the working class which he seeks to control and manipulate"; p. 88. See Harold Perkin, "The Condescension of Posterity: The Recent Historiography of the English Working Class", *Social Science History*, 3:1 (Autumn, 1978), 87–101.

9. Richard Hoggart, *The Uses of Literacy* (London: Penguin, 1971), p. 16.

10. Andrew Sayer, *The Moral Significance of Class* (Cambridge: Cambridge University Press, 2005), p. 207.

11. Robert Tressell, *The Ragged Trousered Philanthropists* (London: Flamingo, 1993), pp. 45–46.

12. Pierre Bourdieu, *Pascalian Meditations* (Cambridge: Polity, 2000), pp. 75–6. In claiming that the less socially empowered are susceptible to social restraints in direct relation to their level of economic disadvantage, this view is naturally controversial. Jan C. C. Rupp characterises Bourdieu's "social space" as "a funnel, in which there is a greater degree of differentiation at higher class levels", warning that he "risks regarding the culture of lower classes as a negatively defined, homogenous mass culture". Jan C. C. Rupp, "Rethinking Cultural and Economic Capital" in *Reworking Class*, ed. John R. Hall (London: Cornell University Press, 1997), pp. 224–225.

13. Pierre Bourdieu, *Outline of Theory of Practice*, p. 73.

14. Walter Greenwood, *Love on the Dole* (London: Jonathan Cape, 1935), p. 138.

15. Anon., "Arts Council ignores his work", *Sunday Independent*, 16 December 1973, p. 9. In an obituary in *The Irish Times*, McKenna's "unapologetically combative stance" was cited as something that "may explain why it was not until 1977 before he received his first commission for a sculpture"; Anon., "James McKenna: Sculptor, playwright and poet with a total commitment to the arts", *The Irish Times*, 21 October 2000, p. 16.

16. *The Scatterin'* was presented by Alan Simpson at the Dublin Theatre Festival of 1960 and was well received, firstly in the Abbey Lecture Hall on 14 September that year. It was also produced in the Theatre Royal, Stratford, and received some excellent reviews. Simpson's collaboration should be seen as indicative of the radical nature of the work – his notoriety for producing *avant-garde* plays courted controversy and resulted in his arrest for "obscenity" in a controversial public spat some years earlier; see Conor Cruise O'Brien, "When the Catholic Church ruled us all", *Sunday Independent*, 5 January 2003, p. 19. The controversy contributed to Simpson's emigration in the 1960s, according to Joan FitzPatrick Dean, in "Irish stage Censorship in the 1950s", *Theatre Survey*, 42:2 (November, 2001), p.159. Simpson established the New Pike in London as a venue for showcasing Irish theatre and also conducted personal academic research on O'Casey.

17. James McKenna, *The Scatterin'* (Kildare: Goldsmith, 1977), p. 7, 26. Further references to this edition are given parenthetically in the text as *SC* etc.

18. John Cook, "Culture, Class and Taste", in *Cultural Studies and the Working Class, Subject to Change*, ed. Sally R. Munt (London: Cassell, 2000), p. 107.

19. James McKenna, "Dublin 58", in *Poems* (Dublin: Goldsmith, 1973), p. 11.

20. Cited in Desmond Egan, "Achievement of James McKenna, Irish Stone Sculptor" <http://www.gerardmanleyhopkins.org/sculptor/achievement.html> [accessed 15 April 2008] (para. 30 of 48).

21. With the leasing, in 1951, of the Queen's theatre to the Abbey, and new management at the Olympia from 1953, the joint phenomena of falling audiences for variety and management preferences for straight theatre played their part in music-hall's decline. See Christopher Morash, *A History of Irish Theatre, 1601–2000* (Cambridge: Cambridge University Press, 2002), p. 221.

22. Anon, "The 'angry' fifties", *Sunday Independent*, 18 Novembers 1973, p. 17; Lar Redmond, *A Walk in Alien Corn* (Dublin: Glendale, 1990), p. 17.

23. Gus Smith, "There's no getting away from violence", *Sunday Independent*, 9 December 1973, p. 19.

24. Des Hickey, "Mr. McKenna among the Teds", *Sunday Independent*, 6 December 1959, p. 20.

25. Denis Donoghue, "Dublin Letter", *The Hudson Review*, 13:4 (Winter, 1960–1961), p. 580; Donoghue dismissed the play as a "derivative piece" from "*Sweeney Agonistes, The Threepenny Opera, The Hostage, The Entertainer, Westside Story* or *The Connection*"; the "local jokes were locally funny," he conceded, "and even the author's self-pity was tolerable". Another anonymous reviewer complimented Simpson's production skills, but condemned the play as an "apologia for the cowardly sadism that Teddy Boys indulge in, led on by the herd instinct, which their ludicrous garments seem to engender in them"; Anon., "The Resurgence In Irish Drama", *The Times*, 28 September 1960, p. 15. The latter review is perhaps indicative of the marginality of Teddy Boy culture.

26. In 1959 McKenna denied he was an "angry young man", associating the term with "cynicism", which was "really only a frozen waste inside you"; Des Hickey, "Mr. McKenna among the Teds", *Sunday Independent*, 6 December 1959, p. 20.

Almost 15 years later, however, he accepted the accuracy of the term; Anon., "The 'angry' fifties", *Sunday Independent*, 18 November 1973, p. 17.

27. Ibid.
28. Séamus O'Kelly, "Theatre Festival", *The Irish Times*, 14 September 1960, p. 6.
29. Ibid.
30. Christopher Morash, "Irish Theatre", in *The Cambridge Companion to Modern Irish Culture*, ed. Joseph N. Cleary, Joe Cleary and Claire Collins (Cambridge: Cambridge University Press, 2005), pp. 322–338.
31. Séamus O'Kelly, "Theatre Festival" in *The Irish Times*, 14 September 1960, p. 6; James McKenna, "Michael Sorohan's Notebook", in *Poems* (Dublin: Goldsmith, 1973), p. 40.
32. Anon., "Festival Playwrights", *The Irish Times*, 17 September 1960, p. 8.
33. McKenna makes a similar point with Patzer's bathetic and hyperbolic dream of owning his own giant scrap yard, which also contrasts tellingly with the grandiose tone of its articulation: "And as the gay vigour of youth leaves my bones," he waxes, "I will make a chariot out of the fragments [of scrap], and leaving this rheumatic world behind, I'll float away off up into the sun; and there I'll end my days in fields of effulgent gold" (*SC*, 15).
34. In an obituary in *The Irish Times*, McKenna was described as "an opponent of abstraction and a committed champion of figuration. He believed art should be accessible, and function as a progressive, egalitarian force in society"; Anon., "James McKenna: Sculptor, playwright and poet with a total commitment to the arts", *The Irish Times*, 21 October 2000, p. 16.
35. Ian Haywood, *Working-Class Fiction: from Chartism to 'Trainspotting'* (Plymouth: Northcote House, 1997), p. 94.
36. James Plunkett, "A Walk Through the Summer", in *James Plunkett, Collected Short Stories* [AU: Please provide the details of the editor(s)](Dublin: Poolbeg, 2000), p. 55.
37. This wailing phrase comes from the 'caoineadh', or lamenting-the-dead tradition in Irish and featured in a 1944 recording of the Irish language writer, Peig Sayers, who is often debunked as the quintessence of pastoral tedium in Irish literature. See Patricia Lysaght, "Caoineadh ós cionn coirp: The lament for the dead in Ireland", *Folklore* 108 (1997), pp. 65–82.
38. Slum clearance was still a major priority in the 1950s, with the Housing White Paper of 1948 being followed by a period of sustained growth in local authority housing, and although output dipped in the late 1950s, the following decade would bring with it the disastrous policy of high-rise that created Ballymun flats in 1964. See Cathal O'Connell, *The State and Housing in Ireland: Ideology, Policy and Practice* (New York: Nova, 2007), pp. 38–43.The relationship between these ghettoised working-class estates and crime was plain to be seen in the coming decades. See also for example Ciaran McCullagh's identification of the "typical Mountjoy male prisoner" of the 1990s, who fits the profile exactly of McKenna's characters of over thirty years earlier: he is "in his early to mid-twenties, from a large family from an urban area [...] the inner city or from one or other of the poorer suburban areas such as Crumlin or Ballymun"; Ciaran McCullagh, *Crime in Ireland* (Cork: Cork University Press, 1996), p. 23.
39. Paul Mercier, *Wasters* (1985, unpublished mss. supplied by the author), pp. 15, 4, 94.
40. Roddy Doyle, *The Van* (London: Vintage, 1988), p. 188.
41. Ibid. 128.

42. Joe O'Byrne, *It Come Up Sun* (unpublished mss. supplied by author and originally staged by Passion Machine Theatre Company, Dublin, in November 2000).

43. Red Magso, the protagonist of Magee's play of the same name, suffered a similar fate. Magee told me he has lost this play. One may also recall the destitute women of Paul Smith's novels in this context. Nuala O'Faoláin quoted in Máirín Johnston, *Alive, Alive O! Recollections and Visions of Dublin Women* (Dublin: Attic, 1990), p. 62.

44. Gerard Mannix Flynn, *James X* (Dublin: Lilliput, 2003), p. 6.

45. John Ryan, *Remembering How We Stood: Bohemian Dublin at the Mid-Century* (Dublin: The Lilliput Press, 1987), p. 38.

46. Robert Collis, *Marrowbone Lane*, p. 10.

47. Val Mulkerns, *Very Like a Whale* (London: John Murray, 1986), pp. 56, 19.

48. Enda Walsh, *Disco Pigs and Sucking Dublin – Two Plays* (London: Nick Hern, 2006), p. 41. Dermot Bolger would adopt a similar pose in his 1999 play, *The Passion of Jerome*, in which the middle-class Jerome suffers stigmata during illicit trips to his brother's Ballymun flat for an extra-marital affair. Jerome suffers for the working-class boy who died in the flat, the nails struck into his hands during supernatural horror scenes symbolising the return of the boy's forgotten story as an act of class vengeance. Jerome never "notice[d]" these people before – "the white sock brigade at job placement interviews" – but the boy forces himself into the businessman's life, imploring him to "suffer for me" to "share this pain". Dermot Bolger, *The Passion of Jerome* (London: Methuen, 1999), pp. 41, 68, 82.

49. While Larkin's childrens' engagement in high-jinx and petty crime mischief in Dublin's Dockland area furnishes fertile material for comedic vignettes, they also show how mass unemployment and limited opportunities lead all too easily into flirtations with crime, something Larkin foreshadows in the final story, "Sanctuary, Sanctuary", which ends with a teenage dance hall fracas and a group of drunken children being lead away by gardaí. This theme recurs in Dermot Bolger's 1980s novel, *Night Shift* (1985), in which "growing stupid on the labour" leaves idle youths with little more to do than play cards and take "the odd stolen car for a spin". Dermot Bolger, *Night Shift* (London: Penguin, 1989), p. 31.

50. Pierre Bourdieu et al., *The Weight of the World: Social Suffering in Contemporary Society*, trans. Priscilla Parkhurst Ferguson (Cambridge: Polity, 2002), p. 51.

51. Such ambiguity is central to Scottish writer James Kelman's Booker Prize winning novel, *How Late it Was, how Late* (1994), in which protagonist and ex-convict Sammy struggles to rationalise his blindness, which is caused by a police beating. He brings the beating on himself by attacking the police, but vacillates between victimhood and self-reproach, not knowing quite how to narrate his own story. "Ye never had any fucking choices", he proclaims to himself at one point, but "it was his own fucking stupit fault anyway", he concedes at another; James Kelman, *How Late It Was, How Late* (London: Minerva, 1995), pp. 32, 99.

52. John Fordham, *James Hanley: Modernism and the Working Class* (Cardiff: Cardiff University Press, 2002), p. 4.

53. 30 per cent of urban males and 26.5 per cent of urban females between 35–39 years of age were unmarried in Ireland in 1951. The marriage rate, both rural and urban, was "low by comparison with other countries". See F. H. A. Aalen, "A Review of Recent Irish Population Trends", *Population Studies*, 17:1 (July 1963), p. 76. Denis Johnston articulated a similarly sardonic attitude to the Catholic Church's inculcation of chastity in his 1958 play, *The Scythe and the Sunset*. As with many retrospective literary treatments of the 1916 Rising,

Johnston deflates Ireland's glorious past by gesturing to its degraded present, the ever-droll doctor Myles MacCarthy remarking of an arguing young couple: "You see. They love each other, but it only embarrasses them. I often wonder how this race of ours has managed to propagate itself at all, with the age of consent at thirty-five." Denis Johnston, *Collected Plays Volume I* (London: Cape, 1959), p. 20.

54. Maura Laverty, excerpt from *Tolka Row* (1950), in *The Field Day Anthology of Irish Writing, V: Irish Women's Writing and Traditions*, ed. Angela Bourke et al. (Cork: Cork University Press, 2002)., pp. 1247–1249. The play has never been published in unabridged form, despite its popularity in the 1950s and its spawning of the more well-known RTÉ soap opera of the same name.

55. Lar Redmond, *A Walk in Alien Corn* (Dublin: Glendale, 1990), p. 15.

56. Lar Redmond, *A Walk in Alien Corn* (Dublin: Glendale, 1990), p. 35.

57. Seán O'Casey, "They Go the Irish", in *They Go, The Irish*, compiled by Leslie Daiken (London: Nicholson & Watson, 1944), p. 9.

58. James McKenna, "Oxford Street is Long", in *Poems* (Dublin: Goldsmith, 1973), p. 21.

59. John Braine, *Room at the Top* (London: Arrow, 2002), p. 96.

60. Ken Gray, "An Outstanding Play", *The Irish Times*, 10 December 1973, p. 10.

61. Scott H. Decker and Barrik Van Winkle, *Life in the Gang: Family, Friends, and Violence* (New York: Cambridge University Press, 1996), p. 134.

62. Qtd. in Des Hickey, "No more begging bowls for Heno Magee", *Sunday Independent*, 31 August 1975, p. 11.

63. This first production in the Peacock Theatre, directed by Roland Jacquarello, was preceded by a Play Circle reading there on 12 April, 1970. At the time Magee attracted similarly phrased plaudits to those for James McKenna, with one critic describing him as "the best Dublin dramatic writer since Behan and O'Casey left us". See Anon., "An Irishman's Diary", *The Irish Times*, 10 April 1970, p. 11. The play was revived a number of times and broadcast on television, by RTÉ, on 5 December 1973. Revivals include one directed by Peter Sheridan at the Olympia Theatre, Dublin, in 1988. Heno Magee, *Hatchet* (Dublin: Gallery, 1978), p. 7; Further references to this edition are given parenthetically in the text as *HAT* etc.

64. Dick Ahlstrom, "'Hatchet' at the Embankment, Tallaght", *The Irish Times*, 28 July 1981, p. 8.

65. Richard Sennett and Jonathan Cobb, *The Hidden Injuries of Class* (Cambridge: Cambridge University Press, 1977), p. 118.

66. Andrew Sayer, *The Moral Significance of Class*, p. 4.

67. Ibid.

68. This is the kind of detrimental, "laddish" class normativity that Paul Willis identifies in his groundbreaking study *Learning to Labour* (1977). Proletarian "lads" reject the effete pursuits of other classes, Willis argues, developing a counter-culture of their own (class), but their inverse snobbery imprisons them in a laddish anti-intellectual habitus; Paul E. Willis *Learning to Labour: How Working Class Kids get Working Class Jobs* (Aldershot: Ashgate, 1993). Becky Francis summarises the term "lad" as evoking "a young, exclusively male, group, and the hedonistic practices popularly associated with such groups (for example, 'having a laugh', alcohol consumption, disruptive behaviour, objectifying women, and an interest in pastimes and subjects constructed as masculine)". See Becky Francis, "Lads, Lasses and (New) Labour: 14–16-Year-Old Students' Responses to

the 'Laddish Behaviour and Boys' Underachievement' Debate", *British Journal of Sociology of Education*, 20:3 (September 1999), p. 357.

69. Dermot Bolger, *Night Shift* (London: Penguin, 1989), pp. 42, 51.

70. Brendan Gleeson, *Breaking Up* (Dublin: Passion Machine, 1988), p. 16.

71. Ibid. 13, 1.

72. Roddy Doyle, *The Woman Who Walked Into Doors* (London: Penguin, 1997), p. 49.

73. Conor McPherson, *Four Plays* (London: Nick Hern, 1999), p. 51; Neville Thompson, *Jackie Loves Johnser OK?* (Dublin: Pollbeg, 1998), p. 16.

74. Roddy Doyle, *The Snapper* (London: Minerva, 1993), p. 39.

75. Robert Collis, *Marrowbone Lane: A Play in Three Acts* (Dublin: Runa Press, 1943), p. 32.

76. In Jim Sheridan's *Mobile Homes* (1976), Scene 2 opens with Helen and Larry bickering – their hopeful attitude in the previous scene suffocating under the weight of financial pressures and substandard living conditions after they move into a grotty caravan. Dermot Bolger's young couple in *Night Shift* also start out in a caravan, and they too fall foul of poverty's impediments. From A. Patrick Wilson's *Victims* (1914) to Paula Meehan's *Mrs Sweeney* (1999), and O'Casey's *Juno and the Paycock* (1924) to Enda Walsh's *Sucking Dublin* (1997), unhappy homes are an abiding emblem of a failed society and, often, of its failed men.

77. Jim Sheridan *Mobile Homes* (Dublin: Irish Writers' Co-operative, 1978), p. 16. This behaviour finds a parallel also in Paul Mercier's 1985 play *Spacers*. Mercier's Thomas, an actor in *Mikado – The Sequel*, a play within the play, fears that "if me mates find out I'm actin' the fairy they'll shove toothpaste up me hole"; he and his fellow actors are later branded "nancies". Thomas is one of the lead actors in the play, a bizarre pastiche of the original *Mikado* (1885, by Arthur S. Sullivan and W. S. Gilbert), martial arts cinema and the local tale of "a junkie and a bum" who becomes a vigilante. Chas, a security guard, who writes the farcical script, fantasises vicariously through his protagonist, "Jimmy the Vigilante", about having the power to "change the world". But the revelation of his own subjection to "post traumatic stress disease", following an in-store attack on him by thieves, underscores his own social impotence and the pathetic lack of power that inspires this macho "vigilante opus". The risible melodramatic cries of his femme fatale, Stella, about being a victim of "the hideous cycle of crime", suffering "at the hands of delinquents", mask their author's (Chas's) unspoken pain. Gilbert and Sullivan used meiosis to drastically understate the tyrannies their play portrayed; so too does Mercier. Paul Mercier, *Spacers* (1985, unpublished mss. provided by author), pp. 6, 35, 100, 132, 40.

78. Doyle, *Brownbread and War*, pp. 9, 12.

79. A similar scenario occurs later still in Mark O'Rowe's comic-tragic play *From Both Hips* (1997), in which the central character, Paul, has been the subject of an accidental garda shooting, during which the garda urinates uncontrollably in his trousers in a fit of fear. Paul's adventurist and "jealous" fascination with the Drugs Squad garda's glamorous job betrays his own lack of agency in society as a working-class man. Mark O'Rowe, *From Both Hips: Two Plays* (London: Nick Hern, 1999), p. 81.

80. Kane Archer, "'Hatchet' at the Embankment," *The Irish Times*, 16 October 1975, p. 10.

81. When Hatchet and his mother argue, Joey also pleads that the argument "wasn't Nellie's fault" and when an earlier fight threatens to explode he suggests, "c'mon we go for a drink" (*Hat*, 72, 32).

82. Sid Chaplin, *The Day of the Sardine* (London: Panther, 1965).

83. Ibid., pp. 21–22.

84. Hunter, Charles, "Heno Magee and the mean streets of 'Hatchet'", *The Irish Times*, 2 April 1988, p. 12.

85. Thomas Malthus's influential 1798 pamphlet, "An Essay on the Principle of Population", which predicted starvation as the result of population growth among the "improvident" poor, was a foundational text in right-wing political theory, and lead to the establishment of the 1834 Poor Law Amendment Act which buttressed paternalistic attitudes to the working class. Ian Haywood indentifies such attitudes, particularly in late 19th-century fiction, as presenting a "pseudo-anthropological Other world, whose primitivist freedoms from moral restraint makes them objects of fear and desire to bourgeois culture [...] its focus on squalid brutality and dehumanized, 'determined' subjects detracted from the laying bare of history surrounding this graphically realized canvas of working-class experience"; see Ian Haywood, *Working Class Fiction: From Chartism to 'Trainspotting'*, p. 13.

86. Rosie in Sean O'Casey's *The Plough and the Stars* (1926), Lily in James Plunkett's *Strumpet City* (1969), Maire in Lee Dunne's *Does Your Mother* (1970), Rose in Paul Smith's *Annie* (1972), are all instances of women who conform to this trope of the "fallen woman" in literature of the working class. Their sexual immorality is explicitly linked to poverty in each case.

87. A similar use of song was employed later on by Roddy Doyle in his BBC-RTÉ drama *Family* (1994), when, in the fourth episode, Paula Spencer sings a love song that jars with the reality of her loveless and violent relationship.

88. Lar Redmond, *Show us the Moon*, (Dingle: Brandon, 1988), p. 28.

89. Gus Smith, "Peacock premiere", *Sunday Independent*, 7 May 1972, p. 15. Smith is accompanied somewhat in this analysis by Robert Welch, who writes that "Magee, in his vigorous demotic dialogue, creates a raw and forceful set of people, animated by sensation, and indifferent to anything remotely resembling finer feelings". However, Welch also viewed the play as indicative of a cultural shift in the Abbey: "The play also showed that there was a new daring in evidence in the Abbey's programme as the theatre gradually gained in confidence in the 1970s". Robert Welch, *The Abbey Theatre, 1899–1999: Form and Pressure* (Oxford: Oxford University Press, 1999), p. 203.

90. Gus Smith, "Peacock premiere", *Sunday Independent*, 7 May 1972, p. 15.

91. Chaplin, *The Day of the Sardine*, p. 70.

92. The play was first produced at the Eblana Theatre (Dublin) by Trio Productions, on 4 September 1976. The novel of 1965 sold over one million copies around the world and was made into a Hollywood movie. The *Irish Times* reviewer, Ken Gray, found the novel unrealistic, especially the idea, which Dunne took from real events in his own youth, that a "stout full-breasted matron" in her forties would pay for sex with a "scrawny urchin [...] to satisfy her lusts"; Ken Gray, "Fiction", *The Irish Times*, 9 October 1965, p. 8. David Nowlan equally saw a work of "creaking improbability", "careering uncertainly from some good bawdry to the most maudlin of melodrama"; David Nowlan, "'Goodbye to the Hill' at the Eblana", *The Irish Times*, 5 September 1978, p. 8.

93. Jason O'Toole, "From the Hill to Hollywood: A conversation with Lee Dunne", *The Dublin Quarterly* (June-August 2005) <http://www.dublinquarterly.com/04/int_ldunne.html> [accessed 17 April 2008] (para. 13 of 28)

94. Fintan O'Toole, "Happenings on the hill", *The Irish Times*, 5 September 1995, p. 19; O'Toole goes on to compare this "pioneer" stylistically to Ernest Hemingway and Raymond Chandler.

95. Mary Leland, "Goodbye to the Hill", *The Irish Times*, 6 October 1975, p. 10.

96. Anon., "An Irishman's Diary", *The Irish Times*, 1 September 1978, p. 9. Dunne's play was still refused a touring grant from the Arts Council as late as 1993.

97. John Fiske, *Understanding Popular Culture* (London: Routledge, 1991), p. 123.

98. Interview by the present author with Lee Dunne, 27 November 2007.

99. A. P. Wilson, *Liberty Hall Plays No. 1: Victims and Poached* [two plays] (Dublin: Liberty Hall Plays, n.d.), pp. 1, 2.

100. Terry Eagleton, *Heathcliff and the Great Hunger* (London: Verso, 1996), p. 303.

101. Mary Russell, "'Goodbye to the Hill' and hello to a 'Mousetrap'", *The Irish Times*, 9 July 1992, p. 11.

102. Gerry Colgan, "Return to the Hill", *The Irish Times*, 29 August 1995, p. 10.

103. Sandra Woolridge, "Tough as old boots", *Southern Star*, 6 March 1993, p. 9.

104. Anon., "An Irishman's Diary", *The Irish Times*, 28 September 1968, p. 9.

105. Lee Dunne, "Is there such a thing as serendipity?" *The Irish Times*, 29 July 1985, p. 13.

106. Henry Kelly, "A Life of Writing", *The Irish Times*, 16 November 1974, p. 6.

107. Ibid.

108. Patricia Deevy, "Goodbye to the anger", *Sunday Independent,* section People, 16 August 1992, p. 6.

109. Jason O'Toole, "From the Hill to Hollywood: A conversation with Lee Dunne", *The Dublin Quarterly* (June-August 2005) <http://www.dublinquarterly.com/04/int_ldunne.html> [accessed 17 April 2008] (para. 9 of 28).

110. Dunne had not read Patrick Kavanagh's epic poem when he wrote the original novel; email correspondence with the present author, 3 September 2008.

111. Roddy Doyle, *The Dead Republic* (London: Jonathan Cape, 2010), pp. 158–160.

112. Lee Dunne, *Goodbye to the Hill: A Stage Play*, (manuscript supplied by author in electronic format), p. 58; further references are cited parenthetically in the text as *GH* etc.

113. Robert Tressell, *The Ragged Trousered Philanthropists* (London: Flamingo, 1993), pp. 267–268, 18.

114. *Down the Corner*. Dir. Joe Comerford. Ballyfermot Community Arts Workshop Productions. 1977.

115. Walter Greenwood, *Love on the Dole* (Harmondsworth: Penguin, 1969), p. 24.

116. Ian Haywood, *Working Class Fiction from Chartism to Trainspotting* (Plymouth: Northcote, 1997), p. 94.

117. [Emphasis added.]

118. Dominic Behan, *Tell Dublin I Miss Her* (New York: G.P. Putnam, 1962), p. 42.

119. James Plunkett, *James Plunkett, Collected Short Stories* (Dublin: Poolbeg, 2000), pp. 142, 148.

120. Ibid. 145.

121. Ibid. 149, 152.

122. See chapters seven and eight of Lee Dunne, *No Time for Innocence* (Dublin: Gill & Macmillan, 2000), esp. pp. 72–80.

123. Interview by the present author with Lee Dunne, 27 November 2007.

124. Thomas Halper writes that the notion of the "deserving poor" emerges from the Protestant ethic of individualism and is integral to bourgeois thinking, from early industrialisation into modern times. The "deserving poor" are "thought to have accepted the dominant business values, remaining poor through no real fault of their own" (Halper, 72). Halper writes: "The deserving poor's acceptance of the system – as manifested in their apparent belief in the value of hard work, their refusal to question the larger economic and social system, their unwillingness to complain publicly about their condition, and their obvious gratitude for aid from their betters – helped to convince the nonpoor that society was just" (76); Paddy manages to use Hayes's need for this bourgeois self-justification as an effective weapon in his own Machiavellian battle for social advancement; Thomas Halper, "The Poor as Pawns: The New 'Deserving Poor' & the Old Author(s)", *Polity*, 6:1 (Autumn 1973), pp. 71–86.

125. Ibid. pp. 73–75.

126. Ibid., p. 74.

127. Oliver St. John Gogarty, *The Plays of Oliver St. John Gogarty* (Delaware: Proscenium, 1973), p. 21.

128. James Stephens, *The Uncollected Prose of James Stephens: Volume 2*, ed. Patrick McFate (London: Gill and Macmillan, 1983), p. 172.

129. Gogarty, *The Plays of Oliver St. John Gogarty*, p. 23.

130. Ibid., pp. 73, 74. George Orwell identified this mixture of moral and physical class loathing as something intrinsic to bourgeois socialisation, asserting that the "middle-class child is taught almost simultaneously to wash his neck, to be ready to die for his country, and to despise the 'lower classes'"; George Orwell, *The Road to Wigan Pier* (New York: Berkley, 1961), pp. 112, 115.

131. Moira J. Maguire, *Precarious Childhood in Post-Independence Ireland* (Manchester: Manchester University Press, 2009), p. 33.

132. Dermot Bolger, *Night Shift* (London: Penguin, 1989), p. 87.

133. Irvine Welsh, *Trainspotting* (London: Vintage, 2001), p. 184.

134. John Braine, *Room at the Top*, p. 219.

135. A. P. Wilson, "Jack Hanlon's Part", *The Slough*, p. 3.

136. Dunne's own battle with alcoholism is dealt with at greater length in his autobiographies and fictionalised in the novels, *Paddy Maguire is Dead* and *Barleycorn Blues*. He wrote a number of provocative opinion pieces in newspapers during the 1970s and 1980s on the matter. Two medical directors at separate hospitals in Dublin even ventured that his "dramatic autobiographical account" of addiction should be published "in booklet form". See "Dunne on Alcoholism" (letter), *The Irish Times* (30 November 1973), p. 13.

137. A.P. Wilson, "Jack Hanlon's Part", *The Slough*, p. 2.

138. Sean O'Faolain, "Fifty Years of Irish Writing", *Irish Writing in the Twentieth Century: A Reader*, ed. David Pierce (Cork: Cork University Press, 2000), pp. 740–747 (p. 743); originally published in *Studies*, 51, (1962), pp. 93–105.

139. Ibid; Ibid. 744.

140. Ibid.

141. Bourdieu, *Distinction*, pp. 41–42.

142. Quote attributed to Stephen O'Connor by Victoria White, "FRONT/row", *The Irish Times*, 18 January 2001, p. 16.

143. John Osborne, *Look Back in Anger* (London: Faber & Faber, 1978), p. 84.

144. Ibid. 89–90.

3   From Rocking the Cradle to Rocking the System: Writing Working-Class Women

1. Pierre Bourdieu, *Distinction – A Social Critique of the Judgement of Taste*, trans. Richard Nice (London: Routledge, 1998), p. 34.
2. Declan Kiberd, *Inventing Ireland* (London: Vintage, 1996), p. 220.
3. Mikhail Bakhtin, *Problems of Dostoevsky's Poetics*, trans. Caryl Emerson (Minnesota: University of Minnesota Press, 2003), pp. 130, 124.
4. Ibid., p. 123.
5. Ibid., pp. 123, 124.
6. Ibid., p. 123.
7. Julia Kristeva, "Word, Dialogue, and the Novel", in *Desire in Language: A Semiotic Approach to Literature and Art*, ed. Leon S. Roudiez, trans. Thomas Gora et al. (New York: Columbia University Press, 1980), p. 71.
8. David Lloyd, "The Subaltern in Motion: Subalternity, the Popular and Irish Working-class History", *Postcolonial Studies* 8: 4 (2005), p. 422.
9. Nancy Glazener, "Dialogic Subversion: Bakhtin, the Novel and Gertrude Stein", in *Bakhtin and Cultural Theory*, ed. Ken Hirschkop and David Shepherd (Manchester: Manchester University Press, 2001), p. 160.
10. Jeremy Lane, "Sociology and Dialogics: Pierre Bourdieu, Mikhail Bakhtin and the Critique of Formalist Aesthetics", in *Face to Face: Bakhtin in Russia and the West*, ed. Carol Adlam et al. (Sheffield: Sheffield Academic Press, 1997), p. 330.
11. Ibid., p. 332.
12. Ibid., p. 335.
13. Glazener, "Dialogic subversion: Bakhtin, the novel and Gertrude Stein," p. 159, 160.
14. Ibid. p. 160.
15. Myrtle Hill, *Women in Ireland: A Century of Change* (Belfast: Blackstaff, 2003).
16. Mary Robinson, when elected in 1990, congratulated "mná na hÉireann, who instead of rocking the cradle, rocked the system." Quoted in Ibid., p. 235.
17. Ibid., p. 8.
18. Kevin C. Kearns, *Dublin's Lost Heroines: Mammies and Grannies in a Vanished City* (Dublin: Gill and Macmillan, 2004), p. xxii.
19. Ibid., pp. xiii–xiv.
20. See Ibid., p. xxi, xxvii.
21. See Maryann Valiulis, "Power, Gender and Identity in the Irish Free State", *Journal of Women's History*, 6/7 (Winter/Spring 1994-5), 117–136.
22. Margaret Ward, *Hanna Sheehy Skeffington: A Life* (Cork: Attic Press, 1997), p. 304.
23. Hill, *Women in Ireland*, p. 100.
24. Ibid.
25. Caitríona Clear, *Women of the House: Women's Household Work in Ireland 1922–1961* (Dublin: Irish Academic Press, 2000), p. 13.
26. Joan McKiernan and Monica McWilliams, "Women, Religion and Violence in the Family", in *Women and Irish Society: A Sociological Reader*, ed. Anne Byrne and Madeline Leonard (Belfast: Beyond the Pale, 1997), pp. 327–341 (p. 327).
27. Jenny Beale, *Women in Ireland: Voices of Change* (Dublin: Gill and Macmillan 1986), p. 140.
28. Caitríona Clear, *Women of the House*, p. 58.
29. Ibid.

30. Tom Garvin, *Preventing the Future: Why was Ireland So Poor for So Long?* (Dublin: Gill and Macmillan, 2005), p. 216.

31. Anthony Burgess, "In the twilight zone", *The Observer*, 18 November 1962, p. 25.

32. See Moira Verschoyle, "Shining Offbeat", *The Irish Times*, 1 December 1962, p. 9.; See Aosdána biography of Smith: <http://aosdana.artscouncil.ie/Members/Literature/Smith-(2).aspx> [accessed 24 June 2008]. Smith's mother's maiden name was also, coincidentally, Kate O'Brien.

33. John Jordan, "Slumlands Tragedy", *The Irish Times*, 3 March 1962, p. 9. Jordan was also friendly with Smith. According to Eibhear Walshe, both, with John Broderick, were part of a "gay men's sub culture [in Dublin] where writing and alcohol was the primary driving forces and Kate O'Brien fitted right into this"; Eibhear Walshe, "Invisible Irelands: Kate O'Brien's Lesbian and Gay Social Formations in London and Ireland in the Twentieth Century" in *SQS*, January 2006, p. 45.

34. See Alla Sarukhanyan, "Irish Literature in Russia", *The Irish Times*, 4 July 1968, p. 13; see also Seamus Ó Coigligh, "Irish writing a la Russe", *The Irish Times*, 21 July 1966, p. 8.

35. James Stern indicated this to be the case in his review; James Stern, "The Ordeal of Molly Baines", *New York Times*, 17 September 1961, p. 4. See also the International Association for the Study of Irish Literature newsletter of July 1997, People section, which states that the novel "tells the story of [Smith's] mother"; <http://www.iasil.org/newsletter/archive/newsletter1997/07_peopl.html> [accessed 10 March 2008] (para. 11 of 16).

36. Des Hickey, "Success for the boy who ran away at eight", *Sunday Independent*, 14 September 1975, p. 8.

37. With a "do-it-yourself" education, he admitted, even as an accomplished novelist, to some basic educational gaps, including not being able to recite the alphabet or the multiplication tables. This may of course, to the sceptical, recall the kind of myth-making O'Casey indulged in with his inventive autobiographies, but it is surely true that Smith suffered severe deprivation. See Paul Smith, "A Dublin Memoir", *The Irish Times*, 5 November 1975, p. 10.

38. Des Hickey, "Success for the boy who ran away at eight", *Sunday Independent*, 14 September 1975, p. 8.

39. Paul Smith, "A Dublin Memoir", *The Irish Times*, 5 November 1975, p. 10.

40. Ibid.

41. He received high praise indeed from some of his contemporaries outside of Ireland. "Dorothy Parker compared him to O'Casey; Cecil Day Lewis claimed he left most of his English contemporaries groping on the ropes; Carson McCullers said he was to be 'praised and wondered at'", Des Hickey recalled; Des Hickey, "Success for the boy who ran away at eight", *Sunday Independent*, 14 September 1975, p. 8.

42. Eveleen Coyle, book editor and publicist, named *The Countrywoman* as her Book of the Century in 1999. See "Books of the Year", *The Irish Times*, 4 December 1999, p. 2. Smith's novels include *Esther's Altar* (1959), *The Countrywoman* (1962), *The Stubborn Season* (1962), *'Stravaganza* (1963), *Annie* (1972) and *Come Trailing Blood* (a revised version of Esther's Altar, 1977). He also wrote plays, including an adaptation of the *Esther's Altar* for BBC Television, and a stage version, *Totem Pole* (1985), for the Los Angeles Actors' Theatre. He wrote *Miss Lemon* (New York, Shelter West Company) in 1986 and *Trudy on Sunday* (New York, Upstate

Repertory Company) the following year. Neither of these were published. An adaptation of *The Countrywoman* was commissioned for Siobhán McKenna to act in, but she died shortly afterwards. Smith himself died in January 1996.

43. Des Hickey, "Success for the boy who ran away at eight", p. 8.
44. Eileen Battersby, "Death of a realist", *The Irish Times*, 18 January 1997, p. 9.
45. Robert Collis, *Marrowbone Lane: A Play in Three Acts* (Dublin: Runa Press, 1943), p. 9.
46. P. T. Hughes, "Slum life in the troubled twenties", *Sunday Independent*, 18 February 1962, p. 15.
47. Anon. "Williams' play banned", *The Irish Times*, 14 June 1962, p. 11. *The Way to a Happy Marriage* was written by Ruth Martin.
48. Robert Collis, *Marrowbone Lane*, p. 15
49. Typified by Coventry Patmore's 1854 poem, "Angel in the House", the phrase has been extrapolated to represent a wider phenomenon of Victorian views on women's roles in society. Virginia Woolf famously invoked the term when she opined that "killing the Angel in the House" is part of the proper mission of the woman writer; see Virginia Woolf, "Professions for Women", in *Collected Essays* (London: Hogarth Press, 1966), p. 285.
50. David Lloyd, "The Subaltern in Motion: Subalternity, the Popular and Irish Working-class History", *Postcolonial Studies* 8:4 (2005), p. 422. See introduction for discussion of Lloyd's subaltern theory.
51. Rex is Latin for "king", while aurealis is the Latin for "gold", an ironic comment on the priest's revered status, and perhaps his wealth. "Tithe" would seem to infer the latter, as it refers to the voluntary contributions or "tithes" levied historically by the Christian churches.
52. Eileen Battersby, "Death of a realist", p. 9.
53. Social historian Kevin C. Kearns's writes of how women were constantly required to "negotiate with, and sometimes bodily confront, various authorities" like Bedell. This "was a perpetual worry for mothers"; Kevin C. Kearns, *Dublin's Lost Heroines: Mammies and Grannies in a Vanished City* (Dublin: Gill and Macmillan, 2004), p. 9.
54. A.P. Wilson, "Mrs. Kelly's Part Act III", *The Slough* (Dublin: Abbey Theatre Papers, 1914; National Library of Ireland Mss. Dept.), p. 11.
55. Joan McKiernan and Monica McWilliams, "Women Religion and Violence in the Family", in *Women and Irish Society: A Sociological Reader*, ed. Anne Byrne and Madeleine Leonard (Belfast: Beyond the Pale, 1997), pp. 328, 338.
56. Thomas J. O'Hanlon, *The Irish: Portrait of a People* (New York: Harper & Row, 1975), p. 150; Like Fr Tithe's abductors, McQuaid even had "a squad of ambulatory censors under his direction [who] patrolled the streets to ensure that displays [in shop windows] of ladies' underwear conformed to some mysterious clerical standard". McQuaid, who wielded considerable influence in Dublin during his tenure, from 1940 to 1972 (during which *The Countrywoman* was written), let "no aspect of sexual life" escape his scrutiny; Ibid. Though "doomed to failure" McQuaid's "gargantuan attempt to control Dublin as though he were the parish priest of a huge Cootehill [...] worked, after a fashion, for a generation", as Garvin further recalls. See Tom Garvin, *Preventing the Future: Why was Ireland So Poor for So Long* (Dublin: Gill and Macmillan, 2004), p. 195.
57. Qtd. in Pat O'Connor, *Emerging Voices: Women in Contemporary Irish Society* (Dublin: Institute of Public Administration, 1998). Kevin C. Kearns argues that within marriage the Church even condoned marital rape; Kevin C. Kearns, *Dublin's Lost Heroines*, pp. 78–79.

58. James Stephens, "Sawdust", in *The Uncollected Prose of James Stephens: Volume 2*, ed. Patrick McFate (London: Gill and Macmillan, 1983), pp. 152–153.
59. Many years later this contention would still be true according to Thomas Kinsella. In his 1990 poem, "Social Work", there is a palpable sense of vexation as an unnamed community campaign finds little favour with Dublin Corporation officials. A priest is present but silent at a community meeting, but is shown to control the officials' actions later on when they are depicted "nodding" to his commands; Thomas Kinsella, "Social Work", in *Collected Poems 1956–2001* (Manchester: Carcanet, 2001), p. 295.
60. According to Myrtle Hill, 56 per cent of lone mothers opted for adoption in 1961, as compared to only 6.7 per cent thirty years later; Myrtle Hill, *Women in Ireland: A Century of Change*, p. 194.
61. Even the religious Mrs Baines briefly considers an abortion of a late child, but rejects the idea because it is "against the canons of the church that said you failed in your duty to God by not having as many children as he saw fit to bless you with" (*CW*, p. 153). Mrs Kinsella, by contrast, dismisses this edict as folly; she surmises that Baines would "never have an abortion, the poor fool!" (*CW*, p. 31).
62. *Up the Junction* was published in 1963, then screened as a Ken Loach television drama for the BBC's *Wednesday Play* in 1965; *Saturday Night, Sunday Morning* was first published in 1958, then made a film, directed by Karel Reisz, in 1960. Both works were to the forefront of a movement in British writing and film towards working-class, "slice-of-life" representation. This incorporated the "Angry Young Man" writing of Sillitoe himself, Kinsgley Amis, John Osborne and John Braine, and other works falling under various genre-terms like "Kitchen Sink" and "British New Wave". Issues of sex, unwanted pregnancy and abortion were dealt with in a serious and often controversial manner by these writers.
63. It might be noted in this regard that while official censorship lasted from 1929 to 1967 in the Irish Republic, advertisements for abortion clinics were still being erased from Irish editions of English magazines in the 1980s.
64. Kevin C. Kearns, *Dublin's Lost Heroines*, p. 83; Ibid., p. 81.
65. Ibid.; Ibid., p. 82.
66. Catherine Dunne, *A Name for Himself* (London: Vintage, 1999), p. 23.
67. It is a way out of the poverty trap in James Stephens' *The Charwoman's Daughter* (1912), in which Mrs Makebelieve tells her daughter that "some one going along the street may take a fancy to you and marry you", leading to her "ease" and the "enlargement of her own dignity". James Stephens, *James Stephens: A Selection* (London: Macmillan, 1962), p. 16.
68. Pio was to be made a saint by the Catholic Church in 2002. He first claimed to have experienced stigmata in 1918.
69. Luke Gibbons, "Coming out of Hibernation? The Myth of Modernity in Irish Culture", in *Across the Frontiers: Ireland in the 1990s*, ed. Richard Kearney (Dublin: Wolfhound, 1988), p. 208.
70. The *Pericope Adulterae* is the New Testament passage, John 7:53-8:11, which describes the confrontation between Christ and the Pharisees over whether an adulteress should be stoned, from which the aphorism "to cast the first stone" is derived.
71. "Analogous to music and chanting, rather than a language of rational analysis", jouissance, associated with the feminist theories of Julia Kristeva and Luce Irigaray, "thus connects the woman's body and language, by rendering audible and visible the underbelly of consciousness as a different language, one that reflects emotional, visionary, and fragmentary aspects of existence. The language of subconsciousness, [*jouissance* is] akin to music on the one hand and

madness on the other"; Paula M. Cooey, *Religious Imagination and the Body: A Feminist Analysis* (Oxford: Oxford University Press, 1994), p. 23.

72. Irigaray uses the term "autoeroticism" to describe women's desire as something that "does not speak the same language as man's desire", for while man requires, sexually, "an instrument in order to touch himself: his hand, woman's genitals, language", a woman is autoerotic by virtue of her sexuality "without mediation". In a manner, Cocky's "stigmata" is such an experience, for her husband is present only in her thoughts. Her autoerotic sexual self-fulfilment is graphically demonstrative of a feminine language beyond men; Luce Irigaray, "The Sex Which is Not One", trans. C. Reeder, in *New French Feminisms*, ed. E. Marks and I. de Courtivron (Brighton: Harvester Press, 1981), pp. 100–101.

73. Sandra Gilbert and Susan Gubar, *The Madwoman in the Attic: The Woman Writer and the Nineteenth-Century Literary Imagination* (New Haven: Yale University Press, 1979), p. 78.

74. Interview conducted with Peter Sheridan on Friday, 9 September 2005.

75. Rosemarie Putnam Tong, *Feminist Thought: A More Comprehensive Introduction* (Oxford: Westview Press, 1998), p. 49.

76. Kevin Kearns, *Dublin's Lost Heroines*, p. xviii.

77. Lar Redmond, *Show us the Moon* (Dingle: Brandon, 1988), p. 33.

78. Sean O'Casey, *Plays* (London: Faber and Faber, 1998), p. 131.

79. Gerard Mannix Flynn, *James X* (Dublin: The Lilliput Press, 2003), p. 19.

80. Richard Hoggart, *The Uses of Literacy* (London: Chatto and Windus, 1957), p. 48.

81. Walter Greenwood, *Love on the Dole* (Harmondsworth: Penguin, 1969), p. 21.

82. Dunn's depictions of domestic violence in *Up the Junction* (1963) were particularly shocking in their brutality. In Barker's *Union Street* (1982) and *Blow Your House Down* (1984), male violence is a common occurrence; for Sillitoe's Arthur Seaton, violence is part of the fabric of social life, indeed even fun, in *Saturday Night, Sunday Morning* (1958).

83. John Benyon, *Masculinities and Culture* (Buckingham: Open University Press, 2002), p. 82.

84. Roland Barthes, *Mythologies*, trans. Annette Lavers (London: Vintage, 1993).

85. Male violence is often something to be expected, even revered, in Dublin's writing of working-class life. In Aidan Parkinson's *Going Places* (1991), female bus conductor Lena Mitchell finds that her retired trade unionist father's reputation for belligerence is a subject of awed admiration for her male Dublin Bus colleagues. A legendary hard man whose mantra was "I'm right [...] and anyone says I'm wrong [...] needs a face lift", Mitchell is recalled with respect by men who talk of him "beating the shite" out of a man who disagreed with him. "He's off his head now, so I'm glad yis have nice memories," Lena retorts, suggesting the new generation of women share no such sense of awe. Aidan Parkinson, *Going Places* (Dublin: Passion Machine, 1991), pp. 9–10.

86. Roddy Doyle, *Brownbread and War* (London: Penguin, 1994), p. 147, 191.

87. Heno Magee, *Hatchet* (Dublin: Gallery, 1978), p. 23. The utter contempt Steve, in Enda Walsh's *Sucking Dublin* (1997), shows for his "dosey cow" partner and her dreams of having children makes the same point. Enda Walsh, *Disco Pigs and Sucking Dublin: Two Plays* (London: Nick Hern, 2006), pp. 51–52.

88. Ann Wilson Schaef, *Women's Reality: An Emerging Female System in a White Male Society* (San Francisco: Harper, 1992).

89. Kevin C. Kearns, *Dublin's Lost Heroines*, p. 61.

90. Brendan O'Carroll, *The Mammy* (Dublin: O'Brien, 1999), p. 13.
91. Neville Thompson, *Jackie Loves Johnser OK?* (Dublin: Poolbeg, 1998), p. 188.
92. Perry Share, Hilary Tovey and Mary P. Corcoran, *A Sociology of Ireland* (Dublin: Gill & Macmillan, 2007), p. 189.
93. See Luce Irigaray, "Commodities Amongst Themselves," in *Literary Theory: An Anthology*, ed. Julie Rivkin and Michael Ryan, p. 574.
94. Pat Barker, *Union Street* (London: Virago, 1982), p. 53.
95. Ibid., pp. 57, 32.
96. Dorothy Nelson, *In Night's City* (Dublin: Wolfhound, 1982), pp. 99, 111, 102.
97. Interview conducted with Peter Sheridan on Friday, 9 September 2005.
98. Val Mulkerns, *Very Like a Whale* (London: John Murray, 1986), pp. 64, 56.
99. Roddy Doyle, *The Commitments* (London: Vintage, 1998), p. 78.
100. Judity Fetterly, "On the Politics of Literature", in *Literary Theory: An Anthology*, pp. 561–569.
101. Luce Irigaray, "The Power of Discourse and the Subordination of the Feminine", in *Literary Theory: An Anthology*, p. 571.
102. Simone de Beauvoir has used this terminology in assessing patriarchal cultures in which "humanity is male and man defines woman not in herself but as relative to him; she is not regarded as an autonomous being [...] is simply what man decrees; thus she is called 'the sex', by which is meant that she appears essentially to the male as a sexual being [...] He is the subject, he is the Absolute – she is the Other"; Simone de Beauvoir, *The Second Sex*, trans. H. M. Parshley (London: Jonathan Cape, 1953), p. xix.
103. Eve Ensler, *The Vagina Monologues: The V-Day Edition* (New York: Villard, 2001), p. xxiv.
104. Nelson, *In Night's City*, p. 104.
105. Gloria Steinem, in her foreword to *The Vagina Monologues,* talks of coming from the " 'down there' generation" in which women's sexual organs were spoken of only "rarely and in a hushed voice". Ibid., p. ix.
106. Ibid., p. xxxii. Ensler recalls the twenty-five hundred people in a New York City event chanting "vagina" in unison in 1997 (the year in which *Big Fat Love* is set), and notes the repossession of formerly negative terms for progressive ends by feminists; for instance, there is now a "Cunt Workshop" at Wesleyan University; Ibid., p. xxviii.
107. It is noteworthy here that this abstract exercise parallels some of the chapters in *The Vagina Monologues,* in which women are asked "if your vagina got dressed, what would it wear?" and "what does your vagina smell like?" Ibid., pp. 15, 93. Also, one may recall the title of Jeanette Winterson's exploration of working-class lesbianism and evangelical repression in *Oranges are not the only fruit* (1985). In that novel oranges symbolise the conservatism of Jeanette's fanatically religious mother, who believes they *are* the only fruit.
108. Ibid., p. xxxii.
109. Cora Kaplan, "Language and Gender", in *Papers on Patriarchy* (Sussex: Women's Publishing Collective, 1976), p. 36.
110. Elisabeth Badinter, *XY: On Masculine Identity*, trans. Lydia Davis (New York: Columbia University Press, 1995), p. 45; Pierre Bourdieu, *Masculine Domination*, trans. Richard Nice (Stanford: Stanford University Press, 2001), p. 63.
111. Elaine Showalter, "Feminist Criticism in the Wilderness", *Critical Inquiry* 8:2 (Winter 1981), p. 191.
112. Gloria Stein, "Foreword," in Eve Ensler, *The Vagina Monologues*, p. xix.

113. Hélène Cixous, "Castration of Decapitation?", *Signs* 7:1, trans. Annette Kuhn (1981), p. 54.
114. Roddy Doyle, *The Woman Who Walked into Doors* (London: Penguin, 1997), p. 184.
115. Ibid., p. 187.
116. Pat Barker, *A Century's Daughter* (London: Virago, 1986), p. 215.
117. Sheila Rowbotham, *Hidden from History: 300 Years of Women's Oppression and the Fight against It* (London: Pluto, 1973).
118. Interview conducted with Peter Sheridan on Friday, 9 September 2005.
119. The emotive term "abandon" clearly carries potent resonance as the anathema of whatever women are supposed to do, part of the pathologised vilification of bad mothers Valerie Walkerdine notes in *Schoolgirl Fictions* (1990). In Paul Mercier's play, *Drowning* (1984), this point is also made when Ma Burns, the victim of domestic violence, disavows her family altogether, and seemingly rejects also the stigma of the runaway mother: "This isn't my house [...] These aren't my family". But Ma Burns ends up the subject of another social stigma, as a "mentler" "pop[ping] pills like they were smarties" in a mental asylum"; Paul Mercier, *Drowning* (1984, unpublished mss. provided by author), pp. 35, 37.
120. Paula Meehan, *The Man Who Was Marked by Winter*, ed. Peter Fallon (Meath: Gallery, 1991), p. 17.
121. Xaviere Gauthier, "Is There Such a Thing as Women's Writing?" in *New French Feminisms* (Brighton: Harvester Press, 1980), p. 162.

4   Industry and the City: Workers in Struggle

1. Peter Beresford Ellis, *A History of the Irish Working Class* (Dublin: Pluto, 1985), p. 184; Desmond Harding, *Writing the City: Urban Visions & Literary Modernism* (London: Routledge, 2003), p. 42.
2. Ken Worpole, *Dockers and Detectives – Popular Reading: Popular Writing* (London: Verso, 1983), p. 79.
3. Terry McCarthy, *Outcast Dublin, 1900–1914* (London: Labour History Museum Pamphlets, 1980).
4. Diarmaid Ferriter, *The Transformation of Ireland: 1900–2000* (London: Profile, 2004), p. 173.
5. Ellis, *A History of the Irish Working Class*, p. 184.
6. F.S.L. Lyons perhaps best summates Larkin's controversial, polarising personality by describing him as "the archetypal bull in a china shop and it was a moot point whether irate industrialists or staid trade unionists were more alarmed by his irruption onto the Irish scene"; F.S.L. Lyons, *Ireland Since the Famine* (London: Fontana, 1985), p. 277.
7. Ferriter, *The Transformation of Ireland*, p. 166.
8. Ibid., p. 31.
9. Indeed, because of their interaction with foreign workers and its importation of radical ideas, trade unionism found particular sympathy among dockworkers, not only in Dublin but throughout Europe; See Dick Geary, "Working-Class Identities in Europe, 1850s-1930s", *The Australian Journal of Politics and History* 45:1 (1999), p. 20.
10. Carl Boggs, *Gramsci's Marxism* (London: Pluto Press, 1976), p. 108.
11. E.P. Thompson, *The Making of the English Working Class* (London: Penguin, 1980), p. 781.

12. Raymond Williams, *Marxism and Literature* (Oxford: Oxford University Press, 1992), p. 109.
13. James Plunkett, *Strumpet City* (London: Hutchinson, 1969), p. 19; all subsequent citations of this edition are indicated in the text in parentheses by *SC* etc.
14. John Fordham, *James Hanley: Modernism and the Working Class* (Cardiff: Cardiff University Press, 2002), p. 235.
15. W. B. Yeats, *Autobiographies* (London: Macmillan, 1955), p. 199.
16. Mikhail Bakhtin, *Problems of Dostoevsky's Poetics*, trans. Caryl Emerson (Minnesota: University of Minnesota Press, 2003), pp. 123, 125, 124.
17. Ibid., p. 125.
18. Interestingly, the real tenement collapse, on which Plunkett based this event, caused the deaths of Christy Brown's grandparents and his mother's siblings. On 2 September 1913, two tenements that housed more than 40 people between them collapsed in Dublin's Church Street. City authorities had inspected and declared the same buildings safe only a fortnight before the collapse. Many were injured and seven died. Christy Brown's mother, who lived there, was among the survivors, but her parents and all her siblings were killed; See Georgina Louise Hambleton, *Christy Brown – The Life that Inspired My Left Foot*, (London: Mainstream, 2007), pp. 18–19. How poetic and auspicious that Brown would release his own great tribute to working-class Dublin, *Down All the Days*, in 1970, a year after Plunkett published his. In another curious association, Christy Brown's beloved doctor, Robert Collis, released a play in 1943 which would infer similar corrupt dealings between local authorities and slum landlords, this time in the 1920s Free State. His characters in *Marrowbone Lane* reside in a tenement that Dublin Corporation had "condemned two years ago", but the local authority maintains the studied unconcern for the poor of its imperial antecedents. Robert Collis, *Marrowbone Lane: A Play in Three Acts* (Dublin: Runa Press, 1943), p. 21.
19. See Georg Lukacs, *The Historical Novel*, trans. Hannah and Stanley Mitchell (London: Merlin Press Ltd., 1962), p. 36.
20. Timothy Paul Roberts, "Little terrors: the child's threat to social order in the Victorian bildungsroman" (unpublished doctoral thesis, University of New South Wales, 2005) http://www.library.unsw.edu.au/~thesis/adt-NUN/uploads/approved/adt-NUN20060310.114803/public/01front.pdf [accessed 10 October 2010], p. 23.
21. Jonathan Joseph, *Hegemony: A Realist Analysis* (London: Routledge, 2002), p. 47.
22. Thomas Kilroy, *Talbot's Box* (Dublin: Gallery, 1979), p. 18.
23. See chapter 22 of Elizabeth Gaskell's *North and South*, ed. Dorothy Collin (Harmondsworth: Penguin, 1970).
24. Ibid., p. 235.
25. Geoffrey Pearson, *Hooligan: A History of Respectable Fears* (London: Macmillan, 1988), p. 168.
26. Ibid. Locusts are symbols of God's wrath in the Bible. He instructs Moses to punish the Egyptians by summoning a swarm of locusts, and he also tells Solomon that he will punish his people with a locust plague; Revelations 9. 1–11.
27. Kari E. Lokke, *Tracing Women's Romanticism: Gender, History and Transcendence* (New York: Routledge, 2004), p. 4.
28. David Trotter, *The English Novel in History, 1895–1920* (New York: Routledge, 1993), p. 34.
29. Judith Plotz, *Romanticism and the Vocation of Childhood* (Basingstoke: Macmillan, 2000), p. 5; Ibid., p. 30. [Emphasis in original.]

30. Christy Browne's *Down All the Days*, Lee Dunne's *Goodbye to the Hill*, Roddy Doyle's *Paddy Clarke, Ha Ha Ha* (1993), Mannix Flynn's *Nothing to Say* (1983) and *James X* (2003), Dermot Bolger's *The Woman's Daughter* and *The Journey Home* (1990), all invoke this loss of childhood innocence to indicate an equivalent loss of social "innocence".
31. Carolyn Steedman, *Landscape for a Good Woman: A Story of Two Lives* (London: Virago, 1986), pp. 127–128.
32. Diane Reay, "Children's Urban Landscapes: Configurations of Class and Place", in *Cultural Studies and the Working Class, Subject to Change*, ed. Sally R. Munt (London: Cassell, 2000), p. 156.
33. I am thinking here, for instance, of the generic child compelled to find acceptance in society: Dickens' orphans or victims of troublesome childhoods in *Nicholas Nickelby* (1839), *David Copperfield* (1850) and *Great Expectations* (1860); the narrative of hard knocks reproduced by Somerset Maughan in Philip Carey (*Human Bondage* (1915)). Most novels in this genre sustain a linear narrative of initiation or progression, from Charlotte Brontë's *Jane Eyre* (1847), with the titular protagonist's ultimate union with Rochester and enlightenment in forgiving her cruel aunt, to novels like Kingley Amis' *Lucky Jim* (1954), with the albeit comic union of protagonist James Dixon with a good job and a good woman.
34. A.P. Wilson, "Tom Robinson's Part Act I", *The Slough* (Dublin: Abbey Theatre Papers, 1914; National Library of Ireland Mss. Dept.), p. 2, 3; Ibid. "Peg Hanlon's Part Act III", p. 5.
35. Oliver St. John Gogarty, *The Plays of Oliver St. John Gogarty* (Delaware: Proscenium, 1973), p. 23. [Emphasis in original.]
36. Christy Brown, *Wild Grow the Lilies* (London: Minerva, 1990), p. 41.
37. Pat Larkin, *The Coalboat Kids and Other Stories* (Dublin: Eprint, 2007), p. 10. One of the scavenging children, Two Slices, ends up badly injured while foraging for scrap on a ship; see. Ibid., pp. 80–81.
38. Paul Sheehan, *Modernism, Narrative and Humanism* (Cambridge: Cambridge University Press, 2002), p. 2.
39. Ibid., p. 4.
40. William E. Cain, *Figures of Finance Capitalism: Writing, Class, and Capital in the Age of Dickens* (New York: Routledge, 2003), p. 174.
41. One of these dislodged, erratic types is a Gissingesque symbol of the senseless self-abuse of the poor in pleasing the rich, selling her ability to "munch glass [...] to amuse the laundered people in the big demesnes" (*SSM*, p. 113). Another "told fortunes with a ball of hair cut from the stomach of a cat" (*SSM*, p. 113). Her futile and eccentric attempts to foretell the future are a dramatic symbol of the failure of reason itself.
42. Franco Moretti, *The Way of the World: The Bildungsroman in European Culture*, trans. Albert Sbragia (New York: Verso, 2000), p. ix; Carolyn Lesjak, *Working Fictions: A Genealogy of the Victorian Novel* (London: Duke University Press, 2006), pp. 16, 89.
43. Franco Moretti, *The Way of the World*, p. 213.
44. James Stephens, *James Stephens: A Selection* (London: Macmillan, 1962), p. 56.
45. Ibid., p. 76.
46. Publius Ovidius Naso, *Metamorphoses*, trans. H. T. Riley (London: George Bell and Sons, 1898).
47. Ibid., p. 125.

48. Lukács's classification of the socialist *Bildungsromans* is synopsised by Sylvia Jenkins Cook: "They take up the life of the hero or heroine at a point where the conventional bildungsroman usually ends: with the acceptance of a traditional role in society or complete alienation from it. Then the characters are drawn into an increasing involvement with new social forces, which brings on a series of crises of consciousness"; Sylvia Jenkins Cook, *From Tobacco Road to Route 66: The Southern Poor White in Fiction* (Chapel Hill, NC: University of North Carolina Press, 1976), p. 92.
49. Susan Fraiman, *Unbecoming Women: British Women Writers and the Novel of Development* (New York: Columbia University Press, 1993), p. xi.
50. Ibid., pp. 53, 140.
51. Patrick MacGill, *Children of the Dead End* (London: Jenkins, 1914), p. 111.
52. Stephens, *James Stephens*, p. 49.
53. See John Lynch, *A Tale of Three Cities: Comparative Studies in Working-Class Life* (London: Macmillan, 1998), esp. pp. 105–106. For most children in these decades working life began at 14 years of age; many young men were made redundant at 18 by employers who refused to pay adult wages.
54. Benedict Anderson, *Imagined Communities: Reflections on the Origin and Spread of Nationalism* (London: Verso, 1991).
55. Ibid., p. 77.
56. Trotter, *The English Novel in History, 1895–1920*, p. 30.

5 Prison Stories: Writing Dublin at its Limits

1. Declan Kiberd, *Irish Classics* (London: Granta, 2001), p. 334
2. Ibid., p. 338; Oscar Wilde, "The Ballad of Reading Gaol" in *Complete Works of Oscar Wilde* (London: Collins, 2001), p. 858.
3. John Fordham, *James Hanley: Modernism and the Working Class* (Cardiff: Cardiff University Press), p. 4.
4. Wilde, "The Ballad of Reading Gaol", p. 857.
5. Frederick Engels, *The Peasant War in Germany* (New York: International Publishers, 2000), p. xii.
6. Qtd. in John Anthony Cuddon, *A Dictionary of Literary Terms* (London: Deutsch, 1979), p. 731.
7. "Letter to Ferdinand Lassalle", 8 May 1859, in *Marxism and Art, Writings on Aesthetics and Criticism*, ed. Berel Lang and Forrest Williams (New York: David McKay, 1972), pp. 48–50.
8. See John J. White, *Bertold Brecht's Dramatic Theory* (Suffolk: Camden House, 2004), esp. p. 198 for more on the "lehrstuck", and pp. 120–26 on "verfremdung".
9. *Mother Courage and Her Children* (1939), for example, uses characters with placards that explicitly comment on the events of the play, along with an anachronistic timeframe (ostensibly a remote seventeenth century war, but inferentially the contemporaneous Nazi invasion of Poland) and unrealistic props (a tree for an entire forest, for instance), which have the effect of distancing audiences from events on stage. *The Threepenny Opera* (1928), an earlier play, employs slogans on placards and uses an unrealistic ending to question the discourse of the play itself.
10. Terry Eagleton, *Literary Theory: An Introduction* (Oxford: Blackwell, 2003), p. 162.

11. Robert Welch, *The Abbey Theatre, 1899–1999: Form and Pressure* (Oxford: Oxford University Press, 1999), pp. 164–165.
12. John Brannigan, *Brendan Behan: Cultural Nationalism and the Revisionist Writer* (Dublin: Four Courts, 2002), p. 79.
13. Brendan Behan, *Behan: The Complete Plays* (London: Methuen, 2000), p. 39; all further references to this play are indicated in the main text in parentheses by *QF* etc.
14. Michel Foucault, *Discipline and Punish: The Birth of the Prison*, trans. Alan Sheridan (Penguin: London, 1991), pp. 195–228.
15. Pat Barker, *The Eye in the Door* (London: Penguin, 1994), p. 93.
16. Michel Foucault, *Discipline and Punish*, p. 217.
17. Corporate crime fails to "mobilise the stigma of criminality", because mostly it doesn't get punished by the courts. "In those few cases that come to the attention of the courts," McCullagh adds, "offenders are 'let off' with a fine". This anomaly has more to do with the class of the criminal than the class of crime, he concludes: "[It is] in some contrast to the way in which the criminality of the working class is dealt with. At the most basic level there is a somewhat greater willingness to use prison as the sanction for the offences they commit"; Ciaran McCullagh, "Getting The Criminals We Want: The Social Production of the Criminal Population", in *Irish Society: Sociological Perspectives*, ed. Patrick Clancy et al. (Dublin: Institute of Public Administration, 1999), p. 424.
18. Leslie J. Moran, "Homophobic Violence: The Hidden Injuries of Class", in *Cultural Studies and the Working Class*, ed. Sally R. Munt (London: Cassell, 2000), p. 209.
19. *Inside*. Prod. Noel O'Briain. RTÉ. 1985; see Sheehan, pp. 140–142, for discussion of this somewhat dreary effort on the part of the national broadcaster to engage issues of contemporary urban experience; Helena Sheehan, *Irish Television Drama: A Society and its Stories* (Dublin: RTÉ, 1987; re-published in a revised edition on CD-ROM, 2004).
20. Declan Kiberd, *Inventing* Ireland, p. 513; Jean Genet, *The Maids and Deathwatch: Two Plays*, trans. Bernard Frechtman (New York: Grove Press, 1962), pp. 103, 115.
21. Ibid., p. 157.
22. Gerard Mannix Flynn, *James X* (Dublin: Lilliput, 2003), p. 43.
23. Qtd. in Georg Lukács, *The Historical Novel*, trans. Hannah Mitchell and Stanley Mitchell (Nebraska: Nebraska University Press, 1983), p. 130. [Emphasis added.]
24. Peter Sheridan, "Author's Note", *The Liberty Suit* (Dublin: Co-op Books, 1978); all page references for this play are hereafter cited in the main text in parentheses as *LS* etc. Mannix Flynn's credit in co-authoring the play was inexplicably missing from this publication.
25. Karl Marx, *Capital, the Communist Manifesto and Other Writings*, ed. Max Eastman (New York: The Modern Library, 1959), p. 180.
26. Mannix Flynn, *James X*, p. 42.
27. Foucault, *Discipline and* Punish, p. 179.
28. Ibid., p. 266.
29. Harold Heslop, *The Gate of a Strange Field* (London: Brentano, 1929), p. 112. It also recalls something of the dismissive attitude of Communist advocate Jim, in Maura Laverty's *Liffey Lane*, who fumes at a fellow tenement dweller's incomprehension of his ideology: "Wasn't James Connolly the eejut of a man to die for the likes of you?"; Maura Laverty, *Liffey Lane* (London: Longmans, Green, 1947), p. 42.

30. Conor McCarthy observes that, if the writers of the "Dublin Renaissance" felt "profoundly alienated" from literary tradition, they were "more at home with the range of mass cultural references (television, rock music, film, Anglo-American youth culture"; Conor McCarthy, *Modernisation, Crisis and Culture in Ireland* (Dublin: Four Courts, 2000), p. 135.

31. Again, there is a parallel with Brecht who – unlike the disdainful theorists of the Frankfurt School – could enjoy Hollywood gangster films and the delights of popular music, as well as the *Communist Manifesto*.

32. Paula Meehan, "The Apprentice", in *Return and No Blame* (Dublin: Beaver Row Press, 1984), p. 28.

33. W.B. Yeats, *W.B. Yeats: A Critical Edition of the Major Works*, ed. Edward Larrissy (Oxford: Oxford University Press, 1997), p. 87.

34. Meehan, "The Apprentice", in *Return and No Blame*, p. 27.

35. Meehan's contrast between Yeats's "swanlike women" and her own impoverished characters pointedly invokes Yeats's representation of Maud Gonne as a "Ledaean body", and then, by contrast, as a figure "hollow of cheek as though it drank the wind". Her women are emaciated by physical privation of history's "whippings", whereas his idealised Gonne is immersed in history's "mess of shadows", as a spectral figure that has taken the metaphysical world "for its meat". The deflationary invocation of Yeats marks a disdain for the ethereal, unworldly imagery of Yeatsian aesthetics, and a preference for social engagement. Ironically, it is in performing his own duties of social engagement as a senator that Yeats conceives his otherworldly poem. See "Among School Children" in *W.B. Yeats: A Critical Edition of the Major Works*, pp. 113–115.

36. Yeats, "Leda and the Swan", Ibid., p. 113.

37. Interview by present author with Paula Meehan, 11 May 2005.

38. Paula Meehan, *Cell* (Dublin: New Island, 2000), p. 7; all page references for this play are hereafter indicated in the main text in parentheses by *Cell* etc.

39. In the interview Meehan spoke of the endemic fear and ignorance surrounding HIV in the Women's Prison, which she observed while conducting educational workshops on the issue.

40. James Joyce, *A Portrait of the Artist As a Young Man* (London: Penguin, 1996), p. 231.

41. Mark O'Rowe, *From Both Hips: Two Plays* (London: Nick Hern, 1999), pp. 149–150. [Emphasis in original.]

42. Paula Meehan, "She-Who-Walks-Among-The-People", in *Pillow Talk* (Oldcastle, Meath: Gallery Books, 2000), p. 60.

43. Ibid., p. 61.

44. See William S. Sax, *The Gods at Play: Lila in South East Asia* (Oxford: Oxford University Press, 1995) and Norvin Hein, "The Rām Līlā", *The Journal of American Folklore* 71:281, Traditional India: Structure and Change (July-September 1958), pp. 279–304.

45. Farley Richmond, "Some Religious Aspects of Indian Traditional Theatre", *The Drama Review* 15:2 (spring 1971), p. 131.

46. Interview by present author with Paula Meehan, 11 May 2005.

47. Directed by Georg Staudacher, in Theater Kosmos, Bregenz, premiering on 23 September 2004; photos taken of the Austrian set are still available on the theatre website, <http://www.theaterkosmos.at/conts/06archiv/2004_03/01.htm> [accessed 25 July 2008], and reveal a distinctly Brechtian use of lighting, photographic projections and props.

48. E-mail correspondence from Meehan, 3 July 2008.

49. Meehan, "Intruders", in *Return and no Blame*, pp. 37–38.
50. Ibid., p. 37.
51. Ibid., p. 38.
52. The Forum for Peace and Reconciliation was established as a means of furthering the Irish Peace Process in 1994, following the Downing Street Declaration. The term "peace and reconciliation" thereafter became one of the many (hackneyed) phrases of Irish political discourse.
53. Frederick Engels, *The Peasant War in Germany* (New York: International Publishers, 2000), p. xii.
54. Karl Marx, *Capital, the Communist Manifesto and Other Writings*, ed. Max Eastman (New York: The Modern Library, 1959), p. 180.
55. Karl Marx, *The Eighteenth Brumaire of Louis Bonaparte* (New York: International Publishers, 1963; orig. 1852), p. 75.
56. Lydia Morris, *Dangerous Classes: The Underclass and Social Citizenship* (New York: Routledge, 1994), p. 15.
57. Peter Stallybrass, "Marx and Heterogeneity: Thinking the Lumpenproletariat", *Representations*, 31, Special Issue: The Margins of Identity in Nineteenth-Century England, (Summer 1990), p. 84.
58. Ibid., p. 85.
59. A number of studies have confirmed that there is a broad class correspondence between those imprisoned in Irish jails. Typical prisoners are "young, unemployed and under-educated", part of the poorest of the working class according to studies conducted in Ireland from the 1980s and 1990s; See Ciaran McCullagh, "Getting The Criminals We Want: The Social Production of the Criminal Population", in *Irish Society: Sociological Perspectives*, ed. Patrick Clancy et al. (Dublin: Institute of Public Administration, 1999), p. 410.
60. Karl Marx and Frederick Engels, *The German Ideology*, ed. C. J. Arthur (London: Lawrence & Wishart, 2004), p. 47.

6   Return of the Oppressed: Sexual Repression, Culture and Class

1. Christy Brown, *Down All the Days* (London: Pan Books, 1972); Dermot Bolger, *The Journey Home* (London: Flamingo, 2003). Further references to these editions are indicated by *DAD* and *JH* etc., respectively, in the text.
2. Ferdia Mac Anna, "The Dublin Renaissance: An Essay on Modern Dublin and Dublin Writers", *The Irish Review*, 10 (Spring 1991), pp. 14–30.
3. Ibid., p. 15, 16.
4. Pierre Bourdieu, *Distinction – A Social Critique of the Judgement of Taste*, trans. Richard Nice (London: Routledge, 1998), p. 41.
5. Ibid., p. 16.
6. Ibid., p. 18.
7. Qtd. in D. Keith Peacock, *Harold Pinter and the New British Theatre* (Westport, CT: Greenwood, 1997), p. 1.
8. Jeremy Ridgman, "Inside the Liberal Heartland: Television and the Popular Imagination in the 1960s in *Cultural Revolution? The Challenge of the Arts in the 1960s*, ed. Bart Moore-Gilbert and John Seed (New York: Routledge, 1992), p. 152.
9. Qtd. in Tom Inglis, *Lessons in Irish Sexuality* (Dublin: UCD Press, 1998), p. 31.
10. Alexander Humphries, *New Dubliners* (New York: Fordham University Press, 1966), p. 232.

11. Inglis, *Lessons in Irish Sexuality*, pp. 31–32, 94, 140.

12. Diarmaid Ferriter, *Occasions of Sin: Sex and Society in Modern Ireland* (London: Profile, 2009), p. 325.

13. Ibid.

14. See Ferriter, *Occasions of Sin*, pp. 348–349; Lee Dunne, *Goodbye to the Hill* (Dublin: Poolbeg, 2005), p. 71.

15. Michel Peillon, *Contemporary Irish Society: An Introduction* (Dublin: Gill and Macmillan, 1982), p. 35.

16. Liam O'Flaherty, *The Assassin* (Dublin: Wolfhound, 1998), p. 81.

17. Qtd. in Georgina Louise Hambleton, *Christy Brown – The Life that Inspired My Left Foot* (London: Mainstream, 2007), p. 140.

18. While the novel refers to its disabled protagonist as "the boy" and never directly refers to the Brown family, it is largely autobiographical.

19. Richard Hoggart, *The Uses of Literacy: Changing Patterns in English Mass Culture* (Boston: Beacon Press, 1961), p. 110.

20. Kershner contends that, "in the represented world of Brown's novel overt political issues play little part, as if the world of the Dublin slums were immune to political change, or to history itself." This seems inaccurate, however, considering the abounding political and historical references of the book; R. Brandon Kershner, "History as Nightmare: Joyce's *Portrait* to Christy Brown", in *Joyce and the Subject of History*, ed. Mark A. Wollaeger, Victor Luftig and Robert Spoo (Michigan: University of Michigan, 1996), p. 39.

21. Christy Brown, *Wild Grow the Lilies* (London: Minerva, 1990), p. 17.

22. Brendan Kennelly, "City of Talk", in *Dublines*, ed. Katie Donovan and Brendan Kennelly (Bloodaxe: Newcastle upon Tyne, 1996), p. 12.

23. Maura Laverty, *Liffey Lane* (London: Longmans, Green, 1947), p. 28.

24. Ibid., p. 43.

25. Bourdieu, *Distinction*, p. 5.

26. Seamus Heaney, "Digging", in *On Opened Ground: Poems 1966–1996* (London: Faber and Faber, 1998), p. 31; Thomas Kinsella, "His Father's Hands", in *A Dublin Documentary* (Dublin: O'Brien, 2006), p. 31.

27. Lar Redmond, *Emerald Square* (Dublin: Glendale, 1990), p. 312.

28. Laverty, *Liffey Lane*, p. 36.

29. Neville Thompson, *Jackie Loves Johnser OK?* (Dublin: Pollberg, 1998), p. 6.

30. Hambleton, *Christy Brown*, p. 136.

31. Nancy J. Lane, "A Theology of Anger When Living with Disability", in *The Psychological and Social Impact of Disability*, ed. Robert P. Marinelli and Arthur E. Dell Orto (New York: Springer, 1999), p. 183.

32. Bourdieu, *Distinction*, p. 7.

33. Inglis, *Lessons in Irish Sexuality*, p. 35.

34. Lar Redmond, *A Walk in Alien Corn* (Dublin: Glendale, 1990), p. 62.

35. This iconoclastic juxtaposition recurs in Brown's work, for example in *Wild Grow the Lilies* (1976), where Babysoft discovers her "oul' ram of a Da" with another woman, while her mother is in labour, "working away like billyo screwed into her, bejaysus, under the picture of the Sacred Heart". Brown, *Wild Grow the Lilies*, p. 152.

36. Gerard Mannix Flynn, *James X* (Dublin: Lilliput, 2003), p. 30; Dorothy Nelson, *In Nights City* (Dublin: Wolfhound, 1982), p. 35.

37. The Catholic iconography of Mariology represents the *Mater Dolorosa* in images with her heart pierced by seven swords, each representing one of her biblical sorrows. *See* Carol M. Schuler, "The Seven Sorrows of the Virgin: Popular Culture

and Cultic Imagery in Pre-Reformation Europe", *Simiolus: Netherlands Quarterly for the History of Art*, 21:1/2 (1992), pp. 5–28.

38. Kershner, "History As Nightmare, p. 37; James Joyce, *A Portrait of the Artist As a Young Man* (London: Penguin, 1996), p. 157.
39. Christy Brown, "Multum in Parvo", in *Collected Poems: Christy Brown* (London: Secker & Warburg, 1982), p. 27.
40. Brown also suffered from severe dysarthria, which impaired his speech.
41. Both Frank McGuinness and John Banville found this scene particularly evocative. See Hambleton, *Christy Brown*, p. 150.
42. Ibid., p. 140.
43. Patrick Brown, known locally as "Squabbler", was a notorious hard-chaw, given, as Noel Pearson would recall, to settle "everything with a head-butt"; Hambleton, *Christy Brown*, p. 158.
44. Thomas Kilroy, *Talbot's Box* (Dublin: Gallery, 1979), p. 25.
45. Dorothy Nelson, *In Night's City* (Dublin: Wolfhound, 1982), p. 64.
46. This may also, again, be in reference to Joyce. Frank Delaney noted of *Ulysses* that if Leopold Bloom's movements are traced on a map they form a shape akin to a question mark. Brown again sees the shape in a taxi driver's ear towards the end of the book; See Frank Delaney, *James Joyce's Odyssey: A Guide to the Dublin of Ulysses* (New York: Holt, 1982).
47. Kershner, "History as Nightmare", p. 44.
48. Hambleton notes that Christy's self-portraits "often combine his own image with that of Christ weeping or bleeding"; Hambleton, *Christy Brown*, p. 134.
49. In 1973, Brown would write of similar desires in a letter to his close confidant and brother Seán. He was "driven to mad acts in [his] longing to approach them and absorb myself in their lives"; qtd. in Ibid., p. 31.
50. As Hambleton notes, Brown "wanted more than anything" to "produce a piece of art that would last in time"; Ibid., p. 105.
51. John Fordham, *James Hanley: Modernism and the Working Class* (Cardiff: Cardiff University Press, 2002), p. 82.
52. Hambleton sees the ubiquitous hawk symbolism in his work as expressions of his feelings as "the outsider quietly observing from afar"; Ibid., p. 32.
53. Qtd. in Carol Meinhardt, "Books, Films, and Culture: Reading in the Classroom", *English Journal* 80:1 (January, 1991), p. 84.
54. James Joyce, *Ulysses* (London: Penguin, 1992), p. 137.
55. In a letter to his brother, Seán, Christy had spoken of his father, and then, in similar terms, of "trying to avoid shadows, like any other man, I suppose, standing and trying to survive in my own little truth". In the same letter, he had spoken of feeling "weak, terribly weak" and fearing he would "give way", that life would become "too much". These feelings reflect the sense he expresses in the novel of his father's legacy as an imposing shadow that he struggles, falteringly and fearfully, to escape. Hambleton, *Christy Brown*, p. 141.
56. Joyce, *A Portrait of the Artist As a Young Man*, p. 288.
57. Ibid., p. 287. Brown uses similar imagery to that of Flann O'Brien, in *At Swim-Two-Birds*, who has his student narrator see himself in a mirror "supplied gratis by Messrs Watkins, Jameson and Pim", bearing a "brief letterpress in reference to a proprietary brand of ale"; Flann O'Brien, *At Swim-Two Birds* (Dublin: Penguin, 1992), p. 11. Both budding writers view themselves, self-deprecatingly and jocosely, through references to that great artistic enabler, alcohol. O'Brien had even characterised the Irish writer as a "drunk in the darkness of a railway

tunnel for days, waiting for the coming of dawn"; qtd. in Keith M. Booker, "The Bicycle and Descartes: Epistemology in the Fiction of Beckett and O'Brien", *Eire-Ireland: A Journal Of Irish Studies* 26:1 (Spring 1991), p. 79.

58. Christy Brown qtd. in Hambleton, *Christy Brown – The Life that Inspired My Left Foot*, p. 90.

59. Ray Ryan, "The Republic and Ireland: Pluralism, Politics, and Narrative Form", in *Writing in the Irish Republic: Literature, Culture, Politics 1949–1999*, ed. Ray Ryan (London: Macmillan, 2000), p. 84.

60. Lynn Connolly, *The Mun, Growing Up in Ballymun* (Dublin: Gill and Macmillan, 2006), p. 117, 120. Bolger would explore this deterioration of the flat complexes in 2004 with his play *From These Green Heights*, and four years later in another play, *The Consequences of Lightning*.

61. Dermot Bolger, *In High Germany* (Dublin: New Island, 1989), p. 38.

62. Dermot Bolger, *Night Shift* (London: Penguin, 1989), p. 27.

63. Declan Kiberd, *Inventing Ireland* (London: Vintage, 1996), p. 609; Paul Mercier, *Wasters* (1985, unpublished mss. supplied by the author), p. 94.

64. Jim Sheridan, *Mobile Homes* (Dublin: Irish Writers' Co-operative, 1978), p. 53.

65. James McKenna, "Crisis", a poster issued by the Goldsmith Press, n. d. My dating of this poem to the mid-seventies is based on its inclusion with another publication of the Goldsmith Press from 1975 in the Trinity College archives. See also "The Goldsmith Press Calendar 1975", on which the month of January is illustrated by McKenna's poem "The Dance of Art". The same sense of fragmentation is to be observed in Neil Jordan's Dublin labourer, in *Night in Tunisia* (1976), cast upon the social melting pot of London's "acquisitive metropolis", having "realized that he would never know" the people about him; Neil Jordan, *Collected Fiction* (London: Vintage, 1997), p. 10, 14.

66. Colin Coulter, "Introduction" to *The End of Irish History? Critical Reflections on the Celtic Tiger*, ed. Colin Coulter and Steve Coleman (Manchester: Manchester University Press, 2003), p. 3.

67. Television documentaries played an important role in this process. The groundbreaking 1999 documentary series, *States of Fear*, revealed how the Irish Rainbow Coalition government censored sections of the damning Madonna House Report (1996), which focussed on abuses committed in the 1980s and 1990s. The report blamed abuse on managerial failures by the Sisters of Charity order running the Dublin institution. But no such cover-up could stem the flow of revelations. In 1997, Louis Lentin had produced an exploration of abuse survivors' campaigner Christine Buckley's experience of institutional abuse, entitled *Dear Daughter*, which illustrated the regime of ritualised punishment at St Vincent's Industrial School, Goldenbridge, in the 1950s and 1960s. A year later, Channel 4 aired its documentary, *Witness: Sex in a Cold Climate*, regarding the Magdalene asylums in 1940s Ireland. Between them, and through harrowing individual testimonies, these programmes had revealed to huge audiences what had gone on over a fifty-year period. A new mood for transparency in abuse cases had developed over these years, leading to the establishment of inquires that have illustrated in panoptic detail the enormous scale of institutional abuse.

68. "Wed 20 May: Child Abuse." *Nightly News with Vincent Browne*. TV3, Dublin. 20 May 2009; <http://www.tv3.ie/videos.php?video=9205&locID=1.65.169&page=5> [accessed 22 July 2009].

69. Anon., "Shattered Lives", *Irish Examiner,* 21 May 2009, p. 1.

70. "Wed 20 May: Child Abuse." *Nightly News with Vincent Browne*.

71. Fintan O'Toole, "Law of anarchy, cruelty of care", *The Irish Times*, 23 May 2009, p. 39.
72. Ibid.
73. Geoffrey Pearson, *Hooligan: A History of Respectable Fears* (London: Macmillan, 1988), pp. 229–30.
74. O'Toole, "Law of anarchy, cruelty of care", p. 39.
75. Mary Raftery and Eoin O'Sullivan, *Suffer the Little Children: The Inside Story of Ireland's Industrial Schools* (Dublin: New Island, 1999), p. 12. [Emphasis added.]
76. Ibid., p. 13
77. Ibid., p. 64.
78. Laverty, *Liffey Lane*, pp. 34, 50.
79. Michael R. Molino "The 'House of a Hundred Windows': Industrial Schools in Irish Writing", *New Hibernia Review* 5:1 (2001), pp. 33–52 (p. 41).
80. Gerry Smyth uses this term to describe the new radical, liberal thrust to Irish writing in 'the decade and a half leading up to the millennium'; Gerry Smyth, *The Novel and the Nation: Studies in the New Irish Fiction* (London: Pluto Press, 1997), p. 7.
81. Dermot Bolger, *The Journey Home* (London: Flamingo, 2003). Further references to this edition are indicated in parentheses in the main text, by *JH* etc.
82. Dermot Bolger, *Invisible Dublin: A Journey through Dublin's Suburbs* (Dublin: Raven Arts, 1991), p. 12.
83. Ruth Barton, *Irish National Cinema* (London: Routledge, 2005), p. 86.
84. Diarmaid Ferriter, *The Transformation of Ireland: 1900–2000* (London: Profile, 2004), p. 664.
85. See Roddy Doyle, *The Dead Republic* (London: Jonathan Cape, 2010), pp. 158–160.
86. Ibid., p. 250.
87. Lar Redmond, *Show Us the Moon* (Dingle: Brandon, 1988), pp. 11, 12.
88. Seán O'Casey, *Collected Plays: Volume One* (London: Macmillan, 1950), p. 232.
89. Conor McCarthy, "Ideology and Geography in Dermot Bolger's The Journey Home", *Irish University Review*, 27:1 (Spring/Summer 1997), pp. 98–110 (p. 103). However, McCarthy very forcefully argues the political inconsistency of Bolger's polarisation of nationalism and modernisation; see pp. 103–105.
90. Linden Peach, *The Contemporary Irish Novel: Critical Readings* (Basingstoke: Palgrave, 2004), p. 42.
91. Interview with the present author, 24 August 2007.
92. Damien Shortt contends that because Pascal's attack emerges from self-repression, and is thus an effect of social conservatism, Bolger is saved from the charge of homophobia. However, this argument elides the fact that homosexuality is overwhelmingly associated with capitalist greed, mental illness and sheer malevolence in the novel. See Damien Shortt, "Dermot Bolger: Gender Performance and Society" in *New Voices in Irish Literary Criticism: Ireland in Theory*, ed. Cathy McGlynn and Paula Murphy (New York: Mellen, 2007), pp. 151–166 (pp. 163–164).
93. Ian Haywood, *Working Class Fiction from Chartism to Trainspotting* (Plymouth: Northcote, 1997), p. 130.
94. Conor McCarthy uses these terms in arguing that there is a latent and hypocritical ruralism in Bolger's somewhat confused retreat from modernity (while simultaneously pretending to champion the urban world); McCarthy, p. 110. Michael

Böss criticises McCarthy and Kiberd, in turn, for their negative commentary on Bolger, postulating (both intriguingly and preposterously, in my view) that their contributions are evidence that 'Irish literary criticism is strongly [and wrongly] political compared to literary criticism in the rest of Europe'; Michael Böss, 'Home from Europe: Modernity and the Reappropriation of the Past in Bolger's Early Novels', in *Engaging Modernity: Readings of Irish Politics, Culture and Literature at the Turn of the Century,* ed. Michael Böss and Eamon Maher (Dublin: Veritas, 2003), pp. 153–166 (p. 165).

95. Declan Kiberd, *Inventing Ireland: The Literature of the Modern Nation* (London: Vintage, 1996), p. 609.
96. Patricia Craig, "Ireland", in *The Oxford Guide to Contemporary Writing,* ed. John Sturrock (Oxford: Oxford University Press, 1996), pp. 221–237 (p. 234).
97. McCarthy, 'Ideology and Geography in Dermot Bolger's The Journey Home', p. 104.
98. Ibid.
99. Ulrike Paschel, *No Mean City? The Image of Dublin in the Novels of Dermot Bolger, Roddy Doyle, and Val Mulkerns* (Frankfurt am Main: P. Lang, 1998), p. 46. However, Paschel proceeds to contradict himself, later arguing that in Bolger Dublin's 'underbelly' is depicted with 'brutal honesty and realism'; p. 62.
100. John Ardagh, *Ireland and the Irish: Portrait of a Changing Society* (London: Penguin, 1995), p. 248.
101. Jim O'Hanlon, 'Dermot Bolger in Conversation with Jim O'Hanlon', in *Theatre Talk: Voices of Irish Theatre Practitioners,* ed. Lilian Chambers (Dublin: Carysfort, 2000), pp. 29–42 (p. 30).
102. Interview with the present author, 24 August 2007. Salò was itself based on the novel *The 120 Days of Sodom* (1785) by the French writer Marquis de Sade.
103. As Ingrid Von Rosenberg notes, "ever since Wollstonecraft's *The Wrongs of Woman,* mental asylums have been used in literature as places symbolizing the unjust limitations imposed on women by society"; Ingrid Von Rosenberg, "The Fiction of Agnes Owens", in *British Industrial Fictions* ed. by H. Gustav Klaus and Stephen Knight (Cardiff: University of Wales, 2000), pp. 193–205 (p. 204).
104. Robert Collis, *Marrowbone Lane: A Play in Three Acts* (Dublin: Runa Press, 1943), p. 48, 63.
105. Interview with the present author, 24 August 2007.
106. Michael R. Molino, 'The House of a Hundred Windows', p. 33
107. Interview with the present author, 24 August 2007.
108. Qtd. in Paschel, *No Mean City?,* p. 143.
109. Paschel, p. 143.
110. Interview with the present author, 24 August 2007.
111. This term is taken from the unpublished manuscript of a conference paper delivered by Shaun Richards in 1992; qtd. in McCarthy, *Modernisation, Crisis and Culture in Ireland,* p. 149. McCarthy argues that Bolger's backlash against the Republic is "just as partial as anything purveyed by Yeats or Synge".
112. Neil Corcoran, *After Yeats and Joyce* (Oxford: Oxford University Press, 1997), p. 127.
113. Terry Eagleton, *Heathcliff and the Great Hunger* (London: Verso, 1996), p. 47.
114. Lane, "A Theology of Anger When Living with Disability", p. 183.
115. Hambleton, *Christy Brown,* pp. 191–192.
116. Ibid., p. 127.

117. William Trevor, "The snarling, yelling world of real Dublin", *Irish Times Saturday Review*, 16 May 1970, p. 1.

7 Revising the Revolution: Roddy Doyle's *A Star Called Henry*, Historiography, Politics and Proletarian Consciousness

1. Seán O'Casey, *Collected Plays Vol. 2* (London: Macmillan, 1949), p. 331.
2. M.A.G. Ó Tuathaigh, "Irish Historical 'Revisionism': State of the Art or Ideological Project?" in *Interpreting Irish History,* ed. Ciaran Brady (Dublin: Irish Academic Press, 1994), p. 321.
3. Brendan Bradshaw, for instance, conceptualises three phases to revisionism in his essay "Nationalism and Historical Scholarship in Modern Ireland", in *Interpreting Irish History,* ed. Ciaran Brady (Dublin: Irish Academic Press, 1994), pp. 122–145.
4. John Hutchinson, "Irish Nationalism", in *The Making of Modern Irish History: Revisionism and the Revisionist Controversy,* ed. D. George Boyce and Alan O'Day (New York: Routledge, 1996), p. 102.
5. T.W. Moody, "Irish History and Irish Mythology", in *Interpreting Irish History,* ed. Conor Brady (Dublin: Irish Academic Press, 1994), p. 86. See also Ciarán Brady, " 'Constructive and Instrumental': The Dilemma of Ireland's First 'New Historians'," Ibid., pp. 3–31.
6. F.S.L. Lyons, "The Meaning of Independence", in *The Irish Parliamentary Tradition,* ed. Brian Farrell (Dublin: Gill and Macmillan, 1973), p. 223. In his essay, "Irish Historical 'Revisionism': State of the Art or Ideological Project?" in *Interpreting Irish History,* p. 311, Ó Tuathaigh also notes the explosive effects of the conflict post-1969 on revisionist discourse.
7. Roddy Doyle, *The Dead Republic* (London: Jonathan Cape, 2010), p. 194.
8. Boyce and O'Day use this term in connection with revisionism; D. George Boyce and Alan O'Day, "Introduction" to *The Making of Modern Irish History: Revisionism and the Revisionist Controversy* (London: Routledge, 1996), p. 2.
9. Moody outlines the history of the project in T.W. Moody, "A New History of Ireland", *Irish History Studies,* XVI (1969), pp. 241–257.
10. T.W. Moody, *The Ulster Question: 1603–1973* (Cork: Mercier Press, 1974).
11. Kevin Whelan, "The Revisionist Debate in Ireland", *Boundary 2,* 31:1 (2004), p. 190.
12. Paul Bew, "The National Question, Land, and 'Revisionism': Some reflections" in *The Making of Modern Irish History: Revisionism and the Revisionist Controversy,* p. 90. Bradshaw, "Nationalism and Historical Scholarship in Modern Ireland", pp. 124.
13. Edward Said, *Orientalism* (London: Penguin, 2003), p. 10.
14. Boyce, "Past and Present Revisionism and the Northern Ireland Troubles", p. 222.
15. Ibid., p. 224.
16. Terry Eagleton, *Heathcliff and the Great Hunger* (London: Verso, 1996), pp. 58–59.
17. Kevin Whelan, "Come All You Staunch Revisionists: Towards a Post-revisionist Agenda for Irish History", *Irish Reporter,* 2 (1991), p. 26.
18. Eagleton, *Heathcliff and the Great Hunger,* p. 43.

19. John Hill, "Images of Violence", in *Cinema in Ireland,* ed. Kevin Rockett, Luke Gibbons and John Hill (London: Croom Helm, 1987), pp. 147–193; Martin McLoone, *Irish Film: The Emergence of a Contemporary Cinema* (London: The British Film Institute, 2000); Patrick Magee, *Gangsters or Guerrillas? – Representations of Irish Republicans in 'Troubles Fiction'* (Belfast: Beyond the Pale, 2001); Ed Moloney, *A Secret History of the IRA* (London: Allen Lane, 2002), p. xiii.
20. Stephen J. Costello, *The Irish Soul in Dialogue* (Dublin: The Liffey Press, 2001), p. 90; Roddy Doyle, *A Star Called Henry* (London: Vintage, 2000), p. 1; page numbers hereafter cited in the main text in parentheses.
21. Rüdiger Imhof, *The Modern Irish Novel: Irish Novelists After 1945* (Dublin: Wolfhound Press, 2002), p. 263.
22. Brian Donnelly, "Roddy Doyle: From Barrytown to the GPO", *Irish University Review,* 30:1 (Spring/Summer 2000), pp. 17–31.
23. Imhof, *The Modern Irish Novel,* p. 256; Ibid., p. 263.
24. Ibid., p. 264.
25. See Rüdiger Imhof, *John Banville: A Critical Introduction* (Dublin: Wolfhound, 1989).
26. Jennifer M. Jeffers, *The Irish Novel at the End of the Twentieth Century: Gender, Bodies, and Power* (New York: Palgrave, 2002), p. 131.
27. Ibid.
28. Costello, *The Irish Soul in Dialogue,* p. 90.
29. Dermot McCarthy, *Roddy Doyle: Raining on the Parade* (Dublin: The Liffey Press, 2003), p. 198.
30. Ibid., p. 199.
31. Thomas Kilroy, *Talbot's Box* (Dublin: Gallery, 1979), p. 58.
32. Ibid., p. 31.
33. Linda Hutcheon, *The Politics of Postmodernism* (London: Routledge, 2002), p. 79.
34. Qtd. in Eagleton, *Heathcliff and the Great Hunger,* p. 311.
35. David Lloyd, *Anomalous States: Irish Writing and the Post-colonial Moment* (Dublin: Lilliput, 1993), p. 124.
36. Gerry Smyth, *The Novel and the Nation: Studies in the New Irish Fiction* (London: Pluto Press, 1997), p 107.
37. Georg Lukács, "The Historical Novel", in *Literary Theory: An Anthology,* ed. Julie Rivkin and Michael Ryan (Oxford: Blackwell Publishing, 1998), p. 292.
38. Tom Garvin, *Preventing the Future: Why Was Ireland So Poor for So Long* (Dublin: Gill and Macmillan, 2004), p. 160.
39. Benedict Anderson, *Imagined Communities* (London: Verso, 1991).
40. Jeffers, *The Irish Novel at the End of the Twentieth Century,* p. 132.
41. Cited in Stephen Slemon, "Post-Colonial Critical Theories", in *Postcolonial Discourse: An Anthology,* ed. Gregory Castle (Oxford: Blackwell, 2001), p. 110; original in Veena Das, "Subaltern as Perspective", in *Subaltern Studies VI: Writings in South Asian History and Society,* ed. Ranajit Guha (New Delhi: Oxford University Press, 1989), p. 314.
42. Ranajit Guha, "The Prose of Counter Insurgency", in *Postcolonial Discourses: An Anthology,* ed. Gregory Castle (Oxford: Blackwell, 2001), p. 120.
43. David Lloyd, *Irish Times: Temporalities of Modernity,* ed. by Seamus Deane and Breandán Mac Suibhne (Dublin: Field Day, 2008), p. 121.
44. Denis Johnston, *Collected Plays: Volume 1* (London: Jonathan Cape, 1960), p. 30.
45. McCarthy, *Raining on the Parade,* p. 217.
46. Cliff Slaughter, *Marxism, Ideology and Literature* (London: Macmillan, 1980), p. 26.

47. Anthony Giddens, "Class Structuration and Class Consciousness", in *Classes, Power and Conflict,* ed. Anthony Giddens and David Held (London: Macmillan, 1990), p. 164.
48. Erik Olin Wright, *Class Counts: Comparative studies in Class Analysis* (Cambridge: Cambridge University Press, 1997), p. 388.
49. Thompson indeed warned against "a static view of class", postulating that it "is a relationship, not a thing"; E.P. Thompson, *The Making of the English Working Class* (London: Penguin, 1980), pp. 9, 10. Bourdieu argued that "organic individuality [...] can never [be] entirely removed from the sociological discourse"; Pierre, Bourdieu, *Outline of Theory of Practice,* trans. by Richard Nice (London: Cambridge University Press, 1977), p. 86.
50. Liam O'Flaherty, *The Informer* (London: New English Library, 1980), p. 169.
51. Ibid., pp. 50, 82, 107, 108.
52. *The Wind that Shakes the Barley.* Dir. Ken Loach. BIM Distribuzione. 2006.
53. John Hill, "Images of Violence", p. 184.
54. Martin McLoone, *Irish Film: The Emergence of a Contemporary Cinema,* p. 62.
55. Ibid.
56. Neil Jordan, *The Crying Game* (London: Vintage, 1993), p. 16.
57. One is reminded too of O'Flaherty's cynical rebel leader's words of contumely for his soldiers, the "stupid carrot heads [...] Theirs is the bravery of the dull-witted ox"; but he also opines paradoxically that "a man must be intelligent to be brave"; Liam O'Flaherty, *The Informer,* p. 162.
58. Eve Patten, "Fiction in Conflict: Northern Ireland's Prodigal Novelists", in *Peripheral Visions of Irish Nationhood in Contemporary British Fiction,* ed. I.A. Bell (Cardiff: University of Wales Press, 1995), p. 129.
59. Richard Hoggart, *The Uses of Literacy* (Harmondsworth: Penguin, 1962), p. 198.
60. *Nothing Personal.* Dir. Thaddeus O'Sullivan. British Screen Productions. 1995.
61. McLoone, *Irish Film,* p. 60.
62. Doyle, *The Dead Republic,* p. 211.
63. Roddy Doyle, *The Woman Who Walked Into Doors* (London: Penguin, 1997), p. 180.
64. W.B. Yeats, "Remorse for Intemperate Speech", *The Winding Stair and Other Poems* (New York: Macmillan, 1933), pp. 58–59.
65. Deane, "Wherever Green is Read", p. 236.
66. Guha, "The Prose of Counter Insurgency", p. 121.
67. Seamus Deane, "Roddy's Troubles: Who needs blarney in the middle of a civil war?", *The Guardian,* 9 September 1999, p. 8
68. Roddy Doyle, *The Commitments* (London: Heinemann, 1988), p. 24.
69. For contemporary commentary on *Family,* see, for example, the *Irish Times* editorial of Saturday 28 May 1994, p. 11. See also Helena Sheehan, *The Continuing Story of Irish Television Drama: Tracking the Tiger* (Dublin: Four Courts Press, 2004), pp. 72–75.
70. Costello, *The Irish Soul in Dialogue,* p. 93.
71. Ibid., p. 91.
72. Doyle, *The Commitments,* p. 9.
73. *The Commitments.* Dir. Alan Parker. Beacon. 1991.
74. O'Flaherty, *The Assassin* (Dublin: Wolfhound, 1998), p. 51, 55.
75. E. J. Hobsbawm, "Working Classes and Nations", *Saothar* 8 (1982), p. 85.
76. James Connolly, *Erin's Hope* (1909) <http://www.ex.ac.uk/Projects/meia/connolly/Archive/jceh00.htm> [accessed 20 February 2005].

77. James Connolly, *Collected Works, Volume Two* (Dublin: New Books, 1987), p. 13.
78. Slaughter, *Marxism, Ideology and Literature*, p. 11.
79. Doyle, *The Dead Republic*, p. 315.
80. Ibid., pp. 316, 315.
81. Ibid., p. 317.
82. Ibid., p. 242.
83. Eagleton, *Heathcliff and the Great Hunger*, p. 289.
84. Ibid., pp. 228, 229.
85. Derek Hand, "A Star Called Henry: Volume One of The Last Roundup", *Saothar* 25 (2000), p. 91.
86. Ibid., pp. 314, 329.
87. Dermot Bolger, *Night Shift* (London: Penguin, 1989), p. 35.
88. E.H. Carr, *What Is History?* (London: Penguin Books, 1987), p. 23.
89. Qtd. in Patricia Craig's review of "Michael Harnett's *Collected Poems*", *Times Literary Supplement*, 3 May 2002, p. 24.
90. W.B. Yeats, "Easter 1916", *W. B. Yeats: A Critical Edition of the Major Works*, ed. Edward Larrissy (Oxford: Oxford University Press, 1997), p. 87.

Conclusion

1. Roddy Doyle, "Introduction" in *Brown Bread and War* (Harmondsworth: Penguin, 1994), p. 1.
2. Brendan Behan, *The Letters of Brendan Behan*, ed. E.H. Mikhail (Montreal: McGill-Queen's, 1992), p. 45.
3. Oliver St. John Gogarty, *The Plays of Oliver St. John Gogarty* (Delaware: Proscenium, 1973), p. 47.
4. Ibid., p. 49.
5. Terry Eagleton, *The Ideology of the Aesthetic* (Oxford: Blackwell, 1990), p. 42.
6. James Wickham, "The New Irish Working Class?", *Saothar* 6 (1980), p. 85.
7. Donagh MacDonagh, *Happy as Larry* (London: Maurice Fridberg, 1946).
8. Ibid. pp. 65–66.
9. Heno Magee, *Hatchet* (Dublin: Gallery, 1978).
10. Interview with the present author, 28 August 2007.
11. Roddy Doyle, *The Snapper* (London: Minerva, 1993), pp. 188–189.
12. Roddy Doyle, *The Van* (London: Vintage, 1998), p. 254.
13. Catherine Dunne, *A Name for Himself* (London: Vintage, 1999), p. 7.
14. Patrick Freyne, "I've always been very keen on speaking truth to power", *The Sunday Tribune*, T2 magazine, 3 January 2010, p. 8.
15. Ibid.
16. Helena Sheehan, *Irish Television Drama: A Society and its Stories* (Dublin: RTÉ, 1987; re-published in a revised edition on CD-ROM, 2004), p. 204. The national broadcaster's inadequacy in terms of representing working class life was not lost on the public or those working within it, Sheehan observed: "This was the source of a great deal of dissatisfaction with RTÉ. Although everyone in RTÉ saw the problem, there was difficulty in generating an effective response to it. Both inside and outside RTÉ, it was asked: Why, in a time of rising unemployment, was there no Irish *Boys from the Blackstuff*? Why, in a period of mounting crime and social indiscipline, was there no Irish *Hill Street Blues*? Why, with all the interesting storylines inherent in earning a living, raising a family, understanding the world and coming to terms with the complexities of

urban life, could RTÉ generate no Irish equivalent to *East Enders* or *Brookside*?";
Ibid.

17. Helena Sheehan, *The Continuing Story of Irish Television Drama: Tracking the Tiger* (Dublin: Four Courts Press, 2004), p. 41.

18. Interview conducted by the present author with Peter Sheridan on Friday, 9 September 2005.

19. Peter Sheridan, "The 40-year-old Thorn", *The Irish Times* (28 January 2006), "Weekend", p. 7.

20. Thomas Kilroy, *Talbot's Box* (Dublin: Gallery, 1979), pp. 30–31.

21. Ibid., pp. 31–32.

22. Maura Laverty had raised this issue earlier with her novel *Liffey Lane* (London: Longmans, Green, 1947), in which a poor family is forced to send a child to the Finglas Industrial School due to their inability to care for him.

23. Gerard Mannix Flynn, *James X* (Dublin: Lilliput, 2003), p. 28.

24. Dorothy Nelson, *In Night's City* (Dublin: Wolfhound, 1982), p. 7.

25. Ibid.

26. Ibid., p. 30.

27. Ibid., p. 48.

28. Michel Peillon, *Contemporary Irish Society: An Introduction* (Dublin: Gill and Macmillan, 1982), p. 35.

29. Terry Eagleton, *The Function of Criticism, from 'The Spectator' to Post-Structuralism* (London: Verso, 1984), p. 36.

30. Ferdia Mac Anna, "The Dublin Renaissance: An essay on modern Dublin and Dublin writers", *The Irish Review*, 10 (Spring 1991), p. 15.

31. Ibid., pp. 23, 24.

32. Ibid., p. 28.

33. Ibid.

34. Mac Anna extrapolates the important tenets of this writing as follows: that it is "primarily a literature of social disenchantment" (without mentioning class), that its "sources are essentially non-traditional, even anti-literary" and that there is a characteristically "ferocious unrelenting energy that is focused directly on stripping away the façade to get at the realities of life in modern Dublin"; Ibid., p. 29.

35. Doyle, *Brownbread and War*, p. 11.

36. Ibid., p. 21.

37. Ibid.

38. Marshall W. Fishwick, *Seven Pillars of Popular Culture* (London: Greenwood, 1985), p. 25.

39. Bolger, *The Journey Home*, p. 195.

40. Paula Meehan, *Mysteries of the Home* (Newcastle: Bloodaxe, 1996), p. 38.

41. Paul Mercier, *Drowning* (1984, unpublished mss. provided by the author), pp. 3, 9.

42. Conor McPherson, *Plays: Two* (London: Nick Hern, 2004), p. 127.

43. bell hooks, *Outlaw Culture: Resisting Representations* (London: Routledge, 1994),
44. In the original production, the actress was Polish, but O'Byrne's lack of specificity infers that the part could be played by an immigrant from another country.

45. Joe O'Byrne, *It Come Up Sun* (2000, unpublished mss. supplied by the author), p. 13.

46. Ibid., pp. 24, 25.

47. Ibid., p. 36.
48. Ken Harmon, *Done Up Like a Kipper* (Dublin: Arts Council, 2002), p. 16.
49. Ibid., p. 64.
50. Ibid., p. 86.
51. Ibid., pp. 66, 86.
52. The diversification of Dublin's working-class recurs as a theme in Roddy Doyle's recent collection of short stories *The Deportees* (2007), and in his collaboration with Bisi Adigun on a rewrite of *The Playboy of the Western World* (2007), in which Christy Mahon is replaced by Nigerian Christopher Malomo seeking refuge in a Dublin pub. This theme recurs also in Lance Daly's recent film *Kisses* (2008), where abused Tallaght children Kylie and Dylan enlist the help of a Brazilian boatman in their joint escape from dysfunctional homes.
53. Dermot Bolger, *The Passion of Jerome* (London: Methuen, 1999), p. 39.
54. Herbert Goldstone, *In Search of Community: The Achievement of Seán O'Casey* (Dublin: Mercier, 1972), pp. 5–6.
55. Peter Hitchcock, "They Must Be Represented? Problems in Theories of Working-Class Representation", *PMLA*, 115:1 (January 2000), pp. 27–28.
56. David Lloyd, "The Subaltern in Motion: Subalternity, the Popular and Irish Working-class History", *Postcolonial Studies* 8:4 (2005), p. 434.
57. Fintan Lane, *The Origins of Modern Irish Socialism 1881–1896* (Cork: Cork University Press, 1997), pp. 3–4.

Bibliography

Aalen, F.H.A., "A Review of Recent Irish Population Trends", *Population Studies*, 17:1 (July 1963), pp. 73–78

Adorno, Theodor W., *Philosophy of Modern Music* (London: Continuum, 2002)

Ahlstrom, Dick, "'Hatchet' at the Embankment, Tallaght", *The Irish Times*, 28 July 1981, p. 8

Allen, Kieran, *Fianna Fáil and Irish Labour: 1926 to the present* (London: Pluto, 1997)

—— "The Celtic Tiger, Inequality and Social Partnership", *Administration*, 47:2 (Summer 1999), pp. 31–55

—— *The Celtic Tiger: The Myth of Social Partnership in Ireland* (Manchester: Manchester University Press, 2000)

Althusser, Louis, "Ideology and the Ideological State Apparatuses", in *Cultural Theory and Popular Culture: A Reader*, ed. John Storey (London: Harvester Wheatsheaf, 1994), pp. 336–346

—— *For Marx*, trans. Ben Brewster (London: Verso, 2005)

Anderson, Benedict, *Imagined Communities: Reflections on the Origin and Spread of Nationalism* (London: Verso, 1991)

Anon., "Williams' play banned", *The Irish Times*, 14 June 1962, p. 11

Anon., "An Irishman's Diary", *The Irish Times*, 1 September 1978, p. 8

Anon., "An Irishman's Diary", *The Irish Times*, 10 April 1970, p. 11

Anon., "An Irishman's Diary", *The Irish Times*, 25 August 1960, p. 8

Anon., "An Irishman's Diary", *The Irish Times*, 28 September 1968, p. 9

Anon., "Arts Council ignores his work", *Sunday Independent*, 16 December 1973, p. 9

Anon., "Festival Playwrights", *The Irish Times*, 17 September 1960, p. 8

Anon., "James McKenna: Sculptor, playwright and poet with a total commitment to the arts", *The Irish Times*, 21 October 2000, p. 16

Anon., "The 'angry' fifties", *Sunday Independent*, 18 November 1973, p. 17

Anon., "The Resurgence In Irish Drama", *The Times*, 28 September, 1960, p. 15

Appignanesi, Richard et al., *Introducing Postmodernism* (London: Icon, 2003)

Archer, Kane, "'Hatchet' at the Embankment", *The Irish Times*, 16 October 1975, p. 10

Ardagh, John, *Ireland and the Irish: Portrait of a Changing Society* (London: Penguin, 1995)

Ashraf, Mary, *Political Verse and Song from Britain and Ireland* (London: Lawrence and Wishart, 1975)

Avrich, Paul, "The Legacy of Bakunin", *Russian Review*, 29:2 (April, 1970), pp. 129–142

Badinter, Elisabeth, *XY: On Masculine Identity*, trans. Lydia Davis (New York: Columbia University Press, 1995)

Bakhtin, Mikhail M., *Problems of Dostoevsky's Poetics*, ed. and trans. Caryl Emerson (Minneapolis: University of Minnesota Press, 2003)

—— "The Bildungsroman and Its Significance in the History of Realism (Toward a Historical Typology of the Novel)" in *Speech Genres and Other Late Essays*, trans. Vern W. McGee and ed. Caryl Emerson and Michael Holmquist (Austin: University of Texas, 1986), pp. 10–59

Balibar, Etienne, "The Basic Concepts of Historical Materialism", in *Reading Capital*, ed. Louis Althusser and Etienne Balibar (London: New Left, 1972), pp. 199–308

Barker, Pat, *A Century's Daughter* (London: Virago, 1986)

—— *Union Street* (London: Virago, 2001)

—— *The Eye in the Door* (London: Penguin, 1994)

Barry, Sebastian, *A Long, Long Way* (London: Faber, 2006)

Barry, Ursula, "The Republic of Ireland: The Politics of Sexuality" in *The Field Day Anthology of Irish Writing, V: Irish Women's Writing and Traditions,* ed. Angela Bourke et al. (New York: Field Day, 2002)

Barthes, Roland, *Mythologies,* trans. Annette Lavers (London: Vintage, 1993)

Barton, Ruth, *Irish National Cinema* (London: Routledge, 2005)

Battersby, Eileen, "Death of a Realist", *Irish Times, Weekend,* (18 Janurary 1997), p. 9

Beale, Jenny, *Women in Ireland: Voices of Change* (Dublin: Gill and Macmillan, 1986)

Behan, Brendan, *After the Wake: Twenty-one Prose Works Including Previously Unpublished Material* (Dublin: O'Brien, 1981)

—— *An Giall: Poems and a Play in Irish* (Dublin: Gallery, 1981)

—— *Behan: The Complete Plays* (London: Methuen, 2000)

—— *Borstal Boy* (London: Hutchinson, 1958)

—— *Brendan Behan's Island: an Irish Sketch-book* (London: Hutchinson, 1962)

—— *Brendan Behan's New York* (London: Hutchinson, 1964)

—— *Confessions of an Irish Rebel* (London: Arrow, 1990)

—— *Hold Your Hour and Have Another* (London: Hutchinson, 1963)

—— *Moving Out and A Garden Party: Two Plays* (Dixon, CA: Proscenium, 1967)

—— *Richard's Cork Leg* (London: Eyre Methuen, 1973)

—— *The Dubbalin Man* (Dublin: A. & A. Farmar, 1997)

—— *The Hostage* (London: Methuen, 1958)

—— *The King of Ireland's Son* (London: Andersen, 1996)

—— *The Letters of Brendan Behan*, ed. E. H. Mikhail (Montreal: McGill-Queen's, 1992)

—— *The Quare Fellow: A Comedy-drama* (London: Methuen, 1956)

—— *The Scarperer* (New York: Doubleday, 1964)

—— *The Wit of Brendan Behan,* compiled by Sean McCann (London: Leslie Frewin, 1968)

Behan, Brian with Aubrey Dillon Malone, *The Brothers Behan* (Dublin: Blackhall, 1998)

Behan, Dominic, *Teems of Times and Happy Returns* (London: Heinemann, 1961)

—— *Tell Dublin I Miss Her* (New York: G. P. Putnam, 1962)

Benjamin, Walter, "On the Concept of History", in *Walter Benjamin: Selected Writings Volume 4: 1938–1940* (Harvard: Harvard University Press, 2003), pp. 389–400

Benyon, John, *Masculinities and Culture* (Buckingham: Open University, 2002)

Beresford-Ellis, Peter, "Revisionism in Irish Historical Writing: The New Anti-nationalist School of Historians" (1989) <http://www.etext.org/Politics/INAC/historical.revisionism> [accessed 4 April 2005]

—— *A History of the Irish Working Class* (Dublin: Pluto, 1989)

Bew, Paul , "The National Question, Land, and 'Revisionism': Some reflections" in *The Making of Modern Irish History: Revisionism and the Revisionist Controversy,* ed. D. George Boyce, and Alan O'Day (London: Routledge, 1996), pp. 90–99

Bhabha, Homi K., "Remembering Fanon: Self, Psyche and the Colonial Condition" in *Colonial Discourse and Postcolonial Theory,* ed. Patrick Williams and Laura Chrisman (New York: Columbia University Press, 1994), pp. 112–123

Bhabha, Homi K., *The Location Of Culture* (London: Routledge, 1994)

Boggs, Carl, *Gramsci's Marxism* (London: Pluto, 1976)

Boland, Eavan, "Dublin's Advocate" *This Week* (Dublin: 12 October 1972), pp. 40–42

Bolger, Dermot, *A Dublin Quartet: 'Blinded by Light', 'In High Germany', 'The Holy Ground', and 'One Last White Horse'* (Harmondsworth: Penguin, 1992)

—— *Emily's Shoes* (London: Viking/Penguin, 1992)

—— ed. *Finbar's Hotel* (Dublin: New Island, 1997)

—— *Finglas Lilies* (Dublin: Raven Arts, 1980)

—— *In High Germany* (Dublin: New Island, 1989)

—— *Internal Exiles* (Dublin: Raven Arts, 1986)

—— ed. *Invisible Cities: The New Dubliners: A Journey through Unofficial Dublin* (Dublin: Raven Arts, 1998)

—— *Invisible Dublin: A Journey through Dublin's Suburbs* (Dublin: Raven Arts, 1991)

—— *Leinster Street Ghosts* (Dublin: Raven Arts, 1989)

—— *Never a Dull Moment* (Dublin: Raven Arts, 1979)

—— *Night Shift* (London: Penguin, 1993)

—— *No Waiting America* (Dublin: Raven Arts, 1982)

—— *The Chosen Moment* (Dublin: New Island, 2004)

—— *The Crack in the Emerald: New Irish Plays* (London: Nick Hern, 1994)

—— *The Habit of Flesh* (Dublin: Raven Arts, 1979)

—— *The Journey Home* (London: Flamingo, 2003)

—— *The Lament for Arthur Cleary* (Dublin: Dolmen, 1989)

—— *The Passion of Jerome* (London: Methuen, 1999)

—— *The Picador Book of Contemporary Irish Fiction* (London: Picador, 1993)

—— *The Reed Bed* (Oldcastle: Gallery, 2000)

—— *The Woman's Daughter* (London: Viking/Penguin, 1991)

—— *Two Plays: April Bright & Blinded by the Light* (Dublin: New Island, 1997)

Booker, Keith M. "Late Capitalism Comes to Dublin: 'American' Popular Culture in the Novels of Roddy Doyle" *ARIEL: A Review of International English Literature* (July 1997), pp. 27–45

—— "The Bicycle and Descartes: Epistemology in the Fiction of Beckett and O'Brien", *Eire-Ireland: A Journal Of Irish Studies,* 26:1 (Spring 1991), pp. 76–94

Boomtown Rats, Rat Trap, A Tonic for the Troops, (Ensign, 1978) <http://www.lyricstime.com/boomtown-rats-rat-trap-lyrics.html> [accessed 1 April, 2008]

Borel, Françoise, " 'I Am Without a Name', The Fiction of Christy Brown" in *The Irish Novel in Our Time,* ed. Patrick Rafroidi and Maurice Harmon (Lille: l'Université de Lille, 1976), pp. 287–295

Böss, Michael, "Home from Europe: Modernity and the Reappropriation of the Past in Bolger's Early Novels", in *Engaging Modernity: Readings of Irish Politics, Culture and Literature at the Turn of the Century,* ed. Michael Böss and Eamon Maher (Dublin: Veritas, 2003), pp. 153–166

Bourdieu, Pierre, *Distinction: A Social Critique of the Judgement of Taste,* trans. Richard Nice (London: Routledge, 1998)

—— *Masculine Domination* trans. Richard Nice (Stanford: Stanford University Press, 2001)

—— *Outline of Theory of Practice,* trans. Richard Nice (London: Cambridge University Press, 1977)

—— *Pascalian Meditations* (Cambridge: Polity, 2000)

—— et al. *The Weight of the World: Social Suffering in Contemporary Society,* trans. Priscilla Parkhurst Ferguson (Cambridge: Polity, 2002)

Bowen, Elizabeth, *The Last September* (London: Vintage, 1998)

Boyce, D. George and Alan O'Day, eds. *The Making of Modern Irish History: Revisionism and the Revisionist Controversy* (New York: Routledge, 1996)

Bradshaw, Brendan, "Nationalism and Historical Scholarship in Modern Ireland" in *Interpreting Irish History*, ed. Conor Brady (Dublin: Irish Academic Press, 1994), pp. 122–145

Bradshaw, Nick, "Doyle's Dubliners", *Details*, (February 1994), 128–130

Brady, Ciaran, " 'Constructive and Instrumental': The Dilemma of Ireland's first 'New Historians' " in *Interpreting Irish History*, ed. Ciaran Brady (Dublin: Irish Academic Press, 1994), pp. 3–31

Bramsbäck, Birgit, *James Stephens: A Literary and Bibliographical Study* (Dublin: Hodges Figgis, 1959)

Brannick, Teresa, Francis Devine and Aidan Kelly, "Social Statistics for Labour Historians: Strike Statistics, 1922–99", *Saothar* 25 (2000), 114–120

Brannigan, John, *Brendan Behan: Cultural Nationalism and the Revisionist Writer* (Dublin: Four Courts, 2002)

Breen, Richard and Christopher T. Whelan, *Social Mobility and Social Class in Ireland* (Dublin: Gill & Macmillan, 1996)

Bromley, Roger, "The Theme That Dare Not Speak Its Name: Class and Recent British Film", in *Cultural Studies and the Working Class, Subject to Change*, ed. Sally R. Munt (London: Cassell, 2000), pp. 51–68

Brown, Christy, *A Shadow on Summer* (London: Secker & Warburg, 1973)

—— *Background Music: Poems* (London: Secker & Warburg, 1973)

—— *Collected Poems: Christy Brown* (London: Secker & Warburg, 1982)

—— *Come Softly to My Wake* (London: Secker & Warburg, 1971)

—— *Down All the Days* (London: Pan, 1972)

—— *My Left Foot* (Cork: Mercier, 1964)

—— *Of Snails and Skylarks* (London: Secker & Warburg, 1978)

—— *Wild Grow the Lilies* (London: Secker & Warburg, 1976)

Brown, Kenneth D., "Trade Unionism in Ireland", *Saothar* 5 (1979), pp. 56–60

Brown, Terence, *Ireland: A Social and Cultural History, 1922–2002* (London: Harper Perennial, 2004)

Burgess, Anthony, "In the twilight zone", *The Observer*, 18 November 1962, p. 25

Cahalan, James, "Review of Farewell Companions", *Eire-Ireland* 13:2 (Summer 1978), pp. 127–130

—— "The Making of *Strumpet City*: James Plunkett and the Historical Vision" *Éire-Ireland* 13:4 (Winter 1978), pp. 81–100

Cain, William E., *Figures of Finance Capitalism: Writing, Class, and Capital in the Age of Dickens* (New York: Routledge, 2003)

Callan, Patrick, "The Political War Ballads of Sean O'Casey, 1916–18", *Irish University Review*, 13:2 (Autumn, 1983), 168–179

Carpentiere, Godeleine, "Dublin and the Drama of Larkinism: James Plunkett's Strumpet City", in *The Irish Novel in Our Time*, ed. Patrick Rafroidi and Maurice Harmon (Lille: l'Université de Lille, 1975), pp. 209–217

Carr, E. H. *What is History?* (London: Penguin, 1987)

Chaplin, Sid, *The Day of the Sardine* (London: Panther, 1965)

Chaudhry,Yug Mohit, *Yeats, the Irish Literary Revival and the Politics of Print* (Cork: Cork University Press, 2001)

Chomsky, Noam, *Pirates and Emperors, Old and New: International Terrorism in the Real World* (London: Pluto, 2002)

Cixous, Hélène, "Castration of Decapitation?" *Signs 7.1*, trans. Annette Kuhn (1981), 41–55

Clancy, Patrick, *College Entry in Focus: A Fourth National Survey of Access to Higher Education* (Dublin: HEA, 2001) <http://extranet.hea.ie/uploads/pdf/Clancymaster%20.pdf> [accessed 2 December 2008]

—— "Education Policy", in *Contemporary Irish Social Policy*, ed. Suzanne Quin, Patricia Kennedy, Gabriel Kiely and Anne O'Donnell (Dublin: UCD, 1999), pp. 72–107

Clarke, Austin, "Tales from Dublin", *The Times Literary Supplement*, 6 September 1963, p. 674

Clarke, Desmond, *Ireland in Fiction: A Guide to Irish Novels, Tales, Romances and Folklore* (Cork: Royal Carbery, 1985)

Clear, Caitriona, *Women of the House: Women's Household Work in Ireland 1926–1961* (Dublin: Irish Academic Press, 2000)

Cohen, Nick, *What's Left? How Liberals Lost their Way* (London: Fourth Estate, 2007)

Colgan, Gerry, "Return to the Hill", *The Irish Times*, 29 August 1995, p. 10

Collins, Micheál, Seán Healy and Brigid Reynolds (eds), *An Agenda for a New Ireland: Policies to Ensure Economic Development, Social Equity and Sustainability, Socio-Economic Review 2010* (Dublin: Social Justice Ireland, 2010)

Collis, Robert, *Marrowbone Lane: A Play in Three Acts* (Dublin: Runa, 1943)

The Commitments. Dir. Alan Parker. Beacon. 1991.

Comerford, Joe, *Down the Corner* (written by Noel McFarlane). Dir. Joe Comerford. Ballyfermot Community Arts Workshop Productions. 1977.

—— *Inside*. Prod. Noel O'Briain. RTÉ. 1985

Connolly, James, *Collected Works, Volume I* (Dublin: New Books, 1987)

—— *Collected Works, Volume II* (Dublin: New Books, 1987)

—— *Erin's Hope* (1909) <http://www.ex.ac.uk/Projects/meia/connolly/Archive/jceh00.htm> [accessed 20 February 2005]

Cooey, Paula M., *Religious Imagination and the Body: A Feminist Analysis* (Oxford: Oxford University Press, 1994)

Cook, Guy, *The Discourse of Advertising* (London: Routledge, 2001)

Cook, John, "Culture, Class and Taste", in *Cultural Studies and the Working Class, Subject to Change*, ed. Sally R. Munt (London: Cassell, 2000), pp. 97–112

Cook, Sylvia Jenkins, *From Tobacco Road to Route 66: The Southern Poor White in Fiction* (Chapel Hill, NC: University of North Carolina, 1976)

Cookman, Anthony Victor, "A Master of the Theatre", *The Times Literary Supplement*, 4 August 1960, p. 22

Corcoran, Neil, *After Yeats and Joyce* (Oxford: Oxford University Press, 1997)

Corkery, Daniel, *The Hidden Ireland: a Study of Gaelic Munster in the Eighteenth Century* (Dublin: Gill and Son, 1967, orig. 1924)

Cosgrove, Brian, "Roddy Doyle's Backward Look: Tradition and Modernity in *Paddy Clarke Ha Ha Ha*", in Studies, 85:339, pp. 231–242

Costello, Stephen J., *The Irish Soul in Dialogue* (Dublin: Liffey, 2001)

Coulter, Colin and Steve Coleman, (eds) *The End of Irish History? Critical Reflections on the Celtic Tiger* (Manchester: Manchester University Press, 2003)

Craig, Patricia, "Ireland", in *The Oxford Guide to Contemporary Writing*, ed. John Sturrock (Oxford: Oxford University Press, 1996), pp. 221–237

—— "Michael Harnett's Collected Poems", *Times Literary Supplement*, 3 May 2002, p. 24

Crist, Raymond E., "Migration and Population Change in the Irish Republic", *American Journal of Economics and Sociology*, 30:3 (July, 1971), 253–258

Crompton, Rosemary and Gareth Jones, *White-Collar Proletariat: Deskilling and Gender in Clerical Work* (London: Macmillan, 1984)

Cronin, Anthony, *An Irish Eye* (Dingle: Brandon, 1985)

—— *Dead as Doornails: A Chronicle of Life* (Dublin: Dolmen, 1976)

Crosbie, Paddy, *"Your Dinner's Poured Out!": Boyhood in the Twenties in a Dublin that Has Disappeared* (Dublin: O'Brien, 1981)

Crosland, Charles Anthony Raven, *The Future of Socialism* (London: Cape, 1957)

Cruise O'Brien, Conor, "When the Catholic Church ruled us all", *Sunday Independent*, 5 January 2003, p. 19

—— *States of Ireland* (St. Alban's: Panther, 1974)

Cuddon, John Anthony, *A Dictionary of Literary Terms* (London: Deutsch, 1979)

Cullen, Bill, *It's a Long Way From Penny Apples* (London: Hodder & Stoughton, 2002)

Cusack, Cyril, "In the Beginning Was O'Casey", *Irish University Review: A Journal of Irish Studies* (October, 1980), 17–24

Daly, Mary E., *Dublin, the Deposed Capital: A Social and Economic History, 1860–1914* (Cork: Cork University Press, 1984)

—— *The Slow Failure: Population Decline and Independent Ireland, 1920–1973* (Wisconsin: University of Wisconsin, 2006)

Das, Veena, "Subaltern as Perspective", in *Subaltern Studies VI: Writings in South Asian History and Society*, ed. Ranajit Guha (New Delhi: Oxford University Press, 1989), pp. 310–328

Davies, Tony, "Unfinished Business: Realism and Working-Class Writing", in *The British Working-Class Novel in the Twentieth Century*, ed. Jeremy Hawthorn (London: Arnold, 1984), pp. 20–35

De Beauvoir, Simone, *The Second Sex*, trans. H. M. Parshley (London: Jonathan Cape, 1953)

De Botton, Alain, *Status Anxiety* (New York: Pantheon, 2004)

De Búrca, Séamus, *Brendan Behan: A Memoir* (Dublin: P. J. Bourke, 1985)

Dean, Joan FitzPatrick, "Irish stage censorship in the 1950s", *Theatre Survey*, 42:2 (November, 2001), pp. 137–164

Deane, Seamus, *Celtic Revivals* (London: Faber & Faber, 1985)

—— *Nationalism, Colonialism and Literature: Nationalism, Irony and Commitment* (Derry: Field Day, 1988)

—— "O'Casey and Yeats: Exemplary Dramatists", in *Celtic Revivals: Essays in Modern Irish Literature 1880–1980* (London: Faber 1985), pp.108–122

—— *Reading in the Dark* (London: Vintage, 1997)

—— "Roddy's Troubles: Who Needs Blarney in the Middle of a Civil War", *The Guardian* section Saturday Review, 4 September 1999, p. 8

—— *Strange Country: Modernity and Nationhood in Irish Writing since 1790* (Oxford: Clarendon, 1998)

—— "Wherever Green Is Read", in *Interpreting Irish History: The Debate on Historical Revisionism*, ed. Ciaran Brady (Dublin: Irish Academic Press, 1994), pp. 234–244

Deevy, Patricia, "Goodbye to the Anger", *Sunday Independent*, section People, 16 August 1992, p. 6

Delaney, Frank, *James Joyce's Odyssey: A Guide to the Dublin of Ulysses* (New York: Holt, 1982)

Delaney, Shelagh, *A Taste of Honey* (London: Methuen, 1959)

Delanty, G. and P. O'Mahony, *Rethinking Irish History: Nationalism, Identity and Ideology* (Basingstoke: Macmillan, 1998)

Deleuze, Gilles and Félix Guattari, *A Thousand Plateaus: Capitalism and Schizophrenia* (London: Athlone, 1988)

Derrida, Jacques, *The Other Heading: Reflections on Today's Europe* (Bloomington: Indiana University Press, 1992)

Devlin, Edith Newman, *Speaking Volumes: A Dublin Childhood* (Belfast: Blackstaff, 2000)

Dickinson, Page Lawrence, *The Dublin of Yesterday* (London: Methuen, 1929)

Donnelly, Brian, "Roddy Doyle: From Barrytown to the GPO", *Irish University Review: A Journal of Irish Studies* (Spring–Summer, 2000), pp. 17–31

Donoghue, Denis, "Another Country", *New York Review of Books*, 3 February 1994, pp. 3–6

—— "Dublin Letter", *The Hudson Review* 13:4 (Winter, 1960–1961), pp. 579–585

Doyle, Paul A., *Liam O'Flaherty* (New York: Twayne, 1971)

Doyle, Roddy, *A Star Called Henry* (London: Jonathan Cape, 1999)

—— *Brownbread and War* (London: Penguin, 1994)

—— "Chapter One" in *Yeats is Dead! A Mystery by Fifteen Irish Writers*, ed. Joseph O'Connor (London: Jonathan Cape, 2001), pp. 3–20

—— *The Commitments* (London: Vintage, 1998)

—— *The Dead Republic* (London: Jonathan Cape, 2010)

—— *The Deportees and Other Stories* (London: Jonathan Cape, 2007)

—— "The Dinner" in *The New Yorker* (23 February, 2001), pp. 72–81

—— *Family*, BBC, 1994, teleplay

—— *Guess Who's Coming to Dinner* (London: Secker & Warburg, 2001)

—— *Paddy Clarke Ha Ha Ha* (London: Minerva, 1994)

—— *Rory & Ita* (London: Jonathan Cape, 2002)

—— *The Snapper* (London: Heinemann, 1988)

—— *The Van* (London: Vintage, 1998)

—— *The Woman Who Walked into Doors* (London: Penguin, 1997)

Dunn, Nell, *Up the Junction* (London: Virago, 1998)

Dunne, Catherine, *A Name for Himself* (London: Vintage, 1999)

Dunne, Lee, *A Bed in the Sticks* (London: Hutchinson 1968)

—— *Barleycorn Blues* (Dublin: Poolbeg, 2004)

—— *Does Your Mother* (London: Arrow, 1970)

—— *Goodbye to the Hill* (London: Hutchinson, 1965)

—— "Is There Such a Thing as Serendipity?" *The Irish Times*, 29 July 1985, p. 13

—— *Maggie's Story* (London: Futura, 1975)

—— *Midnight Cabbie* (London: Coronet, 1974)

—— *No Time for Innocence* (Dublin: Gill & Macmillan, 2000)

—— *Paddy Maguire is Dead* (London: Arrow, 1972)

—— *Paddy Maguire is Dead: the Curious Adventures of an Irishman Abroad* (London: Arrow, 1972)

Dunne, Tom, "New Histories: Beyond Revisionism", *The Irish Review*, 12 (1992), pp. 1–12

Dunphy, Richard, *The Making of Fianna Fáil Power in Ireland, 1923–1948* (Oxford: Clarendon, 2005)

Durcan, Paul, *A Snail in My Prime* (London: Blackstaff, 1993)

Eagleton, Terry, *Crazy John and the Bishop and Other Essays on Irish Culture* (Cork: Cork University Press, 1998)

—— *Criticism and Ideology: A Study in Marxist Literary Theory* (London: Verso, 2006)

—— *Heathcliff and the Great Hunger* (London: Verso, 1996)

—— *Ideology: An Introduction* (London: Verso, 1991)

—— *Literary Theory: An Introduction* (Oxford: Blackwell, 2003)

Eagleton, Terry, *Marxism and Literary Criticism* (Los Angeles: University of California Press, 1976)

—— *Saints and Scholars* (London: Futura, 1990)

—— *The Function of Criticism, from 'The Spectator' to Post-Structuralism* (London: Verso, 1984)

—— *The Ideology of the Aesthetic* (Oxford: Blackwell, 1990)

Eco, Umberto, "Irony and 'Double Coding': Postmodernism, Irony, the Enjoyable" in *Postmodernism and the Contemporary Novel: A Reader*, ed. Bran Nicol (Edinburgh: Edinburgh University Press, 2002), pp. 110–112

Edwards, Ruth Dudley, "Though Rich and Famous He Still Cares", *Literary Review* (September 1999), pp. 47–48

Egan, Desmond, "Achievement of James McKenna, Irish Stone Sculptor" <http://www.gerardmanleyhopkins.org/sculptor/achievement.html> [accessed 15 April 2008]

—— "Appreciation: James McKenna", *The Irish Times*, 14 November 2000, p. 17

Engels, Frederick, "Dialectical Materialism", in *Ludwig Feuerbach and the Outcome of Classical German Philosophy*, ed. by C. P. Dutt (New York: International Publishers, 1996), pp. 42–63

—— "Letter to Joseph Bloch", in *Cultural Theory and Popular Culture: A Reader*, ed. John Storey (London : Harvester Wheatsheaf, 1994), pp. 71–72

—— *The Condition of the Working Class in England*, trans. by Victor Kiernan (London: Penguin, 1987)

—— *The Peasant War in Germany* (New York: International Publishers, 2000)

Ensler, Eve, *The Vagina Monologues: The V-Day Edition* (New York: Villard, 2001)

Fagan, Honor, *Culture, Politics and Irish School Dropouts* (London: Bergin and Garvey, 1995)

Fagan, Terry, *All around the Diamond* (Dublin: North Inner City Folklore Project, 1994)

—— *Down by the Dockside: Reminiscences from Sheriff Street* (Dublin: North Inner City Folklore Project, 1995)

—— *Monto: Madams, Murder and Black Coddle* (Dublin: North Inner City Folklore Project, 2000)

—— *Those Were the Days* (Dublin: North Inner City Folklore Project, 1992)

Fallon, Brian, *An Age of Innocence: Irish Culture 1930–1960* (Dublin: Gill and Macmillan, 1998)

Fanning, Ronan, " 'The Great Enchantment': Uses and Abuses of Modern Irish History" in *Interpreting Irish History*, ed. Conor Brady (Dublin: Irish Academic Press, 1994), pp. 146–158

Fanon, Frantz, *The Wretched of the Earth* (London: Penguin, 2001)

Farrell, Brian, "The Context of Three Elections" in *Ireland at the Polls, 1981, 1982, and 1987: A Study of Four General Elections*, ed. Howard Penniman and Brian Farrell (Durham: Duke University Press, 1987), pp. 1–30

Fay, Liam, "What's the Story?" Interview with Roddy Doyle in *Hot Press*, 3 April 1996, p. 12

Fennell, Desmond, "Against Revisionism" in *Interpreting Irish History*, ed. Ciarán Brady (Dublin: Irish Academic Press, 1994), pp. 183–190

Ferriter, Diarmaid, *Occasions of Sin: Sex and Society in Modern Ireland* (London: Profile, 2009)

—— *The Transformation of Ireland: 1900–2000* (London: Profile, 2004)

Fetterly, Judith, "On the Politics of Literature", in *Literary Theory: An Anthology*, ed. Julie Rivkin and Michael Ryan (Malden: Blackwell, 1998), 561–569

Fishwick, Marshall W., *Seven Pillars of Popular Culture* (London: Greenwood, 1985)

Fitzgerald, Mary, "How the Abbey Said No: Readers' Reports and the Rejection of The Silver Tassie" in *O'Casey Annual, No. 1*, ed. Robert G. Lowery (Atlantic Highlands, NJ: Humanities, 1982)

Flannery, Eoin, "External Association", *Third Text*, 19:5, pp. 449–459

—— "Outside in the Theory Machine: Ireland in the World of Post-Colonial Studies", *Studies: An Irish Quarterly Review*, 92:368 (winter 2003), pp. 359–369

Flood, Vincent, *The Last Corporation Man* (Dublin: Bobdog, 1998)

Flynn, Gerard Mannix, *James X* (Dublin: Lilliput, 2003)

—— *Nothing to Say* (Dublin: Lilliput, 2003)

Flynn, Seán and Gráinne Faller, "Over 60% of Top Schools Limit Admission to Certain Groups", *Irish Times*, 4 December 2008, p. 1

Foley, Barbara, "Generic and Doctrinal Politics in the Proletarian Bildungsroman", in *Understanding Narrative*, ed. by James Phelan and Peter J. Rabinowitz (Columbus: Ohio State University Press, 1994), pp. 43–64

Foran, Charles, "The Troubles of Roddy Doyle" *Saturday Night* (April 1996), pp. 58–62

Fordham, John, *James Hanley: Modernism and the Working Class* (Cardiff: Cardiff University Press, 2002)

Foster, R. F., *Modern Ireland: 1600–1972* (London: Penguin, 1989)

—— "Roddy and the Ragged-Trousered Revolutionary", *The Guardian*, 29 August, 1999 <http://books.guardian.co.uk/reviews/generalfiction/0,6121,97001,00.html> [accessed 14 June 2005]

Foucault, Michel, *Discipline and Punish: The Birth of the Prison*, trans. Alan Sheridan (Penguin: London, 1991)

Fox, Pamela, *Class Fictions: Shame and Resistance in the British Working-Class Novel, 1890–1945*, (London: Duke University Press, 1994)

Fraiman, Susan, *Unbecoming Women: British Women Writers and the Novel of Development* (New York: Columbia University Press, 1993)

Francis, Becky, "Lads, Lasses and (New) Labour: 14-16-Year-Old Students' Responses to the 'Laddish Behaviour and Boys' Underachievement' Debate", *British Journal of Sociology of Education*, 20:3 (September 1999), pp. 355–371

Frayne, John P., *Sean O'Casey* (New York: Columbia University Press, 1976)

French, Billy, *The Journeyman: A Builder's Life* (Dublin: Wolfhound, 2002)

Freyne, Patrick, "I've Always Been Very Keen on Speaking Truth to Power", *The Sunday Tribune*, T2 magazine, 3 January 2010

Friberg, Hedda, *An Old Order and a New: The Split World of Liam O'Flaherty's Novels* (Uppsala: Uppsala University, 1996)

Fuery, Patrick, and Nick Mansfield, *Cultural Studies and Critical Theory*. 2nd ed. (Oxford, UK, New York: Oxford University Press, 2000)

Garvin, Tom, "A Quiet Revolution: The Remaking of Irish Political Culture", in *Writing in the Irish Republic*, ed. Ray Ryan (London: Macmillan, 2000), pp. 187–203

—— *Nationalist Revolutionaries in Ireland 1858–1928* (Oxford: Clarendon, 1987)

—— *Preventing the Future: Why was Ireland So Poor for So Long?* (Dublin: Gill & Macmillan, 2004)

—— "Revolution? Revolutions are what Happens to Wheels – the Phenomenon of Revolution, Irish Style" in *The Irish Revolution 1913–23*, ed. Joost Augusteijn (Basingstoke: Palgrave, 2002)

Gaskell, Elizabeth, *North and South*, ed. Dorothy Collin (Harmondsworth: Penguin, 1970)

Gauthier, Xaviere, "Is There such a Thing as Women's Writing?" in New French Feminisms (Brighton: Harvestor, 1980), pp. 161–164.

Geary, Dick, "Working-Class Identities in Europe, 1850s–1930s", *The Australian Journal of Politics and History* 45:1 (1999), pp. 24–25

Genet, Jean, *The Maids and Deathwatch: Two Plays*, trans. Bernard Frechtman (New York: Grove, 1962)

Gibbons, Luke, "Coming out of Hibernation? The Myth of Modernity in Irish Culture", in *Across the Frontiers: Ireland in the 1990s*, ed. Richard Kearney (Dublin: Wolfhound, 1988), pp. 205–218

Giddens, Anthony, "Class Structuration and Class Consciousness" in *Classes, Power and Conflict*, ed. Anthony Giddens and David Held (London: Macmillan, 1990), pp. 157–174

—— *The Constitution of Society* (Oxford: Polity, 1984)

Gilbert, Sandra and Susan Gubar's study, *The Madwoman in the Attic: The Woman Writer and the Nineteenth-Century Literary Imagination* (New Haven: Yale University Press, 1979)

Girvin, Brian, "Industrialisation and the Irish Working Class Since 1922", *Saothar* 10 (1986), 31–42

Gkotzaridis, Evi, *Trials of Irish History: Genesis and Evolution of a Reappraisal, 1938–2000* (London: Routledge, 2006)

Glazener, Nancy, "Dialogic Subversion: Bakhtin, the Novel and Gertrude Stein", in *Bakhtin and Cultural Theory*, ed. Ken Hirschkop and David Shepherd (Manchester: Manchester University Press, 2001), pp. 155–176

Gleeson, Brendan, *Breaking Up* (Dublin: Passion Machine, 1988)

Gogarty, Oliver St. John, *As I Was Going Down Sackville Street: A Phantasy in Fact* (London: Sphere, 1980)

—— *The Plays of Oliver St. John Gogarty* (Delaware: Proscenium, 1973)

Goldstone, Herbert, *In Search of Community: The Achievement of Seán O'Casey* (Dublin: Mercier, 1972)

Gonzalez, Alexander, "Liam O'Flaherty's Urban Short Stories", *Etudes Irlandaises: Revue Francaise d'Histoire, Civilisation et Litterature de l'Irlande* (June 1987) pp. 85–91

Gonzalez, Rosa, "James Plunkett", in *Ireland in Writing: Interviews with Writers and Academics*, ed. Jacqueline Hurtley et al. (Amsterdam, Netherlands: Rodopi, 1998) pp. 110–122

—— "'Writing out of One's Own Experience': An Interview with James Plunkett" *Revista Alicantina de Estudios Ingleses* (November 1992), pp. 185–194

Gramsci, Antonio, *A Gramsci Reader*, ed. by David Forgacs (London: Lawrence and Wishart, 1988)

Gray, Ken, "An Outstanding Play", *The Irish Times*, 10 December 1973, p. 10

—— "Fiction", *The Irish Times*, 9 October 1965, p. 8

Greenwood, Walter, *Love on the Dole* (Harmondsworth: Penguin, 1969)

Grene, Nicholas, *The Politics of Irish Drama: Plays in Context from Boucicault to Friel* (Cambridge: Cambridge University Press, 1999)

Guha, Ranajit, "The Prose of Counter Insurgency" in *Postcolonial Discourses, An Anthology*, ed. Gregory Castle (Oxford: Blackwell, 2001), pp. 119–150

Hall, John R., "The Reworking of Class Analysis", in *Reworking Class*, ed. John R. Hall (London: Cornell University Press, 1997), pp. 1–37

Hall, Stuart, "Culture, the Media and the 'Ideological Effect'", in *Mass Communications and Society*, ed. J. Curran et al. (London: Edward Arnold, 1977)

Halper, Thomas, "The Poor as Pawns: The New 'Deserving Poor' & the Old Author(s)", *Polity*, 6:1 (Autumn 1973), pp. 71–86

Hambleton, Georgina Louise, *Christy Brown: The Life that Inspired My Left Foot* (London: Mainstream, 2007)

Hamilton, Richard F., *The Bourgeois Epoch: Marx and Engels on Britain, France, and Germany* (Chapel Hill, NC: University of North Carolina, 1991)

Hanafin, Joan and Anne Lynch, "Peripheral Voices: Parental Involvement, Social Class, and Educational Disadvantage", *British Journal of Sociology of Education*, 23:1 (March 2002), pp. 35–49

Harding, Desmond, *Writing the City: Urban Visions & Literary Modernism* (London: Routledge, 2003)

Harmon, Ken, *Done Up Like a Kipper* (Dublin: Arts Council, 2002)

Haywood, Ian, *Working-Class Fiction: From Chartism to 'Trainspotting'* (Plymouth: Northcote House, 1997)

Heaney, Seamus, *On Opened Ground: Poems 1966–1996* (London: Faber and Faber, 1998)

Hein, Norvin, "The Rām Līlā", *The Journal of American Folklore*, 71:281, Traditional India: Structure and Change (July–September 1958), pp. 279–304

Heslop, Harold, *The Gate of a Strange Field* (London: Brentano, 1929)

Hickey, Des, "Mr. McKenna among the Teds", *Sunday Independent*, 6 December 1959, p. 20

—— "No more begging bowls for Heno Magee", *Sunday Independent*, 31 August 1975, p. 11

—— "Success for the boy who ran away at eight", *Sunday Independent*, 14 September 1975, p. 8

Hill, John, "Images of Violence", in *Cinema in Ireland,* ed. Kevin Rockett, Luke Gibbons and John Hill (London: Croom Helm, 1987), pp. 147–193

Hill, Myrtle, *Women in Ireland: A Century of Change* (Belfast: Blackstaff, 2003)

Hilliard, Christopher, *To Exercise Our Talents: The Democratization of Writing in Britain* (London: Harvard University Press, 2006)

Hitchcock, Peter, "They Must Be Represented? Problems in Theories of Working-Class Representation", *PMLA* 115:1 (January 2000), pp. 20–32

Hobsbawm, E. J., "Working Classes and Nations", *Saothar* 8 (1982), pp. 75–85

Hogan, Robert, *The Modern Irish Drama: A Documentary History IV: The Rise of the Realists 1910–1915* (Dublin: Dolmen, 1979)

Hoggart, Richard, *The Uses of Literacy: Changing Patterns in English Mass Culture* (Boston: Beacon, 1961)

hooks, bell, *Feminist Theory: From Margin to Center* (Boston: South End, 1984)

—— *Outlaw Culture: Resisting Representations* (London: Routledge, 1994)

—— "Postmodern Blackness" in *Colonial Discourse and Post-Colonial Theory*, ed. Patrick Williams and Laura Chrisman (New York: Columbia University Press, 1994), pp. 421–427

Hornsby-Smith, Michael P. and Angela Dale, "The Assimilation of Irish Immigrants in England", *The British Journal of Sociology*, 39:4 (December 1988), pp. 519–544

Howell, David, *A Lost Left: Three Studies in Socialism and Nationalism* (Manchester: Manchester University Press, 1986)

Huddart, David, *Homi K. Bhabha* (London: Routledge, 2005)

Hughes, P.T., "Slum life in the troubled twenties", *Sunday Independent*, 18 February, 1962, p. 15

Humphries, Alexander, *New Dubliners* (New York: Fordham University Press, 1966)

Hunter, Charles, "Heno Magee and the mean streets of 'Hatchet' ", *The Irish Times*, 2 April 1988, p. 12

Hutcheon, Linda, *A Poetics of Postmodernism* (New York: Routledge, 1988)

—— "Circling the Downspout of Empire", in *Past the Last Post*, ed. Ian Adam and Helen Tiffin (Hemel Hempstead: Harvester Wheatsheaf, 1991), pp. 29–41

—— *The Politics of Postmodernism* (London: Routledge, 2002)

Hutchinson, John, "Irish Nationalism", in *The Making of Modern Irish History: Revisionism and the Revisionist Controversy*, ed. D. George Boyce and Alan O'Day (New York: Routledge, 1996), pp. 100–119

Imhof, Rüdiger, *The Modern Irish Novel: Irish Novelists After 1945* (Dublin: Wolfhound, 2002)

Inglis, Tom, *Lessons in Irish Sexuality* (Dublin: UCD, 1998)

Irigaray, Luce, "Commodities Amongst Themselves", in *Literary Theory: An Anthology*, ed. Julie Rivkin and Michael Ryan (Oxford: Blackwell, 1998), pp. 574–577

—— *Speculum of the Other Woman*, trans. Gillian C. Gill. (Ithaca: Cornell University Press, 1985)

—— "The Power of Discourse and the Subordination of the Feminine", in *Literary Theory: An Anthology*, ed. Julie Rivkin and Michael Ryan (Oxford: Blackwell, 1998), pp. 570–573

—— "The Sex Which is Not One", trans. C. Reeder, in *New French Feminisms*, ed. E. Marks and I. de Courtivron (Brighton: Harvester, 1981), pp. 99–110

Jackson, Ellen-Raïssa, "Gender, Violence and Hybridity: Reading the Postcolonial in Three Irish Novels", *Irish Studies Review* (August 1999), pp. 221–231

Jameson, Frederic, "The Cultural Logic of Late Capitalism", in *Postmodernism and the Contemporary Novel: A Reader,* ed. Brian Nicol (Edinburgh: Edinburgh University Press, 2002), pp. 20–39

—— "Third World Literature in the Era of Multinational Capitalism", in *Social Text* 15 (Fall 1986), pp. 65–88

Jeffers, Jennifer M., *The Irish Novel at the End of the Twentieth Century* (New York: Palgrave, 2002)

Johnson, James H., "Population Changes in Ireland, 1951–1961", *The Geographical Journal*, 129:2 (June, 1963), pp. 167–174

Johnston, Denis, *Collected Plays Volume I* (London: Cape, 1959)

Johnston, Máirín, *Alive Alive O! Recollections and Visions of Dublin Women* (Dublin: Attic, 1990)

Jones, Lewis, *We Live* (London: Lawrence & Wishart, 1978)

Jordan, Anthony J., *Christy Brown's Women* (Dublin: Westport, 1998)

Jordan, John, "Slumlands Tragedy", *The Irish Times*, 3 March 1962, p. 9

Jordan, Neil, *Collected Fiction* (London: Vintage, 1997)

—— *The Crying Game* (London: Vintage, 1993)

Joseph, Jonathan, *Hegemony: A Realist Analysis* (London: Routledge, 2002)

Joyce, James, *A Portrait of the Artist as a Young Man* (London: Penguin, 1996)

—— *Ulysses* (London: Penguin, 1992)

Kaplan, Cora, "Language and Gender", in *Papers on Patriarchy* (Sussex: Women's Publishing Collective, 1976), pp. 21–37

Katznelson, Ira and Aristide R. Zolberg, *Working-Class Formation: Nineteenth Century Patterns in Western Europe and the United States* (Princeton: Princeton University Press, 1986)

Kearney, Colbert, *The Glamour of Grammar: Orality and Politics and the Emergence of Sean O'Casey* (London: Greenwood, 2000)

—— *The Writings of Brendan Behan* (Dublin: Gill and Macmillan, 1997)

Kearney, Hugh, "The Irish and Their History", in *Interpreting Irish History: The Debate on Historical Revisionism*, ed. Ciaran Brady (Dublin: Irish Academic Press, 1994), pp. 246–52

Kearney, Richard, *Postnationalist Ireland: Politics, Culture, Philosophy* (London: Routledge, 1997)

Kearns, Kevin C., *Dublin's Lost Heroines: Mammies and Grannies in a Vanished City* (Dublin: Gill and Macmillan, 2004)
—— *Dublin Pub Life and Lore: An Oral History* (Dublin: Gill & Macmillan, 1996)
—— *Dublin Street Life and Lore: An Oral History* (Dun Laoghaire: Glendale,1991)
—— *Dublin Tenement Life: An Oral History* (Dublin: Gill & Macmillan, 1994)
—— *Dublin Voices: An Oral Folk History* (Dublin: Gill & Macmillan, 2001)
—— "Industrialization and Regional Development in Ireland, 1958–72", *American Journal of Economics and Sociology*, 33:3 (July, 1974), pp. 299–316
—— *Streets Broad and Narrow: Images of Vanishing Dublin* (Dublin: Gill & Macmillan, 2000)
Kelly, Bill, *Me Darlin' Dublin's Dead & Gone* (Swords, Co. Dublin: Ward River, 1983)
Kelly, Henry, "A Life of Writing", *The Irish Times*, 16 November 1974, p. 6
Kelly, Shirley, "Shirley Kelly talks to popular comic novelist Roddy Doyle", *Writer's Monthly* (September 1992), pp. 4–8
Kelman, James, *A Disaffection* (London: Vintage, 1999)
—— *How Late It Was, How Late* (London: Minerva, 1995)
Kennedy, Kieran A. Thomas Giblin, and Deirdre McHugh, *The Economic Development of Ireland in the Twentieth Century* (London: Routledge, 1988)
Kennedy, Maev, "Arts and Studies: The sculptor goes electioneering", *The Irish Times*, 15 June 1977, p. 10
Kennedy, Tom, ed. *Victorian Dublin* (Dublin: Albertine Kennedy, 1980)
Kennelly, Brendan, "City of Talk", in *Dublines*, ed. Katie Donovan and Brendan Kennelly (Bloodaxe: Newcastle upon Tyne, 1996), pp. 11–13
—— and Katie Donovan eds., *Dublines* (Newcastle upon Tyne: Bloodaxe, 1996)
Kershner, R. Brandon, "History as Nightmare: Joyce's Portrait to Christy Brown", in *Joyce and the Subject of History*, ed. Mark A. Wollaeger, Victor Luftig and Robert Spoo (Michigan: University of Michigan, 1996)
Kiberd, Declan, *Inventing Ireland: The Literature of the Modern Nation* (London: Vintage, 1996)
—— *Irish Classics* (London: Granta, 2001)
Kilmurray, Evanne, *Fight, Starve or Emigrate: A History of the Irish Unemployed Movements in the 1950s* (Dublin: Larkin Unemployed Centre, 1988)
Kilroy, James F. "Setting the Standards: Writers of the 1920s and 1930s", in *The Irish Short Story: A Critical History*, ed. James F. Kilroy (Boston: Twayne, 1984), pp. 103–104
Kilroy, Thomas, *Talbot's Box* (Dublin: Gallery, 1979)
Kindienst, Patricia, "The Voice of the Shuttle is Ours", originally published in *The Stanford Literature Review* 1 (1984), pp. 25–53 <http://www.english.ucsb.edu/faculty/ayliu/research/klindienst.html> [accessed 5 January, 2006]
Kinsella, Thomas, *A Dublin Documentary* (Dublin: O'Brien, 2006)
—— *Collected Poems 1956–2001* (Manchester: Carcanet, 2001)
Kirby, Peadar, *The Celtic Tiger in Distress: Growth with Inequality in Ireland* (New York: Palgrave, 2002)
Klaus, H. Gustav, *The Socialist Novel in Britain: Towards the Recovery of a Tradition* (Brighton: Harvester, 1982)
Kosok, Heinz, *O'Casey the Dramatist* (London: Smythe, 1985)
—— "The Silver Tassie and British Plays of the First World War", *Arbeiten aus Anglistik und Amerikanistik* (October, 1985), pp. 91–96
Krause, David, "Introduction to The Risen People: A Play by Jim Plunkett", *Journal of Irish Literature* (January 1992), pp. 3–10
—— ed., *The Letters of Sean O'Casey, IV: 1959–64* (Washington, DC: Catholic University of America, 1992)

—— "The Risen O'Casey: Some Marxist and Irish Ironies", *The O'Casey Annual*, 3 (1984), pp. 134–168

Kristeva, Julia, "Word, Dialogue, and the Novel," in *Desire in Language: A Semiotic Approach to Literature and Art*, ed. Leon S. Roudiez, trans. Thomas Gora et al. (New York: Columbia University Press, 1980), pp. 64–91

La Haine. Dir. Mathieu Kassovitz. Canal. 1995

Lane, Fintan, *The Origins of Modern Irish Socialism 1881–1896* (Cork: Cork University Press, 1997)

—— and Emmet O'Connor, "Speed the Plough", *Saothar* 26 (2001), pp. 3–4

Lane, Jeremy, "Sociology and Dialogics: Pierre Bourdieu, Mikhail Bakhtin and the Critique of Formalist Aesthetics", in *Face to Face: Bakhtin in Russia and the West*, ed. Carol Adlam et al. (Sheffield: Sheffield Academic Press, 1997), pp. 329–346

Lane, Nancy J., "A Theology of Anger When Living with Disability", in *The Psychological and Social Impact of Disability*, ed. Robert P. Marinelli and Arthur E. Dell Orto (New York: Springer, 1999), pp. 173–186

Lash, Scott, *Sociology of Postmodernism* (London: Routledge, 1990)

Laverty, Maura, *Liffey Lane* (London: Longmans, Green, 1947)

Lawler, Steph, "Escape and Escapism: Representing Working-Class Women", in *Cultural Studies and the Working Class, Subject to Change*, ed. Sally R. Munt (London: Cassell, 2000), pp. 113–128

Leland, Mary, "Goodbye to the Hill", *The Irish Times*, 6 October 1975, p. 10

LeMoncheck, Linda, *Loose Women, Lecherous Men: A Feminist Philosophy of Sex* (Oxford: Oxford University Press, 1997)

Lesjak, Carolyn, *Working Fictions: A Genealogy of the Victorian Novel* (London: Duke University Press, 2006)

Levitas, Ben, "Plumbing the Depths: Irish Realism and the Working Class from Shaw to O'Casey", *Irish University Review: A Journal of Irish Studies* (Spring–Summer 2003), pp. 133–149

Lloyd, David, *Anomalous States: Irish Writing and the Post-colonial Moment* (Dublin: Lilliput, 1993)

—— *Irish Times: Temporalities of Modernity*, ed. by Seamus Deane and Breandán Mac Suibhne (Dublin: Field Day, 2008)

—— "The Subaltern in Motion: Subalternity, the Popular and Irish Working-class History", *Postcolonial Studies* 8:4 (2005), pp. 421–437

Lokke, Kari E., *Tracing Women's Romanticism: Gender, History and Transcendence* (New York: Routledge, 2004)

Lowery, Robert, "The Socialist Legacy of Seán O'Casey", *The Crane Bag*, 7:1 (1983), pp. 128–134

Luddy, Maria, *Women in Ireland* (Cork: Cork University Press, 1995)

Lukács, Georg, *History and Class Consciousness: Studies in Marxist Dialectics* (London: Merlin, 1971)

—— "Tolstoy and the Development of Realism", from *Studies in European Realism* (1950), reprinted in *Marxist on Literature: An Anthology* (Harmondsworth: Pelican 1977), pp. 283–284

—— *The Historical Novel*, trans. Hannah and Stanley Mitchell (London: Merlin, 1962)

Lynch, John, *A Tale of Three Cities: Comparative Studies in Working-Class Life* (Basingstoke: Macmillan, 1998)

Lynch, Kathleen, *Equality in Education* (Dublin: Gill and Macmillan, 1999)

—— and Anne Lodge, *Equality and Power in Schools: Redistribution, Recognition, and Representation* (London: Routledge, 2002)

Lynch, Rachel Sealey, " 'Soft Talk' and 'An Alien Grip': Gallagher's Rhetoric of Control in O'Flaherty's The Informer", *Journal of Irish Literature* (Fall Winter 1993), pp. 260–268

Lyons, F.S.L., *Ireland since the Famine* (London: Fontana, 1985)

Lyons, F.S.L., "The Meaning of Independence" in *The Irish Parliamentary Tradition*, ed. Brian Farrell (Dublin: Gill and Macmillan, 1973), pp. 223–225

Lysaght, Patricia, "Caoineadh ós cionn coirp: The lament for the dead in Ireland", *Folklore*, 108 (1997), pp. 65–82

Mac Anna, Ferdia, "The Dublin Renaissance: An Essay on Modern Dublin and Dublin Writers", *The Irish Review*, 10 (Spring 1991), pp. 14–30

Mac Intyre, Thomas, "Some Notes on the Stories of James Plunkett", *Studies* (Autumn 1958), pp. 323–327

Mac Piarais, Micheál, "Postmodern and Postcolonial Tensions in Flann O'Brien's *At Swim-Two-Birds*", in *New Voices in Irish Literary Criticism: Ireland in Theory*, ed. Cathy McGlynn and Paula Murphy (Lewiston, New York: Edwin Mellen, 2007), pp. 57–71

MacDonagh, Donagh, *Happy as Larry* (London: Maurice Fridberg, 1946)

MacGill, Patrick, *Children of the Dead End* (London: Jenkins, 1914)

Magee, Heno, *Hatchet* (Dublin: Gallery, 1978)

Magee, Patrick, *Gangsters or Guerillas? Representations of Irish Republicans in 'Troubles Fiction'* (Belfast: Beyond the Pale, 2001)

Maguire, Moira J., *Precarious Childhood in Post-independence Ireland* (Manchester: Manchester University Press, 2009)

Mallet, Serge, *Essays on the New Working Class*, ed. Dick Howard and Dean Savage (St. Louis: Teleos, 1975)

Maloney, Caitríona, *Irish Women Writers Speak Out: Voices from the Field* (Syracuse, New York: Syracuse, 2003)

Maloney, Ed, *A Secret History of the IRA* (London: Allen Lane, 2002)

Margulies, Martin B., *The Early Life of Sean O'Casey* (Dublin: Dolmen, 1971)

Marmot, Michael, *Status Syndrome* (London: Bloomsbury, 2004)

Marsh, Ian and Mike Keating, *Sociology: Making Sense of Society* (Harlow: Prentice Hall, 2006)

Marshall, Gordon, *Repositioning Class: Social Inequality in Industrial Societies* (London: Sage, 1997)

Martin, Augustine, *James Stephens: A Critical Study* (Dublin: Gill and Macmillan, 1977)

Martinez, Theresa, "Popular Culture as Oppositional Culture: Rap as Resistance", *Sociological Perspectives*, 40:2 (1997), pp. 276–279

Marx, Karl, "Preface to *A Contribution to the Critique of Political Economy*", in *Karl Marx: Selected Writings* (Indianapolis: Hackett, 1994), pp. 209–213

—— *Capital: A Critique of Political Economy*, trans. David Fernbach, 3 vols. (London: Penguin, 1993)

—— *Karl Marx: Selected Writings*, ed. Lawrence Hugh Simon (Indianapolis: Hackett, 2000)

—— *Capital, The Communist Manifesto and Other Writings*, ed. Max Eastman (New York: The Modern Library, 1959)

—— and Frederick Engels, *The German Ideology*, ed. C. J. Arthur (London: Lawrence & Wishart, 2004)

McAnna, Ferdia, "The Dublin Renaissance: An Essay on Modern Dublin and Dublin Writers", *The Irish Review*, 10 (Spring 1991), pp. 14–30

McCann, Sean, *The World of Sean O'Casey* (London: Four Square, 1966)

McCarthy, Charles, *The Decade of Upheaval: Irish Trade Unions in the Nineteen Sixties* (Dublin: Institute of Public Administration, 1973)

McCarthy, Conor, "Ideology and Geography in Dermot Bolger's The Journey Home", *Irish University Review*, 27:1 (Spring/Summer 1997), pp. 98–110

McCarthy, Conor, *Modernisation, Crisis and Culture in Ireland, 1969–1992* (Dublin: Four Courts, 2000)

McCarthy, Dermot, *Roddy Doyle: Raining on the Parade* (Dublin: Liffey, 2003)

McCloone, Martin, *Irish Film: The Emergence of a Contemporary Cinema* (London: The British Film Institute, 2000)

McCullagh, Ciaran, *Crime in Ireland* (Cork: Cork University Press, 1996)

—— "Getting The Criminals We Want: The Social Production of the Criminal Population", in *Irish Society: Sociological Perspectives*, ed. Patrick Clancy et al. (Dublin: Institute of Public Administration, 1999), pp. 410–431

McDonald, Ronan, "Sean O'Casey's Dublin Trilogy: Disillusionment to Delusion", in *The Cambridge Companion to Twentieth-Century Irish Drama* ed. Shaun Richards (Cambridge: Cambridge University Press, 2004), pp. 136–149

McFate, Patricia, *The Writings of James Stephens: Variations on a Theme of Love* (London: Macmillan, 1979)

McGarry, Fearghal, "Radical Politics in Interwar Ireland", in *Politics and the Irish Working Class, 1830–1945*, ed. Fintan Lane and Donal Ó Drisceoil, pp. 207–227

McGlynn, Mary, "'But I Keep on Thinking and I'll Never Come to a Tidy Ending': Roddy Doyle's Useful Nostalgia", *Literature Interpretation Theory* (July 1999) 10:1, pp. 87–105

McGuire, Violet, "The Departure", in *They Go, The Irish*, compiled by Leslie Daiken (London: Nicholson & Watson, 1944), pp. 82–85

McHugh, Roger, "'Always Complainin': The Politics of Young Sean", *Irish University Review*, 10:1 (Spring, 1980), pp. 91–97

McKenna, James, *Abbey Ambiguities* (n. p: n. pub., May 1980, pamphlet)

—— *Poems* (Dublin: Goldsmith, 1973)

—— *The Scatterin'* (Kildare: Goldsmith, 1977)

McKiernan, Joan and Monica McWilliams, "Women Religion and Violence in the Family", in *Women and Irish Society: A Sociological Reader*, ed. Anne Byrne and Madeleine Leonard (Belfast: Beyond the Pale, 1997), pp. 327–341

McLoone, Martin, "Strumpet City: The Urban Working Class on Television", in *Television and Irish Society: 21 Years of Irish Television*, ed. Martin McLoone and John McMahon (Dublin: RTÉ/IFI, 1984), pp. 53–89

McMullan, Anna, (ed. and intro.) "Contemporary Women Playwrights" in *The Field Day Anthology of Irish Writing V: Irish Women's Writing and Traditions*, Angela Bourke et al. eds. (New York: Field Day, 2002), pp. 1234–1246

McPherson, Conor, *Four Plays* (London: Nick Hern, 1999)

McWilliams, David, *The Pope's Children: The Irish Economic Triumph and the Rise of Ireland's New Elite* (NJ: Wiley, 2008)

Meaney, Geraldine, (ed. and intro.) "Identity and Opposition: Women's Writing, 1890–1960" in *The Field Day Anthology of Irish Writing, V: Irish Women's Writing and Traditions*, ed. Angela Bourke et al. (New York: Field Day, 2002), pp. 1069–1073

Medhurst, Andy, "If Anywhere: Class Identifications and Cultural Studies Academics", in *Cultural Studies and the Working Class, Subject to Change*, ed. Sally R. Munt (London: Cassell, 2000), pp. 19–35

Meehan, Paula, *Dharmakaya* (Manchester: Carcanet, 2000)

—— *Cell* (Dublin: New Island, 2000)

—— *Mrs Sweeney* (Dublin: New Island, 1999)
—— *Mysteries of the Home: A Selection of Poems* (Newcastle-upon-Tyne: Bloodaxe, 1996)
—— *Pillow Talk* (Oldcastle, Meath: Gallery, 2000, orig. 1994)
Meehan, Paula, *Reading the Sky* (Dublin: Beaver Row, 1986)
—— *Return and No Blame* (Dublin: Beaver Row, 1984)
—— *The Man Who Was Marked by Winter* (Oldcastle, Meath: Gallery, 1991)
Meinhardt, Carol, "Books, Films, and Culture: Reading in the Classroom", *English Journal*, 80:1 (January, 1991), pp. 82–87
Mercier, Paul, *Drowning* (1984), unpublished mss. provided by author
—— *Studs* (1986), unpublished mss. supplied by the author
—— *Spacers* (1985), unpublished mss. provided by author
—— *Wasters* (1985), unpublished mss. supplied by the author
Mikhail, E. H., *The Art of Brendan Behan* (London: Vision, 1979)
—— *Brendan Behan: An Annotated Bibliography of Criticism* (London: Macmillan, 1980)
—— *Brendan Behan: Interviews and Recollections* (London: Macmillan, 1982)
Milne, Michael, "Soccer and the Dublin Working Class", *Saothar*, 8 (1982), pp. 97–101
Milner, Andrew, *Class* (London: Sage, 1999)
Mitchell, Arthur, "George Orwell & Sean O'Casey: Two Prickly Characters Intersect", *History Ireland*, 6:3 (Autumn, 1998), pp. 44–46
Mitchell, Jack, *The Essential O'Casey: A Study of the Twelve Major Plays of Seán O' Casey* (New York: International Publishers, 1980)
Montague, John, *Collected Poems* (Oldcastle: Gallery, 1995)
Moody, T.W., "A New History of Ireland", *Irish History Studies*, xvi (1969), pp. 241–257
—— "Irish History and Irish Mythology", in *Interpreting Irish History*, ed. Conor Brady (Dublin: Irish Academic Press, 1994), pp. 71–86
—— *The Ulster Question: 1603–1973* (Cork: Mercier, 1974)
Moran, Leslie J., "Homophobic Violence: The Hidden Injuries of Class" in *Cultural Studies and the Working Class*, ed. Sally R. Munt (London: Cassell, 2000), pp. 206–218
Morash, Christopher, *A History of Irish Theatre, 1601–2000* (Cambridge: Cambridge University Press, 2002)
Moretti, Franco, *The Way of the World: The Bildungsroman in European Culture*, trans. Albert Sbragia (New York: Verso, 2000)
Morris, Lydia, *Dangerous Classes: The Underclass and Social Citizenship* (New York: Routledge, 1994)
Mulkerns, Val, *Very Like a Whale* (London: John Murray, 1986)
Mullan, Don, *Eyewitness Bloody Sunday: The Truth* (Dublin: Wolfhound, 1997)
Munt, Sally R., "Introduction", in *Cultural Studies and the Working Class, Subject to Change*, ed. Sally R. Munt (London: Cassell, 2000), pp. 1–16
Murphy, Cormac, "Revolution and Radicalism in County Dublin, 1913–21" in *Aspects of Irish Studies*, ed. Myrtle Hill et al. (Belfast: The Institute of Irish Studies, Queen's University, 1990), pp. 17–24
Murphy, Jimmy, *Two Plays, The Kings of the Kilburn High Road, Brothers of the Brush* (London: Oberon, 2001)
Murray, Christopher, "O'Casey as Critic", *Canadian Journal of Irish Studies* (December 1992), pp. 58–67
—— "O'Casey's 'The Drums of Father Ned' in Context", in *A Century of Irish Drama: Widening the stage*, ed. Stephen Watt, Eileen M. Morgan, Shakir M. Mustafa (Bloomington: Indiana University Press, 2000), pp. 117–129
—— *Sean O'Casey: Writer at Work, A Biography* (Dublin: Gill and Macmillan, 2004)

—— *Twentieth-Century Irish Drama: Mirror up to Nation* (Syracuse, NY: Syracuse University Press, 1997)

Mustafa, Shakir. "Saying 'No' to Politics: Sean O'Casey's Dublin Trilogy", in Stephen Watt et al. eds. *A Century of Irish Drama: Widening the Stage* (Bloomington: Indiana University Press, 2000), pp. 95–113

Nelson, Dorothy, *In Night's City* (Dublin: Wolfhound, 1982)

Newsinger, John, "'In the Hunger-Cry of the Nation's Poor is Heard the Voice of Ireland': Sean O'Casey and Politics 1908–1916", *Journal of Contemporary History*, 20:2 (April 1985), pp. 221–240

—— "Sean O'Casey, Larkinism and Literature", *Irish Studies Review* (December 2004), pp. 283–292

—— "The Priest in the Irish Novel: James Plunkett's Strumpet City", *Etudes Irlandaises: Revue Francaise d'Histoire, Civilisation et Litterature de l' Irlande* (December 1989), pp. 65–76

Nicci, Gerrard, "What keeps Roddy rooted?", *The Observer*, 15 April 2001, p. 22 <http://books.guardian.co.uk/departments/generalfiction/story/0,6000,473369,0. html> [accessed 27 April 2005]

Nowlan, David, "'Goodbye to the Hill' at the Eblana", *The Irish Times*, 5 September 1978, p. 8

Ó Coigligh, Seamus, "Irish writing a la Russe", *The Irish Times*, 21 July 1966, p. 8

Ó Faoláin, Dónal and Vivian Uibh Eachach, *Féile Zozimus: The Man, the Myth, the Genius: Brendan Behan* (Baile Átha Cliath: Gael-Linn, 1993)

Ó Ríordáin, Seán, *Scáthán Véarsaí* (Baile Átha Cliath: Sáirséal, Ó Marcaigh, 1985)

Ó Tuathaigh, M.A.G., "Irish Historical 'Revisionism': State of the Art or Ideological Project?" in *Interpreting Irish History*, ed. Conor Brady (Dublin: Irish Academic, 1994), pp. 306–329

O'Beirne, Michael, *And the Moon at Night: A Dubliner's Story* (Belfast: Blackstaff, 1981)

—— *Mister: A Dublin Childhood* (Belfast: Blackstaff, 1979)

O'Brien, Flann, *At Swim-Two Birds* (Dublin: Penguin Books, 1992)

O'Brien, Joseph V., *'Dear, Dirty Dublin': A City in Distress, 1899–1916* (London: California University Press, 1982)

O'Brien, Tony, "What about Bob...?", *Irish Independent*, 17 August 1994, p. 26

Ó Broin, Eoin, *Sinn Féin and the Politics of Left Republicanism* (London: Pluto, 2009)

O'Byrne, Joe, *It Come Up Sun*, 2000, unpublished mss. supplied by author

—— *The Clearing Station*, 2001, unpublished mss. supplied by author

O'Carroll, Brendan, *The Mammy* (Dublin: O'Brien, 1999)

O'Casey, Seán, *Autobiographies* (London: Pan, 1980)

—— Sean, *Autobiography Volume 4: Inishfallen Fare Thee Well* (London: Pan, 1972)

—— *Blasts and Benedictions: Articles and Stories* (London: Macmillan, 1967)

—— *Collected Plays* (London: Macmillan, 1949)

—— *Collected Plays, Volume One* (London: Macmillan, 1950)

—— *Collected Plays, Volume Two* (London: Macmillan, 1951)

—— *Inishfallen Fare Thee Well* (London: Pan, 1972; orig. 1949)

—— *Mirror in My House: Autobiographies of Sean O'Casey*, 2 vols (New York: Macmillan, 1956)

—— *Plays* (London: Faber and Faber, 1998)

—— *Red Roses for Me: A Play in Four Acts* (New York: Macmillan, 1943)

—— *The Bishop's Bonfire: A Sad Play Within the Tune of a Polka* (London: Macmillan, 1955)

—— *The Complete Plays of Sean O'Casey* (London: Macmillan, 1984)

—— *The Flying Wasp* (London: Macmillan, 1937)

O'Casey, Seán, *The Green Crow* (London: W. H. Allen, 1957)

—— *The Harvest Festival: A Play in Three Acts* (Gerrard's Cross: Smythe, 1980)

—— *The Story of the Irish Citizen Army* (London: Journeyman, 1980)

—— "They Go, The Irish", in *They Go, The Irish*, compiled by Leslie Daiken (London: Nicholson & Watson, 1944), pp. 7–15

—— *Three Plays* (London: Papermac, 1994)

—— *Under a Coloured Cap: Articles Merry and Mournful with Comments and a Song* (London: Macmillan, 1963)

—— *Within the Gates: A Play of Four Scenes in a London Park* (London: Macmillan, 1934)

O'Connell, Cathal, *The State and Housing in Ireland: Ideology, Policy and Practice* (New York: Nova, 2007)

O'Connor, Emmet, *A Labour History of Ireland, 1824–1960* (Dublin: Gill & Macmillan, 1992)

—— "Labour and Politics, 1830–1945: Colonisation and Mental Colonisation", in *Politics and the Irish Working Class, 1830–1945*, ed. Fintan Lane and Donal Ó Drisceoil (London: Palgrave, 2005), pp. 27–43

O'Connor, Garry, *Sean O'Casey: A Life* (London: Paladin, 1989)

O'Connor, Pat, *Emerging Voices: Women in Contemporary Irish Society* (Dublin: Institute of Public Administration, 1998)

O'Connor, Ulick, *Brendan Behan* (London: Coronet, 1970)

O'Donnell, Hugh, *11 Emerald Street* (London: Vintage, 2005)

O'Donovan, John, *Life by the Liffey: A Kaleidoscope of Dubliners* (Dublin: Gill and Macmillan, 1986)

O'Dowd, Mary, ed. and intro. "Interpreting the Past: Women's History and Women Historians, 1840–1945" in *The Field Day Anthology of Irish Writing, V: Irish Women's Writing and Traditions*, ed. Angela Bourke et al. (New York: Field Day, 2002), pp. 1102–1105

O'Faolain, Sean, "Fifty Years of Irish Writing", *Irish Writing in the Twentieth Century: A Reader*, ed. David Pierce (Cork: Cork University Press, 2000), pp. 740–747

O'Flaherty, Liam, *Insurrection* (London: Landsborough, 1959)

—— *Short Stories* (Sevenoaks: Sceptre, 1990)

—— *The Assassin* (Dublin: Wolfhound, 1998)

—— *The Informer* (London: New English, 1980)

O'Hanlon, Jim, "Dermot Bolger in Conversation with Jim O'Hanlon", in *Theatre Talk: Voices of Irish Theatre Practitioners*, ed. Lilian Chambers (Dublin: Carysfort, 2000), pp. 29–42

O'Hanlon, Thomas J., *The Irish: Portrait of a People* (New York: Harper & Row, 1975)

O'Hare, Shawn, "An Interview with James Plunkett", *The Journal of Irish Literature*, 23:3 (September 1993), pp. 99–111

O'Kelly, Séamus, "Theatre Festival", *The Irish Times*, 14 September 1960, p. 6

O'Riordan, John, "The Garlanded Horror of War: Reflections on The Silver Tassie", *Sean O'Casey Review*, 5 (1978), pp. 23–28

O'Sullivan, Denis, "The Ideational Base of Irish Educational Policy", in *Irish Educational Policy: Process and Substance*, ed. D. G. Mulcahy and Denis O'Sullivan (Dublin: Institute of Public Administration, 1989), pp. 219–274

O'Sullivan, Michael G., *Brendan Behan: A Life* (Dublin: Blackwater, 1997)

O'Toole, Fintan, "Boxers offer a window into our marginalised society", *The Irish Times*, 26 August 2008, p. 13

—— "Going West: The Country versus the City in Irish Writing", *Crane Bag*, 9:2 (1985), pp. 111–116

O'Toole, Fintan, "Happenings on the Hill", *The Irish Times*, 5 September 1995, p. 19

—— *Irish Times Book of the Century* (Dublin: Gill & Macmillan, 1999)

—— "Working-Class Dublin on Screen: The Roddy Doyle Films", *Cineaste: America' s Leading Magazine on the Art and Politics of the Cinema*, 24:2–3 (1999), pp. 36–39

O'Toole, Jason, "From the Hill to Hollywood: A Conversation with Lee Dunne", *The Dublin Quarterly*, (June–August 2005) <http://www.dublinquarterly.com/04/int_ ldunne.html> [accessed 17 April 2008]

Organisation for Economic Co-operation and Development, *Higher Education in Ireland: Reviews of National Policies for Education* (Paris: OECD, 2006)

Ormsby, Frank, "The Short Stories of James Plunkett", *The Honest Ulsterman* (December 1969), pp. 10–16

Orwell, George, "The Proletarian Writer", discussion between George Orwell and Desmond Hawkins, broadcast 6 December 1940; published in *The Listener*, 19 December 1940, republished in *Orwell and the Dispossessed*, ed. by Peter Davison (London: Penguin, 2001), pp. 283–291

—— *The Road to Wigan Pier* (New York: Berkley, 1961)

Osborne, John, *Look Back in Anger* (London: Faber & Faber, 1978)

Ovidius Naso, Publius, *Metamorphoses*, trans. H. T. Riley (London: George Bell and Sons, 1898)

Parkinson, Aidan, *Going Places* (Dublin: Passion Machine, 1991)

Paschel, Ulrike, *No Mean City? The Image of Dublin in the Novels of Dermot Bolger, Roddy Doyle, and Val Mulkerns* (Frankfurt am Main: P. Lang, 1998)

Patten, Eve, "Fiction in Conflict: Northern Ireland's prodigal novelists" in *Peripheral Visions of Nationhood in Contemporary British Fiction*, ed. I. A. Bell (Cardiff: University of Wales, 1995)

Payne, G., "Social Mobility", *The British Journal of Sociology*, 40:3 (September 1989), pp. 471–492

Peach, Linden, *The Contemporary Irish Novel: Critical Readings* (Basingstoke: Palgrave, 2004)

Peacock, D. Keith, *Harold Pinter and the New British Theatre* (Westport, CT: Greenwood, 1997)

Pearson, Geoffrey, *Hooligan: A History of Respectable Fears* (London: Macmillan, 1988)

Peillon, Michel, *Contemporary Irish Society: An Introduction* (Dublin: Gill and Macmillan, 1982)

Pelletier, Martine, "Dermot Bolger's Drama" in *Irish Theatre Stuff: Critical Essays on Contemporary Irish Theatre*, ed. Eamonn Jordan (Dublin: Carysfort, 2000), pp. 34–46

Perkin, Harold, "The Condescension of Posterity: The Recent Historiography of the English Working Class", *Social Science History*, 3:1 (Autumn 1978), pp. 87–101

—— *The Rise of Professional Society: England since 1880* (London: Routledge, 1989)

Persson, Ake, "Polishing the Working Class? A Sociolinguistic Reading of Roddy Doyle's Barrytown Trilogy and Later Fiction", *Nordic Irish Studies*, 2:1 (2003), pp. 47–56

Peter Stallybrass, "Marx and Heterogeneity: Thinking the Lumpenproletariat", *Representations*, 31, Special Issue: The Margins of Identity in Nineteenth-Century England, (Summer 1990), pp. 69–95

Petocz, Agnes, *Freud, Psychoanalysis, and Symbolism* (Cambridge: Cambridge University Press, 1999)

Phillips, Paul, *Marx and Engels on Law and Laws,* (Oxford: Robertson, 1980)

Pilkington, Lionel, *Theatre and State in Twentieth-Century Ireland: Cultivating the People* (London: Routledge, 2001)

Plekhanov, G. V., *Fundamental Problems of Marxism*, trans. Julius Katzer (Moscow: Progress, 1977)

Plotz, Judith, *Romanticism and the Vocation of Childhood* (Basingstoke: Macmillan, 2000)

Plunkett, James, "A Walk Through the Summer", in *James Plunkett, Collected Short Stories* (Dublin: Poolbeg, 2000), pp. 34–63

—— *Big Jim: A Play for Radio* (Dublin: Martin O'Donnell, 1955)

—— *Boy on the Back Wall and Other Essays* (Dublin: Poolbeg, 1987)

—— *Collected Short Stories* (Dublin: Poolbeg, 1977)

—— *Eagles and the Trumpets and Other Stories* (Dublin: Bell, 1954)

—— *Farewell Companions* (London: Hutchinson, 1977)

—— "Homecoming: A Play for Broadcasting", *The Bell*, (June 1954), pp. 11–32

—— *James Plunkett: Collected Short Stories* (Dublin: Poolbeg, 2000)

—— *Strumpet City* (London: Hutchinson, 1969)

—— "The Boy on the Capstan", *Threshold*, (Spring/Summer 1961), pp. 7–14

—— *The Circus Animals* (London: Hutchinson, 1990)

—— "The Mad Barber", *Irish Bookman*, (February 1947), pp. 26–38

—— "The Mother", *The Bell*, (November 1942), pp. 99–108

—— "The Parrot of Digges Street", *Irish Bookman*, (December 1947), pp. 33–45

—— *The Risen People* (Dublin: Irish Writers' Co-op., 1978)

—— *The Trusting and the Maimed* (London: Arrow, 1969)

—— "Working class", *The Bell* (October 1943), pp. 96–102

—— "Yours Respectfully", *New Realities* (Dublin 1972), pp. 29–34

Poulantzas, Nicos, *Classes in Contemporary Capitalism*, trans. D. Fernbach (London: New Left, 1975)

Pound, Catherine, "No Bibles", *Cascando*, 5/6 (1996), pp. 66–69

Puirséil, Niamh, *The Irish Labour Party 1922–1973* (Dublin: UCD, 2007)

Quinn, Antoinette, "Ireland/Herland: Women and Literary Nationalism, 1845–1916" in *The Field Day Anthology of Irish Writing V: Irish Women's Writing and Traditions*, Angela Bourke et al. eds. (New York: Field Day, 2002), pp. 895–900

Quinn, Eithne, *Nuthin' but a "G" Thang: The Culture and Commerce of Gangsta Rap* (New York: Columbia University Press, 2005)

Quinney, Richard, *Class, State and Crime: On the Theory and Practice of Criminal Justice* (London: Longman, 1978)

Radio Teilifís Éireann, *Seven Ages* Dir. Seán Ó Mordha (Radio Teilifís Éireann, 2000)

Reay, Diane, "Children's Urban Landscapes: Configurations of Class and Place", in *Cultural Studies and the Working Class, Subject to Change*, ed. Sally R. Munt (London: Cassell, 2000), pp. 151–164

Redmond, Lar, *A Walk in Alien Corn* (Dublin: Glendale, 1990)

—— *Emerald Square* (Dublin: Glendale, 1990)

—— *Show us the Moon* (Dingle: Brandon, 1988)

Reynolds, Margaret and Jonathan Noakes, *Roddy Doyle: The Barrytown Trilogy: The Commitments, The Snapper, The Van, Paddy Clarke Ha Ha Ha, The Woman who Walked into Doors* (London: Vintage, 2004)

Richmond, Farley, "Some Religious Aspects of Indian Traditional Theatre", *The Drama Review*, 15:2 (Spring 1971), pp. 123–131

Ridgman, Jeremy, "Inside the Liberal Heartland: Television and the Popular Imagination in the 1960s", in *Cultural Revolution? The Challenge of the Arts in the 1960s*, ed. Bart Moore-Gilbert and John Seed (New York: Routledge, 1992), pp. 139–159

Ritchie, Harry, *Success Stories: Literature and the Media in England, 1950–1959* (London: Faber and Faber, 1988)

Roberts, Timothy Paul, "Little Terrors: The child's threat to social order in the Victorian bildungsroman" (unpublished doctoral thesis, University of New South Wales, 2005) <http://www.library.unsw.edu.au/~thesis/adt-NUN/uploads/approved/adt-NUN20060310.114803/public/01front.pdf> [accessed 3 October 2008]

Roland Barthes, *S/Z*, trans. Richard Miller (Oxford: Blackwell, 1990)

Rollins, Ronald G, "O'Casey, Yeats, and Behan: A Prismatic View of the 1916 Easter Rising", *Sean O'Casey Review*, 2 (1976), pp. 196–207

Rowbotham, Sheila, *Hidden from History: 300 Years of Women's Oppression and the Fight Against It* (London: Pluto, 1973)

Rupp, Jan C.C., "Rethinking Cultural and Economic Capital" in *Reworking Class*, ed. John R. Hall (London: Cornell University Press, 1997), pp. 221–242

Russell, George (A.E.), *Some Unpublished Letters from AE to James Stephens* (Dublin: Cuala, 1979)

Russell, Mary, " 'Goodbye to the Hill' and hello to a 'Mousetrap' ", *The Irish Times*, 9 July 1992, p. 11

Ryan, John, *Remembering How We Stood: Bohemian Dublin at the Mid-Century* (Dublin: Lilliput, 1987)

Ryan, Ray, "The Republic and Ireland: Pluralism, Politics, and Narrative Form", in *Writing in the Irish Republic: Literature, Culture, Politics 1949–1999*, ed. Ray Ryan (London: Macmillan, 2000), pp. 82–100

Said, Edward, "Discrepant Experiences" in *Postcolonial Discourse: An Anthology*, ed. Gregory Castle (Oxford: Blackwell, 2001), pp. 26–37

—— *Orientalism* (London: Penguin, 2003)

Sangari, Kumkum, *Politics of the Possible* (New Delhi: Tulika, 1999)

Sarukhanyan, Allan, "Irish Literature in Russia", *The Irish Times*, 4 July 1968, p. 13

Savage, Michael, "Space, Network and Class Formation" in *Social Class and Marxism: Defences and Challenges,* ed. Neville Kirk (Hants, Aldershot: Scolar, 1996)

Sax, William S., *The Gods at Play: Lila in South East Asia* (Oxford: Oxford University Press, 1995)

Sayer, Andrew, *The Moral Significance of Class* (Cambridge: Cambridge University Press, 2005)

Schrank, Bernice, "O'Casey's The Silver Tassie: From Manuscripts to Published Texts", *Bulletin of Research in the Humanities*, 87:2–3 (1986–1987), pp. 237–250

—— "Performing Political Opposition: Sean O'Casey's Late Plays and the Demise of Eamon de Valera", *BELLS: Barcelona English Language and Literature Studies*, 11 (2000), pp. 199–216.

—— *Sean O'Casey: A Research and Production Sourcebook* (London: Greenwood, 1996)

—— "Sean O'Casey (1880–1964)", in *Irish Playwrights, 1880–1995: A Research and Production Sourcebook,* ed. Bernice Schrank and William Demastes (Westport, CT: Greenwood, 1997), pp. 253–269

Schuler, Carol M., "The Seven Sorrows of the Virgin: Popular Culture and Cultic Imagery in Pre-Reformation Europe", *Simiolus: Netherlands Quarterly for the History of Art*, 21:1/2 (1992), pp. 5–28

Scott, James C., *Domination and the Arts of Resistance: Hidden Transcripts* (New Haven: Yale University Press, 1990)

Sennett, Richard and Jonathan Cobb, *The Hidden Injuries of Class* (Cambridge: Cambridge University Press, 1977)

Share, Perry, Hilary Tovey and Mary P. Corcoran, *A Sociology of Ireland* (Dublin: Gill & Macmillan, 2007)

Shaw, George Bernard, *Shaw: An Autobiography* (New York: Weybright and Talley, 1969)

Sheehan, Helena, *Irish Television Drama: A Society and its Stories* (Dublin: RTÉ, 1987; re-published in a revised edition on CD-ROM, 2004)

—— *The Continuing Story of Irish Television Drama: Tracking the Tiger* (Dublin: Four Courts, 2004)

Sheehan, Paul, *Modernism, Narrative and Humanism* (Cambridge: Cambridge University Press, 2002)

Sheridan, Jim, *Mobile Homes* (Dublin: Irish Writers' Co-operative, 1978)

Sheridan, Peter, *Big Fat Love: A Novel* (Dublin: Tivoli, 2003)

—— *Emigrants* (Dublin: Co-op Books, 1979)

—— *Forty-Seven Roses: A Memoir* (London: Macmillan, 2001)

—— *Old Money, New Money* (Dublin: New Island, 2000)

—— (with Gerard Mannix Flynn) *The Liberty Suit* (Dublin: Co-op Books, 1978)

—— "The 40-year-old Thorn", *The Irish Times* (28 Jan. 2006), "Weekend", p. 7

—— *44: A Dublin Memoir* (London: Macmillan, 1999)

Shortt, Damien, "Dermot Bolger: Gender Performance and Society" in *New Voices in Irish Literary Criticism: Ireland in Theory*, ed. Cathy McGlynn and Paula Murphy (Lewiston, New York: Edwin Mellen, 2007), pp. 151–166

Showalter, Elaine, "Feminist Criticism in the Wilderness", *Critical Inquiry*, 8:2 (Winter 1981), pp. 179–205

Sillitoe, Alan, *The Loneliness of the Long Distance Runner* (London: Flamingo, 1993)

—— *The Writer's Dilemma* (London, 1961)

—— *Saturday Night and Sunday Morning* (London: Flamingo, 1994)

Silverman, Marilyn, *An Irish Working Class: Explorations in Political Economy and Hegemony, 1800–1950* (Toronto: Toronto University Press, 2001)

Simpson, Alan, *Beckett and Behan and a Theatre in Dublin* (London: Routledge and Kegan Paul, 1962)

Simpson, Anne, *Blooming Dublin: Choice, Change and Contradictions* (Edinburgh: Mainstream, 1991)

Skeggs, Beverly, "Classifying Practices: Representations, Capitals and Recognitions", in *Class Matters: 'Working-Class' Women's Perspectives on Social Class*, ed. Pat Mahony and Christine Zmroczek (London: Taylor & Francis, 1997), pp. 123–139

Slaughter, Cliff, *Marxism, Ideology and Literature* (London: Macmillan, 1980)

Slemon, Stephen, "Modernism's Last Post", in *Past the Last Post*, ed. Ian Adam and Helen Tiffin (Hemel Hempstead: Harvester Wheatsheaf, 1991), pp. 1–11

—— "Post-Colonial Critical Theories", in *Postcolonial Discourse: An Anthology*, ed. Gregory Castle (Oxford: Blackwell, 2001), pp. 99–116

Smith, Dorothy, *The Everyday World as Problematic: A Feminist Sociology* (Boston: Northeastern University Press, 1987), p. 107

Smith, Gus, "Peacock premiere", *Sunday Independent*, 7 May 1972, p. 15

—— "There's no getting away from violence", *Sunday Independent*, 9 December 1973, p. 19

Smith, Paul, "A Dublin Memoir", *The Irish Times*, 5 November 1975, p. 10

—— *Come Trailing Blood* (London: Quartet, 1977)

—— *Stravanga* (London: Heinemann, 1963)

—— *Summer Sang in Me* (London: Quartet, 1975)

—— *The Countrywoman* (London: Quartet, 1975)

—— *The Stubborn Season* (London: Heinemann, 1961)

Smyth, Emer and Damian F. Hannan, "Education and Inequality", in *Bust to Boom? The Irish Experience of Growth and Inequality*, ed. Brian Nolan, Philip J. O'Connell and Christopher T. Whelan (Dublin: Institute of Public Administration, 2000), pp. 109–126

Smyth, Gerry, *The Novel and the Nation: Studies in New Irish Fiction* (London: Pluto, 1997)

Snee, Carole, "Working-Class Literature or Proletarian Writing?", in *Culture and Crisis in Britain in the Thirties*, ed. by Jon Clark et al. (London: Lawrence and Wishart, 1979), pp.165–192

Somers, Margaret R., "Deconstructing and Reconstructing Class Formation Theory: Narrativity, Relational Analysis, and Social Theory", in *Reconstructing Class*, ed. John R. Hall (London: Cornell University Press, 1997), pp. 73–105

Somerville-Large, Peter, *Dublin* (London: H. Hamilton, 1979)

—— *Dublin: the First Thousand Years* (Belfast: Appletree, 1988)

Spivak, Gayatri Chakravorty, "Can the Subaltern Speak?", abridged in *Colonial Discourse and Post-Colonial Theory: A Reader*, ed. Patrick Williams and Laura Chrisman (Hemel Hempstead: Harvester Wheatsheaf, 1993), pp. 66–111

—— "Scattered Speculations on the Subaltern and the Popular", *Postcolonial Studies* 8:4 (2005), pp. 475–486

Spring, Brian, *The Charwoman's Daughter* (Dublin: Helicon, 1979)

Stephens, James, *Collected Poems* (London: Macmillan, 1965)

—— *Deirdre* (New York: Macmillan, 1970)

—— *Desire and Other Stories* (Co. Dublin: Poolbeg, 1980)

—— *Here are Ladies* (New York: Macmillan, 1928)

—— *James Stephens: A Selection* (London: Macmillan, 1962)

—— *Kings and the Moon* (New York: Macmillan, 1938)

—— *Letters of James Stephens* (London: Macmillan, 1974)

—— *Reincarnations* (London: Macmillan, 1918)

—— "Sawdust", in *The Uncollected Prose of James Stephens: Volume 2*, ed. Patrick McFate (London: Gill and Macmillan, 1983), pp. 149–153

—— *Strict Joy: Poems* (New York: Macmillan, 1931)

—— *The Adventures of Seumas Beg and The Rocky Road to Dublin* (London: Macmillan, 1916)

—— *The Charwoman's Daughter* (Dublin: Scepter, 1966)

—— *The Crock of Gold* (London: Pan, 1965)

—— *The Demi-Gods* (Dublin: Butler Sims, 1982)

—— *The Hill of Vision* (Dublin: Maunsel, 1912)

—— *The Insurrection in Dublin* (Gerrards Cross, Dublin: Colin Smythe, 1992)

—— *The Lover Who Lost* (National Library of Ireland: Abbey Theatre Mss., microfiche, n.d.)

—— "The Thieves", in *The Uncollected Prose of James Stephens: Volume 2*, ed. Patrick McFate (London: Gill and Macmillan, 1983), pp. 170–176

—— *The Uncollected Prose of James Stephens*, ed. Patrick McFate (London: Gill and Macmillan, 1983)

Stern, James, "The Ordeal of Molly Baines", *New York Times*, section Book Reviews, 17 September 1961, p. 4

Stevenson, John, "Social Aspects of the Industrial Revolution", in *The Industrial Revolution and British Society*, ed. Patrick O'Brien and Roland Quinault, (Cambridge: Cambridge University Press, 1993), pp. 229–253

Stewart, Victoria, *About O'Casey: the Playwright and the Work* (London: Faber & Faber, 2006)

Taylor, Charles, "The Salon Interview: Roddy Doyle", <www.salon.com/books/feature/999/10/28/doyle/index2.html> [accessed 28 October 1999]

Tew, Philip, "The Lexicon of Youth in Mac Laverty, Bolger, and Doyle: Theorizing Contemporary Irish Fiction via Lefebvre's Tenth Prelude", *The Hungarian Journal of English and American Studies*, 5:1 (1999), pp. 181–197

The Wind that Shakes the Barley. Dir. Ken Loach. BIM Distribuzione. 2006

Thompson, E. P., *The Making of the English Working Class* (London: Penguin 1980)

—— *The Poverty of Theory and Other Essays* (London: Merlin, 1978)

Thompson, Neville, *Jackie Loves Johnser OK?* (Dublin: Pollbeg, 1998)

—— *Streetwise: Stories from an Irish prison* (Dublin: Mainstream, 2005)

—— *Two Birds / One Stoned* (Dublin: Poolbeg, 1999)

Tong, Rosemarie Putnam, *Feminist Thought: A More Comprehensive Introduction* (Oxford: Westview, 1998)

Tressell, Robert, *The Ragged Trousered Philanthropists* (London: Flamingo, 1993, orig. 1914)

Trevor, William, "The Snarling, Yelling World of Real Dublin", *Irish Times*, section Saturday Review, 16 May 1970, p. 1

Trotsky, Leon, *Literature and Revolution*, trans. Rose Strunsky (Michigan: Ann Arbor, 1971)

—— *The Struggle against Fascism in Germany* (New York: Pathfinder, 1971)

Trotter, David, *The English Novel in History, 1895–1920* (New York: Routledge, 1993)

U2, *Running to Stand Still*, *The Joshua Tree* (Island, 1987)

Valiulis, Maryann, "Power, Gender and Identity in the Irish Free State", *Journal of Women's History*, 6/7 (Winter/Spring 1994–5), pp. 117–136

Verschoyle, Moira, "Shining Offbeat", *The Irish Times*, 1 December 1962, p. 9

Von Rosenberg, Ingrid, "The Fiction of Agnes Owens", in *British Industrial Fictions* ed. H. Gustav Klaus and Stephen Knight (Cardiff: University of Wales, 2000), pp. 193–205

Walkerdine, Valerie, *Schoolgirl Fictions* (London: Verso, 1990)

Walsh, Enda, *Disco Pigs and Sucking Dublin: Two Plays* (London: Nick Hern, 2006)

Walshe, Eibhear, "Invisible Irelands: Kate O'Brien's Lesbian and Gay Social Formations in London and Ireland in the Twentieth Century", *SQS*, 1, (January 2006), pp. 39–48

Walshe, John, "Fee Schools Stretch Lead in Race for Top Courses", *Irish Independent*, 4 December 2008, p. 1

Ward, Margaret, *Hanna Sheehy Skeffington: A Life* (Cork: Attic, 1997)

Welch, Robert, *The Abbey Theatre, 1899–1999: Form and Pressure* (Oxford: Oxford University Press, 1999)

Whelan, Christopher T., and Richard Layte, "Opportunities for All in the New Ireland?", in *Best of Times? The Social Impact of the Celtic Tiger*, ed. Tony Fahey, Helen Russell and Christopher T. Whelan (Dublin: Institute of Public Administration, 2007), pp. 67–85

Whelan, Kevin, "Clio agus Caitlín Ní Uallacháin" in *Oghma 2*, ed. Seosamh Ó Murchú et al. (Dublin, 1990), pp. 9–19

—— "Come All You Staunch Revisionists: Towards a Post-revisionist Agenda for Irish History", *Irish Reporter*, 2 (1991), pp. 23–26

—— "The Revisionist Debate in Ireland", *Boundary 2*, 31:1 (2004), pp. 179–205

White, Caramine, *Reading Roddy Doyle* (New York: Syracuse, 2001)

White, John J., *Bertold Brecht's Dramatic Theory* (Suffolk: Camden, 2004)

White, Victoria, "FRONT/row", *The Irish Times*, 18 January 2001, p. 16

Wickham, James, "The New Irish Working Class?", *Saothar*, 6 (1980), pp. 81–88

—— "The Politics of Dependent Capitalism: International Capital and the Nation State", in *Ireland: Divided Nation, Divided Class*, ed. Austen Morgan and Bob Purdie (London: Ink Links, 1980), pp. 53–73

Wilde, Oscar, *Complete Works of Oscar Wilde* (London: Collins, 2001)

Wilkinson, Ellen, *Clash* (London: Virago, 1989)

Williams, Raymond, *Culture and Materialism* (London: Verso, 2005)

—— *Marxism and Literature* (Oxford: Oxford University Press, 1992)

—— "Notes on Marxism in Britain since 1945", in *Problems in Materialism and Culture: Selected Essays* (London: Verso, 1980), pp. 233–251

Willis, Paul E., *Learning to Labour: How Working Class Kids Get Working Class Jobs* (Aldershot: Ashgate, 1993, orig. 1977)

Wilson, A. P., *Liberty Hall Plays No. 1: Victims and Poached* (Dublin: Liberty Hall Players, n. d.)

—— *The Slough* (Dublin: Abbey Theatre Papers, 1914; National Library of Ireland Mss. Dept.)

Wilson, Donald Douglas, *Sean O'Casey's Tragi-Comic Vision* (New York: Revisionist, 1976)

Wilson Schaef, Ann, *Women's Reality: An Emerging Female System in a White Male Society* (San Francisco: Harper, 1992)

Woolridge, Sandra, "Tough as old boots", *Southern Star*, 6 March 1993, p. 9

Wright, Chrissie, *Paddy Clarke Ha Ha Ha* (London: Longman, 1999)

Wright, Erik Olin, *Class Counts: Comparative Studies in Class Analysis* (Cambridge: Cambridge University Press, 1997)

—— *Classes* (London: Verso, 1985)

—— *Interrogating Inequality: Essays on Class Analysis, Socialism and Marxism* (London: Verso, 1994)

—— "Rethinking, Once Again, the Concept of Class Structure" in *The Debate on Classes*, ed. Erik Olin Wright (London: Verso, 1989), pp. 269–348

—— "Rethinking, Once Again, the Concept of Class Structure", abridged by Maureen Sullivan in *Reworking Class*, ed. John R. Hall (London: Cornell University Press, 1997), pp. 41–72

Yeates, Pádraig, *Lockout: Dublin 1913* (Dublin: Gill and Macmillan, 2000)

Yeats, W. B., *Autobiographies* (London: Macmillan, 1955)

—— *The Collected Works of W. B. Yeats*, ed. David R. Clark and Rosalind E. Clark, Vol. II (Basingstoke: Palgrave, 2001)

—— *The Winding Stair and Other Poems* (New York: Macmillan, 1933)

—— *W. B. Yeats: A Critical Edition of the Major Works*, ed. Edward Larrissy (Oxford: Oxford University Press, 1997)

Young, Robert J. C., *Postcolonialism: An Historical Introduction* (Oxford: Blackwell, 2001)

Younge, Gary, "A Star Called Roddy", *The Guardian*, section Weekend, 29 August 1999, p. 16

Zimmermann, Georges Denis, *Songs of Irish Rebellion: Irish Political Street Ballads and Rebel Songs* (Dublin: Four Courts, 2002)

Index

corruption, 185–186, 215
Cox, Laurence, 264
Craig, Patricia, 216
Crime, 78–79, 80–84, 109, 171–172,
    168–190, 277, 278, 296
Cronin, Anthony, 14
Cruise O'Brien, Conor, 224, 225, 226
Cullen, L.M., 226
Cultural Studies, 2–3, 24

Daingean Reformatory, 178
Daly, Lance, *Kisses*, 157, 307
Damer Theatre, 79
Das, Veena, 233
Davies, Tony, 40
de Beauvoir, Simone, 289
de Botton, Alain, 269
de Valera, Éamon, 16, 17, 51, 68, 120,
    228, 241, 250, 254
Deane, Seamus, 57, 239
Delaney, Shelagh
    A Taste of Honey, 93
Dickens, Charles, 105, 117, 163, 292
Dobrolyubov, Nikolay, 38
Doheny, John, 47
Donoghue, Denis, 77
Dostoyevsky, Fyodor, 117
Douglas, Aileen, 264–265
Doyle, Roddy
    A Star Called Henry, 62, 70, 146, 161,
        194, 222–246, 247–248, 251
    Barrytown Trilogy, 89, 144, 189, 192
    Brownbread, 90, 217, 253
    The Commitments, 135, 240–241
    The Dead Republic, 49, 213, 222–223,
        224
    The Deportees, 240
    and education system, 27
    Family, 240
    and form, 227–229
    and history of the working class, 229,
        244
    The Last Roundup, 98, 244, 252–253
    magic realism, use of, 227–228
    and masculinity, 89
    and nationalism, 230–246
    Paula Spencer, 110
    The Playboy of the Western World, 240
    politics, 229–246
    and revisionism, 223–227

The Snapper, 110, 194, 240, 249
The Van, 81, 249
The Woman Who Walked into Doors,
    27, 63, 89, 110, 130, 131, 139,
    237, 240
War, 131
drugs,183, 184, 185–186, 188
    anti-drugs activism, 18, 26
Dublin and Monaghan bombings, 224
The Dubliners, 118
Duffy, Joe, 249–250
Dunlop, Joe
    Inside, 172
Dunn, Nell, 30
    Poor Cow, 131
    Up the Junction, 123, 130, 192
Dunne, Catherine
    A Name for Himself, 26, 124, 249
Dunne, Lee, 25, 54, 63, 66, 97, 192
    and alcoholism, 283
    and censorship, 95
    Does Your Mother, 59, 72, 98
    and emigration, 97, 107–108
    Goodbye to the Hill, 73, 75–76, 95–109,
        191, 193, 194, 253, 255
    and masculinity, 102–103
    and nationalism, 98–99
    Paddy, 95
    and popular/mass culture, 100–101
    and theatrical snobbery, 96–97
Dunnes Stores strike, 29–30

Eagleton, Terry, 1, 24, 26, 38, 41, 49–50,
    168, 220, 226, 245, 248, 252
    Saints and Scholars, 49–50
Eblana Theatre, 95
education system
    and class, 22–24
    curriculum issues, 23, 24–25, 264–265
    impact of free post-primary
        education, 19, 22
    Investment in Education report, 19, 23
    in literature, 26–28
    and working-class life, 19, 22–23
Edwards, Owen Dudley, 224
Edwards, Robert Dudley, 223–224
Eliot, George, 165
    The Mill on the Floss, 162, 163
Embankment Theatre, 87
emigration, 56, 73, 77, 83, 84–86, 119

Haywood, Ian, 281
Heaney, Seamus, 197
hegemony, concept of, 39, 44
Heinemann, Margot
   The Adventurers, 107
Herman, Mark
   Brassed Off, 135
Heslop, Harold
   The Gate of a Strange Field, 180
Hill, John, 226, 237
Hilliard, Christopher, 68
Hines, Barry, 68
   A Kestrel for a Knave, 93, 109
Hitchcock, Peter, 257
Hobsbawm, Eric, 47
Hoggart, Richard, 24, 28, 43, 74–75,
   130, 195, 196, 237, 257
Holderness, Graham, 40
homosexuality, 172, 214, 217, 219
hooks, bell, 255–256
Horkheimer, Max, 196
Howell, David, 46
Humphries, Alexander, 19, 192
Hutcheon, Linda, 229
Hutchinson, John, 224

IRA (Irish Republican Army), 13, 52,
   177, 225, 230, 234, 236, 238, 244
IRB (Irish Republican Brotherhood), 52,
   53
Imhof, Rüdiger, 227
immigration, 240, 256–257
Inglis, Tom, 192, 199
institutional abuse, 192–193, 209–211
Ionesco, Eugène, 172
Irigaray, Luce, 134, 136
Irish Christian Front, 15, 69
Irish Church Missions, 64, 70
Irish Citizen Army (ICA), 213, 236, 242
Irish Historical Studies, 223–224
Irish Labour History Museum, 24
Irish Labour History Society, 24
Irish Labour Party, 14–15, 17
Irish Socialist, 29
Irish Socialist Republican Party
   (ISRP), 15
Irish Worker, 13
ITGWU (Irish Transport and General
   Workers' Union), 13, 145
ITUC (Irish Trade Union Congress), 15

Jackson, Alvin, 47
Jacquarello, Roland, 279
Jeffers, Jennifer M., 228, 233
Jenkins Cook, Sylvia, 293
Johnson, Samuel, 189
Johnson, Tom, 14
Johnston, Denis, 73, 234
Jordan, John, 117
Jordan, Neil, 237
   Night in Tunisia, 299
Joseph, Jonathan, 152
Joyce, James, 52, 183, 247
   A Portrait, 200, 206
   Ulysses, 201, 205–206

Kant, Immanuel, 43
Kaplan, Cora, 137
Kassovitz, Mathieu
   La Haine, 43, 84
Kavanagh, Patrick, 66, 98
Kearns, Kevin C., 11, 22–23, 114–115,
   116, 132
Kelman, James
   A Disaffection, 28
   How Late it Was, How Late, 278
Kennelly, Brendan, 196
Kershner, R. Brandon, 196, 200, 203
Kiberd, Declan, 65, 72, 167, 172,
   207, 216
Kiely, Benedict
   Proxopera, 237
Kilroy, Thomas, 247
   Talbot's Box, 153, 202, 228, 251
Kinsella, Thomas, 27, 30, 197, 287
Kirby, Peadar, 22
Kisses, see Daly, Lance
Kitchen Sink writing, 77, 94, 118, 192,
   287
Klaus, H. Gustav, 42
Krause, David, 69
Kristeva, Julia, 111, 287–288
Kuznitsa, 35

Lane, Jeremy, 112
Lane, Fintan, 11, 23, 257–258
Lane, Nancy J., 198
Larkin, James, 12–13, 14, 47, 135, 144,
   145–146, 152, 154, 155, 195,
   242, 270
Larkin, Pat